seven deadly sins

VOL 3.

ALSO BY ROBIN WASSERMAN

Hacking Harvard

The Cold Awakening trilogy:

Frozen

Shattered

Torn

Seven Deadly Sins Vol. 1
Lust & Envy

Seven Deadly Sins Vol. 2
Pride & Wrath

Seven Deadly Sins Vol. 3
Sloth, Gluttony, & Greed

seven deadly sins

VOL 3.
SLOTH, GLUTTONY & GREED

ROBIN WASSERMAN

Simon Pulse
New York   London   Toronto   Sydney   New Delhi

This book is a work of fiction. Any references to historical events,
real people, or real locales are used fictitiously. Other names, characters,
places, and incidents are the product of the author's imagination,
and any resemblance to actual events or locales or persons,
living or dead, is entirely coincidental.

SIMON PULSE

An imprint of Simon & Schuster Children's Publishing Division
1230 Avenue of the Americas, New York, NY 10020
First Simon Pulse paperback edition October 2013
Sloth copyright © 2006 by Robin Wasserman
Gluttony copyright © 2007 by Robin Wasserman
Greed copyright © 2007 by Robin Wasserman
All rights reserved, including the right of reproduction
in whole or in part in any form.
SIMON PULSE and colophon are registered trademarks
of Simon & Schuster, Inc.
For information about special discounts for bulk purchases,
please contact Simon & Schuster Special Sales at 1-866-506-1949
or business@simonandschuster.com.
The Simon & Schuster Speakers Bureau can bring authors to
your live event. For more information or to book an event contact the
Simon & Schuster Speakers Bureau at 1-866-248-3049
or visit our website at www.simonspeakers.com.
Designed by Mike Rosamilia
The text of this book was set in JansonText LT.
Manufactured in the United States of America
2 4 6 8 10 9 7 5 3 1
Library of Congress Control Number 2013931937
ISBN 978-1-4424-7508-3

seven deadly sins

SLOTH

For Aunt Sherry and Uncle Jim,
and for Brandon,
who likes to sleep

How heavy do I journey on the way
When what I seek, my weary travel's end,
Doth teach that ease and that repose to say,
"Thus far the miles are measured from thy friend."
—William Shakespeare, "Sonnet 50"

Nothing to do
Nowhere to go
I wanna be sedated
—The Ramones, "I Wanna Be Sedated"

chapter one

"I'M IN HEAVEN," HARPER MOANED AS THE MASSEUR kneaded his supple fingers into the small of her back. "You were right, this is exactly what we needed."

Kaia shooed away her own masseur and turned over onto her back, almost purring with pleasure as the sun warmed her face. "I'm always right."

"I wouldn't go that far," Harper snarked, but there was no venom in her tone. The afternoon sun had leached away most of her will to wound—and a half hour under Henri's magic fingers had taken care of the rest. "Mmmmm, could life get any better?"

"Yoo are steeel verreee tense," Henri told her in his heavy French accent.

"And yoo are steeel verreee sexeeeee," Kaia murmured, in an impeccable accent of her own. The girls exchanged a glance as the hunky but clueless Henri smoothed a palmful of warm lotion across Harper's back.

"Zhees weeel help you reeelax," he assured her. As if anyone could relax with a voice like that purring in her ear. "I leave you ladies now. *Au revoir, mes chéries.*"

"*Arrivederci*, Henri!" Harper cried, giggling at the rhyme.

"That's Italian," Kaia sneered. "Idiot."

"Who cares?" Harper countered. "Snob."

"Loser."

"Bitch." Harper narrowly held back a grin.

"Slut." Kaia's eyes twinkled.

"Damn right!" Harper pulled herself upright and raised her mojito in the air. Kaia did the same, and they clinked the plastic cocktail glasses together. "To us. Good thing we found each other—"

"—since no one else could stand us," Kaia finished, and they burst into laughter.

It was the kind of day where the clouds look painted onto the sky. The scene was straight out of a travel brochure—five star all the way, of course. Storybook blue sky, turquoise ocean lapping away at the nearby shore, gleaming white sand beach, and a warm tropical breeze rustling through their hair, carrying the distant strains of a reggae band. The girls stretched out on their deck chairs, their every need attended to by a flotilla of servants.

"I could stay here forever." Harper sighed. She let her leg slip off the chair and dug her bare toe into the sand, burrowing it deeper and deeper into the cool, dark ground. "I wish we never had to go back."

"I don't know about you," Kaia drawled, "but I don't *have* to do anything."

"Right," Harper snorted. "The great and powerful Kaia Sellers, with the world at her fingertips. As if you can ditch real life and just stay here in paradise."

"I can do anything I want. Haven't you figured that out yet?"

Harper rolled her eyes.

"Why not?" Kaia continued. "What do I have to go back for? What do you? Isn't that why we came out here in the first place, to leave all that shit behind?"

Harper sighed. "You're right. And it worked. I can barely even remember what we were escaping from, and—" Her eyes widened. "You're bleeding." A small trail of blood trickled down Kaia's temple; Harper raised her hand to her own face, as if expecting to feel a similar wound.

Kaia frowned for a moment, dabbing her head with a

napkin. "Just a mosquito bite," she said with a shrug. She took a closer look at Harper, whose face had gone pale. "You were totally freaked, weren't you?"

"No," Harper lied. "It's just gross. All these bugs . . ." She swatted at a mosquito that had just landed on her bare leg, then another whizzing past her nose. "They're everywhere."

"Easy way to fix that." Kaia stood up, her bronze Dolce bikini blending seamlessly into her deep tan. "Come on." Without waiting to see if her orders were followed—after all, they always were—she bounded toward the shoreline, kicking up a spray of sand in her wake.

Harper raced after her, and they reached the ocean's edge at the same moment. Harper stopped short as a wave of icy water splashed against her ankles, but Kaia didn't even hesitate. She waded out, the water rising above her calves, her knees, her thighs, and then, submerged to her waist, she turned and flashed Harper a smile. It was the eager, mischievous grin of a little kid sneaking into the deep end even though she's not quite sure how to swim. Harper waved, frozen in place, unable to force herself to go any deeper into the churning water, unwilling to go back.

Kaia took a deep breath, closed her eyes, and dove under the surface, her arms slicing through the water, pulling her into the deep. She resurfaced, gasping for air, and leaned back into an easy float, the salt water buoying her body, the gentle waves bouncing her up and down. Harper's shouts, dim and incoherent, blew past with the wind, but Kaia dipped her head back and the roaring water in her ears drowned out the noise.

Harper stood in the same spot, the tide carving deep rivulets around her feet as the waves washed in and back out again. The wind picked up, but the sky remained clear and blue. Harper stood, and Harper watched, and Kaia floated farther and farther out to sea—

And then she woke up.

She'd hoped the dreams would stop once she weaned herself off the Percodan. They hadn't. Just like the phantom pains that still tore through her legs when she tried to sleep, they'd outstayed their welcome.

For a long time, the pain had kept her awake.

Ambien had helped with that, the little pink pills that carried her mind away. But when sleep came, so did the dreams. They weren't always nightmares. Sometimes they were nice, carrying her away to somewhere warm and safe. Those were the worst. Because always, in the end, she woke up.

It was better just not to sleep.

But she needed her strength, they were always telling her. *For what?* she wanted to ask. For tolerating her disgustingly bubbly physical therapist? For avoiding phone calls and turning away visitors? For limping from her bedroom to the kitchen and back again? For zoning out through a *Little House on the Prairie* marathon because she was too lazy to change the channel? For turning two weeks of recuperation into four, inventing excuse after excuse until she no longer knew how much of the pain was real and how much was just expedient?

Maybe they were right. Because her strength had finally given out. She'd run out of imagined excuses, and the big day had arrived: back to school.

She'd already picked out the perfect outfit: an eggplant-colored peasant top with a tight bodice and sufficiently low neckline, a tan ruffled skirt that flared out at the bottom, and, just for added panache, a thin, gauzy black scarf woven through with sparkly silver.

After a long, too-hot shower, she slipped into the outfit, certain it made the right statement: *I'm back.* She brushed out her hair and mechanically applied her eye shadow, mascara, a touch of gloss, barely looking in the mirror; it was as if she went through the routine every morning, and this weren't the first time she'd dispensed with her cozy gray sweats since—

Since the accident. Since what had happened.

It still hurt her to say the words. It hurt to think them. And that was unacceptable. She couldn't afford to indulge in that kind of frailty, especially not today, when everyone would surely be staring at her, the walking wounded, waiting for a sign of weakness.

So she'd been practicing. Every day, she forced herself to think the unthinkable, to speak the hateful words aloud. She whispered them to herself before she drifted off to sleep, in hopes of forestalling the dreams. She murmured them while watching TV, while waiting for the doctor, while pushing her untouched food around on the plate—she had once shouted them at top volume, her stereo turned up loud enough to drown out her voice.

Speaking the truth didn't make it seem any more real. In fact, it sounded just as strange, just as surreal, each time it trickled off her tongue. And it always hurt. But she was hurting *herself*, and that gave her power. It made her feel strong, reminding her that there was nothing left to be afraid of.

She said them to herself now, as she hovered in the doorway, gathering her strength to face the day. The first day. She ran a hand through her hair, willing it not to shake. She zipped up the new boots that rose just high enough to cover the bandage on her left calf. She applied a final layer of Tarte gloss, then practiced her smile. It had to look perfect. Everything had to look perfect.

She took a deep breath and held herself very still. And then, softly but firmly, she said it:

"Kaia is dead."

And with that, Harper Grace was ready to go.

"Haven High!
Haven High!
Haven High!"

Beth Manning did her best to hold back a sigh at the roars of the crowd. When she'd volunteered to organize Senior Spirit Week, she hadn't taken into account the fact that it would require so much . . . spirit. That meant mustering up some kind of enthusiasm for the place she was most desperate to leave.

But that was her penance, right?

She forced herself to smile as she handed out the carefully crafted info packets to the rest of the Senior Spirit team. Too many tasks and not enough people meant Beth had been up for two days straight pulling things together; despite a morning espresso and a late-morning Red Bull, her energy level was still in the toilet.

"Let's hear it for the senior class!" she shouted now into the microphone, tossing back her long blond hair and aiming a blazing smile out at the crowd. She pumped her fist in the air, trying to ignore the embarrassment creeping over her. So she sounded like a cheerleader. So what? "Are you ready for an awesome end to an awesome year?" she cried.

College apps were in. Decisions were pending. Grades

were irrelevant. And, as tradition dictated, the senior class was treated to a whirlwind of activity: a senior auction, a community service day, a school spirit day, student-teacher sports challenges—day after day of celebration, kicked off by this inane afternoon rally. An official Haven High welcome to the beginning of the end, capped off by a very unofficial blow-out party

There'd be a lot of hangovers in the next couple weeks.

And a lot of girls weeping and guys manfully slapping one another on the back as the realization began to sink in: High school came with an expiration date.

It couldn't arrive soon enough, Beth thought, as she announced the schedule of upcoming activities in the perkiest voice she could muster.

Once, she would have enjoyed all of this. Even the marching band's off-key rendition of the school song. Even the cheerleaders firing up the crowd and the jocks preening under the spotlight. Especially the jocks—one of them in particular. Beth had been eager for college; she'd spent half her life preparing—studying, working, saving, dreaming—but she hadn't been eager to leave behind everything and everyone she knew. She would have mourned and celebrated with the rest of them, cheered and shouted and wept and hugged until it was all over.

But that was before.

As she stepped away from the microphone to let the

student council president make his speech, Beth's gaze skimmed across the crowd—until, without meaning to, she locked eyes with Harper. Only for a second. Then a lock of curly auburn hair fell across Harper's face, hiding it from view, and Beth looked away.

One glance had been enough to confirm it: The queen was back. Her lady-in-waiting Miranda hovered dutifully by her side, and in the row behind them, fallen courtier Adam, angling to get back into his lady's good graces. It was as if nothing had ever happened, and from the self-assured smile on Harper's face, Beth could tell that was just the way she liked it. Surely it would only be a matter of time before Harper and Adam picked up where they left off—

Stop, she reminded herself. She was done with all that bitterness, anger, and—she could admit it now—jealousy. She was better than that. And she owed Harper the benefit of the doubt, even if her former rival could never know why. She owed everyone the benefit of the doubt; that's what she had decided on that day last month. When you've screwed up everything, not just stepped over but set fire to the line, you needed all the good karma you could get. When you can't apologize for what you've done, and you can't fix it, all you can do is forgive others, and try to make everything better. And Beth was trying, starting with herself.

Even when it was hard; even when it seemed impossible.

After the accident, things are strange for days. Silent, still, as if a loud voice could break through the fragile frame of reality that they were slowly trying to rebuild. Eyes are rimmed with red, hands tremble, empty spaces sprinkle the classroom—absent faces who couldn't bear to stare at the chair that will stay empty forever.

Beth wants to stare at the chair in French class, but she sits in the front. So all she can do is tune out the substitute and imagine it behind her. And in her imagination, the seat is filled.

I'm not responsible, *Beth tells herself. It has become her mantra.* Not my fault. Not my fault.

But that feels like a lie. A comforting lie, supported by cool logic and endless rationales, but a lie nonetheless. There are too many what-ifs. What if Harper had been in the school, rather than in the car? What if Kaia had gone inside, rather than drive away? What if Harper hadn't had such a reason to escape?

Step one to being a better person: Forgive. She sees Adam every day at her locker, and on the fourth day, she talks to him.

"I'm not angry anymore," she says, wishing that it were true. "I don't hate you. Life's too short."

And it is. But when she looks at him, all she can think about is his bare body on top of Kaia's, the things they must have done together. And when he beams and hugs her, she can't forget that he pledged his love, then betrayed her. He slept with Kaia. She can't forgive that, not really.

Of course, she forgives Kaia, she reminds herself. Of course.

Next up is Kane.

"Apology accepted," she says, although he never apologized. He wrecked her life—tricked Adam into dumping her, fooled her into turning to Kane for comfort, trashing her reputation when the truth came out—and he walked away unscathed. Kaia helped. Not because there was anything in it for her; just for the fun of it. Just to see what would happen.

"I hope we can be friends," Beth says, hoping she never has to speak to him again.

Kane nods and walks away. He knows a lie when he sees it.

Beth smiles as she closes her locker. She smiles as she waves at someone across the hall.

She should start smiling more, she decides. Being a better person is supposed to feel good; she should look the part.

A round of applause snapped Beth back to the present, and she realized it was time to step up to the mic and wrap things up. "Welcome to senior spring," she announced, her voice nearly lost amid the cheers. "Let's get ready for the best time of our lives!"

"Is everything okay?" Miranda asked again.

Harper nodded, shifting her position on the narrow metal bench. The bleachers couldn't be very comfortable for her, Miranda suddenly realized, feeling like an idiot. Her leg was still healing, and with a sore neck and back . . .

"Do you want to take off?" Miranda asked. "We don't have to stay if you don't—"

"I'm fine," Harper said quietly. She stared straight ahead, as if mesmerized by Beth's ridiculous speech. A few months ago, the two of them would have been soaking up every absurd word, adding ammunition to their anti-Beth arsenal. Later Miranda would have them both cracking up over her Beth impersonation, complete with bright smile and frequent hair toss.

Or more likely, they would have skipped the rally altogether, snuck off campus to gossip and complain, then drunk a toast to their high school days drawing to a party-filled close.

Instead, Harper had insisted on attending. It was her first day back, and maybe she'd been looking forward to the crowds and excitement, or maybe she'd just wanted to get it over with; Miranda didn't know. She hadn't asked.

"Do you need anything?" she asked instead. "I could get us something to drink, or—"

"No. I'm fine."

"Are you sure?"

"Miranda, *I'm fine*," Harper snapped. "Can you give it a rest?"

"I'm sorry, I—"

"No, I'm sorry." Harper shifted in her seat again, rubbing her lower back. Miranda successfully resisted the urge to comment. "Really." Harper smiled—and maybe someone who hadn't been her best friend for almost a decade would have bought it. "I'm just . . . can we talk about something else? Please." It wasn't a request. It was an order.

No problem; Miranda was used to talking about something else. It's all they'd been doing since that first day, when Harper had finally agreed to visitors. Miranda had been on her best behavior; and she'd stayed that way.

Among the questions she knew better than to ask:

How do you feel?

What's it like?

Do you miss her?

What were you on, and why, when you humiliated yourself in front of the whole school?

Why did you get into the car? Where were you going?

What really happened?

It had been a long month of unspoken rules, and Miranda was almost grateful for them, as if they were bright flags dotting a minefield, warning her where not to step.

They never spoke Kaia's name.

They never talked about the fight, the betrayal that Miranda had forgiven the moment her phone rang with the news.

It made things easier. Like now—Miranda knew better than to mention the last time she'd been in this auditorium, shivering in an upper row of the bleachers while student after student somberly spoke of Kaia's grace and fortitude. Her beauty, her wit, her style—they never mentioned her cruelty or her penchant for causing misery, the way she thrived on other people's pain. They never mentioned the rumors swirling around her relationship with a certain former French teacher, lying in a hospital bed of his own, Kaia's fingerprints found at the scene of the apparent crime.

A wreath of flowers had lain at the center of the court, right where the Haven High mascot was currently doing cartwheels to rally the crowd. An enormous photograph of Kaia, bundled up in cashmere with windblown hair and rosy cheeks, had stood behind the podium, where Beth now raised her hands and clasped them in triumph. Kaia's father had already left town, maybe for good; Harper was still in the hospital. Miranda had sat alone, trying to force her mind to appreciate the tragedy of wasted youth, to force herself to weep or shake like all those girls who'd never even spoken to Kaia, who knew her only as the new-ish girl with the Marc Jacobs bag—unlike Miranda, who'd shared drinks with Kaia, shared a limo with Kaia, shared a best friend with Kaia.

Kaia, who was now dead.

That should mean something. It should be a turning point, one of those moments that make you see the world in a new way

But everything had seemed pretty much the same to Miranda, except that now the second-tier girls had a new strategy for sneaking onto the A-list; they'd been unable to befriend Kaia in life, but now there was nothing to stop them. It was still the same game, and it didn't interest her.

She'd thought instead about Harper, who, she'd been told, was in stable condition and recovering well. No visitors allowed, patient's orders.

She'd thought about how strange it was to see her math teacher cry.

She'd thought about whether her chem test that day would be cancelled.

And that was about it.

"So I've decided I hate all my clothes," Miranda said now, plucking at her pale blue T-shirt that had been washed so many times, she could no longer tell when it was inside out. "We're talking serious fashion emergency—and you know what that means. . . ."

Harper didn't say anything.

"Shopping spree," Miranda chirped. "You, me, Grace's finest clothing stores, and, of course"—she patted her purse—"Mom's gold card."

A faint smile crept across Harper's face. "I could use some new . . ."

"Everything?" Miranda prompted.

"You know it." She rolled her eyes. "Not that anything

in this town would be worth buying—you know Grace."

"It's a total fashion—" Miranda cut herself off just in time. *Train wreck*, she'd been about to say. "Wreck" was too close to "collision." Accident. And that was another thing on the list of what they couldn't discuss. "Wasteland," she said instead. "I guess if you want, we could drive down Route 53 and pick up some swank duds at Walmart. . . ."

Harper laughed, and it actually sounded real. "I'll pass, thanks. Hopefully Classic Rags will have some good stuff, and we can check out—oh."

"What?"

"It's nothing." Harper glanced off to the side. "It's just, I'm supposed to go to physical therapy this afternoon . . . but it's totally stupid. I can just blow it off."

"No!"

Harper's eyes widened, and Miranda softened her tone. "I just mean, no, you should go. We can shop any-time. You have to take care of yourself."

"It's really no big deal," Harper argued. Her fingers tightened around the edge of the bleacher seat.

"But you really should—"

"I guess, maybe. . . ."

"Unless there's some reason you actually want to—"

"Forget it." Harper stood up, wincing a bit as she put weight on her left leg. "You're right, we can shop another time. I'll see you later, okay?"

"Where are you going?" Miranda jumped up from her seat. "I'll come with you."

"I've got some stuff to do," Harper said, already walking away. "You should stick around here."

Once again, it wasn't a request. It was an order.

"Where are you taking me?" the redhead giggled as Kane Geary led her, blindfolded, down the empty hallway.

"That's for me to know"—he kissed the back of her neck, then ran his fingers lightly down her spine, relishing the burst of shivers it caused—"and you to find out. Come on"—Sarah? Stella? Susan?—"babe. Time to make your dreams come true."

He pulled her along faster, but she tugged back, slowing them down. "I can't see anything," she reminded him, squeezing his hand. "I'm going to trip."

"I'd never let you fall," he assured her. "Don't you trust me?"

She laughed. "I'm not that stupid."

Kane begged to differ. But not out loud.

"How about you take off the blindfold and just tell me where you're taking me?"

"Where's the fun in that?" Kane shook his head. "I've got a better idea." He hoisted her over his shoulder. Once she stopped wriggling and giggling, she lay pressed against him, her arms wrapped around his waist and her lips nuzzling the small of his back.

"All the blood's rushing to my head, Kane," she complained, "so you'd better hurry."

But he stopped.

A month ago, Kaia's locker had been transformed into a makeshift shrine, with a rainbow of cards and angel pictures adorning the front, above an ever-growing pile of flowers and teddy bears. There were notes, bracelets, magazine cutouts, candles—an endless supply of sentimental crap—but no photos. None of the mourners had any pictures of Kaia; none of them even knew her.

Even Kane had no pictures. Back in the fall, he, Kaia, and Harper had staged an illicit photo shoot, a faux hookup between Harper and Kane captured on film—and later doctored to make it appear that Beth was the one in his arms. Kane still had the original images stored away for a rainy day; but Kaia had stayed behind the lens. And Kane's mental picture was blurry. He remembered the way she'd felt, the one night they spent together—he remembered her lips, her skin, her sighs. But the room had been dark, and she'd been gone by morning.

For the first few days, there had been a strange zone of silence around her locker—you dropped your voice when you passed by, or you avoided it altogether. But then it faded into the background, just one of those things you barely noticed as you hurried down the hall.

Even Kane, who noticed everything, had successfully blocked it out after a few days of cringing and sneering. He'd almost forgotten it was there. And now it really wasn't.

The collage of cards and pictures had disappeared, with only a few stray, peeling strips of tape to remember them by. The pile of junk was gone—only a single teddy bear and a couple of votive candles remained, and as Kane watched, they too were swept up by the janitor, deposited in a large bin, and wheeled away.

Now it was just any other locker. Reduce, reuse, recycle.

"Kane, what is it?" the redhead asked, tickling his side. "Are we here? Wherever we are?"

"No, we're not here," he said, still staring at the locker. "We're nowhere."

It's just a locker, he told himself. *She doesn't need it anymore.*

He put the redhead back on her feet, tipped her blindfolded head toward his, and gave her a long kiss. Then he put his arm around her shoulder and guided her away from the locker, down the hall, toward the empty boiler room, where he'd prepared his standard romantic spread.

"We're two of a kind," Kaia had once told him. Meaning: icy, detached, heartless. Winners, who didn't need anyone else's approval to be happy, who sought out what they wanted and took it. Who didn't look back.

Wouldn't it be a fitting tribute to prove her right?

chapter two

ADAM WAS WAITING ON HIS FRONT STOOP WHEN
the car pulled into the driveway.

At first, he didn't move, just watched as Mrs. Grace
climbed out of the rusty Volvo, then scurried around to
the passenger's side to help her daughter.

Harper shrugged her off.

If you didn't know her, she would have looked perfectly
normal, Adam mused. Aside from a few fading scratches
on her face and neck, and a long scar on her left arm, she
looked totally fine. The same. And from a distance, you
couldn't even see that much; he'd only noticed the scar
this afternoon at the rally, sitting behind her, close enough

to see the thin white line arcing across her unusually pale skin, close enough for her to see him—and turn away.

From this distance, all he could see was her wild hair curling around her face, and the syncopated rhythm of her walk—not the familiar stride of superiority, as if she were a wealthy landowner touring her property, but a more tentative, irregular gait, small nervous steps that favored her right leg.

He called out; she didn't stop. But she was moving slowly enough that he could catch her.

"Adam, what a pleasant surprise," Amanda Grace said, favoring him with her unintentionally condescending smile—at least, he'd always assumed it was unintentional. Amanda Grace had always been nothing but kind to the boy next door, and probably had no idea how obvious her disdain for his mother or his circumstances truly was.

By any objective standard, her family was worse off than his—after all, his mother was the top Realtor in town, while the Graces ran a dry cleaners that even in good years barely broke even. But Adam and his trailer park refugee mother had poor white trash written all over them—and his mother's not-so-circumspect bed-hopping didn't help matters—while the Graces had their name.

It was pretty much all they had, aside from the stately but dilapidated home left over from boom times, but in the town of Grace, California, surrounded by Grace

Library, Grace Hospital, Grace Retirement Village, their name was enough.

"Would you like to come inside, Adam?" she asked, putting a hand on Harper's shoulder; Harper squirmed away. "I'm sure you could use a home-cooked meal."

"I'm sure he's got other plans," Harper said, her glare making it clear to Adam that if he didn't, he'd better make some.

"In that case, I'll give you two a chance to talk. Don't stay out too long, hon," she cautioned Harper as she stepped inside the house. "You need your rest."

"I'm *fine*, Mother."

Adam tasted victory. He was sure Harper had been about to duck inside as well—but now that her mother had cautioned her, Adam knew she'd stay out as long as possible. Even if it meant talking to him.

"What do you want?" she asked, and again, if you didn't know her, you'd think her voice perfectly pleasant. But Adam knew her—had grown up with her, briefly dated her, been betrayed by her, was finished with her—or so he'd thought, until he realized what "finished" could mean.

"Just wanted to see how you're doing," he said. "You haven't been returning my phone calls, and this afternoon we . . . didn't get a chance to talk." Because she'd kept her back to him the whole time and had left as quickly as she could.

"How sweet," she said coolly. "Thank you for asking. I'm fine, as you can see. So . . . ?"

"So?" he repeated hopefully, after a long pause.

"*So* is there anything else?"

"Oh." Adam looked down at his scuffed sneakers. "I thought we could hang out," he suggested. "We could go get some coffee, or just, you know, go out back. On the rock."

On our *rock*, he wanted to say, the large, flat bed of granite that separated their two backyards, where they'd played G.I. Joes, shared their secrets, kissed under the moonlight.

"I'm not really in the rock-sitting mood," she told him.

"Then let's go out," he pressed. "There's some band playing at the Lost and Found, and—"

"What band?"

Was that honest curiosity in her voice?

"Something like Blind Rabbits. Or maybe Blind Apes? I don't know—it's just some guys from school, and I'm sure they suck, but—"

"What do you want from me, Adam?" The curiosity—and all other emotion—was gone from her face. And in its blankness, it looked familiar. It looked like Kaia.

"Nothing. Just—I thought we could have some fun together. I want . . ." Screw the casual act, he decided. Nothing between them had ever been casual, and she couldn't change that just by pretending they were strangers. "I want to be there for you, Gracie." She flinched at the sound of her old nickname, but her face stayed blank. "I want to be your friend."

"You can't always get what you want," she half said, half sang, in a tuneless rendition of the Rolling Stones lyric. "And I'm not granting wishes these days. Sorry."

"I'm sorry too."

He has never seen her look so small, or so pale. She is swaddled in white sheets, her bandaged arms exposed and lying flat at her sides. He tries to ignore the tubes and wires, the intimidating machines with their flashing lights and insistent beeping.

Her eyes are closed. She's only sleeping, he tells himself.

But it's difficult to believe that when she's so pale and still.

The last time he spoke to her, he told her she was worthless—that he would be better off without her in his life. Everyone would be better off, he'd suggested. She told him she loved him. And he told her it wasn't love—it couldn't be, because she didn't have that in her. He'd sent her away.

And then she'd appeared onstage, drugged out and miserable, begging him to take her back in front of the whole school.

He'd been humiliated. Enraged. Until he got the phone call.

He sits down on the small plastic folding chair next to her bed and cradles her hand in his, careful not to move her arm. He doesn't want to hurt her. She doesn't wake up.

The room is empty. Her parents are in the cafeteria. The nurse just left. Adam is alone, and he can say what he needs to say. Even if she can't hear him.

"Please be okay," he begs her. "I need you."

He wishes she would open her eyes. Or squeeze his hand.

Talk to her, they'd told him. It can help.

"Remember when we were in fourth grade and I forgot my permission slip for that trip to the amusement park?" he asks. He feels stupid, even though there's no one to hear. But he keeps going. "And I started crying in front of everyone when Mrs. Webber told me I couldn't go? You tore your permission slip in half so you'd have to stay there with me. You missed out on your first roller coaster—" He stops and closes his eyes. He doesn't want to remember. "Just for me," he whispers. He wants to lay his head on her chest and listen to her heartbeat, confirm that it's steady and strong. But there are too many bandages and wires, and he's afraid he could hurt her. Even more.

He leans down, his face close to hers, and for a moment he is tempted to kiss her, convinced that, like Sleeping Beauty, the touch of his lips might bring her back. Instead, he rests his head on the pillow next to hers and whispers. He asks her to wake up. He tells her, again, that he needs her.

Still, she sleeps.

Adam lies motionless for a moment, watching her breathe, soothed by the rhythmic rise and fall of the white sheets. Then he sits up, stands, and says good-bye.

"I've got to go," he says. "I'm sorry. But I'll be back tomorrow."

If he had forgiven her sooner, and she hadn't made that speech . . .

If he had caught her before she had run out of the building . . .

If he had followed her to the parking lot, stopped her from getting into the car . . .

He knows she can't hear him, but he says it again. "I'm sorry."

"Nothing to be sorry about," Harper said, and the artificially casual tone was back in her voice. "I've got all the friends I need right now, and like I say, I'm fine, so you can forget that whole guilty conscience thing."

"That's not—"

"Better get inside now," she said, staring at a point over his shoulder. "Or my mother will send the dogs out for me. Thanks for stopping by."

"Harper, if we could just—"

"See you around." She turned her back on him and walked inside the house.

Adam wasn't ready to go home. No one was waiting for him there. So he circled around the back of his house and hoisted himself up onto their rock. He could see Harper's bedroom window; the shades were drawn. He lay back against the cool granite, staring up at the hazy sky, tinged with a grayish purple.

He thought he should be angry, or sorry, or hopeless. But he was just tired. He closed his eyes, and waited for sleep.

"Dude, get up!"

"Whuh . . . ?" Reed Sawyer propped himself up and shook his head, trying to get his bearings. A thick fog hung over his brain, courtesy of a mid-afternoon toke and nap session. But gradually, the blur of noise and color resolved itself into comprehensible details, and the world clicked back into place.

The cold, hard metal beneath him—the hood of his bandmate's car.

The loud voice harshing his buzz, the heavy hand shaking him awake—said bandmate.

The big emergency—a gig, their first in weeks. Tonight. Now.

Reed nodded to himself as the facts crawled back into his brain. He lay back against the hood and pulled out another joint. His fingers fumbled with the lighter, but it lit up, and a moment later, so did he.

He sucked in and grinned. That first lungful was his favorite part, the sweet familiar burn spreading through his body. Peace.

"What's with you—get the hell up!" The hand was shaking him again. His eyes had slipped closed without him noticing. Things were easier in the dark.

"Chill, Fish," he groaned. "I'm up."

"The gear's packed up, we've got to go," Fish complained. "What's with you, man? Do you *want* to be late?"

Did he want to be late? Reed didn't want . . . anything. To want, you had to think about the future, you had to think outside the moment. Reed drew in another lungful of smoke. Thinking about the future only led you to the past; it was safer to stay in the present.

"I'm coming," he said, digging into the pocket of his jeans to make sure he had his lucky guitar pick. "In a minute."

"Right." Fish grabbed his arm and dragged him up. "Get your ass off my car. You're coming now." He rolled his eyes and, with a laugh, grabbed the joint out of Reed's hand. "Didn't your mother ever teach you to share?"

As they ambled toward the van, Fish babbled about the gig, about possibilities, new songs, recording, making it big. Pointless dreams, Reed realized that now. But he kept his mouth shut.

The band didn't seem to matter much to him these days. Nothing did. Not since—

Before it happened, he'd almost gotten himself kicked out of school. He'd refused to apologize for something he hadn't done. It had seemed so important then: upholding his honor. Telling the truth.

At the thought of it, Reed almost laughed. What the

hell was the difference? That's what he'd figured out, after the accident. It didn't matter what you did or didn't do. If life wanted to kick you in the ass, no one could stop it. If the universe wanted to take away the one thing that mattered . . .

So he'd given in. He confessed, he took the suspension, went back to school. It was what everyone wanted, and that made it easy. He hadn't stopped to think about what he wanted. Because he didn't want anything. Not anymore.

"We got a surprise for you." Fish ran a hand through his greasy blond hair—he'd decided the tousled, wind-blown look would get him more girls. Stuck at the back of the stage, behind the drums, only his head was visible, he always pointed out. He couldn't do anything about his face, but the hair was a constant work in progress.

"Uh-huh."

"Aren't you curious?"

"No."

"You don't want a surprise?" Fish asked, sounding put out.

"Do I get a choice?"

Fish shrugged. "Good point." They'd reached the van, and Reed headed toward the driver's seat, as always. But Fish pushed him toward the back. "Not today. I'm driving, Hale has shotgun. You're in back."

Reed shook his head and slung himself into the van—

nearly landing in the lap of a tall, skinny brunette who was sprawled along the length of the backseat. Her legs were nearly bare, along with the rest of her.

"Uh . . . Fish?"

"Surprise!" Hale chuckled and twisted around to face the backseat. "Reed, meet Sandra. We thought she could cheer you up. She's a *big* fan." Hale's hands flickered briefly at his chest, universal code for bigness of a certain shape and form. Reed didn't need the tip. Sandra was bulging out of a tight leather halter top, her breasts seeming ready to escape at any moment.

"The boys told me I could ride along with you," Sandra said, in a soft, flighty voice. "Hope you don't mind."

He didn't want to touch her; but she was lying across his seat and showed no sign of moving. He nudged her gently and squeezed himself in. She grabbed his hand. "I love guitarists," she said, massaging his fingers. "Such a strong grip, all that flexibility—"

"Let's get going," Reed said. He leaned against the dirty window and stared out at the dull scenery. He tried to ignore the pressure of Sandra's body leaning against his, and the way her fingers were playing up and down his thigh. The bar was close. They'd be there soon.

"Whatcha thinking about?" she asked, after a few minutes of silence.

"Nothing."

He wished it were true. But every time he tried to wipe his mind, the words came back. Her voice. It was his own fault—he'd listened to the voice mail, the last voice mail, so often that he'd memorized it. And even now, wishing he could forget it, he couldn't stop hearing her voice.

Reed, I don't know if you want to hear this, but I need to tell you that I'm sorry. I was wrong, about everything.

Then there was a pause, and a loud, deep breath.

I'm sure you don't want to talk to me, but—

Her voice shook on the word.

I need to talk to you, to explain. Just call me back. Please. Because I—

Another pause. And this one was the worst, because he would never know what Kaia was about to say. And because he knew the last two words would be the last, and she would never know if he accepted them.

I'm sorry.

The joint was burned out, and he lit another one.

"The strong, silent type," Sandra said, winding her finger through one of his curls. "I like." She edged closer.

He inhaled deeply, blew out a puff of smoke, and waited for the calm to settle over him again. There was no other escape.

The timing was suspicious. An hour after the Adam encounter and Miranda called, suggesting—*quelle coïncidence!*—a night out at the Lost and Found to see the Blind Monkeys. Harper may have taken a hiatus from scheming, but she recognized the signs; so Miranda and Adam were teaming up to drag her out of the house and back to "normal" life? So be it. She had her own reasons for wanting to suffer through a Blind Monkeys performance; and if she ran into Adam, at least she'd be ready.

She just wasn't ready to face the *rest* of the senior class, Miranda having neglected to mention that the band was playing the official opening event for Senior Spirit Week. That meant crowds, noise, gossip, a night of public posturing . . . and no alcohol to dull the pain. At the request of Haven High, the Lost and Found had gone dry for the night, and Harper was left with few options. She and Miranda pulled two chairs up to a tiny, filthy table and set down their Cokes.

"This sucks," she complained, trying to make herself heard over the noise passing as music that was blasting out of a nearby speaker.

"What?" Miranda mouthed.

"This sucks!" Harper shouted. Miranda just shook her head, miming frustration. It was too loud for anything else. "I shouldn't have come," Harper said at normal volume, relishing the strange sensation of knowing no one would hear. "I hate—" She stopped, as the lyrics became clear.

Get out of my dreams.
Get out of my head.
Will I have to stick around this hell,
When I'm the one who's dead?

It was a shit song, but she knew who'd written it, and why. She'd wanted to see him—not *speak* to him, of course, but just watch him. Reed Sawyer, Kaia's . . . whatever. He was hunched over the mic, dark, shaggy hair falling across his glassy eyes, his voice coarse and throaty, scraping across the so-called melody.

She'd seen this band play once before, she suddenly realized. Months before, she'd come here with Adam, desperately hoping he would finally make his move, ending their friendship and starting something new. She'd come with Adam—but she'd left alone. And Adam had left with Kaia. Harper had cried and raged, while Kaia had whisked Adam away to an abandoned motel, laid him back on a sunken mattress, and fulfilled his fantasies.

Harper could still picture them together in a dark recess of the bar, Kaia's hands in his hair, Kaia's tongue in his mouth. And the Blind Monkeys blasting in the background, shaking the floor as Harper stood perfectly still, trying not to scream.

That bitch, Harper thought, before she could stop herself. Then she felt sick. *I never should have come back here.*

"I have to get out of here," she told Miranda. But Miranda only looked at her quizzically and took another sip of her soda. "I HAVE TO GO!"

Miranda nodded and, totally misunderstanding, pointed off to the left, toward the bathrooms.

Harper already knew where they were. It's where Adam had gone that night. He'd stood up from their table, headed for the bathrooms—and had never come back.

Maybe he'd had the right idea.

She made it outside before realizing she had nowhere to go. Miranda had the car keys, and it was too far to walk—especially when everything already felt so sore. Maybe it would be enough to stand outside, breathe some of that fresh air everyone always claimed was so helpful. She could wait it out. Maybe, eventually, she'd be able to go back inside.

Maybe not.

Harper leaned against the dank brick wall of the bar, not caring about the gunk that would surely rub off on her gauzy white shirt. Her leg hurt, her head hurt, and she needed some support. The wall would have to do.

"Who let you back out on the streets?" Kane smirked and leaned an arm against the wall, giving Harper a sardonic grin.

"What's it to you?"

"Just need to know who I should complain to," he teased. She rolled her eyes and turned away—he was sure it was to hide a smile. "Good to see you up and out, Grace."

"Miss me?" she asked, arching an eyebrow.

"I wouldn't say that—but you know I've got a low tolerance for boredom. And you definitely make things interesting."

"Gosh, I'm overwhelmed by your kindness and affection. Is this the part where you hug me and ask me how I'm doing?" Her tone was mocking, but Kane could tell she expected exactly that—and dreaded it.

Instead, he laughed. "You *have* been away for a long time," he said, shaking his head. "Why would I want to know how you're doing? I just want to know if you've got a cigarette."

That earned him his first real smile. And a pack of Camel Reds. He pulled one out, tossed the pack back to her, and took his time lighting up. "So . . . ," he finally said. "Are we going in, or what?"

She waved lazily toward the entrance. "You go. Say hi to the pep squad for me. And enjoy your ginger ale."

"Meaning?"

"Meaning I'd rather bash my head into this wall than go back inside," she said bitterly. "But hey, be my guest."

"Better idea." He wiggled his eyebrows at her and

cocked his head toward the parking lot. Translation: *Let's get out of here and get into some trouble.* "You in?"

"Let me just text Miranda," she said, whipping out her phone, "and then"—she did some rapid-fire typing and put it away again—"we're out of here."

She stumbled on the way to the car, and he caught her before she fell; but he resisted the urge to help her inside the silver Camaro. She was back on two feet again—she could do it herself. Or at least, he concluded, she thought she could. He slammed the door shut, started the car, slipped in his favorite CD and turned the pulsing rock beat up to top volume, and they were off.

Grace was a dead-end town whose residents led dead-end lives—meaning there were plenty of dark, dingy spots where you could drown your sorrows. And none of them carded.

They ended up nestled in a booth in the back of the Tavern, a nondescript bar and grill for the over-forty set, complete with a washed-out seventies decor and surly middle-aged waitresses who'd been working there since the decorations were new.

Privacy guaranteed, or your money back.

Harper, after downing half a gin and tonic—her first in weeks—was already slurring her words. Kane, more on half-formed instinct than out of any reason or desire, had opted for root beer.

"When did you join AA?" Harper joked, flopping

forward in her chair and propping her head in her hands. "Gonna leave me all alone to drown my sorrows?"

"Someone's got to drive you home," he pointed out as she downed the rest of her drink and waved the waitress over for another one.

"S'okay, I'm used to alone," she slurred, as if she hadn't heard him. "I mean, they're always there, *everyone's* always there, staring at me. Alone is good. They should all go away."

"You want me to stop staring at you?"

She let out a sharp bark of laughter, then slapped her hand over his. "Not you. You're the only one. You . . ." She stopped talking, distracted by the prospect of fishing the slice of lime out of the bottom of her glass.

"I . . . ?" he prodded.

"What? Oh. You don't give me that 'How are you doing' shit or 'Isn't it terrible aren't you traumatized what can I do' blah blah blah." She made a fake vomiting noise. "You don't care about what I do, you don't care about anyone but yourself. Thank God."

"Uh, thank you?" he asked sardonically. He leaned forward. This was the moment, he realized. Kane hated nothing more than not having the answers, and ever since that day in the hospital, he'd had nothing but questions. Her guard was down. She would answer. "Where'd you get the drugs, Grace?"

"Huh?"

"That day. The speech. What were you high on? And why?"

She shook her head furiously. "Not you, too!" But after a flicker of anger, she sighed loudly and slumped down in her chair. "Nothing," she said. "I told you. I told them. Nothing."

"Come on, Grace," he pushed. "They found them in your system. Everyone saw you up onstage—I heard what a head-case you were." *And I saw the way you pulled out of the parking lot. I saw the car skid out, I saw you drive away.* "You were on *something*."

She shrugged her shoulders. "Believe me. Don't believe me. Who cares. And what's the difference? It's over now."

"Yeah, I guess. What's the difference?"

He is sitting in the waiting room, breathing shallowly. The scent of citrus-scented air freshener is overwhelming—but not enough to mask the smells beneath it. Old age, decay, vomit, blood, death. He hates hospitals. He hasn't been in one since he was a kid, sitting by his mother's bed, pretending not to know his father was crying out in the hall.

It's too soon, too fast, and no one knows everything, but as always, Kane knows enough. He has his sources.

One crash. Two girls, both thrown from the car. One with traces of psychotropic drugs in her bloodstream. One dead.

"*Mr. Geary.*"

The cop sits down across from him. It's a woman, which he's not expecting. She's short and stocky in a dark gray blazer, her hair pulled back in a tight bun. Right out of central casting, he thinks. Not a coincidence—she probably takes her cues from Law & Order.

The thought depresses him.

"*I'm told that you have some information that can be of assistance to us, Mr. Geary.*"

She has a sexy voice.

He shrugs. "*I saw them leave the school,*" *he says.*

"*Can you describe what you saw?*" *She doesn't ask what he was doing loitering on the back steps when the rest of the school was stuffed into the auditorium for a mandatory assembly.*

"*Harper ran out of the school.*"

"*How did she appear?*"

"*What do you mean?*" *He knows. But he's not in the mood to help.*

"*Did she seem upset? Disoriented? Ineb—*"

"*She seemed in a hurry. She didn't stop to talk. She ran down to the parking lot. Kaia was standing there, by her car.*"

"*What was she doing?*"

The question hadn't occurred to Kane before. He didn't know the answer. He never would. "*Standing. Staring. They talked for a while. Then they got into the car and drove away.*"

"*Who was driving?*"

It is the question he has been waiting for. She asks it casually, as if uninterested in the answer. He responds the same way, without pause, without hesitation, without thinking of Harper grabbing the keys, jumping inside, and tearing out of the lot.

"Kaia," he says with certainty. "It was her father's Beamer. She always drove."

They believe him. The evidence has all burned away. There's only his word. And when Harper wakes up, groggy and confused, she believes him too.

"I can't remember," she says, her voice soft but angry. These days, she is always angry. "Nothing. Just school, that morning, then . . . here. I can't remember." She closes her eyes and knits her brow. She can't rub her forehead—her arms are caught in a web of wires and tubes. He surprises himself, pressing his palm to her head, brushing her hair off her face.

"There's nothing to remember," he tells her. "You two got into the car. And Kaia drove away."

It's the last time he sees her. Soon she's done with visitors, except Miranda. But he knows she believes him.

They all do.

Some days, he even believes himself

He drove Harper home, stopping only once for her to hop out and throw up in some bushes.

"Sorry," she said weakly, climbing back into the car.

"We've all been there," he assured her. "Just as long as you don't hurl in my car." He patted the dashboard fondly.

"Then I dump you out on the side of the road and you can find your own way home."

She chuckled—then moaned and leaned forward, cradling her head in her arms as if the laughter made her brain hurt. He knew the feeling. "That's what I love about you," she said in a muffled voice. "There's no confusion about where your loyalties lie. You look out for your car—"

"Of course."

"You look out for yourself—"

"Naturally."

"And the rest of us can find our own way home."

"You know me too well, Grace." His fingers tightened around the steering wheel. "You always have."

chapter three

"CAN I CARRY YOUR BOOKS FOR YOU?"

"Can I get you a soda?"

"Could I stand in line and get you some lunch?"

"She said *I* could stand in line!"

"But you got to drop her stuff at her locker—"

"Girls!" Harper massaged her temples as the two girls abruptly stopped their bickering.

"What is it?"

"What do you need?"

She sighed. She'd been waiting for this moment for three years, ever since she'd spent one eternal day sophomore year traipsing around after a bitchy blond senior with an undeserved superiority complex. King and Queen for a Day was a senior tradition—on paper, it meant that each underclassmen showered his or her designated senior with affection and treats. In reality, it meant spending the day being primped and pampered by your own personal servant—or, in Harper's case, two.

Who knew being waited on hand and foot could be so exhausting?

Of course, perhaps she could have enjoyed the novelty of the experience a bit more had the two underclassmen in question not spent the better part of the year following her around and imitating her every move. A theme song from one of those old nick@nite shows floated into her head: *They laugh alike, they walk alike, at times they even talk alike—you can lose your mind . . .*"

That sounded about right. And now Mini-Me and her best friend Mini-She were stuck to her like glue, jockeying for the right to clean off her cafeteria seat. *The best time of my life?* Harper thought dryly. *Starting when?*

"Why don't you go get me something from the vending machine," she suggested to Mini-She, then turned to Mini-Me. "And you can go buy me some lunch."

"Coke? Diet Coke? Sprite? Vitamin Water? Gatorade? Snapple?"

"Salad? Meat loaf? Meat loaf and salad? And what kind

of dressing? And what if there are fries? Or some kind of vegetable? Or—?"

"Vitamin water. Salad, make sure it's not just lettuce, Italian dressing. And—" It was going to be a long day; she deserved a treat. "Plenty of fries."

They were gone, and she was left with a blessed silence, so sweet that she was disinclined to scope out the cafeteria and find herself an appropriately high-powered table; better just to stand to the side for a moment and try to gather her strength. She'd been working on her icy, expressionless face, and she deployed it now. You never knew who was watching.

She didn't notice him at first—people like that flew below her radar; and even when she registered his presence, dimly, all she noticed were the ripped jeans and the scuffed sneakers, the long hair and the grease-stained fingers, and she expected him to pass her by.

It wasn't until he spoke that she looked at his face.

"Hey." He slouched against a wall and tilted his head down, looking at her briefly, then looking away again, as if stealing glances at the sun.

"Hey." No stolen glances here; she stared, unabashedly, trying to figure out what Kaia had seen in him. There must have been something, but it was well disguised. True, his black T-shirt hugged some impressive arm muscles, and he did have that whole dark, sullen man of mystery thing going for him. But judging from the smell, the only mystery was how he'd managed to afford so much pot.

Probably grew his own, Harper decided. That's what they always did on TV.

She knew she should say something caustic and send him away; he wasn't the type she should be seen talking to, especially not now, with her reputation on the bubble. But she was too curious to hear what he was going to say—and how *she* was going to respond.

"I'm Reed," he said.

"Yeah, I know."

"Kaia and me, we—"

"Yeah, I know that, too." She didn't, not really. Kaia had never talked much about her life. But she'd dropped enough hints, and Harper had witnessed one kiss steamy enough to confirm that *something* was going on.

"I want to ask . . . I need to know . . ."

She felt a fist tighten around her heart. She'd been waiting for this, she realized. He would want to know all about it, what happened, every detail. *Did she suffer? Did she scream? Did she know?*

I don't remember! Harper wanted to shout. *I know what you know. Leave me alone.* But she stayed silent and kept her placid, patient smile fixed on her face. Maybe she wanted him to ask. At the very least, she could understand why he wanted to know: She did too.

"Were you two, like, friends?"

"What?" It was so far from what she'd been expecting that it took her a moment to process.

"I don't know, I just thought—how are you, uh, doing?"

Harper let out a ragged breath, a precursor to a laugh or a sob—she wasn't sure which. What did he want, some kind of partner in crime for his adventures in grieving? As if the two of them would walk off hand in hand somewhere and cry on each other's shoulders? As if she could ever open up to someone like him?

If not him, then who?

"Uh, anyway, if you ever need, like, to talk—" He put a hand on her shoulder. A wave of emotion washed through her, and it wasn't the annoyance or revulsion she would have expected. It was comfort—and gratitude. *You too*, she wanted to say. But she couldn't force the words out.

"Ex*cuse* me?" Mini-She slammed three bottles down on the table and advanced toward Reed, hands on hips. "What are *you* doing here?"

"Am I hallucinating, or are you, like, touching her?" Mini-Me chimed in, sliding a heaping lunch tray next to the drinks and joining her co-clone.

"You must be hallucinating," Mini-She pointed out, "because no way would someone like *him* be bothering someone like *us.*"

"Don't you have, like, an engine to build?" Mini-Me asked. "Or some fires to set?"

"He's probably just begging for funds for his next pot buy," Mini-She suggested. She waved disdainfully. "Sorry, but charity hour's over for the day. Better luck next time."

Harper wanted to stop them, but if she did that, and took a stand, it would surely mean something—and she didn't have the energy to find out what.

"Yeah . . . ," Reed mumbled. "This was a mistake. Later."

"Try never!" Mini-Me called as he ambled away. Then she burst into giggles. "God, Harper, were you actually *talking* to that waste of space?"

"You're such an airhead," Mini-She taunted her friend. "She's Queen for a Day, remember? She was just waiting around for us to get rid of him for her."

"Which, by the way, you're welcome." Mini-Me did an exaggerated curtsy. "We're at your service, as always."

"Great job," Harper said weakly. She slumped into a chair at the nearest table. The giggle twins bounced down beside her.

"They didn't have Vitamin Water," Mini-She explained, pushing a handful of bottles across the table. "So I got you some Sprite, and Diet Coke, and some

Poland Spring, and I can go back if you want something else. . . ."

"And the salad looked kind of dingy," Mini-Me added, setting a tray in front of Harper. It was piled high with a lump of brownish slime, surrounded by heaps of creamy beige sludge. "So I got you the . . . well, I'm not sure what it is, but there's plenty of protein. And then I got the mashed potatoes instead of the fries, you know, so there'd still be something healthy. . . ."

They gazed at her from across the table, identical expressions of nervous excitement trembling on their faces.

Harper felt sick at the thought of eating anything, especially the steaming heap sitting before her. She felt even sicker at the thought of sending the idiots away with a bitchy comment or two—much as she longed for some alone time, their words to Reed still hung in the air. They'd just been imitating her; she couldn't bring herself to repay the favor.

"This is great, guys," she said instead. "Everything's fine. Thanks." She grabbed the Sprite and took a fake sip. Ten minutes, she promised herself, and then she'd be up and out.

"You okay, Harper? You look kind of pale."

"Yeah, and no offense, but you're a little, like, sweaty. You sure you're okay?"

The more times she had to say it, the bigger the lie. But it's not like she had any other option.

"No worries," she assured them. "I'm fine."

"Beth, we still need a head for this article," the copy editor called out.

"And we're missing a photo for the Valentine's Day piece," the features editor called from the other side of the room.

Beth typed faster, trying to load in the changes to the front-page layout so she could deal with the hundred other things on her to-do list. It was times like this, rushing back and forth across the newsroom, slurping coffee, cutting and pasting, slapping on headlines, tweaking leads, and refereeing the occasional game of Nerf basketball, that she felt like a real editor in chief, the nerve center of a well-oiled fact-finding machine.

Then she remembered that, despite her best efforts, the paper rarely came out more than once a month—and when it did appear, its heartfelt missives on Homecoming Day hairdos and the debate team's latest victory ended up littering the floor of the cafeteria, crumpled and tossed aside before anyone had bothered to read them.

They weren't a complete failure, she reminded herself. They'd managed to get a special Kaia memorial supplement out a couple weeks ago, filling it—despite the short notice and lack of sources—with photos, poems, and the occasional testimonial from someone who professed to have known and loved "that dear, departed soul." Several of Beth's teachers had complimented her on the fine tribute. It wasn't the kind of compliment from which you could draw much joy—especially when you were still swimming in guilt.

Now things were back to normal, if you could call it normal when your front page featured an article about the sordid criminal past of the paper's former sponsor. Beth should have been pleased: It was just the kind of hard news she'd always imagined importing to the *Haven Gazette* when she finally took the reigns. Along with all her other big plans, that dream had fallen by the wayside back in the fall, after her encounter with Mr. Powell.

Perhaps it was only fitting that, courtesy of Mr. Powell and his misdeeds, the *Gazette* was finally reporting something that mattered.

Beth had long dreamed of covering a story like this, rich with tantalizing details and actual import. But not *this* story. She hadn't rushed an issue into print, hadn't assigned anyone to pester the cops or the administration for details. Instead, she'd just picked up the story that had run in the *Grace Herald* earlier that month. It would be reprinted verbatim. And it would have to do.

STUDENT-TEACHER SCANDAL
ROCKS HAVEN HIGH

Police uncover secret identity as French teach skips town

By Milton Jeffries
Staff writer, *Grace Herald*

Massachusetts state police are pursuing Jack Powell, aka Julian Payne, for questioning in regard to two statutory rape cases allegedly involving the former Haven High School French teacher. Grace police are similarly eager to question him regarding his relationship with Kaia Sellers, a Haven High senior who was killed in a hit-and-run the same week Powell fled town. Police have ruled the incident an accident and concluded it was unconnected.

Powell joined the Haven High faculty in the fall, professing several years of teaching experience and proffering impeccable–and apparently forged–references. The first indication that anything was amiss came in late January, when an anonymous tip led paramedics to discover Powell unconscious in his apartment. Kaia Sellers's fingerprints were found at the scene, but she was killed the next day, before she could be questioned. Powell's fingerprints, when run through a national database, revealed him to be Julian Payne, a British citizen who had disappeared from Stonehill, Massachusetts, six months earlier when allegations were made against him by two unnamed teenage girls.

Authorities at Stonehill Academy say that both girls are well-behaved, honor roll students who are to be commended for speaking out against their teacher. "We're all grateful that they had the courage [to turn Payne in] and prevent this from happening again," said Stonehill principal Patrick Darnton.

In Grace, area parents have expressed deep concern that a teacher with his background could have been employed by the high school; district officials say they had no sign Powell was not what he seemed.

Powell left the hospital, against medical advice, before Grace police were able to detain him. He has not been seen since.

She doesn't know why she came.

Hospitals have always seemed dirty to her, grimy, as if the grayish tinge to the walls and the floor were just germs made visible, layers of illness, fluids, and death that had built up over the years.

Still, she comes here often, forces herself to suffer through the candy striping, pediatric parties, holiday gift distributions. She knows where the bedpans are stored and which nurses ignore the call light. And she knows where all the exits are; from the moment she steps inside, she is always planning her escape.

She has come to see Harper, but she doesn't know why, and she doesn't have the nerve to go through with it. She steps off the elevator and starts down the hallway, but there is Adam, hovering outside the room next to the Graces, whom she recognizes because, in a small town, there is no one you don't know. She stops. She has nothing to say to any of these people. She has nothing to apologize for.

She has everything to apologize for.

Before she knows what she's doing, she turns around, is back at the elevators, pressing the button, waiting. It has been like this all week. Doing things without knowing why. Making decisions without even noticing. She wonders if she is in shock. Not over Kaia's death—none of that seems real yet; it all has the feel of a bad movie she wandered into that will surely end soon. No, if she is in shock, it is over what she has done, which is all too real and tangible, like the empty box on the edge of her nightstand that used to contain two yellow pills. She should throw it out, now that it's not just a box—now that it's evidence—but she can't bring herself to do so.

The elevator doors open and she steps on blindly, just as she does everything, which is why she doesn't see him until the doors close and it's too late.

"Now this is a pleasant surprise," he says, in the soft British accent she still hears in her nightmares. "And here I thought I'd have to leave without saying good-bye."

She ignores him. There is a vent in the ceiling of the elevator, and from a certain angle she can see through the slits and watch the walls of the shaft sliding by. There is a fan in the vent, its sharp blades spinning fast enough that they would slice off a finger if she were tall enough to reach.

"I'm fine, thanks for asking," he says. Unable to help herself, she glances toward him. There is a large white bandage on his forehead. His skin is pale. "Just a concussion, nothing to worry about."

"I wasn't," she says sharply.

He smiles at her, and then his face goes flaccid, his eyes flutter, and he stumbles backward, slamming into the console of buttons, catching himself just before he slumps to the floor. The elevator jerks to a stop. Beth says nothing, does nothing. He breathes deeply once, twice, as if willing the color back into his face and the strength back into his body. His head lolls to one side, and he grasps the railing on the wall for support. There is nothing Beth can do to help; she need not feel guilty for doing nothing.

She feels guilty for being glad about it.

More deep breaths, and soon, his face is no longer white, and the smile is back. And the elevator is not moving.

"I'm fine now," Powell says, touching his forehead gently. "Happens sometimes."

She doesn't say anything.

He steps away from the wall to look at the console. "I must have hit the emergency stop button. Not to worry, I'll have us moving again. Momentarily."

"You just need to flip the lever," Beth says, hating to acknowledge him but needing to escape. "It'll start up again."

Instead, he turns his back on the console and steps toward her. She jerks away, but of course, there is nowhere to go. Beth, who knows all the exits, knows that better than anyone.

"You're never sorry?" he asks, and he sounds almost plaintive.

"For what?"

"You misjudge me, you know." His voice is soft, and his eyes kind, as they were at the beginning, when the two of them worked long hours in the tiny newsroom, bent over layouts, their heads together. She'd called him Jack, cried on his shoulder, imagined what it might be like were she ten years older. She was no longer fooled. "We understood each other, or we could have. I could have taught you a lot. I could have been a friend. Things might have been . . ." He looks off to the side and sighs. "Different."

"Flip the lever," she says through gritted teeth. "Now."

"Scared?" He takes two rapid steps toward her and, before she can move, he's planted his arms on either side of her, pinning her against the wall. She is trembling. "You're a smart girl." His face is inches from hers, his breath sour. She knows she should do something. Spit. Scream. But she's frozen. "I could do anything." He leans closer, his eyes locked with hers. When their lips are about to touch, he stops. "But I won't."

His arms drop to his sides, and he steps backward again. "Disappointed?"

"Go to hell."

He shakes his head. "There's a part of you, Beth, that wants it. I knew it the moment we kissed—"

"When you *kissed* me," *she snaps.*

"When we *kissed, I could tell. You want a lot of things you're not allowing yourself to want. You don't let yourself do anything about it, but that doesn't change the facts."*

"You don't know anything about me," she whispers. Her throat is tight, as if she's having one of those dreams where she wants to scream but can't make a sound.

"I know girls," he says, nodding. A lock of brown hair flops over his eyes, and he brushes it away. The gesture reminds her of an old Hugh Grant movie. Adorable British charmer fumbles through life and gets the girl. She'd wanted a romantic-comedy life, maybe. But she hadn't wanted him, she insisted to herself, not really. She hadn't wanted this. "And I know you. You may be fooling everyone else with that good-girl act, Beth, but you can't fool me. I'm just sorry you felt you had to try."

He flips the lever, and the elevator jerks into motion.

As the doors open, he gives her a cheery salute. "Until we meet again . . . and something tells me we will."

She doesn't say good-bye.

Anyone with information about the whereabouts of Jack Powell or knowledge of his relationship with the late Kaia Sellers should contact the Grace Township Police Department, 555-0145.

"Beth, are we set with that article? We've got to lock the front page," the deputy editor reminded her.

She had an hour left before the paper went in for final proofing, then she had a history presentation to give, and afterward would rush off for yet another job interview, then home, where she could divide the rest of her night between studying for her math test, babysitting her little brothers, and working the phones to finalize logistics for Spirit Day and the senior auction.

She didn't have time to linger over Powell anymore. She clicks a button on the mouse and locks the article. "This one's set," she told her deputy. "Let's move on."

Miranda heard the chorus of blondes before she saw them, and their voices—high, flirtatious, infused with a permanent giggle and inevitably ending on a question mark—told her everything she needed to know. As she rounded the corner and approached the lockers, one look confirmed her suspicions. A harem of sophomores, outfitted in standard uniform: high boots, short skirt, tight shirt, and enough makeup to paint a house.

And there was Kane, towering above them, intense brown eyes sparkling under his chiseled brow, and his smile . . . that smile was going to destroy her, Miranda often thought. It filled her daydreams—all her dreams, in fact—and rendered her powerless.

She was no better than any of these girls, except that she kept her simpering to herself. And look where it got her: They fluttered around the flame, and she lurked in the shadows, just passing through, nothing to see here but dull, drab Miranda.

She would just keep her head down, she told herself. Walk quickly and quietly down the hall and slip into study hall without anyone noticing her.

"Yo, Stevens! What's the hurry?"

She turned toward the syrupy smooth voice and at the sight of his familiar smirk was helpless not to favor him with one of her own.

"Looks like you've got your hands full at the moment," she told him, flicking a hand toward the girls.

"Beauties fit for a king, don't you think?" He gave them a magnanimous wave. "Ladies, you can take your leave for the moment—"

"But Kane, we're here to serve you," one of the blondes reminded him in a throaty voice.

"What if there's something you need?" another asked.

"And we can provide *anything* you need," the first reminded him.

"I'm sure Stevens here will take good care of me while you're gone."

The pom-pom posse looked her up and down. "Doubtful," one of them grouched. But they knew their role in this little drama: They followed orders and disappeared.

"That," Miranda began, shaking her head, "may be

the most disgusting display I have ever seen."

Kane shrugged. "Give them a break—they're young, impressionable, and hey, it's hard not to go weak in the knees when you're in the presence of greatness."

"I'm not talking about them, your highness," Miranda snorted. "I'm talking about you. Could you be any more of a pig?"

He curled an arm around her shoulders and tugged her toward him. "You know you love it."

"How do you fit that huge ego into that tiny car of yours?" she teased.

"How do you fit that huge chip on your shoulder into that teeny tiny T-shirt?" he retorted.

Miranda blushed, pretending not to notice that *he'd* noticed her unusually snug shirt—though, of course, why else had she worn it?

"Don't give me that modest act," he chided her. "You know you look good." His hand glided down her back and Miranda caught her breath. "Sure you don't want to . . ."

God, did she want to. "We talked about this," she reminded him. She patted him on the shoulder and shook her head sympathetically. "It's so sad—no impulse control. Good thing I'm around to remind you of the rules."

"Rules are made to be—"

"Followed," she cut in. "Otherwise, why make them?"

And she was the one who'd made them, of course,

much as she hated them. It was funny: She'd spent years hoping that Kane would notice that she'd grown past the tomboy phase and had actually sprouted a chest (sort of) and a healthy sex drive (at least when he was around). And now that he had finally noticed her—finally *kissed* her— she spent half her time fighting him off.

Okay, not so funny—more like tragic. But his brilliant friends-with-benefits plan had a few holes. One gaping hole, actually—the one that would appear after Miranda's heart shriveled up and disappeared, as it surely would after a few weeks, when Kane got bored of his no-strings-attached foreplay and moved on to his next conquest. She wanted more than that—she *deserved* more than that, she told herself, though she wasn't quite sure she believed it. She'd like to think she was pushing him away to preserve her dignity, but really, it was just self-protection.

So when he'd made a move, she'd made a rule:

No kissing.

Also: No fondling, flirting, or foreplay. No stroking, no tickling, no grabbing.

No fun, he'd pointed out. But then he'd shrugged and laughed. Your game, your rules, he'd said.

Since then, they'd gone back to their default mode of snarky banter—with a twist. Now half the time the banter was tinged with sexual innuendo, and occasionally, when bored, Kane seemed to enjoy testing their new boundaries. "Does this count as a kiss?" he'd ask, playfully whispering in her ear with his lips against her skin. "Is this stroking, or just heavy petting?" he'd tease, smoothing down her long, reddish hair.

Sometimes, she suspected that knowing she was off limits actually made him want her more; sometimes she suspected that had been her plan all along.

In the meantime, she pretended it was all a game, one whose outcome didn't faze her one way or the other. She pretended that, like him, she was putting aside lust for the good of their growing friendship; hoping he'd never suspect the true four-letter L word that lay behind it all. It was torture, but the sting was sweet and sharp, like when you bit your tongue and then couldn't stop worrying the tender spot against your teeth, half enjoying the taste of pain.

"When are you going to loosen up, Stevens?" he asked, heaving a sigh that she knew was all for show.

"As soon as you grow up, Geary."

"Never!" He leaped back with a look of horror, then whipped out a pen and posed, brandishing it as if it were a sword. "Just call me Peter Pan."

Miranda grinned despite herself. "My very own lost boy. Aren't I lucky?"

"And you, lovely lady, can be my Wendy . . . or perhaps you'd prefer Tinker Bell?"

"Tinker Bell? Give me a break." Miranda winked; then, in a single, lightning-quick gesture, snatched the pen out of his hand while circling behind him, wrapped an arm around his waist, and pressed the edge of the pen against his neck as if it were a blade. "More like Captain Hook."

"Mr. Morgan," the secretary said, eyeing him suspiciously, "she'll see you now. Go right in."

Adam sighed and stuffed his iPod back into his back-pack. Secretaries used to love him—but then, that was back when he only got called down to the administrative wing to pick up his latest trophy or talk to some local reporter about breaking an all-school record. He was even trotted out at the occasional school board meeting, an example for the community, of Haven High's "exceptional athletic organization." But ever since starting an on-court brawl and getting suspended for a week, Adam had noticed a definite chill in his relationship with the administration, including the secretaries.

That's all behind me now, Adam reminded himself. He'd been angry—*too* angry—for a long time. After everything had happened, he'd resolved to get some control over himself. Forgive, forget, chill out. Get his act together. And it was working . . . so far.

He slung his backpack over one shoulder and stood up, trudging slowly toward the guidance counselor's door. Of all the doors in all the offices in all Haven High, this was his least favorite. Ms. Campbell didn't care if he'd broken the butterfly relay record or led the basketball team to its first regional championship in a decade. All she ever wanted to talk about was his classes, his work, his SATs—and all she ever wanted to know was how he could accept being so subpar. She wouldn't accept it, she always promised him. What she didn't get was that *he* didn't accept it, either. But he didn't know what else he was supposed to do.

"Come in, Adam. Sit down." She waved him in, offering him a decrepit hard candy from the overflowing china dish at the edge of her desk. He waved it away. An elderly, overweight woman whose gray hair and wire-rimmed glasses gave her an unfortunate resemblance to Ben Franklin, Ms. Campbell served as a part-time health teacher, part-time English teacher, part-time PTA liaison, and full-time busybody. She'd been the Haven High guidance counselor for thirty years—which made a fair number of students question her guidance-giving credentials. Not to mention her sanity. Three decades in Haven's hallowed halls wouldn't represent a bright future; it sounded more like a prison sentence.

Ms. Campbell pushed a mound of clutter across her desk—Adam caught a snow globe moments before it crashed to the ground—making room for his permanent file. She flipped it open and peered at him over the rims of her glasses.

"How are things going, Adam?" she asked, frowning. "Anything happening in your life? Any concerns you'd like to express?"

Was anything happening? Aside from his two best friends teaming up to ruin his life? Aside from breaking up with one girl, falling in love with another, then breaking up again, all in the space of a month? Aside from one of those girls almost dying in a car crash and then refusing to speak to him?

And, oh yeah, aside from the fact that the girl to whom he'd lost his virginity had ended up *dead*, and he was still having dreams about the night he'd spent with her— dreams that turned into nightmares as her flesh burned away in his arms?

Aside from that?

"Nothing much." Adam shrugged. "Just, you know, the usual."

"Well, *I* have some concerns," she said. "Maybe we can talk about that." She began flipping through the file. "Your grades have never been . . . let's just say you've never worked up to your full potential."

Guidance counselors loved that kind of talk. Potential. Aspirations. Opportunity. None of it meant anything to Adam. It was all just a bunch of abstract bullshit designed to make you play along with their game and do whatever they said. He didn't need the stress; he was happy just hanging with his friends and playing ball, and the rest would take care of itself.

"But this year, your teachers have alerted me to a distinct dip in your grades," Ms. Campbell said. She looked up from the file and fixed him with a sharp gaze. "Are you aware that you're failing most of your classes?"

"Uh . . . no." He began to tense up, realizing this wasn't going to be some generic meeting he could just ignore. He'd never had the best grades—but he'd never failed before, either. Of course, in the past, he'd had Beth by his side, forcing him to get the work done, and to do it right. Now he was on his own.

"What are your plans for the future, Adam?"

"The future?" Another one of those words guidance counselors liked to toss around, as if the future was really something you could plan for. If he'd learned anything this year, he'd learned that was a joke.

"Next year. We've only got a few months until graduation. Have you thought at all about what you're going to do?"

Adam shifted uncomfortably in his seat. He preferred not to think about graduation, and the gray space that lay beyond it. He'd ignored the whole college applications thing. There was always community college, down the road in Ludlow, or the state school in Borrega. More school just seemed like a waste of time. He liked being outside. He liked playing ball. He liked working with his hands. College wasn't going to help much with any of that.

"There's plenty of time," he muttered.

"Too many people your age don't consider the future," she lectured. "You're just aimless wanderers, stuck in the moment, as if nothing's ever going to change, as if you'll never have any responsibilities. These days it's all about instant gratification, what can I have *right now*. And what with all the drugs, alcohol, sex . . ."

After an uncomfortably long pause, Adam wondered whether she was waiting for him to respond.

"Uh . . . Ms. Campbell?" She nodded expectantly. "I guess, I'm, uh, not sure where you're going with this?"

She snapped the file shut and stood up. "Where I'm going is this," she said in an unusually firm voice. "Your grades are atrocious, and you're in danger of failing the year. I'm assigning you a tutor, and with some hard work, I hope you'll be able to dig yourself out of this hole."

"A tutor?" He was aware of the whiny note that had crept into his voice, but couldn't help himself. How lame could you get? "Do I have to?"

"You don't *have* to do anything, Adam."

He smiled in relief.

"But without a tutor, your grades won't improve. And if your grades don't improve, *soon*, you can stop worrying about your future. Because you're not going to graduate."

Miranda was about to open the stall door when she heard their voices. Mini-She's was a bit higher than Mini-Me's, but otherwise, they were interchangeable. Just like the rest of them.

"She's such a bitch."

"Totally."

"Do you think she even knows what people are saying about her?"

A sigh. "It's tragic."

"Totally."

"I mean, she was the shit."

"Definitely."

"But all that crazy stuff last month?"

"Total meltdown."

"And poor Kaia . . ."

"She probably went crazy and ran them both off the road."

A moment of silence.

"That was all really sad."

"Yeah."

"That was kind of a hot skirt she was wearing today, though. Think it would look good on me?"

"Totally. And I was thinking I might pick up one of those tank tops—"

"You bitch! I was all over that."

"No prob, I'll go green, you stick with the blue."

Giggles.

"I feel kind of bad for her, you know?"

"Oh, yeah, me too, of course."

"That's why I'm totally going to stick by her."

"Oh, yeah, me too, of course."

"It's like a community service project or something."

"God, that's sad."

"Tragic."

"Good thing she's got friends like us."

"Totally."

The door banged shut, and then there was silence.

Miranda held her breath and opened the door of the stall. The girls' room was empty. She squirted some soap into her hands, ran them under the hot water, and waited.

She'd just reached for a paper towel when a second stall door opened, and Harper finally emerged.

Harper washed her hands in silence. Miranda could tell she was nibbling on the inside of her left cheek, a nervous habit. She bent down, and then flipped her head up again, her hair flying back down to her shoulders. She ran a hand through, fluffing up the sides and smoothing it down at the roots. "I'm thinking of getting it cut," Harper said finally. "Nothing too dramatic, though."

"Sounds good," Miranda said, waiting for some kind of explosion.

Harper pulled out a tube of cherry-colored lipstick.

"Nice color," Miranda told her. "New?"

"Yeah. Want to try?"

"I don't know." She looked in the mirror, giving her limp hair a disdainful flip. Cherry and orange didn't seem like a match made in heaven. "Think it would look good on me?"

Harper tossed over the tube, then raised her eyebrows and gave Miranda a weak half smile. "Totally."

chapter four

IT WASN'T EASY TO SURPRISE KANE GEARY. WHEN
you assume that everyone in the world is out for themselves, not much happens that you don't see coming.

But this was most definitely unexpected.

Beth sat at a table just in front of the school doors,
handing out Haven High pennants and wrist bands to
any seniors who'd forgotten to dress in Haven's school
colors—rust and mud—for Spirit Day; the most festively
adorned, psychotically spirited senior would win some
kind of fabulous grand prize.

Kane wore a navy button-down shirt and Michael
Kors jeans.

He didn't do spirit.

Harper was a few feet ahead of him, walking quickly with her head down, taking a few final puffs on her cigarette before entering the school. Kane, who noticed everything, caught Beth looking away as she approached—no surprise there. Harper, on the other hand, barely noticed the table of paraphernalia or the blond beauty staffing it. She just took one last drag and carelessly flicked the cigarette away—too carelessly, it turned out, as it tumbled through the air, right into Ms. Barbini's back.

Never a good idea to pelt the teachers with cigarettes—tempting as it often was—but Ms. Barbini, the no-nonsense, no-deodorant geometry teacher, was a particularly poor choice. She whirled around, bent down, and picked up the incriminating butt between her thumb and index finger, then glared at Harper, who had frozen in place.

"Who threw this?" she asked, in a tone that suggested she need not wait for an answer.

Kane was close enough to see Harper roll her eyes, open her mouth . . . and snap it shut again as Beth leaped to her feet.

"I did, Ms. Barbini," she announced.

Surprise.

Kane and Ms. Barbini goggled at her; Harper's face remained expressionless, as if she were watching a rather boring show on TV and was just waiting for a commercial.

"You?" the teacher said incredulously.

"Me."

"Can I go now?" Harper asked. "Wouldn't want to be late for homeroom." She shot a hostile glare at Beth—a silent message that looked less like *thank you* and more like *your choice, your funeral*—and, without waiting for an answer, limped up the stairs and disappeared inside the school.

"I'm very disappointed in you, Ms. Manning. Smoking on school grounds?" The teacher whipped out a small pink pad and began to scribble. "That's two days' detention." She thrust the detention slip at Beth and, after giving her a disdainful scowl, followed in Harper's footsteps up the stairs and through the heavy wooden doors.

It had been a late night, and Kane had almost cut homeroom to sleep in—good thing he'd made the "responsible" choice, as nothing cured a hangover like a good mystery. And there was nothing more mysterious than Beth taking the fall for her mortal enemy.

"Now *that* was interesting," he said, sauntering up to Beth's table. He swept aside a swath of orange and brown crap and hopped on, half standing, half sitting, and all in Beth's face.

"Good morning," she chirped, her face a gruesome imitation of a smile. "Would you like a pennant?"

"I'd like to know if you're lobbying for sainthood."

The smile collapsed into a frown—this one looked real. "Get off of there." A pause. "Please."

"She's not going to thank you," Kane pointed out. "But you know that. And you've got no reason to want to help her, unless maybe you just feel sorry for her . . . but even the kind and generous Beth Manning wouldn't go *that* far." He leaned toward her, squinting as if to peer more deeply into her eyes and uncover the real motive.

"Can you just leave me alone?" Beth snapped. Her face was turning pale, and she looked nervously down at the stack of papers she was shuffling and reshuffling as she spoke.

"If I didn't know better, I'd think you owed her in some way," Kane mused. "But what could *you* possibly owe *Harper?*"

At first, he'd just been enjoying himself watching her squirm—but Kane was beginning to suspect that his instincts were right, and something really was going on here. And it turned out that accompanying his natural curiosity was an uncharacteristically sincere urge to protect Harper from whatever it might be. The second surprise of the morning.

"Just drop it," she pleaded in a choked voice. "Just go away."

"Where's all this hostility coming from?" He gave her

a wounded look. "I thought we were supposed to be *friends* now—isn't that what you said?"

"Forget what I—"

"Is this jerk bothering you?"

Ah, the knight in shining armor, Kane thought, without turning around. Just in time.

"Chill out, buddy," he told Adam. "Your ex and I are just having a little chat." Kane stopped, and then, laughing as if the thought had just occurred to him, continued, "I guess she's *my* ex too. Share and share alike."

"Get out of here, Kane." Adam grabbed him roughly by the shoulder and pulled him off the table. Kane wrestled his arm away, but that was it. He didn't leave; he also didn't fight back. Adam was the one with the problem, Adam was the one with the grudge—Adam was the one who, despite an apology and plenty of time, refused to get over it. He liked to act the wounded party, but he was the one who'd called an official end to their friendship. Over a *girl*. Adam was the one who just couldn't deal.

"You okay, Beth?" he asked now, pulling that Mr. Sensitive act the girls couldn't get enough of. (Except for Beth, Kane noted with more than a flicker of pride—thanks in part to him, she'd had plenty.)

"I don't need you to protect me," she snapped, rising from the table.

"Can't you both see that I'm busy?" she cried suddenly. "I'm taking care of a million things, and the two of you . . ." She slammed down the cover of her thick binder and grabbed it off the table, hugging it to her chest.

"Beth—" Adam smiled and held up his hands in supplication.

"No. Not now. Just leave me alone. *Both* of you." No one moved. "No? Fine, then I'll do it for you."

She spun away, her blond hair whipping against Kane's face, and walked off.

Kane and Adam stared at each other, Adam looking like he'd just taken a swig of sour milk.

"So," he said finally, rubbing a hand against his close-cropped blond hair.

"Yeah," Kane agreed.

"What did you—?"

"Hey, nothing," Kane protested quickly, shaking his head. "She's just wound too tight."

"Ya think?" Adam laughed, sounding not particularly happy, but not particularly angry, either, which was a change. "I'm starting to think all girls are crazy. She 'forgive' you, too?"

Kane nodded, and the two exchanged a wry smile, their first in weeks. "Wonder what she acts like when she holds a grudge."

✤   ✤   ✤

Adam was waiting for his tutor in the "computer lab" (really a closet-size space with a couple of stone-age PCs) when Miranda wandered in.

Great. Just great.

He'd hoped to keep the whole humiliating tutor thing under wraps, but if Miranda got wind of it, surely she'd run straight to Harper—who, in her current mood, might spread it all over school.

More good luck for me, he thought sourly.

"Hey, Adam." Miranda didn't look particularly surprised to see him, just uncomfortable. "What's up?"

"Just waiting for someone," he said brusquely, hoping she'd take the hint and leave.

And then the other shoe dropped—on his head.

"Uh, yeah . . . I know." She gave him a tight smile, and the truth sunk in.

"You're my tutor?"

"Guilty." Miranda rubbed the back of her neck and hovered in the doorway. "Look, if this is too weird for you or anything, I'm sure you could get them to assign you someone else—"

"No, no," he said without thinking, not wanting to be rude. But, on second thought . . . he'd known Miranda for years, and though they'd never been close, they'd always had one big thing in common: Harper.

Maybe this wasn't such bad luck after all.

"I'm glad it's you," he told her, "and not some jerk who'd go bragging to the honor society about what an idiot I am."

Miranda set her stuff down and pulled up a chair. "You're not an idiot," she said firmly.

Adam spit out a laugh. "I can see Campbell didn't give you the full story. Trust me," he boasted, clasping his hands together over his head like a champion, "you're looking at the official winner of the Haven High dumbass award."

"I'm sure it's not that bad," Miranda said, grinning. Adam was suddenly certain that she didn't know he was on the verge of not graduating; he wasn't about to fill her in.

"So, where should we start?" she asked.

He shrugged. "I guess I've got a math test this week," he mumbled. Most of his friends were in calc or pre-calc this year, but he was stuck taking basic algebra. It was really for juniors—and it was still way over his head.

"Cool, I love math." As the words slipped out, Miranda looked up, horrified. "You tell anyone I just said that and I'll have to kill you."

"How about a deal?" he suggested. "You keep this whole tutoring thing to yourself and I won't tell anyone that you're secretly a total geek."

They grinned, and shook on it.

That was the end of the fun—Miranda dove right into

the work, struggling to explain to Adam how to apply the quadratic formula and what it meant when an equation had an imaginary solution. But he couldn't focus, and not just because it all sounded like a foreign language.

"How is she?" he asked suddenly, looking up from the books.

Miranda didn't even pretend to be confused. "She's okay. . . ." She sighed. "That's what she says, at least. I don't ask anymore. It's just . . . it's better that way, you know?"

"Yeah." He didn't know, of course. But he knew Harper, so he could imagine.

"Have you talked to her? I mean, have you two been . . . ?"

"You don't know?" Adam wrinkled his forehead. "I thought girls talked all that stuff to death."

"Well, lately . . ."

"Yeah," he said again. "Lately." He wouldn't make her say it. "She won't talk to me," he admitted. "I don't know why."

But that was a lie, wasn't it? He knew exactly why—he couldn't accept it.

She looks much better this time. Her skin is pink, her breathing strong and steady, the machines gone. And her eyes are open.

For two days, she refused to see anyone. And then, today, he was summoned.

She waves weakly when he comes into the room. She doesn't smile.

"You look good, kid," he says. Comparatively, it is true.

"They say I'm going home tomorrow."

"Great!" His smile feels fake. Hers is nonexistent.

He comes over to the bed and leans over, giving her a kiss on the forehead. "I'm really glad you're okay, Harper," he says softly. "I'm—" He doesn't know how to talk about it, what it felt like to lie awake in bed worrying about her, not knowing, waiting for something to happen, desperately hoping it wouldn't, but even more desperate for the weird, endless, torturous limbo of waiting to just end. One way or another. He doesn't want to ask if she heard all the things he told her when her eyes were closed, because he's afraid that she did—and afraid that she didn't. "We were all really worried," he says finally, hiding in the "we."

"I didn't think you'd come," she says dully. "I thought you hated me."

"Of course I don't hate you," he says, his voice too jolly. She winces. He knows he's trying too hard; he just doesn't know what he's trying to do. He pulls a familiar chair up to the bed. He doesn't take her hand. "Look, things got all screwed up at the end there, and I . . . we both said a lot of things that . . . you know, we probably shouldn't have."

"Mostly you said a lot of things," she reminds him. "I just said I'm sorry."

She'd said it over and over again; he hadn't wanted to listen.

"I know. I know you are," he tells her. "I get that now. And I forgive you."

"Really?" Her eyes widen. She tries to sit up in bed, and her face twists in pain. He touches her shoulder, gently, helping her to lie back. She reaches out, touches his face. "Everything I did, I just did it because—"

"I know."

The tension disappears from her face. "Then it's okay," she murmurs, almost to herself. "Then at least something is . . ."

He leans in closer, struggling to hear—and she kisses him.

He jerks away.

He does it without even thinking.

He hasn't thought any of it through, he realizes now. And now it's too late.

"What?" There is a new pain on her face. "What is it?"

"Gracie, when I said—I didn't mean—"

"You said you forgave me, Ad," she says softly, as if maybe he forgot, and this is all a simple misunderstanding. "So that's it. We can start again. No more lies, no more—"

"No." He doesn't know he's going to say it before the word pops out, but he means it. "I want us to be friends again, Harper, I really do. But anything else . . . I think we work better, just as friends. When we tried to have more"— When *you* had *to have more, he doesn't say—"things got messy."*

"But it was all a mistake!" she protests, her voice scratchy and weak. "I explained that. I apologized, a million times. And you just want to go back? Like none of it ever happened? Like you never told me that you—"

"None of it was real." He tries not to look away. He wants so much to make her smile; but he can't tell her what she wants to hear. "When we were together, it was all a lie." The words are harsh, but his voice is gentle. He doesn't want to hurt her. "Everything you said was based on lies—and everything I said, that was just because I believed them."

She sags back against the pillows, her face returning to the dull, expressionless mask she'd worn when he came in.

Stop, he tells himself, horrified. Look what he's said, what he's done. He has to fix it—fix her.

"Gracie, you're my best friend," he says, and now he does take her hand. He can feel her pulling away, but he squeezes tighter, and she doesn't have the strength. "I miss that. I miss you. We tried the whole dating thing, and it didn't work out. It doesn't matter why, or whose fault it is. It just didn't. But that doesn't mean—"

"Get out," she says flatly.

"What?"

"I don't need this."

"I don't understand," he says, trying not to.

"You don't forgive me," she says bitterly. "You still think I'm not good enough for you, that I'm this manipulative slut who can't be trusted. That's what you told me, isn't it? That I'm this terrible person, all rotted on the inside?"

"But I was wrong," he protests. "I didn't mean it."

"Right." Her voice swells, and he realizes that even now, hurt, powerless, confined to a bed, she has power. She is still, after all, Harper Grace. "You meant it. Then. So what's changed now? You see me lying here and you feel sorry for me? You figure poor little Harper needs a nice pick-me-up in her bed of pain? And what? I'm supposed to be grateful for your pity?" Her voice is shaking, but her eyes are dry. And he knows that she will never let him see her pain.

"It's not pity," he argues.

"Yeah, but it's not—" She stops herself. There is a long silence. "You don't have to worry about me," she says finally. "I'm fine. You did your little good deed by coming here, so you can forget your guilty conscience."

It would be so easy to fix this, he thinks. All he has to do is take her back, tell her he loves her and he understands everything she did to him. Tell her he's ready to start over again, that the past doesn't matter.

But it does matter. A car crash can't erase anything that happened, or the choices that she made; it doesn't change the kind of person she is, it doesn't make it any easier to trust her again.

"You should get some rest," he says. "We can talk about this tomorrow. I'll come back and—"

"Don't."

"I want to."

"I don't care." She turns her head away from him and closes her eyes. They're done.

"She's feeling a lot better," Miranda said, shrugging. "I'm sure pretty soon everything else will be back to normal. And the two of you . . ."

"I don't know," he said dubiously, although he had the same hope. It's why he kept trying, in hopes that, if nothing else, she'd eventually get tired of pushing him away.

"I could tell her you were asking," Miranda offered.

"No, don't bother." He looked down at his notebook, where a mess of numbers and letters sprinkled the page in an incomprehensible pattern. "Maybe we should just get back to work."

After all, nothing in his life made much sense anymore; at least when it came to algebra, there was an answer key in the back of the book.

Beth pressed her foot down on the gas pedal, nudging the car just over the speed limit, and tried not to think about the two meetings she was blowing off or the stack of homework she'd face when she got home again. Today had gone from bad—an encounter with Kane that had rattled her even more than her first ever detention slip—to worse as she'd bombed a pop quiz, forgotten her gym uniform, and almost lost the Spirit Day prizes. She'd found them at the last minute, but had been forced to miss the culminating Spirit Rally in favor of her first detention, where she'd cowered in the back row under the glare of a tall, gaunt boy with pale skin and greasy hair who kept whispering something about how hot she'd look in leather.

It would be nice to say it had all been worth it, that she'd managed to erase some part of her imagined debt to Harper, and she was able to start feeling good about herself again, or at the very least that she could put the day behind her, sleep long and hard, and hope the next day would be better.

But she just felt unsteady. Maybe it was the detention, maybe it was the four cups of coffee she'd downed since morning, maybe it was Kane—her *supplier*, she reminded herself. She tried to shut it out, but the image popped into her mind yet again: the empty box on her nightstand. Kane was the only one who knew about it—the only one who could ever suspect what she'd done.

And if he hadn't given her the pills, she reminded herself, none of this would have happened. She hated him— almost as much as she hated herself.

Little wonder that she couldn't face her meeting, haggling with a bunch of overly enthusiastic volunteers about how to stage the next day's auction, where to hang the banners, which last-minute details to delegate and which to ditch. It was too depressing, especially since she used to be one of them, trying hard, worrying, taking all that nervous energy left over from waiting for college decisions and funneling it into something productive and mildly entertaining. Now she was just acting the part. And it was getting old.

She couldn't face going home; the house was always either too full of people, noise, and clutter to think straight, or it was empty and too quiet.

So she'd driven away, following the familiar curves until she reached the spot that guaranteed her a quiet place to think. She felt guilty there, as if she were trespassing, especially in those moments when she was overcome by self-pity—it felt wrong, feeling sorry for herself, there of all places. But she couldn't help it. And as time passed, it became the only place that could help.

The road curved, and the thin white cross appeared. Beth pulled her car onto the shoulder and parked. She hesitated for a moment, staring through the windshield at the small wooden cross stuck into the brush-covered ground, the withering bunches of flowers gathered around it. It looked almost lonely, dwarfed by the vast emptiness of the surrounding desert. From this distance she couldn't see the name scratched into the wood, but she imagined she could. She had traced her fingers over the letters often enough.

Beth didn't know who had erected the small memorial—Kaia's father, from the few glimpses she'd gotten before he left town, didn't seem the type. And there were few other candidates. She got out of the car and walked slowly over to the cross, then sat on the ground in front of it, not caring if she got dirt all over her jeans. She'd brought along her ancient, beat-up iPod, and now she switched it on, sliding the headphones over her head and tuning out the world.

The first time she'd come, she had wandered through the brush, looking for signs that something had happened here. And she'd found them—small spots of scorched earth, scratches and gouges in the ground, a smear of rubber on the road, a jagged chunk of metal, twisted and torn beyond recognition. But all of that was gone now; or, at least, Beth no longer had any urge to look. Now she just sat and stared, sometimes at the roughly engraved letters—just KAIA, no dates, no messages, no last name—sometimes at the empty road and still scenery, disturbed only by the occasional eighteen-wheeler barreling through, sometimes at the sky. She chose her music at random, though most of the songs in her collection were weepy women, singer-songwriters warbling about lost love, so there was rarely much surprise. Today, however, she'd started playing a Black Keys album—something Adam had given her in hopes of giving her some kind of music makeover. She'd never really listened to it. But today, somehow, it worked.

It's not my fault, she told herself, trying to dislodge the mountain of guilt. There was no cause and effect. No connection. She'd drugged Harper; Kaia had crashed a car. It was a coincidence, nothing more. A bad driver, speeding down the road, slamming into the BMW, disappearing. It was an accident—just bad luck. *Not my fault.* Harper was fine. Harper was healthy. Whatever Beth had done, there'd been no permanent consequences.

What happened to Kaia was permanent, but—*not my fault.*

She didn't know how long she'd been sitting there when she felt the hand on her shoulder. She tipped her head back and looked up into the deepest brown eyes she'd ever seen. She took in his warm, crooked smile, the tendrils of dark, curly hair that flopped over his eyes, the smudge of grease just above his chin . . . and then it all came together into a familiar face, and she jerked away.

"Hey," he said, his voice warm and gravelly, as if he'd just rolled out of bed. "Sorry." He sat down next to her. "Didn't mean to scare you."

"You didn't," Beth said, pulling off her headphones. She couldn't look at him.

Reed flicked his eyes toward the cross. "I didn't know anyone else came here," he said. "Didn't think anyone cared." He spoke slowly, pausing between each word as if part of him preferred the silence. "I didn't know you two were friends."

Beth couldn't bring herself to say that they weren't, that Kaia had zoomed to the top of Beth's enemies list by sleeping with her boyfriend; she couldn't admit the hours she'd spent wishing Kaia Sellers out of existence. But she also didn't want to lie.

"I'm Reed," he said, breaking the awkward silence. "Maybe you don't remember, but we met a while ago, before . . ." He reached for her hand and shook it, an oddly formal gesture considering they were sitting across from each other in the dirt on the side of a highway. His hand was warm, his grip tight; she didn't want to let go.

"I remember." She'd been upset, and he'd cheered her up, somehow—she couldn't remember now. Couldn't even remember what she'd been so upset about. It felt like a different lifetime. "I should go," she said suddenly, realizing he probably wanted to be alone—she didn't belong. "Do you want me to—?"

"I should take off," he said at the same time. They both stopped talking and laughed, then, shooting a guilty glance at the thin, white cross, fell into silence again.

"Really, I should go," she insisted.

"No, stay." He sighed and rubbed a worn spot on the knee of his jeans where the denim was about to tear apart. "Please."

Beth nodded, feeling her chest tighten. *It's not my fault. I didn't do this.*

The sun was already setting, but it was a cloudless day, so there was no brilliant sunset, only a steadily deepening haze as the sun dipped beneath the horizon. Reed dug around in his pocket and pulled out a flat, grayish stone, its edges rounded and its top streaked with red. He stood up, placed it in front of the cross, where it was lost amid the bouquets of dying flowers. Then he sat down again and gave Beth a half smile. "I saw it, somewhere, that people do that. And I just thought it was, you know, a good thing to do."

Beth opened her mouth to say, "That's nice." Instead, she let out a gasping sob and burst into tears.

"Hey," Reed said, sounding alarmed. "Hey, don't—"

Beth had squeezed her eyes shut, willing the tears to stop, so she didn't see him leaning toward her. She just felt his strong arms pull her in, pressing her head against his chest.

"It's okay," he murmured, stroking her hair. "It's okay."

He smelled sweet and smoky and, as her gasps quieted, she could hear his heart beat.

"I miss her too," he whispered.

Oh, God.

"I'm sorry," she blurted, her voice muffled by his shirt.

She pushed him away and stood up. "I have to go, I'm sorry." By the time he stood up, she'd already started running toward her car, tears blinding her vision.

She didn't know if he was trying to follow her, and as she started the car and tore out onto the road, she forced herself not to care. She never should have allowed him to comfort her like that, and she couldn't let it happen again.

She didn't deserve it.

Harper jerked awake, her breath ragged, sweat pouring down her face. She turned over to check the clock: 2:46 a.m. Four hours to go before the rest of the house woke up, and she would hear some noises other than her pounding heart.

She felt like she was still trapped in the nightmare; the dark shadows of her room seemed alive with possibility, as if the childhood monsters she'd once feared had returned to haunt her. But that was just the dream talking, she reminded herself. And nightmares weren't real.

Except.

Except that her nightmares were memories that fled as soon as she opened her eyes. All she had were glimpses: the scream of tearing metal, the stench of smoke, the heavy weight on her chest that made it hurt to breathe. Her pillow was damp, maybe with sweat—she rubbed her eyes—maybe with tears.

She should be used to it by now, and she ran through her regular routine: Lying still, on her back, eyes fixed on the ceiling, counting her breaths. It was supposed to relax her and lull her back to sleep, but this time, it relaxed some protective barrier in her mind, and the images of her nightmare came flooding back.

Harper sat up. "No." It was halfway between a plea and a moan. "Please."

But the truth slammed into her. She squeezed her eyes shut and fell forward, clapping a hand over her mouth, fighting against her sudden nausea.

Deep breaths, she told herself, trying to stop shaking.

It was only a dream.

Except it wasn't a dream and she *couldn't* breathe. She felt like someone had shoved a gasoline-soaked rag into her mouth and she was choking on rough cotton and toxic fumes.

If it was true, she thought, *I'd light the match.*

She'd waited so long to remember, but now she fought against it; maybe she could hide in the dark, she told herself, slip back into sleep, and wake up the next morning, everything safely forgotten.

But she stood up and fumbled her way toward the desk, refusing to turn on a light—that would make it too real. Blinking back tears, she found the business card and brought it back to her bed, reading the numbers by the dim light of her clock radio. Her fingers hesitated over the buttons on her cell. She had to do it now, she told herself; in the morning, in the light, she'd be too afraid.

The phone rang and rang, and then, just before she was about to hang up, the voice mail kicked in.

"This is Detective Sharon Wells. Leave your name and phone number after the beep. If this is an emergency, please call 911."

"This is Harper Grace," she said quickly, thinking, *This* is *an emergency.* She tried not to let her voice shake. "You told me to call you if I remembered anything. About, you know, the accident. And. I did."

Harper snapped the phone shut and dove back into bed, burrowing under the covers. She squeezed her eyes closed but couldn't force the images out of her brain.

Kaia laughing.

The truck barreling toward them.

Music pumping.

Brakes squealing.

And Harper's hands wrapped around the wheel.

chapter five

"I NEED TO TALK TO YOU. *NOW*," HARPER HISSED.

Pretending not to notice the urgency in her voice, Kane tossed some books into his locker and eased the door shut. "At your service," he told her, leaning against the cool metal and waiting for her to unload.

"Not here." She looked up and down the hallway—students were trickling into the classrooms and there wasn't a teacher in sight. "Come on."

Not like he had much choice in the matter. She grabbed his sleeve and dragged him down the hall, slipping through a side door and depositing him on a small landing behind the history wing. It was an emergency exit whose alarm had been conveniently disabled, and since the stairwell down led to a narrow plot of cement bordered by a concrete retention wall, it was unlikely they'd be noticed.

"So what's the emergency?" He perched on the railing and, letting himself tip backward, idly wondered how far he'd be able to lean before gravity pulled him all the way down.

"You want to tell me again what you saw?" Harper asked, pacing back and forth on the narrow landing. Her hair, more unruly than usual, flowed out behind her, and Kane suddenly noticed that she wasn't wearing any makeup. His grin faded; Harper didn't go for the natural look. Ever.

"Saw when?" he asked. "You're going to have to give me a little more to go on here."

"The accident." She spit out. "In the parking lot, the day—you know when. What you told the cops. Tell me."

Kane stretched his mouth wide open, cracking his jaw, then sighed. "I saw Kaia drive up to the school," he began in a mechanical voice. The recitation of events had by now become so familiar, he'd memorized the spiel. "I saw you run out of the school. You talked for a while. Then you got into the car and Kaia drove away."

"Bullshit!" Harper snapped. "Want to try again?"

"That's the only story I've got," Kane protested. "So unless you want me to make something up . . ."

"You? Lie?" She made a noise that could have been a laugh. "Wouldn't want to make you do that."

She stopped pacing suddenly, and slumped against the brick wall of the school, facing Kane. Her chest shuddered as she gasped for air; how fast did you have to be breathing, Kane wondered, before you were officially hyperventilating?

"Chill out, Grace. What's with you?"

"What did you *see*, Kane? Not what you told the police. What *happened?*"

She knew something, he could hear it in her tone. Kane swung off the railing and approached her. "What. Are. You. Talking. About," he said, slowly and clearly, overenunciating, hoping that if he couldn't tease away her mood, he could piss her off enough that she'd snap out of it.

"When I woke up in the hospital, I didn't remember anything that happened," Harper said.

"I know." He said it casually, as if it were no big deal that she was talking about this, despite the fact that until now, it had been clearly marked as off-limits, surrounded by conversational barbed wire.

"They just told me what—" She closed her eyes for a moment and, drawing in a deep breath, set her mouth in a firm line as if readying herself for a blow. "They told me she died. She was driving, there was some other car, there was a crash, and she . . . died."

"It sucks." Kane shifted his weight back and forth, waiting for the point.

"Why'd you do it?" she asked softly.

"*What?*"

"That's what I don't get. What's in it for you?"

"What the hell are you talking about, Harper?"

"I remembered."

Now Kane closed his eyes, then opened them again, searching her face for . . . uncertainty? Vulnerability? Gratitude? He didn't know, and whatever he was looking for, it wasn't there. Her face was angry, and that was it.

"Last night," she said, "I had a nightmare, and then when I woke up—"

He relaxed. "Just a dream, then." Kane forced a laugh. "Grace, I know it's tough not to know what happened, but just because you have a nightmare doesn't mean—"

"I *know* what happened. It was my fault. It was me."

He put his hands on her shoulders and gave her a soft shake. "Nothing was your fault, Grace. You don't know what you're saying."

"I know exactly what I'm saying!" she cried, pushing him away. "I was driving!"

"Shut up!" he hissed, glancing around to make sure no one had heard. "You can't go around saying things like that," he told her softly, urgently. "You know they found drugs in your system. If people thought . . ." Did she not get how dangerous this was? Did she not understand what she was playing around with?

She rolled her eyes. "What's the difference? Everyone's going to know soon enough. The cops will make sure of that."

"The *cops?*" He grabbed her again, and this time, when she tried to push him away, he gripped tighter, pushing her up against the wall. "What did you do?"

"Nothing," she admitted. "Yet. But I have to tell them."

"Are you fucking insane?" He rubbed his fingers against the bridge of his nose, searching for a way to make her understand. "Whatever you think you remember, Grace, you've got to just forget about it. This isn't something to screw around with."

"I don't *think* I remember, Kane. I *know* what happened. And I know what you saw. I just don't know why you lied about it."

Join the club, Kane thought bitterly. It was his general policy not to get involved, and yet he'd opened his big mouth, spit out a single lie, and now it was too late. He was involved.

And, even more puzzling: He didn't completely regret it.

"Grace, listen to me, okay?" He leaned against the wall next to her and stared off into the grayish morning haze.

"I'm trying to help you, so you have to listen to me. You *cannot* talk to the cops. You'll ruin your life."

"So?" she muttered. "I ruined hers."

Kane pretended not to hear. "At least don't do anything yet," he insisted. "Just think about it. Give yourself some time. Don't be an idiot about this. It's too big."

"And why should I listen to you?" Her voice had lost its anger and was now just a flat, tired-sounding monotone.

Because I'm your friend, he wanted to tell her. *Because someone has to look out for you since you're doing such a shit job of it yourself* "I know about getting into trouble," he said wryly "And I know about getting *out* of it."

"Maybe I don't want to get out of it," Harper snapped, opening the emergency exit door and slipping back inside the school. "Maybe I just want what I deserve."

Beth shoved her fist against her mouth to stifle a scream. Then she bit down, hard, tears springing to her eyes—not from the pain.

Above her, she could hear Kane pacing back and forth on the landing, muttering to himself. She couldn't make out his words, but then, it didn't matter—she'd already heard enough. Beth tugged her knees to her chest and wrapped her arms around them tight, rocking back and forth, trying to drive the new knowledge out of her brain.

She'd cut class for the first time ever, needing to be alone. Kane had shown her the spot, long ago. That day, they had lounged on the landing, kissing in the sun. Today she had slunk down the rickety stairs and retreated to the dank, narrow space below. She had pressed herself up against the concrete retention wall, closed her eyes, and hoped, just for a few minutes, to hide from her life.

But the truth had found her.

Harper had been driving the car.

Harper had been drugged up, and Harper had gotten behind the wheel.

Kaia was dead. And Beth was to blame.

It was that simple.

Not my fault, she'd insisted, over and over again. The mantra had been a wall between her and an ocean of terror and guilt.

And now the wall had crumbled. And she was drowning. She couldn't think, couldn't move, couldn't do anything but rock back and forth as two words battered her brain.

My fault. My fault. My fault. Her lips moved, but no sound came out, not because she had no air left but because she was a coward. Kane was still up there. She could—*should*—stand up and scream out the truth about what she'd done, but the thought of moving made her dizzy. "Give yourself some time," Kane had told Harper, and it was as if he'd been talking to Beth.

And in a way, he had—he'd been talking to Kaia's killer. *Me.*

She needed to slow down; she needed to think.

"Shit!" Kane's voice. There was a loud clang, as if he'd kicked the railing. Then the door opened, closed. And she was alone.

I killed her, Beth thought, testing the way the words sounded in her head. She almost laughed out loud; it sounded ridiculous. She'd never stolen anything, never gotten a speeding ticket, never been in a fight, still felt guilty when she lied to her parents. She was responsible, she was caring—she was *good.* And yet . . .

She squeezed her eyes shut and held her breath, willing herself to wake up and discover that the last month had been a stupid nightmare, that the box of pills was still sitting on her nightstand and Kaia was still alive. She would do anything, give up anything, to go backward. Maybe, if she wished for it hard enough, if she made enough silent promises, she could open her eyes and be back in January. None of this seemed real, anyway; maybe it wasn't.

She opened her eyes and she was still huddled on the ground, facing a blank wall. Nothing had changed.

It didn't matter what she'd meant to do, she told herself. All that mattered were the consequences.

You say you're a good person, she thought. *Prove it.*

Beth stood up, hyperconscious of every breath, as if without constant monitoring she might forget to take another one. She trudged up the stairs and opened the door, squeezing the handle so tightly that it left an angry red slash across her palm. Now what? She would have to find Harper, or maybe the principal—or maybe she should just go directly to the police. She didn't know how these things worked, aside from the stray detail she'd picked up from *Law & Order* reruns.

She almost burst into laughter again, and stopped herself just in time, fearing that once she started, she might never stop. She was losing it.

"Hey, watch it!"

Someone slammed past her as she stumbled blindly down the hall, and she suddenly realized that she was surrounded by people. The bell must have rung. She should be getting to her second-period class. She wouldn't want to get in trouble for being late—

The crazy laughter threatened to bubble up again, as she remembered herself. What was detention, compared to a jail sentence? What was facing down an angry teacher, compared to facing down the knowledge that she was a killer?

"Beth! Thank God I found you—" A short girl with dirty blond hair grabbed her and pulled her over toward the wall, out of the stream of students. It took a moment for Beth to register her identity: Hilary, the perky vice-chair of the Senior Spirit committee. "Listen, we have to talk; the auction this afternoon's going to be a total disaster if we don't figure this stuff out."

"What?" Beth asked weakly, backing away.

"The *auction*," Hilary repeated. "You missed the meeting yesterday, and we still need to get final approval on the list of participants and talk to Mr. Grady about—"

"I really . . . I really can't deal with this right now," Beth protested. "I've got to . . . I can't talk."

"Okay, okay, then let's pick a time to meet." Her words tumbled out at lightning speed, and Beth could barely follow her; or maybe Beth's mind was staging a slowdown. "I can't do third period because I have a test, but maybe I could get out of fourth if I got Grady to sign off on it or fifth period lunch—when are you free?"

"I don't . . ." Beth tried to battle her way through the fog and come up with something coherent to say. She had a test next period, she realized, and a project to present in the next, and at lunch she was supposed to be assigning articles for the next edition of the *Gazette* and then doing an extra credit project for chem lab, and—and she gasped. Because all of that was irrelevant now. If she walked down the hall and into the principal's office and turned herself in, it wouldn't matter that she'd skipped her calculus test or ditched a newspaper meeting. She felt like she was living out two lives—or worse, was split between two levels of reality, and one was about to consume the other. She was about to lose everything, and the weight of what she'd done and what she needed to do pressed down on her like a vise, squeezing her chest until it felt like her organs would mash together and it would all finally stop.

"Beth? Are you okay? You look a little . . . pale."

The voice sounded like it was coming from a great distance. "I'm fine," Beth said, and her own voice sounded even farther away. She tried to say something else, but she couldn't breathe, much less speak. Hilary's concerned face slowly faded out of view as her field of vision turned to white, then gray, like poor TV reception breaking the world down into a blank screen of scrambled light. Beth felt her control slipping away and, along with it, her panic.

Maybe now I don't have to decide what happens next, she thought as her knees buckled and Hilary caught her just before her head smacked against the linoleum floor. Someone somewhere was shouting and footsteps were pounding and Beth didn't care about any of it anymore. She just closed her eyes and let it all fade away. *Maybe this is the end.*

She might have made it out safely if her phone hadn't rung. Harper had persevered through the morning and made it to lunch—largely because her mother had driven her to school and she didn't have any way of getting home early that didn't involve throwing herself on some-one's (read: Miranda's) mercy. But class was torture, as was lunch, a silent staring contest between Miranda and Harper, ensconced across the room from their usual table—the better to avoid Kane—neither commenting on the change or on much of anything beyond that night's history homework and the possibility of their gym teacher having another nervous breakdown.

By the time the bell rang, Harper had resolved to get out, somehow. She didn't want to drag Miranda along, as that would involve offering some kind of explanation—painful but true, or false but exhausting—and her leg still hurt too much to make the long walk home. But surely, if she could just sneak off campus, she could find a nice, quiet place to hide and wait for the day to officially end. Thanks to the senior auction, the end would come more quickly than usual, and her mother wouldn't think anything of it if Harper called home asking for an early pickup. (An even earlier pickup, courtesy of a never-fail headache-cramps-dizziness combo and a trip to the nurse's office, had crossed her mind, but she'd quickly vetoed it. These days, her mother would just drag her straight to the doctor for excessive testing and monitoring, a fate worse than school, if such a thing were possible.)

So she got rid of Miranda, tossed her uneaten lunch, and followed the crowd out of the cafeteria and down the hall, hoping to slip outside unnoticed. She had just stepped outside, smiling at the rush of cool air against her face, when her phone rang.

Harper cursed, knowing she shouldn't have turned it on after class, but she hadn't been able to resist.

Restricted number.

She didn't need a number to tell her it was Detective Wells—and if she just answered now and told the truth, all this would be over. But she couldn't do it. She stopped walking and slouched against the wall, staring at the flashing red light on the top of her phone; part of her wanted to throw it against the concrete pavement as hard as she could and watch it shatter, as if that would be the end of anything.

It was her own fault that she didn't hear him coming.

"Harper Grace? Is that you? What are you doing out here?"

Mr. Grady was a round little man with a rapid-fire smile and a walrus mustache who'd never forgotten the glory days of his high school drama career and now never missed the chance for a performance, onstage or off. Harper avoided him whenever possible.

She slipped the phone back into her bag, only half grateful that the decision, for the moment, had been made for her.

"Good lord, Harper, whatever has come over you, you look pale as a ghost!" Mr. Grady boomed, his voice tinged with a vaguely British, entirely fake accent that he claimed to have picked up during his "time abroad." (Harper and Miranda had always suspected he'd picked it up from one too many nights on the couch in front of *Masterpiece Theatre*.)

"Just getting some air," Harper said with a sigh, already resigned to her fate: school.

"Good, good," Mr. Grady said, bouncing up and down on the balls of his feet. "Always best to energize yourself before a performance, I always say. Now, you'll need a pass so you don't get in trouble for being late."

"Uh . . . performance?" She realized as soon as she said it that she should have just kept silent; he was already fumbling with a pad of hall passes, and she didn't want to endanger her Get Out of Detention Free card by pointing out that he was possibly insane, certainly mistaken.

"Well, perhaps not in the *technical* sense of the word," Mr. Grady admitted, winking at her, "but I won't tell if you won't. After all, people like you and I know that any public appearance is a performance, don't we?" He handed her the hall pass and then, before she could escape, placed a hand on her shoulder. "I have to admit, Harper, I'm surprised to see you getting back on the horse so quickly, after your rather . . . unfortunate turn at the podium last month. And to put yourself out there in the service of your fellow students? Magnificent, young lady, simply magnificent!"

At the thought of her "unfortunate turn," Harper almost gagged; she remembered little more than the glare of the spotlight, the murmurs of the audience, and the sense that everything was spiraling out of control. But the days before her speech were still clear in her mind, and they'd all been colored with an overwhelming fear of public speaking; for a million reasons, it wasn't an experience she was planning to repeat anytime soon.

"What are you talking about, Mr. Grady?" She pulled away from him; it was bad enough when anyone touched her, these days. But nothing skeeved her out more than the familiar well-meaning shoulder grip, usually deployed by middle-aged men barred—by decorum, circumstance, Harper's hostile glare, or their own awkwardness—from anything more openly affectionate. "How exactly am I serving my fellow students?"

"At this afternoon's auction, of course!" He tapped his clipboard. "I've got you down right here: dinner date with Harper Grace. Should go for a pretty penny, I'd wager, a popular girl like you."

"What?! No. No way. That's a mistake. I never signed up for—"

"Now, now, don't be nervous. It's a little late to back out now."

Her stomach churned, waiting for her to decide on an emotion—she was torn between fear (of having to go through with it) and loathing (for the demonic loser who'd signed her up). But neither of those would be of much help now. "Actually, Mr. Grady, I'm really going to have to—back out, I mean." She gave him a weak, brave smile and put her hand to her head. "I'm just not feeling very well, and actually, I was headed off to the nurse." Better to be fussed over by her mother and a team of hack doctors than to have to parade around on an auction block in front of the whole senior class, most of whom would undoubtedly be hoping—and waiting—for her to humiliate herself once again.

The sympathy ploy might have worked on some teachers, but the oblivious Grady was too intent on insuring that everything followed his script and the show went on. "Nonsense!" he cried, flinging his hands in the air. "Stage fright, preshow jitters, that's all. I've seen it a million times before. Nothing to worry about. This will do you good." He put one hand on each of her shoulders, squeezed tight, and steered her firmly back into the school. "I expect to see you backstage in an hour, Harper. *No excuses.* This is going to be just the medicine you need."

"But Mr. Grady—" she protested, cursing the pleading tone in her voice and wondering what had happened to the authoritative, autocratic Harper Grace who could have any teacher wrapped around her little finger in under ten minutes. Another by-product of her "unfortunate turn" at the podium, she supposed, and the "unfortunate" events that followed. The teachers all looked at her with pity now, and a bit of wariness; they *watched* her, as if last month's disaster had just been the beginning, and the full saga of destruction had yet to play out.

"I'd hate to have to give you detention for backing out on your responsibilities," he warned her in a jolly voice. "But I will, if need be. It's for your own good, after all. Now, now, nothing to be afraid of," he said, depositing her in front of her classroom. "As the bard says, 'All the world's a stage'! So really, we're all performing, all the time. Even now."

Thanks for the heads up, Harper thought bitterly. *Now tell me something I don't know.*

"I've got thirty, do I hear thirty-five?"

"Thirty-five!" a high, desperate voice shouted from the back.

Mr. Grady beamed and waved his gavel in the air. "That's thirty-five from the lovely lady in the back. Do I hear forty?"

"Forty!"

"Forty-five!"

"Fifty!"

"Fifty dollars!" Grady boomed. "We can do better than that." Silence from the crowd. "Let me remind you ladies that you're not just purchasing a lesson in driving a stick shift, you're purchasing the company of this handsome young man for one entire afternoon. Now that *must* be worth at least fifty-five dollars!"

It was worth twice that, Miranda thought, smiling at Kane's obvious discomfort up onstage as Mr. Grady whipped the crowd into a frenzy. But if even if she hadn't maxed out her allowance for the last few weeks, she wouldn't have allowed herself to place a bid. That was most definitely against the rules.

"Seventy-five dollars!" someone yelled. Miranda whipped around to her left and spotted Cheryl Sheppard, a ditzy brunette with a double-D chest and an even bigger wallet, waving her hand in the air.

"Seventy-five dollars!" Mr. Grady announced, fanning himself as if the bid had caused some kind of heat stroke. "Do I hear more?"

There were some murmured complaints from the crowd, but no one spoke up.

"Going once?"

"Going twice?"

Crack! Miranda jumped as the gavel slammed against the podium. "Sold, to the young woman in blue."

Kane grinned and gave Cheryl a cocky wave before strutting offstage. At least that solved the mystery of why he would have deigned to participate in this kind of thing to begin with. Kane was the opposite of a joiner; he was the guy that—at least in junior high—joiners used to run away from for fear of wedgies. But Miranda supposed that the chance to watch a room full of girls practically throw money at the stage just for the privilege of spending an afternoon with him had been too much to resist.

And she didn't care, she told herself. This was yet another example of why Kane was the last person she should waste her time thinking about—evidence, as if she needed any more, that just because he'd finally noticed her lips were good for more than snarky banter didn't mean he wanted anything more, or ever would. She should just smile and clap unenthusiastically, as she had after Lark Madison's brownie-baking lesson went for twenty bucks and Scott Pearson's old golf clubs went for fifty. *Pretend you care that your class is raising some money*, she reminded herself. *Pretend you don't care about* him.

"Now that you ladies have had your turn, it's time for the fellows to pull out your wallets, because next up, we have the beautiful Harper Grace."

Miranda almost choked.

Grady waved his hand toward the wings. Nothing happened. Nodding his head at someone behind the curtain, he beckoned frantically, then turned back to the audience. "As I was saying, the beautiful Harper Grace." Harper walked slowly and confidently toward the center of the stage, where she rejected his offer of a chair and stood with her hands on her hips, facing down the crowd. "She's auctioning off one dinner date, at the restaurant of your choice. Shall we start the bidding at thirty dollars?"

What the hell are you doing? Miranda asked silently, wishing she could send her best friend—if that was even the name for it these days—a telepathic message. She willed Harper to seek her out in the crowd, hoping that, if they made some eye contact, Harper could give her some kind of sign that would explain how she'd ended up as the poster girl for Grady's manic auctioneering. But Harper wasn't making eye contact with her, or anyone. She'd fixed her eyes on a point in the back of the room, above the heads of the audience, and remained frozen, expression serene, mouth fixed in a Mona Lisa smile. She looked almost as if she wanted to be up there; which, Miranda supposed, must somehow be the case.

"Do I hear thirty dollars?"

Miranda suddenly realized that the auditorium was silent. Not just normal high school assembly quiet, where the air still buzzed with gossip and commentary, but the eerie, ominous *Who died?* quiet of the kind you find in lame horror movies, when the heroine puts her hand on the doorknob, just before it turns beneath her grasp and the spooky sound track kicks in.

"Okay . . . do I hear twenty-five dollars? Twenty-five dollars for a night on the town with Harper Grace?"

More silence. Miranda wanted to place a bid herself, just to end the misery, but that, obviously, would be the most humiliating blow of all. She kept her mouth shut. And onstage, Harper seemed barely aware of her surroundings or Grady's swiftly fading enthusiasm. She just smiled.

"Twenty-five dollars!" a nasal voice called out from the front row. Miranda didn't have to crane her neck to see the bidder; she would recognize Lester Lawrence's voice anywhere after sophomore year, when he'd called every Tuesday night for three months, waiting for her to change her mind about a date and succumb to his well-hidden charms. Harper didn't even wince.

"Thirty dollars!" A Texan twang from the back, owned by Horace Wheeler, who also owned an extensive gun collection he was fond of exhibiting to creeped-out visitors who'd made the mistake of stopping by his parents' Wild West–themed ranch.

Out of the frying pan, into the firing range.

"I have thirty dollars," Grady said, feigning excitement. "Do I hear more? Going once? Going twice?" He was talking quickly, as if eager to end the awkwardness and move right along to the next victim.

"A hundred dollars!" someone shouted.

Harper flinched.

Oh, no. Miranda slumped down in her seat, shaking her head. He really was the dumbass of the year.

"A hundred dollars!" Grady repeated, a smile radiating across his face. "Going once? Going twice? Sold, to our very own basketball champion!"

Oh, Adam, she moaned silently. *You poor idiot.*

He'd just wasted a hundred dollars on what he probably thought was the ultimate chivalrous gesture, sweeping in to rescue Harper from her humiliation, saving the day as all heroes can't help but do. And he'd obviously failed to notice that the rest of the school would see it as nothing more than a hundred-dollar pity date, a fresh sign of just how far the mighty Harper had fallen.

Miranda knew how much Harper hated to be rescued; she knew better than most, since she'd been trying to do exactly that for a month now, to no avail. The harder you pushed, the faster Harper ran away, and poor, oblivious Adam had just guaranteed a record-breaking sprint.

Not that you'd know it from looking at her, of course. As Grady banged the gavel to a smattering of applause and a growing tide of laughter, Harper just gave the audience a curt nod, as if she'd done them all a favor by gracing them with her presence but was too polite to accept their gratitude. Then she turned on her heel and walked off toward the wings, where, Miranda knew, she would remain calm and dry-eyed, proud to the bitter end.

Miranda was the one who bent over in her seat, burying her head in her hands, ignoring the arrival of Inez Thompson onstage to auction off a painting from her father's gallery of cheesy desert-sunset paintings. Feeling like she'd been the one to stand up onstage weathering the silence, wishing that she could have been the one, or could at least have done something, *anything* to help, rather than, as always, remaining quiet and ineffectual in the face of Harper's pain, she squeezed her lips together against a wave of nausea.

This was how it always was in their friendship: Miranda waiting on the sidelines, while Harper fought the battles and reaped the rewards. It was better that way, Miranda had always told herself. Harper was the strong one, who could take anything, as she'd just proven to herself and everyone watching.

Miranda was the one who cringed at every blow, as if she were the one being struck. And when it was all over and Harper was left battered but still standing, Miranda was the one who cried.

Beth woke up as someone laid a cool, damp washcloth across her head, but she didn't open her eyes. It was too easy just to lie there, on the small cot in the nurse's office, and let someone take care of her. The nurse's small radio was set to an easy-listening station, and the numbing sound of light jazz, punctuated only by occasional static or a soporific DJ, had lulled Beth to sleep shortly after the nurse laid her down for "a little R & R." She would have been happy to stay that way. But the cot was uncomfortable, the washcloth was dripping down her face, and eventually, as Beth shifted around, trying to force her body back to sleep, the nurse realized that her patient was finally awake.

"Feeling better, dear?" she asked, sounding significantly more sympathetic and nurselike than she had the last time Beth encountered her, trying to teach sex-ed to a horde of hormonally crazed teenagers. She seemed much more relaxed and competent here in her natural habitat. "Ready to sit up?"

Beth had only passed out for a few seconds, but when she awoke to find herself flat on her back in the middle of the hallway, twenty or thirty faces gawking down at her, the nurse had insisted on taking her down to the office. Beth wasn't about to resist; her mind was still sluggish and fuzzy, and she was happy to leave it that way for as long as possible.

They didn't trust her to drive herself home; probably for the best—she didn't trust herself. And she couldn't pull her parents out of work and make them lose a day's pay just because she couldn't handle her stress. She'd be burden enough, once they found out the truth. So the nurse had let her recuperate in her office for the rest of the day, and Beth had stayed there, sleeping on and off, hiding out from her tests and her projects and her meetings and her decisions until the final bell rang and it was time to escape.

"I'm feeling a lot better," she said truthfully. "Thanks for letting me hang out here."

"Are you sure?" The nurse frowned with concern. "I still think I should send you on to a doctor, have someone check you out."

"No, no, I'm fine," Beth protested. "I didn't eat anything this morning, and it just . . . got to me. Really. I feel okay now."

She had a job interview after school, one that might actually pay off, and she couldn't miss it, anxiety attack or not. *Except I don't need the job now, do I?* she asked herself. What would she do with spending money in reform school? Or prison?

But she forced herself to stop thinking about what she'd heard that morning, and what she was going to do about it. She needed to be rational and plan her next move, and to do that, she had to make it through the rest of the day. Tonight, she promised herself, she would figure everything out. She would find a way to live with herself—she would have to.

Beth waved off the nurse's concerns and gathered her stuff, then, steeling herself, rejoined the outside world. Managing to make it down to the parking lot without speaking to anyone—not too difficult, considering that she'd run out of friends weeks ago and so only needed to dodge the handful of acquaintances who needed something from her—she got into her car and wrapped her hands around the wheel.

I could crash too, she told herself. *I could pull out onto the road and crash into anything. No drugs, just me. Just an accident. It could happen to anyone.*

But it was no comfort; yes, some deaths were random, some accidents were really just that. But some effects had causes—some victims had killers.

"Stop," she ordered herself again, aloud in the empty car. She couldn't think about it while she was driving, not unless she really did want to crash into something. (And she didn't, she assured herself. Much as she hated herself and what she'd done, it would never come to that.)

By the time she'd pulled into the lot of Guido's Pizza, she'd reassembled herself into some semblance of calm. She smoothed down her hair and did a quick mirror check: She wasn't exactly decked out in a suit and heels for her interview, but then, given Guido's usual T-shirt and grease-smeared apron, her faux cashmere and khakis would probably do the job.

Just keep it together, she begged herself. *Just for one more hour, keep it together.*

And she did, all the way across the parking lot, up to

the door of the restaurant, where she almost slammed into a guy backing out the door carrying a large stack of pizza boxes.

He turned around to apologize—and she nearly lost it.

"Hey," Reed said, his smile just peeking out over the top of the boxes.

"Hey." Her heart slammed against her chest. Would he be able to tell, just by looking at her? she wondered. Was her guilt painted across her face?

"Listen, about yesterday . . ."

"I've gotta go," Beth said quickly, clenching her stomach and trying to keep her lower lip from trembling. She brushed past him and stepped inside, immediately blasted by a wave of garlic that made her want to throw up.

"See you later?" he called hopefully as the door shut behind her.

Beth pressed both hands to her face and took a deep breath. *God, I hope not.*

chapter six

IT TURNED OUT THAT "GUIDO" WAS ACTUALLY ROY, a sixty-two-year-old widower from Vegas who, having a hankering for small-town life, had moved west to find himself. He'd found Grace instead, a go-nowhere, do-nothing town in dire need of a pizza parlor, however mediocre.

And that's pretty much all Beth took in from his half-hour monologue as she trembled in the chair across from him, willing him to continue talking so that she wouldn't have to speak. It was hard enough to listen when there were so many loud thoughts crowding into her head.

"My daughter, she wanted me to move in with her

and her husband. They fixed up the room over the garage real nice."

My life is over.

"I raised her right—but that's no life for a man, livin' off his daughter, wasting away the days starin' at someone else's walls."

My life should *be over. I killed her.*

"It'd be different if there were grandkids, but you know how it is today, no one's got any time for family. 'What's the hurry, Dad?' she keeps asking me. 'What are you waiting for?' I say, but she just laughs, and that husband of hers . . . it's not my place to say, but if you ask me, he doesn't want the bother."

I didn't mean to.

"He's not a worker, that one. Never did a day's hard work in his life. Not like me. Twenty-five years at the casino and now here I am, shoveling the pizzas every day, and let me tell you, life couldn't get much better."

But it's still my fault.

"Couldn't get much worse, either, if you know what I mean. That's life, eh? Gotta take that shit and turn it into gold, I always say. And it's not so bad. Rent's low, sun's always shining, and customers know better than to talk back."

Ruining my life won't change anything.

"'Course, can't say as I don't miss the old days. Vegas

now? That's nothin' but a theme park. But in my day . . . yeah, you had your mob, and you had your corruption—but you also had your strippers and your showgirls and your cocktail waitresses. And then there was my Molly. . . ."

I don't even know what really happened.

"So what's your story? I got your resume here, and I see you got plenty of experience serving. But why ditch the cushy diner job and come here? Don't know as I'd see this place as a step up."

I know what happened.

"Beth? You still with me?"

Beth tuned back in to realize that a large, calloused hand was waving in front of her face. "Oh . . . sorry. Yes."

"So?"

She tucked her hair behind her ears, a nervous habit. "So . . . I'm, uh . . ." She wasn't good at bluffing, even on a good day. And this had not been a good day. "I didn't quite hear what you asked."

He gave her a friendly smile. "Nerves got you, eh? Take your time. A few deep breaths never hurt anyone."

She tried to follow his suggestion, but the heavy scent of garlic made her head pound. She didn't know why he was being so nice to her. She didn't know why *anyone* would be nice to her anymore.

"I asked why you wanted this job," he repeated.

But Beth couldn't concentrate on sounding responsible or eager to work in a grease-stained pit. She just shrugged. "I think it would be . . . I mean, I like pizza, and . . ." She'd prepared a perfect answer the night before—but it had escaped from her mind, and now she had nothing. She held her hands out in surrender. "I need the money."

He grinned. "Who doesn't? And why'd you leave your last job?"

Another perfect answer that she no longer had. "Creative differences?" she said instead, giving Roy a hopeful smile.

"Gonna have to ask you to be more specific on that one, hon."

"Well . . ." She giggled nervously, her eyes tearing up. "I dumped a milk shake on one of the customers."

"Can't say as clumsiness is something I look for in a waitress," he said, tipping his head to the side. "But I'm no ballerina myself, if you know what I mean."

"No," she said quickly. "No, I did it on purpose. I just dumped it on his head. It felt great." Her giggles grew into full-scale laughter, the kind that steals control of your limbs and your better judgment. There was no joy in the spasms rocketing through her body, just an explosion of all the tension she'd been storing since morning—once it started coming out, she couldn't figure out how to shove it back in again. She flopped around on the chair, heaving with hysteria, gasping for breath, until finally Roy's frozen scowl brought her back to reality.

"Look, I don't know what the joke is," he said, standing up, "but I really don't have time for this kind of thing."

"No!" she cried, leaping up. "No joke. This isn't me—I'm a great employee, really, just give me another chance, I really need this job, I've tried everywhere else in town—"

His expression warmed, but he shook his head. "I'm sorry. I am. But I can't hire you just because I feel bad for you—I need someone reliable, and it's pretty clear that you're—"

"Not," she finished for him. It would have been hilarious if it hadn't been so sad. Reliable was all she'd ever been. Good ol' reliable Beth. And now she didn't even have that. She slumped down over the table, her head resting on her arms and her arms resting on something wet and sticky, but she didn't cry. She'd been holding it all in for hours now, and it seemed the tears had all dried up.

When she felt the hand on her shoulder, she knew who it was, and she knew she should stand up and rush out of the restaurant without even looking at him, but she was too weak and too selfish, and so she lifted her head up and smiled. "Hey. Again."

"You're having a bad week," Reed said, without a question in his voice. "Come on." He grabbed her arm gently and pulled her out of the chair, walking her toward the door. She let herself go limp, happy for a moment to be a marionette and let someone else pull the strings.

Once outside, he sat her down on the bumper of his truck, then perched up on the hood.

"I should go," she mumbled, avoiding eye contact. "I should get out of here."

"Slow down." He pulled something out of his pocket—a small, squished paper tube, and offered it to her. "This always helps," he explained.

Drugs, she thought, and the hysterical laughter threatened to burble out of her again. *Why does every guy I'm with keep shoving drugs in my face? Doesn't he know what could happen?* That shut down the laughter impulse immediately; Reed, better than anyone, knew what could happen. She waved the joint away and sighed heavily.

"What is it?" he asked, his soft, concerned voice so incongruous against his punk rock wardrobe and apathetic pose. "What's going on?"

"Nothing. I just screwed up my interview," she admitted. "And everything."

Reed laughed, a slow, honeyed chuckle. "Don't worry about 'Guido.' He's a pushover. I'll talk to him, vouch for you—he listens to me."

"Why bother?" she asked. "You don't even know me."

"So tell me."

"What?"

"About you."

So she told him about how she made up stories for her little brothers when they had trouble falling asleep, and about the stacks of blank journals that were piled up on her bookshelf, each with two or three entries she'd written before getting distracted and giving up. He told her that he'd taught himself to play the guitar when he was twelve, when the school had started using the music room for detention overflow. She admitted that she liked Joni Mitchell, Tori Amos, Ani DiFranco—the sappier, the better. He admitted that he hated the whole girl-power, singer-songwriter, release-your-inner-woman genre, but recommended Fiona Apple and Liz Phair to bulk up her collection.

They didn't talk about Kaia.

Reed was lying back on the hood of the truck, staring up at the darkening sky. Beth couldn't stop watching him, the way he moved his body with such fluid carelessness, as if he didn't care where it ended up. The cuffs of his jeans were fraying, and his sockless ankles peeked out above his scuffed black sneakers. Beth resisted the crazy urge to touch them.

"I should take off," she said, realizing that the sky was fully dark—her brother's babysitter would be eager to leave, and her parents would be expecting to find dinner on the table when they got home from work.

"Wait—" He grabbed her wrist, and she gasped as the touch sent a chill racing up her arm. Their eyes locked, and neither of them spoke for a long moment. She had time to notice that his skin was softer than she'd expected, and then, abruptly, he pulled away. "If you need me . . ." He dug a scrap of paper and a stubby pencil out of his back pocket. She now knew he always kept one on hand, for times when a strain of melody popped into his head and he needed to record it before it disappeared. He scrawled down a number and handed it to her.

Beth knew she shouldn't take it; she should never have allowed herself to lean on Reed, even for an afternoon. But she let him hand it to her, and she let herself smile when their fingers touched.

"Why are you doing this?" she asked.

"What?"

"Being so . . . *nice.*"

"Because you—" He stopped in the middle of a word, closed his mouth, and looked beyond her for a moment, out to the dark horizon beyond Guido's pizza shack. She wondered if he was thinking about that day on the side of the highway—and she wondered if letting him believe in it, and believe in her, counted as a lie. "Because you look like you could use it."

She couldn't stand it anymore. "Reed, I should tell you—"

"I gotta go." He gave her an awkward wave before sliding into the driver's seat.

"Wait—"

But before she could say anything more, he shut the door and drove away.

"A little to the left, farther, no, now to the right, faster, faster, okay . . . not there—now! That's it! *Yes!*"

"Awesome!" Miranda cried, tossing down the controller and shooting her fists in the air. "I rock!"

"You really do," Adam marveled. He threw himself back on the couch, kicking his feet up on the coffee table. "Who knew?"

"High score!" Miranda cheered, pointing at the screen. "See that? I got the high score."

"Mmph," Adam grunted.

"Oh, don't get cranky just because you got beat by a girl." Miranda tapped her thumb against the buttons until her initials were correctly entered in as a testament to her glory. "Where has this game been all my life?" She glanced over at Adam, giving him a playful grin. "Think I could convince the phys ed department to give me some sort of credit for playing Trails Evolution?"

"*Trials* Evolution," Adam corrected her. "You've really never played before?"

Miranda shook her head. "My cousin gave me his old

PlayStation, but that was, like, when I was a kid. And it broke after a couple days. This is much cooler."

"Okay, so what's next? Resident Evil or NBA 2K13?"

Miranda checked her watch and her eyes bugged out. "Adam, we've been playing for *two hours*." She hadn't even noticed the time passing, which was pretty much a miracle since the first ten minutes in Adam's living room had dragged on forever. Without Harper around, the two had nothing to say to each other; all the more reason to consider Xbox 360 a gift from the gods.

"Yeah? So?" Adam hopped off the couch. "Hungry? I could order a pizza, and I think we've got some chips or something—"

"Adam, we haven't even started looking at math," she pointed out. "What about your test?"

"What about *your* high score?" he countered. "You really gonna leave it undefended and let me kick your ass?" He plopped down on the floor beside her, lifting a controller and restarting the game.

"But . . ." Miranda stopped. If he didn't want to work, it was his funeral, right? she told herself. And after all, just one more game wouldn't hurt. . . .

They spent another hour glued to the screen, switching from Trials to Resident Evil to NBA 2K13 before they were interrupted again.

"No fair!" she yelled as he sank yet another three-pointer.

"You're captain of the basketball team and I'm barely five feet tall—how am I supposed to block your shots?"

"Miranda, it's a video game," he reminded her. "Your guy's about seven feet tall and he was last year's MVP. I think it's a pretty fair matchup."

She was about to confess that she didn't actually understand the rules of basketball—a fatal weakness no matter how many all-stars her cyber-team was fielding—when her phone rang. She paused the game and checked her phone. Harper.

Adam caught the name on the screen and gave her a pained nod. "You take it. I'll practice my free throws."

Miranda answered. "Hey, what's up?" she asked, pretending it was no big deal that Harper had called, though Harper *never* called, not anymore.

"Nothing. I just . . . can you talk?"

"Of course."

"What are you doing?"

"Nothing much. Just hanging out." It wasn't really a lie, Miranda told herself. And it was for a good cause—if she admitted she was busy, Harper would probably just use it as an excuse to hang up again. And if she admitted she was at Adam's house, fraternizing with the enemy . . . she'd have to explain what she was doing there, and Adam had asked her to keep that quiet and, all in all, it was easier just to be vague. "How about you?"

"Thinking."

"You?" Miranda asked, automatically slipping into sarcasm before she remembered that the old days were over.

But Harper laughed. "Crazy, I know. I need to ask you something. Do you think—"

"Woo hoo! High score, baby!"

Miranda winced as Adam's shouts echoed through the empty house.

"What was that?" Harper asked.

"What?" Miranda said. "I didn't say anything."

"The champion returns!"

"Is that Adam?" Harper asked, continuing on before Miranda had a chance to answer. "It is. What's Adam doing there?"

Miranda sighed. It would have been easier to ignore the whole thing, but she wasn't about to lie now, no matter what Adam had asked of her. It's not like he had anything to be embarrassed about—it was just Harper. "Actually, I'm at his house," she admitted.

Harper didn't say anything, and for a moment Miranda worried that the line had gone dead.

"Hello? Harper?"

"You're next door," she finally said in a low monotone. She didn't ask why.

Miranda laughed nervously. "It's not like we're hanging out, like we're friends or something. I have to be here—I mean, I don't *have* to, like it's some horrible ordeal. Actually, when you called, he was teaching me how to play some video game, which actually turned out to be fun—crazy, huh?"

"Wild."

She was babbling, the words spilling out before she had time to think better of it. Which was ridiculous, because there was no need to be nervous—it's not like she had snuck over here behind Harper's back. Yes, she'd walked thirty minutes instead of driving over, but not because she didn't want Harper to spot her car, she reasoned. It was just a beautiful day, and she needed the exercise, and . . . it's not like everything she did had to do with Harper, she insisted silently

It's not like Harper had any right to care.

"But, really, we're supposed to be studying," she tried again. "See, Adam—"

"Miranda."

She stopped talking abruptly, as if Harper had flipped a switch.

"I don't want to hear it," Harper continued. "What do I care if the two of you want to hang out?"

"But we're not hanging out, I'm—"

"I don't want to bother you," Harper said loudly, talking over her. "Sorry I called. Talk to you later."

"Score!" Adam cried from the living room, just as the

phone went dead. Miranda hit end and pressed it against her forehead. However irrational it may have been, she felt like that was her one chance to fix things—and she'd blown it.

Reed hadn't set out with a destination in mind; he'd just wanted to take the edge off his strangely unsettled mood. He felt like he'd forgotten something important, but his thoughts were too jumbled to pin down what it was. So he decided to ignore it and take a drive. He wasn't too surprised to see where he'd ended up. He made a sharp right and pulled off onto the small access road that led straight to the glass monstrosity. He'd always hated this house, with its jutting corners and its smooth, shiny facade. It looked like a machine, some gruesome futuristic gadget blown up to unnatural size and dropped into the middle of the desert. It looked *wrong*, its sleek silver lines out of place in the rolling beiges of the desert landscape.

Kaia had always complained about the scenery—or, as she was quick to point out, lack thereof. They'd stood on her deck and looked out at the deserted space surrounding her house, and she'd seen nothing but an ocean of beige. She'd called it a wasteland, but only because she didn't see that what was sparse and clean could also be beautiful, precisely because it had nothing to hide. He hadn't had the words to explain it to her, however, so he'd just shrugged, and then kissed her.

She hated the house, too, but for different reasons. It was her outpost of civilization, true, but it was also her prison, and she resented its cream-colored walls and architecturally avant-garde floor plan, and even its size. She'd explained to him that her mother's penthouse apartment back home could fit into one wing of her father's mansion, and that the giant empty house swallowed her up and made her feel small and alone. It was the same way Reed felt about the desert, except he liked it.

Now the house really was empty. The windows had been dark and the driveway empty for weeks, until one day, Reed arrived to discover that the windows had been boarded up and a large FOR SALE sign planted in the absurdly well-manicured front lawn. But Reed kept coming back. He didn't have anything left of Kaia except his swiftly fading memories. He dreaded the day he forgot how her pale cheeks reddened when she laughed, or the hoarse sound in her voice when she'd just woken up; the house helped him remember.

"Don't I get some?" Kaia asks, grabbing his hand before he can bring the joint to his lips.

"You don't smoke," Reed reminds her.

"I know," she says, snatching it away and tossing it to

the ground. "And neither should you. It makes you sound like an idiot."

"Doesn't take much," he mutters.

"Shut up."

"What?"

"Clueless smile?" She grazes her fingers across his lips. "Hot. Self-deprecation? Not."

They are lying on a blanket in front of the old Grace mines. It has become "their place," a phrase neither of them will say out loud because, as Kaia often points out, this is not 1957 and they are not teenyboppers in love. But nonetheless, it is their place; ever since Reed brought her here for the first time, he has been unable to think of it as anything else. He has been coming here since he was a kid, biking out along the deserted stretch of highway long before he had his driver's license, enjoying the sense of freedom and power that came from getting away from the safe and the familiar and getting by on his own. But now, when he comes on his own, as he still does, something feels off. The cavernous warehouses, the decaying machinery, and the welcome darkness of the mines themselves are no longer enough. He misses Kaia; it has been only a couple weeks since they toppled to the happier side of the love-hate fence, but already he has got- ten used to having her around.

Today they skipped school and drove out here instead. They lie next to each other, staring up at the sky, swapping the occa- sional insult and listening to each other breathe. He doesn't know what he's doing with her—rich, stuck-up, spoiled, beautiful. And she's made it clear that she doesn't know what she's doing with him. Neither of them care.

"Don't try to reform me," he warns her. "It won't take."

She rolls over onto her side, propping herself up to look at him. Her fingers toy with the curls falling over his forehead, and a smile plays at the corners of her lip. "Don't worry," she assures him. "You're good just the way you are."

"And how's that?"

"Hmmm . . . dirty." She rubs his chest, where a long, dark grease stain stretches across his shirt. "Smelly." She buries her face in his neck and breathes in deeply. "Grungy." She pulls his hands toward her face and kisses the tips of his fingers, ignoring the dirt lodged under each nail. "Mine."

He grabs her around the waist and rolls her over on top of him, lifting his head up to meet her lips. They kiss with their eyes open, and he can see himself reflected in her pupils. Her weight flattens him against the ground and he lets his head fall back as she spreads his arms out and entwines her fingers in his.

They stop kissing after only a few minutes, but she continues to lie on him, resting her head on his chest.

"Happy?" he asks, because he knows she never is.

"Shhh. I'm listening."

"To what?"

"Your heartbeat," she whispers. They are both still. Then she laughs. "Did I just say that? What the hell are you doing

to me?" She sighs and tries to roll off of him, but he wraps his arms around her and holds her in place.

"Turning you into a sap," he teases. "I like it."

"Don't try to reform me," she tells him. "It won't take."

"Don't worry," he says, echoing her words as she echoed his. "You're good just the way you are."

Too late, he forgets how she hates compliments from him, even in jest.

"It's getting cold," she says, and he can feel her muscles tense. "I'm getting out of here."

"Don't," he tells her. "Stay."

She breathes deeply, and as her chest expands, it pushes against his, forcing their breathing to fall into the same rhythm. "I don't know what we're doing here," she says, touching the side of his face.

"Who cares?" he asks, laying his hand over hers. "Don't go."

She kisses him, hard, her tongue prying his lips open and slipping in, her hands gathering the light cotton blanket into tight fists. This time she closes her eyes, but he keeps his open. He can't stop watching her, as if part of him harbors the child-like belief that if he closes his eyes, she might actually disappear.

He looked up at the sound of a siren—it blipped once, like a horn blast, as if to alert him that he was totally screwed, without waking the neighbors. (Not that there were any.) The flashing lights of the approaching car cast a yellowish-orange tinge over everything as Reed scrambled to stow his pot deep in the glove compartment and popped a breath mint, not that it would be of much help. Everything about him reeked of stoner, and even though he'd had his last joint an hour or two ago and was as alert as he ever got these days, if the cops wanted to bust him, they would. It's not like they hadn't done it before.

The car pulled onto the shoulder just behind his, and a figure stepped out. As he approached, Reed was surprised to note that it wasn't Sal or Eddie, the two beat cops who loved nothing more than handing out parking tickets and hassling "street punks," aka anyone under the age of eighteen who didn't dress like they were auditioning for an Abercrombie ad. Sal and Eddie had, until recently, been actual street punks—or, as close as Grace got to urban blight—until their shoplifting had gotten them banned from pretty much every store on Main Street, and a number of drunken brawls had had the same effect on their barhopping days. They'd joined the police force for the thrill of running red lights; the guns were just a bonus.

This cop, an overweight guy in his mid-forties with a mustache and an eye-twitch, tapped on Reed's window. "Whatever you're up to, forget about it," he snapped, once Reed had rolled the window down. "Just get out of here."

That wasn't a cop uniform, Reed suddenly realized. It was gray, not navy blue, and a narrow label above the shirt pocket read CAPSTONE SECURITY. "What's it to you?" he asked. Sucking up to authority figures was bad enough; sucking up to a paunchy rent-a-cop who probably had a stash of his own hidden in the cruiser next to his mail-ordered Taser gun? Not gonna happen.

"Gimme a break, kid." The guy leaned against the truck, casually letting his jacket fall open to reveal the holster strapped underneath. It wasn't holding a Taser gun. "You think I'm out here in Crapville, USA, for my health? They pay plenty to run punks like you off the property— so I'm telling you. Get."

"No one lives here anymore," Reed pointed out.

"Don't mean no one owns it." He glanced up at the deserted mansion and scowled. "And the guy who does is plenty pissed off. There've been some break-ins—but I don't suppose you'd know anything about that, eh?"

Reed just stared blankly at him.

"Yeah. Of course not. But now I'm here, and I've got my instructions."

"Yeah?"

"No lurkers. No prowlers. No squatters. No punks." He squinted into the truck and stared pointedly at a glass pipe that had rolled onto the floor. "I don't care which one you are. Just get going and don't come back."

"Or what?" Reed asked, something in him spoiling for a fight. "You'll call in the *real* cops?"

"Don't need 'em," the guy said, ambling away from the window. But he didn't head back to his car—instead, he circled the front of the truck and, looking up to give Reed a jaunty grin, smashed in the front headlight.

"Dude! What the hell are you doing?"

"Take my advice, kid. Just get out of here," the guy yelled, waving with his arm still and his fingers glued together in the universal sign for *buh-bye*. "Just drive away and don't look back."

"Harper, can you come down here for a second?" Her mother's normally lilting voice had a steely undertone that suggested her options were limited.

"Great, more family together time," Harper muttered, burned out on bonding after a night that had already included ice-cream sundaes and four rounds of Boggle. Ever since the accident, her parents had gone into maximum overdrive on the TLC front—failing to realize that, to Harper, tender loving care involved a few drinks, a sugar high, and plenty of uninterrupted alone time. Tonight the plan had been simple: barricade herself in her room, blast some Belle and Sebastian, bury her head under a pillow, and try to plan out her next step. She'd been a master strategist, once, and though it seemed like too long ago to remember, she was certain the skills had just gone into hibernation, waiting for a more hospitable climate before they re-emerged to save her. Family fun time didn't fit into her schedule.

"What?" she grunted as she trudged down the stairs. She stopped, midway down, catching sight of Kane's smooth hair and smoother style. He gave her a reptilian grin, then offered her parents a far warmer expression, compassion oozing from every orifice.

"It's just so good to see her up and around again," he told her parents, as if she weren't even in the room.

"Yes, *she's* thrilled to pieces," Harper said dryly. "What the hell do you want?"

"Harper!" Her mother shot her a scandalized look. Much as Harper despised the depths to which her family had sunk over the generations, from American-style royalty (read: outrageously wealthy with an attitude to match) to middle-middle-class plodders carrying the torch of small-town mediocrity, Amanda Grace hated it more. So much so that she refused to acknowledge that the family she'd married into no longer guarded the flame of civility amongst the heathens of the Wild West. "People look to us," she'd often told a young Harper, lost in delusions of mannered grandeur, "and it's important we live up to expectations." Miss Manners had nothing on Amanda Grace; Emily Post would have been booted from the house for rude behavior. And a solicitous attitude toward guests, from visiting dignitaries (in her dreams) to collection agencies (a walking, and frequent, nightmare) was rule number one. Apparently even in her fragile, post-invalid state, Harper was still expected to abide by the Grace code of etiquette.

"As I was saying, Kane, it's so lovely of you to drop by," her mother said, placing a deceptively firm hand on Harper's shoulder. "*Isn't* it?"

"Lovely," Harper echoed. Her mother got a dutiful smile; Kane got the death glare.

"How are you feeling, sweetie?" her mother asked, releasing her grip.

"Fine." Harper scowled; if only everyone would stop asking her that a hundred times a day, maybe she'd actually have a prayer of it being true. Though that was doubtful, she conceded. How fine could she be when the most important moment of her life was lost in some fog of forgetfulness and the only glimpses her memory chose to grant her were the ones that proved she probably didn't deserve to live?

"That's great!" Amanda Grace turned to Kane. "I think it's a fine idea, then, as long as you don't have her out too late."

"Excuse me?" Harper snapped. "Could everyone stop talking about me like I'm invisible and—" She caught sight of her mother's face and forced herself to soften her tone. "What's a fine idea, *Kane*?"

"Well, *Harper*—" He winked at her, acknowledgment of the fact that he almost never used her first name and its appearance only confirmed that everything following would be a show put on for the sake of her parents. "I was just telling your parents that I thought you might enjoy it if I took you out for some coffee—"

"Decaf," her father interjected.

"Right, of course, decaf." Kane shrugged and gave everyone an "Aw shucks, aren't I a heck of a guy" look. "You've been cooped up in the house for so long, and we get so little chance to catch up in school, that I thought it might be nice. As long as your parents are okay with it, of course."

"It's quite refreshing," her father said, beaming. "Most of the time, you kids just dash off to some place or another and no one knows what the hell"—this time her father was the one who drew the patented Amanda glare—"I mean, heck, you're up to. I hope you know what a good friend you've got here, Harp. I think this one's a keeper."

"Oh, don't worry, I know exactly what I've got here," Harper said through gritted teeth. *Nice job with the Eddie Haskell impression*, she thought. *I'm suffocating in smarm.* Kane always boasted he could read minds—let him read that.

"I'm kind of tired, actually," she said, faking a yawn. "I was thinking I'd just stay here tonight . . ."

"You're spending too much time up in your room," her mother said, and behind the polite facade Harper could read real concern in her voice. "It'll be good for you to get out. Get back to—"

"Okay. Okay, fine, whatever," Harper cut in, knowing that if one more person suggested that things could ever be normal again, she might spit, or scream, or simply collapse, any one of which was definitely a Grace etiquette *don't*. With a sigh, she slipped into a pair of green flip-flops and grabbed a faded gray hoodie from the closet. Her mother hated it—so much the better.

"Now, remember, don't be back too late," Amanda Grace reminded them as Kane escorted her out, hands tightly gripping her arm and waist.

"So now you're kidnapping me?" Harper asked as soon as they were safely in the car. "General havoc and mischief making getting too boring for you, so you're moving on to felonies?"

"I don't know what you're talking about," Kane said in his parent-proof, silky smooth voice. "I just wanted to spend some time with my good friend Harper, who's so recently been having such a tough time of it." There was a pause, then, *"Oof!"*

Kane talked tough, but shove a sharp elbow into his gut and he'd fold like a poker player with no face cards.

"What the hell was that for?" he asked, rubbing his

side and giving her a wounded look. "You know I bruise easily."

"Gosh, I'm awfully sorry," Harper whined, pouring on some false solicitation of her own. "Whatever was I thinking?" Then she whacked him in the chest. "What the hell were you thinking? Since when do you ask my parents for my hand in coffee?"

"If I called and asked if you wanted to go out tonight, what would you have said?"

"You're assuming I would have picked up the phone?"

"Exactly," he concluded in an irritatingly reasonable voice. "You would have made the wrong choice. *Again.* So this time, I decided not to give you one."

"Fine." Harper leaned back against the seat and rolled her eyes toward the ceiling. "So where are you taking me? Bourquin's, at least? I can't drink that shit coffee they have at the diner."

He shook his head. "Guess again."

"*So* not in the mood for games, Kane. And you know exactly why."

"This isn't a game, Grace—you're the one who hasn't figured that out yet. You'll see where we're going soon enough."

She crossed her arms and turned toward the window. "Fine."

"Fine."

They drove in silence for several minutes. The radio might at least have lightened things up or offered them something neutral to argue about, but Kane made no move to switch it on and Harper wasn't about to do anything that might signify her willing participation in this ridiculous adventure.

They swung into a small parking lot and Kane turned off the car. "We're here."

"And where is . . . oh." They had pulled up in front of a large, boxy building, its face a windowless wall of institutional gray. A single door, also gray, stood square in the middle, and over it hung a neon blue-and-white sign that would have been enough to scare away most visitors if the decor hadn't already done the job: POLICE.

"What the hell is this, Kane?" Harper's eyes flicked toward her bag, half expecting her phone to ring as if Detective Wells, who'd already left four or five messages for her over the course of the day, could somehow sense that she was nearby. Maybe she wouldn't bother to call—Harper turned back to the window, gaze fixed on the solid-looking door, wondering if it would swing open. Who would they send out to escort her inside, where she belonged? "Why would you bring me here?"

Kane shrugged, but this time there was nothing *aw-shucks* about it. "You're the one who said you wanted to talk to the cops. I thought I'd help you out. You want to confess your sins? You want to ruin your life? Go ahead."

"This isn't how it works," she retorted, struggling against encroaching panic. "This isn't—what do you want me to do, just march in there and say, 'Hey, just FYI, I was the one driving the car'?"

"You don't think they'd be interested to hear it?"

"This is what you want me to do?" Harper asked, her hand gripping the door handle.

"Isn't it what *you* want to do?" Kane sneered.

"It's the right thing. . . ."

"Absolutely. So go ahead."

"I'm just not . . . "

"No time like the present, Grace." Kane opened his own door—and at the sound of the latch releasing and the outside air rushing in, Harper almost gasped. "I'll go with you, if you want. Should be quite a show."

She couldn't say anything; she didn't move.

"What are you waiting for? They're right inside, just—"

"Stop!" she shouted, slapping her hand over her eyes so he wouldn't see the tears. "Why are you doing this?"

He slammed the door. "Why are *you* doing this?" he shouted, and it was the first time she could remember ever hearing him raise his voice. "What the hell are you trying to do to yourself?"

"What do you care?" she mumbled, still hiding her face.

"This is real, Harper. Look out there." When she didn't move, he grabbed her hands roughly and pulled them away from her eyes, jerking her head toward the police station. "*Look.* This isn't *Law & Order.* This is your life."

"It was her life too," Harper said, almost too softly to hear.

"You don't know what happened," Kane said in an almost bored voice, as if he'd gotten tired of ticking off the items on the list. He'd stopped shouting and had released his grip on Harper's wrists, and was now staring straight ahead, his hands loosely resting on the wheel. "You don't remember anything about the accident—" She tried to interrupt, but he talked over her. "*Except* a few things you *think* you remember but could just be part of some Vicodin-induced nightmare."

"Percodan," she corrected him.

"Whatever. Okay, so you were driving. So what? There were drugs in your system—you don't know how they got there. You were going somewhere—you don't know where. Kaia's fingerprints were found all over that perv's apartment after he turned up with his head beat in—you don't know why. Another car forced you off the road—you don't know who. You don't know *anything* except that if you tell them you were behind that wheel, they'll crucify you."

"I know it's my fault," she said stubbornly.

"You don't know *anything*," he repeated loudly, over-enunciating each syllable.

And I can't stand it, she admitted, but only to herself.

"I'm not saying we can't figure it out," he suggested, turning toward her and slinging his arm across the back of her seat. "Do some investigating, poke around—you and me against the world, like the good old days?"

"So this isn't *Law & Order*, but now you want me to go all Veronica Mars on you?" Harper asked wryly.

"That's kind of a chick show." Kane smirked. "I was thinking more *CSI*. Or *Scooby-Doo* . . . you'd look pretty smoking in that purple dress, and I don't know"—he peered at himself in the rearview mirror—"think I could pull off an ascot?"

"This isn't funny," she said dully.

"I'm serious, Grace—if you want to know what happened, we can figure it out. *They* can't," he added, pointing toward the station. "They won't need to, because they'll have you. But we can fix things, and get them back to normal."

"Take me home," she told him, not wanting to think any more about the accident, or any of it.

He ignored her. "Start with the drugs—that's the key. Are you sure you didn't take *anything*?"

She remembered Kaia handing her two white pills:

Xanax. She remembered popping them into her mouth and stepping onstage, and her world falling apart. But that couldn't be right.

"Take me home," she insisted, louder.

"Promise me you won't go to the cops," he retorted.

"I still don't get why you care."

"You don't have to," he said, looking away. "Just promise." She had already promised herself that she would do the right thing; tonight was supposed to have been about figuring out what that was. Kane was the last person to go to for that kind of help. *On the other hand*, she thought, torn between horror and bemusement, *who else have I got?*

"I'll do whatever I decide to do, Kane. Take me home."

Kane banged a fist against the steering wheel, then visibly steadied himself, taking two deep breaths before turning to her with a serene smile. "Fine, Grace. Do what you need to do. It's your funeral."

But that was just the problem—maybe it should have been. But it wasn't.

chapter seven

THE NEWSPAPER STAFF WAS AT THE HOSPITAL, reading picture books to sick children.

The cast of the school musical was performing excerpts from *Oklahoma!* at the Grace Retirement Village.

The French club was distributing meals—with a side of croissants, but no wine—to invalids and shut-ins.

Community Service Day was a success, and any senior with a conscience or a guilt complex was devoting the morning to helping others. The only seniors left in class were the ones too lazy to make the effort and too dim to realize that even cleaning bedpans or trimming nose hairs would be preferable to spending the morning in school.

And then there was Beth.

She'd organized the event, worked with the hospital administrators and the town hall community liaison, shined with pride at adding a socially responsible activity to the spirit week agenda, and planned to lead the charge with a quick visit to the Grace animal shelter and a stop at the hospital children's wing, culminating in a triumphant hour of reading to the blind. But instead, she was hiding in an empty classroom, folded over her desk with her head buried in her arms, like she was playing Heads Up, Seven Up all by herself. She'd told her history teacher that she had a headache, but instead of going to the nurse's office, she'd slipped in here and was wiling away her time by listening to her breathing and wondering if Berkeley admitted felons.

She looked up at the sound of a knock on the door. Before she had a chance to come up with a cover story or consider hiding, the door swung open, and Beth was momentarily relieved to realize that it wasn't a teacher, who might demand an explanation for Beth's presence. But her relief was short-lived, as a dour-looking woman with a squarish build, coffee-colored skin, and a pinched, vaguely familiar face stepped into the room—followed by a reluctant Harper Grace.

"I was told this room would be empty," the woman said, her words clipped and precise. "You'll have to go."

The woman sat down on one of the desks and, without bothering to check that Beth would follow her command, focused her attention on Harper.

"I should get back to class," Harper mumbled, still standing in the doorway. Beth had to push past her to get out of the room, a maneuver made more difficult by the fact that Harper didn't edge out of the way, but instead just stood planted in the middle of the doorway.

"Come in, sit down," the woman said, and though her voice was soft, it was far from kind. "You said you needed to talk to me—here I am."

Harper glanced toward Beth for the first time, and Beth recoiled from the look in her eyes, a confusing mixture of *Get out* and, more disturbingly, *Stay*. Beth quickened her step. She shut the door behind her, just slowly enough to hear the woman's final words.

"So, what did you remember about the accident?"

She just *had* to come to school today. She couldn't be bothered to tend to the elderly or wipe the brows of the sick—and apparently, this was her punishment. Detective Wells was perched on the edge of one of the desks, while Harper had squeezed herself into a seat, feeling oddly constrained by the metal rod and flat, narrow desk that wrapped around and held her in place. When they called her out of class, she should have known what was coming, but she'd somehow fooled herself into thinking that Wells was a problem that, if ignored, would go away. Not forever, she'd promised herself, screening the latest of the calls, but just long enough that Harper could have a chance to figure out what she was going to do.

Apparently Detective Wells was working on her own timeline.

"I really don't remember what happened," Harper said uncomfortably. The detective's gaze was making her skin crawl, but the alternative views weren't much better. Whoever usually used this classroom had papered the walls with portraits of historical courage—Martin Luther King, Jr., FDR, Rosa Parks, Winston Churchill (she only recognized that one thanks to the oversize caption)—face after face staring down at her with solemn expectation. All she needed was a big painting of Honest Abe to remind her that *some* people "cannot tell a lie." (Or was it George Washington who'd chopped down his cherry tree and then needlessly confessed? Harper could never remember, but she'd always thought that, in the same position, she would have gorged herself on cherries and then enjoyed a sound sleep in the log cabin without giving her sticky red ax a second thought.)

"You left me a message, Harper, saying that you'd remembered *something*." A ridge of wrinkles spread across the detective's forehead. "I don't know why you wouldn't want to help us out, unless—"

"It's just hard," Harper said quickly. *Shut up*, she told FDR's accusing stare. *At least that's true.* "You know, talking about . . . what happened." After struggling for weeks to maintain a mask of contentment, it was tough to make an abrupt shift to visible vulnerability. But Harper didn't know how else to slow things down.

It worked.

"Just take your time," Detective Wells suggested. She leaned forward. "Anything you remember might help us, even if it seems inconsequential."

Harper took a breath and opened her mouth, then shut it again, stalling for time. *You don't know anything*, Kane had said. She wanted to believe him. "I remembered . . . I thought I remembered that the car that hit us was . . . white."

The detective whipped out a notebook and favored Harper with a wide smile. "That's great—anything else?"

"But then, the next night, I had another dream, and the car was black. I guess it was just a dream. Not, you know, a memory," Harper added, wondering if Grace cops got trained in spotting liars. Detective Wells didn't seem much like a human polygraph machine, but you could never tell. "That's why I was, uh, avoiding your calls. I was embarrassed to waste your time."

"It's not a waste," the detective assured her, without bothering to suppress a disappointed sigh. She shut the notebook and stuffed it back into her bag. "You thought you could help, and you did the right thing. No need to be embarrassed about that."

"So . . ." She wasn't sure she actually wanted to know. "Do you have any leads?" Did they even use that word in real life? she wondered. "You know, about what happened? I mean, the other car?"

She shook her head. "We haven't been able to match the paint samples—the van was red, by the way."

"Oh." She wondered why no one had told her that before. She tried to imagine a red van speeding toward her and tried to picture her hands on the wheel, jerking away; but visualization exercises were tough to do when you had to keep your eyes open and smile at a cranky detective.

"We've ascertained that both vehicles were speeding, and that the collision took place on your side of the road, which implies that the driver of the other vehicle may have strayed into your lane, but I'm afraid that's all we know. So far, of course."

"Of course," Harper repeated, although judging from Detective Wells's hopeless and impersonal tone, she guessed that no one really expected to learn much more. "But if you ever did find the guy . . . ?"

"Hit-and-run is a very serious crime," the detective said, looking up at the posters lining the wall. "He or she would be punished to the fullest extent of the law." She scratched the side of her neck, visibly uncomfortable with what she had to say next. "Look, I know it can be difficult, after a traumatic event like this—especially when no one's taken responsibility, and you have no one to blame. There are people you can talk to, if—"

"I'm fine," Harper half shouted. "Can I go back to class now?"

"Sure. Of course. Thanks for speaking with me."

"Sorry you had to come out here for nothing." As Detective Wells shook her hand and headed for the door, Harper could feel her split-second decision hardening into reality. She could still tell the truth—catch the detective before she walked out the door and explain everything—but then the door shut, and the moment had passed.

These are the things I know, Harper told herself.

1. No one knew she was driving, and Kane would never tell.
2. If the van had been in the wrong lane, the accident would have happened anyway, no matter who was driving.
3. Kaia was dead, and she would stay that way, no matter what anyone did.
4. Kaia didn't believe in self-sacrifice.

That left plenty of gaping holes. She didn't know where she'd gotten the drugs from, or why she had taken them. She didn't know why she and Kaia were on the road in the first place, or where they were going. She didn't know whose fault the accident was, not really, though she could pretend that she did. She didn't know if she believed in Hell, so she obviously didn't know if she'd end up there. And she didn't know if she could live with herself—with what she knew and what she didn't—in the meantime.

I have to, she told herself. *And I will.* She looked again at the posters—JFK, Gandhi, Anne Frank, Charles Lindbergh. They must have been from a set made specially for irony-deficient high school teachers, because they all bore some cheesy-beyond-belief quote designed to inspire students.

The nearest way to glory is to strive to be what you wish to be thought to be. Socrates.

He who fears being conquered is sure of defeat. Napoleon.

It's not good enough that we do our best; sometimes we have to do what is required. Winston Churchill.

That one appealed to her the most.

I will do what I have to do and no matter what, I will survive. Harper Grace.

"Where to?"

Beth leaned her head back against the seat and half-heartedly tried to wipe some of the grime off her window, as if the answer to his question might arise from a better view. "Wherever." The word came out as a sigh, fading to silence before the last syllable.

"Okay." Reed drove in circles for a while. He had nowhere to be. When she'd called, he had been at his father's garage, tinkering with an exhaust system and ready for a break. "Can you come?" she'd asked. And for whatever reason, he'd dropped everything and hopped in the truck. He'd found her slouched at the foot of a tree, just in front of the school, hugging her arms to her chest and shivering. She wouldn't tell him anything, but when he extended a hand to help her into the truck, she squeezed.

It's not like they were friends, he told himself. But she needed something, and he had nothing better to do. He couldn't help but notice that she relaxed into her seat, stretching out along the cracked vinyl, unlike Kaia, who almost always perched on the edge and sat poker-straight in an effort to have as little contact with the "filthy" interior as possible. Beth also hadn't commented on his torn overalls or the smudges of grease splashed across his face and blackening his fingers.

Reed caught himself and, for a moment, felt the urge to stop the car and toss her out on the side of the road. But it passed. "Wanna talk about it?" he asked.

She shook her head. "I don't even want to *think* about it," she said. "Any chance you can take me somewhere where I can do that? Stop thinking?"

She said it bitterly, as if it were an impossible challenge. But she obviously didn't know who she was dealing with.

Reed swung the car around the empty road in a sharp U-turn and pressed down on the gas pedal. She sighed again heavily, and without thinking, he reached over to put a hand on her shoulder, but stopped in midair—maybe because Kaia had trained him well: no greasy fingers on white shirts. Maybe because he didn't want to touch her— or maybe because he did.

He put his hand back on the wheel and began drumming out a light, simple beat. "I know just the place," he assured her. "We'll be there soon." It felt good to have a destination.

Adam crushed the paper into a ball and crammed it into the bottom of his backpack, then butted his head against the door of a nearby locker—stupid idea, since all it produced was a dull thud and a sharp pain, neither of which went very far toward alleviating his frustration.

But a stupid idea seemed appropriate; after all, what other kind did he have?

Fifty-eight percent.

Maybe if he and Miranda had spent more time working and less time playing video games and talking about Harper . . . At the time, it had seemed like the right thing to do. For those few hours, he'd felt more normal and more hopeful than he had in a long time. Though he and Miranda had never been close, they had history—and, more important, they had Harper. He hadn't needed to confide in her, because she already knew how he felt. And he knew she felt the same.

She was a good friend, he'd realized.

Just maybe not a very good tutor.

Or maybe it's just me, Adam thought in disgust. He'd actually studied this time, staring at the equations long enough that at least a few of them should have started to make sense and weld themselves to his brain. But the test had been a page of incomprehensible hieroglyphics, and Adam's answers—what few he bothered to attempt— were mostly random numbers and symbols that he strung together in an approximation of what he thought an alge- bra equation should look like.

Thanks to Mr. Fowler's supersonic grading policy—all tests graded and returned by the end of the school day, courtesy of a team of eager beaver honor students who gave up their lunch period for some extra credit and a superiority complex—he didn't have long to wait for the results. Not that there was much suspense.

Fifty-eight percent. It was scrawled in an angry red, next to a big, circled F and a note reading *Come see me*.

Instead, Adam dumped his stuff in his locker and walked out of school. It was bad enough he'd had to show up in the first place. Haven teachers were "encouraged" to postpone tests and important lessons for Community Service Day, but Adam's math class was for sophomores and juniors. Which meant enduring both a brain-busting test and the curious stares of his classmates who obviously wondered what kind of loser he was to get left so far behind. Now that he was free for the day, he wasn't going back.

He stomped out of the school, the pounding of his footsteps mirrored by the rhythmic battering of a single word against his brain:

Stupid.

Stupid.

Stupid.

Stupid.

His basketball was in the trunk, and the court across from the school parking lot was empty. It was a no-brainer—fortunately, since his brain was otherwise occupied.

Adam dribbled up and down the court, forcing himself to take it slow and easy. At first the word beat louder, in time with the ball slapping his palm and then slamming into the concrete.

STU-pid.

STU-pid.

STU-pid.

But then he sank his first basket. Adam had always

been able to lose himself in the soft sigh of the ball sinking through the net, and today was no different. He emptied his mind and let his body take over, relaxing into the familiar *thwack* and *crack* and *swoosh* that made him feel more alive. Chest heaving, muscles aching, sweat pouring down his face, he didn't notice the time passing or the sky darkening. He stopped only briefly to take a few swigs of water, and again to pull off his shirt and toss it to the sidelines, dimly registering that the scalding afternoon sun had given way to a cool breeze.

He didn't notice Kane step onto the court—it wasn't until the rebound dropped into Kane's hands that Adam looked up. It wasn't the sight of Kane's tall, angular figure poised under the basket that knocked Adam out of the zone; it was the break in the rhythm, when suddenly the expected crack of the ball against pavement was replaced by a soft slap and then silence, as Kane cradled the ball to his chest.

They hadn't faced each other on a basketball court since the game last month, when Adam started a fight with the other team and, in the chaos, flattened Kane, accidentally on purpose. The bruises had taken a couple weeks to fade; Kane's basketball career had dissipated more quickly, as he hadn't returned to practice since.

Kane held the ball and looked at Adam expectantly, his infuriating smirk gone. There were a lot of things Adam could have said—many that he'd said before, many he'd been holding in for a long time:

I thought we were friends.

Did you want Beth, or did you just want to screw with me?

Are you happy now?

We both slept with someone who died. Are you as freaked out by that as I am?

What happens now?

"Check it," he called, reaching for the ball. Kane bounced it toward him. "First to fifteen."

"Make it twenty-one," Kane suggested, chasing after Adam as he dribbled the ball up the court.

Adam feinted left, then went right, darting around Kane, sprinting toward the basket, and sinking an easy layup. "Done," he agreed.

That was the end of the talking. After that it was all grunting and panting, punctuated by the occasional groan of displeasure as a ball rolled off the rim or a hoot of triumph after a wild shot from the three-point line sailed in with nothing but net. An hour passed, and soon they were playing in the shadows, tracking a sound and a silhouette to chase down the ball, shooting as much by feel as by sight.

Kane sank the final shot. "Twenty-one!" he crowed.

He always won. Adam felt the familiar anger bubble up, but instead of exploding, it just popped and drizzled away, like a string of soap bubbles turning to mist. "Good game," he grunted, slapping Kane's sweaty palm. He grabbed his water bottle and dumped it over his head, closing his eyes and tipping his face up to the cool stream.

"Morgan . . . ?" Kane, who looked as sleek and unruffled as when he'd first appeared, tossed Adam his shirt and a second bottle of water. He rubbed his lower back and looked over toward the empty parking lot. "Look. About . . . everything . . ."

"Forget it, Geary." Adam pulled his shirt on over his dripping torso and grabbed the ball out of Kane's loose grip. He rolled it around in his hands, enjoying the familiar grooves and ridges of its rough grain. "Rematch tomorrow?" he suggested. He turned his back on Kane without waiting for an answer and headed for the car.

"Same time, same place," Kane agreed from behind him, and it was impossible to tell whether his unfailingly sardonic tone masked relief, eagerness, apathy, or regret.

Adam bounced the ball a few times, then tossed it high in the air and caught it with his eyes closed, cupping his hands in a loose cradle and stretching them out to where he knew the ball would be. "I'll be there."

"Aw yeah, that's right." The one named Hale clapped his hands together once as Fish hoisted a giant glass tube out of the crawl space behind the lopsided couch. "Give it here, dude."

"Hold your shit," Fish said, flourishing a lighter.

Beth tucked her hair behind her ears and tried not to look nervous.

Get out, her instincts screamed.

"You okay?" Reed asked, as if he could sense her discomfort. It probably wasn't too hard, she realized, since she was squeezed into the corner of the couch, as far away from Fish as she could get, her arms scrunched up against her sides and her mouth glued shut. She nodded.

"Over here, baby," Hale requested, beckoning Fish to hand over the bong.

"Dude, don't you have any manners?" Fish grabbed one of the discarded fast-food wrappers off the ground, scrunched it up, and threw it at his head. "Ladies first." He stretched across the couch and handed the long glass tube to Beth, giving her an encouraging nod. She noticed that his hair was even paler than hers, and almost as long.

"Guys, I don't think . . ." Reed, who was perched on an orange milk crate, leaned forward, speaking softly enough that only Beth could hear. "You don't have to. We can go, if you want."

He'd said the same thing when they'd walked into the house and he'd seen the look on her face. There were some empty rooms upstairs, he'd suggested, if she didn't want to hang with the guys—and then he'd flushed, stumbling over his words, hurrying to explain that he hadn't meant *bedrooms*, not like that. Or they could just go. Anywhere. But for some reason, Beth had insisted they stay, and now here she was, the bong delicately balanced in her hands, nauseating fumes rising toward her, a trippy hip-hop beat shaking the walls—which were covered with fading posters of half-naked women—and for the first time that day, Beth smiled.

"Just tell me what to do," she said firmly. She'd always sworn she wouldn't smoke pot—it was illegal, not to mention dangerous. But she was already a criminal, she reminded herself, and danger didn't scare her anymore— things couldn't get much worse. If she could find a way to turn off her brain, maybe, for a little while, they could actually be better.

Reed didn't try to talk her out of it, and didn't ask about the sudden change of heart. He just rested his hand on top of hers and guided the opening toward her mouth, then gently pressed her finger over a small hole and flicked on the lighter. "Take a deep breath, but don't—"

A spasm of coughing wracked through her body and she inadvertently jerked the bong away, spilling warm, grayish water all over her jeans. "Sorry," she mumbled, her face flushing red.

"No problem. Take a smaller breath the next time," Reed suggested. "And don't uncover the hole until you're ready. Then suck the smoke into your mouth and kind of breathe it down into your lungs."

"Okay, I think—" She broke off as another cough ripped out of her. Reed put his hand on her back, rubbing in small, slow circles.

"Take it easy," he said quietly. "Go slow."

"I'm okay. I'm okay," she protested, straightening up so that he would take his hand away, even though it was the last thing she wanted. "Let me try this again." This time she got a hot lungful down without much coughing. She passed the bong to Fish and leaned back against the couch, waiting for it to take effect.

"Man, this is some good shit!" Fish sputtered as he took his mouth off the tube.

"Totally," Hale agreed after his turn, already looking tuned out to the world.

Reed didn't say anything after his turn, just fixed his eyes on Beth. She looked away, waiting for the room to start spinning or her tongue to start feeling absurdly big. She felt nothing, except the same panic and fear she'd felt for days.

"Time for another little toke," Hale said eagerly, grabbing it back. "Yeah, that's good. Dude, I'm totally high."

"It's like . . . yeah. Cool," Fish agreed.

"Hey, uh . . . Reed's girl, you feeling it?" Hale asked.

Lesson one of getting stoned: Talk about how stoned you are. Beth learned fast. "Yeah," she lied. "It's really wild."

"Dude, Fish, you know what I just realized? You totally look like a girl," Hale cried, a burst of giggles flooding out of him.

Fish ran his fingers through his straggly straw-colored hair as if realizing it was there for the first time, then looked at Beth in wonderment. "Yeah," he agreed. "And I must be hot. Blondes are *hot.*"

Beth laughed weakly and searched herself for hysteria, paranoia, munchies—*something* to testify to the fact that she'd just ingested an illegal substance for the first time in her life. But she felt, if anything, more self-conscious than ever, as if they could all tell that her mind was running at normal speed and that she was, even here, a total fraud.

"You usually don't feel much the first time," Reed confided, again using that just-for-her voice. "You didn't do it wrong."

Once again, he'd known exactly what she was thinking. A horrifying thought occurred to her: What if he really could tell what she was thinking? What if he knew about Harper, and about Kaia, about everything? And even if he didn't, what would happen if he found out?

Maybe this is paranoia, Beth thought, and now a hysterical giggle did escape her. *Maybe I am high.*

"So, you guys, like, live here?" she asked, trying to make her voice sound as slow and foggy as theirs.

"Fish and Hale do," Reed explained. "And I crash here sometimes."

"He brings his *ladies* here," Hale cackled. "All except—"

"Dude, shut up," Fish snapped, pelting him with another fast-food wrapper—this one seemed to have a chunk of something oozing out of it.

"Oh, yeah. Right. Sorry, bro. Didn't mean to—"

"Whatever." Reed turned the stereo up and then threw himself down on the couch in between Beth and Fish. He leaned his head back, closed his eyes, and kicked his legs up on the milk crate. "Awesome song." He sighed.

When in Rome . . . , Beth thought. *Do as the potheads do.* She closed her eyes, kicked her feet up on the same milk crate so that one leg crossed over Reed's, and forced a serene smile. "I'm, uh, totally hungry," she said tentatively "Anyone got anything to eat?"

It was such a relief not to have to screen her calls anymore that Harper forgot to play it safe; she forgot that there were still plenty of things she needed to avoid.

"So, I was thinking, tomorrow night," Adam said as soon as she picked up.

"For what?" She lay on her bed, facing away from the window so she wouldn't be tempted to look out for him, or wonder if he was watching her.

"For our date."

"Adam—" she began warningly.

"I paid good money for that date," he pointed out.

"Don't remind me." Her list of humiliating moments was mounting up daily, but stepping onstage for that auction still hovered near the top. "Let's just forget the whole thing."

"Tomorrow night," Adam said again. "Eight. I'll pick you up."

"I told you that I'm not doing this," Harper told him, but she was too tired to fight. "You and me . . ."

"One night. You owe me that."

She sighed. "Fine. Eight. See you then." He started to say something else, but Harper hung up.

It was barely past nine, but she was already in her pajamas. Her homework lay undone—as usual—in a stack on her desk. Her Thoroughly Depressing Music mix (Anna Nalick, Norah Jones, Belle and Sebastian, Mumford and Sons), was on repeat.

"'*Breathe, just breathe . . . ,*' " she sang along under her breath with the mournful melody. "'*There's a light at each end of this tunnel, you shout 'cause you're just as far in as you'll ever be out . . .* '"

Yeah, right. Everyone had a cliché to offer, and they were all wrong.

Harper was wearing one of Adam's old T-shirts, a Lakers shirt that he'd brought back from his one trip to

L.A. a few years ago. Before going, he'd bragged to half the school about going to see Shaq and Kobe play. His mom was dating some real-estate hotshot she'd met at a conference, and the guy had gotten them floor seats and all-access passes. He might even get into the locker room, Adam had bragged. But on the night of the game, his mom and her bigwig boyfriend had disappeared for the night, leaving Adam back in the hotel room to watch porn and steal candy from the minibar. He showed up at school the next week wearing the Lakers shirt, full of stories about Shaq's giant feet and the way Kobe had winked at him. Harper was the only one he ever trusted with the truth. She'd borrowed the shirt once last summer, after a drunken water balloon fight had gotten out of hand. She never gave it back.

Summer had been easier, she thought, but then stopped herself. Even then, things hadn't been right, not really. Adam had been slobbering over Beth while Harper pretended not to care. She imagined she could still see shallow imprints in the heel of each hand from where she'd dug her nails in every time she saw them together, hoping the pain would distract her. She had thought that if she got rid of Beth, somehow, all her problems would just go away. After all, she was Harper Grace—she wasn't supposed to have problems. Ask anyone. She could still remember when that had been true—not last summer, but the one before that, when everything in her life had still made sense.

Kane measures out a small shot of vodka into each of their plastic cups, then tucks the silver flask back into his pocket. Harper puts an arm around Miranda and leans against Adam and, after they clink glasses, downs the shot in a single gulp. A warm tingle spreads through her.

"This idea wasn't nearly as dumb as I thought it was," she admits to Kane, who has dragged them out to the lame ghost town in the dead of night. He gives her a mock bow. They have snuck inside the fake saloon, squeezing up to a table already occupied by plastic mannequins dressed in cowboy clothing. A frozen bartender stands behind the bar, holding a jug of whiskey that will always remain half empty.

"Agreed," Adam says, clapping Kane on the back. "Excellent plan."

"I'm full of them," Kane brags.

Miranda snorts. "Is that why your head's so big?"

He grabs her and puts her in a loose headlock. "Watch it, Stevens," he warns, "or I might be forced to . . ."

"I'm terrified," *Miranda says sarcastically.* "I'm shaking. What are you going to do?"

Kane doesn't respond, just drives his knuckles into her head and spins. A noogie.

"What are you, ten years old?" *Miranda squeals, convulsing in giggles as he lets her go.*

Adam and Harper exchange a glance and smile.

"So where's your latest conquest?" Kane asks Adam. "I figured you'd bring her along."

Harper suppresses a laugh. Adam doesn't bring his girl-friends out on excursions like this. They're excess baggage. They'd miss the jokes and spoil the flow of banter honed over the years. They are a foursome, and Adam knows better than to screw with that.

"This one's kind of cute," she tells him, ruffling his hair. "A little bland, but—"

"Who needs a personality when you've got a body like that?" Kane points out, giving them an exaggerated leer. "She's hot."

Miranda smacks him on the shoulder. "She must have some personality—after all, she was too clever to fall for your bullshit."

"I just stepped out of the way and let my man here have a shot," Kane says magnanimously.

Adam, Harper notices, says nothing. It's his turn—now is the time when he chimes in about the annoying way she slurps her soup or the nasal sound of her voice. They always have some minor flaw that becomes insurmountable—too much throat clearing, too many pimples, not enough Family Guy trivia— and then he moves on to the next. It is how things work.

"I'm going to do some exploring," he says instead, stand-ing up.

Harper jumps up. "I'll come along. You guys in?"

Kane puts an arm around one of the mannequins. "What? And leave my friend Buffalo Bob here to drink alone?"

Miranda stays too, and Harper and Adam wander out into the darkness. There are no lights, and she can barely see. She takes Adam's hand so they don't get separated. It is warm and his grip is strong, and she is not afraid of falling.

"Where do you want to go?" she asks.

He shrugs. "Dunno. I just needed to get out of there."

They wander aimlessly without speaking, past ramshackle buildings whose hokey labels are too difficult to read in the dark. This is the Adam no one else knows, quiet and thoughtful. To everyone else, he is the hot jock, blond and beautiful. To Harper, he is just Adam, who eats his pizza slices crust first, can recite the alphabet backward, and has a tiny scar just behind his left ear. He always capitalizes the word "summer," and flosses his teeth twice every night because he's terrified of getting a cavity. She knows him better than she's ever known anyone.

"So what's the deal?" she asks, shivering as the wind begins to blow. He puts his arm around her and tugs her toward him. She snuggles into his side, where it's warm.

"With what?"

"With the new girl. Beth. Bad breath? Can't stop clearing her throat? Drools when she kisses?"

"Nah, she's good."

"Come on," she says playfully. "It's always something. You can tell me."

"It's weird, Gracie." His voice isn't playful at all. "It's not like that. She's . . . different."

"Oh, I get it." Harper squeezes her arm around his waist. "You're still in that nauseating 'everything is wonderful' stage. Ah, young lust. So romantic."

"No." He stops walking and drops his arm away from her shoulder. "It really is different this time. It's . . . she's . . ." He holds his hands out to his sides. She can't see his face in the dark. "I can't explain. There's just something about her."

"I understand, Ad." And she does. She throws her arms around him and hugs him tightly. "I'm really happy for you." And she wants to mean it. She knows she should mean it, but as she holds him, her face burrowed into his shoulder, breathing in the familiar mix of fabric softener and a woodsy aftershave, she realizes something important. And then she squeezes tighter. She doesn't want to let go, because when she does, everything will change.

Harper turned out the light and curled up into a ball, trying to sleep. Her leg throbbed and her back ached, and the T-shirt felt uncomfortably tight around her collar. It kept getting caught beneath her weight as she rolled to one side, then the other. It was tugging at her and choking her, keeping her from sinking into sleep. Eventually she wriggled out of it and tossed it to the floor. It didn't even smell like him anymore.

chapter eight

"TELL ME YOU'RE FREE TONIGHT."

"Uh . . . what? Who is this?" But Miranda knew who it was. She would have recognized the voice even if she hadn't recognized the number (which she'd memorized back in ninth grade).

"I'm bored," Kane said, affecting a little kid voice. "Come play with me?"

Her chest tightened, and a warm glow spread through her cheeks. *Not a date*, she reminded herself. But the caution had little effect. He wanted to see her; that had to mean something.

"It's kind of short notice," she pointed out, toying

with him. "A true lady wouldn't accept an offer made in such haste."

"Well then, it's a good thing you're not—"

"Don't even say it," she warned. This whole banter thing was so much easier when he wasn't there to see the crimson flush rising in her cheeks. She could put her hand over the mouthpiece whenever she needed to mask her giggles and gasps. It was easy to sound cool and unconcerned.

He laughed—a rich, warm sound made all the sexier by the knowledge that she'd caused it.

"There's this thing, kind of a pre-party, and it'll probably be lame, but I thought I'd check it out," he explained.

"Pre-party? So I'm not good enough to take to the *actual* party?" She sounded sarcastic, but couldn't help but fear it was true.

"Insecurity doesn't suit you, my dear. The actual party's tomorrow night—this is just a little warm-up."

"Why not?" She tried not to sound too eager.

"Cool. You think you can give me a ride? I figure, in case I get wasted . . ."

Well, that solved the mystery. He just needed a designated driver; it's not that he thought he'd have fun with her, it's that he knew she could be trusted *not* to have any fun. She pressed her palm against the mouthpiece and sighed. It didn't matter why he had called. She would go anyway, just as she would spend the next half hour tormenting herself about what to wear, even though she'd already convinced herself that he didn't want anything from her beyond the occasional ride and no-strings-attached hookup. There was always a chance, and even an eternal pessimist like Miranda couldn't help but cling to that.

Adam brought her to The Whole Enchilada, her favorite restaurant—as Kaia had often pointed out, there was no *good* food in Grace, but the local Mexican food came the closest. Harper hadn't wanted to admit that she was addicted to their guacamole ("could be fresher," according to Kaia) and loved their burritos ("overstuffed"), but both girls agreed that the stale chips and crappy salsa—half as spicy and twice as watery as you'd want—were worth suffering through for the oversize frozen margaritas. They were frothy and sweet, with a double shot of tequila—and served by waiters who could be counted on not to card.

Tonight, Harper sipped a Coke.

She hadn't said much after hello, nor had she bothered to listen as Adam babbled on about his latest basketball game or some lame joke the guys had pulled on their coach. She'd ordered a chicken enchilada, but when it appeared in front of her, she couldn't even imagine eating it. She nibbled at the edges, crunched down on a couple chips, and drank a lot of water. It was a waste of a meal, but then, Adam was paying—so who cared?

"You know, my grandfather died when I was a kid," he said abruptly.

She froze, a forkful of rice halfway to her mouth. She'd been expecting him to bring up Kaia, and she'd readied herself to shoot him down. But she didn't have a contingency plan for this.

"He was the only grandparent I had," Adam continued. "My dad's parents, they kind of . . . disappeared, or something. Before I was born. And my mom's mom died when she was a kid. But my grandfather was around for a while, and when he died, you know, it was really sudden. It sucked."

Harper felt like she was supposed to say something. "Yeah."

"I didn't, uh, I didn't really get it, at first. I was just a kid. I kept asking my mom why we didn't go over to see him anymore, and then she'd just start freaking out and crying. So then after a while, I just stopped asking." He gave her a weird look, half determined and half scared. Harper wondered what he expected now: Did he think that just mentioning someone dying was going to make her cry, and then he'd have to mop up the mess? "I know it's not the same, or anything . . ."

"No," she agreed.

"The worst part was that I was all alone with it, you know? So I just thought, maybe . . ."

She gave him a faint "Where are you going with this?" smile. She wasn't going to make it easier on him.

Adam squirmed in his seat. Touchy-feely stuff wasn't really his style. "You can talk to me. About how you're feeling. About . . . anything."

He wanted to know how she was feeling.

She felt numb.

She felt hollow, like a black hole at her center had sucked away her insides, only no one could tell because the outer shell was still intact.

She felt angry all the time, at Adam, at her parents, at the world, at herself. And she didn't know why.

Her thoughts were jumpy and sluggish at the same time, skipping from subject to subject only because by the time she got to the middle of a thought, she forgot where she'd started or where she was going. So she felt lost.

She felt like crying every time she laughed, and she rarely felt much like laughing.

She felt heavy.

She felt unworthy.

She felt like if someone touched her in the right way, she might disintegrate.

She could turn off the tears and paint on a smile whenever she needed to, which made her wonder if the tears weren't real either. She felt like a fraud.

But she wasn't about to tell him any of that.

"I feel fine," she said coolly. She pushed her plate toward his side of the table. "Want to try some? I'm done."

"BETH!"

"We're BOOOOOOOOOOORED!"

"I'll be down in a minute!" she yelled, gulping down a couple Advil tablets. It was nice that her parents got to spend a romantic evening out on the town while she took care of the twins, she knew—and it wasn't like she could have turned them down, given the fact that she had no other plans—but handling the twins' hyperactive sugar craze was about the last thing she needed right now.

She picked up the envelope and pulled out the letter, even though she didn't need to read it again. It was short, and she'd already memorized it.

No one got mail these days, so although it was probably still too early for college acceptances to arrive, she'd let herself get excited, anyway, just for a moment, when her mother had returned from the mailbox and tossed a letter toward her.

Her first reaction: It was thin. She was screwed.

But then she took a closer look and realized it wasn't from a college at all. Her name and address were hand-written, as was the return address, a P.O. Box in Texas. She didn't know anyone in Texas.

She was mystified, but some part of her—maybe the part that was always watching and worrying these days, waiting for something awful to happen—made her take the letter upstairs so she could open it in private. Her father was at the kitchen table pouring over bills, and her mother had already turned her attention toward the high-maintenance part of the family. When Beth slipped up to her room, no one even noticed.

She'd been up there ever since, coming out only briefly to say good-bye to her parents and receive the standard lecture about emergency contact numbers and keeping the boys away from sugar, fire, and electrical sockets. She'd nodded and pretended to listen, like playing the responsible and dutiful daughter hadn't become more of an act than a reality, and then gone back to her room, figuring the twins could fend for themselves, at least until it was time to heat up some leftover pizza and watch *SpongeBob*.

The letter, more of a note, really, scrawled on a slip of hotel stationery, had come stapled to a familiar clipping from the *Grace Herald*.

STUDENT-TEACHER SCANDAL ROCKS HAVEN HIGH

Two phrases were highlighted in light green:

"We're all grateful that they had the courage [to turn Payne in] and prevent this from happening again,"

and

district officials say they had no sign Powell was not what he seemed

The attached note was only a few lines long: *Good to know I can always count on you . . . to keep your mouth shut. See you soon? JP.*

"Beth!" There was a loud pounding at the door. "Come play with us," Jeff begged—although their voices were as identical as their faces, she was sure it was him. He always took the lead.

"Yeah, or we'll tell Mom!" And that would be Sam, who could always be counted on to tattle.

Beth folded the letter and the clipping and stuffed them back in the envelope, which she stuck in her top desk drawer, beneath a box of paper clips and old stationery. She shouldn't throw it out—what she should do, in fact, was take it to the police and explain everything. But she knew she wouldn't. What if no one believed her story? Or worse, what if everyone did? The way they would all look at her, unable to believe that good, reliable Beth had gotten herself involved in something so publicly tawdry. . . .

And that was just the best-case scenario.

What if Powell came back to town? What if he realized she *wouldn't* keep her mouth shut, and decided to shut it for her?

Or what if the police decided to check into her story and started digging into her life? If anyone started asking questions, if anyone found out about the box of pills, about what she had done—no. She couldn't risk it. She would hold on to the letter, on the off chance that she found some secret store of courage somewhere within her.

But she wasn't holding her breath.

"Okay," she said wearily, opening the door. Jeff and Sam launched themselves at her, each grabbing hold of one of her legs. "What do you two brats want to do?"

"I'm not a brat," Jeff complained, turning his head up and sticking out his lower lip.

"I am!" Sam shouted, and poked Jeff in the shoulder. "See? Brat! Brat! Brat! Brat!" Each time he yelled the word, he poked Jeff again. Jeff scrunched up his face, squinted, turned bright red, and then began to scream.

"Aaaaaaagh!" he shouted, hurling himself toward

Sam with his fingers extended like claws. "I'll get you!" But Sam, sensing that his brother was about to blow, had already taken off down the hall.

Beth sagged against the wall as the two chased each other through the house, hooting and growling. She gave herself two minutes, silently counting off the seconds in her head until she could justify it no longer, and then ran down the hallway, hoping to find a way to tame the wild beasts.

An hour later, she'd gotten them tucked into a blanket on the couch, one on either side of her, both staring blissfully at SpongeBob and friends. It occurred to her that her parents had wanted her to do something constructive with them—the twins each had a thick workbook with "fun" activities about telling time and counting money. But that would require thinking, and none of the Manning children was up to that tonight. It was so much easier just to snuggle on the couch and relax in the flickering light of the TV. Beth tugged the blanket toward her neck and closed her eyes, trying to forget. . . .

"Beth! Wake up!" Jeff shouted, shaking her shoulder. "You're missing the best part."

Her eyes popped open, just in time to see a dark figure creep across the screen, lurching toward a peacefully sleeping child. She must have fallen asleep, and the twins must have taken the opportunity to change the channel, unless this was a Very Special Episode, "SpongeBob Goes on a Killing Spree."

Sam and Jeff burrowed into her sides, pressing her hands over their eyes but peeking out just enough to see what was happening. Beth knew she should change the channel, but she couldn't find the remote, and she didn't really want to get up. . . .

The figure came closer to the sleeping boy, and the eerie music rose in the background.

Closer and closer, until—

"Aaaah!" the boys screamed in unison as a knife slashed down. Beth leaped off the couch and switched off the TV.

"Just a movie," she said cheerfully.

But it was too late. That night, it was impossible to get them to sleep. They wouldn't let her turn out the light, and kept asking if "He" was going to come and get them. Feeling guilty—as if she ever felt any other way, these days—Beth let them sleep in her bed, together, and promised to sit by their sides until they fell asleep.

Eventually, Sam closed his eyes and fell silent, but Jeff couldn't stop whimpering.

"Shhh," Beth said, putting a hand against his forehead. They always looked so small and sweet in their pajamas, tucked under the covers, impossibly innocent about the way anything worked. As if it were the bogeyman they really needed to be afraid of.

"I'm scared," Jeff whispered.

"There's nothing to be scared of," Beth assured him. "I'll protect you."

"Aren't you scared?" he asked, wide-eyed.

"No." She leaned down and kissed his forehead, then kissed Sam, too, gently so that he wouldn't wake up. "I told you, there's nothing to be scared of."

No wonder he couldn't fall asleep; lamer words were never spoken.

Miranda wasn't sure whether the house was abandoned or just a pigsty; it was hard to tell in the candlelight. About thirty people, mostly drunk or high, were scattered around the grounds—smoking in the backyard, making out in the bedrooms, experimenting with mixers in the kitchen. Miranda and Kane were sprawled out on a dusty couch in the living room. They'd snagged the best spot; most of the other couples were stuck lounging on the floor or leaning against each other in secluded corners. It wasn't much like any party Miranda had ever been to; there was very little "partying" going on, as far as she could tell. There wasn't even any music.

Not that she cared, not while Kane leaned against her, one hand cradling a beer and the other idly playing with her hair. Was he desperately wishing he could take her off somewhere private and have his way with her? Was he struggling with his fear of intimacy, wondering if his newly discovered love for her could overpower his nerves, and if he could convince her that he was serious about making things work?

Miranda doubted it, but it was a fun fantasy (courtesy, in part, of an afternoon with *Dr. Phil*). She could lean over and kiss him right now. But she wanted more than that, she reminded herself. She wasn't that kind of girl. Her friendship didn't come with benefits.

"Sorry this sucks," Kane said, his voice slow and heavy the way it got when he was a little drunk. Miranda almost liked him better this way; the cold, sneering veneer fell away and, every once in a while, he was actually nice. She'd always told herself this was the real Kane—alcohol just let him come out and play. "I should have known better."

"It's fine," she assured him. "I'm having fun."

He snorted, almost spitting out his mouthful of beer. "Yeah, right. Tell me something," he said, stretching out along the couch and lying down, his head in her lap. He looked up at her. "This okay?" She nodded, not trusting herself to speak. His hair fell back from his forehead, splaying out across her leg. It was so unbelievably smooth.

"Tell you what?" she asked, resisting the urge to stroke his forehead.

"I don't know," he said, slurring his words slightly. "Why you're so sad."

"I'm not sad," she protested.

He nodded as well as he could with his head resting on her legs. "Are too. Sad Miranda."

"I'm not sad right now," she pointed out, leaning over him so he could see her grin.

He reached up and touched her lips. "Can't fool me."

She didn't know how drunk he was; maybe he wouldn't even remember this in the morning, which would be better. All she knew was that she *was* sad—and it had been a long time since anyone had noticed, or wanted to know why.

"It's Harper," she admitted, feeling a hint of relief now that she'd finally said it out loud, even to Kane, who would probably make a joke out of it as he did about everything else. "Everything I say is wrong, and she doesn't want to talk to me, and it's like we're not even friends anymore." The words came fast and furiously; she'd been afraid that if she said it out loud, she would make it real. But saying it out loud was better than saying it to herself, over and over again.

"She's just . . . upset."

"*I'm* upset!" Miranda exclaimed. She stopped herself and took a deep breath. It felt almost like she was talking to herself. "I want to be a good friend to her, but . . . I also,

I just . . ." She put her hands over her face, humiliated to realize it was wet with tears. "I miss having a best friend," she choked out.

"Hey," he said in alarm, pushing himself up. His breath was sour and his eyes glassy, but she didn't care. "Hey, don't—" He wrapped his arms around her and she clung to him, for once not wondering what he was thinking or wishing she could kiss him. She just closed her eyes and tried to catch her breath. "She'll be back," he promised, and much as she wanted to believe him, she knew he was just saying it. Guys would say anything to get a girl to stop crying.

"I hate being alone," she mumbled into his soggy collar.

He pushed her away, just far enough that he could see her face, and he held her in place so she couldn't look away. "Stevens, you're not," he said firmly.

"I know," she said, nibbling at the edge of her lip. "It's just . . ."

"No. You're *not.*"

She wanted him so much, suddenly, that she couldn't breathe. His lips were half parted, and his eyes, usually so cold, now seemed like warm, inviting pools of deep brown. She bit down on the inside of her cheek, hoping the pain would make her ignore how good, how *safe* it felt to have his arms around her.

Maybe this was right after all; maybe it didn't matter that he was drunk and horny and she was in love—maybe they could meet in the middle, just for tonight.

"I have to go," she said, forcing the words out.

"What?"

"Just for a minute. I just need . . . I need some air. I have to go outside," she said, trying to convince herself as much as anything.

"Do you want me to . . . ?"

"Stay." She put a hand on his bicep and suppressed a shudder. "I'll be right back. And . . . Kane?"

"Yeah, Stevens?"

"Thanks."

Things weren't going as well as he'd expected, although now that dinner was done—Harper's meal nearly untouched, Adam's plate scraped clean—and the bill paid, Adam had to admit that he didn't know what he'd expected. His auction bid had been a spur-of-the-moment thing, but over the last few days he'd built it up in his head into his big last chance. It seemed that, despite his carefully chosen clothes—the light green button-down shirt that she loved and he hated, khakis that usually only left his closet when his mother forced him to go to church—this day was going to end the same as all the rest. Unless he did something.

"I thought we'd walk home," he suggested, hoping to delay the inevitable.

Already halfway to his car, she turned and gave him a weird look. "You didn't even have anything to drink. And, FYI, your car's right here."

"It's such a nice night," he pointed out, fully aware that it was a kind of girly thing to say.

Harper shrugged. "Yeah. Whatever." Translation: *You forced me into this, and I'm just counting the minutes until the night is over.*

They walked along the side of the road in silence. The sidewalks were deserted; most of Grace's nightlife was limited to the dive bars and greasy taverns lining the side streets, and their patrons wouldn't be stumbling out for hours. Main Street—home of assorted failing small businesses and several gas stations—was shuttered and dark. They could have been alone in the world.

Harper shivered, and Adam wondered if she'd had the same thought, or if she was just cold. He didn't ask, nor did he offer his jacket, knowing she'd turn it down.

It took him about ten minutes to work up his courage, then another five to figure out how to express what he needed to say—but when that proved to be a doomed effort, he just started talking. "I miss you, Gracie," he told her.

She didn't even look at him. He stopped walking and grabbed her arm, forcing her to stop too. They stood in the shadows of Shopsin's Shoes, which had closed months before and was now boarded up and empty. Harper tapped her foot and looked over his shoulder.

"I miss you," he said again.

"I'm right here."

"No you're not," he argued.

She crossed her arms and scowled, looking like a pouty child. "Can we *go* now?"

"I want you back."

She rolled her eyes. "As a friend. Yeah. I know."

"What's wrong with that?"

"What's wrong with something more than that?" she challenged him.

"Harper, you know—" He stopped himself. He didn't know how to put it into words, that feeling he got when he felt her getting too close, some strange mix of anger, fear, repulsion—and desire. It was all too much. "We already talked about this," he said vaguely.

"I want to hear you say it," she sneered. "I want to hear you say exactly what you think of me. Exactly what kind of person you think I am."

"I don't . . . I don't know what you want from me."

She took a step toward him, then another. And then suddenly, she was on top of him, her arms threaded through his and her fingers digging into the skin of his lower back, then scraping up his back toward his neck.

"I want *this*," she hissed. She lifted her right leg, rubbing her thigh against him, and she sucked in his lips, nibbling, biting the edges and shoving her tongue into his mouth as her hands began tearing at his hair, squeezing his face and pressing it into hers. There was friction, heat, rubbing, pulling, kneading, sucking, moaning—and then silence as he pushed her away.

"What the hell are you doing?" he asked, his face hot and his breathing rapid. There was something so ugly about her naked need, and it pained him to realize that an angry, primal part of him wanted to grab her back and finish what she'd started.

"You think I'm a slut," she spit out. Her eyes were wide and her face was unnaturally pale, while her voice was nearly an octave higher than usual, which sometimes happened when she got too angry.

"I don't—"

"You *do*. A shallow slut that you can be *just friends* with"—her face contorted in pain at the words—"but why would a slut want to be friends with a guy like you if she can't get something out of it?" She stepped toward him again, and before he could back away, she shoved him in the chest, hard. "All I want is sex, right? *Right*?" Another shove. "And if you can't give it to me, what the hell good are you? Why wouldn't I just go find it somewhere else?"

Maybe that's where she was headed when she stalked away. Adam didn't know, and he didn't follow.

Miranda took a deep breath and stepped back into the house, ready to rejoin the party—or at least rejoin Kane. But her seat was taken. Kane lay in the same position as before, his head now in the lap of a curvy junior cheerleader who was running her fingers lightly up and down his face.

She didn't want to get any closer. But she didn't have much other option, unless she wanted to start up a conversation with the couple making out to her right, or the guy passed out on her left. Kane had a short attention span; maybe he'd just gotten bored while she—perhaps rudely—left him alone. It was possible the girl was just a diversion and he'd get rid of her as soon as he saw Miranda.

But he didn't see Miranda. It would have been pretty much impossible for him, what with the 110-pound cheerleader now attached to his lips. Feeling sickened, Miranda sank back on one of the arms of the couch, trying to look away but compelled to keep glancing at them. Kane wasn't doing much, just lying there, as the girl rubbed his face and started kissing down his neck.

"Hey," he said suddenly, spotting Miranda now that his face was clear. The cheerleader didn't even look up—

she was too busy nuzzling his chest. Kane gave Miranda a lazy grin. "Party's not so bad after all."

Miranda couldn't force her mouth into a smile, so she settled for a thin, wobbly line.

"So, are you—" But Kane broke off into a spasm of laughter as the cheerleader began tickling his sides. "I don't *think* so," he mock growled, and flipped her over on the couch so that he was on top, perfectly positioned for some tickling torture of his own.

It was like Miranda wasn't there anymore.

She tried not to cry.

The room was dark, and nearly silent, but she felt like everyone was staring at her, wondering what that loser was doing. Maybe she looked like some kind of pervert, spying on Kane as he made out with his latest floozy. It's not like she wanted to keep standing there. But she didn't have anywhere else to go.

The minutes dragged by.

And as she stood there, her back unnaturally straight and her hands clenched into fists, her tears dried up. *Screw him*, she thought. Bringing her here, acting like he cared, then ditching her as soon as she left the room. Let him find his own ride home.

"I'm out of here," she said softly, as if experimenting with the words. There was no response from the couple on the couch.

"Kane, I'm out of here," she said, louder this time.

He flicked his gaze up toward her. "Cool. I can get a ride home from . . ."

"Kelli," the junior giggled into his ear. "With an *i*."

Of course. It was always with an *i*.

"Fine," she snapped. He didn't need her; she didn't need him. Whatever. *Screw him. Screw him. Screw him.* "Screw you!" It popped out before she realized she was going to say it, and it felt good. She stood up and strode out of the "party," stepping over two guys passed out on the floor and narrowly avoiding a collision with some jock who was lurching toward the door, his face a disconcerting shade of green.

The car was parked about half a block away, and she walked quickly, her thoughts keeping time with her footsteps. *I don't need him. I don't want him. I don't need him. I don't want him.*

"Hey, Stevens, what gives?"

She whirled around at the touch of his hand on her shoulder and shrugged him off. "Where's your *friend*?" she sneered.

"Are you mad?" His eyes were wide and innocent, but it was hard to tell whether he was playing oblivious for effect or whether the alcohol really had numbed his brain enough to make it true.

She was totally sober, but apparently her judgment

control had forgotten that. "Why would I be mad?" she yelled. "You drag me to this *pit* and then you ditch me for some . . . You're such an asshole!"

"Uh . . ." He looked dazed, as if she'd hit him in the head. Then a slow grin spread across his face. "Jealous, Stevens? Did you think that we . . ."

She told herself not to blush, but she could feel the heat rise in her cheeks. "No! No."

"Then what?"

Her righteous anger faded away, because, of course, she *was* jealous. She was also certain that she had every right to be mad, jealous or not—but she couldn't quite figure out why, not with Kane standing so close and the corners of his eyes crinkling up so hotly. "It was just rude," she complained, hating herself for not being able to hate him. She turned away and kept walking toward her car, ignoring the footsteps that followed behind her.

"What are you doing?" she asked finally as she opened the car door and he stood by the passenger's side, waiting for it to be unlocked.

"What's it look like?"

"Go back to the party," she said, suddenly too tired to fight, with him or with herself.

"I'm going home with you," he said stubbornly. "You're still mad."

"Kane, I'm not mad." She sighed. "Just go back to the party. You're allowed to do whatever you want."

"I want to go home with you," he said. "I didn't mean that the way it sounded . . . unless . . ."

"Forget it, buddy."

"Let's go," he said, getting into the car and snapping on his seat belt.

Miranda shook her head. "I think I can handle the ten-minute drive on my own. Go back to the party."

"Stevens, when are you going to learn? I *am* the party." He leaned across the bucket seats and laid a hand on her thigh. "If you want, we can have a little party of our own. . . ."

She took his hand away, but before she could drop it back to his side, he squeezed and they paused like that, their hands joined in midair. All she could hear was their breathing, hers rapid and fluttery, his labored and heavy. She pressed her lips together and dropped his hand. "Okay, party boy, let's get you home."

She started the ignition, and he flicked a lock of her hair over her shoulder, forcing her to turn toward him again and face his crooked, knowing smirk. "Have it your way, Stevens. But you don't know what you're missing."

Let's see, she thought wryly, *that would be: pain, lust, heartbreak, torture.*

Although, come to think of it, her personal inventory already had plenty of those items in stock. So she wasn't missing a thing.

It didn't seem real and it didn't make sense, but it was happening. Harper pressed herself against the wall. She wanted to look away—she wanted to run away—but her feet were stuck to the floor. She couldn't move, and when she tried to speak, nothing came out.

There was no light in the room, but somehow, she could see everything clearly.

Adam on his back, in his boxers. Kaia straddling him, her head tossed back, her black hair splashed out behind her.

Stop! Harper shouted, and even though her lips didn't move, she could hear the word echoing through the room. Kaia and Adam didn't notice.

"Are you ready?" Kaia whispered. She kissed his chin. She kissed his neck. She licked his nipples, one by one. Adam moaned.

So did Harper.

"I've been waiting for you," Adam said, unlatching her lacy black bra and letting it drop to the floor.

Kaia made a noise that sounded like a purr. "I know." She slipped her fingers under Adam's head and jerked it toward hers, giving him a long, sloppy kiss. Then she turned and looked directly at Harper. "He doesn't want you," she sneered, giving Harper a cruel smile. "He wants me. They all do."

Shut up! Harper screamed silently. It felt like her throat was choked with cotton. She tried to close her eyes, but they wouldn't shut.

Kaia shimmied down Adam's body until she reached the waistband of his boxers. She slipped her thumb between his skin and the cotton and began, ever so slowly, to pull them off.

"I hate you!" Harper shrieked, finding her voice. The words exploded from her lungs and filled the room, which seemed to shake with the noise. Adam half sat up and looked across the room at Harper, shaking his head sadly. Kaia touched his chin to stop the motion, then kissed him again. *"I hate you!"* Harper shouted again, feeling the power of her wrath course through her body.

And then she woke up.

Drenched, shivering beneath her covers, tears streaking her face.

Harper turned over on her stomach, burrowing her face into the pillow. "I'm sorry!" she gasped, fighting for breath. "I'm sorry. I'm sorry. I'm sorry. I'm sorry." She murmured the words over and over again until her breathing slowed and she stopped shaking. But that night, she didn't fall back asleep.

chapter nine

THERE WERE NO INVITATIONS. WORD TRAVELED, and everyone just knew where to show up, and when. Senior Spirit Week was for the teachers and the administration so they could feel good about offering their students some good, clean fun. But everyone knew that senior spring only officially began at midnight, in the midst of debauchery and revels. There was a spot out in the desert, a shallow wash of scrub-brush surrounded by clumps of Joshua trees on one side and a stretch of low, rocky ridges on the other. It was tradition. The cops allowed it. The administration ignored it. Parents pretended it didn't exist—although most of them had been through it themselves, twenty years before. It signified the beginning of the end, a night of wild release that, if all went well, would be whispered about for years. Graduation was a hot, tedious hassle; prom was a chance for girls to spend too much on evening dresses and guys to get that last precollege shot at losing their virginity. *This* was a rite of passage.

Beth had decided not to go.

Then she changed her mind.

After an hour of flip-flopping, she was standing in front of her mirror wearing standard-issue black pants, a shimmery blue scoop-neck top that matched her eyes, and a sparkly bracelet she'd gotten for her birthday last year but never taken out of the box. She swept her hair up into a high, loose ponytail, wishing the long, blond strands would wave or curl or do anything other than fall limply down to her shoulders. She dabbed on some glittery gray eye shadow and a layer of clear gloss.

And she still wasn't sure she was going to leave the house.

Her original plan had been to never leave the house *again*, but that seemed less than feasible.

She'd come up with a variety of rationales:

If she didn't start acting normal, people would suspect something was going on, and she couldn't afford that.

She would likely have a terrible time, so she didn't need to feel guilty.

If she wasn't going to turn herself in—because, she reminded herself, she hadn't intentionally hurt anyone, and not because she was a pathetic coward—she had to start living her life again at some point.

None of them were nearly as persuasive as the deciding factor: Reed's band was playing the party. And, much as she hated to admit it, she wanted to see him again.

There was nothing going on, she assured herself. She and Reed were a nonissue—even if it hadn't been for . . . what had happened with Kaia. Reed was the opposite of her type, and last time she'd played that game, she'd lost big. If she was going to get involved with anyone again, it would be someone sweet and quiet, who was kind to children and animals and cared about getting into college, going to class, and doing the right thing.

Except: Why would someone like that ever want to be involved with her? She wasn't Beth Manning, golden girl, anymore. She'd stopped going to class, probably wouldn't get into college—and had proven once and for all that, unless it was painless, she wouldn't do the right thing.

If she was being honest with herself, she knew she couldn't get involved with anybody. Lonely as she was, she couldn't afford something open, honest, or *real*. She couldn't invite someone into her life and trust him with her secrets and her fears.

Still, she slipped on a jacket and wrapped a pink scarf

around her neck, waved good-bye to her parents, and walked out the door. She'd never heard Reed play before, and she was just curious, she assured herself. Miserable, bored, scared, and curious. That's all there was to it.

Miranda drained her plastic cup and stuck it under the keg, pumping until a frothy flow spurted out. It tasted like shit, but she forced it down, anyway. The world tipped a bit to the left, then righted itself before she could fall over, but she still felt like things would start spinning if she turned her head too fast.

Perfect.

There he was, less than ten feet away, standing at the fringes of a group of jocks trying to set fire to a cactus. He looked disgusted—and hot. Miranda stumbled toward him, sneaking up behind him and slapping her hands over his eyes.

"Geary," she whispered, holding back a giggle. "Guess who?"

He spun around, and she hopped up and gave him an impulsive kiss on the cheek. "I'm drunk," she announced giddily.

He looked her up and down, then patted her on the head. "Thanks, Captain Obvious. I got that."

She felt so free. "You like?" she asked, twirling around to show off her outfit, a dark green corset and very un-Miranda-like skin-tight pants.

"Nice." He ran his hand down the laced up sides of her shirt. "*Very* nice."

Before the party, she'd decided: It doesn't count if you're drunk. Everyone knew this party was about doing things you shouldn't—and so why should she deny herself the one thing she knew she absolutely, under no circumstances, if she wanted to keep her sanity or her dignity, shouldn't do? She just needed to work up a little safety buzz—get just drunk enough to serve as an excuse for anything that might happen. Anything she hoped would happen. She'd thought it all out, and it had made perfect sense.

Four beers later, she was done thinking. "You look good," she said, stepping toward him and nearly falling as the ground shifted beneath her feet. Or, at least, it seemed to. "Whoops," she squeaked as he caught her in his big, strong, muscular, tan arms. "Did I mention I'm a *little* drunk?"

"Did I mention this is a new shirt?" Kane asked wryly. "Don't puke on it."

He slung an arm around her waist and walked her away from the crowd, sitting her down on the ground so she wouldn't have too far to fall.

"Hey!" she called, tugging on the leg of his jeans. "It's lonely down here."

Kane crouched down next to her.

"Hi!" she said in her best sultry voice, leaning toward him.

He flinched away from her breath. "Jesus—did you drink the whole keg?"

This wasn't going right. Miranda struggled to figure out where she'd run off track, but her brain was like a see-saw, swinging wildly back and forth, up and down . . . and at the thought of that, she felt a wave of nausea rise in her. So she stopped thinking again and just blurted something out. "This isn't going right."

Oops.

"What isn't?"

Instead of answering, Miranda leaned against him and let her head drop to her shoulder. "The music's nice, huh?"

Kane glanced over at the Blind Monkeys, who were banging something out that approximated a song. "You call this music?"

"I love your smile," Miranda slurred, touching his lips. "It's so . . . smiley."

He frowned, took her hand, and peered into her eyes. "You in there somewhere, Stevens? 'Cause I think some kind of pod person's taken over your body."

He was so funny. "You're so funny." She laughed, her body twitching uncontrollably, until finally she pressed both her hands against her mouth to stop herself. "D'you want to kiss me?" she asked suddenly, taking her hands away and pursing her lips.

"Uh, Stevens . . ."

"'Cause you can. I'm right here." She let herself fall toward him, but at the last moment, he grabbed her shoulders and held her at arm's length.

"I'm not sure we should—"

"Hey!" she cried, suddenly distracted. "It's Harper!" She started waving wildly. "Harper!" But Harper was too far away. "She's mick of see. I mean. She's sick of me. I mean. You know. What I mean." Some sleazy guy in cargo shorts with a studded collar around his neck was leading Harper away from the band and toward the more private, shadowy area beyond the rocks.

"You know that guy?" Kane asked suspiciously.

Miranda shook her head. The sleazeball swooped in for a kiss and Harper pulled herself away—but she wasn't quick enough. They made out for a minute, and then the guy continued leading her away.

"She's even drunker than me." Miranda giggled, then stopped as a pinhole of light opened up in the dark fog of her mind. "What's she doing with that guy? What if—?" Her happy buzz turned into an angry beehive. "We have to stop her," she said, trying to stand up. She shook her head, but that just made things more jumbled. "We have to go, we have to—"

"Whoa. Better idea." Kane pressed down firmly on her shoulders, settling her back on the ground. "I'll go. You stay."

"But I have to help, I have to—"

"I'm sure it's fine," he assured her. "I'll go. I'll take care of it. Are you okay here?"

"My knight in shining armor." She sighed, a happy glow settling over her again. Kane would take care of everything, and then he'd be back for her.

"Yeah, that's me," he scoffed. "Just try not to wander off and get into trouble before I get back, princess."

As he disappeared into the crowd in search of Harper, Miranda sighed happily and lay back against the ground, staring up at the stars and wondering if she could find the Big Dipper.

He'd be back soon—and she wasn't going anywhere.

Forgive, forget; the wavy lines on my TV
Go dark as you, betray your confidences on—

Reed broke off in disgust. The sound system was crap, and he could barely hear himself sing over the drunken crowd—not to mention the fact that he was pretty sure someone was blasting Beyonce on a stereo not too far away. But that wasn't the real issue.

"Fish!" he snapped, spinning around to look at the

drummer. "What the hell are you doing back there?"

"Man, I forgot what song we were playing." He giggled. "Can you believe that?"

"Dude, you're totally baked!" Hale mocked, waving his guitar over his head. "Awesome."

Reed knocked the microphone away in disgust. "You're both playing for shit. Get it together."

"Take it easy, kid," Fish suggested. "I can fire up another one for you."

"Let's just play," Reed said, half tempted, half disgusted. "'Miles from Home,' okay? On three?" They nodded, and Fish counted off; Hale came into the song a half beat late but at least, Reed told himself, he'd come in at all.

I wanna get away from this place,
I wanna blow my brain, forget your face—

No one had even noticed they were playing again. By the light of the moon, Reed could see a horde of seniors milling about, making out, and lighting things on fire. Up front, next to the platform they'd put together for their stage, their single groupie danced by herself, flinging her tattoo-covered arms in the air in a wild frenzy, despite the slow and moody beat of the music. That was their audience: One goth girl who hated their music but had a not-so-secret crush on Hale.

Reed didn't care.

Same as you always were
Too good too much too fast too far,
And all the knives into my head and all
The holes and all the time to get away—

He knew the lyrics were lame. He didn't care about that, either. The guys all wanted to do cover songs—they'd have wrestling matches over Led Zeppelin versus Coldplay, Bright Eyes versus The Ramones—and then they'd get distracted and Reed would place the only vote that mattered. They played his music. And when he was really in the zone, it was a better high than pot. It was just him and the words and the music. It was cool.

He wasn't in the zone.

And he couldn't stop scanning the crowd.

I wanna get away from this place,
I wanna choke it up and spit in your face—

He stopped singing and held his breath. She was walking through the crowd, which seemed to part slightly as she passed. Her back was to the stage. Her movements were graceful and deliberate, her body slim and perfect. Her sleek black hair spun in the wind as she turned around, and he was about to whisper her name when—

It wasn't her. Of course.

He hadn't believed it, not really, he told himself. But he had. Just for a second, he'd let himself forget—he'd let himself believe that, somehow, it could be her.

"Awesome set!" Fish cried, slamming his stick against one of the cymbals. "Break time."

"Set?" Reed asked, trying to remember himself. "We haven't even gotten through one song."

"Dude, whose fault is that?" Hale asked, giving Reed a pointed look. (As pointed as a look could be when his eyes were half shut.) "I say break time. I've got . . ." He glanced offstage, where goth girl had stripped off her T-shirt to reveal a black leather bikini. She slowly licked her hand, from her palm up to her fingertips, then threw it to Hale as if it were a kiss. "I got stuff to do, kid." Hale ditched the guitar and hopped off the platform, grabbing goth girl and kissing her like he was trying to Hoover her mouth right off her face.

Reed turned to exchange a glance with Fish, but the drummer had already laid his head down on the snare drum and shut his eyes. So much for the gig.

Reed stumbled off the makeshift stage and began to walk without a direction in mind. This wasn't his scene. Some asshole in a letter jacket with a squealing girl slung over his shoulder slammed into him with a glare and a warning. "Watch it, loser!"

Definitely not his scene.

He was well away from the party and halfway to his car when he realized that he wasn't alone. He didn't turn around to see who was following him, figuring that whoever it was would eventually reveal themselves or, preferably, lose interest and wander away.

It took about five minutes.

"Reed?" Her voice was tentative and musical.

He turned around. "Hey." She looked good. Reed hated himself for noticing.

"Leaving?" Beth asked. "It's early."

"Yeah." He shrugged. "I'm just . . ." He wasn't leaving. He had a tent and a sleeping bag in the truck, and he had a plan. He and the guys were going to hike out to somewhere quiet and alone and have a party of their own. But the guys were useless. ". . . you know."

"Yeah." Beth gave him a wry smile. "This isn't really my thing either."

"Really?" She was too blond and beautiful not to be one of *those* girls.

"I hate parties." There was a pause, though not an awkward one. "I guess I'm going too."

"Unless—" He wanted to be alone. But even with her there, he felt alone—in a good way. He didn't have to put on a show. And maybe—he remembered her tears, and the way she'd shaken in his arms—maybe there were some things she could understand. "You want to hang? You know, just for a while?"

Her eyebrows crinkled together, and there was another pause. Maybe she was trying to decide if he was good enough for her, or what the odds were of anyone seeing them together. Reed decided to forget the whole thing. But she spoke before he could. "Yeah. Okay. Let's, uh . . . hang."

"Cool," he said, wondering if that unclenching in his shoulder blades was relief.

"Cool."

"Baby, you are *so hot!*" the guy said, nuzzling his greasy head into Harper's chest. Harpers head lolled back, her eyes half closed. The guy's fingers crept up her thigh and across her stomach and, encountering no resistance, began to unbutton her shirt. "I mean, *damn!*" he exclaimed, catching his first glimpse of her bare cleavage and pale, creamy skin. "Makes me wanna—"

"Hold that thought," Kane drawled, clamping an iron grip around the guy's scrawny shoulders and tossing him away. "We'll get back to you."

"What's it to you?" the loser whined, trying to elbow Kane out of the way. "Jealous? She wants me."

Kane looked down at Harper, sitting cross-legged on the ground, slumped over at the waist now that there was no one left propping her up, her tangled hair falling over her face. She looked limp and pliable, like a doll that would be content however you posed her.

"She doesn't know what she wants," Kane murmured, then turned toward the greasy loser and smiled. He didn't need to raise a fist to convey his warning. "You should probably get out of here, asshole. *Now*."

Kane could have taken the guy in a fight, but he knew it would never come to that. Even a loser like this knew that Kane had all the power, and knew better than to stick around.

"You okay, Grace?" Kane asked, hauling her up. She lifted her head and scowled.

"What are you doing?" she asked, her voice slurred.

"Rescuing you, in case you hadn't noticed."

She shook him away. "I don't need rescuing. I was fine."

"Yeah, you and Drunky McDateRapist were having a grand old time."

"I can hook up with whoever I want."

"Your warm gratitude means the world to me," he said dryly. This knight-in-shining-armor business didn't come with many perks. Probably a good thing: A few more good deeds and his rep would end up in the toilet.

Standing up and arguing seemed to revive her a bit, because the color seeped back into her face and her hand suddenly squeezed down on his. "Let's go!" she cried.

A manic-depressive drunk. Great. *Party on, Kane,* he thought sourly, wondering if it was sexist to believe girls couldn't hold their liquor. Not that he wasn't already an unapologetic sexist—he just liked to be consistent. "Go where?" he asked wearily.

"Dance!" she tugged him toward the whirling crowd, thrashing her head in time to the tinny hip-hop bursting from some cheap speakers. "Come on."

"I don't dance," he reminded her, reluctant to leave her alone again. "How about we go visit your good friend Miranda. She's just over—"

"Shut up and dance with me," she said, threading a finger through his belt loop and pulling him toward her. She ignored the pulsing beat and instead collapsed into his arms, hanging around his neck and swaying back and forth. "Stop rescuing me," she said, her voice muffled by his shirt.

"Stop screwing up," he suggested.

She dragged herself up a few inches and propped her chin up against his chest so that, when he looked down at her, their lips nearly met. "I know what you want," she said, too loudly, a harsh smile twisting her face.

"A private jet? A harem? My own private island?"

"Stop!" she cried, hitting against his chest.

"Stop what?"

"Being nice to me."

Kane tilted his head down enough that their foreheads touched. "I'm never nice. You know that."

Before he knew what was happening, she'd pushed herself up on her toes and kissed him, her hands tightening around his neck. A soft moan escaped her as she pulled away.

"Now I know you're drunk," he joked, his mouth on autopilot as he struggled to plot his next move.

"Shut up," she murmured, kissing his chest, sucking on the bare skin at the nape of his neck.

"You don't know what you're doing, Grace," he warned her, halfheartedly trying to push her away.

"Who cares?" And then her lips were on his again, her tongue probing, her hands massaging his back and then slipping beneath his shirt and clawing against his skin.

If he were a cartoon character, this is the point at which the tiny angel and devil would pop into existence, one perched on each shoulder.

Angel, complete with halo and miniature golden harp: *She's drunk. She's self-destructive. She's out of her mind.*

Devil, with red horns and a familiar smirk: *She's drunk. You're drunk. Let's party. It's all good.*

Angel: *She doesn't really want you.*

Devil: *Everyone wants you. Don't be stupid.*

Angel: *Don't be evil.*

Devil, jabbing him with his tiny pitchfork: *Don't forget*

about that tight ass, and her magic fingers crawling down toward your waistband, and—is that a black thong peeking out over her jeans?

Angel: *Ohhh, definitely a thong. And that ass . . .*

Devil: *Told you so.*

Angel: *And that thing she's doing with your ear?*

Devil: *Do they give gold medals for tongue aerobics?*

Angel, slapping the devil five: *God, she's good.*

Devil: *Hallelujah.*

Kane groaned, half in pleasure and half in torture, as he wrestled with himself (and with Harper). And while he deliberated, she kissed him, and groped him, and he let it happen, their bodies tangling together and his mind's voice growing quieter and quieter, drowned in the force of desperate, physical need.

He'd push her away.

He would.

In a minute.

Miranda wandered unsteadily through the crowd. At least the world had stopped spinning and her head had stopped throbbing. But as her mind and vision cleared, she'd realized she was sitting alone on a rock, waiting for someone who, apparently, wasn't coming back.

She was still drunk enough to go and look for him.

First she flipped open her pocket-size mirror and

checked things out. Eye shadow a little smeared, mascara intact, fresh coat of Midnight Rose–colored lipstick in hopes of looking extra kissable, and she was ready to go.

He wasn't hanging with the stoners, who were sprawled on their backs, passing around a massive bong.

He wasn't, thank God, groping the cheerleaders or charming the prom committee.

He wasn't wandering along the edges of the crowd, looking for her.

He wasn't by the keg, or the speakers, or the jocks, or the trees.

And then time stopped.

She didn't see it as a fluid series of events, but rather as a series of frozen snapshots, flashing in front of her eyes and then fading away:

Kane's back, and a girl's arms roaming across it.

Curly auburn hair falling across a shoulder.

Two faces in profile, eyes closed, tongues locked.

Harper, her eyes open, locked on Miranda. Her smile.

Harper turning away, kissing him again.

Miranda sat down where she'd been standing, Harper and Kane fading from view. All she could see now were people's legs and feet, some walking, some dancing, some standing around, some wrapped up in others. She tried to catch her breath.

She's drunk, Miranda told herself. *Self-destructive. She doesn't know what she's doing.*

But Harper had stopped. Looked at Miranda. Smiled and turned away. She knew exactly what she was doing.

Miranda suddenly felt completely sober and clear. But she couldn't have been, or she wouldn't have stood up and walked purposefully off toward the crops of Joshua trees, where she'd seen half the basketball team breaking bottles and doing keg stands. If she wasn't drunk, where did she get the nerve to wrap her arms around Adam and whisper in his ear, "I need you, now"?

She didn't think about the consequences or fear humiliation. She just acted, tugging him away from the group, deeper into the trees. She didn't need to think. She'd come to this party to give in to her desires. At the time, those had been: longing, lust, hope.

Now they'd been replaced with one: revenge. She didn't pause to acknowledge that to herself or explain it to Adam. She didn't even need to take a deep breath before kissing him. And she had to admit that Harper had been right. The chiseled face and perfect body was a definite turn-on. As was the prospect of smashing Harper's heart to pieces.

"Miranda?" Adam was out of it, completely, his face slack and his words thick. "Whuh?"

"This doesn't have to mean anything," she said, stripping off her shirt. "It's just for fun." She tugged at the edge of his shirt and stumbled against him. "It's a party, right?"

Adam didn't say anything. But he let her tug him down to the ground, and he didn't resist as she ran her fingers through his hair. She didn't know how to seduce someone, or how to follow up the first move with a second one. *Harper* would know.

Harper was probably doing it right now.

She lay down on her side, ignoring the sharp edges digging into her. "Come here," she told Adam, hooking her finger into his collar and jerking him toward her. He toppled over with a grunt, then rolled to face her. "Miranda, I'm not really—"

"You waiting around for Harper?" she snapped, enjoying his wince. Suddenly it seemed like the whole world should share in her pain. *See? I can be just like you,* she told Harper silently. *I can be cold, and I can take what you want.* "She's with Kane. Déjà vu all over again, right?"

"Shuddup."

"Kane gets everything, and you get—"

"Shut up." Louder this time.

"Make me," Miranda challenged, jerking her face toward his. Their noses bumped, and then awkwardly but without hesitation, their lips met.

His face was stubbly and his hair too short. His breath was sour, his kiss was rough, angry, but at least she had *acted.* And her eyes were dry. He grunted like an animal, and she accidentally bit his tongue, and the rocks beneath them felt like they were drawing blood. But she persevered. She closed her eyes, kissed him harder, and tried not to pretend he was someone else.

Beth drew in a breath and tried not to cough out the smoke. "This is harder than it looks," she sputtered, lying back against the sleeping bag.

"You'll get the hang of it," Reed assured her. He lay down next to her, and for a long time all she could hear was their breathing, and the whistling of the wind. "You feeling anything?" he asked.

"I don't know . . ." The words sounded strange, and *felt* strange, as if her tongue had suddenly doubled in size. She stuck it out at him. "Does my tongue look weird?" (This came out sounding more like, "Doz ba tog look eered?") She burst into giggles before he could answer.

"Yeah, you're feeling it," he said, satisfied.

Beth waved her hand in front of her face, marveling at the fact that it was too dark to see. *Maybe I don't have a hand anymore*, she thought. *Maybe I'm just a mind.* The theory seemed startlingly profound, and she was about to explain it to Reed, but the words slipped away from her.

"I never knew why she was with me, you know?" His words seemed like they were dropping out of the sky, unconnected to either of them. "I mean, I'm . . . and she was . . . yeah. Like the way she talked. It was like everything she said came out of a book. Like . . ."

Beth zoned out, just listening to the pleasant rise and fall of his voice, tuning for scattered words and phrases— "never again"; "in the water"; "can't stop"; "sundress"; "going crazy"; and, several times, "why"—but she couldn't focus enough to draw them together into a single thread. Every time she tried, she would realize that the ground was hard and soft at the same time, or that the air tasted like peppermint, and she would wander off into her head.

Until it occurred to her: Maybe he was onto her. Maybe he knew her secret. He knew exactly what she'd done, and what she was hiding, and this was his way of torturing her. Beth jerked herself upright and curled her legs up to her chest, trying to catch her breath. He would pretend to be nice to her, and then, just when she felt safe, he would bring the cage down, trap her in her lies, and destroy her. Which was what she deserved. And of course he hated her. She tried to look at his expression, to see if she could find the hatred in his eyes, but it was too dark. She didn't know what he was thinking, but what if he knew what *she* was thinking? The truth was so obvious, he must know. He must be waiting, biding his time, and then—

"Hey." His hand was on her back. His voice didn't sound angry. "What is it?"

"Nothing," she said quickly, gasping for breath. Would he hear the lies in her voice? "I have to get out of here." Away from him.

She tried to stand up, but he stopped her. "Chill. Wait," he urged. "It's not real, whatever it is. It's just the weed. It's just something that happens." He rubbed her back, and she bent her head to her knees. "Deep breaths," he advised, rubbing her back. "Slow, deep breaths."

"I know you know," she said feverishly. "I know you know I know you know you know you know . . ." She repeated the words so many times, they lost all meaning and became absurd, like a made-up language. "Owyoo no new oh," she said experimentally. It suddenly seemed ridiculous that some noises had so much meaning and others were just noise. "New yo I you?" she asked, bursting into laughter as Reed gaped at her in confusion.

Words were so weird.

"Weird," she said, testing out the sound. "Weeeeeeeeeird."

Reed shook his head, bemused. "Yes, you are."

She lay down again on her back, her breathing slowed and her mind clear. Just like the stars, which seemed so bright, like they were holes in the sky. The desert was cold, and empty, but she didn't feel alone. Even though she couldn't see him, she knew he was there.

The world seemed so huge, and so small at the same time, like she and Reed were the only things in existence. And wouldn't everything be so much easier if that were true. The world felt fresh. The sharp wind against her face, the rough polyester beneath her. Reed's hand brushing, just slightly, against hers—she'd never felt so *there*.

"Are you happy?" she asked.

"No. You?"

"No. But—" She searched for the words that described how she *did* feel, a certainty that she'd never be happy combined with a strange acceptance and even contentment, as if she was floating along and the current was strong but she could trust where it would take her, so she could just close her eyes, sink back, and relax. She felt like she understood everything at once, with a deep clarity—but when she tried to name it, assign words and sentences to the certainty, it flowed away. The closer she drew, the blurrier it got. So she gave up. "But it's okay," she concluded simply.

She heard Reed take a sharp, deep breath and let it out slowly. "Yeah. It's okay. Everything is."

chapter ten

"UHHHHHHHHHHHHHHH." MIRANDA OPENED HER eyes. Her first mistake. The morning light burned.

She twisted her head to the left. Mistake number two. The world spun, her stomach lurched, her muscles screamed. Her cottonmouth filled with the sour taste of bile.

Better not to move.

Go slow, she warned herself. Focused on taking one breath, then another, tried to ignore the throbbing pain in her head. *Take stock:*

Arms and legs: fully functional. Too heavy to move.

Location: burning white sun, jagged rocks digging into her back. So, outside. Somewhere, for some reason.

Miscellaneous: Shirt on the ground. Bra unhooked. Her left arm squashed between her chest and the ground, her right arm propped up on something. Something that moved.

Uh-oh.

Her breathing was like thunder in her ears. She held it. The roaring stopped. And she heard him.

She twisted her head around. "Ooooooooooooh noooooooo." A weak and scratchy wheeze, but still too loud. She winced. He woke.

"Unnnh?" Adam shook his head and propped himself up, then dropped back down to the ground. "What am I . . . what are you . . . ?"

There was a party, Miranda remembered. Images floated across her brain.

Beer. Lots of beer.

Kane's arms holding her up.

More beer.

Kane and . . . A sharp pain cut through the dull throbbing in her head. *Harper.*

The trees. Adam. Unbuttoning her shirt. His tongue . . .

"What did I do?" she whispered. Her throat burned. "Adam," she croaked. His eyes had slipped shut again. His chest was bare. "Adam!"

"Uh?"

Her arm was still lying on top of him. She jerked it

away, heaved herself over onto her back. "Do you remember what . . . what did we . . ." *No. Not possible.* She closed her eyes. *No, no, no. Maybe.* She had to know.

"Did we . . ."

". . . you know?"

Shut up, he thought. Her voice hurt. Everything hurt. Every noise was another bottle broken over his head. And hangovers turned him into an asshole.

Home. That was what he needed. His bed. His dark room. His Ultimate Hangover Cure (milk, orange juice, honey, bananas). Just what the doctor ordered. But that would mean standing up, and he was too tired to move.

And then there was Miranda. Who wouldn't shut up.

"Adam, what *happened*?"

Be nice. "Okay, okay," he groaned. "Just stop yelling. We kissed, okay?"

"*And?*"

"And that's it." Adam opened his eyes again. Her lower lip wobbled, and her eyes bugged out. He sighed. "And then you, uh, kind of puked. A lot."

"Oh, God. On you?"

"Well . . ." He took a big whiff. Almost choked. Yeah, on him. He forced a smile. "No big deal. Really."

"This is so humiliating," Miranda moaned, turning away from him and curling up into a tight ball.

"It's fine." *Comfort her*, he told himself. But that would take so much damn effort. He stifled a yawn. "It's already forgotten."

"We can't tell anyone."

"Yeah."

"*Promise*," Miranda insisted.

"Uh-huh. I promise." He stretched out, feeling like he hadn't moved in months. "We should probably get going."

"Yeah."

Minutes passed. No one spoke. No one moved.

"Or we could just rest for a while," Miranda suggested.

But no one heard. Adam was already asleep.

"Uhhhhhhhhhhhhhh." Beth opened her eyes. Her whole body ached. The thin sleeping bag offered no protection for her from the hard-packed desert gravel. She was tired. Thirsty.

Happy.

My parents are going to kill me.

It didn't seem to matter.

Maybe the pot permanently warped my brain. Maybe I just don't care anymore.

It sounded like heaven.

She had awoken in the night, shivering in the dark. Reed had wrapped an arm around her; she'd snuggled up against his chest. Now she could feel him breathe.

She felt like a stranger. And it felt good. As long as she stayed out here, she could be someone else. She could be the kind of girl who didn't care what happened next.

"Reed?" Her head was nestled into the space beneath his chin. He didn't answer, and she couldn't see his face.

The calm couldn't last forever. But maybe when he woke up, he'd pull out his small plastic bag again. He'd roll the ashy, dark green flakes into a neat white tube. She would inhale more of the magic potion.

I shouldn't . . .

It was a quiet voice, and easy to ignore. To smother, until it stopped flailing and gave up the fight.

She closed her eyes and shifted against him. It felt good—a warm body beside her, the weight of someone's arms around her. She'd been so alone.

She knew she deserved to be alone.

But in the sunrise, in the desert air, in Reed's arms, she could almost allow herself to forget.

"I wish I could tell you the truth," she whispered as he slept. "I wish we could stay here forever."

I have to get out of here, Reed thought. He squeezed his eyes shut. *Don't speak. Don't move.* If she knew he was awake, she'd want to talk. And he wasn't ready.

So he pretended to be asleep. He pretended to be

somewhere else. Not here, lying next to *her*, with his arms around her, breathing in her hair, wishing he could—

Stop.

He wasn't betraying Kaia. Nothing had happened. Nothing had to happen. It was innocent.

But didn't he want more?

Didn't he like the way her body felt against his?

He was comfortable with Beth, safe. He could *talk* to her—in a way he'd never talked to Kaia.

That was the betrayal.

I miss her, he said silently, as he did every morning. And every morning, he woke up with a hole inside of him. Feeling like if he looked down he would see that a part of his chest was just missing, or that his legs had suddenly become transparent. He felt unwhole.

Except that this morning, he didn't.

It didn't feel like Kaia was watching, or that he could ask for forgiveness. She felt far away, like someone he'd imagined. Reed wanted to push Beth aside, stand up, brush off all traces of her, and leave her behind as he drove home, alone. And Reed always did exactly what he wanted.

He kept still. He kept silent. He stayed.

"Uhhhhhhhhhhhhhh." Some asshole was trying to wake her. She'd kick his ass. Except that would mean sitting up.

"Time to get up, Sleeping Beauty," Kane said, standing up and dumping her to the ground. She'd fallen asleep sitting up, leaning against his shoulder, and now she found herself facefirst in the dirt. Asshole was right.

"Aren't you supposed to wake me with a kiss?" Harper groaned.

"I would think you had enough of that last night."

"Uch." Harper spat into the dirt. "Don't remind me."

"Glad to know it was as good for you as it was for me," Kane said dryly, sitting down again, a safe distance away.

Harper stayed where she was. She remembered everything. Unfortunately. "Don't be bitter just because you didn't get anything more than a kiss," she chided him. "I'm sure you'll get over it, in time."

Kane snorted. "I'm the one who pushed *you* away, lovergirl. Or have you forgotten, 'Kane, I want you! I need you! Give it to me now!'?" he asked, affecting a high, nasal voice.

"I did *not,*" Harper said indignantly.

"You tell yourself whatever you need to get by, dearest—we both know what really happened." Kane yawned and pulled a small flask out of his pocket. He took a gulp. "Hair of the dog. Want some?" She waved it away. "How do you feel?" he asked in a softer voice.

Physically, she felt fine.

"I feel like shit," she said, curling up and burying her head in her arms. "Like somebody flushed me down the toilet and I ended up lying in a puddle of crap at the bottom of the sewer system."

In other words, same as always. But he didn't need to know that.

"I'm just going to go back to sleep," she lied, closing her eyes. That was the answer. She'd escape into the hangover. She wouldn't have to talk, she wouldn't have to smile. She could just be—and be miserable.

Her voice faded, and she was out. Kane rolled his eyes. He was wide awake, despite the fact that he'd been sitting up most of the night. Not to keep an eye on her, he told himself. Just because how the hell was he supposed to sleep sitting up, leaning against a giant, lumpy rock, with a girl passed out on top of him.

And not even a real girl—just Harper.

She was a mess. Not that she'd ever admit it. She wasn't a whiner; she didn't cry and cling to you like she'd fall down if you weren't there to hold her up. She'd rather crash.

And let him pick up the pieces.

No one had made him stay, of course. No one was making him stay now. And no one had made him untangle himself from a horny Harper and sit her down on the rocks, forcing her to calm down and stop groping him. He'd ditched the action to tend to her, keeping her out of trouble and pretending he didn't notice her tears. And he had no one to blame but himself.

It was the party of the year, and he'd spent the whole thing tending to drunken *friends*. Being *solicitous*. Exercising *restraint*.

Kane didn't do hangovers. But the thought of all that wasted potential was enough to make him sick.

chapter eleven

ACHY AND BLEARY-EYED, BETH STEPPED THROUGH
her front door—and into an ambush.

"Where the hell have you been?"

"Are you okay?"

"What were you thinking?"

"Why didn't you call?"

Beth sighed, ducked her head, and waited for the yelling to stop.

"Well?" Her father loomed over her, fuming, while
her mother slumped onto the frayed living-room couch,
her eyes rimmed with red. Beth supposed she should
feel sorry for causing concern, but all she had to offer

was surprise and a mild disgust.

"Well what?" she asked. "I told you I was going to a party. I stayed over."

Her father's eyes widened. She knew what they'd been expecting. Sweet, mild-mannered Beth, always responsible and always apologetic. She was sick of it.

"Do you know how we felt when we woke up and saw you never came home last night?" her father boomed. "Do you know what we thought?"

"That you'd actually have to make your own breakfast for once?" Beth snapped, horrified as soon as the words popped out of her mouth. But there was no taking them back, and she didn't particularly want to.

"*What did you say?*"

"You heard me."

"Beth, Beth, sweetie." Her mother shook her head sorrowfully, giving Beth her well-practiced martyr look. "Things around here are hard enough without . . . we really expected more of you."

Beth wanted to kick something. "Too bad!" she cried, all the stress of the last week shooting out of her. "I'm *seventeen*, Mom. I'm not your maid, I'm not your babysitter, I'm not your cook, I'm your *daughter*, and sometimes I screw up. *Deal with it.*"

"That's it!" her father shouted. "Go up to your room.

Your mother and I don't have time to deal with your temper tantrum right now."

Cue the guilt: Her parents both worked triple shifts and were constantly exhausted. The twins took a lot of work. The house was always a mess. It was Beth's responsibility to pitch in and shut up. She knew all that—but today, she just didn't care.

"I'm out of here," she muttered, turning her back on her parents.

"Don't you disobey me," her father warned. "Get back here."

"Or what?" Beth kept her back to him, not wanting him to see the tears threatening to spill out of her eyes. "You'll punish me? You'll disown me? If it turns out I'm not one hundred percent perfect, you'll just stop loving me?"

"Beth, what are you—?" Her mother's voice broke. Beth forced herself not to give in to the inevitable tears. She slipped out the door before her father could issue any more threats or her mother any pleas.

I'm not who they think I am, she told herself, getting into the car without knowing where to go next. *Better they find that out now.*

Tyson versus Holyfield.

Obama versus Romney.

Jennifer versus Angelina.

As all-time grudge matches go, they had nothing on this.

In one corner: Miranda Sellers, five feet of fighting force powered by jealousy, humiliation, a world-class hangover, two months of repressed anger, and eighteen years of repressed everything else.

In the other corner: the undefeated champion Harper Grace, aka the Terminator, aka the Beast, aka the Ice Queen, who would settle for nothing less than unconditional surrender.

Ladies, come out fighting—and try to keep this fair and above the belt.

As if.

Miranda and Harper circled each other warily, each waiting for the other to land the first blow. Harper had the home-court advantage, which only meant that she had nowhere to escape. Miranda had shown up at her door, dragged Harper up to her bedroom, and now, behind closed doors and with a bleary-eyed ferocity, was ready to pounce. On the wall behind her hung a bulletin board covered in photos of the dynamic duo's greatest hits: junior high dances, makeover-themed slumber parties, crappy double dates, and triumphant after-parties. It was a vivid documentary record of their friendship; but at the moment, it was irrelevant.

Miranda swung first. "How could you?" she asked, pacing around Harper in a tight circle.

"What?"

"I saw you with Kane," Miranda snapped. "It was disgusting."

"So?"

"So you know how I feel about him."

Harper landed the first blow. She laughed. "So maybe I don't care."

"That's obvious," Miranda retorted. "You don't care about anything."

Point to Miranda.

"What do you know?" Harper yelled, her face turning red.

"Nothing!" Miranda shouted back. "Because you won't *let* me!" She paused, and sucked in a lungful of air. "I'm supposed to be your best friend," she said quietly.

Harper threw her hands in the air. "Since when? Last month you hated me, this month you love me. Gosh," she said sarcastically, opening her eyes wide in confusion. "I just can't keep track."

"Last month you screwed me over and were a total bitch about it!" Miranda snapped. "This month . . ."

"Yeah." Harper scowled. "This month you're back, because you feel sorry for me. Like I need that!"

The gloves were off.

Miranda wanted to cry. But, instead, she balled up her fists, wishing she could land a real blow.

Harper felt the anger explode from her, and it was such a blissful release to finally let it go that she didn't care who was in the line of fire. She didn't care who she was really angry at—Miranda was there, and she made for an easy target. It just felt so good, after all these weeks, to shout, to scream, to unclench her muscles, to drop the fake smile.

To let herself *feel*.

It was almost worth it.

Even when Miranda pounded her fist against the wall, slammed through the door, and left Harper alone.

Here is what Miranda remembered as she walked down the driveway to her car, trying to keep her face turned away from Adam's house, and trying not to cry:

The sneer on Harper's face and the ice in her eyes.

The sound of Harper laughing at her pain.

And, most of all, Harper's words.

"Maybe if you weren't so goddamn annoying and in my face *all! The! Time!*"

"Stop pretending you can understand anything about me!"

"I don't need your pity and I don't need you!"

And here is what Harper remembered as she sat on the edge of her bed and let the numbness seep back in:

Miranda's eyes blinking back tears.

Miranda's voice shaking as she spit out everything she'd been holding back.

Miranda's attack, the words they both knew were true.

"Why is everything always about *you*?"

"Of course I felt sorry for you—why else would I pretend you weren't such a bitch?"

"I've been your best friend for ten fucking years—you barely even *knew* her!"

Mostly, both girls remembered the end.

"You want to be miserable? You want to be totally self-destructive and pathetic and blow off anyone who tries to help?" Miranda asked, disgusted. "Don't let me stop you."

Harper opened her bedroom door and waved her hand like an usher. "Don't let *me* stop *you* from leaving."

And with that, they were both down for the count.

Reed was on his back under the truck, monkeying with the exhaust system, when she came into the garage. He could only see her feet and ankles: thin, black pumps with a low heel; pale, delicate ankles growing from them, narrow enough that he could probably encircle each with one hand. He'd seen those feet before.

"Hello? Is anybody here? Hello?"

For a moment, Reed considered hiding under the

truck until she gave up and went away. And he might have, if his wrench hadn't slipped out of his fingers and clattered to the floor. After that, he had no choice.

He wheeled himself out from under the truck and sat up, wiping his greasy hands against his jeans. Beth was still wearing the same outfit she'd worn the night before. It had looked perfect at the party; here, surrounded by chains and toolboxes and busted carburetors, it didn't fit.

"What's up?" he asked, not really wanting to know.

Her face was flushed and tearstained, and her hands kept flickering toward her head. She would twirl a strand of hair, tuck it behind her ears, put her arm down, and then, a moment later, start twirling again, as if she couldn't help herself. "I didn't know where else to go," she said simply. "I thought . . ."

She looked so lost and fragile, he just wanted to go to her and hug her. He wanted to fix her problem, whatever it was.

But why? he asked himself. *What's she to you?*

"Can we, uh, go somewhere?" Beth asked, her lip trembling.

Reed shook his head. "I got a lot of stuff to do here," he said. "You know."

"Maybe I could just hang out for a while?" she asked, almost pleading. "I really just need—"

"No." It would be too easy to be happy if she were

there. And he shouldn't be happy, not with someone else. "I told you, I've got stuff to do. You'd be in the way."

"Oh." She looked like he'd punched her. "Okay." She began backing out of the garage, her eyes whipping back and forth, searching fruitlessly for something to focus on. "See you around, I guess."

He shrugged. "Maybe. Whatever."

Then she was gone. He felt like an asshole. And he hurt.

He hadn't lit up since the night before, and now, as the pain crept back into his brain, seemed like as good a time as any. He grabbed his stash out of the glove compartment and wandered outside, sitting on a small ledge behind the garage. He'd have plenty of privacy.

It was a familiar, soothing routine, parsing it out, rolling it up, sealing the blunt with a swift and smooth flick of the tongue.

A few deep breaths and he'd be able to float away, beyond all the pain and all the shit. It would stop hurting.

Reed brought the joint to his lips—and stopped.

He still missed Kaia when he was high. It was a dull, faint throbbing, like a bruise that's turned invisible but has yet to fully heal. Not like now, when the pain was sharp and clear.

The pain was the only thing that was clear, and it burned everything else away. Maybe instead of putting the fire out, this time he should let it burn. He hadn't cried when Kaia died, or yelled or pounded his fist into a glass window, as he'd wanted. He had just smoked up, and that made it all go away.

Just as he'd made Beth go away.

Reed didn't know why he couldn't let her get close.

He didn't know why he couldn't forget the touch of Kaia's fingers on his neck—but could no longer picture her face.

He didn't know if there was some time limit on what he felt, if one day he'd wake up and things would be right again—and he didn't know what he was supposed to do if that never happened.

He stuffed the joint into one pocket, and the plastic bag into another. He was tired of being confused. Maybe, just for a while, he'd stay clear. It was worth a try. And if it was too much, relief was no more than a few lungfuls away.

In the back of Miranda's closet, behind the stash of liquor, cigarettes, old issues of *Cosmo*, and a single pack of condoms that she enjoyed owning but had no expectation of using anytime soon, there was a stack of cardboard boxes. There were seven of them, each labeled in black permanent marker; one for each year, stretching back to sixth grade, and one extra for everything that had come before.

Every year, Miranda set aside an empty desk drawer and filled it with all the detritus of life that most normal people threw out. When the year ended, she dumped the contents into a box and started her collection over again. There were the obvious—ticket stubs, photographs, birthday cards—but everyone with the slightest pack rat tendency saved those. Miranda had an eye for the more subtle mementos: take-out menus, empty cigarette boxes, fliers for concerts she'd never attended, notes passed in class, detention slips, matchbooks, napkins, receipts, anything that might someday bring faded memories back to full color. Her mother liked to call her "the connoisseur of crap," but as Miranda saw it, she was curating the museum of her life.

It was a narrow life, she saw now, sitting on the floor surrounded by half-open boxes and carefully sorted mounds of memories. There was the occasional home-made Valentine's Day card from her little sister, and an entry pass left over from a long-ago family trip to some amusement park that had gone bankrupt only a few months later. But those were the exception; Harper was the rule.

Item: a torn scrap of lined paper, with the initials HG and SP written in neon, encircled by a light blue heart. (Pink had been out that year.) Harper had slipped Miranda the note while their sixth-grade teacher, Ms. Hernandez, had droned on and on about Lewis and Clark. Miranda knew exactly what it meant. For weeks, Harper had been drooling over Scott Pearson, universally acknowledged to be the cutest boy in the sixth grade, except for Craig Jessup, who didn't count because he smelled like mildew. Everyone knew that Scott had been planning to take Harper behind the school at recess and kiss her. They'd disappeared after lunch, right on schedule—and now they were back in the classroom, and here was Harper's note. Miranda got the story on the walk home: He'd kissed her. It was wet, and sloppy, and gross, and now he was her boyfriend. Miranda made Harper promise to tell her every detail of everything that happened, so that she, too, could know what having a boyfriend was like. And Harper came through, recounting every moment she spent with Scott for the nine days their relationship lasted. Then Scott moved on to Leslie Giles, a seventh grader with bigger boobs, and Harper pretended her heart was broken, to get sympathy from every girl in school. Only Miranda got to hear the dirty little secret: Scott had bad breath, kissing was boring, and she was glad to be done with the whole stupid thing.

Item: a wrinkled napkin from High Score, a sports bar that had closed a couple years ago, probably because its TV was only thirty-two inches wide and its waitresses, who mostly looked like they'd been around since the

Eisenhower administration, preferred using it to catch up on SOAPnet reruns of *Dynasty* and *Melrose Place*. For her sixteenth birthday, Harper had given Miranda her very first fake ID. It was crude and cheap, and claimed Miranda was a twenty-one-year-old Virginian named Melanie DeWitt, born May 27, Gemini, residing on Applewood Road, Manassas, Virginia, 20108. All details Miranda had struggled to memorize before they set out to test her new identity at High Score, where it was reputed that they'd let in a second grader if she flashed a homemade library card with her picture taped to it. Miranda was still nervous, forcing Harper to give her a pep talk before they strutted past the bouncer, flashing their ridiculous IDs, and sat down at a bar together for the first time. And despite the gross tables, nasty smells, and cheap beer, it had been the first truly great night of Miranda's life.

Item: a program from the ninth-grade musical, *Oliver!* Miranda had wanted to try out—and, given the size of their school, "try out" really meant "write your name on the list and Mr. Grady will assign you your part." But Harper had labeled it TLFU, Too Lame For Us. Lots of things were TLFU that year, which, not coincidentally, had marked the beginning of Harper's rise to the top of the social stratosphere. White sneakers, boy bands, binders, the color pink (in the previous year, now out once again), eighth-grade boys, PG movies, sparkly nail polish—all TLFU. It was a lot for Miranda to remember, which was why, as in the case of the school musical, Harper had to keep reminding her. But they'd gone to see it, because Harper had scored them an invitation to the cast party, hosted by geeky Mara Schneider, whose brother Max was a junior and topped the official list of high school hunks. Max was supposed to be at the party, but didn't show. Instead, Harper and Miranda got stuck in a corner with Barry and Brett Schanker. Barry had played the Artful Dodger, Brett had played the trumpet in the pit; both were pale, gangly, pockmarked, and intent on getting Harper and Miranda to play Twister with them in Mara Schneider's rec room. Instead, Harper and Miranda had escaped into the backyard, where they'd spent the night dangling their feet in the Schneiders' pool, smoking a full pack of cigarettes (courtesy of Brett Schanker), getting drunk on the hot pink "Kool-Aid-plus" punch, and pretending that they were the only two people there, or at least the only two who mattered. By the end of the night, Miranda had thrown up in the bushes, Harper had nearly fallen into the pool, and, in an act of mad courage (or courageous madness), they'd snuck up to Max's room and snagged a pair of his boxers. (White, size medium, and covered in bright yellow happy faces; Max, they decided, was definitely TLFU.)

Item: a dried carnation from tenth-grade Valentine's Day, left over from the bouquet Harper had given Miranda when she freaked out about not having a boyfriend.

Item: a magazine clipping of a tropical island, where they'd dreamed of someday co-owning a vacation house with their unspeakably wealthy and unbelievably hand-some husbands.

Item: a Scrabble tile, rescued from the trash, after Harper—tired of losing each and every rainy day—had dumped the game.

Item: a thin, green plastic ring purchased for a quar-ter from a gumball machine. They'd each bought one, pledging to wear them forever. Miranda had lost hers first—this was Harper's, because they both knew that Miranda's cardboard boxes were the only place it would be safe.

Miranda rubbed her eyes. She'd been looking through the boxes for hours, as if something in one of them would be able to explain what was happening. But there were no answers, only the record of a friendship that should have been enough.

It was enough for Miranda—it had, for all these years, been nearly everything, and here was the proof. So why did Harper need so much more? And why was she willing to trash it, for Adam, for Kane, for Kaia, for anything?

Miranda had been willing to put everything aside for

Harper's time of need, because that's what best friends do. But it was obvious now: Whatever Harper needed, it wasn't her.

Sometimes, she knew it was a dream while it was happening.

"Where are we?" she asked Kaia, gaping at the tiny huts lining the cobblestone streets. They wound up and around into the hills, giving way to long stretches of emerald-green vineyards. On the other side, the land dropped off abruptly, and at the base of a cliff lapped the waters of a calm, turquoise sea.

"Italy," Kaia said, looking bored. She slipped on a pair of sunglasses, despite the cloudy sky. "A little fishing village on the Riviera."

"But I've never been here," Harper said, confused. She'd never been out of California, not that she would have admitted it to Kaia, with her passport stuffed full of stamps from glamorous getaways to international hot spots.

"I have," Kaia said, shrugging. "It gets old."

"But this is *my* dream," Harper pointed out. She wandered down one of the uneven paths, stopping just before the land dropped off to nothingness. Keeping her back to the town and staring out over the cliff face, she felt like she was on the edge of the world. "How can—?"

"You want to argue?" Kaia asked, stretching out on the ground as if she were at the beach. "Or you want to get a tan?"

Harper tossed a small rock over the edge of the cliff. She tried to follow its way down, but didn't see it land. "What are we doing here? What are *you* doing here? You're . . ."

"Can't say it, can you?" Kaia laughed bitterly. "Dead. Kaput. Kicked the bucket. Passed over to . . . woooooooh . . ." She made her voice dramatically low and solemn, "the *Other Side*."

"I was going to say, 'You're *annoying* me,'" Harper corrected her. "Can't you just leave me alone?"

"I did leave you alone. Isn't that the problem?" Kaia stood up and brushed herself off. "Why else are you acting like such a mental case?" Before Harper could answer— not that she had an answer—Kaia wandered over to a small storefront, where she haggled with a stooped old man. She came back a moment later with an ice-cream cone heaped high with dripping scoops of chocolate and handed it to Harper.

"None for you?" Harper asked.

"Some of us actually *care* about our figures," Kaia said, giving Harper a pointed look. She ignored it and took a big, slippery mouthful. It was chilly and delicious and, just like everything else, seemed somehow more real than waking life. For weeks, everything had looked gray, tasted dull; but here, even the air tasted sweet, and the ocean blazed a brilliant blue.

She stared down at the jagged rocks at the base of the cliff. The waves slammed against them, frothy geysers spurting several feet into the air. Harper crept closer to the edge, feeling a strange sense of power and possibility. Taking another step seemed like such a small, routine choice—she took steps every day, thousands of them—but the next one could launch her into midair, hundreds of feet above the ground.

What happens if you die in a dream? she wondered.

And maybe she wouldn't die at all—maybe the water would cushion her and she would float away. Or maybe, since it was a dream, she would step off the ground and discover she could fly.

She was too afraid to find out.

"I don't blame you." Kaia's voice was almost lost in the thunder of the crashing surf.

Harper didn't turn around. It was all so easy for Kaia. It always had been. She just did whatever the hell she wanted, and then walked away. Disappeared. Harper was the one left to face the consequences. Harper was the one left to bear the pain.

She wanted to scream, as loud as she could, to see if her voice could fill the emptiness that lay before her, the vast ocean and sky bleeding together in a field of blue. She wanted to berate Kaia for leaving, to beg her to come back, to admit the horrible truth: More than anything, she wished she and Kaia had never met. Because then this whole nightmare—before the accident, and after—would disappear. But even though it was a dream, that was no excuse to let things get out of control, or to feel the things she wasn't allowed to feel.

She opened her mouth, intending to apologize—for what she'd done, for what she'd thought, for what she'd wished. But something else leaked out.

"Maybe it doesn't matter," she told Kaia in a tight, level voice. "Maybe I blame *you*."

chapter twelve

IT TURNED OUT SCHOOL WAS JUST AS BORING WHEN you weren't high.

Reed's experiment was in its fifth day, and so far, so . . . okay. He hadn't had any remarkable revelations; his newly clear mind hadn't discovered the meaning of life or the secrets of cold fusion. (Though it did make it a bit easier for him, in remedial physics, to finally figure out what cold fusion was—school was mildly more informative when you bothered to show up to class, rather than skulk in the parking lot.) He hadn't even decided whether his mind was actually clearer, to be honest. Things seemed to move faster, and matter more, but that just meant that more stuff crowded into his head, none of it making much sense.

Fish and Hale were a bit confused, but when weren't they? And they didn't care what he did. "Whatever, dude" was a one-size-fits-all response.

Reed was beginning to realize that no one much cared what he did. The teachers who ignored his absence didn't perk up at his presence. His father was happy as long as he kept his job and stayed out of jail. Fish and Hale just needed someone to snag them the occasional free pizza. Kaia was gone. And Beth . . .

Beth was avoiding him, her face turning red every time their paths crossed. Not that it happened often; she existed in a different world. Usually, people like her didn't even see him—he was a part of the background, like the garbage cans lining the cafeteria or the gum stuck under every desk.

It was okay with Reed. Being invisible made it easier to watch. He saw Beth hovering on the fringes of crowds, always fidgeting, rarely speaking, never setting off on her own. He watched her spend lunch periods in the library, hunched over a book. Once, he glimpsed her slip away to the newspaper office, her hands covering her eyes to mask the tears.

It seemed like her eyes were always on the verge of filling with tears. But maybe that was just because they were such a shimmering, limpid blue.

He didn't even know why he was watching, until the fifth day, when he made his decision.

He ditched school after lunch—that would give him plenty of time to be back before the final bell. It took him about twenty minutes to drive the familiar route, and with every passing mile, the lump of dread in his stomach grew bigger. But at the same time, the closer he got, the more he needed to be there, and the faster he drove.

Reed pulled off onto the shoulder and stared up at the imposing hulk of a building. He'd brought Kaia here, the first time he'd brought her anywhere, back when he'd thought she was just some stuck-up rich bitch. But she'd understood what he saw in the place, and though she never said it, Reed was sure she felt the same way. They'd come out here a lot, sitting silently, staring at the abandoned machinery, the rusted barbed wire, the gaping maw of the mines themselves, and imagining the past.

He hadn't been back since the accident. And he wouldn't be coming back again. He just needed to say good-bye.

He stepped out of the car and forced himself to stare at the spot of their last night here together, as if he could still see the imprint of his blanket on the ground. It hurt like hell. But that was the point.

After a moment, he tore himself away and headed toward the gap-ridden metal fence that surrounded the heart of the refining complex. Ducking through a huge, jagged hole just to the left of a rusted NO TRESPASSING sign, he emerged in the land of forgotten machines. One of the burned-out buildings was missing a large piece of its wall, allowing him to step inside. He wandered past the towering tubes and smokestacks, skirted the giant husks of machines made for smashing and sifting and smelting and sorting, and tried to pretend the whole place didn't feel like it was about to collapse.

In the middle of the refinery he stopped, turning slowly in place, soaking it in. He wanted to remember every detail. But he barely registered the rusted machinery or the blackened walls. He saw only her face.

The pain hit him, raw and scalding. He couldn't stand to be here, surrounded by her absence. He couldn't even think about the time they'd spent here—because when he thought of her now, all he could picture was a burning heap of metal, a lifeless hand, a wooden cross. Someday, maybe, he'd be able to remember the way she was, not the way she ended up. And then he would want something to remember her by.

Reed knelt to the ground and grabbed the first thing he saw: a thin, curved piece of metal half buried in the ground. Half of it was rusted, but the other half was polished smooth and looked almost new. It was about three inches long and an inch wide, and curved at almost a right angle, one end flaring out into a hollow tube shape and the other rounding to form a small, silver sphere. He clenched it in his fist, enjoying the warmth.

It would make a good souvenir. He walked back to the car, hesitating for a moment before he got inside.

"Good-bye," he said aloud, feeling like an idiot.

I'm not coming back, he said silently, wishing he could believe he wasn't just talking to himself. He gripped the small piece of metal tighter, and the flat end dug sharply into his palm. *But I won't forget.*

Bourquins @ 3?

Miranda hadn't expected the text message and didn't know what to do when it arrived. So she fell back on the default option: Obey Harper.

She hadn't responded, but she'd shown up, arriving a few minutes early so she could grab her coffee and be sitting down if and when Harper arrived. She needn't have bothered; Harper, as always, was late.

Harper didn't bother to stop at the counter; she just came straight to the back corner, where Miranda had snagged a table next to the window. The heavy pink drapes were drawn back, and a splash of sunlight fell across her lap. If they stayed long enough, they'd be able to watch the sunset; it didn't seem likely.

Miranda waited. Harper sat down without saying

anything, and for a few moments the two girls just stared at each other. Miranda refused to speak first, no matter how difficult it was to stand the silence.

"So," Harper finally said.

Miranda decided that didn't count, and kept her mouth shut.

After another long pause, Harper rolled her eyes. "Look, I'm sorry. I didn't . . . the thing with Kane, it wasn't . . ."

"So what was it, then?"

Harper shrugged.

"Do you want me to hate you?" Miranda asked— realizing, once the words were out there, that maybe that was exactly it.

Harper looked down at the table. "Do you?" she asked quietly.

Miranda sighed. She scraped her spoon around the bottom of her empty coffee mug, then tapped it a few times against the rim. "No. God, Harp, I love you. Don't you get that?"

Harper didn't look up. She drew her arms close against her body, as if for protection, though Miranda suspected she didn't even realize she was doing it. She held her body rigidly still. She obviously wasn't going to say anything, but Miranda remembered those boxes in the back of her closet, and decided to keep going.

"I'm your best friend," she said simply. "I want to help. I know you don't think I understand, and maybe I don't, but I get that you miss—" Miranda paused. She'd been so wary this month of saying the name by accident, dropping it into conversation and setting off some kind of emotional explosion, that it required a force of will to spit it out now. "*Kaia*. If I don't understand the rest, it's because you don't tell me anything."

Harper was now trembling, and still staring down at the table.

"I can do whatever you need me to do, but you have to *tell* me. Whatever you need, I'm there. But if you don't need me . . ." Miranda took a deep breath. She didn't want to get angry or hysterical—she just needed to get this out so that she would know she'd tried everything she could. "If you want me to stop bothering you, fine. I'll go away. You just—I need to know what you want. Just *say* it."

Harper finally looked up. She took a deep, shuddering breath, opened her mouth, then shut it again.

Long minutes went by, and nothing happened. Miranda shook her head in disgust. She stood up, pushed her chair in, and gave her best friend a curt wave. "See ya."

She'd turned her back and already walked away when Harper finally spoke. "I do . . . I need you."

Miranda turned slowly but didn't come any closer, as if Harper were a wild beast she was liable to frighten away.

"I just need some time, Rand, okay?" Harper was looking down at the table once again, her voice high and tight. "Can you just . . . wait for me?"

It wasn't much, but Miranda suddenly felt weightless. "Sure," she said, trying to sound like the whole thing was no big deal. "And when you're ready—I'll be there."

The truck skidded to a stop a foot in front of her. Reed's face peered out from the open window. "Get in."

"What?" Beth's mind wasn't at its sharpest these days, and, given that it had been days since she'd expected—and hoped—never to see him again, the scene took a moment to process.

"Get in." He leaned across to the passenger door and pushed it open for her. "Come on, trust me."

Never, Beth thought, in the history of the universe, had the words "trust me" led to anything but disaster. But she didn't have particularly far to fall.

She got in.

"I'm sorry," he said. "About before."

"Okay." She waited for him to elaborate, but he was apparently done talking. Beth shrugged and turned to look out the window as the desert streamed by. They drove for a little under an hour, without conversation or music. Beth closed her eyes, listening to the steady hum of the engine and the snap, crackle, pop of rocks and sticks kicked up by the tires and clattering against the underside of the truck. She'd almost drifted off to sleep when the truck made a sharp turn, swinging off the main highway onto a narrow, bumpy dirt road that seemed to wind into an expanse of nothingness.

Beth wondered if she should be concerned—then closed her eyes again and let the bumping and rocking of the truck guide her back toward sleep.

"We're here," Reed suddenly said, pulling to a stop. He grabbed a couple bottles of water from the back and tossed one to Beth. "Let's go."

They were deep in the desert, standing at the foot of an unnaturally smooth, bright white expanse. A dry lake, Beth realized as they hiked across—there were a few of them sprinkled across the area, but she'd only ever seen them from a car window. As they crossed the lake, it appeared on the horizon: an enormous cone, hundreds of feet high and wide, spurting out of a field of jagged, reddish-black rock.

"Salina Crater," Reed said as Beth's eyes widened. "It's prehistoric."

They followed a gently sloping path into the crater's center, climbing over hardened lava rolls and scrambling up a slippery trail toward the top. The afternoon sun beat down on them, and Beth gulped her water greedily, pouring a tiny trickle down the back of her neck. She shivered at the delicious touch of cold. She was breathing too hard to speak, but it didn't matter; the breathtaking size and alien beauty of the place had stolen all her words. It felt like they'd traveled back in time and that, when they emerged at the top of the rim, they would see a panorama of roiling volcanoes and wandering dinosaurs stretched out before them.

There were no dinosaurs, but she still gasped at the view. The white lake stretched out to their left, dwarfing the tiny strip of black that marked the highway, and in the other direction, a range of low, rolling mountains dotted the horizon.

"This is amazing," she breathed. She'd been feeling alone in the world for so long—but now, here, she actually understood what that would mean.

The rim was at least ten feet wide, and Reed sat down toward the outer edge, gesturing for her to join him.

"I can't believe this place," she said quietly, not wanting to disrupt the absolute calm and stillness of the setting.

"My dad told me about it," Reed said. He should have looked totally out of place up here, in his black, ripped punk rock T-shirt and dark, stained jeans. But somehow, he fit perfectly. "I always wanted to check it out, but just never, you know."

"So why today?" she asked. The sun was dipping

toward the horizon, and part of her worried that they should start back down so they wouldn't have to hike in the dark. But she didn't want to go anywhere.

"I wanted to go somewhere new." He chewed on the edge of his thumbnail for a moment, then shook himself. "I wanted to—"

And then his lips brushed against hers, so lightly that, if she'd had her eyes closed, she might have thought she imagined it. They were soft, and tender, and then, before she knew what was happening, they were gone.

"Reed . . ." Beth covered her face with her hands and leaned toward the ground, as if she were praying. What was she supposed to do? Not this—she was certain of that. Not with him.

His hands grabbed hers and gently pried them away from her face.

"You don't even know me," she whispered. "You don't know what I've done."

"I don't care." He was still holding her hands. "Screw the past. We're here, *now*."

"I *want* to tell you . . ." But she knew she couldn't.

"Don't. Let's just . . . be." His lashes were so long and dark, like a girl's. And in his eyes, which she'd once thought were a deep brown, she could now see flecks of blue, green, silver, even violet. He was looking at her like he could see into her—like he knew everything.

Of course he didn't.

But maybe he really didn't want to. Maybe they could make a fresh start, and help each other forget the past; or at least move forward.

"Your move," he said, his lips turning up into a half smile. She moved.

It was the kind of kiss you imagine when you're a kid, dreaming of a fairy tale romance: soft, chaste, quick, and perfect. Beth broke away first. If she was going to do this, she was going to do it slowly.

Reed stood up and took her hand, pulling her off the ground. He led her to the edge of the rim and put his arm around her. She nestled against him, and they stood in silence, watching the sun blaze toward the horizon. The desert stretched on forever, still and silent, miles of emptiness in every direction. It seemed like civilization, and along with it, her life, her problems, and everyone else in the world were just figments of her imagination.

So it was especially strange that, for the first time in months, she felt like she wasn't alone.

Harper huddled under her covers with the phone cradled to her chest for more than an hour before she got up her nerve to call.

He didn't answer, and she almost hung up—but she stopped herself, just in time.

"I know I told you to leave me alone," she said after the beep, talking quickly before she lost her nerve, "but—"

She couldn't say it.

I need you—it wasn't her, no matter how true it might be.

"Just come find me when you get this. Please."

She told him where she'd be, and hung up. Her parents, who'd thankfully given up on the nightly family bonding sessions, were downstairs watching TV and would be only too delighted to let her go out and meet a friend for "coffee," even if it was a school night. Harper promised them she'd be home early, then hurried out to the driveway, forcing herself not to look up at Adam's dark and empty bedroom window.

There were no lights on the road, and she had some trouble finding the right spot, but the thin white cross glowed in the moonlight. Harper hadn't been back since the accident, and in her imagination she'd pictured a burned strip of land strewn with torn metal and ash. But, aside from the small memorial, the spot looked no different from any other stretch along the road.

She sat down on the ground, tugging her sweater around herself, and waited. There was no reason to expect that he'd come. Even if he got her message, the odds were low that he'd bother to show up. Especially after the way she'd treated him these last few weeks.

But she was holding too much inside. If he didn't

show, maybe she could just scream her pain into the night; maybe that would make everything somehow better. She stared at the thin, white wooden boards and wondered why she didn't cry. Being here should offer some kind of release, she thought in frustration. Instead, it just made her feel disconnected; it didn't seem like anything that had happened here could have any connection to her.

The road was empty, and when the headlights appeared on the horizon and drew closer, splashing her with light, she knew he'd come for her. The car pulled off the road and stopped. A door slammed, and footsteps approached.

"Okay, Grace. I'm here. Now what?"

Harper stood up to face Kane. The smirk dropped off his face. "What the hell is wrong?" he asked. "You look like shit."

"Gee, thanks."

"Seriously, Grace, what is it?"

"It's . . . everything." Harper rubbed her hand against the back of her neck, trying to ease the tight knots of muscle. "I just wanted to . . . I need . . . I—" She wanted to tell him everything: how she couldn't even remember what it felt like not to be miserable; how every night she went to sleep dreading the next morning; how she wanted to escape from inside her head and just become someone else, with a normal, happy, guilt-free life. But the words froze somewhere in her throat. "I'm sorry," she said, turning away from him. "I thought I could do this, but I can't." She shook her head. "Sorry I dragged you out here. You should just go."

"I don't think so." Kane grabbed her arm and spun her back around. "Talk to me, Grace. What do you need?"

"What the hell do you care?" she sneered, pulling her arm away.

"I'm beginning to wonder that myself," Kane said, arching an eyebrow, "if this is the thanks I get. . . ."

"Whatever." Harper walked away from him, wishing she could just keep walking, into the darkness, and disappear.

"Hey!" Kane followed. "*Harper!*" he grabbed her again. "Get off of me!"

"I'm not leaving you here alone!" he shouted.

Harper forced a laugh. "As if you care about anyone but yourself."

"Insult me all you want, but I'm not leaving."

She smacked his arm, then his chest. "*I* am."

But Kane threw his arms around her and pressed her fiercely against him.

"Let go of me!" she cried, banging her fists into his back. He ignored her and just held her tighter. "Kane, please! Please. Just let me go."

"And then what? You get to finally be alone? You think I don't know I'm your last stop?" He stopped shouting. "I'm not like the rest of them—you can't push me away. Come on, Grace, you know I always stick around until I get what I want."

She burst into laughter, letting herself sag against him, and in that moment of release, everything she'd been holding down so tightly came flooding to the surface, her laughter quickly turning into gasping, wracking sobs.

And Kane held her as she cried.

"This is natural," she hears the doctor say to her mother as she lies still in the bed, unwilling to move, or speak, or do anything but stare at the ceiling and wait for the nightmare to end. "She's in shock. Give her a chance to absorb things. It's all a part of grieving."

It doesn't feel like grieving. It feels like falling.

"I killed her!" Harper screamed, shaking. "I did it. She's dead. I did it." Tears gushed down her face and she gasped for breath, wishing she could just pass out so the pain would end.

"It was an accident." Kane insisted. "It *wasn't your fault.*"

But she wasn't listening. She was remembering.

They won't tell her what happened to Kaia. They won't tell her anything. Until, one day, when she is "strong enough," they do.

"Kaia didn't . . . didn't make it, hon. I'm so sorry."

Harper doesn't say anything. She doesn't feel anything— just . . . empty. It doesn't seem real. Things like this don't happen to people like her. She doesn't cry.

"It should have been me," she moaned.

"No."

"*Yes.*"

"Harper, no."

The memories flowed faster, beating her back in time through the misery, through the pain.

Everything hurts.

"Where am I?" she asks. Her voice sounds like two pieces of metal scraping together.

"There was an accident," her mother says, hovering over her. "You and Kaia. . . . Do you remember what happened?"

She doesn't remember anything. She feels like the past doesn't exist, that there is only the present—pain and confusion.

It isn't the first thing she asks. But, eventually, it occurs to her: "How's Kaia?"

"It should have been me," she said, letting herself fall limp in his arms. If he hadn't been holding her up, she would have fallen.

"Stop."

"It should've," she insisted.

"It shouldn't have been anyone," Kane said softly, smoothing her hair down.

"I wish I could just go back." She closed her eyes and lay her head against his shoulder. It was wet with her tears.

"It's going to be okay, Grace."

The tires screech as she spins the wheel, but the car won't move fast enough. The van is bearing down, and next to her, Kaia screams and screams as the car shakes with a thunderous impact and rolls off the road. The world spins, Kaia screams, and everything goes dark.

Harper shuddered. "Nothing's ever going to be okay." But her sobs had quieted and she realized she could breathe again. She took a few deep breaths.

"Better?"

"Don't let go," she murmured. Not yet. She wasn't ready.

"Never," he promised.

The wind rushes past them, and Harper can feel everything fall away until nothing is left but a crisp, clear certainty that life is good, and that she is happy. Kaia turns the music up, and they shout the lyrics into the wind, their voices disappearing in the thunder of the engine.

She presses her foot down on the pedal. Faster, faster, the world speeds by, her life fades into the distance, she can leave it behind if she just goes fast enough and far enough.

"Let's never go back!" she shouts to Kaia.

"Never!" Kaia agrees, tossing her head back, laughing.

They have everything they need. A fast car. A sunny day. Freedom. Each other.

She has been so miserable, so angry, so afraid, for so long, and now all that has burned away, and there is only one thing left.

Joy.

seven deadly sins

GLUTTONY

For Richard, David, and Natalie Roher
And for Aunt Susan, who has heard it all—
and is always willing to listen

They are as sick that surfeit
with too much as they that starve with nothing.
—William Shakespeare, *The Merchant of Venice*

I eat too much
I drink too much
I want too much
Too much
—Dave Matthews Band, "Too Much"

chapter one

"ANYTHING WORTH DOING," KANE GEARY INTONED, gulping down a glowing green shot that looked radioactive, "is worth overdoing."

"Thanks for the wisdom, O Wise One." Adam Morgan pressed his hands together and gave Kane an exaggerated bow. "What did I ever do without you to guide me through the mysteries of the universe?"

"Less sarcasm." Kane clinked his shot glass against the half-full pitcher of beer. "More drinking."

It was nearly midnight, and the bar was packed. To their left, a whale-size cowboy in a ten-gallon hat tucked hundred-dollar bills down the cleavage of a harem of spangled showgirls half his age. Against the back wall, a table of white-jumpsuit-clad Elvis impersonators argued loudly about whether *The Ed Sullivan Show* hip swivel properly began with a swing to the left or the right. The bartender, who wore a gold bikini and a cupcake-size hair bun over each ear, would have been the spitting image of Princess Leia—were he not a man. The walls were lined with red velvet and the ceiling covered with mirrors.

Welcome to Vegas.

Adam felt like he'd set foot on an alien planet; Kane, on the other hand, had obviously come home.

"Where do you think Harper and Miranda are?" Adam asked, nursing his beer.

Kane rolled his eyes and spread his arms wide. "Morgan. Dude. Focus. Look around you. This is nirvana. Who the hell cares where the girls are?"

"If they got stuck somewhere—"

"They'll be fine. You're the one I'm worried about." Kane clapped him on the back. "You need another drink, kid. You've got to loosen up."

Adam shook his head. "No more. It's late. And I'm—"

"Lame. Very lame." Kane grabbed Adam's glass and downed the remaining beer in a single gulp. Then he filled it back up to the brim and slammed it down in front of Adam. "But we'll fix that."

"Oh, will we?" Adam asked dryly.

"Adam, my doubting disciple, if there's one thing you learn from me tonight, let it be this." He was silent for a long moment, and Adam began to wonder whether all that beer sloshing around in his brain had swept away his train of thought.

"Yes?" Adam finally said.

Kane leaned across the table, the better to wheeze his sour breath into Adam's face. "This is Vegas, baby." His voice was hushed, almost reverential. "America's Playground. City of Lights. Sin City." He leaned in even closer, as if to whisper a crucial secret. *"This is Vegas, baby!"* Adam recoiled as Kane let loose an ear-piercing whoop of elation. "Live it up!"

"This is definitely *not* Vegas," Harper Grace observed sourly.

Miranda Stevens pulled the car over to the side of the road and shut off the ignition. "Thanks for the news flash," she snapped. "If you hadn't pointed that out, I might have mistaken that"—she gestured toward the hulking mound of rock and dirt jutting out of the desert landscape—"for the Trump Taj Mahal."

"That's in Atlantic City," Harper corrected her.

"Gosh, maybe *that's* where we are," Miranda said in mock revelation. "I knew we shouldn't have taken that left turn. . . ."

Harper tore open a bag of Doritos and kicked her feet up onto the dashboard. "I really hope that's not sarcasm," she said, neglecting to offer Miranda a chip. "Because the person responsible for stranding us here in the middle of East Bumblefuck should probably steer clear of the sarcasm right about now."

Miranda snatched the bag out of Harper's hands, though it was several hours too late to prevent an explosion of orange crumbs all over the front seat of her precious Honda Civic. "And by the person responsible, I assume you're referring to . . . you?"

Harper raised an eyebrow. "Am *I* driving?"

Harper, doing her share of the work? Miranda snorted at the thought of it. "No, of course not. You're just sitting there innocently, with no responsibilities whatsoever, except, oh . . . *reading the map.*"

That shut her up. Miranda's lips curled up in triumph. Beating Harper in an argument was a rare victory, one that she planned to savor, lost in the wilderness or not.

"Okay, let's not panic," Harper finally said, a new, ingratiating tone in her voice. "Look on the bright side. It's your birthday—"

"Not for another twenty-four hours," Miranda corrected her.

"We're bound for Vegas," Harper continued.

"Maybe. *Someday.*"

"And we're not stranded," Harper added, grabbing a map off the floor, seemingly at random, "just—"

"Lost."

"*Detoured.*" Harper spread the map across her lap and began tracing out their route with a perfectly manicured pinkie. "We just need to get back to the main highway," she mumbled, "and if we turn back here and cross over Route 161 . . ."

Miranda sighed and tuned her out, resolving to backtrack to the nearest gas station and get directions from a professional. Professional lukewarm coffee dispenser and stale-candy-bar salesman, maybe, but anything would be better than Harper's geographically challenged attempts to guide them. Especially since Harper periodically forgot whether they should be heading east or west.

This was supposed to be a bonding weekend—or, rather, a re-bonding weekend, given all the tension of the last few months. But it turned out that five hours in a car together didn't exactly make for a BFF bonanza.

Call it the sisterhood of the traveling crankypants.

Miranda turned the key in the ignition, eager to start driving again—somewhere. Anywhere.

A small, suspicious, gurgling sound issued from the motor. Miranda turned the key again. Nothing. With a sinking feeling, she lowered her eyes to the dashboard indicators: specifically, the gas gauge.

Uh-oh.

"Harper?" she said softly, nibbling at the edge of her lower lip.

"Maybe if we circle around to Route 17," Harper muttered, lost in her own cartographic world. "Or if we—wait, am I looking at this upside down?"

"Harper?" A little louder this time.

"Fine, *you* look at it," Harper said in disgust, pushing the wad of paper off her lap. "And if you tell me one more time that I don't know how to read a map, I'm going to scream. It's not like I didn't—"

"Harper!"

"*What?*"

Miranda tore the keys out of the ignition and threw them down on the dash, then leaned her head back against the seat. She closed her eyes. "We're out of gas."

She couldn't see the look on Harper's face. But she could imagine it.

There was a long pause. "So you're telling me—" Harper stopped herself, and Miranda could hear her take a deep breath. Her voice got slightly—very slightly—calmer. "You're telling me that we're out of gas. We're out here in the middle of nowhere, and now we're not just lost—"

"We're stranded," Miranda confirmed. "So, Ms. Look On the Bright Side . . . *now* can we panic?"

✐ ✐ ✐

He woke her with a kiss.

"Whuh? Where . . . ?" Beth Manning opened her eyes, disoriented and unsure why she was sleeping sitting up, lodged into the corner of a van that stunk of pot and sweat socks. But she smiled, nonetheless. It didn't really matter where she was, or how much her neck and back ached— not when Reed Sawyer's chocolate-brown eyes were so close, and his dark curly hair was brushing her skin.

It was the best kind of alarm clock.

"Was I sleeping?" she mumbled, slowly making sense of her surroundings. She remembered piling into the van, nestling into a space, between the guitar cases and the drum, that was just big enough for one—or two, if they sat nearly on top of each other. She had curled under Reed's arm, leaned her head on his shoulder, promised to stay awake for the long drive, and then zoned out, staring at the grayish brown monotony of the landscape speeding by. "Sorry, I guess I must have drifted off."

"No worries," Reed assured her, giving her another quick peck on the lips. "It was cute."

"Yeah, the snoring was adorable!" Hale called from the driver's seat.

That's right, we're not alone, Beth reminded herself. When Reed was around, it seemed like the rest of the world fell away. But in reality, his bandmates, Fish and Hale, were never far behind. Not that Beth was complaining. She was in no position to complain about anything.

"And the drooling," Fish added teasingly. "The drooling was *especially* attractive."

"I did not drool!" Beth cried indignantly.

"Oh, don't worry." Fish, riding shotgun, twisted around toward the back and brandished his phone. "We've got pictures."

"Shut up, losers," Reed snapped. But Beth just smiled, and snuggled into his side, resting her head in the warm and familiar nook between his chest and shoulder. He looped his arm around her and began lightly tracing out patterns on her arm. She shivered.

Without warning, the van made a sharp left turn, veering into a parking lot and screeching to a stop. "Welcome to Vegas, kids," Hale said, with a sharp blast on the horn. "Gateway to stardom."

Stardom couldn't come soon enough, if it would mean an entourage to carry all the instruments and equipment up to the room. Or, even better, a van with a real lock on the doors that would keep out any thieves desperate enough to steal fifteen-year-old half-busted amplifiers. But since they currently had neither roadies nor locking doors, the three members of the Blind Monkeys had to make do with what they had: the combined strength of three scrawny potheads.

And one ever-faithful blond groupie.

"You don't have to help," Reed told her, pulling his guitar case out of the back. Beth was loaded up like a pack-horse with heavy, scuffed-up duffel bags—no one trusted her to carry the real equipment. "You can go check in and we'll meet you inside."

"I'm fine," she protested, ignoring the way the straps dug into her bare shoulder. "I want to help." She was afraid that if she didn't make herself useful, the other guys might realize that she didn't really belong. Reed might finally figure it out himself.

Yes, she was the one who'd found out about that weekend's All-American Band Battle, and she was the one who'd convinced Reed and the guys to enter. But no matter how much she hung out with them, she'd never be one of them, not really.

And she dreaded the day they got sick of her and left her behind.

Alone.

She couldn't stand that. Not again.

Reed shrugged. "Whatever." He slung his guitar case over his shoulder and hoisted an amp, heading across the parking lot. Beth began to follow, but then, as the hotel rose into full view, she stopped. And gasped.

The Camelot was the cheapest hotel almost-but-not-quite-on the Strip; Beth, a Vegas virgin, would have been willing to bet it was also the gaudiest. The gleaming white monstrosity towered over the parking lot—literally, as its twenty stories were sculpted into the guise of a medieval tower, complete with ramparts, turrets, and, down below, a churning, brownish moat. It reminded Beth of a model castle her fourth-grade class had once built from sugar cubes, except that in this version, the royal crest was outlined in neon and featured a ten-foot-tall fluorescent princess wearing a jeweled crown—and little else.

Then there was the pièce de résistance, guarding the palace doors. Beth goggled at the enormous green animatronic dragon swinging its long neck up and down with an alarmingly loud creak each time it shifted direction. Periodically a puff of smoke would issue from its squarish mouth, followed by a warning siren, and then—

WHOOOSH! A flume of fire blasted out of the dragon, a jolt of orange and red billowing several feet out into the night. Beth cringed, imagining she could feel the heat.

"It's not going to eat you," Reed teased, tipping his head toward the front doors, which were now nearly eclipsed by smoke. "Let's make a run for it."

Weighed down by luggage and guitars, it wasn't much of a run, but they eventually made it inside the hotel and up to the room. The Camelot had obviously burned through its decorating budget before furnishing the guest rooms, and the Blind Monkeys had reserved the cheapest one available. It smelled like cigarettes, the toilet was clogged, and the tiny window faced a cement airshaft.

There was one bed.

Harper could barely keep her eyes open, but she wasn't about to fall asleep, not when the skeezy tow-truck driver kept sneaking glances at her cleavage. He'd already offered—twice—to bundle her up in one of his ratty old blankets to protect her from the cold. As if she needed some middle-aged dirt-bucket to tuck her in—as if, in fact, she'd be willing to touch anything in this trash heap on wheels. Touching the seat was bad enough; these pants would need to be burned.

Miranda, on the other hand, apparently had no such qualms. She was totally conked out, her head resting on Harper's shoulder. All that complaining—*Stop spilling crumbs in the car! Stop sticking your head out the window! Stop flashing the other drivers!*—must have worn her out. Or maybe it was just the hour they'd spent shivering in the darkness, waiting for someone to pass by. With no cell reception and no idea how far they were from civilization, they'd been forced to flag down a trucker, crossing their fingers that he wasn't a deranged ax murderer trolling the roads for pretty girls too stupid to fill their gas tanks.

Trucker Hank offered them a ride, and got a quick

thanks but no thanks for his trouble. They may have been stupid, but not that stupid. So instead, the guy promised to check in at the next gas station he passed and send someone back to help them.

"We're going to be out here all night," Miranda had moaned, once the truck's lights had disappeared into the distance.

In fact, it had only been another hour, but that had been long enough. When Leroy had finally arrived with his tow truck, offering to take them and their wounded Civic back to "town," they'd climbed in eagerly, only later realizing that the cab of the truck smelled like roadkill, as did Leroy.

It was a long drive.

"Here we are, gals," he said finally, pulling into a tiny, one-pump gas station that looked like a relic from the stone age—or, at least, the fifties. (Same difference.) Harper poked Miranda to wake her up, and climbed out of the truck, sucking in a deep lungful of the fresh air. She'd been hoping to grab something to eat once they got into town, but . . .

"Where is 'here,' exactly?" she asked dubiously.

"Natchoz, California," he said proudly. "Town center."

"Did he say nachos?" Miranda whispered, half giggling, half yawning. "Think we could find some?"

Doubtful. Harper took another look at the "town center." Aside from the gas station, there was a small shack whose sign read only CAFÉ and . . . that was about it. She was used to lame small towns—being born and bred in Grace, CA, lameness capital of the world, it kind of came with the territory. But this wasn't a town, it was a live-in trash heap with its own mailbox.

Leroy filled up their tank, never taking his eyes off Harper's chest. "That'll be forty-seven bucks, ladies," he finally said, hanging up the nozzle. Harper looked at Miranda; taking her cue, Miranda whipped out a credit card. "No can do." Leroy chuckled. "The machine's busted."

"You can't fix it?" Miranda asked anxiously.

Now the chuckle turned into a roar. "Machine's been busted since 1997. You girls got cash?"

Miranda darted her eyes toward Harper and gave her head a quick shake. Translation: They were totally screwed. Harper's wallet, as usual, was empty; she'd been counting on Kane to front her the cash for the Vegas adventure, and Miranda's credit card to get them through the journey.

So now what?

They could make a run for it—hop in the car and drive away before Leroy knew what hit him.

Or—

"You girls ain't got the cash, I'm thinking you could

make it up to me another way," Leroy said, giving them a nasty grin. "In trade."

Holy shit.

Beth couldn't stop staring at the bed. She snuck a glance at Reed—he was watching it too.

Her mother thought she was spending the weekend at a friend's house—which showed how little her parents knew of her life these days. She was out of friends. Reed was all she had left. If he disappeared . . .

She refused to let herself think about it. But she still couldn't avoid looking at the bed.

Reed had never pushed her, never pressured her, never expected her to move faster than she was comfortable with or go further than she was ready to go. Not like Adam, who'd pretended he would wait forever—but only waited until a better offer came along. And not like Kane, who never wanted to take no for an answer, and who made Beth feel like a con artist, promising something that she was never intending to deliver.

Why did everything always come down to sex?

Reed was different from other guys in a lot of ways, but Beth wasn't stupid. He was still a guy. And sooner or later, he would surely want to know: When? And then: Why not?

She couldn't avoid it forever. And now, here, the bed

filling up half the room, she suspected she couldn't avoid it at all.

"Why don't you guys scope out the casino?" Reed suggested. He shot Beth an easy to interpret look: *Let's ditch these losers, and we can finally be alone.* Part of her couldn't wait—but part of her, as always, was afraid.

"Dude, we have to get ready for tomorrow," Fish pointed out.

"You want to rehearse?" Reed asked incredulously, glancing at the clock. The Blind Monkeys almost never rehearsed—it was one of the reasons they sucked. (Not the only reason, of course: Fish's near total lack of rhythm and Hale's tendency to forget what he was doing in the middle of a song helped too.) "Now?"

"Not rehearse," Fish said, a lopsided grin spreading across his face. *"Prepare."*

Hale got it instantly. They were tuned in to the same wavelength. Or, more accurately, tuned out. "Gotta prepare the *mind*, dude," he said, digging for something in his backpack. "Get in the zone."

He pulled out the bong. Fish whipped out a lighter and cocked his head at Beth and Reed. "You in?"

"I don't know," Reed hedged. "Maybe we should—"

"We're in," Beth interrupted. She plopped down on the edge of the bed and tugged Reed down next to her. She could tell he wanted to get away from the guys—and probably the bong, too. Ever since they'd started dating, Reed had been cutting back on the pot. Way back.

But no matter: Once she'd discovered that one or two puffs of the miracle drug would crush her doubts, calm her terrors, and clear her head, Beth had been more than happy to pick up his slack. She reached for the bong and, like an old pro, inhaled deeply, savoring the burn.

Along with Reed, this was the only thing that had allowed her to make it through the last couple months. This feeling of lightness and freedom, so different from the suffocating guilt and shame that always threatened to crush her. She needed the escape—and if Reed ever found out why, he would leave her, which made her terror absolute.

Fish reached for the bong, but she held tight and, violating etiquette and caution, inhaled another deep lungful. It would be a long weekend—and she needed all the help she could get.

"Now, *this* is more like it," Harper gushed as they turned onto the Strip. "Civilization. Thank God."

"Mmm-hmmm."

"Okay, how much longer are you going to give me the silent treatment?" Harper asked, exasperated. "I already told you I was sorry. How was I supposed to know that you'd find—"

"Don't say it!" Miranda shrieked. "I'm trying to block it out of my mind forever."

"Okay, okay. How was I supposed to know you'd find that *thing* in the sink. I only volunteered to take the toilet because I thought it would be the grosser job, and it is your birthday weekend, after all."

"Celebrate good times," Miranda deadpanned, and suddenly, in sync, they both burst into laughter. "Did all that really happen?" Miranda sputtered through her giggles. "Or was it just some joint hallucination?"

"I'm not hallucinating the smell," Harper gasped, waving her hands under Miranda's nose. "I washed them ten times back there, and they *still* stink."

Miranda wiggled away, trying to focus on the road. "Don't talk to me about smells," she groaned. "It'll just remind me of—"

"Don't even go there," Harper cautioned her. "You're going to make us both sick."

"Again."

It had turned out that paying for the gas "in trade" had meant helping Larry and his half-toothless wife clean up the "café." It had sustained a fair amount of damage during some kind of brawl earlier that evening: truckers versus motorcyclers, with a few local ranchers thrown in for fun. Harper and Miranda had been charged with cleaning the bathroom: It wasn't pretty.

Now safely back in civilization, with its lights, non-toxic air, and toilets complete with modern, functional plumbing, they shook with hysterical laughter, and Harper closed her eyes, soaking in the moment. It may have been the most disgusting night of her life, but things between the two of them were actually starting to feel back to normal. There was a time when Harper had feared they would never be close again, mostly because of the things she'd done and said—and all the things she couldn't bring herself to say. *I'm sorry. I need you.* For years, Harper and Miranda had told each other everything. But now Harper was harboring a secret, and Miranda couldn't ever find out the truth. Harper had to stay silent and guarded, always wondering how it was possible that life could go on, day after day, totally normal, that the people around her could smile and laugh like they didn't know the whole thing could come crashing down at any moment, crushing them all.

Harper had to act like nothing was wrong, like she had forgotten what she had done. She had to pretend that she was as confident and carefree as ever, and hide her terror—and her guilt—from everyone. Even Miranda. Especially Miranda, who knew her the best.

How were they supposed to rebuild a friendship with such a massive lie lodged between them? Harper had almost given up hope. But somehow, they'd found their way back to their bickering, bantering norm, and that meant that the long ride, the many detours, and the adventures in raw sewage had all been worth it.

Well, almost.

When they finally found the hotel, they pulled into the lot without registering much of the medieval tackiness of the garish white tower. It was nearly two in the morning, and they could focus on only two things: a hot shower and a soft bed. Both were now, finally, in reach.

They checked in, ignoring all the other Haven High seniors who littered the hallway—it seemed half the school had hit Vegas for the long weekend, and they were all staying at the Camelot, less for its bargain basement prices than for its widely renowned attitude toward its underage denizens: Don't ask, don't tell.

Usually Harper would have lingered amongst the admiring crowd; she never let a moment in the public spotlight go by without putting on a suitable show. But the fewer people who saw—and smelled—her in this state, the better. The girls trekked down a dingy hallway and arrived in front of room 57. Harper swung the door open to discover a small, squalid room with two full-size beds and little else. Miranda immediately dropped down on the one closest to the door, stretching her arms with a satisfied purr. "I could fall asleep right here, right now."

"Perfect, because I call the first shower," Harper said.

She dumped her bag and rushed to the bathroom before Miranda could object. She could feel the stink and filth crawling over her skin and needed to scrub it away before she could enjoy the fact that she was finally, after a lifetime of waiting, spending the weekend in Las Vegas.

And after nearly drowning in misery for three months, she planned to enjoy the moment as much as humanly possible.

She opened the door of the bathroom, stepped inside—and screamed.

chapter two

ADAM GRABBED A TOWEL AND TRIED TO COVER HIM-
self, but it was too late. Harper had seen everything. Every
tan, muscled, gleaming inch of him. She felt faint, and it
was all she could do not to lunge across the bathroom and
sweep him into her arms, perfect body and all. But she
forced herself to stop, and remember: She and Adam were
no longer best friends, as they'd been for half their lives.
They were no longer in love—*lovers*, she told herself, her
mind lingering on the word—as they'd been for too short
a time. They were . . . nothing. And she intended to treat
him as such.

"What the hell are you doing in our room?" she

snapped, trying to regain her equilibrium. *Don't look at his chest*, she told herself. *Don't look at his shoulders. Don't look at his arms. Don't look* . . . This was maybe not the most effective strategy.

"*Your* room?" Adam tugged the towel tighter around himself and took a step forward, as if to escape the bathroom—which would mean his half-naked body brushing right past Harpers, a fact he seemed to realize just in time. He stopped. "This is *our* room. We checked in hours ago!"

"And 'we' would be . . . ?"

"Me. Kane. We. Our room."

And then it all made sense. "Very funny, Geary," she muttered to herself. "Very cute." When Kane had offered to pay for her and Miranda's room for the weekend, Harper had figured it was just an uncharacteristically gallant gesture, an extravagant birthday present for Miranda. (And not that extravagant: According to the website, rooms at the Camelot went for sixty bucks a night.) She should have known better.

"Harper, look," Adam began, "since you're here, maybe we can—"

"I'm out of here," Harper snapped. Why couldn't Adam just give it up? He couldn't get that if he didn't want a relationship with her, she wasn't about to accept his friendship as a consolation prize. Not when she knew what he *really* thought of her. But he just wouldn't take no for an answer, and kept forcing her into these painful state of the union talks. As if she didn't want him in her life, desperately. As if it didn't kill her to remember all the things he'd said when he'd broken her heart, how he hated her, how he could never trust her again, all because she'd made a few not-so-tiny mistakes. And then his belated and halfhearted offer of forgiveness, just because of the accident, just because she'd gotten hurt and Kaia had—

No. She'd resolved not to think about any of that this weekend. She was taking a vacation from her pain and her guilt and everything else that had been weighing her down. Kane *knew* that, and was still pulling this crap? Unacceptable.

But she should have known better than to expect even a brief escape from Adam. Only one thing would make him give up the fight. If he ever found out what she had done to Kaia, Harper knew that would be the end of it. Of everything. And she wasn't ready for that; all the more reason to get away.

She backed out of the bathroom and, without a word of explanation to Miranda, rushed out of the hotel room in search of her target.

"Harper, wait!" Adam called down the hallway. She glanced over her shoulder and, sure enough, he was standing in the hall in only a towel, flagging her down. She didn't stop—but grinned to herself when she realized that he'd let the door slam and lock behind him.

Just before reaching the elevator, she heard a loud thud and a shouted curse.

Apparently he'd realized it too.

Kane sighed and, reluctantly, tore himself away from the stunning blonde to answer his ringing phone. He allowed Harper about thirty seconds of ranting before cutting her off. "I'll meet you in the lobby in five," he promised, ending the call before she had a chance to respond. He had been expecting her call and, though the face-off could easily be avoided for hours, he preferred to get all potential interruptions out of the way now. The blonde could wait.

This weekend was too important, and his plans too delicate, to risk interference from a wild card like Harper. And from the sound of it, she was about to get pretty wild.

"What the hell were you thinking?" she raged, as soon as he came into sight.

"Nice to see you, too, Grace," Kane said dryly, spreading out on one of the Camelot's threadbare couches. The pattern had likely once been intended to resemble a medieval tapestry, but now it just looked like Technicolor puke. "Have a good drive?"

"Lovely, thanks for asking." As if the sarcasm had

sapped all her energy, she sank into a chair beside him. "Seriously, Kane, what's the deal?"

"The deal with . . . ?"

"Adam? In *my* room? Taking a shower? Any of this ringing a bell?"

Kane smiled innocently. "Adam's up in *our* room—yours, mine, his. Ours. Think of it as one big happy family."

"And it didn't occur to you to mention that this was the plan?"

Kane shrugged. "Did you think I was going to pay for two hotel rooms? I'm not a bank, Grace."

"I—" Her mouth snapped shut, and he knew why. Given that he was footing the bill for the trip, it would be pretty tacky of her to complain about the lodgings. And Harper Grace was never tacky. "I just would have liked some advance notice, that's all," she said sullenly. "You didn't have to ambush me."

"If I'd told you ahead of time, you wouldn't have come," Kane pointed out. Adam and Harper had been feuding for a month now, and Kane was getting sick of it. Not because he felt some goody-two-shoes need to play peacemaker, he told himself. Just because there weren't too many people whose presence he could tolerate; it was troublesome when they refused to share breathing room.

"What do you want me to do?" she asked, a hint

of a whine entering her voice. "Make nice and pretend like nothing ever happened between us? Not gonna happen."

"Not my problem, Grace," Kane told her. "Talk to him, don't talk to him, I don't care." Not much, at least. "But this is the only room you've got, so unless you don't plan on sleeping or bathing this weekend—and, no offense, but I think you're already overdue on the latter— you should probably get used to it."

"But—"

"Gotta go," he said quickly, bouncing off the couch. "The most beautiful blonde in all the land is waiting for her knight in shining armor to arrive. I'm hoping to show up first." He wiggled his eyebrows at her, and, miracle of miracles, she cracked a smile. "Now, your mission, and you have no choice but to accept it: Chill out, shower, then grab Miranda and meet me down here in one hour. We're going out."

Harper checked her watch and rolled her eyes. "Geary, it's the middle of the night, and some of us have been on the road for an eternity."

Kane shook his head. "Grace, this is *Vegas*." Why was he the only person capable of understanding the concept? "Night doesn't exist here. It's a nonstop party, and we're already late."

"I don't know . . ."

"Since when does Harper Grace turn down a party?"

He knew perfectly well since when. That was why he'd insisted she come this weekend and why he'd dragged Adam along for the ride. Harper had been on the sidelines long enough—it was time for her to get back into the game. Whether she wanted to or not.

It was good pot—strong, smooth, decently pure—but not good enough to help Beth sleep through Fish and Hale's impromptu jam session. (Featuring Hale's off-key humming and Fish banging Beth's hairbrush against the wall for a drumbeat.) After an hour of tossing and turning, she finally gave up on trying to sleep—only to discover that Reed was wide awake, lying on his side and staring at her.

"What?" she asked, giggling at the goofy expression on his face.

"Nothing." He gave her a secretive smile, then a kiss. "Let's get out of here."

Still clad in her T-shirt and purple pajama shorts, she crawled out of bed and followed him out the door. They headed downstairs in search of the pool, running into half the Haven High senior class on their way.

Beth didn't care who saw her or how she looked. Only one person's opinion mattered to her these days, and only one person's presence made any difference.

Make that two.

Beth saw her first, and tried to dart down a hallway before they were spotted, but it was too late.

"Well, this is just great," Harper said, lightly smacking her forehead. "As if my weekend weren't perfect enough."

Just ignore her, Beth told herself. She didn't want to get into any more fights with Harper—and not just because she always lost. Yes, Harper had done her best to ruin Beth's life—but Beth's attempt at revenge had nearly succeeded in ruining Harper, permanently. Just as she would always bear the guilt for Kaia's death—*Don't think about that*, she reminded herself—she would always know that Harper could just as easily have been the one who'd died. Harper *was* the one who'd landed in the hospital, gone through painful rehabilitation, emerged pale, withdrawn, and the object of too much curiosity and not a little scorn. They were more than even, although Harper would never—*could* never—know it.

But forgiveness was easier said than done. And even the sight of Harper still made Beth's stomach twist.

"Hey, Harper," she said softly. Reed pressed a hand against her lower back, as if sensing her need for support.

Harper's eyes skimmed over Beth without stopping and zeroed in on Reed. "Having fun with the new girlfriend?" she asked, disdain dripping from her voice. "Guess it's easy for some people to forget."

Harper tried to push past them, but Reed's arm darted

out and grabbed her. *Just let it go*, Beth pleaded silently, wanting only for the moment to end quickly, without bloodshed. But she could tell from the look on his face and the tension in his body that he'd already been wounded.

"I haven't forgotten," he told Harper, in a low, dangerous voice. "Kaia would have—"

"Don't say her name," Harper ordered him, her voice tight and her face strained. "Don't say anything. Just *enjoy* yourself. I'm so sure"—though it wouldn't have seemed possible, her tone grew even more sarcastic—"that's what *she* would have wanted."

A moment later, Harper was gone, and Reed was the one who needed support. But when Beth tried to touch him, he stepped away.

"I'm sorry," she said softly, knowing he wouldn't understand what she was apologizing for.

"It's not you." He wouldn't look at her. "It's nothing."

When they first met, he had talked about Kaia nonstop. But something had changed—Beth never knew what, never wanted to ask. Reed had kissed her and, after that, never spoke of Kaia again. There were moments when his voice drifted off and his eyes stared at something very far away, and she knew, then, that he was wishing for something he couldn't have. But he never said it out loud.

And, though she knew she shouldn't be, Beth was glad. Because the only way she could be with Reed was to force herself to forget. Kaia had died because of her—no, phrasing it that way avoided the truth. She had *killed* Kaia. Accidentally, maybe, but killed nonetheless. And now, reluctantly, guiltily, but undeniably, Beth had taken her place.

She wrapped her fingers around Reed's, half fearing he would pull away. He didn't—but he still wouldn't meet her eyes. "Let's go find the pool," she murmured. He nodded, and she squeezed his hand. He felt so solid, and so safe. He wouldn't disappear, she reassured herself. He would never leave her alone.

Unless he found out the truth.

Then he would be gone forever.

"Down to business," Kane said, rubbing his palms together in anticipation. "How should we kick things off? Blackjack? Poker?"

As Harper and Adam began bickering about where to start—Adam voted blackjack, so Harper, obviously, voted roulette—Miranda lagged behind. She didn't want to admit that she didn't know how to play any of the standard casino games—though she had a vague idea, courtesy of *Ocean's Eleven*, that roulette wouldn't actually require anything other than choosing a color. She'd watched it in anticipation of the big trip, but had been too distracted by George Clooney to glean much more information than that.

She would have been happy enough to spend the whole weekend without coming face-to-face with a dealer, since surely they'd take one look at her height (or lack thereof) and sallow babyface and show her the door. Or whatever it was they did in Vegas when they busted you for a fake ID.

But she didn't want to seem timid or clueless, not in front of Kane—and especially not when he was giving her that anything-goes smile—so she shut up. She was trying to be on her best behavior this weekend. Or rather, her most mature, most carefree, most badass, most Kane-appropriate behavior—especially now that she knew they'd be sharing a room. Okay, so there were two beds and two other people. And Vegas was filled with girls who were much more his type. Maybe it was a statistical impossibility that anything would happen. But Miranda couldn't help letting her imagination have a little fun.

This was, after all, Vegas, where anything could happen . . . which meant that, despite the odds, something *might*.

In the end, they compromised, deciding to start slow, with the slots.

All the action was over at the tables—the slot machines seemed solely the territory of the blue-haired ladies and a few caved-in old men with bad toupees, waiting for the big payoff. Miranda dug into her pocket and pulled out a fistful of quarters, plugging them into a rain-forest-themed machine that touted itself as the Green Monster. She put her hand on the long silver lever, then sucked in her breath as a warm, strong grip closed over hers.

"Feeling lucky, beautiful?" Kane murmured from behind her.

Miranda bit down on the corners of her mouth in a pointless attempt to suppress a smile. Was he, too, thinking about the last time they'd been in a casino together, the last time—the only time—they'd kissed?

Doubtful. For Miranda, it had been the culmination of five years of hoping, dreaming, waiting; for Kane, she knew, it had just been a fast way to liven up a slow afternoon.

Still, he was here, so close that she could feel his chest just grazing her back, and she knew that all she'd have to do was step backward and she would be in his arms.

She stayed where she was, and pulled the lever.

Too late, Miranda thought to wonder: What if she hit the jackpot? If the movies were any guide—and, really, if the movies *weren't* an accurate guide to life, she was totally screwed, since they were pretty much her sole source of information—sirens would blare. Coins would pour out. People would cheer and stare. And the security guards would sweep her away before she could touch a dime.

There was no siren, no jackpot, no cash—and the man

who lurched toward her, his breath reeking of gin and his meaty hands grabbing at her chest, was no security guard.

"You're a liar!" he slurred, his hand tightening around Miranda's shoulder as he staggered against her.

"Get the hell off," Kane snapped, shoving himself against the drunk, who squeezed even tighter, nearly pulling Miranda down with him as he stumbled to the floor. For a moment that lasted too long, she was falling, stubby fingers biting into her skin, a leering smile spreading across the man's scarred face. She tugged, she pulled, but his grasp only tightened, and though she tried to scream, her breath caught in her throat, and he was still pulling her down, still grinning, would never let go, and she was powerless, weak—alone.

And then, just in time, Kane ripped her arm free. Miranda shook him off too, and crossed her arms over her chest, squeezing tight and trying to catch her breath. She told herself that nothing had actually happened. No reason to panic, she was fine.

Too out of it to pull himself up, the guy writhed on his back like a crab, pointing at Miranda and howling, *"Liar!"* She couldn't look away. "You're all liars!"

"Can we get a little help here?" Kane called, waving down a swarm of security guards.

Miranda was dimly aware that Harper and Adam had joined her on either side, that Adam's hand was pressing down firmly, protectively on her shoulder—that she was shaking. But none of it really registered.

"It's all going to come out," the drunk moaned, as the guards hauled him off the floor. "No more secrets," he hissed. "Not here." The guards grabbed his arms and began to drag him away, slicing through the crowd of gamblers and disappearing behind the glittering slot machines. A moment later, his howls faded away. There was only giddy laughter, clanging machines, canned jazz, and the occasional hoot of victory. The sounds of Vegas. Like nothing had ever happened.

"You okay?" they all asked Miranda, who nodded like she was.

She forced a smile. "What an asshole, right?"

Crisis averted, Kane's smirk reappeared. "He's right, you know. About Vegas. Everyone here's a liar, but . . ." He narrowed his eyes and pursed his lips in an exaggerated scowl. "It takes a damn good liar to beat Vegas. This is the city of truth."

Adam dropped his hand from Miranda's shoulder and stepped quickly away, and she wondered whether he was thinking the same thing she was. Their secret—one drunken night together, a hookup she barely remembered, a memory they'd both agreed to forget, to bury forever—could ruin everything. And there was no reason for anyone to ever find out—no reason for *Harper* to find out.

Unless Kane was right. Unless there was something here, something in the air, in the oversize drinks or the adrenaline rush, something that forced secrets into the light. . . . Miranda stole a glance at Harper, whose face was ghostly pale, her eyes darting back and forth between Miranda and Adam, her lip trembling.

And Miranda had a horrible thought. She'd worried for weeks that Harper would find out what had happened, would misinterpret an innocent, unimportant, drunken mistake as something more than it was. Something unforgivable.

But what if all that worrying had been a waste—what if Harper already knew?

All she had wanted was an escape. A return to normalcy.

What an idiot.

Of course Kane was right, Harper thought bleakly. Of course this was where the secrets came out to play— everyone drunk all the time, never sleeping, pushing themselves to the limit, letting their guard down. It was a disaster waiting to happen.

It was *her* disaster. What if they found out somehow? The image forced itself back into her head, the one she'd been trying to forget—the one she'd driven hundreds of miles to escape. Her hands on the wheel, her foot on the gas pedal, the world spinning. The flames.

They all pitied her now, which was bad enough. If they found out she'd been the one behind the wheel, if *Adam* found out . . .

She told herself she didn't care what he thought, not anymore. But she knew he could never forgive her for being a murderer. Why should he? It's not like she had found a way to forgive herself.

Two days, she thought. *Forty-eight hours.* If she could survive, stay sane, stay hidden, keep the real her—the unforgivable her—under wraps for the weekend, it would be a sign. She had hoped for a vacation from the torment of her life, but maybe that wasn't what she needed. Maybe she needed one final test, proof that she could put the past behind her and focus on normal life, that she could live with keeping quiet, that she could go on, even here. She would survive Vegas, and that would be proof—she could survive anything.

"Forget the drama, guys," Kane said, drawing the group toward the exit. "We're wasting valuable party time."

"I'm, uh, thinking I might get some sleep," Miranda said, staring at the ground.

"Yeah." Adam's gaze was fixed on the ceiling.

"Maybe they're right, Kane—" Harper began.

"What the hell is this?" He pointed ahead of them to the giant neon sign blinking a few feet away: MIDNIGHT

MAGIC BUFFET—24-HOUR FEAST. "It's two-for-one drinks night. What are we waiting for?"

"No more drinking tonight," Adam said. "Not for me."

Kane gaped at the three of them as if they'd sprouted antennae. Then he nodded with sudden understanding. "I get it." He grinned. "I spooked you. Look. I'm sure none of us have any secrets. . . ."

He turned to Harper, who met his stare without flinching. He knew what she had to lose—and she knew he was daring her to chicken out.

"But let's just say, hypothetically, we all do," he continued. "So I suggest a pact. We'll hit the buffet and drink to it. Anything we find out about each other this weekend . . . well, it doesn't count. All secrets forgotten as soon as we leave the city limits. After all, what happens in Vegas—"

"I don't drink to lines that are so old, they have mold growing on them," Harper snapped.

"What happens in Vegas *stays* in Vegas," Kane finished, arching an eyebrow. "Agreed?"

They nodded, and they shook on it. Not that it mattered. Harper knew she was the only one with a secret that really meant something—and there was no way in hell she was risking exposure. Pact or no pact.

"Good. Let's get some cocktails and make it official,"

Kane ordered, charging toward the buffet. "Eat, drink, and be merry, folks, for tomorrow—we do it all over again."

Reed was buzzed.

But it wasn't the drugs. It was her. It was the blond hair, the blue eyes, the cotton-candy lips—all of it like a doll, a picture in a magazine. Picture perfect, but so real, and so unpredictable, starting with her inescapable, unbelievable choice: him. From honor roll to rolling blunts, from superstar to slacker?—he didn't even remember how she'd woven her way into his life. She'd just appeared. As if he'd been asleep and then, on waking, there she was. Part of him.

After Kaia . . . Beth had helped him. Not to forget— never, he had promised himself. But Beth had helped him survive the remembering. To live.

He had never asked her why she was hanging around the slums of his life, maybe because he knew it wouldn't last. But Reed had never before cared about the future. Why start now?

"Guess I should have changed into a bathing suit," Beth said, stretching out on the edge of the pool and skimming her bare toes across the water. "We could have gone in the hot tub."

Reed had only ever been in one hot tub in his life, and it was a part of his life that was over now. *It'll be fun,* he heard Kaia's voice say, somewhere in the depths of memory. *Promise.*

"I don't do bathing suits," Reed said, and—except for that one time—it was true. He gestured down to his black AC/DC T-shirt and dark, well-worn jeans, his standard uniform. "This is it."

Beth stood up, her long legs mostly bare beneath the sheer pajama shorts, and joined him on the lounge chair. He scooted over to give her room, but she barely needed any, stretching out alongside him, wrapping an arm over his chest and twining her legs with his. The pool area was nearly empty.

"You can't see the stars here," she mused, resting her cheek against his to look up at the sky. "Too many lights. It's weird."

They'd both grown up under the bright, too-clear desert night sky, where civilization—or what passed for it in Grace—faded away just after nightfall. The city haze was disconcerting, like the sky was closing in on them—or like the stars had disappeared altogether. "Get used to it," he warned her. "Next year . . ."

"Yeah, next year." She fell silent, and in that silence, he saw it all: graduation, summer, and then the day she packed up her stuff and moved to L.A., to college, leaving him to his deadbeat, dead-end life. "About that . . . ," she murmured. "I'm not going."

Reed didn't say anything.

"I'm not—it's not what I want anymore," she said softly, and he could feel her arm tighten around him. She was still searching for the stars. "Maybe if I'd gotten into Berkeley, things would be . . . maybe if a lot of things had happened, or hadn't happened, or—" She stopped, and shivered against him. He began rubbing his hand up and down her arm. "It's not me anymore," she finally said. "It's not what I want."

"So next year, you're just going to . . . ?"

"Stay in Grace. Stay with—" She turned away from the sky, toward him, and rested her hand gently against his cheek. "I know we don't really talk about—I mean, we've never, about next year, but I thought you might . . . be . . . happy."

Happy that she'd given up the only dream she'd ever had, to get the hell out of Grace and move on to something better? Happy that, ever since they'd gotten together, she'd never talked about what she wanted or where she was going, had just lain around on the couch with him listening to his music and smoking his pot? Happy that, unlike him, she had a real future, and she was giving it up?

"Yeah," he said, tipping his head forward and kissing her, still overwhelmed by the taste and feel of her lips, as much as he had been the first time. "I guess I am."

✎ ✎ ✎

They stuffed themselves on prime rib, shrimp cocktail, fresh fruit in a honey-lime yogurt sauce, jalapeño poppers, garlic-roasted pork loin, fried chicken wings, meat loaf, mashed potatoes, several hearty helpings of chocolate cheesecake and, since none of the half-asleep Midnight Magic staffers seemed to doubt their flimsy IDs, several pitchers of beer.

Merry was an understatement.

"Thish is awesome," Miranda slurred as they stumbled up the Strip back to their hotel. All her ridiculous fears about secrets and lies had long since been forgotten. "I love Vegas."

"Viva Las Vegas!" Harper shouted, flinging her arms in the air. "We love you!"

No one even bothered to stare.

"Shhhh!" Miranda spit out the warning, along with a frothy spray of saliva, and gave Harper a light push—or not so light, as it nearly knocked both of them to the ground.

"Steady," Kane cautioned, pulling her back up. Miranda wanted to say something filled with sparkling wit and sex appeal, but the world was spinning and all she could think to say was, "Woo-hoo! Vegas!"

And then she saw it. Saw him. Twenty feet tall, looming over their heads. Jared Max, lead singer of the Crash Burners, her absolute, all-time favorite band. Jared Max was a rock god—hotter than Adam Levine. Hotter than Justin T. Hotter, even, than Kane.

Miranda sank to her knees in the middle of the sidewalk. "Harper," she gasped. "Harper. Look." She pointed, tipping her head away from the billboard as if it blazed like the face of God.

CRASH BURNERS–LIVE
ONE NIGHT ONLY

And a bright yellow band slung across the image, blotting out the drummer's head. SOLD OUT!

"Harper," she moaned. "They're heeeeere. And we're missing it."

Harper joined Miranda on the ground as the guys gaped at them, obviously unable to understand the crisis at hand.

"We're going," Harper said, throwing her arms around Miranda.

"Sold out," Miranda keened, her brain too clogged with fatigue and liquor to form complete sentences, much less rational thought.

"We're going, birthday babe," Harper cried, letting herself fall backward on the sidewalk and squealing as Adam hauled her to her feet. "I promise."

My turn, Miranda thought blissfully, watching Adam prop Harper upright and then turning to stare at Kane, trying to send him a silent message. "Come and get me."

Or had she said that part out loud?

Kane laughed and grabbed her hands, hoisting her up. She didn't want to let go, so instead she let herself sag against him, the Crash Burners and the amazing, inaccessible Jared Max entirely forgotten.

Kane might not have been quite as hot, and he might have been half drunk and all tone deaf, but he was there, he was real and, if only for the too-brief duration of the walk home, he was all hers.

chapter three

"UGH, WHAT TIME IS IT?" HARPER ROLLED OVER IN
the bed and smashed a pillow over her head, trying to
block out the painful morning light.

"Shhh, it's still early, go back to sleep," Miranda
whispered. She climbed slowly and carefully out of bed—
but Harper, half hungover and half drunk, felt every
pitch and roll of the bed, as if she were seaborne. She
had resolved not to drink much the night before—but
the stress in her head and Kane's incessant needling had
proven too much. One beer, she'd told herself. One beer,
and no more.

She could clearly remember gulping it down and, as

the welcome warmth spread through her body, reaching for another. After that, things got a little fuzzy.

Now, too few hours later, even Miranda's careful tip-toes toward the bathroom sounded like elephant footfalls, slamming against the beer-saturated walls of Harper's brain. Forget sleep; it was all she could do to keep her head from exploding.

So she lay awake and very, very still. And she heard everything.

The bathroom door closing.

The water running.

And the unmistakable sound of Miranda puking her guts out.

Harper would know it anywhere.

The toilet flushed and the water kept running—the ever-considerate Miranda would be brushing her teeth now, Harper figured. Gargling mouthwash. And then, right on cue, tiptoeing back to bed.

"You okay?" Harper whispered, rolling toward the edge of the narrow bed to give her friend more room to stretch out.

Miranda smiled ruefully. "Just too much to drink. Sorry for the gross-out factor. Go back to sleep."

But she knew very well that Miranda never threw up when she drank. Harper was self-absorbed, but she wasn't blind. And what she saw was Miranda stuffing her face last night—and unstuffing it in the morning. She didn't do it all the time, not as far as Harper knew, at least. She didn't even do it often—though more often than she had in the fall, before their nightmare year had really begun.

Harper could say something. Miranda always did whatever she said; it formed the basis of their friendship.

But this weekend was supposed to be about making things up to Miranda, celebrating her, not bashing her and her stupid choices. Not driving her away again. Besides, who was she to force Miranda to face reality, when she was doing everything she could to avoid it herself?

Harper took a deep breath and reached out an arm, fully intending to shake her best friend awake. But then her arm dropped to her side, and, feeling suddenly groggy and overwhelmed, she closed her eyes, hoping for sleep.

This . . . *thing*, this problem that Miranda had, it wasn't an emergency, she told herself. She decided to wait until the time was right.

More to the point: She chickened out.

She chose the same no-risk, no-gain approach she took to all her problems these days: ignored it, and hoped it would go away.

Beth was nearly asleep on her feet. They'd crawled out of bed at 7 a.m., hoping to beat the inevitable crowds at the All-American Band Battle registration area. But that was wishful thinking. Judging from the way they looked—and smelled—some of these bands must have camped out in the auditorium all night; Beth and the Blind Monkeys were at least fifty people back in line, which so far had translated into a painful hour of scoping out the competition.

When they finally made it to the small metal folding table at the head of the room, a sullen girl with thick purple eyeliner and matching purple dreads handed Beth a stack of forms without looking up. "Band name?" she asked, sounding almost too bored to bother taking another breath.

Beth looked around at the guys, waiting for one of them to speak, but none of them did. Apparently, she was now groupie, roadie, and form-filler-outer. So much the better. The more responsibilities she had, the more they would need her. "Blind Monkeys," she said, half proud to be a part of something and half embarrassed by the knowledge that, in fact, she wasn't.

The girl scanned her clipboard, then sighed in irritation. "Not on here. Did you send in your preregistration forms?"

"Of course—" Beth started to say. Then she caught the glance exchanged between Fish and Hale. "Guys?"

Fish twirled a strand of his long blond hair; Hale just stared at her blankly. "Did you mail it in?" She'd filled out the forms, signed their names, bought the stamps, put it all together—all they'd had to do was take it to the post office to send it off. She and Reed would have done it themselves, but the guys had volunteered.

"We may have . . ." Fish scuffed his toe against the shiny hardwood floor. "There was this girl . . ."

"And the pizza, dude, don't forget the pizza," Hale added, his face lighting up at the memory.

"Yeah, and then this guy, and we had to get the truck for him—"

"And the girl was hot, man," Hale explained, punching Reed's shoulder. "Smoking hot, you know?"

Reed ran a hand across his face, mashing it against his eyes. "You didn't send it in," he said, without looking. It wasn't a question. "Let's go. We're screwed."

At the sound of Reed's hoarse, gravelly voice, the girl at the table finally looked up. Her eyes widened, and her surly expression morphed into a half smile. "Not so fast, boys," she told them, fingering the black, studded collar that hugged her neck. "You come a long way for this?"

"We were on the road all day yesterday," Beth said. The girl didn't appear to notice. She was too busy staring at Reed. And he'd noticed.

"Can't believe the shitty van made it the whole way," he told her, flashing a rare smile. "We're probably stuck here for good."

The girl leaned forward, giving all of them a good glimpse of the dark crease at the base of her neckline. (Could it still be called a neckline when it dipped nearly to her navel?) "That wouldn't be the worst thing in the world," she said.

"Maybe not," Reed agreed, reaching back and rustling the back of his head, which made his wild black hair fly out in all directions. Beth couldn't help admire the way his sinewy biceps moved between his tight black T-shirt—and she wasn't the only one.

She's flirting with him, Beth thought in disgust. And, what was worse—*he's flirting back.*

"I'm Starla," the girl said, extending a hand to Reed. When he took it, she didn't shake, just gripped his hand firmly, holding it in midair for a too-long moment. "That's Starla with a star." She turned his hand over and, grabbing a ballpoint pen, illustrated on his palm:

STAR*LA

Beth felt like she was going to be sick.

"Reed," he told her, without snatching his hand back.

"And I'm Beth," Beth said, stepping closer to her boyfriend. She wanted to wrap an arm around his shoulder, the universal sign for *He's mine and you can't have him*, but she was afraid of looking petty. And what if he stepped away?

"I might be able to slip you guys into the schedule," Star*la said.

"You won't get in trouble?" Reed asked.

How sweet, Beth thought sourly. *He's looking out for her.* She wasn't usually the jealous type—but then, until recently, she hadn't been the Reed type either. Things change.

"I'm sure it'd be worth it," the girl assured him. "After all, you could be 'America's Next Superstars,'" she said with mock enthusiasm, mouthing the contest slogan.

"Never gonna happen," Reed promised her, though he leaned over the table and began filling out the forms she'd handed him.

"Have a little hope, Reed Sawyer," Star*la said brightly, reading the name upside down off one of the forms. She pulled out a handful of buttons, each bearing the label #32. Two went to Beth, who handed them off to Fish and Hale. Star*la took the third one and pinned it onto Reed's shirt, just below his breastbone. Beth noticed that her fingernails were painted black and a small, thorny rose was tattooed along the length of her inner wrist. She caught Reed noticing it too. "This is Vegas." Star*la slapped her hand flat against his chest. "Anything can happen."

"How can you watch that shit?" Kane flicked his hand toward the TV, where a bright blue squirrel was chasing a talking bird through the magic forest.

"The question is, how can you *not* watch it?" Harper

asked, stretching her legs to the ceiling, then flopping them back down to the bed with a satisfied sigh. "It's Saturday morning. These are Saturday morning cartoons. Had you no childhood? Have you no soul?"

Kane shrugged. When he was a kid, he'd spent Saturday morning helping his brother clear up the remains of last night's partying before their father came home. As for the dubious existence of his soul . . . it wasn't a question for a hungover Saturday morning in Sin City.

"I've got a phone call to make," he told the girls. "If this slacker wakes up"—he gestured at Adam, still conked out in his sleeping bag—"tell him not to touch my after-shave."

"Yeah, we'll make sure he knows your makeup and hair gel is off-limits too, Tyra," Harper mocked. He tossed a pillow at her, hitting Miranda instead. She grabbed it with a giggle and threw it back at him, the worn gray tank top she'd slept in rising up to reveal a taut band of skin above her low-riding boxers.

"Back in a flash, ladies. Try not to miss me too much." He tipped an imaginary hat to them and slipped out to the hallway. Let his friends sleep in and waste the day away watching TV. Kane had been up for an hour or two and was already showered, impeccably dressed, and ready to go. He just had a few details to finalize.

He dialed the number. "I'm here," he said into the

phone, before his contact had a chance to speak. "When can we meet?"

"Do you have the cash?"

"Do you have the stuff?"

There was a pause. "I have what I said I would. You shouldn't have to ask."

Kane always had to ask. "Just tell me where." A few girls he vaguely recognized from Haven High wandered down the hall in their pajamas, giggling and blushing when they spotted him. He waved, flashed the famous smirk, then, as soon as they passed, turned toward the wall and hunched over the phone. Normally he loved nothing more than to see and, more importantly, be seen; but this was nobody's business but his own. "Where and when?"

"Two thirty. At the Fantasia, by the fountain in the rear lobby. You know the place?"

"I'll find it," Kane said, and punched end. He checked his watch: He had almost two hours to kill. Two hours in paradise—not usually the kind of thing he minded. But he was impatient to get the meeting over with, the deal done. He headed back into the room to swig some mouthwash and grab his wallet, his mind already running through all his options for pleasure in the pleasure center of the world.

He never needed a reason to go to Vegas, his haven away from Haven. It had everything he could ever want: booze, blues, girls, gambling, endless possibilities. But a little added incentive never hurt anyone, and as far as he was concerned, there was no better incentive than cold, hard cash.

As much of it as possible.

"What do you mean you're leaving?" Harper pressed herself against the bathroom door, blocking his exit. It was far too early in the morning for her plans to be falling so completely apart.

Kane hoisted himself up onto the bathroom sink and swung his feet off the edge. "I mean, I'm walking out the door, closing it behind me, walking down the hall, getting on the elevator—"

"Shut up," Harper snapped. "It's too early for sarcasm."

"It's past noon," Kane pointed out.

"Whatever. Are you forgetting what we talked about last night?"

Kane tipped his head to the side, tapped his chin, and pretended to think. "World peace?"

He could be such a bastard sometimes—and yet so useful. At least when he decided to play nice. "We talked about the concert tomorrow. The Crash Burners, remember?" His face remained an impenetrable blank. "You promised to help me track down some tickets today. For Miranda?"

Kane shook his head. "Any promises made under the influence are null and void. Look it up in the rulebook."

"Geary, you're *always* under the influence of something or other," Harper pointed out.

He rewarded her with a smile. "And now you understand why I never keep a promise."

"You're pathetic." So much for Miranda's fabulous birthday weekend. So much for *her* promise, drunken or not. What was she supposed to do all day instead: lie around the room feeling sorry for herself?

"And you love it." Kane hopped off the sink and scooped Harper out of the doorway. "Look, I can give you the name of a guy I know, he works the controls at the Oasis Volcano, he'll probably be able to help. Go see him—and bring Adam."

Harper wrinkled her nose. "Why would I do that?" The less time spent with Adam this weekend, the better. It was hard enough shutting him out of her life when he wasn't around. But when he was right in front of her, staring at her with those "love me" puppy-dog eyes, how was she supposed to keep her emotional distance? She was already this close to letting him back in—it was only running into Beth last night that had snapped her back to reality, reminding her that she'd never be able to match up to the pretty princess in Adam's eyes. And she was sick of spending all her energy to claw her way into second place.

"This guy . . . he's got some issues. He won't talk to

strangers—he'll only help you if he thinks he's dealing with me. And unless you want to dress in drag . . ."

Harper rolled her eyes. "I suppose Adam's got a Kane mask stashed away in his suitcase somewhere?"

"I've never met the guy face-to-face," Kane explained. "He does me favors sometimes, when he's in the mood. Just get Adam to say he's me. It'll be almost as good as having the real thing."

"You know what would be even better?" Harper drawled. "*Having* the real thing. You're really going to ditch me and leave me with . . . *him*?"

Kane gave her a condescending pat on the head. "It's for your own good, Grace. So take it or leave it."

She hated to lose. And only Kane knew quite how much—which was why, she was sure, he took such a special pleasure in beating her. "I'll take it." She sighed, then decided to press her luck. "And I'll take something else, too." She opened her palm and held it out in front of him.

"You want me to give you five?" he asked, willfully obtuse. He slapped her palm lightly. "If you insist."

"More than five, Geary. If you're going to send me off on some wild-goose chase looking for your skeezy errand boy, I'm going to need to find a way to keep Miranda occupied. And that's going to cost."

Kane grabbed her hand and, firmly, pushed it back down to her side. "Just take her with you."

"It's got to be a surprise," Harper insisted. "I don't want her to suspect anything."

"And you don't think dragging me into the bathroom and locking the two of us in isn't going to make her just a little suspicious?" Kane asked, raising an eyebrow.

She hated that he could do that. In junior high, she'd spent hours in front of the mirror trying to train her eyebrow muscles to work independently of each other, but she'd failed miserably. Maybe the skill was genetic—if so, Harper guessed, it was probably linked to the genes for selfishness, smugness, asshole-ishness, and all the other qualities Kane Geary carried so proudly.

She couldn't help but admire him.

But that didn't mean she was going to back down.

"Let me worry about that," she told him. "Just help me out with this. If you don't care about helping me, think of Miranda." From the look on his face, Harper knew it was the right card to play. She knew that, no matter how much Miranda might wish for it, there was no way in hell Kane would ever fulfill her sad little romantic fantasy and declare his love. But Kane knew it too, and Harper suspected that somewhere beneath his preening, posing shell, he felt a little sorry.

Apparently not sorry enough. "Nice try. No sale."

Harper shrugged. "Okay."

"Okay?" He peered at her suspiciously.

"Sure." She gave him a perky grin. "No problem. Don't worry about it."

"What's the catch?"

Ah, he knew her so well. "No catch. No hard feelings. I'm sure the three of us will have a lovely day together."

"The three of you?"

"The three of *us*," Harper corrected him. "Miranda, me, and *you*—together. Just like the Three Musketeers. The Supremes. The Three Tenors. You get the idea. One happy threesome—"

Kane's smile twitched, and broadened.

"Not like that, gutter-brain," she snapped. "Like this. You head out on your mysterious mission, we follow. Wherever you go, we go. Whatever you do, we do. And whatever it is you're up to this afternoon, we—"

"Spare me the tedious details, I get it. You win."

She met his bitterness with a beatific smile. "Music to my ears."

"Just take the cash and let me out of here." He pulled out his wallet and handed her a credit card. "Send her to a spa for the afternoon. Girls love that shit, right? Massages, scented candles, mani-pedis, whatever."

Harper bit back the urge to point out that, between the two of them, Kane seemed the far more likely candidate for spa-hopping. From his Theory shirt to his Diesel jeans, he was Grace's only known metrosexual, and damn proud of it. But, credit card not yet in hand, she decided silence might well be the best policy.

He handed her the credit card, along with a scrap of paper bearing the name and number of his "guy," and then, with a final infuriating elevation of his left eyebrow, reached for the doorknob.

"So where *are* you going in such a hurry?" she asked, knowing better but too hungover for caution.

"I'll tell you later," he promised.

Well, that was unexpected.

"Really?"

"No."

The awkwardness was new—but it was getting old.

Last night had been their first uninterrupted stretch of time together in weeks, and Harper's frosty demeanor had given way after the first pitcher of beer. Things had been almost easy between them, and Adam had allowed himself to hope. Until this morning, when she'd once again frozen him out.

Adam knew Harper well enough to understand his odds: hopeless. If he wouldn't give her what she wanted—and he couldn't—she wouldn't give him the satisfaction of revealing how much she needed him. And maybe, these days, it wasn't much at all.

So, after a few frosty unpleasantries, Adam had gone

back to bed. But not to sleep. How was he supposed to sleep, knowing she was sitting only a few feet away from him, maybe waiting for him to say something—or, for all he knew, waiting for him to blink out of existence once and for all.

He didn't even know why she was still there. He had expected her to leave along with Kane and Miranda, but instead, she'd stayed in bed, stretched out with her feet kicking the pillows, staring at the television. *Say something*, he told himself. *Sit up, start a conversation.*

But he didn't know how. Even in the beginning, when they'd first become friends, they had always understood each other. Always known what the other was thinking. It had been effortless. Now, blundering around in the dark, he didn't even know where to start hunting for the light switch.

There had been that brief period of weirdness in fifth grade, when Harper woke up and realized Adam was a boy, and Adam—courtesy of a windy day, a gauzy skirt, and a bout of humiliated tears—clued in to the fact that even tomboys had their girly moments. Harper stopped wrestling him to the ground and demanding the remote control. Adam stopped mixing her dolls with his action figures. Harper stopped using her Fisher-Price telescope to peer in his bedroom window, and Adam started dating a pretty blond sixth grader named Emma Farren, who once poured red paint all over Harper's spelling homework.

It was a long week.

Long and lonely—and before too long, Adam and Harper mutually decided to ignore the sticky boy-girl thing and proceed as if nothing had changed. Which, other than Harper's perfect curves and Adam's elephant-size libido, it hadn't.

Since then, he had always been able to count on her, and she on him. They'd climbed the social ladder together, Adam with the unconscious ease of a blond jock built for adoration, Harper with ruthlessness and a fierce determination. Adam had grown cavalier—with his grades, his games, his girls—and Harper had grown vicious, but they'd stayed loyal to each other. Without question, without doubt, without exception.

And then, in short order, it had all been destroyed.

Adam had fallen in love with Beth; a jealous Harper had torn the two of them apart. Adam, oblivious, had fallen in love all over again, with Harper—or with the Harper he thought he knew. And when the truth came to light, when he realized who Harper had become and what she was capable of, he'd pushed her away.

How was he supposed to know that days later, she would be lying in a hospital bed, pale and unconscious, as he waited and wondered and wished he could take back every word? And what was he supposed to do when she woke up and mistook his concern for forgiveness, when she rejected his offer of friendship because he refused to deliver anything more?

She wanted her boyfriend back; he wanted his best friend back. She couldn't forget how happy they'd been; he couldn't forget what she'd done, how she'd lied. Adam just wanted to go back to the beginning, before things got ugly and cruel—but Harper preferred to go forward, alone.

And now here they were, awkward and miserable. At least, he was miserable. It had been a mistake to let Kane talk him into this trip, into this ridiculous ambush, as if the element of surprise would shake Harper's resolve. He needed to get out of here and forget about the whole thing for a while. He decided he would get up, slip into some clothes and out of the room, so quietly and quickly that she wouldn't have time to react—or, at least, he wouldn't have time to dwell on how she chose not to.

Then, without warning, she spoke.

"I need your help," she said, and he could guess how much effort it cost her to keep her voice casual and even as she uttered her four least favorite words.

He couldn't make a big deal about it. She was on the line, nibbling at the bait—he had to reel her in slowly, before she got spooked.

"Mmmph." He sat up, realizing she must have known all along that he wasn't asleep.

"I got Miranda the full treatment," she said, sounding almost as if she were talking to herself, "which should give us about six hours. But we have to start now."

Maybe he should have resented the fact that she just assumed he would go along with her—but he knew what it meant. She knew she could still count on him when she needed him.

And she needed him now.

Adam suppressed the urge to jump out of bed and embrace her—or, better yet, shake her and force her to admit that her whole act was a sham, and she needed their friendship as much as he did.

Slow and steady, he cautioned himself. *Patience.*

"I was going to watch the game," he complained, grabbing the remote and switching to ESPN.

Harper switched off the TV. "Look, I don't want to spend the day with you any more than you want to spend it with me, but I'm stuck, and I . . ."

"Yeah?"

She propped her hands on her hips and stared down at him impatiently. "Are you going to make me say it again?"

"You . . ."

Harper rolled her eyes.

"You need . . ."

Harper still stayed silent, though Adam was sure he saw the ghost of a smile playing at the edge of her lips.

"You . . . need . . . my . . . help," he concluded trium-phantly.

She sighed. "What you said."

"Well, since you put it so sweetly . . ." Adam climbed out of bed. "I'm all yours."

"Lucky me," she muttered, shutting herself up in the bathroom so she wouldn't have to watch him change.

"Lucky us," Adam said quietly, to himself. She'd opened a door—to possibility, to reconciliation, to the past. No matter what, he wouldn't let it slam shut again.

chapter four

"I JUST DON'T GET IT," MIRANDA SAID AGAIN. "WHAT am I supposed to *do* at a spa?"

Kane shook his head. It was almost charming, her complete lack of comprehension about one of the most fundamental feminine pleasures. He spent most of his life on the arm of beautiful girls who were more primped and pampered than a Westminster Dog Show poodle. Miranda's awkward naïveté was almost charming. "Not my area of expertise," he reminded her—while making a mental note that, speaking of pampering, his nails were looking a little too ragged these days. "I've just been informed that I'm to drop you off at the spa and make sure you go inside. My mission ends there."

"Door to door service? Ooh-la-la."

"Only the best for the birthday girl," he said, leading her to the entrance of Heavenly Helpers. He grabbed her hand and, in his standard farewell gesture—at least when it came to pretty girls—turned it palm down, lifted it, and brushed it with his lips. Most girls giggled at the faux chivalry, but Miranda, despite a faint reddish tinge to her cheeks, didn't crack a smile.

"You're too kind, sir," she said mockingly. And, with a quick flip of the wrist, she brought his hand to her lips and mirrored his gesture.

"And they say chivalry's dead," he joked.

"They say feminism's dead too," she shot back, "but here you are, working nonstop on our behalf."

"I do what I can," he said modestly.

"Kane Geary," she said, presenting him to the non-existent audience with a Vanna White flourish, "helping women one bimbo at a time."

"You wound me, Stevens," he said, clasping his hands to his heart.

"Every chance I get," she agreed. And now, finally, he got a smile.

She wasn't hot, he reflected. Pretty, maybe, in an understated way, if you liked them short, pale, and skinny. Definitely not his type, though he was certain—despite her blustering and her refusal to stage a sequel to their last hookup—she wished she were. But she was a much better kisser than he'd expected, and there were times during these conversational jousts, when her face got flushed, her voice high, and her eyes bright, when he wished he could just drop the game and grab her and—

Whoa. He stopped himself abruptly. That was not a place his mind was supposed to go with Miranda Stevens. Good kisser or not. This was Vegas, land of gold fringe and stiletto heels; he refused to allow Miranda, with her ill-fitting jeans, faded T-shirts, and assorted neuroses, into his fantasies, much less his schedule.

"Door-to-door service, and here's the door," he said, losing the flirtatious tone. "Have fun."

Miranda raised her eyebrows. "Sure you don't want to see for yourself what—"

"Another time," he cut in, before he could get sucked into another round of volleying. He waved and backed away before she could say anything more, and didn't turn around to check that she'd stepped inside the spa, Harper's instructions be damned.

It didn't stop him from being sorry to see her go.

Shake it off he warned himself. *You've got business.*

It was a five-minute drive to the Fantasia—or would have been, had traffic on the Strip not been at a standstill. Kane had never considered himself a small-town guy, even though he'd spent his life in a place where the prairie dog population outnumbered the human one. But he couldn't help gaping at the flashing lights, packed sidewalks, and feverish motion of everyone and everything in sight.

Someday, he vowed, he would live in a place like this; someday, he would run it.

He dropped off the car with the valet and made his way to the back lobby, trying to ignore the many temptations along the way. (Out of the corner of his eye, he caught a glimpse of a redhead with a glass of whiskey in one hand and a deck of cards in the other: one-stop shopping for all his vices.) His contact was already waiting.

"Maryjane420@xmail.com, I presume?" A tall, wispy guy in his early twenties stepped out from behind a column, extending a hand.

Kane noted the guy's woven hemp necklace and scraggly blond goatee—he was a dead ringer for the dealer who'd hooked them up. Not a huge surprise; these Berkeley guys liked to play at being nonconformists, but with the tie-dye and the Birkenstocks, they might as well be wearing a uniform. "Kane," he said, giving the guy a firm handshake. He couldn't afford his customary caustic snark; another temptation to avoid for the sake of business.

"Jackson," the guy replied, flashing a peace sign.

Kane suppressed a snort. If this loser was as happy-go-lucky as he looked, things would go very smoothly indeed.

"So are you the small-talk type, or are you ready to see the merchandise?" Jackson dropped his faded gray backpack to the ground and began to unzip it without waiting for an answer.

"Here?" Kane hissed. His contact had assured him this Jackson guy was 100 percent professional, a safe way to kick his own business up to the next level. But was he too dim to realize that Las Vegas was closed-circuit-TV central? That was the problem with Nor Cal dealers, Kane had found—too much sampling of their own merchandise had fried their brains. Kane, on the other hand, prided himself on restraint. He was only too happy to supply others with whatever they needed, as a gesture of goodwill—and good profit—but he wasn't about to follow them down the rabbit hole.

"Here, there, anywhere," Jackson babbled. "That's the beauty of it." And before Kane could stop him, he pulled something out of his bag. It was about four inches long and wrapped in orange and brown foil.

It was perfect.

"Munchy Way," Kane read off the wrapper, admiring the logo's similarity to the familiar Milky Way swirl. This was even better than he'd hoped.

"And here's a couple Pot-Tarts," Jackson said, pressing a small stack of foil squares into his hand. "For later." He grinned proudly. "Cool, yeah?"

They looked almost real. It was the perfect product for Kane, who was tired of serving as a go-between for his brother's skeevy dealer buddies and their junior high customers. With a gimmick like this, he could attract a bigger crowd, a *better* crowd—and the operation would be all his. He'd pocket all the money, carry all the risk; and, with no one else involved, he could be sure that the risks were kept to an absolute minimum.

Kane didn't trust anyone but himself—but he trusted himself absolutely.

He ripped open the foil and took a bite. It was the familiar gooey chocolate goodness—with an equally familiar, almost bitter undertaste.

"I've got Rasta Reese's, Buddafingers, Puff-a-Mint Patties, whatever you need," Jackson told him, zipping the bag shut.

"This could work," Kane mused, hoping to disguise his enthusiasm. Jackson might have been a dippy hippie, but he was also a pro; this was, on the other hand, Kane's first big buy, and he wanted to do it right. "What's your price?"

"Not so fast," Jackson said, and the foggy expression vanished, replaced by a look that was sharp, canny, and hungry. "I don't know you, I don't know if I can trust you. I definitely don't need you. So why don't you start by telling me what *you* can do for *me*."

The rapid shift caught Kane off guard, but not for long. "Meaning?"

"Meaning, if you want in, I'm going to need some insurance—and I'm going to need some incentive."

It turned out that the Oasis Volcano was really a giant fountain with reddish water cascading down its sides and spurts of fire shooting out of the top. Like everything else in Vegas, Harper was discovering, the plastic mountain was impressive until you got up close—then it was just tacky and sad.

"One thing I forgot to tell you," Harper said as they approached the operator's booth in search of Kane's "guy." She hadn't forgotten—she'd just been trying to keep conversation to a minimum until absolutely necessary. "You're Kane."

Adam wrinkled his forehead. "Try again. I'm *Adam*."

She used to think it was so cute when he tried to be funny—even when he failed. Especially when he failed.

"This guy will only talk to Kane, but they've never met face-to-face," she explained impatiently. "Kane called and told him we were coming—I mean, that he was coming. You know what I mean. So you're just going to have to play the part."

"I'm going to have to play the part . . ." he prompted, his eyes twinkling.

She sighed. Magic word time. "Please."

The operator's booth was stationed in the back of the volcano, behind a low fence that Adam vaulted easily. He reached out his arms for Harper. "Want help?"

"I got it, thanks," she said brusquely, and scrabbled over, catching the edge of her shirt in one of the barbs. She didn't notice until she slid down to the other side and her shirt, still caught at the top of the fence, flew up over her head. Harper slammed her arms over her chest, trying to tug the shirt down with one hand and extricate herself with the other, a move that would have been possible only if she'd picked up some triple-jointed tricks from the local Cirque du Soleil troupe.

"Still got it?" Adam asked, standing a couple feet away with his arms folded.

"I'm just—almost—" After nearly stretching her arm out of its socket, Harper gave in to the inevitable. "Get me off this thing, will you?" And a frustrated moment later, "Please?"

Adam stood in front of her and, reaching an arm around either side, fumbled with the back of her shirt. It seemed to take a very long time, and Harper spent it trying not to notice that his head was so close to hers that she could smell his shampoo. She didn't want to meet his eyes—or worse, let her gaze travel down his body, lingering on her favorite parts—but she refused to look away.

"You're free," he told her. But she was still locked into place by his arms on either side.

She ducked underneath and escaped. "Let's do this."

"I'm Kane?" he asked, as she knocked on the window of the tiny booth.

"You're Kane," she confirmed, crossing her fingers. Adam's idea of acting usually involved bad foreign accents and funny hats. This could end poorly.

The door swung open, and a bulky guy with acne and a shaved head beckoned them inside. "Yo, Jenkins, dude, how's it hanging?" Adam asked, giving the guy one of those handshake/slap/snap things wannabe skater dudes exchange on MTV.

Harper tried not to roll her eyes. This could end *very* poorly.

"I'm Carl," the guy said, extending a hand to Harper. "Carl Jenkins. Kane's told me how much he likes beautiful women, but . . . wow."

Harper knew she was supposed to be flattered, not grossed out. Fortunately, she was a better actor than Adam. Practice makes perfect, right?

"That's so sweet, Carl," she said, giving his hand a gentle squeeze before dropping it (and resisting the urge to wipe the grease off on her jeans).

"You mackin' on my lady?" Adam asked, wrapping an arm around Harper's waist. Without warning, he began to tickle her side—she squealed and sprung away. "You know you want me, Mandy," he said, grabbing her hand and pulling her back against him. "I mean, uh, Sandy. I mean . . ." Adam gave Carl an exaggerated wink, and then shrugged. "Who can keep track? All I know is, she sure does come in handy!"

"I can imagine," Carl said, with a low whistle. "You're like my hero, man."

"That's why they call me LL-Cool K," Adam joked. "Ladies *Love* Cool Kane."

Oh. My. God. Harper buried her face in Adam's shoulder as the giggles burst out of her, hoping Carl would mistake it for a sudden burst of affection for her man. She only wished Kane could be here to see exactly what Adam thought of him.

And imagining that, she began to laugh even harder.

Adam patted her heaving shoulders. "Her pet cat died this morning," he explained. "Her name was Lady. So every time she hears the word, well . . ." He dropped his voice to a loud whisper. "You know girls."

After a moment, Harper regained control of herself and looked up, her face stained with laughter-induced tears. Perfect. "I'll miss her a lot," she said, her breath still ragged and torn by the occasional leftover giggle. "But at least I've got Kane here to comfort me." She patted him back. Hard.

"But there's only one thing that would *really* comfort her, Jenkins, you know what I mean?" Adam winked.

"Oh . . . uh . . . I'd give you some privacy, but I can't leave the booth—but there's this storage room in the lobby where no one goes and—"

"Ew—no!" Harper shivered. She didn't want any part of Carl's gross fantasies. "I mean, that's not what he meant. Tell him, *Kane*."

"Tickets," Adam said, and now he was the one choking back laughter. Harper could feel his body tremble. "For the Crash Burners tomorrow night—they're her favorite. And when we talked on the phone, you said . . . ?"

"Oh, yeah." Carl rubbed the back of his neck. "Look man, I know I owe you, for that other thing you did."

"Yeah, uh, that thing. That was rough," Adam said quickly. "You definitely owe me, Jenkins."

"And I thought I could deliver, but turns out these tickets are impossible to get."

"There's nothing you can do?" Harper asked, dropping the damsel-in-distress act. "There's got to be *something*."

"There's one person who might be able to help you," Carl said, giving Harper a shy smile. He tore out a page from his magazine—*Guns & Ammo*, Harper noted with displeasure—and scrawled down a name and address on the back. "She works at the Stratosphere, up top, on the coaster. Tell her I sent you, and maybe you'll get what you're looking for."

Adam made another attempt at the lame handshake combo. "Thanks, dude. I'll remember this."

"So next time I need, you know . . . you'll . . . you know?"

"Oh, totally." Adam gave him a mock salute. "You're my guy."

"Awesome."

"Yeah, yeah, totally awesome," Harper added, impatient to get going. "Great to meet you and all, but we've got to . . ."

"Yeah." Carl checked his watch. "Holy shit, it's time for the eruption. I've gotta kick you guys out. But stick around, you'll love it."

Adam escorted Harper out, and, since the fence unlocked from the inside, they made it back to the tourist zone unscathed.

"What was *that*?" Harper asked, bursting into laughter once they were a safe distance away.

"What?"

"*That! You* were supposed to be acting like Kane, not like . . . like some *Saturday Night Live* lounge lizard."

"He bought it, didn't he?" Adam asked indignantly.

"Ladies *love* cool Kane." Harper shook with laughter, and soon Adam joined in. "Seriously? LL-Cool K? I mean, *seriously*?"

Adam shrugged and gave a gee-whiz smile. "What can I say? The ladies love me."

Something about the line stopped her cold, and her smile faded away. "We should get going," she said, already feeling the distance beginning to grow between them. "We don't have all day."

"Wait." He reached for her arm, but pulled back just as his fingers grazed her skin. "Wait," he said again. "Let's at least stay for the show."

As he spoke, a loud rumbling began deep inside the volcano, which looked even faker now that Harper had seen the switches, dials, and the guy who made it run. But it couldn't hurt to stay for just a few minutes and see what the big deal was.

They inched closer to the front of the crowd, stealing a spot on the guardrail at the edge of the fountain pool, and waited. Soon the volcano began bubbling and burbling, and then a huge plume of flame burst out of the top, followed by a geyser of red water, arcing out of the crater mouth and out toward the crowd.

Harper leaped back. Adam, too slow on the uptake, merely stared slack-jawed at the sky as a wall of bloodred water crashed down on him.

Another burst of flame, a puff of smoke, and the eruption had ended. Adam rubbed the water out of his eyes and began wringing out his sopping T-shirt. "That was . . ."

He looked down at himself, soaked to the skin. ". . . unexpected."

Harper felt another surge of giggles rippling through her. It felt good to laugh again. "I don't know why you didn't see it coming," she sputtered. "You said it yourself, LL-Cool Kane. Lava Loves Cool Kane!"

"Very funny," Adam growled. "You know what's even funnier?" He lunged toward her and gave himself a mighty shake. Water flew everywhere.

"Watch it!" she cried, twisting away.

"I think you mean, watch *out*!" He chuckled, and lunged toward her again, wrapping his arms around her and pressing her against his soaking body. She struggled playfully for a moment, but these were arms that regularly shot fifty free throws a day. They didn't give. "Thanks for helping me dry off," he teased, rubbing his wet arms up and down her back.

"Thanks for ruining my outfit," she complained, but she stopped struggling. He didn't understand how hard it was for her, having him so near, touching her, *holding* her, and knowing that he didn't mean it, didn't want her.

Knowing that he didn't think she was worthy of him—and that he was right.

The moment she let down her guard and let him in, just a little, waves of pain came along for the ride.

Let go of me, she thought, but couldn't force herself to say, even though it would be for her own good.

Adam held on tight.

Reed slammed his hand down on the guitar strings in disgust. "Fish, you're still coming in a beat too late after the bridge!"

Fish snorted and pointed at Hale. "If this dude would actually follow my cues, I wouldn't have to—"

"If you picked up the tempo and—"

"At least I'm not playing in the wrong key," Fish shot back.

"At least I'm *playing*—a monkey could bang sticks together. What I do takes talent," Hale argued.

"You're right," Fish agreed, slamming his stick against the cymbal. "Too bad you don't have any."

Bah-dum-bum. Beth shifted in the folding chair, searching for some position that wouldn't leave the metal bar digging into her lower back. Star*la had squeezed them into a rehearsal room in the basement of the Fantasia for some last-minute fine-tuning—but so far, the band had barely managed to make it through a single song.

"Maybe you guys should take a break?" Beth suggested.

Fish and Hale exchanged a glance. "Dude, can you tell your girlfriend to chill?" Fish said quietly to Reed—but not quietly enough.

"She's kind of freaking me out, just staring at us like that," Hale added.

"She's right here, guys," Beth said loudly. "She can hear everything you say."

"Dude, it's just that—"

"Forget it." Beth stood up, realizing that her left foot had fallen asleep. She stamped it against the ground, trying to get rid of the pins and needles. "I'm going to take a walk."

Reed hurried over to her and tipped his head against hers so that their foreheads met. "You don't have to go," he said softly. "They're just . . . we kinda suck right now, and—"

She ran her hand lightly up the back of his neck, playing with some loose strands of curly hair. "You guys are great," she assured him. "You just need practice. And you don't need me throwing things off."

Reed kissed her on the cheek. "I need you."

She laughed and, for a moment, was tempted to stay—but she knew better. "Yes—but you don't need me right now. You need to practice."

Reed crinkled his nose, the way he always did when he was surprised. "You know what?"

"What?"

His answer was a kiss.

Beth left—reluctantly—and wandered through the

cavernous lobby, barely noticing the people she passed by. She still saw Reed's face in front of her, looking at her like she could do no wrong. He was the first person she'd ever been with who didn't judge, didn't impose, didn't expect. It wasn't even that he wanted her to be happy—which was something she couldn't do, not even for him—it was enough that she did what she wanted, and that she wanted to be with him.

It made her feel like a fraud. She could hear the clock ticking in the back of her mind, and time was running out. Eventually, she would be exposed. When his arms were around her, she could relax. But every time she left his side, the fear descended like a black curtain. Would he be there when she came back?

She knew it was crazy to wonder.

But maybe it was even crazier not to prepare herself for the inevitable. Because one day, he wouldn't.

She needed some fresh air. But the hotel was like a maze, hallways leading to stairways leading to more hallways, all of which seemed to lead directly back to the gaping mouth of the casino.

"Didn't think you were the gambling type," someone said from behind her.

She didn't have to turn around to put a face to the voice—and didn't *want* to turn around, since it was a face she never wanted to see again.

"Of course, I didn't think you were the druggie type either, not after that whole Just Say No lecture on New Year's Eve," Kane sneered. "So I guess nothing should surprise me now."

Beth braced herself for attack. Since their breakup several months before, she and Kane had been at war—and things had only gotten worse since Kaia's accident. He always looked at her suspiciously, as if he could see her guilt. So, just in case, she tried not to look at him at all. "Leave me alone, Kane," she said wearily. "I'm not in the mood."

"Maybe I can help with that." Until he spoke, she hadn't even noticed the guy standing next to Kane. Maybe because he looked about as un-Kane-like as you could get, from his baggy patchwork jeans to the henna tattoo crawling across his neck. "Guaranteed mood enhancement," the guy said, handing her a chocolate bar. "Instant happiness, or your money back."

It would take more than chocolate to guarantee her happiness, especially with Kane on the prowl. Beth waved the candy away. "Thanks, but—"

"Don't waste your time," Kane sneered. "She's morally opposed to . . . well, pretty much all of life's pleasures, wouldn't you say?"

The guy pressed the candy bar into her hand and wrapped her fingers around it, holding on for several moments too long. "I'm sure that's not true," he said, and something about his tone made Beth uneasy. She pulled her hand away.

"No, it's true," she assured him. "Kane's right. You're always right, aren't you?" she asked, aiming for sarcasm but achieving only fear.

"I was wrong about *you*," he pointed out.

Not wrong enough. He'd been right to think that she was naive enough, stupid enough to fall for his sympathetic act, straight into his arms. And he'd been right to think that he could string her along for weeks, charming her with smiles and kisses and extravagant gifts and suckering her into trusting him.

He'd just been wrong to think that when the truth came out, she'd slink away peacefully, never to be heard from again.

"Turns out this little holier-than-thou act is just a pose," Kane said. "Turns out she's just as selfish, weak, and indulgent as the rest of us—she's just not as good at it."

Beth thought about her single-minded pursuit of revenge against the people who'd ruined her life: Harper. Kane. Adam. Kaia. She'd indulged her rage, overruled the weak protests of her conscience, selfishly ignored the consequences. She'd done it all incompetently—and someone had died.

Kane didn't know it, but he was right yet again.

✢ ✢ ✢

Reed wished he hadn't let her leave. The music still sucked, Fish and Hale still bugged—nothing was different without her there.

Except him, and not for the better.

He let Fish and Hale take off, and then he wandered off, half hoping he would find her, knowing it was unlikely. There were too many people, a crowd of strangers crushing past him. And she wasn't answering her cell.

Eventually Reed headed back to the practice room, knowing she would show up eventually. And for a second, when he opened the door and saw a figure inside cleaning things up, he thought he wouldn't have to wait.

Then he took in the dark dreads, the tattoo, the wicked smile. "Hey, Star*la," he said, leaning in the doorway. "Thanks again for the space."

"You remembered." She turned to face him, and caught him staring at the pale purple snake tattoo that twisted around her waist and climbed upward, disappearing beneath the tight black shirt.

"Tough to forget a name like that," Reed told her, his face growing a little warm. Did she realize that they didn't make girls like her back home? That if someone had asked him, last year, to describe his ideal woman, she would have looked like the front-woman of some rock funk punk band, moved like someone born onstage, spoke like music was pounding in her brain, and smiled like she knew a secret that was too good not to spill and too dangerous not to keep?

He'd thought girls like that only existed in magazines and wannabe rock star fantasies. But here she was, in the tattoo-covered, multipierced flesh.

It didn't matter what he'd wanted a year ago, he reminded himself. He'd been a kid, and now . . . a lot had changed.

But it didn't stop him from staring at her as if she were some mythical creature he'd brought to life with the power of his mind. Maybe anything was possible. Dragons. Giants. Centaurs.

And Star*las.

"I was looking for you, actually," Star*la said.

"Yeah?" Had his voice just cracked? She was surely only a year or two older than him; but he suddenly felt like he was thirteen again, covered in zits and begging his father for a real guitar.

"I just downloaded this new song and I thought you might like it," she said.

"Why?" Shit, that was rude. "I mean, what made you think that I'd . . . ?"

"I was standing outside listening to you guys practice. Does that bother you?" she asked defiantly.

Only because they sucked. "Whatever. What did you think?" Bad idea, he told himself. This girl was obviously totally into the music scene here—and *here* was about as far as you could get from home, where the Blind Monkeys were the only rock band in thirty miles, which meant they played every gig from birthday parties to funerals, despite their general level of suckitude. Star*la, clearly, would have higher standards.

She laughed. "I *thought* you might like this song I just downloaded. So . . . wanna hear it?" She pulled an iPod Touch out of her pocket—exactly the model he'd been craving but couldn't afford, not when all his extra cash went to fixing the van and helping his dad with the never-ending stack of bills.

Reed nodded, not wanting to risk another humiliating falsetto moment. He reached out for the iPod, but instead she just gave him one earbud and stuck the other in her own ear. Tethered together, they sat down on the floor, backs pressed against the wall, legs pulled up to their chests, and arms just barely touching. She pressed play.

A scorching chord blasted through the buds. A sharp, syncopated beat charged after it, overlain by a twangy acoustic guitar solo—and then, without warning, the band plugged in. And the song took off. Reed closed his eyes, letting the music storm through him, banging his head lightly back against the wall in time with the drums, his fingers flickering as if plucking and strumming invisible strings.

Everything disappeared but the music—and then the music stopped.

The first thing he registered, as the song came to an end: He and Star*la had leaned in toward each other, their cheeks and temples pressing together as they lost themselves in sound.

The second thing: Beth's face in the doorway.

She just looked lost.

chapter five

"WE'RE GOING TO DIE." HARPER GRIPPED THE BAR until her knuckles turned white. One loose screw was all it would take to send her plummeting. She looked down—despite every instinct in her body screaming not to. The people were the size of pinheads. She wondered which one she would land on. "We are *so* going to die."

"It's just a ride," Adam pointed out, stretching back in the roller-coaster seat as if it were a lounge chair and grinning up at the sky. (The clouds seemed—to Harper, at least—unnaturally close.) "Enjoy it."

"I was enjoying standing flat on the ground," Harper snapped, as the car continued its slow, terrifying creep up the track. They were tilted back at nearly a right angle, and the ascent seemed to last forever. Which would have been okay with Harper, except for one little problem: What goes up, must come down. Fast. "I was enjoying the view from nine hundred feet up without feeling the asinine desire to get on a *roller coaster* that some *idiot* thought it would be neat to build on top of a building." She closed her eyes.

"You're the one who wanted to suck up to the girl at the controls," Adam pointed out.

"How are we supposed to suck up to her from here?" Harper shot back. "How are we supposed to enjoy a concert when we're splattered on the ground a thousand feet down?"

"Why do you always have to look on the dark side of everything?" Adam complained.

"Why do you have to act like everything's a game? Some things aren't fun."

"*I'm* having fun," Adam countered.

"And that's all that counts?" Harper asked.

"*You're* going to lecture *me* about being self-centered?"

"I'm—" Harper's next words flew out of her mouth and her mind as the cars rolled over the peak of the incline and . . .

"*Aaaaaaaaaah!*" she shrieked as they whipped through the air, the wind slicing her cheeks and her head pressed back flat against the seat. They zoomed down the track, up a hill, around a loop, the sky beneath her and the ground above, her hair flying everywhere and her stomach knocking around, banging her intestines, crushing her lungs. She kept her eyes squeezed shut and screamed and screamed, waiting for the nightmare to end until, with a heart-stopping jolt, it did.

Harper took a deep breath, then another. "Are we alive?" she whispered, her eyes still shut tight.

"You were really scared, weren't you?" Adam said, and she could hear the surprise in his voice. She would have shot back some snide comment about how he might have picked up on that from the hundred times she'd said it, back when he was dragging her into the seat. But she didn't have the energy. She was too relieved that it was over, and they were still alive.

There was nothing fun about screaming metal, uncontrollable speed, spinning and plunging and waiting for the crash.

At least, not when you'd been through the real thing.

Harper realized that her hands were still gripping the thin metal bar, and they weren't alone. Adam's left hand was wrapped over the top of her right one, his grip warm and firm, as if he'd meant to keep her safe.

He let go first.

✒ ✒ ✒

"Here at Heavenly Helpers, it's all about *you*," the attendant had chirped. "What *you* want, what *you* need, whatever makes *you* happy."

It had, in fact, sounded a bit like heaven to Miranda, whose life was usually all about anyone and everyone else. But the spa's slogan soon proved more fiction than fact, since whatever made Miranda happy most definitely did *not* include the Heavenly Peace Floral Skin Resurfacing and Pore Varnish facial.

"For your skin, dear," the woman had chirped as she slapped and pulled Miranda's face, then rubbed on a layer of acidic slime, ignoring Miranda's protestations. "Those pores are enormous, and caked with bacteria—when was your last facial?"

How about never?

Nor would she have chosen the Warming Stone Mint Massage with Body Wrap.

"It's a must!" The burly male masseur said, bustling her off to the steam room after a painful and slightly embarrassing hour of rubbing, pinching, and moisturizing. "The heat and the aromatherapy will fuse together in a blessed blend of healing vapors. It's unforgettable!"

But as far as Miranda was concerned, it was just hot and boring. And when she emerged, still covered in a thin film of all-organic mint-infused mud and smelling like a bag of potpourri, she felt neither relaxed nor rejuvenated. She just felt slimy.

"Isn't this heavenly?" the woman to her left asked as they lay back on over-padded chairs, cucumbers covering their eyes and gauzy netting draped down over their bodies as if to protect them from mosquito sized bad karma.

"Mmm-hmmm," Miranda mumbled, trying not to seem ungrateful for her birthday present, even though the stranger in the next chair obviously had no idea who Harper was or why it would matter that Miranda feigned gratitude. "It's great." She couldn't help but wonder what Harper was thinking. Didn't her best friend know her at all? Maybe, just *maybe*, if they'd done this together, they could have laughed at the manicurist's beehive hairdo and tag-team flirted with the hot masseur. But Harper apparently preferred to spend the day without her, and Miranda was left to spend her last day as a seventeen-year-old alone, getting scolded.

The manicurist scolded her for biting her nails; the facialist scolded her for poor skin hygiene; the masseur scolded her for letting stress build up in her muscles and tie knots in her back.

Try living my life, she'd wanted to tell him. *And then talk to me about stress management.*

"My sister and I come here every year," the woman confided. "Our husbands go off and gamble or"—she tittered—"at least that's what they tell us they're doing. And we come here. It's a tradition—we've been doing it for years."

"Mmm-hmmm," Miranda mumbled again, wondering how she was supposed to relax when they stuck her in the relaxation room with someone who wouldn't leave her alone.

"Who are you here with, dear?" the woman asked.

The door opened before Miranda was forced to admit the truth: She was alone.

"Miranda Stevens?" a scratchy voice called out. "Time for your wax."

Miranda sat up and peeled the cucumber slices off her eyes, delighted to be leaving the so-called soothing sounds of the rain forest and her Chatty Cathy meditation-mate. Delighted, that is, until the woman's words sunk in. She'd seen "bikini wax" on the schedule the spa had handed her when she first walked in. But she'd elected to ignore it. She'd never had one before, and would have been more than happy to leave it at that.

But that wasn't the kind of happiness the Heavenly Helpers were shooting for.

"Nonsense," the attendant told Miranda when she tried to talk her way out of the appointment. "It's very freeing. And your boyfriend will love it."

Miranda was all for the "if you build it, he will come"

theory of boyfriend hunting, but as far as she was concerned, that applied to things like chic hairstyles and sexy miniskirts. A freshly waxed bikini line wouldn't turn her into much of an irresistible draw unless she started parading around town in a bikini . . . in which case, unwanted hair would be the least of her concerns.

Still, she lay down on the table, as the waxer insisted, wearing only her bra and underwear and feeling strangely like she was at the doctor: chilly, exposed, vulnerable, and slightly bored.

The attendant approached carrying a long strip and a brush dripping with wax, then stared down at Miranda with disdain. "You'll have to take those off," she said.

"Take what off?" There wasn't much to choose from. She pointed at her bra. "You mean . . ."

"No." The attendant scowled, as if she had better things to do than waste her time with wax neophytes who didn't know the dress code. She pointed down at Miranda's pale blue bikini briefs. "You're blocking my access."

"But they're bikini," Miranda protested. "So it should be—"

"We do *Brazilian* waxes here," the woman informed her. In the midst of her confusion, Miranda noted that the waxer could use some wax herself on her upper lip; she decided not to mention it.

"I don't . . . is that some special type of . . . ?"

The woman rolled her eyes. "We wax it all, honey. We leave you completely bare."

"*Completely* . . . bare?" Miranda repeated, understanding dawning over her, swiftly followed by horror.

"Completely bare. Down there."

And that's when Miranda got the hell out.

"You guys have a fun ride?" Carl's friend Esther gave her replacement a quick wave and laced her arms through Harper's and Adam's, leading them to the opposite end of the roof.

"I did," Adam began, "but I think Harper—"

"It was great," Harper cut in. "Thanks so much for the free ride. Adam was just—"

"Thought his name was Kane?" Esther cut in.

"It is," Harper said quickly. "Adam's just his middle name. I call him that to bug him. Uh . . . anyway, he was just telling me how grateful he was for the free ride. Weren't you?" She glared at him, as if he was failing to get the message.

Which, apparently, he was, because Adam had no idea what he was supposed to say next. "Um, yeah, thanks. It was great."

"Cool." Esther pulled out a pack of cigarettes. She took one out, then tipped the pack toward Harper and Adam, who both shook their heads. Shrugging, she hunched over, trying to protect her lighter from the wind. "I hate it up here," she complained. "It takes the whole damn break to light the thing up," she complained.

"Adam can help you," Harper said quickly.

I can? Adam mouthed. Harper just grabbed the lighter and tossed it to him and, with luck, he got the flame lit and held it to Esther's cigarette.

She leaned against the railing, tipped her head back, and sucked in one long drag, then another. Finally, she seemed to remember she wasn't alone. "So, Carl sent you?" Esther asked. She gave Adam an appraising look, then grinned. "Lucky me."

Adam had been off the dating market for a while, but he knew flirting when he saw it. Harper's expression remained neutral, as if she hadn't noticed—or didn't care.

"So what can I do for you?" Esther asked.

Adam waited for Harper to speak, but when she didn't, he stepped in. "Well, this is a little awkward, but—"

"Just tell her," Harper said quickly. She gave Esther a half smile. "He can be a little shy, especially around cute girls."

What? Before he could say anything, Harper gave him the signal they'd used when they were kids whenever an intruder had walked in on one of their clubhouse meetings (membership was exclusive, limited to Harper and Adam). She made a fist with her right hand and, tucking her fingers under her chin, pressed her thumb to her lips. Meaning: *Shut the hell up. Now.*

Esther fluffed her hair out and tipped her head to one side. "So you think I'm cute?" She ran her hand lightly across Adam's bicep. "You're not too bad yourself."

Adam got the plan: Flirt with her, charm her, then get the tickets out of her. And given Esther's long, tan legs peeking out from beneath her short sundress, her pert nose, big brown eyes, and full lips, the mission shouldn't have been much of a burden.

But it still felt like one. Not because he wasn't attracted to her, and not because he felt guilty—just because he didn't feel like flirting.

He would do it, anyway, for Harper.

"Esther's a great name," he said, the best he could come up with on short notice. "It's unusual. But really pretty."

She shrugged. "It's my grandmother's," she said. "Most of my friends call me Estie."

Adam flashed a grin. "Okay, *Estie.* So, say I just got into town and I'm looking for something fun to do—any recommendations?"

"Why recommend when I could show?" she asked, stepping forward and looping an arm around Adam's shoulder. "Where should we go first?"

"Uh, don't you have to work?" Harper asked, sounding a little cranky.

"I can switch shifts," Estie said. "It's not every day that a guy this cute walks into my life." She tousled Adam's hair, and he squirmed away. "Aw, he *is* shy, just like you said. So adorable!"

"Yeah. Adorable," Harper muttered. "The thing is, we've got stuff to do—"

"We're on vacation," Adam pointed out. "We've got plenty of time. So, Estie, where shall we go?"

"The gondola rides at the Venetian are über-romantic," she told him, then frowned at Harper. "They only seat two, though, so you should probably stay here. It was nice to meet you, though. Come on, Adam—Kane—whoever you are."

Estie grabbed Adam's hand and began tugging him toward the elevator doors. He gave Harper a helpless look, then followed.

Harper didn't look in the mood to help; she looked in the mood to attack. "No!" Estie and Adam froze. "He can't go with you."

"He can't?"

"I can't?"

"And why not?" Estie asked.

"Because he's—we're—he was just—you just can't," she sputtered, slapping the railing for emphasis. "Just tell her you have to *go*."

Estie burst into laughter. "That took longer than I thought," she exclaimed.

"What?" Harper and Adam asked together, completely confused.

"Carl called me to tell me you guys were coming over here, and that you were looking for Crash Burners tickets," Estie admitted. "Trying to flirt them out of me?" She shook her head at Adam. "That's low."

Harper sagged back against the railing, looking half relieved and half humiliated. Adam was still just confused. "How did you know that's what I was trying to do?" His flirting skills had never let him down in the past—but maybe it *wasn't* like riding a bicycle, after all.

"Come on, you guys are obviously together."

Adam and Harper just looked at each other, then back at Estie. "Us?" Adam asked incredulously. "Did Carl tell you that?"

"No, it's just obvious," Estie said. "You are, aren't you?"

Adam wondered which part of the hostile, nonstop bickering, no-touching interactions between him and Harper could have screamed "relationship."

"Definitely not," he said firmly. "No way."

"Seriously?" Estie looked back and forth between the two of them. "Well, then, you should be."

Adam laughed—and then, too late, caught the look on Harper's face. He wanted to apologize; he hadn't been laughing at the idea of the two of them together. It was just the whole awkward, painful, utterly ridiculous situation. But he couldn't say any of that in front of a stranger. And even if he'd been alone, he suspected he couldn't have explained it, anyway. He wouldn't have known how.

"Man, I was so sure there was something between you guys," Estie said.

Harper looked over the railing, out at the sprawling strip of lights and people far beneath them. "Trust me," she said in a flat voice. "You couldn't be more wrong."

"That's my final offer," Kane said firmly. "Take it or—"

"I'll take it." Jackson, who'd proved a shrewder negotiator than Kane had expected, extended his hand, then whipped it away again just as Kane was about to shake. "On one condition."

"Try me." The price was right, the wrappers were flawless, and there was no way Kane was going to screw up his first big deal.

"Hook me up with your hot, blond friend."

Kane let out a whoosh of air. He wanted to say yes. He would have *loved* to say yes, for more reasons than one. But . . .

"No can do." Kane slumped down on one of the lobby chairs. "In case you didn't notice, she hates me."

Jackson nodded and raised his eyebrows. "That's what made her so hot. Spicy food and spicy women—that's what it's all about, am I right?"

Being so close to a black hole of classlessness made Kane's skin crawl. But his facade—smooth, polite, mildly bored, and immune to shock—was well worn and impossible to shake. "You know it," he agreed, baring his teeth in the imitation of a smile. "But Beth's about as spicy as vanilla pudding. You wouldn't be interested. Trust me."

"And you know this because . . . ?"

"Let's just say, been there, done that." Kane winced at the sleaze, but pushed on. "If you know what I mean."

"Really?" Jackson's eyes widened, and he held out his palm for Kane to slap. *"Nice."*

"Not really," Kane said wryly. "So do we have a deal?"

"I don't know." Jackson laced his fingers together and stretched his arms out in front of him, a yawn contorting his face. "I was really counting on Barbie to sweeten the pot. Now, I don't know . . ."

"Wait. You say you like bitter, argumentative girls?" He was getting an idea. He didn't much like it, but that didn't keep him from recognizing its genius.

"You know it," Jackson said eagerly, leaning forward. "You got someone else?"

"How do you feel about sarcasm?"

"Love it."

"How about pessimism?" Kane continued.

"Hot."

"Insults? Arguments? The burning need to always get the last word?"

Jackson rubbed his palms together. "Bring it on. So what's she look like?"

Kane wasn't the type to grapple with indecision. He usually knocked it out in a single punch and vaulted right over it. But this time, something made him pause, at least for a moment.

But it was no more than that.

"Well, let me ask you this," he finally said, a plan coalescing. "How do you feel about redheads?"

"Excrement."

"Simply awful."

"The worst I've ever seen."

"You should sue your guitar teacher for criminal incompetence."

Beth cringed at every word out of the judges' mouths. Reed, Fish, and Hale, on the other hand, stood lined up at the edge of the stage, taking it all without a single change in facial expression. Beth knew that, were she up there, listening to a panel of so-called experts bash her talent and smash her dreams, she'd be a wreck. In tears, inconsolable; but Reed looked as if he was barely listening, and the other two followed his cue.

The All-American Band Battle had introduced a new

judging tactic this year—if you could call a total rip-off of a played-out reality TV show "new." The organizers had assembled a team of experts—the Gee Whiz Kids, a pop foursome with pseudo-indie cred and a cult following, in town to open for the Crash Burners—and given them free reign to bash the bands in front of the audience. Beth had been watching for an hour and she had yet to see the panel give anyone a thumbs up. That said, she'd also not seen a single band come in for the beating that the Blind Monkeys were taking. Not even close.

"Can you even call that music?" asked one of the Gee Whiz Kids who—certainly to the delight of the organizers—had a possibly authentic British accent. "Because I call it noise, plain and simple."

"And the song? What *was* that?" another asked. "No, really, I'm asking—you, lead singer guy, where the hell did you get that?"

Reed leaned into the mic. "I wrote it," he said, looking out into the audience and meeting Beth's eyes. She knew the lyrics by heart:

> *I don't know where you are,*
> *but I'm there with you.*
> *Your lips, your tongue, your fire*
> *It's all I wanna do . . .*

She'd often wondered whether he had written it about her—for heir—but she'd never had the nerve to ask. Still, the song was one of her favorites.

"It's rubbish," the vaguely British guy snapped, dismissing it with a wave of his hand. "Pointless lyrics, bad rhymes, sappy sentiment. This isn't nursery school."

"And it's not a karaoke bar!" one of the other judges chimed in; he'd used the same line on almost every band. Apparently, he thought it quite clever. So did Beth . . . or at least she had, the first time she'd heard it, back before Simon Cowell had stopped recycling put-downs. A million times later, with the phrase spilling from the mouth of an already washed-up wannabe, and aimed at her boyfriend, she was less than amused.

"Judges?" British guy asked, turning to face the panel. "What do you say?" By the rules of the competition, the four of them would now vote on whether to pass the Blind Monkeys on to the next round or eject them from the competition. Beth wasn't waiting on the edge of her seat.

Judge #1: "They're out."

Judge #2: "So far out, they're almost in again . . . but, not."

Hilarious, Beth thought. *Somebody get this guy on* Letterman.

Judge #3: "Out. Go find a karaoke bar and leave us alone."

Judge #4, with a smart British lilt that gave Beth a

serious case of déjà vu: "Out. Best of luck, fellows. You're going to need it."

As the guys filed offstage, Beth rushed out of the auditorium and hurried to meet them at the stage door. Her heart ached for Reed. She just wanted to find him, comfort him, fix him. Strong as he was, he couldn't have escaped something like that without breaking. He had comforted her so many times, mostly without even knowing why, and without asking. He would just let her cry in his arms, clinging to him, unable to tell him the reason for fear it would drive him away.

He never seemed to need her, not the way she needed him. But maybe now she could pay him back.

Not that she was glad, she told herself. Not that she would ever want him to fail. She just wanted her chance to prove how much she cared about him—and this was it. She would reassure him that *she* knew he was amazing, no matter what anyone else thought.

And they would both remember that he needed her too.

"I'm so sorry!" she cried, as soon as he emerged from backstage. Fish and Hale followed behind, laughing— Beth wasn't surprised. They had no ambition; there was nothing to be crushed. But Reed looked even paler than usual, drawn into himself. "You were so amazing. I don't know what they were talking about."

She tried to hug him, but he neatly sidestepped her.

"They were right," he said in a hollow, wooden voice. "We played like ass. And the song—"

"I love that song," she assured him, compromising by stepping behind him and putting her arms around his waist, pressing her head against his shoulder blades.

"It's crap."

"No—"

"Beth. Just—" He pulled her arms apart and stepped away. "Just let it go. It's fine. They were right. I'm over it."

"Reed . . . " She wanted to touch him again, to remind him that she was there—that he wanted her there—but forced herself not to push. "It's just one opinion."

"Actually, it's four." His laugh was short and off-key.

"Maybe it was just—"

"Yo, tough break." Star*la rounded the corner and gave Reed a sympathetic punch on the shoulder. She waved at the guys, but didn't acknowledge Beth.

"You were watching?" Reed's voice shot to a higher octave and, though it might have been Beth's imagination, he seemed to stand slightly straighter. Taller. "We were playing like shit today."

Beth put her hand on his shoulder. "No you—"

"Yeah," Star*la interrupted. "It happens. But the song's not bad—ever think about switching it up in the bridge, have your drummer shift to 4/4 and then maybe jumping a key?"

To Beth, it all sounded like a foreign language. But

Reed suddenly brightened up. "That's not bad," he mused. "Fish, you get that?"

"Yeah, I heard. Could work."

"And I was thinking, maybe in that first verse . . ."

Beth tuned out. She stared at the floor. Counted the lights in the ceiling. Tried not to notice that Reed and Star*la looked like a matching pair in their vintage tees and black denim, while Beth looked like a refugee from a J. Crew clearance sale. She'd always thought that belly button piercings looked kind of slutty, but on Star*la . . . well, slutty, yes. But she couldn't help notice that Reed's eyes kept dropping down to the glint of silver that poked out above her low-riding jeans. *Stop worrying*, she told herself. *Reed isn't Adam. He would never . . .*

She didn't even want to put it into words, because that might make it real.

"Beth, sound okay to you?"

"What?" He was looking at her again, waiting for an answer. But to what?

"Star*la's done here and she says she can show us some bar downtown where all the locals hang out. You want to?" Reed had never expected anything from her before, but now it was clear: He expected an answer, and he expected it to be a yes.

"I don't have my ID on me," she said hesitantly, thankful that it was true.

"No problem." Star*la grinned. "This isn't an ID kind of place. You'll see."

"Beth?" Reed curled his arm around her waist and tugged her toward him. "If you don't want to, we don't have to, but . . ."

"No. Sounds great," she said, hoping she seemed sincere. She'd wanted to help him, and if this is what it took to cheer him up—if *Star*la* cheered him up, with her stupid piercings and her tattoos and her oh-so-happening bar scene—then that's what it took. Tonight wasn't about Beth; it was about Reed. She had no reason to feel threatened, she reminded herself. And even if she did, she wasn't going to let that stand in his way.

chapter six

THEY STRODE UP TO THE HOTEL CHECK-IN DESK hand in hand, identical love-struck smiles painted on their faces. "This is a bad idea," Adam muttered out of the side of his mouth, trying not to let the happy expression falter.

"It's our best shot," Harper countered, through gritted teeth. "Just act happy."

"I'm not that good an actor."

Estie hadn't been able to help them with the concert tickets, but she had offered them a lead: The hotel that was hosting the concert often reserved a few free event passes for especially cute honeymooners.

So here they were, glowing with fake love and walking

on artificial sunshine. A chipper brunette named Margie—
at least, according to her I'M MARGIE, TELL ME HOW I CAN
HELP name tag—greeted them at the desk.

"Yes?" she asked.

They'd agreed it would be best not to come right out
and ask for the tickets, at least not at first. Better to be so
insufferably adorable that Margie had no choice but to
reward them.

"We just wanted to thank y'all for letting us stay
in your lovely hotel on our special weekend," Harper
said, the Southern accent pouring out before she realized what she was doing. "Sweetie pie here is just loving
every minute of it." She nuzzled her face into Adam's
neck—pausing for a moment to enjoy the familiar scent,
woodsy and clean. It had been so long since they'd . . .

No. This was no time for sappy love-struck nostalgia:
It was a time for romance.

"I could just take you back to the room right now,"
she murmured, then turned back to Margie, confiding,
"We've barely left the room all weekend. You know how
it is."

The look on Margie's face said no, she didn't know
how it was, nor did she want to. "Glad you're enjoying
your stay with us," she said tentatively. "So this is a special
weekend for you?"

"Me and the wife just got hitched!" Adam said, lifting

Harper up and whirling her around. "She's my wife! Woo!"

Harper resisted the urge to smack him. She'd said act cute, adorable—not wasted. He was acting like he was at a tailgate party. Though she had to admit, it was indeed pretty damn cute. •

"So, newlyweds," Margie said, sounding less than enthused. "Congratulations."

Harper gave Adam a quick kiss on the cheek. "I wanted a simple church wedding, back home, but my man here, he's just obsessed."

"Obsessed?" Adam and Margie asked together.

"With Elvis. So of course we just had to come to Vegas and get hitched at the Hunka Hunka Chapel of Love, and you"—she dug her finger gently into Adam's chest— "looked so handsome in your white jumpsuit and those sexy sunglasses."

"Well, uh"—Adam gave her his best Elvis lip-curl— "thank you, thank you very much." Beneath the counter, Adam gave Harper a quick pinch just above the hip, and she bit her lip to keep from squealing. He knew that was where she was most ticklish; he was *trying* to make her laugh. It wasn't going to work. "I'm just sorry about last night," he said.

"Uh, last night?"

"You know." He lowered his voice to a stage whisper. "When we were in bed and . . . I called you *Priscilla*."

Now Harper nearly did laugh. But, instead, she gave him a light slap across the face. "You're going to bring that up in front of a stranger?" she cried. "You *know* I'll never be able to measure up to her. I try and I try, I got the implants and the new hairdo and—"

"Give it a rest, guys," Margie snapped, the help-me-help-you grin gone from her face.

"What?" Harper asked, trying to look innocent.

"You heard about the free tickets for newlyweds, right? You think you're the first couple to try this?" She rolled her eyes. "You're just the worst."

Harper glanced at Adam, briefly considered trying to bluff it out, then shrugged in defeat. "So much for my acting career." She hoped she sounded sufficiently breezy. It wouldn't do to let either of them know how much she'd been counting on these tickets—how she'd decided that one grand gesture for Miranda would, just maybe, erase everything Harper had done to her this year, and let them start fresh. And more than that—chasing down the tickets had helped distract her from thing things that actually mattered. But that was over now.

She tugged at Adam's shirt. "Come on, let's get out of here."

He shook her off and planted his hands on the fake wooden desk. "Isn't there anything you can do?"

Margie blew out an exasperated sigh. "I don't have

time for this. Come on, listen to your girlfriend—give up."

And for a moment, Adam looked like he was considering it. Then his jaw tightened—it was so imperceptible that someone else might not have noticed. But Harper knew what to watch for. And she was always watching.

"I know you're busy," Adam said. "I know you don't have time for a couple of high school kids trying to score free tickets. But just listen to me. We need this. *She* needs this." Harper froze, but he didn't try to touch her, or even look at her. "And it's none of your business why, so you're just going to have to trust me. She has gone through way more shit this year than anyone should ever have to, and I'm not saying she can't take it, because she can, and she *has*, and she doesn't complain, and she never asks for help and—" He paused, and took a deep breath, then another, and when he spoke again, his voice had lost some of its volume, but none of its intensity. "And now she's asking for this one thing," he said slowly. "And I wish I could give it to her. I really wish—" Harper was staring at the ground, but she could feel him watching her. "But I can't. *You* can. Please."

Margie tore herself away from Adam's face and looked over at Harper, who forced herself to meet her gaze. *Do not cry*, she commanded herself. She refused to be pitied, not by some random hotel clerk, not by Adam, not by anyone. *Just breathe.*

Finally, Margie's expression softened and she nodded. "I'm not supposed to do this, but . . ."

Adam snatched the tickets out of her hand and passed them to Harper, who stayed still and silent, just focusing on keeping her composure.

Adam pulled her away, and they walked through the lobby in silence. Finally, outside the hotel, Harper stopped. "Adam, I . . ." She chewed on the inside of her cheek, trying to figure out how to say what she wanted to say—how to thank him for helping her, despite the way she'd treated him, despite what she'd done to him, despite everything. She glanced down at the tickets, still unable to believe that they'd actually, finally succeeded. "Adam, I just want to say—holy shit!"

"What?"

Without a word, she handed him one of the tickets. He looked down, then back up at her, his mouth a perfect O of horror.

Margie had scored them second-row seats to a one night only, sold-out concert:

The Ninth Annual Viva Las Vegas International Elvis Extravaganza.

Thank you, Margie. Thank you very much.

If there had been papers, they would have been signed, sealed, and delivered. But this was a handshake business, and hands had been shook. As Kane led Jackson through the Camelot's lobby in search of the pool—in search of Miranda, who'd been only too happy to agree to meet him and his "friend"—Kane couldn't help but feel extremely pleased with himself. Even more than usual.

He'd suckered Jackson into agreeing to the deal, for the sole concession of introducing him to a hot redhead— an introduction, and nothing more. After that, they were on their own. So it wasn't like he was selling out Miranda, he told himself. More like he was using her as bait—bait that was in no danger of even a nibble, since obviously once Jackson saw her, the whole sordid business would be over with. Not that Miranda was some kind of guy repellant. But Jackson wasn't going to waste his Vegas weekend on a mousy, bookish stringbean, no matter how entertaining, and Kane doubted whether Miranda would last more than ten minutes with the smooth-talking, peace-loving, hemp-weaving Jackson before getting up and out.

No harm, no foul, and plenty of money soon to be rolling in. All in all, Kane decided, a good day's work.

"So how do I get in good with this chick?" Jackson asked, as they stepped onto the pool deck.

Calling her *chick* would surely be a great place to start, Kane thought in amusement. This could be more fun than he'd thought.

The pool area was mostly empty. A few kids were play-

ing Marco Polo in the shallow end, splashing and screaming. Kane caught one kid cheating—climbing out of the
pool and running to the other end before diving back in,
just as he was about to get tagged. Underhanded—and
brilliant. It brought back fond memories.

"I don't see her," he said, wondering if it had taken her
longer to get back from the spa than she'd expected. His gaze
skimmed across a row of women lying in the shade: old lady
with her knitting, desperate housewife with curves several
sizes bigger than her suit, skinny twelve-year-old trying to
look like Britney, and . . . whoa. Kane nodded appreciatively
and drank in a pair of perfect, delicate feet, each toe painted
a deep shade of red, slim, pale legs, lime green bikini board
shorts, a flat, taut midriff and barely there bikini top and—

Their eyes met, and she propped herself up and waved.

"Tell me that's your redhead," Jackson said in a
hushed voice.

Kane could hardly believe it, but . . . "Yeah. That's
Miranda."

Jackson slapped him on the back. "Nice, dude. I knew
I had a good feeling about you. Let's do this."

Kane led Jackson over and they sat down on an adja-
cent chair. He couldn't stop staring: Everything about her
looked the same as always. She was still just Miranda—
but looking at her from across the pool, as if she were a
stranger, it had been . . . deeply weird. He tried to shake it

off. Bikini or not, pedicure or not, sexy half smile or not, this was still Miranda. *Just* Miranda.

"Stevens, I'd like you to meet a good friend of mine," he said as she set down her book and extended a hand.

"*You* can call me Miranda," she told the drug dealer, touching her face self-consciously. Her skin looked almost like it was glowing.

"Jackson," he said, shaking her hand. The dealer checked out her book. "*Anna Karenina?*" he asked, raising his eyebrows. "Not quite beach reading."

Miranda waved her hand toward the giant waterslide and the plastic palm trees. "Not quite the beach," she pointed out.

"It's one of my favorites," Jackson told her. "I love the way Tolstoy uses the theme of the moving train to propel us through the book."

"Really?" Miranda asked, her eyes widening in surprise.

"Really?" Kane echoed. What was going on here?

Jackson began explaining his take on Tolstoy and why he preferred him to Dostoyevsky ("*Crime and Punishment* is thought-provoking, to be sure, but *War and Peace* changed my life. . . .") but liked Chekhov best of all, especially on his "dark days." Miranda listened in rapt amazement.

Kane couldn't bring himself to listen at all. Nor did he pay much attention when Miranda offered her own criticisms of the novel and then shifted from fiction to current events, analyzing the latest move by the Russian president, while Jackson jumped in with a comparison to nineteenth-century geopolitics. Instead, Kane watched. He watched Miranda nervously play with her hands, picking at her cuticles with sudden, sneaky plucks as if no one could see. He noticed her smoothing down her hair and grazing her fingers across her lips, and he noted that when Jackson made her laugh, he briefly rested his hand on her skin—first on her arm, then on her thigh. Kane spotted her blushing, and caught Jackson sneaking more than one glance at the low neckline of the bikini, always darting his eyes back up to Miranda's before she picked up on his distraction.

And finally, he couldn't take it anymore.

"Jackson, can I talk to you for a minute?" he asked.

"Kinda busy here," Jackson said, without turning his gaze from Miranda.

"It's important." Kane stood up and waited for Jackson to follow. "We'll be back in one minute, Stevens. Promise." He pulled Jackson across the deck to the other side of the pool, where the Marco Polo game had morphed into net-less water volleyball. "What are you doing?" he hissed.

"Reeling in the catch of the day," Jackson leered. "You were right, she's as spicy as they come."

Kane winced. This had to be handled delicately—but it had to be handled. "But all that stuff about Tolstoy, politics—where did you . . . ?"

"You gotta play to the audience," Jackson explained. "Let them think you're on the same wavelength, and then—" He shook his head. "You think all this hippie crap is my idea? My girlfriend's all peace, love, happiness, bullshit—but if it keeps her happy to dress me like granola boy, well, you do what you gotta do, am I right?"

"Your . . . girlfriend?" Kane wondered why his brain was moving so much more slowly than usual.

"Yeah, she's getting in on Monday. But till then, I figure I can have a little fun, and Miranda's perfect—or she will be, once she loosens up a little."

"Look, Jackson, I know I said she was your type, but I really don't think—"

"I owe you one," Jackson said, clapping Kane on the back. "But now, how about you get out of here and leave us to it."

Kane was stuck. He couldn't afford to alienate Jackson—but he couldn't just let Miranda walk into the lion's den wearing a necklace of raw meat.

You don't owe anything to anyone, he reminded himself.

Words to live by—words he always *had* lived by—but that didn't make them true.

The Tonky Honk was half bar, half coffeehouse, and all hipster. The nexus of the Vegas indie rock scene—at least, according to Star*la, a self-described expert—it was packed, even in the middle of the afternoon, with world-weary aspiring poets sipping anise and off-duty house bands knocking back shots. Papers lined with song lyrics and guitar chords lined the walls, a floor-to-ceiling tribute to a million impossible dreams. And, on a small stage in a dark recess of the bar, a four-piece band played interminable songs about flat tires and worn-out toothbrushes, each bleeding into the next in a tedious litany of trivial torments. According to Star*la, the Tonky Honk was a Vegas institution, occasionally attracting legends like Tony Bennett for a post-concert drink. (Reluctant to admit she didn't know who that was, Beth just ooh'd and aah'd along with the rest of them.)

Beth slumped in the corner of a back booth sipping a weak espresso while the guys drowned their sorrows in a seemingly bottomless bottle of whiskey. Star*la, of course, matched them drink for drink.

She was regaling them with backstage stories about a bunch of bands Beth had never heard of, all of whom had apparently passed through Vegas—and through Star*la—in the past year. Fish, Hale, and Reed couldn't get enough of it.

"So, what kind of stuff do you listen to?" Star*la suddenly asked Beth.

She flushed, and tucked a lock of blond hair behind her ear. "I, uh, you know. Whatever." She wasn't about to say the words "Tori Amos" or "Sarah McLachlan" in a place like this.

Reed nudged her. "You know you love all those weepy girls," he told her. "Dar Williams. Ani DiFranco. And, of course—"

"Let me guess," Star*la said. "Tori Amos."

Beth's face turned bright red as everyone else at the table burst into laughter. She didn't even get what was so funny—or so lame—about her taste, but that was probably part of the problem. "That's not all I like," she said defensively. She brushed some stray curls out of Reed's face. "You know I love your stuff."

Reed raised his glass in a drunken toast. "To Beth, our one and only fan!" He clinked her glass loudly, his whiskey splashing over the side and spattering into her cup.

Beth's first impulse was to comfort him; Star*la's, apparently, was to ridicule. "Is he always such a whiny baby?" she asked Beth, as if to forge some kind of sisterhood. Beth just shrugged and looked away. "You know what you need?" Star*la asked.

Reed, Hale, and Fish exchanged a glance, and then chorused, "Another drink!"

"Not quite." Star*la hopped up from the table. "Be right back." She jogged toward the bar and began an animated conversation with the bartender. The boys watched, though Beth was unsure whether they were wondering about her plan or admiring the way she filled out her jeans.

Reed's hand was resting on Beth's inner thigh, and the warm pressure on her leg should have been comforting: He was with her, and that's all that mattered. But his mind was somewhere else.

"It's all set," Star*la said, bounding back to the table. "The guys are a little sensitive about other people touching their instruments, but they've got no problem with Reed doing it."

"With Reed doing what?" Beth asked.

"Jamming with them," Star*la explained, as if it had been obvious.

"You crazy?" Reed asked.

"Do a couple songs," she urged him. "Get back on the horse. They'll play anything you want—they know no one's listening. Hey!" she turned to Beth. "Why don't you go too?"

"Uh . . . what?" Beth cringed under Star*la's gaze, feeling herself slide down a bit in the seat and wishing she could go all the way, right under the table.

"A duet!" Star*la exclaimed. "It would be great. Like karaoke, right?"

Beth winced at the word, but the guys burst into laughter.

"Awesome!" Fish said, apparently—and unusually—

not too stoned to follow along with the conversation. "Go for it."

"Yeah, man, you and your girlfriend, rocking out," Hale agreed. "That's hot."

Hale thought everything was hot.

Reed turned to her, a questioning look on his face. "It could be . . ."

"No." The word slipped out before she had a chance to think; but really, it was the only possible option. Beth didn't sing in public. She didn't even sing in the shower. Not that she had a terrible voice—but the thought of anyone hearing her sing, much less watching her stand up on a stage, under the spotlight, staring at her, judging her, laughing at her—even imagining it made her want to throw up. "I can't."

"Sure you can," Reed encouraged her. He stood up and tugged at her arm. "It'll be fun." She could tell by his glazed look and careful enunciation that he was drunk. Otherwise, she was sure, he would never push the issue. He should, by now, know her well enough to understand why going up on that stage would be a walking nightmare for her. "It'll be fun. You and me. C'mon."

"I can't sing," she protested, shaking him off.

"Anyone can sing!" He grabbed her again, pulling her out of the seat. She stumbled into his arms.

"No!" She shook him off. "I *can't!*"

"Let it go, Reed," Star*la said, touching his shoulder. "She doesn't want to." She turned toward Beth and apologized, but Beth barely heard—she was too busy wondering why a single word from Star*la had been enough to get him to stop. And wondering whether Beth had really *wanted* him to stop. Maybe if he'd kept pushing, she would have given in and followed him up to the stage. And maybe that would have been for the best. "Come on," Star*la said, guiding him away from the table. "I'll go with you."

Of course she would.

Reed took the stage and, giving a few quiet instructions to the band, leaned into the mic and began to sing. Beth expected him to do the same number the Blind Monkeys had performed that afternoon, but instead, the band launched into a Rolling Stones cover. "'*When I'm driving in my car,*'" Reed sang, "'*and that man comes on the radio . . .*'"

Beth drew in a sharp breath. It was the perfect song for him—his voice, scratchy and low, massaged the words, rising and falling with the melody, sometimes straying off the beat, forging ahead and then falling behind. She closed her eyes, letting his voice surround, drawing it inside her. He stumbled over the words and as the music swept past him, a rich, deep, *female* voice took over, picking up where he'd left off and carrying the song until Reed could join back in.

Beth opened her eyes and there they were, hunched over the microphone together, voices melding together, faces beaming, Star*la's dreads whipping through the air as she flung her head back and forth, his curls flying, their hands both gripping the mic stand, nearly touching, their bodies dancing them toward each other, then away, then back again, ever closer to embrace.

"*I can't get no, satisfaction,*" they howled, and Beth looked away, suddenly feeling like *she* was the interloper, catching the two of them in an intensely private moment, invading a closed-off world. "*'Cause I try, and I try, and I try, and I tryyyyyyyy . . .*"

Reed would never cheat on her, but nothing he could do with Star*la behind her back would be as raw and sensual as what he was doing right now, onstage, in front of all these people, letting himself go and charging through the music, stomping with the beat, losing control, with her. Beth and Reed were never that free with each other, that close, swept away, because Beth couldn't afford to lose control. She always had to keep a piece of herself—the most important piece—locked away.

But that's just an excuse, Beth thought, placing her mug carefully on the table and standing up. Fish and Hale, mesmerized, didn't even notice. Her reluctance—her *inability*—to get up on that stage didn't have anything to do with keeping secrets. She had to admit it to herself, as she slipped quietly away from the table, moving toward the exit, knowing she wouldn't be missed. She wasn't holding herself back for the sake of caution or self-protection.

It was just fear.

"So I have to ask—what's with the tie-dye?" Miranda didn't even hesitate to say it. For some reason, nervous paranoia had yet to set in. Maybe because she was on vacation, in a strange place with a strange guy, with no baggage and no expectations for the future, nothing to risk and nothing to lose—or maybe it was just Jackson. She felt comfortable with him, free to speak her mind. It wasn't like they'd settled into some cozy conversational groove, pretending they'd known each other forever; it was more that there seemed no danger that she could say the wrong thing. She could somehow tell that he was enjoying everything that popped out of her mouth. The feeling was mutual.

He was fascinating, funny, and—once you got past the wispy goatee and overgrown hair—adorable.

"You know Berkeley." He shrugged. "It's illegal there not to wear some kind of tie-dye or peace sign on at least one part of your body."

In fact, she didn't know Berkeley—pretty much didn't know anywhere beyond the claustrophobic confines of Grace, CA. Which was why she couldn't believe that this guy, this *college* guy, was wasting his time on her.

"Hate to mention this to you, but you're not in Berkeley anymore," she pointed out.

If this had been Kane she was talking to, he would have immediately wondered whether that was a veiled invitation to take his shirt off. And then he promptly would have obliged.

But it wasn't Kane—after hanging out for a few minutes he'd obviously decided he had something better to do. Jackson just plucked at the edge of the multicolored shirt. "Yeah, but it's all I've got," he said without a hint of self-consciousness. "I'm just not that into clothes. Or appearances, you know?"

Maybe that was why he was still talking to her, Miranda concluded, despite the fact that she was wearing a bikini that exposed more of her flab and cellulite than she'd ever allowed anyone to see. (She had intended to cover up before Kane and his friend arrived, determined not to let him see the humiliating bulges and sags, but—unwilling as ever to accommodate her hopes—he'd arrived early.)

"So what *are* you into?" she pressed. "Other than Tolstoy and world peace, of course."

"What am I into?" Jackson tipped his head back to catch the fading light of the afternoon sun. "The taste of cold beer at a baseball game, when the score is tied and your team has one man on base and two outs," he said.

"Discovering a new band, just after they've found their sound, but before they sign away their souls to the radio gods. Poems that make no fucking sense but still manage to blow your mind. And"—he gave her a mischievous smile—"good conversation with pretty girls."

Miranda felt the heat rising to her cheeks. "In that case, what are you doing here?" she joked.

He didn't laugh. "Having an amazing afternoon," he told her, with a totally straight face.

Miranda didn't know what to make of it. A cute, smart, older guy, giving her two compliments in a row as if it was nothing? Guys her age didn't talk like that—at least, not to her.

So, instead of responding, she just laughed nervously and turned toward the pool. "The water looks so tempting when you can't go in, doesn't it?" she asked. "Even though you know it's just going to be cold and over-chlorinated, from here it looks so insanely refreshing, like we're in some kind of beer commercial."

"Who says we can't go in?" Jackson asked, appearing not to care that she'd randomly changed the subject.

"Well, I guess I *could*," Miranda allowed, though she had no intention of doing anything of the sort. "But I think you've got a small problem."

"And that would be?"

"Shirt? Jeans? Shoes? Unless you're going to dive in

like this, or—" She stopped, realizing that she didn't know this guy well enough to suggest a skinny-dip, even as a joke. "I'd say swimming is out."

"You don't think I'd jump in with my clothes on?" Jackson asked.

"Now *that*, I'd love to see," Miranda said, laughing. The only people left at the pool were a few little kids and their nervous mothers, who she guessed wouldn't take too kindly to some random college student throwing himself in fully clothed. (Although this was Vegas—surely it wouldn't be the first time.)

"What do I get?" Jackson sat up and leaned forward. Their knees were almost touching.

"Get for what?"

"For jumping in the pool and soaking myself, just for your amusement," he explained, staring at her so intensely, she had to force herself not to look away.

"I don't know. A dollar?"

"How about you go out with me tonight?" he suggested, his grin stretching nearly to his ears.

"I barely know you," Miranda said, as her brain furiously tried to process the request. He wanted to go out? With her? Like, on a date? Would it *be* a date? What else could it be? "For all I know, you're some psychotic ax murderer trolling cheap hotels looking for redheads to chop up for your salad. I watch *CSI*."

"I don't think your buddy Kane would have introduced you to an ax murderer," Jackson pointed out. "And
I've never seen *CSI*, but I can assure you that I'm a veg-
etarian. Only thing in my salad is lettuce and tofu."

She was supposed to meet up with Harper for the
night—although, Miranda reminded herself, Harper had
ditched her that morning and probably never looked back.
And she would be the first person to urge Miranda to go
on a date. She always pushed Miranda toward every guy
who crossed her path—every guy, that is, except Kane.
The ultimate lost cause.

Miranda had to admit that she'd been hoping to spend
the night hanging out with him—along with Harper and
Adam, of course, but that was a coupling-off waiting to
happen and, if it did, she'd be left alone with Kane. In a
place where, according to him, anything could happen.

Anything like what? she asked herself. *What the hell am
I waiting for?* Kane had, several months before, finally seen
her as something more than boring Miranda, just one of
the guys. He'd taken her out, he'd *kissed* her—and that had
been the end of it. The moment she'd spent all those years
dreaming of had come, and then gone, almost as quickly. So
what did she think was going to happen next? That one day,
he would just wake up and realize what he'd been missing?

In less than eight hours, she would be eighteen years
old. Did she really want to kick off another year of her life

sitting in a corner, waiting for Kane to notice her?

Hadn't she had enough?

"Okay," she said finally. "If you actually jump in that pool, then yes, I'll go out with you tonight."

With a holler, he jumped up and raced toward the pool. Miranda felt a warm tingling spread through her body at the thought that this guy was really going to go through with it, just to get a date with her. He stood on the edge and turned to face her, flashing her a peace sign.

"You won't be sorry!" he shouted, then spun around and, with an enormous splash, did a perfect belly flop into the deep end.

She was only sorry she'd hesitated.

The balcony was too high up for Kane to hear what was going on.

Still, he managed to get the general idea.

Bad enough that their conversation stretched on for more than an hour. Worse yet that, after the lame pool stunt, Miranda rushed to the edge holding a towel, then wrapped it around him, rubbing his back for warmth.

The final blow: Jackson ditched the towel and, still dripping, took Miranda's hand. She let him, and they walked off together.

Kane had tried to call her cell, hoping to whisper

a warning in her ear, but she wasn't answering. Too engrossed, apparently, by Jackson's pathetic sideshow. How could she fall for his act? She was too sharp for that, too guarded. Maybe, Kane thought, she was just playing Jackson, waiting for the right moment to make her move.

But Kane was forced to admit it was unlikely. Miranda might have been sharp when it came to calculus homework or Trivial Pursuit, but when it came to guys, she was clueless. He knew that firsthand.

Kane tightened his grip on the balcony railing, choosing not to wonder why he cared, or why it sickened him to see that slimeball holding Miranda's hand. This wasn't jealousy, and it certainly wasn't self-sacrifice—he wasn't planning to risk his own standing with Jackson to protect Miranda from her own mistakes.

But he couldn't stop thinking about it. Kane, who had always believed his only responsibility was to have fun and his only obligation was to himself, felt responsible for the situation. Obligated to Miranda.

To *Miranda*, of all people.

She was a good friend. She was, on the whole, more tolerable to be around than nearly anyone he knew. She let him get away with anything—though never without a sharp rebuke that cut deeper than she knew. And, clueless or not, she didn't deserve Jackson. Staging a rescue attempt would be totally inconvenient—and, for all he knew, unwelcome. But it was also the right thing to do.

There was just one problem: Kane had wide variety of skills, talents, and areas of expertise.

Doing the right thing definitely wasn't one of them.

chapter seven

AS SOON AS SHE STEPPED OUTSIDE THE CLUB, BETH realized she had no idea how to get back to the hotel. They'd driven over in Star*la's car, and she didn't have enough cash on her for a taxi. Even if she could get a cab driver to take her to a bank and wait while she hit the ATM, there wouldn't be much point: Her tiny savings account was even emptier than usual. She'd drained it for gas and food money, figuring this trip would be worth it.

After all, now that she'd decided to take college off the table, what was the point in saving her money? What was she saving it *for*?

Emergencies, perhaps. Like this one.

A screeching crowd of girls burst out of the bar, slamming into Beth as they charged toward the street. She stumbled backward, catching herself just before she fell.

"Watch yourself!" a tall, skinny girl in knee-high leather boots yelled. "You're in the way!"

That part, she'd already figured out.

Maybe she could walk back. Beth knew this wasn't like home, where everything was within a couple miles of everything else. It could take all night—but she had nowhere else to be. Nor was she in any particular hurry to get back to the hotel room, because then she'd have to address the question: What next? Reed would have to return eventually. (Beth tried to ignore the persistent voice in her head pointing out that, no, Reed didn't *have* to come back—not if he got a better offer.)

Unable to decide and unwilling to turn back, she stood in front of the bar, watching the traffic crawl by.

She didn't hear his footsteps behind her, but she recognized his voice when he whispered her name. She still flinched when he put his arms around her and leaned his chin on her shoulder.

"What's going on?" Reed asked. His hair brushed against her neck. "Where'd you go?"

Beth didn't know how to answer. Now that she had to put it into words, her fears seemed ridiculous.

"I'm not feeling well," she lied.

"So you leave without saying good-bye?" He turned her around to face him. Their noses were almost touching. "How were you going to get back?"

Beth shrugged.

"What's really going on?"

She looked away. "Nothing."

He took her chin and tipped her face up so she couldn't avoid his dark eyes. "Tell me."

Beth took a deep breath. "When I saw you with *her*, I just thought—"

With both hands, Reed, smoothed down her hair, then pressed her head against his chest. His T-shirt was so old and worn that the cotton felt like skin. "I'm sorry."

Her eyes widened. She'd been expecting denials, laughter, maybe even ridicule. Anything but a simple apology. Guys didn't work that way. "For what?"

"For making you think that anything could ever—"

"She's just so much more . . . like you," Beth said weakly, wondering why she was encouraging the idea. "She—she fits in. And I . . ."

"You fit," Reed assured her. "Here." He laced his arms around her waist and held tight.

"That's not what I mean," Beth protested.

"But that's what matters." When she didn't answer him, he ran a hand through his tangles of black curls. "Look. I know I don't . . ." He pressed his lips together and closed his eyes. When he opened them, she realized she could see her reflection. "All this—" He waved his arm at the club, the people, and, somewhere inside, Star*la. "You're right, it's me. And you're different. But that's why . . .You make *me* want to be different, you know? You make me think I can be better, that, like, I should be better. And . . ." He rubbed his hand against her back in a slow, soft circle. "You get that there's something else, something beside all this. I don't have to *be* anyone for you. All these people? They think they know, but they don't get it. They don't get *me*. You do."

It was the most he'd ever said to her at once. She tipped her head up to him, but before she could respond, he leaned down and kissed her. She closed her eyes, and the world beyond his lips disappeared.

"This is what I want," Reed told her. "You. Believe me?"

Beth realized she did. And always had. Reed was so open about everything. He never did anything he didn't want to do, he never shaded the truth, and he never broke his word.

And that was the problem. Because Beth could never tell the real truth, and everything she said and did, every kiss, every smile was a lie. She didn't deserve to be with Reed, the one person in the world who had the most reason to hate her, but she was too weak to push him away. At the beginning, Beth had promised herself that she would end this before she got in too deep. But she'd let it go on, and now she couldn't imagine how she would make it through a day without Reed. He couldn't ever find out about her ever-present misery; but she couldn't survive it without him.

She was too much of a coward to let him go. But if he'd done it for her, she realized, that would have been it. An easy way out. If he had pushed her aside for Star*la, it would have destroyed her—but at least it would all be over, and she would no longer need to pretend to be happy or ignore the suffocating guilt.

She had *wanted* her suspicions to come true, wanted him to cheat on her. It would have been hard, but not as hard as telling the truth. This way—the Star*la way—she could have just slipped out the back and faded from his life. No messy scenes, no recriminations, no admissions. No pain.

"Beth?" he asked again when she didn't answer. "Do you believe me?"

She couldn't trust herself to speak, so she just nodded.

"Come back to the hotel with me," he suggested. "Let's forget this whole shitty day ever happened, and start over. Okay?"

I don't deserve you, she wanted to say. *I deserve to stay here, walking the streets, alone and miserable. I deserve to be alone forever.*

But she was weak. Too weak to confess her crime, too terrified to face her punishment. So she nodded again, and took his hand.

Kane had orchestrated his share of schemes, but he wasn't used to sneaking around to carry them out. He'd always preferred the bold lie to the snoop and spy—but in this case, it couldn't be helped. Miranda wasn't answering her cell, and if Jackson caught sight of him, the deal could be thrown into jeopardy. So Kane was reduced to stalking from afar.

The things I do for—He caught himself then, not having an easy word to fill in the blank. He could be out drinking, gambling, hooking up, living it up, and instead he was threading his way through a crowded street, always staying at least ten feet behind his prey, ducking behind corners and into alleys when it seemed they might be onto him. It was on the cusp of being humiliating, and Kane still wasn't quite sure why he was bothering. So he put the question out of his mind and focused on the chase.

They began the date at Sunset Terrace, a nauseatingly romantic bar overlooking the Strip. Miranda and Jackson placed their orders, then took their drinks out onto the wide outdoor deck, walking a little too closely together for Kane's comfort.

No matter. Kane knew just how to handle this—Jackson had made it easy on him.

He strode up to the bar, keeping a laserlike focus on the couple to make sure they didn't glance back inside, then beckoned the bartender toward him. "So, when did they pass the law?" he asked. "I would have thrown a party."

The bartender, a brawny guy in a light blue polo shirt and ill-fitting slacks, slung a towel over his shoulder and scowled at Kane. "What law?"

"The law lowering the drinking age." Kane gave him a serene, wide-eyed smile.

"What the hell are you talking about?"

Now Kane shrugged. The sneaking around part had been ignominious, but this was pure fun. "I just assumed," he said innocently. "After all, I know that girl over there"—he pointed at Miranda—"and she's only seventeen. But since you served her, anyway . . ." Kane had been watching closely enough to know that Miranda hadn't even had to flash her pathetic fake ID. "It's weird, though, since I probably would have heard about a new law like that, what with my dad being on the state liquor board and all."

Bingo.

"Shit." The bartender's jaw dropped, and he stepped out from behind the bar.

Kane winked at him. "Don't tell her I tipped you off, and no one has to know you're serving anyone old enough to walk "

"Deal," the bartender agreed. As he stalked off toward Beth and Jackson, Kane ducked out of the bar and positioned himself behind a large column just outside the entrance. He wished he could have stayed to watch the fall-out, but he had a rich imagination.

His hopes were confirmed a moment later, when the bartender appeared in the doorway, one hand wrapped tightly around Jackson's arm, the other firmly at Miranda's shoulder blades. "Nice try, kiddies," he growled, pushing them both onto the street. "Come back when she's potty-trained."

Kane was close enough to hear Miranda apologize— and close enough to see that Jackson wasn't about to give up that easily.

"No worries," he assured her, rubbing her shoulder in sympathy.

A weasel, Kane thought, but an effective one.

"If you want to go," Miranda began, "I totally—"

"*We're* going," Jackson told her. "And I know just the place."

They set off and, with a deep sigh, Kane followed. So the game wouldn't end as quickly as Kane would have liked, but it would still certainly end in his favor. Jackson didn't know who he was playing against.

In fact, to Kane's great benefit, Jackson didn't know he was playing at all. And that was Kane's favorite way to win.

"I *cannot* believe you talked me into this," Harper groused as a line of Elvises spread out across the stage in a Rockettes-like kickline.

Adam clinked his glass against her Blue Hawaii daiquiri and took a sip from his All Shook Up vodka tonic. It was just as disgusting as it looked. "How can you not be enjoying this?" he asked, grinning widely. When Miranda had called to cancel that night's prebirthday dinner, it had taken Adam only twenty minutes of concentrated wheedling to convince Harper that the Elvis Extravaganza might be their best bet.

Not that Adam had nurtured any particular desire to see a two-hour parade of Elvis impersonators, spanning the eras from *Ed Sullivan Show* chic to bloated 70s white jumpsuits. But he also hadn't wanted the day to end.

They were the youngest people in the hall by more than a decade. But thanks to their new friend Margie, their free tickets placed them at a small table only a few feet from the stage. Adam could almost see his reflection in the fat Elvises' oversize sunglasses and gold medallion belts.

It was gaudy, tacky, and so noisy, he feared he'd be hearing "Jailhouse Rock" echo in his ears for weeks. But

Harper wasn't arguing with him, attacking him, or running away from him, so Adam concluded it was worth it.

"Remind you of anything?" he asked suddenly. The so-called music was so loud that no one could hear them talking, even at normal volume—they could barely hear themselves. "Sixth grade?"

She looked puzzled for a second, then burst into laughter. "Oh my God, I can't believe you remember that."

Their teacher had been one of those naive, over-eager, twenty-two-year-olds who had yet to realize that Grace, CA, was about as dead as dead ends could get. Ms. Carpenter had quickly tired of the explorers, the Civil War, and the Great Depression, and had skipped forward to what she saw as the fundamental development of American history: the creation of rock-'n'-roll. They'd formed groups, and each had been charged with reenacting a performance of some famous group from the past. Complete with costumes and offbeat lip-synching.

"If you'd just listened to me in the first place," Harper said, giggling, "it never would have happened."

"If I'd listened to you in the first place, I would have ended up wearing a dress." Harper had done her best to convince Adam to join up with her and Miranda . . . to perform as The Supremes. By the time Harper pulled out the spangly sequined miniskirts she had discovered in her parents' attic, Adam was out the door and halfway down the block.

He'd opted to go solo, and there was only one true option: Elvis Presley, the King. His rendition of "Jailhouse Rock" had brought the audience to its feet within seconds. (Not much of an accomplishment, considering the audience was made up entirely of sixth graders—half of whom already wanted to date him.) Harper had helped him tape black stripes to his white shirt for an excellent convict effect, and choreographed a dance for him. It all went perfectly . . . until he climbed up on his chair, kicked his leg out while strumming his air guitar—and slipped off the chair, flipping through the air and landing in a tangled, broken heap.

He'd hobbled around on crutches for the next two months, with a broken ankle almost as painful as his new nickname: the Klutz King.

"I still blame you," Adam said, waving an accusing finger in Harper's face. "If you hadn't suckered me into doing that stupid chair dance—"

"If *you* hadn't fallen on your ass—"

"I might never have become the man I am today," Adam concluded jokingly. He clapped Harper on the back. "I guess I owe it all to you."

Her grin faded suddenly, and she looked away, taking a long sip of the drink that looked even more disgusting than his. "Yeah."

"What's wrong?"

"Nothing." But she lowered her head, letting her wild wavy hair fall across her eyes. He knew it wasn't accidental. She was hiding.

"What is it, Gracie?" He hesitated, remembering that the last time he'd tried using his childhood nickname for her, she'd blasted him for his presumption that their history together still mattered. "What's wrong?" He used to be able to read her, and know why she was upset almost before she did. But this year, too much had happened—too much had changed. "Is it the tickets?" he guessed. "Miranda will never even know you were trying to get them for her. So she won't be disappointed. I'm sure we can think of something else great to surprise her with."

Harper laughed, but it was a sad sound. "I don't care about the stupid tickets," she admitted, her voice muffled. She was speaking so softly, he could barely hear her over the music, but what she said next was clear enough that he could almost read her lips. "It's . . . you. I miss you."

His first sensation: relief. Pure and overwhelming. Adam had to grip the edge of his chair to hold himself still. He didn't know what to say next. Their friendship—what was left of it—was so fragile, he feared that the wrong words could smash it beyond repair. "I—"

But before he could say anything, right or wrong, one of the white jumpsuit Elvises hopped off the stage and strolled right up to their table, close enough that Adam could see the plastic studs holding the rhinestones in place. "How about a serenade for our young lovers here?" the Elvis asked, and the audience roared with approval. Harper's face flushed red, and Adam wished he could hide under the table—or, better yet, shove the Elvis under there until he and Harper had safely left the building. But they did nothing, and Elvis began to sing.

"*Love me tender,*" he crooned. "*Love me true . . .*"

Adam buried his face in his hands, but it didn't make the nightmare end.

"*For my darlin' I love you. And I always will.*"

". . . and let's just say that I will never again bite into something without checking to see if it's still breathing," Jackson concluded, shaking his head as if in dismay at his own foolishness.

Miranda laughed—perhaps a little harder than the story merited, but then, she was spending her birthday with a cute older guy who, in his own words, thought she was "adorable," "hilarious," and "fantastic." A little extra laughter was a small price to pay. "That's unbelievable," she said, gasping for breath.

"I swear." Jackson put a hand over his heart. "It happened exactly like I said."

When they'd been booted out of the bar, Miranda had been sure her date was over before it even began, but Jackson had just shrugged and escorted her down the strip to Killian's, a dark, opulent, outrageously Irish pub with thick burgers, heaping plates of mashed potatoes, and towering mugs of beer. Miranda stuck to salad and soda.

"I'm really glad you agreed to come out with me tonight," Jackson told her.

Miranda searched for a suitably snappy response, but under the table she suddenly felt the light touch of a hand on her knee, and her witty bravado melted away. "Me too," she said sincerely, and, though it felt unthinkably bold, she rested her hand on top of his, lightly twining their fingers. Jackson stared at her so intensely that she was tempted to look away, but she knew that in a situation like this, she was supposed to meet his eyes. So she forced herself to do it.

He's gazing *at me*, the overanalytical part of her mind that refused to shut up observed. *I never thought anyone would do that.* It was only a few hours to her birthday, and Miranda allowed herself to hope that she would get to start off her eighteenth year in the best way imaginable: with a kiss.

"Can I get you anything else?" the waitress asked, appearing as if from nowhere. She was dressed in green from head to toe, and wore a four-leaf clover beret over her bright red—certainly dyed—hair. "Some more water?"

"We're fine," Jackson said, but she had already leaned in to start pouring.

"Jesus!" he screeched, as half a pitcher of ice water sloshed into his lap. He jumped up, but it was too late—a large dark spot was quickly spreading across the front of his pants.

"Oh, I'm so sorry!" the waitress cried, slipping out of the fake Irish brogue she'd adopted for the rest of their meal. "Here, let me—" She leaned toward him to start patting him down with a napkin, but Jackson squirmed away.

"I got it," he snapped. Sliding out of the booth. "Miranda, I've got to—"

"Go," she urged him, marveling at how quickly her perfect date could go south. Not that it was a surprise. The perfection of the afternoon had seemed bizarre. It was all too unbelievably smooth and perfect to be true. This comedy of errors, on the other hand, was totally in keeping with the way Miranda's life usually went. "I think the bathroom's that way." She pointed, but he was already gone. *He'll come back in a minute*, she assured herself, but she couldn't make herself believe it.

"Clumsy waitress, eh?" a familiar voice chuckled from the next booth over. Miranda peeked her head over the top of her booth to see Kane staring up at her. He shook his head. "It's so hard to find good help these days."

As always, she felt an unmitigated blast of joy at seeing him—so it took her a moment to wonder at his presence. "What are you doing here?" she finally asked.

"You're not answering your phone," he pointed out.

"I'm on a *date*."

He smirked. "Yeah. I caught that. How's it going?"

"It's going great," she boasted. "Fantastically. Best date I ever had." Mostly because all her other dates had sucked. But that wasn't the point. The point was to let Kane know that he wasn't welcome to crash this one.

Even if, secretly, possibly, he was.

"I was afraid of that."

"Afraid of what? That I'd actually have a good time?" Dare she allow herself to hope that he was jealous? *Stop*, she instructed herself. *It doesn't matter. I'm here with Jackson.* Jackson was cute, smart, sweet, and, though he wasn't Kane, he had one important thing going for him that Kane didn't: He wanted to be with Miranda.

"He's bad news," Kane told her. "Don't trust him. I'd leave now, if I were you, now that I've given you the chance."

"Now that you've . . . ?" The pieces fell into place: the suddenly clumsy waitress. The fact that Kane just *happened* to be sitting at the next table. Maybe even the bartender who'd randomly thrown them out of the bar. "Are you trying to ruin my life? Or just my night?"

"Just trying to help," Kane said. "Get away from him. He's—uh-oh. Don't tell him I was here." Before she could say anything else, Kane had ducked out of the booth and disappeared into a corridor. And then Jackson was back.

"Well, I've gone from soggy to damp," Jackson said ruefully, sliding back into his seat. "So that's an improvement. Still, maybe after dinner we could stop by my room, just to grab a change of clothes. If you're up for it, I mean."

It didn't make any sense. This was Kane's friend; Kane was the one who'd introduced them. He'd vouched for Jackson. And now he was trying to torpedo the date? It was as if he was jealous, but he *couldn't* be jealous. And it didn't matter either way. It didn't matter what his reasoning was. She'd wasted enough of her time worrying about Kane—this was her chance to actually be happy, even if it was just for the night. She wasn't going to screw it up. "Sure, as soon as we're done here, we should definitely hit your room so you can get out of those wet pants." She giggled as they both realized the implications of what she'd just said. They weren't altogether unintentional.

Miranda was about to continue, to tell Jackson about the strange encounter she'd had while he was drying off, so that they could laugh about and then dismiss Kane's ludicrous scheming. But Kane had asked her not to say anything.

And though she didn't owe him anything, didn't care

what he wanted, and refused to spend another moment thinking about him, she kept her mouth shut.

Her skin was so soft.

Everything about her was perfect. That sweet, lilting voice that sang whenever she spoke. Her hair, which fell through his fingers like it had no substance, no weight, but was made of golden light. Her lips, which were now pressed against his neck, and her fingers, which crawled down his bare chest and massaged his back. Her pale blue eyes, closed now, shaded by delicate eyelids rimmed by eyelashes so light, they were nearly invisible.

But it was her skin that Reed loved the most. The cheap hotel sheets were scratchy, but her pale, creamy skin was unbelievably soft and smooth, as if it had never been exposed to the outside world. Reed loved the way it felt against his cheek, his lips, his fingertips, his body—always wondering how something that delicately perfect could exist. And how it could be within his grasp.

She moaned softly, and shivered as he traced his fingers lightly down the small of her back. He grabbed her waist, gently tipping her onto her back and rolling on top of her, so their chests breathed together and their lips met. He supported his weight on his elbows, so as not to crush her, and stared down at her.

Whatever doubts he'd had at the beginning, whatever guilt he'd struggled with, he was past that now. He had no regrets.

"Do you . . . do you want to?" she whispered suddenly, her eyes still closed.

"Want to what?" He kissed her cheek, then her forehead, her nose, and, finally, her lips.

"You know." She opened her eyes. A tear was pooling in one of the corners. "I don't know if you brought . . . protection." It sounded like she had to choke the word out. "But if you did, maybe we should—"

Reed rolled off of her and propped himself up on his side. "Where's this coming from?"

Beth tucked a strand of hair behind her ear and, instead of turning to face him, stayed on her back, staring up at the cracked ceiling. "I know I said I didn't want to, not yet, but that was before . . ."

"Before what?" When she didn't answer, he sat up, and pulled her up too. "Before *what*?"

"You're just really good to me, and I thought—" She took his hand in hers. "I want to make you happy."

"You think *this* will make me happy?" he asked incredulously, his voice rising. "You're doing this as if—as if you owe me something? Do you think I'm that kind of guy? That I'd ever want you to—"

"Are you mad?" Her voice sounded like a child's.

"Of course not!" He forced himself to stop and take a few deep breaths. "I just don't get it. Why would you think . . . I told you I'd wait. I told you I didn't care."

"I know. But . . ."

She didn't need to say it out loud. He got it: She hadn't believed him.

Reed didn't know much about Beth's past, so he didn't know who had screwed her over so badly, or how. But something must have happened to make her so unwilling to trust that someone would wait for her.

"Why now?" he asked. "Why tonight?"

"Because I don't deserve you," she admitted. "And I just thought maybe . . . I don't know." She threw herself back down on the bed, face first, her head buried in her arms. "I don't get why you want . . . I don't know why anyone would want to be with me," she mumbled, her voice muffled by the sheets. Her body trembled, and Reed wondered if she was crying.

It didn't make sense. He was the stoner. The dumbass. The loser. She was smart, beautiful, perfect. Grace's princess. He was the one who didn't belong in the picture, who was undeserving. How could someone so smart miss something so obvious?

"Come on," he said. She didn't sit up, just shook her head, still hiding her face as if afraid to show him her tears. "Come on," he repeated. "For me."

Finally, she lifted her head, wiping clumsily at her tears like a little kid. Her makeup smeared across her face. "Where?"

"You'll see."

He took her by the hand and led her out of the room, down the hall to the elevators and, when they'd stepped inside, pressed the button for the top floor. Moments later they stepped out onto an identical hallway, and Reed, once again leading the way, guided Beth down to the opposite end and through a half-hidden door.

"I did a little exploring," Reed explained as they entered the dark, cramped stairwell, though she hadn't asked, or even spoken since they'd left the room. "Found something I thought you'd like." They climbed up two flights of stairs, pushed through a heavy door at the top, and found themselves standing on the roof, surrounded by the tall silhouettes of the Camelot's fake turrets. "Come on," he urged Beth, leading her toward the edge. She followed as if she'd lost all momentum of her own—as if, were he to let go, she would stand motionless until given another command.

They stood at the rim of the roof, the lights of Vegas spread out beneath them like stolen gems spilled onto a sheet of black velvet. A small smile crept onto Beth's face, still streaked with mascara-stained tears.

"Remember that first day, on the crater?" Reed asked.

She nodded. They had hiked up to the top and, surrounded by miles of empty desert wilderness, had decided to take a chance. Together. Reed realized he was breathing quickly and tried to calm himself down. He'd been steeling himself to do this at some point in the weekend—but now that he was actually here, and the words he'd never said before were ready to come out, he could barely speak. "Beth, since then, being with you—it's not what I expected. It's—" He hadn't rehearsed; that would have been lame. But now that he was here, he almost wished he'd prepared something to say. When he wrote a song, the words always came pouring out. But actually *talking* about the way he felt—especially to someone else—was different. It was almost impossible.

He had to try.

"I used to think it was just something people said, you know? Some obligation, but it didn't mean anything." He knew he wasn't making much sense, but it was a place to start, and she was listening. "I didn't care. And when I met you, I didn't care about anything. And then . . ." He put his arms around her shoulders, resting his hands loosely at the nape of her neck. "Now. It's different. You know?"

"I don't . . . I don't get what you're trying to say," Beth said slowly, her face pale. "Are you breaking up with me?"

"No. No!" This was going all wrong. Reed wished

he'd had a joint ahead of time, because then he wouldn't care so much and it wouldn't matter if it came out wrong. But then, it wouldn't have mattered at all—that's how it had always been, before her.

Sober was hard, but if he was going to do this—do this and *mean* it—it was necessary.

"I'm trying to tell you—" He couldn't look at her while he was saying it, so he turned to face the endless spread of lights, grasping her hand as he waited for the words to come. "I think . . . I love you."

Silence.

"Beth. I love you." It was easier this time. There was no more doubt.

But she didn't say anything. Finally, he dared to look at her—and she seemed so terrified, so appalled, that he quickly looked away.

"You can't," she whispered. "Take it back."

But Reed couldn't. "I love you," he said again.

She touched his cheek, gently, with that impossibly soft skin. "Reed . . ." He waited for her to say it back, to say *anything*. But instead, she let out a loud, anguished sob—and bolted.

"Beth!"

But she didn't hesitate, or look back. She raced across the roof, flung the door open and, just like that, she was gone.

chapter eight

EVEN AFTER THEY'D STEPPED OUTSIDE THE BUILD-
ing and into the relatively quiet night, Harper imagined
she could still hear the oversynthesized chords of the love
song echoing in her ears. It made the awkward silence a
little easier to take.

"So," Adam finally said.

"So."

About a foot of distance lay between them, which
seemed safest. Adam leaned against the wall of the hotel,
the flashing Elvis billboard casting a series of red and
gold lights across his face. He watched her as if expecting
something.

She knew she was supposed to start. After all, she'd been the one to push him away. It was just that now she couldn't quite remember why.

He raised an arm and leaned it against the wall, his biceps bulging with even the small movement. And Harper imagined what it would feel like to have those biceps encircling her; to have free range to stroke his arms and lean against his chest and—

So that, obviously, was problem number one. Could she handle having him in her life without having *all* of him? It had been hard enough before, when all she'd had was her imagination. Now she had memories, and they were more insistent. They were more real.

But it had never been about that, or only that. It had been about Adam, the only person she could truly count on, the one who knew every detail of her past and was present in every dream of her future. She'd been miserable these last few months, and now that pain seemed pointless, the time wasted.

"You miss me," Adam prompted, when it became obvious that she wasn't going to begin.

Harper attempted a blasé expression. "You can be useful," she told him. "Occasionally."

Adam took a step toward her. "So, does that mean we can end this thing?" he asked casually.

Harper shrugged. "I guess."

"And you and me . . ."

"Yeah." Harper allowed herself a smile. "We're okay." That was the great thing about being friends with guys: They didn't need any of that sappy "I'm so sorry," "No, *I'm* so sorry" crap. They could just shrug and move on. Move forward.

Now Harper took a step, and they met in the middle. She wanted to wait for Adam to move first, but her patience ran short, and she threw her arms around his waist, pressing her head against his chest, feeling like she had come home. Adam wrapped her into a tight bear hug, his cheek pressed against the top of her head.

"I really did miss you," she murmured, thinking it would be too soft for him to hear.

"I know," he whispered back. Then, louder, in a more teasing voice, "You know you can't live without me."

No, she couldn't.

When they finally broke from the hug, he didn't release her, just loosened his arms enough that she could lean away from his body and look up at him. The Vegas night was lit by enough neon to see every chiseled feature of his face in sharp relief, from his squarish, dimpled chin to his regal brow line and deep-set eyes. But Harper barely noticed any of that; he wasn't an assemblage of perfect pieces. He was just her best friend. "Adam, I—"

He kissed her.

Not on the forehead, not on the cheek. On the lips.

And not slowly, not gently, but hard, desperate, hungry. She closed her eyes and sucked his lower lip, nearly gasping as his tongue crept past her teeth and met hers, his breathing sped up, hers nearly stopped, and she drank him in. He tasted the same.

And then it was over, and just as roughly as he'd grabbed her, he pushed her away.

"What was—?" Harper, still stunned—and already missing his touch—tried to catch her breath.

"I don't know. I don't know." Adam was panting, leaning his fists against the wall. "I'm sorry, I don't—"

"You said you didn't want that. This," Harper reminded him. "You said friends." He couldn't trust her enough for a relationship, he'd told her. Things would get too messy, and they would lose each other again.

"I know what I said!" he snapped. Then he pressed a hand to his forehead. "I'm sorry. I don't . . . you were there, and it just felt . . ."

"Yeah." She wanted to touch him, but—she didn't want to touch him, not if it meant scaring him away. "We can just . . . forget it. If you want." *No, no, no*, she pleaded silently. *Say no*.

"Maybe. But . . ."

"But?" She tried to keep the tinge of hope out of her voice.

Harper leaned against the wall next to him, their faces once again only inches apart.

"If we did this—I mean, if we were going to do this, we'd have to decide," Adam said. "You know? It can't be . . ."

"Casual."

He took her hand, then dropped it a moment later and shoved his hands in his pockets. "I missed you too, Gracie. And I—I *miss* you. But when we were together, like that, it just . . ."

"I know."

"Everything got so fucked up."

Because of me, Harper thought. Adam was kind enough not to say it; but she knew he was thinking it too. He had to be. "Maybe we should just . . . forget it. Or, take some time."

"Yeah." He nodded to himself. "Maybe. That would be good. But . . ." He took her hand again, and this time, he pressed it to his chest, then tugged her toward him. Their lips nearly met when, with all the strength she could muster, Harper pushed him away. It nearly wasn't enough.

"No," she said firmly. "You should go."

"This could be the right thing," Adam told her. "Maybe I was wrong before, and this—maybe it could work."

She wanted to stay—she wanted to kiss him again, to make him remember what he was missing and convince him that he needed it as much as she did. But if he wasn't sure yet, then she couldn't risk it. If she let him back in and he changed his mind again—it would be too hard. For both of them.

Restraint wasn't in Harper's repertoire. But she could try. "You need to know," she told him. "You need to be sure."

"What if I told you I was sure?"

"Then you'd be lying."

He let out a pained laugh. "I hate that you know me like this."

"You love it."

"Yeah." He reached over and twisted his finger through her hair. "What time is it?"

She checked her cell. "Almost nine." Strange, it seemed later.

"Okay. You think. I'll think. And we'll meet later—"

"At midnight," Harper suggested. "But before you go, there's something . . . you need to know. . . ." She wanted to tell him her secret—to tell him the truth about Kaia, and the accident. He deserved to know who she really was, and he deserved the chance to push her away.

And maybe . . . he deserved the chance to forgive.

"What?" he asked, after a long pause.

But she couldn't do it. She would, she promised herself, but only when she knew what was at stake. If he decided that he needed her as much as she needed him, then she would know she could trust him to keep her secret. Maybe she could even trust him not to leave her. But it was too soon—he was still unsure of what he wanted. So she couldn't take the risk. "Nothing," she said quickly. "Save it for midnight."

"Where?"

Harper scanned the skyline, and her gaze stumbled over the towering replica of the Empire State Building. It reminded her of some movie—some lame romantic comedy, probably, but certainly one with a happy ending. And she could use that kind of luck. She pointed. "Up there, on the roof. Whatever you decide."

"I'll be there," he promised. "And Harper . . ." He gripped her shoulders. "Whatever happens next, we need to make it work. Because this friendship—you . . ."

"I know," she assured him. "You don't have to say it."

"Yes, I do." He hugged her again, his strong arms locking her into the embrace. "This friendship is everything, Gracie. I'm not losing you again."

Miranda finished the meal still hungry, so she allowed Jackson to talk her into dessert: a massive ice-cream sundae with three scoops of chocolate chip ice cream, a hearty helping of chocolate hazelnut sauce topped by two cherries, all piled atop a freshly baked double fudge brownie.

Miranda had promised herself she would only have a couple bites—but it was already half gone.

"This is amazing," she moaned as another gulp of icy sweetness slid down her throat. And she wasn't just talking about the food. Kane's bizarre interruptions aside, the night had gone remarkably well. It was the kind of date other people had: normal, pleasant, engrossing and, hopefully, all leading up to a goodnight kiss. Or more.

This wasn't the way Miranda's life usually went, but it was, after all, almost her birthday. Maybe the universe was giving her a present.

"*You're* amazing," Jackson told her, and scooped his spoon into the heaping sundae, then brought it to her lips. She sucked down another mouthful and, smiling at him, licked her lips. When Harper did that kind of thing, she always made it look incredibly sexy. Miranda suspected she just looked like a messy eater—but then, that's what she was, so it couldn't be helped. "Uh, you've still got a little on your face. . . ."

"Where?" Miranda asked, turning red. She slid her napkin across her lips and looked up at him. "Better?"

Jackson laughed. "Not really. There's still a little, just above your lips—no, not there—no, to the left . . . here." He leaned across the table and gave her such a soft, brief kiss that she could almost believe she'd imagined it.

"Mmmm," he said, licking his own lips with a satisfied grin. "Sweet."

Miranda didn't know what to do. She brushed her fingers against her lips, as if to check that the smear of ice cream was really gone—or to find some trace evidence of his kiss. Her fingertips tingled.

They stared at each other, Miranda blushing and Jackson playing with the peace sign that hung on a chain around his neck. "You wanna get out of here?" Jackson finally said. "We could . . . go somewhere."

From the burning sensation in her cheeks, Miranda guessed that they had just turned from pale pink to fire engine red. But Jackson didn't seem to care. "I guess," she told him. "I'd like that."

Jackson gestured to the waitress that she should bring over the bill, but when she returned, she wasn't alone. "This gentleman would like to speak with you," she said, stepping aside to make way for a short, squat guy in a security guard uniform. He pointed at Jackson's backpack.

"Open the bag for me, sir."

Jackson stood up, but made no motion toward his backpack. "What's this about?"

"I said, open the bag, *sir*. Or I'll open it for you."

"You can't just come here and—"

The security guy lunged for the bag and ripped it open before Jackson could stop him. He plunged his hand inside and pulled out a stack of candy bars and several plastic bags filled with green flakes. It looked like oregano. But Miranda knew it wasn't.

Jackson did a 180, dropping the offended bravado and starting to whine. "Look, man, give me a break, it's just my private stash, and I'm just trying to have a good time here—"

The security guard shook his head and waved the baggie in his face. "I don't think so, kid. You got a lot of shit in here. This looks like intent to distribute, to me. And you know what that means."

Miranda sat dumbstruck as the long arm of the law—or, in this case, the short, hairy arm—reached out, grabbed her date, and dragged him out of the restaurant, backpack and all. "Babe, I'm sorry!" Jackson cried as they hustled him away. "I'll call you. . . ."

In a moment he was gone, and she was left alone at an empty table, waiting for the check—which she would now have to cover herself. The whole restaurant was staring at her like she'd just turned green and sprouted antennae. "Happy birthday to me," she muttered.

"It's not midnight yet," a voice pointed out. "There's still time for things to pick up."

"Did you do this?" she asked as Kane slid into the seat across from her, an even smugger than usual grin painted across his face. "Are you fucking kidding me? *Did you do this?*"

She'd never been so angry with him—she'd never been angry at him at all, in fact, since usually his careless smirk and halfhearted apologies charmed the emotion out of her before it had a chance to take root. But charm could only go so far.

"It was for your own good, Stevens."

"Oh, really?" The sarcasm felt good, like she was in control again. And when he flinched at the cool anger in her voice, that was even better. "And how exactly do you figure that?"

"He was a dealer, Stevens."

"So you got him arrested?" It's not that Miranda wanted to date a drug dealer—and, she had to admit, there was a ring of truth in Kane's words, especially given what she'd just seen of his supply—but still, he hadn't seemed like a bad guy. And he'd kissed her.

"The security guard's a friend of mine," Kane explained. "He'll take him outside, give him a good scare, confiscate his stash, then let him go. Don't worry about him—he's not worth your time."

"What do you know?" she retorted.

"I know he has a girlfriend."

"You're lying."

"No."

It was like getting punched in the stomach. "Oh." She sank back in her seat, stared up at the ceiling, and wondered how she could have been so stupid.

"I didn't know," Kane said. "Not at first, and then—it was too late."

"Uh-huh." She'd been so excited, imagining that a cute college guy might actually be interested. And what did he turn out to be? A drug dealer with a girlfriend. Killing time. "So, what? He was just using me or something?" Why even bother, Miranda wondered. It's not like she was hot—it's not like this city wasn't filled with beautiful women. Why pick on Miranda, unless he just got some sadistic joy out of stringing her along and watching her get her pathetic little hopes up? "So this was all some kind of game?" she guessed bitterly, trying to make her lower lip stop trembling. She didn't want Kane to know how close she was to tears. "Get the pathetic loser to fall for him, go back to his room, and then—?"

"No, that's not it," Kane said quickly. He slid across to the other side of the booth and put an arm around her. "He really liked you. He did." But she could hear the lie in his words. "He wasn't good enough for you, Stevens."

"I guess no one is," Miranda spit out. "Maybe *that's* my problem. That's why I'm always ending up alone. I'm just too fabulous, right?" She closed her eyes and pressed a hand across her face, hoping he wouldn't notice her sniffling. "I'm not going to thank you, you know," she informed him, trying to sound strong.

"Wouldn't expect you to."

"You don't need to pull asinine stunts like that just to rescue me from my own idiocy. I'm a big girl."

"The biggest. Elephantine."

A giggle sputtered out through her tears. "Shut up."

"I often say to myself, 'That Miranda, she is truly an Amazonian giant among men. Doesn't need any help from anyone, and too big to fit inside normal-size buildings. It's—'"

"*Shut up*," she repeated, laughing and elbowing him in the side.

"That's better." He gave her a soft shove back. "So what now?"

Miranda tried to gather herself together. She took a deep breath. "I guess I should call Harper and tell her the date . . . ended early. She'll probably want to hang out." She reached for her phone, but he caught her wrist.

"What's your hurry?"

"You have a better idea?" she asked. He hadn't yet let go of her wrist.

"Always. We get out of here, and I make things up to you." He raised an eyebrow. "Think you'll be able to forgive me?"

"Maybe," she allowed. "If you behave."

The charming smile returned with a vengeance. "Not a chance."

She didn't know what she was doing or where she was going, she just knew that she had to get away. He couldn't be in love with her. He *couldn't.*

Beth burst through the doors of the hotel and huddled under the front awning, shaking, barely aware of the tears streaming down her face. She curled her hands into fists, digging her nails into her palms, as if the pain would make things clearer. It didn't. He was in love with her.

She had killed his girlfriend.

He was in love with her.

She was a murderer.

As soon as the words were out of his mouth, Beth had known that her time was up. She had to confess everything. But it was too hard.

She hated herself for her weakness, and for her terror. Was she in love with him, too?

She didn't allow herself to wonder.

A tall, too-skinny guy wandered up to her and, though she couldn't face anyone, she didn't have the will to turn away. "No one that pretty should be that sad," he told her.

Beth took a closer look at his familiar face. It was the guy she'd seen earlier, with Kane. As if the night wasn't bad enough. "Are you staying here?" *Or just following me?*

"Looking for someone," the guy muttered. "But she's not here. Lucky I found you."

"Can you just leave me alone?" Beth wasn't even sure she meant it. At least talking to him was helping to drive Reed's words out of her mind. *I love you.* How could she believe that when she hated herself so much? Who could ever love her, once they knew what she really was?

"Whatever. But first." He reached into his pocket and pulled out a lumpy, misshapen joint. "Pigs got everything else, but this one's special. Guaranteed to brighten your night. My treat."

Common sense would tell her not to accept drugs from strangers—especially strangers who associated with Kane. But common sense had gone to sleep for the night, and Beth needed something to get her through the next minute, and the one after that. She reached for the joint. The guy handed it to her, then, as she turned to go, he grabbed her other hand, squeezing tight. "Not so fast. I'm not done with you."

Whatever he was about to do, she deserved worse. So she didn't pull back, didn't scream, didn't show a hint of fear. She wasn't feeling any. She felt dead inside, flat and hopeless. Her mind flashed a danger sign, but her body and her emotions refused to react. Whatever happened, would happen.

The guy reached into his pocket again, and Beth saw a glint of metal.

He pulled out a lighter, stuck the joint between her

lips, and lit the tip. "Enjoy the night," he said, already walking away. "Someone should."

She drew in deep, gulping down the bitter smoke. And again. A burning cloud filled her lungs, searing her insides, and it almost made her smile. Because she knew that soon the cloudy haze would descend and she wouldn't have to worry about anything anymore, not for a long while.

Her muscles went loose as her senses intensified, and the world seemed to get stronger and brighter with every breath. The joint burned out, but the lights and colors around her continued to brighten, until the world seemed to pulse with a rippling energy that drew the earth and sky together into a living creature poised to consume her.

This was new. And it felt wrong.

Beth turned to look for Kane's friend, but he was gone, disappeared into the crowd, and as she turned in a slow circle searching for him, she found she couldn't stop, and her spinning grew faster and faster until she was whirling wildly, her hands outstretched and her face tipped up to the sky. She stumbled as the ground tilted toward her, then rolled away, and as she flung her arms out for balance, she saw an impossible trail of blue tracing through the air following her movements. Suddenly the colors were everywhere, bursting out of people's heads like a Crayola explosion, wiggling and swirling through the air until mixing into a thick, heavy, mud-colored fog that pressed down upon her until she fell to the ground under its weight.

She pressed herself against the wall, crawling, almost slithering, around the corner, out of sight, hiding from whatever was out there, watching, waiting. And in the darkness of the alley, she curled into a tight ball, pressing her legs against her chest and digging her chin into them, trying to think. But her thoughts kept bobbing to the surface and dipping below again, just before she could pluck them away . . . they were too fast, she was too slow.

This isn't pot.

He loves me.

I killed her.

What if they find me?

What is this?

What's happening to me?

What will happen to me?

Help . . .

That was the right thought, the important one, the one she should turn into words and scream aloud before she got dragged under, but it was so hard to focus, and before she could speak, the idea drifted away.

So did she.

chapter nine

IT WAS ALL CLEAR TO HIM NOW.

Standing so close to Harper, breathing in her perfume, it had been too hard to think rationally. But a couple hours of wandering the streets had given Adam everything he needed to be certain.

It was a frightening choice. Sticking to friendship would be the safe move, that much was obvious. But what if Harper was supposed to be the one?

Not that Adam believed in that cheesy shit. That was for girls, long-distance commercials, and Valentine's Day. Still, he couldn't forget how happy he'd been for those few weeks they were together, and how right it had felt to hold her again.

But on the other hand—and it seemed there was always another hand—coming together had nearly blown them apart for good. He had meant what he'd told her in the hospital, months before: He loved her, he forgave her, but he wasn't ready to trust her. He couldn't force himself to forget the lies she'd told and the pain she'd caused. She'd manipulated him and destroyed his relationship with Beth, all to get what she wanted.

And, despite how easy it was to believe otherwise when looking into her eyes, he suspected she'd be willing to do it all over again.

Within minutes of leaving her side, he'd known exactly what to do. An hour later, he'd changed his mind, just as sure that he was right. Eventually, he'd gone back to the hotel room—half hoping to run into Kane or Miranda, *someone* he could ask for advice, even though he knew that no one could help. Not with this. The room had been empty, and he lay down on the bed, closed his eyes, and tried to decide what he wanted.

Was it more important to be happy? Or to protect himself from being miserable?

It was almost midnight, and he finally knew the

answer. He just didn't know what Harper would do when she heard it.

He had intended to walk to their rendezvous point— the New York–New York hotel, with its neon and plaster skyline, was less than a mile away. But now it was too late for that. So instead he was forced to wait in front of the hotel for the taxi, shifting his weight back and forth, nervously wondering how the night would end.

If he hadn't been looking for something, anything, to take his mind off of things, he might never have heard the noise, a soft, muffled whimpering, like an injured animal. He almost certainly wouldn't have gone in search of its source. And so he would never have discovered the girl huddled in the alley, dirty-blond hair spilling in a thick curtain around her face, her hands wrapped around her knees. She was rocking back and forth, muttering the same phrase over and over again, until the words blended together into a string of nonsense syllables.

"I did it. I did it. I didit. I didit. IdiditIdiditIdidit . . ."

He should have recognized the voice, or the hair, or the way her fingers trembled as they clasped her lower legs and pulled them tighter to her chest. But it wasn't until he put a hand on her shoulder, leaned down, and asked if she was all right that the girl tilted her head up, just a bit, but just enough, for him to understand.

"Oh my God." Adam staggered backward with the shock. "Beth? What happened? Are you . . . okay?" He was almost afraid to hear the answer to the first question. The answer to the second was pointlessly obvious.

"Reed?" she whispered.

"It's Adam." The kernel of terror within him began to blossom.

She stared up at him and squinted as if she didn't recognize him. "What's going on? What are you what am I you need to go. I did it I did it I did it . . ."

Her pupils were overdilated, and her whole body was shaking. "Hey. Shhh, calm down." He put his arms around her and tried to help her stand up. "It's going to be okay." But was it? "Come on, let's get you up."

She resisted at first, curling tighter into herself, her muscles straining against his touch. Then, suddenly, all the tension flooded out of her, and she sagged in his arms. He stood, and she leaned against him, still conscious but no longer trembling. Her face was streaked with tears. "Is this what it was like for her?" she asked him plaintively, tugging at his collar. "Oh God, did I do this to her? How could I do this?"

"I don't understand," Adam said gently, but she didn't seem to hear him.

"I did it. I deserve it. Ohgodohgodohgodohgod—" Her voice broke off into a heaving sob, and she buried her head in his shoulder. He stroked her hair and tried not to panic. Should he call 911? Should he find a doctor, get her to a hospital? Or just inside and up to the room? She didn't seem hurt, but—something was obviously wrong. Seriously wrong.

Upstairs, he decided. Calm her down, figure out what's happening, and then deal with it.

"It's okay, I'm here," he whispered, stroking her hair and trying to calm her sobs. He guided her into the lobby and toward the elevator bank, not even noticing the crowd's curious stares. He didn't have the mental space to worry about anything now except for Beth, and making sure she was okay.

"Where are we going?" she whispered. "Where are you taking me?"

"Somewhere safe," he promised. The room was still empty. He led her inside and sat her down on the bed. She didn't curl up again, or lie down. She just sat where he'd placed her, still clinging to him. He sat down beside her and gathered her in his arms.

"Don't hate me," she begged. "Not you, too. Please."

"Of course not." He kissed the top of her head. "I could never hate you."

"Don't leave me."

"I won't."

"I'm sorry for before," she said. "I shouldn't have let

you say it. I should never have let you. And then I left. You should have left me."

"Don't worry." Adam wasn't even sure she knew who he was, much less what she was saying. "Don't apologize."

"But *I'm sorry!*" she wailed.

"I forgive you. I do. For everything."

"I love you, too," she said, throwing her arms around his neck and laying her head against his chest. "I should have said it. I love you, too."

He didn't know what to do, so he held her until she stopped crying. And when she did, he still held her, and listened intently to her shallow but even breaths, wishing that he could save her from whatever was tearing her apart.

He didn't notice the time passing, and when his cell phone rang, again and again, he barely heard it. His world had narrowed to a single point, and a single mission: protecting Beth.

She needed him. And for now, that was all that mattered.

It wasn't like him to be late.

The balcony atop the fake Empire State Building was nearly empty this time of night, and Harper leaned against the railing looking out over the lights, wondering.

She dialed his number again, but he still didn't pick up.

Maybe something happened to him, she thought. But she knew nothing had. He had obviously made his decision, and couldn't even be bothered to tell her to her face. *Maybe there's still a chance*, she told herself. *It's possible.*

But he was almost an hour late. This was Vegas, a town full of dreamers hoping that their big win would come through despite million-to-one odds. They stayed at the table hour after hour, night after night, waiting for their luck to turn.

Harper was a realist; she knew when to fold.

She just couldn't bring herself to leave—because giving up would mean admitting that Adam didn't want her, that he didn't even think enough of her to explain why. So much for the friendship he refused to lose; so much for the two of them being all that mattered.

The city twinkled below her, and Harper wondered what the view might be like from the real Empire State Building, so much taller than this lame cardboard copy. She'd only seen it in movies, but Kaia, who never tired of reminiscing about her hometown, had once tried to describe it. "You can imagine you're standing at the edge of the world," she had said. By day, you would see Central Park in one direction—and here, thanks to Kaia's descriptions, Harper always imagined an overgrown jungle brimming with out-of-work artists, horny couples, and needle junkies. From the other end, Kaia claimed, you could see across the whole island of Manhattan, down to its narrow tip and beyond. "You can even see *Brooklyn*," Kaia had said in a hushed voice, as if Brooklyn were an exotic foreign land of hidden wonders.

But the view during the day was nothing compared with the view at night, when the city lit up and you could chart the lives of a million people by the flickering and streaming of an infinity of lights.

Standing here in the dark, bracing against the wind and watching the neon flash and shimmer, it was easy to imagine she was thousands of miles away, somewhere *real*. She thought that if she tried hard enough, she could probably convince herself that Kaia was standing next to her in the darkness. But Harper was still a realist—and Kaia was still dead.

"He's not coming," she said aloud, testing out the sound of the words. She knew she should leave and get on with her night—but that would mean getting on with her *life*. Without Adam. And she wasn't ready for that.

"He's not coming," she said again, louder.

There was no one there to hear her, and no one to know that she decided not to leave. Not yet. Long ago, Adam had asked her to trust him, and to trust their friendship. She would wait, just a little longer.

Maybe she was wrong, and he hadn't abandoned her.

Maybe he was coming after all. So she held on to the railing, looked out at the landscape that glittered like a desert sky, and waited.

If he cared about her at all, he would come.

The world faded in.

Bright seeped into shadow, light searing her eyes and then disappearing into a dark cloud. She felt like she was flying. She felt like she was sailing. She felt like she was drowning.

She felt still and safe, wrapped in his arms.

"Beth."

My name. But the voice was distant, and her words were lost.

"Beth!"

She smiled, and fingers pressed against her lips. Her fingers, warm and damp. His fingers on her forehead.

Hello? But she spoke only in her head, the words flashing against her brain, bright gold against a deep grey emptiness. *Don't go.*

Silence, and the fear overtook her. Alone, she would float away. No one to keep her safe, no one to tie her down, free to fly, free to crash. Crash—and burn, as the car had burned.

As her head burned, raging hot, flames licking her body and, alone, no one would notice, no one would save her and she would burn.

"Beth . . ."

But she wasn't alone. He was still there. His arms. His heartbeat. His face, too bright for her to see. His voice, familiar, indistinct. She had lost his name, lost herself, but he would find her. He would keep her safe.

And the world faded out.

"That is *disgusting*!" Miranda cried, puckering her cheeks and reaching frantically for a glass of water. She took a swig, then another to wash the taste of Kane's scotch out of her mouth. "You can't drink that."

"Not only will I drink it, but for your viewing pleasure, I'll drink it in a single gulp." Kane had whisked her out of the restaurant and taken her to an enormous bar that looked like the inside of an airport terminal. What it lacked in ambiance, it made up for in mug size.

"Not possible," Miranda decreed, glancing skeptically at Kane's oversize glass filled with Glenlivet aged to taste-bud-killing perfection.

"Wanna bet?"

Miranda nodded. "I win, you answer a question. Any question."

Kane rolled his eyes. "Remind me to bet you more often. And if I win . . . well, since you've chosen truth, I guess I'll take dare."

"Dare me to what?"

"To be decided later. After I win. You in?"

Miranda glanced down at the glass again, then up at his cocksure face. "I'm in."

Kane shrugged. "Your funeral." He slapped his palm down on the table and, with his other hand, grabbed the glass, tipped his head back, and poured the scotch down his throat. Just before the glass emptied, a spasm of coughing wracked his body, and he spit out the final mouthful—right in Miranda's face.

"I was wrong," she said wryly as she dried herself off with a soggy napkin. "There is something more disgusting than *drinking* scotch."

"I don't get it," Kane mumbled.

"Well, when you spit liquor in someone's face, it is traditional to apologize," Miranda explained. "I know it's a difficult and foreign ritual to understand, but maybe you should just go with it—"

"No, I mean, I never lose," he complained. "There must be something wrong with this glass. And you distracted me, Stevens."

"Yes, I've oft been told that my beauty is enough to drive men to distraction," she joked. "Now, back to business. The question."

Kane sighed and leaned back in his chair, still looking confused. "Fire away."

Under ordinary circumstances, she wouldn't have

had the nerve, but she was a little tipsy and even more exhausted, and the combination made her brave. "Why'd you really ruin my date?"

"I told you already, Stevens, the guy was a jerk—"

"Yes, but what made that your problem? I'm sure you've got plenty of things you could have been doing tonight. Why waste your time rescuing me from the dangers of a three-course meal?"

"I don't know what you want me to say," he shot back. "I already told you everything."

"Were you . . . jealous?"

Kane leaned forward, and the sulky expression melted away. His eyes narrowed, and his lips pulled back to reveal gleaming white teeth; everything about the look screamed *challenge*. "And what if I was?"

"Well . . ." She didn't have an answer for that one. In her mind, she hadn't gotten past asking the question. "I don't . . . uh . . ."

"That's what I thought." He looked down at his watch. "It's 12:58," he told her. "You know what that means."

"You have somewhere better to be?"

"It means it's officially tomorrow." He clinked her glass. "And you're officially eighteen. Happy birthday, Stevens. Ready for your present?"

"You didn't have to—"

But she stopped speaking, somehow knowing what

he was going to do before he did it. So when his face came toward her, she was expecting it, and when his lips touched hers, she was ready—but that couldn't keep her from getting swept away.

When Beth opened her eyes again, she was lying with her head on Adam's lap, and his arms were still around her. This time, she knew him. "Hey," she said weakly. "What happened?"

"Beth?" He peered down at her nervously, his face crinkled with concern. "Are you—do you know who I am?"

"Of course." She tried to sit up but, still a little woozy, fell back against his side. He held her steady, his grip firm. "How did I get here?" For a moment, she wondered if the last several months had been a long nightmare from which she was finally waking, safe in Adam's arms. But then she remembered—running away from Reed, talking to someone outside the hotel, taking . . . something.

It was all real. Her acts; her lies.

"I didn't know what happened to you. I found you in the alley," Adam said, sounding sick and broken. "And you were . . . it wasn't good."

"Nothing happened. I—I took something," Beth admitted. She rested the back of her hand against her throbbing forehead. "It was stupid. But I think . . . I think

I'm okay." She didn't feel okay. She felt weak and shaky, scared that if she didn't hold tight to each word, her thoughts would fly away again, stranding her in darkness and confusion. She couldn't go back there again.

"I was worried." Adam hugged her and pressed his cheek against the top of her head. The pressure felt like an iron barbell, but Beth didn't say anything. Pain or not, she liked knowing he was there. "You really scared me."

"I scared myself," she said, trying to laugh it off. But there was no relief in her voice. As her mind woke up, so did her memory. Not just of the night, but of the year—everything was equally sharp, as if it had all happened at the same time, was still happening. Adam calling her a slut. Harper tearing away everything that meant anything to her. Kaia sleeping with Adam. And the rage, the terrible rage that had swept through her and driven her to get revenge. Kaia's death. Reed's pain. Beth's lie.

It was all jumbled in her mind, screaming for attention, and a part of her longed to be back in the silent dark.

"Hey, what is it?" Adam stroked her face, and Beth realized she was crying. She shook her head, but didn't want to speak. She didn't know what would come out.

"I can't tell you," she whispered. "I can't tell anyone."

"You can tell me anything." He wiped away another tear from her cheek. "Is it Reed? Did he . . . do something?"

"No!" She jerked her face away from him. "It was me. I did . . . it doesn't matter now. I can't change anything."

"Maybe I can help."

Beth wanted to laugh. It was such a genuine offer, and such a pointless one. No one could help her, not now. No one could change what she'd done. She searched for the words that would convince him she was okay, so that he could go on with his night and stop showering her with even more care and attention that she didn't deserve. She knew it should only make her feel worse, and hated that it didn't.

In fact, he was helping just by being there. Holding her.

Then the room door swung open—and he let go.

"Harper!" he cried, pulling away from Beth and jumping to his feet. "Oh, shit!"

"It's lovely to see you, too," Harper drawled, her eyes skimming over Beth. They paused only for a second, but it was long enough. Beth could feel Harper's gaze slicing into her, peeling back all her layers until she was left exposed, naked, a shivering mass of raw pain. Harper's expression didn't change, and she moved on.

"I didn't mean that," Adam babbled, "I just meant, I was surprised to see you here—"

"Of course you were, since we were meeting up there," Harper pointed out. There was a strange note in her voice, Beth realized. Something almost human. Almost like . . .

pain. "Of course, I was surprised too . . . when you didn't show. But now I get it. You found a better option." She glared at Beth, her eyes narrowed and her teeth bared. "I didn't mean to interrupt—I'll just grab my jacket and get out of your hair."

"It's not like that, Harper, I just forgot, and—"

"Oh, *that* makes me feel a *lot* better. I'm standing up there like an idiot, waiting around, wondering if you were dead or something, because surely nothing but that would have kept you away, not after all that 'I'll never lose you again' *crap*."

"It wasn't crap," he said quietly.

"Good luck explaining that to your new girlfriend."

"That's not what's going on here," he insisted. "If you'd just give me a chance . . ." Beth expected him to move toward Harper, to do *something*, to force her to understand. But, instead, he just remained where he was, standing in front of the bed, his arms dangling loosely, one of them still brushing Beth's shoulder.

"I *gave* you a chance, and *you forgot*," Harper snapped.

"That's not fair!"

"You want to talk *fair*? You want to sit *here*, with *her*, and talk *fair*?"

"I don't even know why—"

"*STOP!*"

Beth wondered why they had both frozen and turned

to stare at her. Then she realized that she was the one who had screamed.

She couldn't stand it anymore; she couldn't ruin anything else with her lies and her cowardice. Everything was falling apart around her, and all this destruction, all this pain, it was because of her. She was done. Whatever had happened to her tonight, whatever she had taken, it had apparently had an effect. The terror was still there, but it was quieter, farther away, like her mind had sunk into a deep sea, and all the excuses, all the rationalizations, all the terrifying consequences were muffled by the dark, still waters.

She couldn't stand the twisted pain on Adam's face and the hatred in Harper's eyes, and she couldn't stand her own weakness. Not anymore.

"Adam's only here with me because I lied to him," Beth said. She barely spoke above a whisper, but there must have been something in her voice, or in her face, that commanded attention. Harper and Adam didn't interrupt; they barely moved. "If he knew the truth, he would—" She held her breath until the urge to sob passed. "He would hate me. He should hate me."

Adam still didn't speak, but he sat down again on the edge of the bed and took her hand, pressing it gently. Beth wanted to pull away, but speaking was hard enough. She couldn't move. "I lied to everyone. At least, I didn't tell the truth. Harper, I didn't tell you what happened, and now you think that it was your fault and I wanted to tell you, I did, because I am *so* sorry, even if that sounds stupid and small to say, it's true, I would do anything to change what happened, and if I could I would you have to believe that—"

"*Beth!* What the hell are you talking about?" Harper's hand was trembling, and Beth wondered if some part of her already knew.

It didn't make it any easier to say it out loud.

Beth allowed herself a moment to hope that speaking the truth would change everything: It would lift the cloud of guilt and let her breathe again. It would make up for what she'd done, *redeem* her so that she could enjoy her life again, allow herself to be happy. Maybe it wasn't just a cliché—maybe the truth really would set her free.

The moment passed. And it didn't matter, not anymore. Maybe nothing could save her now. But she had to try.

"I did it." In her mind, Beth delivered the news standing up, facing Harper with strength and dignity, a noble image of apology and disgrace. In reality, she pressed her face into her hands, her shoulders shaking with suppressed sobs, her nose stuffed, her cheeks wet, her voice muffled. "I spiked your drink, Harper. Before the speech. Before the accident." A wave of nausea swept through her, and she fell forward, her head spinning like she was going to pass out. Hunched over, she couldn't see Harper's reaction, didn't even know if Adam was still by her side. A dull, roaring thunder filled her ears. She couldn't even hear her own voice, and wasn't sure if she was speaking at all anymore, or whether she was confessing in her own head.

Maybe, she thought, as the world spun around her, fading in and out of a gray mist, this is all still just a dream.

Still, she forced the words out. Each one hurt, as if scraping a razor blade across her tongue on the way out.

"It was me."

She was no longer in the hotel room; she was back at school, a small pill warm in her hands, slipping into a mug of coffee. Dissolving. Disappearing.

"I did it."

She was on an empty road, standing over a scorched patch of ground, everything matted down. Burned out. Dead. She choked on an acrid stench of smoke and gasoline.

"I killed Kaia."

She stopped waiting to wake up.

chapter ten

FIRST CAME THE RELIEF.

Then came the rage.

Harper pressed herself flat against the wall, her nails digging into the cheap paint. She imagined they were digging into Beth's big blue Bambi eyes. She wanted to claw them out.

I didn't kill her. Every night as Harper went to sleep, she felt her hands on the steering wheel; she heard the crunch of metal, and the screams. But all of it had been a lie. It might as well have been Beth at that wheel; it might as well have been a gun in Beth's hand. *It wasn't my fault,* Harper thought in wonderment.

It was hers.

"I don't . . . I don't understand," Adam stuttered. Harper realized he was still sitting next to Beth on the bed—next to a killer. Their hands were clasped together. She held herself still, and tried to resist the urge to attack. "How could you . . . what do you mean you killed her?" Adam said. "You weren't even there, and—I thought Kaia was driving the car?"

"I was driving," Harper said flatly. The words had been trapped in her for so long, poisoning everything. And now they didn't even matter.

And Beth had known all along, she realized. Beth had known, and let Harper believe . . .

She almost hadn't survived the guilt. She had almost drowned. And Beth held the life preserver in her arms, saw her flailing—and turned away.

"I was driving," she said again, louder this time. The words gave her power. "But this—" Bitch. Psycho. Murderer. "*You.* You put something in my drink. And you let me get up there in front of all those people and make an ass of myself. Then you let me get into a car. You just let—" She gasped, remembering the sirens, remembering the screams. "You just let it happen."

"I'm sorry . . . !" Beth wailed, her words trailing off into an incoherent moan. She tipped over onto her side and curled up into a tight fetal ball, shaking. Adam leaned over her, stroking her head.

"What the hell, are you doing?" Harper asked Adam. "Didn't you hear her? She *killed* Kaia. And she let me think that I—what are you doing?"

"We have to give her a chance to explain," Adam said softly, as if Beth were a child who'd just confessed to breaking Harper's favorite lamp. "This doesn't make any sense, and she . . . it's *Beth*. She's a good person. There must be some explanation, some—"

"There's nothing!" Harper shrieked. She felt like she'd slipped into some parallel universe where everyone but her was insane. How could he not see what was going on, and who he was comforting? How could he not care what she'd done to Kaia—to *Harper*? "There's no excuse. There's nothing she can say. She did it. She deserves to cry. She deserves to be miserable. She deserves to go to hell, and you should leave her the hell alone."

Adam looked at her helplessly. "Don't say that. I can't. She's still . . . whatever she did, I still care about her. I can't just leave her here, like this." He rubbed his hand slowly across Beth's heaving shoulders. She didn't appear to notice.

Harper's stomach contracted, and tears of rage sprung to the eyes. Adam was a caring, responsible guy. It was one of the reasons she loved him. But this was ridiculous. He was *Harper's* best friend—or he was supposed to be. He was supposed to love her. Protect her. Support her.

He was supposed to be on Harper's side. But here he was, embracing the enemy.

"I made a mistake," Harper reminded him, "because I *loved* you—and you threw me out of your life. You told me I was a horrible person, that you could never trust me again. Because I made a fucking mistake. But she . . . she *kills* someone, and you just . . . shrug?" Harper forced her voice not to tremble. She walked slowly to the door, turning away from Adam and placing her hand on the knob. "If you ever cared about me, you wouldn't be able to look at her. You'd leave her here to rot. You'd leave right now."

"Don't say that, Harper," Adam pleaded. "Please. Don't make me . . ."

Don't make me choose. That's what he'd been about to say. And a chasm of black, bottomless darkness opened up inside Harper. Because if he thought he had to choose—if he thought, now, after hearing the truth, that there *was* a choice, that he had any option but one—then it was already over.

"She needs someone right now, Gracie. I can't leave her alone."

I *need you*, Harper thought bitterly. But she didn't say it out loud. He shouldn't need to hear it. "I'm leaving. Come if you want. Stay if you want."

Harper opened the door, stepped through, and closed it behind her.

She didn't need to look back to know what he'd decided.

✿ ✿ ✿

Adam couldn't believe she was gone.

He couldn't believe any of this. Things like this didn't happen. Not to him.

He was having trouble processing. Beth had spiked Harper's drink. Harper had gotten into the car. And Kaia had—

None of it made any sense. Beth was so gentle, such a good person, always doing the right thing, guiding him in the right direction. He'd been with her for almost two years, and he knew what kind of person she was. The kind that would never do anything like this. Never.

Unless she'd been pushed past her breaking point. Unless something had happened—some*one* had pushed her so hard, hurt her so badly, that she'd broken.

Maybe me. He remembered pushing her away, cursing her, hating her for something she hadn't done. He remembered sleeping with Kaia—and breaking Beth's heart.

He looked down at Beth, who was sobbing into the comforter, her hands balled up tight and thumping softly against the bed, her eyes squeezed shut. She needed him.

But what if he needed Harper?

He owed Harper his loyalty. He owed Beth his help, maybe even his forgiveness. What did he owe himself?

"Leave me alone," Beth mumbled, her arm spasming

out as if to shoo him away. "You shouldn't be here."

Adam knew that he should, and that whatever Beth said, she knew it too. But he couldn't stop staring at the door. And, eventually, he couldn't stop himself from standing up, walking over, and opening it.

He looked up and down the hallway. Only a few minutes had passed, but he had waited too long. She was gone.

She probably hadn't gone far—he was sure he could find her. But he could still hear Beth weeping, back in the room. She was crushed. Damaged. Helpless. And Adam still cared about her, enough to cringe at her whimpering. Enough to want to hold her and give her comfort, maybe even forgiveness, if that's what it would take.

"Shhh, I'm back," he told her, gathering her up in his arms.

"No."

"Yes. And I'm not leaving you."

Beth was weak, and she needed him *now*. Harper was strong.

She could wait.

The kiss hadn't lasted long enough.

One moment he'd had his arms around her, his lips pressed to Miranda's, his eyes closed while hers stared, wide open, memorized the tiny dips and crinkles in the skin around his left eye. The next moment, which came far too quickly, Kane had pulled away, and they were seated across from each other again, as if nothing had happened.

Maybe nothing had, and her obsession with Kane had finally swept away her last grip on reality. But she didn't think so.

What did it mean?

Nothing?

Everything?

She was afraid of the answer, reluctant to ask. Harper saved her the trouble.

"Thank God you're here!" she cried, flinging her arms around Miranda. "I don't know what to do. I don't know what just happened. I just, I don't knooooooooow."

Miranda let her best friend cry against her shoulder, trying not to regret the fact that she'd left Harper a message to explain where she was or to wonder whether her brand-new, now-tear-stained birthday shirt was dry-clean-only. She certainly tried not to resent the fact that Harper's latest melodrama was interrupting—well, she didn't know what it was, but that was the point.

Above all else, Miranda was a good friend, and good friends listened. They sometimes snuck glances out of the corner of their eye at tall, well-built Greek gods in training, and sometimes got distracted wondering how to kiss that hot smirk off a certain hot face—but mostly, they listened. Or at least pretended to.

"What's wrong now?" Miranda asked, lightly patting Harper's back.

And then Harper began to tell her story, and as the details poured out, Miranda no longer needed to pretend.

"Kaia's dead, and now Beth's just lying there, crying, like *I'm* supposed to feel sorry for *her*," Harper concluded, taking a long gulp of Miranda's drink and then, finishing it, grabbed Kane's out of his hand and downed that one too. "And Adam's just taking it. Like he doesn't care. That she *killed* someone. That she drugged me. That . . ." Harper sagged against Miranda, moaning as if all the words had leaked out of her. Then she burst into tears.

"I don't believe it," Miranda said, shaking her head.

"I do." Kane had been so silent that Miranda had almost forgotten he was there. He was holding himself very still, his fingers pinching the bridge of his nose. "I should have known," he said, so quietly that she could barely hear him. "I should have figured it out."

"But it doesn't make any sense," Miranda countered. "Where would she even get the drugs, and how would she, how could she do something so . . ." But she was beginning to remember how it had felt, those days and weeks after Harper betrayed her—and how Beth's pain had cut so much deeper. How Beth's lust for revenge had overwhelmed them both. And Miranda had been more than happy to let Beth talk her into anything. She had so desperately wanted to lash out, to hurt Harper the way she'd been hurt. If Beth had come to Miranda with the plan—the plan she must have thought would be harmless—would Miranda have talked her out of it?

Or would she have gone along for the ride?

Harper didn't know how long she had been crying. She'd held it together as she walked out of the hotel room, strode down the hall, waited impatiently for the elevator—maybe because she had still hoped Adam would follow.

But he didn't. And when the elevator doors closed her in, she lost it. She'd been crying ever since. Crying and drinking, drinking and crying, and even though she was in public, and she could feel Miranda and Kane staring down at her, for once, she didn't care. What did it matter what they thought—what anyone thought?

She was in a strange city, surrounded by foreign people and places, and her world was shattered.

It shouldn't matter, she told herself. Losing Adam. She'd been through worse. She'd lost more than that. She'd survived.

But it all added up. And just knowing what Beth had done, knowing she was up there in the room, with Adam, that the two of them were . . . together . . . it felt like a knife digging into her side, carving out pieces of flesh. Soon there would be nothing left.

She felt a light touch on her shoulder. At least she still had Miranda. She felt a gush of gratitude. "Harper, come on, let's get out of here," her friend—the only one who *hadn't* betrayed her—said gently.

"I can't go back to the hotel," Harper moaned. "Not when he's there. With her."

"Okay. Okay, then, let's just go somewhere more private, get you . . . cleaned up."

Dimly, Harper realized she must look like shit. And probably the whole bar was staring at the crazy girl, wondering what was wrong with her.

Someone spiked my drink, Harper thought giddily. *Call the cops.*

She didn't care about any of it, but she let Miranda pull her out of the chair and guide her toward the back of the bar. Kane kept his hand on her lower back, keeping her steady. She wanted to tell him she didn't need his help, but she couldn't choke the words out.

"I'm going to take her in here," Miranda said, and Harper realized she was talking to Kane. She was talking as if Harper couldn't hear her, couldn't speak or act for herself.

Miranda pushed open the door to the women's room, and Kane caught Harper's hand, pulling her toward him. He placed a hand on each of her shoulders and held her firmly. He looked blurry and out of focus, but she knew it was just the tears. "We'll figure this out, Grace," he said. "It's all going to be fine."

He'd always been a good liar.

Miranda led her inside the empty bathroom and left Kane outside to guard the door. Harper, usually unwilling to touch anything in a public restroom without several layers of paper towel between her and the germs of the masses, hopped up on the edge of the sink and leaned back against the mirror.

"This is it," she said dejectedly, trying to pull herself back together. "He's gone. I have to deal."

"He's not gone," Miranda pointed out. "He's back in the room right now, probably wondering where you are. You sure he didn't call you?"

Harper shrugged. He had called. Seven times. She hadn't answered. "I don't care if he's looking for me. He stayed with her, after what she did. He *stayed with her*."

"Is that really so unforgivable?"

"Rand, after what she did to me?"

"She didn't do it to *you*," Miranda said flatly. A look of horror flashed across her face. "I'm sorry, I didn't mean it to sound like—"

"Yeah. You did." Harper hung her head down and wiped away the last of her tears. "I get it. I'm selfish. It's all about me. Whatever. This isn't about me, I get that. It's about Kaia. No, screw that. It's about Beth, and what she did—and how she lied about it. She hurt so many people, Rand. And a few little tears and it's like, *poof.* Adam forgives and forgets. He never forgave *me*."

"I know." Miranda put an arm around Harper's shoulders. "I know it feels like he's choosing Beth over you—"

"Because he *is*," Harper said sullenly. At least she was finally getting it.

"But maybe . . ."

"What?"

Miranda opened her mouth. Shut it again. "Never mind."

"Just tell me!"

"Maybe it's not as simple as you're making it out to be," Miranda suggested.

"She spiked my drink because she wanted to humiliate me. She wanted to ruin my life, and ended up killing Kaia. She's a *murderer*. What's simpler than that?"

"But she didn't *mean* for it to happen." Miranda smoothed Harper's hair down and rubbed a hand across her back. "It was an accident."

Harper laughed bitterly through her tears. "An accident. Right. The only accident is that Kaia's the one who ended up dead. You know the little psycho was hoping it was me."

Miranda sighed. "No. She didn't want you dead. She just wanted . . ."

"What are you, a mind reader now? How could you know what she wanted? She's crazy. She's evil. She *wanted* me dead. And she almost got it."

Miranda took a deep breath. "Harper, I think all Adam's trying to do is look at it from her side. He's not betraying you. He's just . . . well, imagine what she must have been feeling—what could have made her do something so stupid."

"What the hell are you trying to say?" But it was obvious. Harper would never have thought Miranda would have the nerve for bullshit like this. Kane, maybe. But not Miranda. Never Miranda. But if this was where she wanted to go, Harper was damn well going to make sure she went all the way "Do you mean *what* made her—or *who* made her?"

"She was hurting," Miranda said. "And . . . I can kind of imagine how she felt." Harper could tell from her expression that Miranda was remembering her own pain; she was remembering her own anger. At Harper. "Maybe she just wanted to strike back, hurt someone the way she—"

"Maybe I *deserved* it," Harper snapped. "That's what you're trying to say, isn't it? Maybe you agree with her—maybe *you* wish I was the one who'd died!"

Miranda flinched, and her lip began to quiver the way it always did just before she started to cry "Don't say that.

You know that's not what I mean. I'm not trying to hurt you." She tried to touch Harper again, but wised up when she caught the look on Harper's face. She stepped away. But she refused to stop. "I know you don't want to believe this. I know you want it to be simple, and have Beth be evil, and everyone on your side—"

"Because that's the truth," Harper insisted. "That's reality."

"Or maybe that's just what you want to be true, because then you wouldn't have to face the fact that maybe you—"

"You want to talk about what's true?" Harper said, hopping off the sink and charging toward Miranda. She couldn't let the conversation go any further—she didn't know what would happen if she let Miranda finish her thought. "*You're* going to tell *me* about making my own reality? Avoiding the harsh glare of truth?" She forced a bitter laugh. "That's hilarious. That is fucking hilarious."

"Harper, I'm just trying to—"

"And here, of all places." Harper spun around, flinging her arms out toward the filthy stalls. The anger coursing through her felt good. It swept away the misery, and gave her strength. Power. "You think I don't know what you're doing, rushing off to the bathroom after every meal? You think I haven't figured out your pathetic little problem, even if you want to pretend it doesn't exist?"

"That's ridiculous, Harper, I do not—"

"What was that about facing the truth? Oh, 'I don't want to hurt you,'" Harper said, pouring a bucket of fake sympathy into her voice, "'but it'll be *good* for you to face reality.' Life isn't always what you *want* it to be, after all. You want to be sexy, desirable, and stick thin—but instead all you are is a pathetic closet-case bulimic who's so incompetent at keeping your oh-so-special secret that the whole world knows what a head-case you are."

"Harper, stop it," Miranda whispered, backing away. "Please."

"And if you want to talk hard truths, here's another one," Harper yelled. "Kane will never love you. He knows how you feel, and he's playing with you. Like a toy. Get it? You're a joke to him. You're nothing."

Harper wanted to stop herself now. She'd gone too far. She pressed her hand against her lips, to stop the flood of words. But the dam wouldn't hold for more than a second. Screaming at Miranda, forcing the tears out of her, was the only way to drown out everything that Miranda had said. And everything she hadn't said.

Because Harper could fill in the blanks.

You wouldn't have to face the fact that maybe you caused this.

Beth would never have done it, if it hadn't been for you.

Kaia might still be alive if it hadn't been for you.

You destroyed everything good in Beth's life—what did you expect her to do?

You still got in the car. You're still the one who was behind the wheel.

"Shut up!" she screamed, even though Miranda hadn't said anything. "You've been following after Kane like a sick little groupie for all these years, and where has it gotten you? You're alone, you're bitter, and you puke your guts out every day like the before version of some Oprah charity project. And you want to lecture *me* about avoiding the truth? You make me sick."

Miranda fled, flinging open the door—and slamming into Kane, who was waiting just outside. It was obvious he'd heard everything. She took one look at him, let out a thin cry of despair, and ran away. "Miranda!" he called. "Wait—" But she kept running.

Kane stared after her for a moment, then turned slowly toward Harper. "How could you?" he asked, his voice icy.

She just wanted to crawl into a corner and die. "Kane, I—"

"Don't." He'd never looked at her that way before: stern and serious. Disappointed. "Just don't." And he spun around and left her behind.

Harper gulped in one deep breath after another, trying to summon up the strength to figure out what to do.

She needed to do *something*. She needed to fix this, fix everything. But it was all so screwed up. How could all of her friends turn on her like that—why couldn't they see that Beth was the enemy? Why were they so ready to give her their sympathy and to leave Harper to fend for herself?

You drove them away, a voice in her head pointed out.

But that wasn't what she wanted to hear. She wanted to hear someone rage against Beth for what she'd done. She wanted to hear that she wasn't the only one who cried herself to sleep most nights, imagining that she could still hear Kaia's icy laugh.

Or Kaia's screams.

She wanted someone to blame for everything that had happened. She wanted someone to punish.

And though her friends may have abandoned her, she suddenly realized that she wasn't alone.

It took a few phone calls and a little detective work, but in Grace, CA, there were far fewer than six degrees of separation between Harper and, well, anyone. She had the phone number in under five minutes. It only rang once.

"Beth?" a voice asked hopefully. "Where did you—"

"It's not Beth," she snapped. "Is this Reed?"

"Yeah, but who—"

"This is Harper Grace. We need to talk."

Sleep was impossible. But Beth had gotten good at pretending. She lay on her side, Adam's arm curled protectively around her, his face pressed against her shoulder, and kept her eyes closed, listening to his steady breathing. Her arm was twisted at an odd angle and had long ago fallen asleep; her neck ached, and she longed for a tissue with which to blow her stuffed-up nose or to clean the dried tears off her face. But she didn't want to move, lest she wake him.

She didn't want him to leave.

Because she was so intently focused on Adam—the comforting pressure of his body, the soft, snuffling sounds he made as he slept, the tickle of his hot breath on her neck—she didn't hear the door inch open, or the footsteps creep toward the bed. And because she had her eyes closed, she didn't see the figure standing over her, fists clenched.

But she smelled him. Stale coffee, cigarettes, motor oil, and the faint sweetness of fresh-grown marijuana. She squeezed her eyes shut even tighter, hoping he would believe the pose and go away, so she wouldn't have to face him—not like this.

"Is this a fucking joke?" he growled loudly.

Adam jerked awake and stared groggily at the intruder. Beth opened her eyes and sat up, wondering how much he knew, and how much she would have the courage to tell him.

"We fell asleep," she lied. "But nothing happened. Adam was just—"

"You think I give a shit what you do with him?" Reed's

voice, usually so warm and slow, pelted her like hail, rapid and unforgiving. "You can screw every guy in town, for all I care. You can fucking *die*, for all I care."

And she knew that he knew.

"Don't talk to her like that," Adam said, about to stand up. Beth put a hand on his back.

"Let me," she told him. This was her battle to lose. "Reed . . ." Her voice sounded strangled. Which is how she felt. "I wanted to tell you myself—"

"I *comforted* you," he spit out, looking disgusted. "I touched you, I held you, I let myself—" He sagged against the wall and wiped the back of his hand against his mouth, as if to wipe the memory of her off his lips.

"How did you find out?" she asked in a whisper.

Harper stepped through the open door. "I told him." She glared smugly at Adam. Beth didn't turn to see his reaction. She didn't care about anything right now but making Reed understand.

"It was an accident," she told him, the tears returning even though she thought she'd wept herself dry. "It was a mistake. I should have told you. I know. But . . ."

"But you didn't."

"Because I thought you'd hate me!" she cried.

"You were right."

"Reed . . ." Beth lunged toward him, then, pulling him toward her, wrapped her arms around him and clutched his worn cotton T-shirt in tight fists so he couldn't escape. She expected him to push her away, but he didn't move, just stood there in her embrace, his arms at his sides, his head staring straight ahead over her shoulder, motionless, like a mannequin. She glanced over at Harper, hating to do this in front of her. But she had no choice. "Up on the roof, I only ran away because—because I was afraid of this. I told you! I told you I didn't deserve you, that you didn't really know me. . . ."

"So this is my fault for not believing you?"

"No! No, that's not what I mean." She clutched him tighter and closed her eyes again, trying to memorize everything about his body, knowing this might be her last chance. "I just don't want you to think that I was . . . I wanted to stay with you. I didn't want any of this to happen. I wanted to tell you . . ." She lowered her voice so that only he would hear. "I'm in love with you, too."

There was no answer.

"Reed? Did you hear me? I *love* you. And maybe we can find a way—"

He didn't push her away, or touch her at all, but somehow he stepped out of the embrace, so quickly that Beth found herself holding empty air.

"You make me sick." His voice was hoarse and expressionless. "There's no way. There's nothing."

"But after everything we—"

"Don't you get it? There *is* no we. None of it happened—none of it was real. It was all a lie."

"It wasn't! You have to believe me," she begged, "it was all real. And everything I said was true, except—"

"You're a liar," he said flatly. "You're a killer. You . . . you took her away from me, and then thought you could just *replace* her? You're psychotic."

"I love you," she told him again, this time loud and clear. She knew now that it didn't matter, that he was already gone, but she needed to say the words. She needed them to hang in the air so that there was at least some record of the last good thing in her life, before it faded away.

"I don't even know you," he shot back. "I don't want to." He pressed his hand over his eyes and hunched forward, as if he were struck by a sudden sharp pain. Beth moved toward him again, but Harper was quicker. She materialized by his side; he took her hand.

Beth felt like her own hand had been dipped in acid.

"I'm sorry," she said again, the words now sounding meaningless even to her.

"Save it," Harper sneered, leading Reed to the door. She was no longer holding his hand; now her arm was loosely wrapped around his waist. Beth didn't want to look, but she couldn't help herself. "No one wants to hear your lame apologies." Harper paused in the doorway and glared once again at Adam. "Some things are unforgivable."

chapter eleven

SEX ON THE BEACH.

Tequila Sunrise.

Alabama Slammer.

Cosmopolitan.

Appletini.

Mojito.

Kamikaze.

The city was drowning in cocktails, and Harper planned to try them all. The world tipped and turned, spun and sloshed, and she poured another drink down her throat, and another. She drenched her doubts in tequila, showered her guilt with vodka, poured Captain Morgan rum all over the flames that still burst out of a crumpled car, washed Kaia's wounds in a bath of gin.

Harper wobbled down the Strip, a yard-long margarita in one hand, emptiness in the other. She sucked on the straw. One gulp for Adam, who would never choose her. One for Miranda, who now understood the pain of truth. And the rest for Kaia, who'd left her behind to face it all, alone.

She wobbled. She stumbled. She fell, into the arms of a stranger. His hands were strong, his face gentle, familiar.

"Watch out," he told her, and she'd heard his voice on the radio, she'd seen his eyes on a billboard. She'd longed for this opportunity—in what seemed like another life. "Too much to drink?" the famous addict asked her.

Too much would never be enough.

"No such thing," she mumbled.

"Can I help?"

Front-row tickets, Harper wanted to say. *Backstage passes. For me and my best friends.*

Twenty-four hours ago, it was all she'd wanted. Now she just wanted him to leave her alone. She wanted to forget. She wanted to black out the world.

She wanted another drink.

"I said, can I help?"

She shook her head. The world shook too. The dizziness spun her around, dragged her stomach to her feet.

The buzzing in her ears finally blocked out all the words she refused to hear, and a dark fog crowded her vision. She opened her mouth—

And threw up all over the famous man's leather boots.

She felt better. Empty. And that meant she could start all over again. She held out her glass, slurred out the words.

"Fill 'er up."

"Fill 'er up," Miranda told the man with the ladle. The hot fudge sauce came pouring down over four scoops of coffee mocha ice cream with chocolate chips, rainbow sprinkles, Heath Bar crumbles, sliced banana, almond crumbles, Oreo wedges, and three Reese's peanut butter cups. Miranda stuck a cherry on top.

Then she dug in.

She sat at an empty table, hunched over her tray, and shoveled the food down her throat. She should, more than anything, put the spoon down, stand up from the table, and walk out of the buffet; she should prove Harper wrong, once and for all. But her fingers still gripped the spoon and the ice cream still filled her mouth, sliding down her throat though she barely tasted its sweetness or noticed the cold.

And when it was done, she would have more. She would pile her tray high with black-bottom brownies, cream-centered doughnuts, oversize peanut butter cookies, chocolate truffles, vanilla wafers, raspberry sherbet, apple pie, strawberry shortcake, rice pudding, Oreo cheesecake, cherry tarts, and a chocolate soufflé.

She would stuff it in, wash it down, smear her face and hands with chocolate, drop crumbs all over her lap, keep her head down to avoid the stares. She would curse Harper for driving her to a piggish extreme, and then she would curse herself for her weakness, her disgusting desires, and the bottomless hunger that showed no mercy and had no end.

And when she stopped, sick and bloated but still starving, still empty, and still alone, she would hate herself even more. She would feel the fat surging under her skin like an insect infestation. Her stomach would twist and spasm and her body would scream in protest, until she submitted to the inevitable.

She would lock herself in a dirty stall. Pull her hair back into a sloppy ponytail. Lean over the toilet bowl. Promise herself this was the last time. And then stick her finger down her throat.

She could see it all playing out, just as it had too many times before. But even that wasn't enough to make her put the spoon down. Not as long as she could still picture Kane's face or hear Harper's voice.

She knew she would eventually have to figure out

what to do next, and face up to her life—and her problems. But in the meantime, she would chew and swallow, chew and swallow, until mouthful by mouthful, she filled herself up.

Blondes and brunettes, C-cups and D-cups, strippers and hookers, showgirls and show-offs, the menu was complete, and available à la carte or as an all-you-can-eat buffet. Vegas wasn't picky, and neither were its women.

But Adam's appetite was gone. He felt gutted, wrecked—like this place had chewed him up and spit him out.

Harper had walked away from him; a moment later, Beth had run. And he'd let them both leave. Because he was an idiot—and now he needed to fix his mistake. He needed to find them.

One blonde, five foot four, bright blue eyes, and snow-white skin.

One brunette, wild curly hair with reddish streaks, a wicked smile, just the right curves.

Two women who wanted nothing to do with him. Lost amidst a sea of others who couldn't get enough.

"Don't look so sad, sweetie."

"Want me to cheer you up?"

"Sure I'm not what you're looking for?"

"I'm all yours, baby."

But he didn't want her. He didn't want any of them. He waded through the redheads, threaded his way through a cloud of blondes, strained to see over the Amazonian warriors of a women's basketball team, all outfitted in lime green tank tops and short-shorts that hugged their tightly muscled thighs.

They were barely people to him anymore, just a moving mass of soft parts and honeyed voices. And yet he watched them all, because somewhere in the crowd of hair and lips and chests and hips, he would find something he recognized—maybe a strand of silky blond. Maybe the curving corner of a smug grin, or a pinkie with a razor-thin scar from a sixth-grade art project gone awry.

They were out there, somewhere, one running away from him, the other running away from everything.

There were hundreds of places they could hide; millions of faces to sift through. And he didn't even know where to start.

He knew he'd been dealt a bad hand—but everything was riding on this one, and he wasn't about to fold.

"Fold." Kane threw his cards down in disgust and moved along to the next table. The games blurred together, and still, he played—he bet, he checked, he passed, he raised, he called, and he lost.

His head wasn't in the game.

He tossed a few chips on the blackjack table. "Hit me." A five of clubs slapped down on the table. "Hit me again." A nine of hearts. "Again." Jack of spades.

Bust.

She meant nothing to him, he told himself. Or at least, nothing much. She was just a girl, an automatic no-value discard in the poker hand of life. He wouldn't let himself get fooled into caring, not again. It was a sucker's bet—the house always won, and losing hurt.

It was why he loved to watch the high rollers throwing their thousand-dollar chips down and walking away with a wink and a shrug. Nothing broke them, nothing even dented. Because they never let the game matter. The good ones chose their table carefully, played the odds, risked only what they could afford to lose, and ditched a cold deck without looking back. It was the only way to play.

"Hit me," Kane said again as the dealer shuffled through a fresh deck. Queen of hearts. "Hit me again." King of spades.

Bust.

The best players—the counters—could play several games at once, shifting their focus from one to the other, never letting the money ride too long or leaving while the deck was still hot. Kane did the same thing—just not with cards.

He kept his options open, and his women wanting more. He could spot a winning bet from a mile away, recognized every tell, knew when to smile, when to kiss, when to get the hell out. He could lay down his money and spin the wheel, because with nothing invested, he had nothing to lose.

And so he never lost.

Miranda should be no different. She was, in fact, that most elusive of bets: the sure thing. She knew his game all too well, yet still wanted to play. Because, like the worst of gamblers—like the degenerate losers who stayed at the table as their chips disappeared, waiting in vain to throw that lucky seven and shooting snake eyes every time—she had hope. She expected the next hand—*her* hand—to be different. She actually thought it was possible to beat the house.

Which should have made it incredibly easy for Kane to clean up, and that was the problem: Beating Miranda—*playing* Miranda—would feel like losing. The danger sign blinked brightly. Once emotions got involved, the game was over. You got distracted, you got sloppy and, much like tonight, you walked away with empty pockets.

Or, if you got very lucky, you hit the jackpot.

Kane hated to admit it, but when it came to Miranda, he couldn't hedge his bets. She was an all-or-nothing proposition. And maybe it was time for him to ante up.

> *You promised all or nothing, babe,*
> *You said our bodies fit.*
> *You lied and tore my heart out,*
> *And I don't give a shit!*

Reed's hand was numb, his fingers stinging, his voice hoarse. He leaned into the mic and beat his guitar into submission, letting the rage and pain and misery churn through him and explode into the air.

> *Love me, leave me, kill me dead.*
> *Your voice is like a knife,*
> *Your tears are mud, your hands are claws.*
> *Get the hell out of my life!*

It hurt. It burned. But he wrapped his voice around the notes and let the words slice and stab at an invisible enemy, and though he wasn't drunk and wasn't high, the world seemed miles down as the music carried him up and out, a wall of sound that sucked him in and blasted him out the other side, enraged, exhausted, spent.

> *Forget it forget me forget you forget,*

See your face and I wish I was blind.
Your love and your hate and your lies and your
rage,
And you're driving me out of my mind.

The club had been dark and empty when he arrived—but Star*la had a key. He played and stomped and sang and raged and she closed her eyes, swaying to the music, her body twisting and waving with the sounds, and though he could block out the world, he couldn't miss her hips and her flying hair and her lips, stained with black gloss and mouthing his words.

And then somehow she was on the stage, her body grinding against his, their hips thrusting together as the chords piled on top of one another. And the feel of her flesh and the grip of her hand around his wrist and her breath on his neck reminded him of everything he wanted to forget—everything he wanted to destroy.

He played louder, he sang louder, but the music fell away and the blessed amnesia of sound disappeared and all he could see was Beth's face, her strangled voice, her tears. He tried to lose himself in the thunder of the guitar and the roar of his own voice, but hers was louder and he had to listen.

Please.

Forgive me.

And then Star*la's hands were on his waist and creeping up beneath his shirt, climbing on bare skin, rubbing his chest, and he laid down his guitar and turned to face her, but he wasn't seeing her.

Her black fingernails scraped against his face; he saw only pastel pink, felt silky skin.

Her black hair whipped across his neck; he saw shimmering gold, like strands of sun.

Her eyes, so dark, almost purple, closed; he saw pale blue irises, wide open, alert. He saw tears.

He closed his eyes and when his lips met hers, Beth's face finally disappeared and her voice faded away, and the rage boiling within him spilled out through his hands and his lips and his body. She shoved him up against the wall and dug her elbows into him, pinning him down, and he sucked her lips and bit her earlobe and she scraped her fingers up and down his back until his skin felt raw.

The wall of sound returned. She was like music, a raging, pumping punk anthem come to life in his arms. She kissed his chest and kneaded his flesh and he needed hers. He wanted to sing—he wanted to scream. Their bodies blended together like a perfect chord, and he let himself forget everything but the ceaseless rhythm, the pounding, pulsing beat.

He let himself get lost.

ℒ   ℒ   ℒ

I once was lost, but now am found, Beth sang to herself, tune-lessly. She almost giggled, wavering on the edge of hysteria, stepping back from the ledge just in time. She had been confused for so long. Lost, searching for the right path, the right direction, the first step back toward normalcy, to forgiveness, to sanity. Even, someday, to happiness.

And now she understood. She'd found the path, *her* path. It led to a dead end.

Just like Kaia's.

She had been drowning in self-pity, struggling and flailing, fighting the inevitable. It had been exhausting—and now that it had ended, she realized that fighting had been her first mistake. Exhausted, she had submitted to the hopelessness. And now she was finally at peace.

She leaned against the railing, looking out over the sparkling city. Had it been only hours since she'd stood up here with Reed, then fled, uselessly postponing her fate? She felt like a different person now. Because now she understood.

This is it, she told herself. *This is how it always will be.* And this was what she deserved. Reed's disgust and disdain, his hand in Harper's. It was easier to take than what she had seen on Adam's face: sympathy. Concern. A hint of forgiveness. She couldn't let herself fall into the trap, not again. She couldn't seek comfort, or hope for rescue.

She couldn't change what had happened, and she couldn't save herself. But she could at least end the pain. She gripped the railing and looked down, but it was too dark to see anything but the blinking lights smeared across the landscape.

The first step would be hard.

She wondered if it would hurt. Even if it did, it would be fast, and then it would be over. And that was all she wanted—an ending. She couldn't fight the current, not anymore, and she refused to drag Adam down with her when she finally sank to the bottom.

It would be quiet there. It would finally be over.

And justice would be served.

chapter twelve

SAYING GOOD-BYE DIDN'T TAKE AS LONG AS SHE'D expected.

It was a short list, which only reminded her of how little she was leaving behind.

Beth's fingers didn't even tremble as she dialed in the numbers that would take her straight to voice mail. She couldn't face anyone, but she still needed to say she was sorry, one last time.

"It's Harper. Do your best, and if you're lucky, I might call you back."

Beep.

"Harper . . . this is Beth." She took a deep, shuddery

breath. "Please don't hang up before you listen to this. I know you'll never understand what I did, and I know you hate me, so I'm not asking you to forgive me. I just want you to know I'm sorry. More than I can ever say. I—" Her voice caught, and she gripped the phone tighter, fixing her gaze on the horizon and forcing herself to stay calm, make it through. "Just take care of Adam. I-I'm glad he'll have you."

One down. Two to go.

Adam's was easier, somehow, maybe because she was only saying what she'd said so many times before. Or maybe because she hadn't hurt him as badly, and didn't owe him as much.

"Hey, it's Adam, you missed me now, but I'll catch you later."

She sighed a little at the sound of his voice, the light Southern accent infusing each word with the hint of a warm smile. "I'm sorry for all the things we said to each other," she told him, wondering when he would hear her words. "And for all the time we wasted being angry. Maybe if I hadn't been so angry, things would have . . . a lot would have been different. We were really good, Ad, and I just want you to know, whatever happened, I still love you. Not like, you know, the way we were, but I'll always—" She stopped. *Always* didn't mean much. Not anymore. "I just hope you don't forget the way things used to be. Before. And Adam . . . thank you. For tonight and . . . just for being . . . you."

Then she waited. For ten minutes, then twenty. Hoping that it would get easier. But when it didn't, she knew she couldn't wait any longer. Reed had gotten a new phone the month before, but rarely remembered to turn it on. "Why bother?" he'd always asked Beth. "The only person I want to talk to is already here." She didn't want to just leave him a message; she wanted to talk to him. Not because she thought she'd be able to change anything—she was past that kind of stupid hope—but just because she wanted to hear his voice again. Even if he was angry, even if he told her again how much he hated her, she wanted to hear him say her name.

He didn't answer.

"You know who it is and you know what you want. Speak."

But Beth didn't know what she wanted. "Reed. Reed . . ." Saying his name was all it took, and she burst into tears. She pressed a hand over the receiver, hoping to muffle her sobs, and quickly choked them back, forcing herself to talk. "It's beautiful here," she said in a thin, tight voice, trying to work up to saying something that actually mattered. "It makes me think of you. It makes me think . . . I'm not sorry, not about us. I shouldn't have lied, and I shouldn't have—I did a terrible thing. I know you hate me. I know you can never forgive me. You shouldn't. I hate myself for what I did to you. But . . . I love you. And I know what I have to do now." She shut her eyes against the lights and tried to picture his face—but all she could see was Kaia. "I can't stand what I did to you, to—" She hiccupped through her tears and had to pause to catch her breath. "What I did to all of you. Not anymore. I'm sorry. For Kaia, and for us. For everything. Just try to remember that—and maybe someday you'll even believe it."

She hung up the phone before she realized that she'd forgotten to say the most important thing of all, maybe because saying it out loud would make it true, and she wasn't ready for that yet. She needed more time. Not much, just a few more minutes of breathing deeply and staring up at the sky and holding on.

A few more minutes, and she would be ready to say good-bye.

Miranda felt sick. The food still churning in her stomach, she could feel the fat moving in, unpacking, making itself at home. She needed to do something about it. But before she could, her phone rang. And, glancing down at the screen, she discovered what sick *really* meant.

"Stevens, we need to talk," he said as soon she picked

up the phone, giving her an extra couple of seconds to decide what to say. It wasn't enough.

"Kane . . . I . . ." Her face blazed red just thinking about him and what he'd overheard. There was no way she could face him.

"Meet me back at the hotel, by the pool," he ordered.

There was no way she could disobey.

"Half an hour? You'll be there?" he pressed.

She nodded.

"Well?"

She suddenly realized he couldn't see her through the phone. Thank God. "Yeah. Half an hour." She hung up and, nibbling at the edge of her thumbnail, wondered what would happen next. The options:

He wanted to let her down gently. Which would be humiliating, excruciating.

He wanted to pretend nothing had happened. Which might be better—or even worse.

He wanted to tell her he was madly in love with her, and now that he knew she felt the same way, they could—

She forced herself to stop. She'd promised herself no more lame daydreaming. And it was nearly morning—she was too tired to lie to herself anymore. Kane Geary didn't lurk around in corners, afraid of his feelings, pathetically waiting for a sign.

No, that's me, she thought wryly. When Kane saw what he wanted, he took it.

And he'd already chosen to leave Miranda on the shelf.

She considered ditching him, just sneaking back up to the room and finally getting some sleep. But she never considered it very seriously—doom-and-gloom expectations or not, she needed to know what he wanted. And she needed to prove to herself that she could handle it.

He got there first; maybe he'd already been there when he called. He was sitting on the edge of the pool, his jeans rolled up and his feet dangling in the water. He had his back to her, and Miranda assumed he hadn't seen her come in—but after she'd stood in the entranceway for several long minutes, he called out her name.

"Come here," he urged. "I won't bite."

She slipped her sandals off and sat down next to him, cringing as the unheated water lapped over her toes.

"You just have to get used to it," he told her. "Then it feels good."

"I guess I can get used to anything."

There was about half a foot of space between them, except at their fingertips. Her right hand and his left hand were both pressed flat on the damp cement, less than half an inch apart.

Miranda put her hands in her lap and tried not to pick at her nails.

Silence.

"So," Kane finally said, staring straight out at the water. "Our friends are pretty fucked up, huh?"

Miranda's tension spurted out of her in a loud snort. *Very attractive*, she told herself irritably. *Lovely.*

"Yeah." Miranda kicked her feet lightly in the water. "I just can't believe Beth . . ."

Kane tipped his head back, as if to look up at the stars, but they were covered by a reddish haze. "I should have figured it out. Maybe I should have seen it coming."

"If anyone should have, *I* should have," Miranda countered. "I knew how angry she was about what Harper—"

"What *we* did to her," Kane corrected her.

Miranda barely heard. "But I should never have said that to Harper. I thought it would help, but . . . she was so upset and miserable, and I had to go and tell her it was all her fault."

"You didn't tell her that."

"Yeah, but I might as well have. It's what she heard. And it's no wonder she said all those—" Miranda kicked herself. She'd steered the conversation exactly where she didn't want it to go.

"You told her the truth," Kane insisted. "Beth wouldn't have . . . done what she did if . . ."

Miranda shrugged. "But that doesn't mean I had to say it."

"I gave her the drugs," Kane said suddenly, in a very quiet voice. She spun to look at him, and he met her gaze.

"What?"

"I gave her the drugs," he repeated, more steadily. "As a present. I thought . . . it doesn't matter what I thought. I didn't expect her to keep them. Or use them. But I gave them to her. And I helped ruin her life. Hell, I started the whole thing. Which I guess makes me to blame too."

Miranda didn't know what to say.

"Doesn't it?" he asked, his voice rising.

She shook her head, then caught herself. "Yes."

He nodded once and let his head hang low with his chin resting against his chest and his shoulders slumped. It was a pose she'd never seen his body make before, so it took her a moment to identify it: defeat. Miranda lifted her hand and, with painful slowness, reached out for his shoulder. But she stopped, just before she touched him, her fingers trembling. She put her arm down, and they sat in silence.

Something jerked him out of a fitful sleep, but by the time he sat up in bed, whatever it was—the noise, the movement, *something*—was gone. Reed looked around, bleary-eyed and confused. The blinds were mostly drawn, but a thin band of darkness beneath the cheap cotton suggested that morning hadn't yet arrived. His lips were dry and cracked, head foggy, and a sour taste filled his mouth. And the bed was strange, unfamiliar, as was the room. . . .

Oh.

He lay back against the uneven mattress and shut his eyes, as if that could block out the reality he was beginning to remember. He was in Vegas. With Beth. But Beth had—

You're a fool, Kaia's voice told him scornfully. *You fell for it. You fell for* her—*after* me?

He wanted to hate Beth: for Kaia's sake, and for his own. But lying there in the dark, it didn't seem possible. And he hated himself for his failure.

Something began to buzz, and he felt a steady vibration against his hip. His phone, alerting him to a message—its ringing must have woken him up. He picked it up, and even the dim light of the screen was blinding in the total darkness. There was one voice mail, and as he listened to it, he realized his hand was shaking.

He wanted to hang up in the middle; he wanted to hang up as soon as he heard her voice. But he listened to the whole thing. And he couldn't help but remember: Kaia had left him a voice mail too, once. She had begged his forgiveness. And she had died before he could deliver.

He could picture Beth's face, her lips trembling, tears magnifying her eyes to look like pure blue reflecting pools. She just wanted him to try to understand.

"I can't," he whispered, dropping the phone to his side. "I just can't."

"Hey . . . it's the middle of the night," a girl's voice complained. "Go back to sleep." Star*la rolled toward him and draped an arm across his bare chest. She pressed her lips against the nape of his neck, and he felt her tongue darting back and forth, as if tapping out a private message in Morse code. He resisted the urge to push her away.

What did I do? he asked himself silently. But it was a rhetorical question. He remembered everything.

"Sorry I woke you," he murmured, holding himself very still.

"Everything okay?"

He grunted a yes.

"Well, since we're both awake . . ." She began playing with the dark curls of hair on his chest and then, slowly, her fingers began walking their way south. "Want to play?"

Though he didn't want to touch her, he grabbed her hand and tucked it against his chest. "Let's just go back to sleep."

"Mmmm, sounds good." She yawned, then nuzzled into his back; moments later her breathing had settled into a deep and steady rhythm. He dropped her hand and lay quietly with his eyes wide open, staring at nothing. There was something about Beth's message. Something wrong.

I know what I have to do.

Try to remember.

It wasn't his problem anymore; *she* wasn't his problem anymore. Reed closed his eyes and breathed in deeply, counting the seconds. Then breathed out. One. Two. Three. In. One. Two. Three. Out . . .

Sleep would come eventually, he told himself. And if it didn't, there was always the fail-safe option, a small plastic bag with just enough left to help him zone out and forget.

But the voice mail kept replaying itself in his head. Not Beth's—Kaia's.

When he'd gotten Kaia's message, he had thought about calling her back—but decided against it. He would forgive her, he'd already decided. But he wasn't ready to talk to her, not yet. And there had been no hurry.

He'd just assumed they had plenty of time.

When Kane finally lifted his head again, she couldn't read his expression. His eyes were half closed, and his face impassive, hidden in shadow. He rested his hand on her knee and a warm heat radiated out from the point of contact up and down her leg. "Thanks."

"For what?"

"For telling the truth. Like always."

"Kane, I—"

"Stevens, I—"

They laughed, and Miranda gestured that he should speak first.

"I got you something." He pulled a small white, scrunched-up paper bag out of his pocket. "For your birthday. Since you're having such an awesome celebratory weekend so far."

She shrugged. "It's not like it's your fault. It all just happened."

"I am the one who ruined your date," he pointed out.

"Is that a note of *apology* I hear in your voice?" she joked, pressing the back of her hand against her forehead. "Do I have a fever? Because I think I'm hallucinating."

"Shut up and open it," he said, shoving the bag into her hands.

"Lovely wrapping job." She needed the sarcasm. It kept all the real emotions away. Miranda delicately peeled open the mouth of the bag and reached inside, pulling out a necklace of cheap, chunky plastic beads, painted in bright colors and attached to a label marked AUTHENTIC NATIVE AMERICAN JEWELRY. It was about as authentic as an aluminum Christmas tree—and just as tacky. "It's . . . uh . . . nice. Thank you?"

"I saw it and thought of you," he said proudly. "I knew you'd love it."

Miranda knew she probably shouldn't take it as an insult; but, looking down at the garish piece of pseudo-jewelry, it was hard not to. "It was very . . . sweet of you to get me something, Kane. You shouldn't have. I mean, you *really* shouldn't have."

Kane burst into laughter. "Stop looking so appalled, Stevens. I know it's gruesome. It's not like I'm expecting you to like it."

"Oh, thank God." She waved it through the air, giggling as the beads clanked loudly together; wear this and she'd become a human maraca. "But then . . . what's it for?"

"I found it in the gift shop," he explained. "And it reminded me of—"

"The gift shop at the Rising Sun," she cut in. Where they'd spent twenty minutes mocking the jewelry. Kane had strung the ugliest necklace they could find around her neck—and then they'd kissed. "I can't believe you remember that."

"I can't believe *you* forgot."

Miranda didn't want him to know that she remembered every second of that day, that she could show him every point on her skin his hands and lips had touched.

"We picked out a necklace," Kane reminded her, "and I put it around your neck—" He took the garish chain of beads out of her hands and latched it around her neck, pausing as his fingers fumbled with the clasp and brushed against her skin. "Like this. And then we stared at each other." His forearms rested on her shoulders, locking her in. She could see her reflection in his eyes. "Like this. And you got all awkward and sarcastic . . ."

"That's me," she joked, trying to smile, "ruining things like always."

"And I wouldn't let you." He moved closer, never taking his eyes off of hers. "I told you how beautiful your lips are—"

"No, you didn't."

"So you *do* remember," he crowed, raising an eyebrow.

"No, I just know I wouldn't have gone for a lame line like that," Miranda countered.

"Girls love my lines," he said, close enough that she could feel his breath on her lips, close enough that she couldn't see his mouth moving because his enormous, dark brown eyes filled her field of vision.

"I'm different," she reminded him.

"I know. That's why, instead, I just—"And the distance between them disappeared as he kissed her. Everything disappeared other than his lips, and the touch of his skin as she stroked her hand across his cheek. His teeth, nibbling at her earlobe. Her tongue, lightly grazing his neck. His breathing, heavy and fast, her quiet gasp as his warm hand slipped beneath her shirt and pressed against the skin of her lower back.

And then reality came rushing back, and she pushed him away.

Right into the pool.

"Oh, no!" She jumped to her feet as he flailed about, finally finding his footing and standing up in the waist-deep water, drenched. "I can't believe I just did that, I'm so sorry, I—"

"It's fine," he assured her, holding out his hand. "Help me up?"

She should have seen it coming. She'd seen enough movies. But she still took his hand—and, like clockwork, he pulled her in after him. The cold water slapped her in the face, spun her upside down, and when she found the surface, shivering and gasping, she was alert again, aware enough to stay away.

"Now you want to tell me why we're both in the pool?" Kane requested, wading toward her. She backed away.

"You pulled me in!"

"You pushed me first."

"Good point."

Kane sliced through the water and, before she could get away, wrapped his arms around her.

"Let go," she said, and it sounded less like an order than a question.

"You're shivering," he pointed out.

"And you're soaking wet, so I don't see how that's helping."

"Why did you push me away?" he asked, his lips at her ear.

Miranda didn't say anything.

"I thought we were having fun," he prodded. "Weren't you having fun?"

She nodded, even though he couldn't see her face. Her chin dug into his shoulder; he'd get the idea.

"So why push me away?"

"You know why," she said quietly. He was right, she was shivering—but not because of the cold.

"No."

"Yes you do! Please don't make me say it."

"Miranda, I don't . . . ?"

"You heard Harper." She tried to slide out of his embrace, but he wouldn't let her. He only let go a little, so he could see her face. That was worse. "You *know* why I . . ." Miranda just wanted to look away, to *be* away, but the best she could do was squeeze her eyes shut so she didn't have to see him looking at her. "I can't do casual. Not with you. It's too hard."

"And what if I don't want casual?"

She didn't want to understand his meaning, because it was too dangerous. If she was wrong . . .

"Open your eyes, Miranda."

She shook her head.

"Open them, or I'm kissing you again," he threatened. She opened her eyes.

"Let's try this," he told her. He wasn't smirking, or

even smiling. "You. Me. For real. Let's just do it."

"But . . . why?" Was this some kind of pity thing? Didn't he know how much worse that would make everything in the morning, when the dream ended and she woke up?

"Because you want to. And because . . . I want to." He didn't sound sure, but he looked it.

"It would never work."

"Probably not. But Stevens, why not take a chance for once?"

It was easy for him to say. He wasn't the one with everything to lose.

On the other hand . . . what did *she* have to lose, she asked herself, when she had so little to start with?

She'd spent so long convincing herself that this moment would never happen, and now here it was—and she almost hadn't recognized it. She was terrified; but that was no excuse.

"Okay."

"Okay?" he repeated, his irresistible smile finally making an appearance. "You'll deign to give me a shot?"

It was hard for her to speak, since she was barely breathing. "I guess you lucked out. So . . . what now? Should we, uh, talk about what we're going to—"

He pressed his right hand to her lips, then, lightly, traced a path across her cheek, to the tip of her ear, then down along the edge of her jaw, coming to rest with his fingers just beneath her chin. "Enough talking," he told her. "We have a deal—now we celebrate."

The water was still ice cold, but as he leaned down and kissed her, his soaking hair dripping down her face, his wet T-shirt sticking to her skin, she felt perfectly warm.

And though the water was only waist deep and her feet were firmly planted on the floor of the pool, she felt like she was floating.

Beth didn't know why she answered the phone. She supposed it was a reflex, left over from her old life. She couldn't have been hoping that there was still a chance— that someone could say something that would make a difference. Even if there was someone who could reach out to her through the phone and explain to her how to fix things, this wasn't going to be that kind of call.

Beth had seen the name on the screen and she picked it up, anyway, but that didn't mean she was ready to talk. She lifted the phone to her ear but remained silent, trying to decide whether to hang up.

"I can hear you breathing." Harper's voice was low and cold. It reminded Beth of someone, though at first she couldn't figure out who. Then it came to her: Kaia. "I know you're there. Beth. *Beth.* Say something."

What do you want? It took her a moment to realize

she'd only mouthed the words, and no sound had come out. She tried again. "What do you want?" It was barely more than a whisper, but it was enough.

"What do I want? What do *I* want?" Beth held the phone away from her ear, but could still hear Harper's tinny laugh. "You're the one who called me, remember? Oh no, wait, you didn't *call* me, you left a message. Like a coward. Afraid to face me, Beth? Too afraid I'll tell you what I really think of you?"

"I think I've got that figured out already."

Just hang up the phone, she told herself, *and you can end this for good.*

"Don't pretend you know what I think," Harper snapped. "If you knew anything, you wouldn't leave some stupid message whining about how sorry you are, like that's going to change anything. You don't get to do that."

"What should I do, Harper?" she asked, trying to sound tough, but failing miserably. "You tell me."

"Grow a fucking spine for once, how about that? You face me. You face me and tell me what you did—"

"I already told you."

"You tell me again, and you tell me how *sorry* you are," she sneered, "and then you listen when I tell you exactly where to stick your useless apologies. *You. Face. Me.*"

"I can't."

"Where are you?"

Beth didn't say anything.

"Where the hell are you!" Harper screamed, the last word sliding into a shriek of rage.

Beth just wanted it to stop; she wanted everything to stop. "I'm on the roof," she whispered. "At the hotel. On the roof."

"Stay there," Harper commanded in a dangerous voice. "I'm coming."

Beth hung up.

Why? she asked herself, the panic rising. Why tell her, when it would be impossible to face her without disintegrating? Just one more stupid decision in a lifetime of them. Harper would arrive soon, and Beth knew what she would say. And it would all be true. "Coward." "Bitch." *"Murderer."* There would be no one to calm Harper down, and no one to hold Beth and assure her—lie to her—that it would be all right. There was no one left at all. The fear and loneliness threatened to overwhelm her—and then she remembered.

It didn't matter how angry Harper was. It didn't matter what she wanted to say.

Because by the time she got there, it would be too late. It would be over.

chapter thirteen

THE PHONE CALL SOBERED HER UP. HARPER RAN the entire way back to the Camelot, fearing that Beth would lose her nerve and disappear. And as she reached the top of the stairs, she discovered she'd been right to worry: The roof was empty.

Screw it, Harper thought in disgust. She should have known better. For all she knew, Beth had never been here in the first place. Maybe she'd thought it would be fun to send Harper on a wild-goose chase. She was probably downstairs in the room—*Harper's* room—right now, enjoying a good night's sleep. Or worse, she was down there awake, and she wasn't alone.

Harper refused to consider the possibility. Not because it wasn't likely, but because she'd done enough vomiting for the night.

She hesitated on the rooftop, trying to plan out her next move, and that's when she saw it: a hint of blond, just behind the walled edge of the roof.

The Camelot rooftop was shaped like a turret, with a flat, round top surrounded by a thin, waist-high wall of fake brick, assembled in a cutout pattern that looked like jack-o'-lantern teeth. The gaps were wide enough to sit on—and low enough to climb through.

Harper took a few quiet steps across the roof, as the tip of a blond head dipped below the brick and then, a few seconds later, bobbed into sight again. It wasn't until Harper reached the opposite end that she got a good view of what was happening: Beth had climbed over the wall and found footing on a narrow ledge that ran around the outside of the turret. She was pressing herself flat against the fake brick, one hand clutching an ugly plaster gargoyle, the other balled into a fist.

"You can do it," she murmured to herself. "Come on. Come on. Do it."

"Holy shit." The words popped out of Harper's mouth before she could stop herself. "Beth, what the hell are you doing?"

Beth twisted her head up to see Harper, who caught

her breath, as it looked for a moment that the movement might shift Beth's balance enough to send her flying. "You weren't supposed to see this." She turned away again, and stared down—*way* down—at the ground. "But I couldn't—"

"Then what was the plan, genius?" Harper snapped. "I was supposed to come back here and find you all splattered and bloody on the ground?" Beth flinched, and Harper pressed on. "Yes, splattered and *bloody*—what did you think would happen if you do something stupid like this? You float to the ground on a magical cloud and ride off into the sunset? Are you nuts? Oh wait, what am I saying? Look where we are. Of *course* you're freaking nuts."

Stop, she begged herself. *Just shut up. Tell her not to jump. Tell her it will all be okay.* Harper knew her role in this script, and the ineffectual clichés she was supposed to utter. She was supposed to play the hero, to save Beth— and the thought enraged her. Where was Beth when Kaia needed saving?

Where was Beth when Harper was lying on the ground in pain, choking on smoke, waiting for sirens, waiting to hear Kaia scream, or move, or breathe?

"I don't owe you anything," she cried. "Do you hear me? I owe you *nothing*!"

Beth didn't respond. From where she was standing, Harper could see Beth's arm shaking and her grip on the gargoyle slip, then tighten. She could see the tears running down Beth's face, and the way the ball of her left foot stuck out over the edge. And, if Harper leaned over, she could see all the way down, to the half-empty parking lot below. She could see the spot where Beth would land.

If.

Harper wondered if it would be possible to survive a drop like that, and wondered how you would land. If you dove forward, would you smash into the pavement gracefully, like a diver hitting an empty pool, arms first, crumpling into the cement, and then head, then body? Or would you twirl through the air in some accidental acrobatics and fall flat, a cement belly flop? An old Looney Tunes image flashed through her head, and for a second, she pictured a deep, Beth-shaped hole in the ground, Beth standing up and brushing herself off, flat as a pancake but otherwise intact.

This is real, Harper had to remind herself. The edge was real. The drop was real. The ground was real. She could climb onto the wall and all it would take was one step, and everything would end. No equipment necessary. *This is real.*

"Beth. Don't." Her voice had none of the sugary sweetness of some touchy-feely suicide hotline. Harper, in fact, couldn't associate the word "suicide" with this scene—that was a textbook word, a TV word, something ordered and comprehensible that happened to fictional characters and crazy teenagers on some other town's local news. This was too messy to have a label, especially a label that predicted, *required*, a certain end. This was just some nameless thing that was happening, and she wanted it to stop. "Come back up here. We'll talk."

"You don't want to talk to me," Beth said dully.

"Yes, of course, I do."

"You hate me."

"No," Harper protested. Lied. "I forgive you. I accept your apology. Just come back up here. We'll figure it out."

She wanted to mean it, but she couldn't, and it showed. "Look, let me call someone," she suggested. "Reed or—" Even now, she couldn't say it. "Someone."

"No!" Beth twisted around in alarm, again almost losing her grip. "Don't call anyone! And don't lie to me."

You're the liar, Harper wanted to say. The hypocrite, the crusader for truth and justice, the perfect, principled princess, little miss can't be wrong. What a joke—what a fraud she had turned out to be. No one had ever guessed at what lay beneath the blond hair and blue eyes.

But had it always been there? Harper wondered. Or had circumstances created it?

Circumstances. Such a bland, passive, forgiving word. Circumstances, like heartbreak, manipulation, humiliation. Circumstances, as if they were beyond human control. As if, in the end, there was no one to blame.

Circumstances had propelled Beth over the wall, onto the narrow ledge, to the limits of sanity and the cusp of disaster. Circumstances had left only Harper as her would-be savior.

Circumstances, it seemed, were out to get them both.

"What do you want me to say?" Harper asked wearily. "What are you waiting to hear? Can we just cut to it?"

"I know what you're thinking. You're thinking how pathetic I am. I can't even do *this* right."

Harper didn't allow herself to question whether it was true. "You're not pathetic, Beth."

"I said don't lie to me!" she wailed.

"I don't know what else I'm supposed to say here."

"Try the truth," Beth suggested bitterly.

"I can't."

"Because you know what you'd have to say. Because you *want* me to jump."

The unspoken accusation: *You want me to die.*

Harper wanted to deny it. She didn't want to hate anyone that much. Death was too final. She got that now, finally understood that Kaia was never coming back.

But Kaia didn't have to die, she reminded herself. They could call it an accident all they wanted, but that didn't make sense. Nothing so huge, and so horrible, could be so random; it didn't feel right. There had to be a reason—there had to be someone to blame.

And didn't that mean someone should have to pay?

"Let me in!" Reed shouted, pounding harder on the door. "Come on, wake up! Let me in!" Finally, just as he'd accepted the fact that no one was there, the door swung open, Adam in its wake.

"What?"

Now that he was here, Reed almost didn't want to ask the question. What she wanted to do was her business. But he had to make sure. "Is Beth here?"

"What's it look like?" Adam stepped aside and ushered Reed into the empty hotel room. Unless she was hiding in the closet, Beth wasn't there.

He checked, just to make sure. The closet was empty.

"Where is she?" Reed asked.

"Hell if I know. I thought she was with you."

"Why? Did she say something?"

Adam stifled a yawn. "When she ran out of here, I figured she was looking for you. Guess not."

"If you hear from her, can you just tell her to call me?" Reed said, trying to keep the worry out of his voice. "I need to see her."

"Why? So you can mess with her head some more? Maybe get her high again? That worked great the last time. If I hear from her, I'll tell her she's better off without you. Or maybe she's finally figured that out for herself."

Reed wasn't big on physical violence. Especially when it came to all-star athletes who could bench-press cars. But he didn't even stop to think before grabbing Adam's shoulders and pushing him up against the wall. "This isn't a joke. I need to find her."

Adam took a deep breath, then another. "Look, asshole, you want to take your hands off me," he said, in a deliberate and measured voice. *"Now."*

Reed let his arms drop, and sagged against the door frame. "If you hear from her. Please."

Adam's scowl shrunk almost imperceptibly. "I'm not going to hear from her. She's not answering her phone. But . . ." He grabbed for his cell. "Let me call again and—shit."

"What?"

"There's a message—I must have fallen asleep, missed the call. Hold on." He dialed into his voice mail, his eyes widening as he listened to the message. He closed the phone, then hurled it against the mattress. "What the hell are you doing, Beth!"

"What did she say?" Reed asked urgently, though he could guess.

"She—it doesn't matter. It's personal. But . . . I need to get out of here. Find her."

"I'm coming with you."

"Whatever." Adam grabbed his jacket and his room key, opened the door, then doubled back to slip into his sneakers. Reed waited impatiently in the hallway, but Adam paused, just before stepping through the threshold. "You don't think she . . . I mean, she wouldn't . . ."

Reed was trying not to think at all. "Let's just find her," he suggested, striding down the hallway without waiting to see if Adam would follow. "Soon."

"You want the truth? Fine. Truth."

Beth dug her fingers into the pitted stone of the gargoyle and tried not to shut her eyes against the stinging wind. She wanted to see everything, even if it hurt.

"The truth is, I hate you," Harper shouted down.

Big surprise there.

"I've always hated you. You're weak, you're bland, you're spineless, you act like you're this model of virtue who always does the right thing, as if you get to look down on the rest of us because you never make any mistakes. Everything about you is a lie."

"Is this supposed to be helping?" Beth could feel the loose gravel between her left foot and wondered how big a gust of wind would be required to push her off balance. At least that way she wouldn't have to do it herself.

This was humiliating. She'd lowered herself down

here, she'd made peace with her decision, and then—she'd frozen. Unwilling to go back up, unable to let herself go down, she'd stood in this gusty limbo for what felt like hours—until Harper arrived, apparently determined to ship her straight to hell.

"Why should I help you, after what you did to me? And to *her*?"

"You shouldn't!" Beth cried, her voice carried away on the wind, so that she didn't know whether or not she would even be heard. "No one should. That's the point."

"That's *my* point!" Harper shouted back. "Can't you come up with anything better than that? Can't you even defend yourself?"

"What am I supposed to say? I did it." After keeping it trapped inside all this time, it almost felt good to say it—to shout it—to know that when she did fall, it would be without secrets.

"You could say Kaia was a bitch who slept with your boyfriend. You could say *I'm* a bitch who tried to ruin your life and drive you crazy—that I *did* drive you crazy, and you were just trying to get back at me. You could say you weren't the one who was driving the car."

Her perch was precarious, and she didn't dare look up again to see Harper's face. And Beth's imagination wasn't rich enough to come up with something that matched the odd mixture of rage, hysteria, and regret in her voice.

"I can't blame anyone else," Beth insisted. "I did it. I killed her. And this is the only way to make things right . . . even."

"Maybe you don't get to just blame yourself!" Harper yelled. "Maybe you don't get to decide who's guilty."

"So I'm supposed to blame you? For almost getting yourself killed? You want to join me down here?"

"You'd like that, wouldn't you? Because that would make everything neat and even again, right? Because you can't stand a fucking mess."

"I can't stand—"

"You can't stand to face it. To *deal* with it. You think you're doing the right thing? You're just doing what you always do, taking the easy way out. Look, you did something horrible. And maybe I . . ."

Now Beth did look up, just enough to see Harper leaning over the wall, her hair flying across her face, close enough to touch.

"I did something horrible too," Harper concluded. "But that doesn't mean, that *can't* mean—this. Kaia's dead. But we're not, and—"

"And that's not fair!" Beth screamed.

"Oh, grow up! Life isn't fair, you're not perfect, everything sucks—get the hell over it."

Beth wanted to believe her. She wanted to relieve her burden, hand out the blame like a pile of Christmas presents, climb back up onto the roof, go inside the hotel, and go on with the rest of her life as if nothing had ever happened. But . . .

"Harper, I don't know if I can."

The hallways were choked with clumps of drunken Haven seniors, talking, smoking, drinking, and grabbing at Adam as he pushed past. Everyone wanted something from him, and he just wanted to get away. He threaded his way through the crowd, tuning out the chatter and ignoring the gossip until one line finally penetrated:

"Dude, did you hear? There's some crazy chick up on the roof and it looks like she might jump!"

It felt like a pair of iron hands had wrapped around his throat and started to squeeze.

Nothing to do with me, he assured himself. *No one I know.* But as a flood of people crowded toward the elevators, he shoved them all out of the way, hurtling down the hall in the opposite direction, searching for Reed, knowing that he shouldn't waste the time but not wanting to go up there and face whatever there was to face alone.

And Reed deserved to know.

Adam found him, and without explanation—and maybe no explanation was needed, because maybe they had already known—they bypassed the clogged elevators and raced up the stairs, flight after flight, panting but never flagging, Adam several lengths ahead but pausing when he reached the top. They passed through the door together. A crowd of witnesses clustered in front of the door, hushed but disengaged, like they were watching it all unfold on reality TV. Adam knew he should push his way through the crowd, but he couldn't help it. He hesitated.

Beside him, Reed hadn't moved either.

All they had now were their fears—and a little hope. But when they saw what was really going on, there would be no more space for either. There would only be reality. And Adam wasn't ready to face it. Not yet.

"Beth, listen to me," Harper insisted with a new urgency, realizing somehow that this conversation—though it seemed too civilized a term for whatever was going on between them—was nearing its end, one way or another. "Maybe I started this, maybe you did, it doesn't matter— the point is, this can't be how this is supposed to end."

This. If she were stronger, maybe she could be clearer. *This never-ending nightmare of hatred and revenge and misery and death.*

And if she were bolder, maybe she could be more accurate. *I started it. You can't be the one to finish it.*

"You hate me," Beth whined. "I don't know why you even want . . . why you even care—"

"You hate me too," Harper pointed out. "You hated Kaia. But it didn't mean you wanted her—"

"No. No! I didn't want that. I never meant for it to happen. I swear. I promise. It just . . ."

"Happened. I know." And she wasn't just saying it. She could still hate Beth, blame Beth; she could still blame herself. She did. But—

That was the thing. There were no *buts*. No excuses. No explanations. No apologies that could ever be enough. No way to make things right again, no way to make things even. And trying to do that, trying to go backward, reliving the moment over and over again, trying to justify and understand and escape the guilt—it didn't work. It left you on a ledge, twenty stories up, staring down at an empty parking lot, working up the courage to die.

There was no going backward, only forward. There could be no forgiveness, only acceptance. *This* had happened. And that wasn't going to change. So it was either live with the consequences, bear the guilt, and keep going—or the ledge. The parking lot. The other choice.

"This won't fix anything, Beth. This won't make anything even. You're not making up for what you did— you're just running away."

"So what am I supposed to do?"

"Stay. Fight. Feel guilty. Feel miserable. Hate me. Hate yourself. *Live*." Harper hesitated. She had never told anyone what it was like, how bad it got at night, when she felt trapped inside her own body, when she wanted to punish herself, tear her own skin away or just crawl into a dark corner in the back of her mind, disappear into oblivion. But maybe Beth already knew. "It's impossible. Painful. And sometimes you . . . *I* just want it to fucking end. But I . . ."

"You what?"

"I keep going. I make it through a day, and then I make it through the next one. I don't give up. I try."

"What if I can't?" Beth's voice was almost too quiet to hear. Maybe it was the wind. "What if I'm not as . . . strong as you? What if I just can't?"

Harper paused, but it was too late for lies; there'd been too much truth. "Then I guess you give up," she said bitterly. "I guess you quit. You jump. But don't pretend that's some twisted kind of justice. Don't tell yourself that you're doing the right thing. Just . . . please. Don't."

He had expected to recognize the figure on the edge, he had expected the terror and the shock and the nausea. But he hadn't expected this.

"Harper?"

The night folded in on itself, and, as if the last several nightmarish hours had never happened, he imagined for a moment that he was on a different roof, alone, and Harper was still waiting for him.

I never gave up on you, he told her silently. *On us.*

He had been so certain of his decision, so eager to find her, hold her, start all over again with a perfect kiss that would heal all their wounds. And then—circumstances had gotten in the way.

Apparently she wasn't waiting for him anymore. Apparently, she'd given up.

Before he could move, Harper had swung herself half over the wall. He opened his mouth to scream, but only a hoarse moan dribbled out, like he was in a dream. And it felt like a dream, everything moving so slowly, yet inexorably, toward a point he could see so vividly, it felt like it had already happened, and there was nothing he could do.

"No," he begged, but only in a whisper.

And then he saw a hand clasping Harper's, and a blond head emerging over the wall. From this distance he couldn't see her face, but he could picture the limpid blue eyes, and he could imagine the tears. Harper clutched her hand, pulled her over the wall, and back to safety. They stood there frozen for a moment, silhouetted against the neon skyline, holding hands like two paper dolls, in peril of blowing away. And then their hands dropped. Beth took a step forward, then another, and collapsed to the ground, shaking, her sobs echoing across the night.

Adam gave himself a moment to let the relief sink in, a moment of joy. And then he began to run.

It had all happened too fast, over before Reed even understood what was at stake, and what he'd almost lost. He'd seen her hair, her pale skin almost gleaming, and just like that, she'd been back on solid ground. And she needed him.

I loved you, he thought.

I hate you.

She'd taken Kaia away from him. She'd taken everything away, not just Kaia, but herself. She had been too good for him, too much for him, but she had loved him, and it had made the world glow—and it had all been a lie.

And yet.

She was still here. He had almost lost her, as he'd lost Kaia. But she was still here. Alive. Needing him. Maybe she wasn't the person he'd thought she was. But maybe—and he hated himself for thinking it, because it was a betrayal, it was treason—maybe it didn't matter.

She was still Beth, and she was still alive.

Maybe it's not too late.

And then it was.

By the time he took a step forward, Adam was already halfway across the roof. By the time he took another, Adam had scooped her up in his arms. Adam had pressed her head against his shoulder. Adam had saved the day.

Reed knew she could see him, and he waited for her to push Adam aside. To walk across the roof and apologize one more time, to give him a chance to forgive—and maybe this time he could. But she held Adam tight, and buried her face in his shoulder.

I loved you, Reed thought as he backed away through the crowd, through the doorway, inside, away. *I could have loved you. I love you.*

He didn't know which it was.

He didn't know where he was going.

He didn't care.

She had stupidly thought he was coming for her.

Harper had stood against the wall, eyes shut, breaths coming in deep, erratic gasps as the tension leaked out of her. Her hand had tightened, as if she still held Beth, knowing what would happen if she let go, and how easy it would be. Knowing she never would. She had, after a moment, taken in the crowd hovering fearfully by the stairwell, and tried to collect her energy to decide what to tell them.

It was Beth's story—Beth's show—but Harper knew she would have to direct it herself. She would dole out the details. She would handle the spin. She would make sure no one ever knew the truth. Because she could—because she was still standing, and Beth was crumpled on the ground, waiting for rescue.

Harper had done enough.

And then she saw Adam, and knew he had finally come for her. It was the wrong roof, the wrong time, but he was here, and she was ready. She'd meant what she'd told Beth, about forgiveness, about moving forward—now that he was here, she was ready to start again.

He had run toward her, and it seemed to take forever, his movements in slow motion, like the hero's run through a meadow in a cheesy movie, except that it didn't seem cheesy to Harper, it just seemed romantic. Perfect.

And then she realized she was in the wrong movie. She wasn't the heroine, and this wasn't her happy ending.

She was a cameo role, a plot device.

He swept Beth into his arms and she hung limp against him, her body curled up in his embrace.

Harper remembered telling Beth to get a spine, and realized it would be a useless purchase: She already had everything she needed to hold herself up. Adam hugged her, and rubbed her back, and from where she was standing, Harper could see her trembling, could hear her sobs.

Harper, on the other hand, held herself perfectly still. She forced herself to breathe evenly. She forced her eyes not to tear—she'd had plenty of practice.

And by the time Adam thought to look over at her, Beth's slim body draped across his chest, her hair spilling down his arm, Harper knew she had attained just the right look. The look that said, with ferocious determination, *I don't care.*

It all fell away as soon as she met his eyes. They looked haunted. She felt the tears spring into her own, and she was glad for the wall behind her, holding her upright. He gave her a half smile, one she recognized from years of friendship, the one he'd pulled out when he broke her Barbie doll or mashed a snowball into her face and given her a bloody nose. It said, *I'm sorry. I didn't mean to. I wish it had happened another way.*

He opened his mouth, as if to speak. But they had known each other for so long, they didn't need words.

She could, if she allowed herself, read the truth in his face. Whatever it was.

She needs me now, but I *need you. Just wait.*

Or maybe:

I choose her. Again.

Harper, he mouthed silently. *Please.*

She could know everything, if she wanted to. Just from watching his face, looking in his eyes. But whatever he had to say to her, it wouldn't change the fact that his arms were still wrapped around Beth. That Harper stood off to the side, watching, alone.

She might need to wait a lifetime, or maybe just a day.

But she was Harper Grace, and she was tired of waiting. He'd made his choice. Now it was her turn.

And she turned away.

chapter fourteen

HOME.

It was a six-hour drive, without traffic. Time he needed, to think. To figure things out. But he was having some trouble with that.

The thinking.

It was all muddled in his brain, the last twenty-four hours, the fear and the relief and the regret all bleeding together into a muddy, impenetrable sludge. Adam clenched the wheel tightly. He'd driven Kane's car plenty of times before, but never without Kane in the passenger's seat, hounding him to speed up, warning him of the penalties of living life in the slow lane—and the even graver penalties of denting Kane's Camaro.

But Kane was riding home in Miranda's car, with Harper. Where Adam was no longer welcome.

It was easy to zone out, to listen to the gravel under the wheels and the wind against the dash. It was easy to pretend that by the time he got home, everything that had happened would be forgotten. Life would return to normal.

But he knew it was a lie. Harper wouldn't forgive him, not this time—at least, not unless he was willing to meet her demands. And he couldn't. He had responsibilities now, and he couldn't walk away, even if it meant losing—

No. He wouldn't think about that. He couldn't afford to. Not when Beth sat beside him, her eyes closed, her face still stained with tears. What he wanted, what he'd lost, it wasn't important now. Beth was the one in trouble—and someone had to make sure that, whatever happened, she never ended up on that roof again. She was weak, in need. He was strong, and he could be there for her.

He *would*.

He was glad she'd finally fallen asleep in the passenger's seat, glad she felt comfortable enough—safe enough—to close her eyes and escape from everything, at least for a few hours. If only he could do the same.

❧ ❧ ❧

Love.

Was it possible? *I'm in love*, Miranda thought, pretending she was saying it casually, the way you'd say, *I have a toothache* or *I'm hungry*. Like it was something that happened to you all the time. Like it wasn't something you'd been dreaming of for years, all the while forcing yourself to stop, knowing that you had no chance of ever getting the thing you most desperately wanted.

I got it, though. She turned toward Kane, who took his eyes off the road just long enough to give her a warm smile. *I got* him.

She knew she needed to slow down. She wasn't in love—or, at least, *he* wasn't in love, not yet, and until both people felt the same way, it didn't count. She knew that better than anyone, since she was the one who'd been longing, for all these years, watching him from a distance, waiting for him to notice.

She still didn't understand why he suddenly had.

She should be cautious. She understood that. He hadn't made her any promises, hadn't talked about the future. Yes, he had implied that there was now *something* where there had been nothing, but they were on vacation. It was Vegas, where anything goes. What would he want from her when they got back home? What if he didn't want anything?

But her doubts couldn't make much of a dent in her happiness. Not even Harper, moody and silent in the backseat, could do that. Miranda had already forgiven her best friend—in the mood she was in, she would have forgiven anyone anything—but much as she wanted to, she couldn't force herself to wallow in Harper's misery. She didn't have room for it in her brain.

Her body glowed with the memory of Kane's touch, and she touched him now, just because she could. His hand rested on the gearshift, and, still a little terrified, she wrapped hers around it. He smiled at her again.

She was allowed to touch him now, whenever she wanted. She was allowed to kiss him. Maybe she was even allowed to fall in love with him.

Miranda wasn't stupid. She knew she was getting ahead of herself, that things were too new, too uncertain, that if she let herself go too far too fast, she could end up getting hurt.

But with their hands pressed together, none of that seemed to matter. When Kane smiled at her—with that look in his eye, the one she'd always been waiting for, the one that said *I want* you—she couldn't help it.

She felt like she would never hurt again.

Maybe.

That's what Kane kept telling himself. He didn't *know* it was a bad decision; he wasn't *sure* it was going to lead to disaster. Yes, there was that feeling in his gut, that *Oh, shit* feeling that had never steered him wrong before. But backing down just because he expected disaster? That would be giving in to fear. And that was unacceptable.

She kept darting glances at him, nervous, adoring looks. *Smile back*, he instructed himself. *Play along.*

Except that he wasn't playing, not this time—and that was the problem.

Miranda was the one he should be worried about. She was fragile, even if she pretended not to be. He knew he could hurt her—he knew exactly how to do it. And this whole thing, this ludicrously bad idea he'd had, it was probably a good way to start.

And yet . . .

Maybe it was a worthwhile experiment. That's how he would look at it: an experiment. Nothing less, nothing more. Maybe he could let someone in, maybe she really was different from the rest of them, the girls he strung along until they got too close, or he got too bored.

It's not like he had proposed or anything. A kiss was not a promise. A beginning didn't have to last forever.

Stop making such a big deal out of this, he thought, focusing on the road. He wouldn't look at her again, not for a while. He would concentrate on the road ahead of them, on the wide, cement path stretching to the horizon. He would clear his mind and analyze his options. He would *not* panic.

And by the time they got back home, maybe he would have an answer. He would have figured out how to make this thing work—or, at least, whether he wanted to try. *What happens in Vegas . . .* he reminded himself. It could be a mistake, trying to bring a piece of the city home with them. The two of them together, it had made sense back there—but that was a foreign land. A million miles away from Grace, CA. Who knew what would happen when they tried to fit themselves back into their old lives—together.

It could work, he decided, feeling her watching him again.

Maybe.

Empty.

It was as if someone had carved out her insides and dumped them in the garbage. Or maybe they were leaking out, slowly but steadily, because the farther away they got from Vegas, the emptier Harper felt. It was as if she'd left behind everything that had ever mattered to her, and part of her wanted to scream at Kane, beg him to stop the car, turn around, take her back.

But a U-turn wouldn't help—what she needed was a time machine.

It was so strange, being back in the car again, back on the same highway, as if nothing had changed, when everything had. She was in the backseat now, while Kane and Miranda sat together in the front, not talking, just exchanging sly little glances, speaking to each other in that silent language that all couples have. The wordless communion that left everyone else out in the cold. Harper wanted to be happy for them, but she didn't have it in her. All she could see was the potential for pain; all she could believe was that, in the end, everyone ended up alone.

She had been so optimistic on the way to Vegas, stupidly thinking that she could find happiness there, that Sin City would somehow show her a way to wash herself of her sins.

They say you can find anything in Vegas, but all she'd found were answers. She knew whom to blame now. She knew who was on her side—and who wasn't.

Harper stared out the window, out at the desert flatness, remembering how much Kaia had hated the unchanging scenery, with its dusty infinities and scraggly brush, as if the land had a skin condition. The ground was pitted and pockmarked. Diseased.

She closed her eyes, trying to regain the certainty she'd felt up on that roof, her belief in the necessity of moving forward. And maybe it was possible. They had hours left on the road, time enough to cleanse herself. She would leave her emotional baggage in Vegas, and arrive back in Grace refreshed and renewed.

She would leave behind the anger, the pain of betrayal, the misguided hope, the guilt, the bitterness. And, hardest of all, most important of all, she would leave behind the love. She would leave Adam; she would stop clinging to the past and stop hoping they could go back.

But if she succeeded, if she really could leave it all behind . . . what would she have left?

Lost.

"Shit!" Reed pounded the wheel in frustration. He'd just passed the same crappy Howard Johnson for the third time in a row. Confirmation that he was no closer to the highway entrance than he'd been an hour ago. A fucking waste of time, just like the entire weekend, he thought.

Except not a total waste—at least he'd found out the truth. That was something.

He cursed the guys for ditching him—they'd hooked up with a couple of Haven High's hottest stoner girls and were staying in town an extra night. How was he supposed to read the map and drive at the same time without crashing into the side of the damn Howard Johnson?

Maybe it wouldn't be the worst thing in the world, he thought.

Then hated himself for thinking it.

He pulled the van into a gas station, intending to ask for directions. But instead of getting out, he just sat there, resting his head against the cool leather steering wheel. Then he lit a joint and let his mind drift.

Maybe this was a sign. Maybe he was supposed to be lost, stranded in Vegas, hundreds of miles from home. It wasn't much of a home, not now, after Kaia . . . after Beth.

He'd gambled and he'd lost. Big. He'd lost it all. He could start over again in Vegas. Wait tables, get a cheap apartment, start up a new band. Track down Star*la. He could make a new life for himself.

He knew it wasn't realistic. It wasn't going to happen. But it was nice to imagine, just for a while. It was nice to ignore the future, the crap he would face when he got back to Grace, the pain that would slice through the fog as soon as the buzz wore off.

Eventually, he'd go inside, get directions, hit the highway, drive home. He just didn't know why. He'd lost it all this weekend, so what did he have to go back for?

Nothing.

Hope.

Beth had thought she would never experience it again. And maybe you couldn't call it hope yet, not quite. It was just a tiny kernel of an emotion, buried so far down that she wouldn't have known it was there if she hadn't been so raw, if everything she thought or felt hadn't screamed for attention. There was still so much pain, fear, sorrow, and, as always, guilt—but now there was something else, too. A tiny bright spot, a fresh breath. An expectation that maybe, just maybe, the worst was behind her.

Hope.

Her terrible secret had come out, she had been exposed—and then accused, and then abandoned. But not completely. She squeezed her hand into a fist, remembering how tightly Harper had grabbed her, how Beth hadn't wanted to let go. Harper wanted her to live.

And, as she had realized on that roof, staring down at the cement, willing herself to take the step, Beth wanted it too.

Adam hadn't spoken, not since they'd gotten onto the highway. And Beth didn't know what to say, so eventually she had closed her eyes and pretended to sleep. She didn't know what was going to happen next, when they got home, when she had to face Harper again. When she had to face the absence of Reed, who she knew would never come back to her.

Adam, she thought. *Remember Adam.* She could hear him breathing next to her. She could smell his familiar, comfortable scent, and knew that if she put her hand on his, he wouldn't pull away. He wasn't repulsed by her. He didn't hate her. He wanted to help—he wanted to forgive.

He didn't think she was worthless. And that was a start.

It seemed silly to hope, to think that anything good could happen or that her life could return to some kind of even balance, something tolerable, not weighed down by guilt and misery. But she couldn't help it. Behind her, Vegas was dipping beneath the horizon, and it felt like all the horrible things she'd done—or, at least, that one horrible thing she'd done—was receding along with it.

Maybe Harper had been right.

Beth didn't deserve happiness, forgiveness, or peace.

But maybe somehow she would find them anyway.

seven deadly sins

GREED

For Susie

I grant him bloody,
Luxurious, avaricious, false, deceitful,
Sudden, malicious, smacking of every sin
That has a name.
—William Shakespeare, *Macbeth*

✳

All the riches, baby, won't mean anything
All the riches, baby, don't bring what your love can bring.
—Gwen Stefani, "Rich Girl"

chapter one

"MIRROR MIRROR, ON THE WALL," BETH MANNING whispered, "who's the fairest of them all?"

The mirror was silent.

She laughed softly at her own silliness—then froze, realizing that this was the first time in a long time she'd seen a real smile on her face. The girl in the mirror looked unfazed, like smiling was something she did every day. The girl in the mirror, her long blond hair wrapped into an elegant slipknot, her lips brushed a pale pink, her blue eye shadow as shimmery as her strapless blue gown, looked like she didn't have a worry in the world. She looked like the kind of girl who frolicked in enchanted forests, transformed toads into princes, talked to mirrors and expected them to talk back.

She looked happy.

Beth wished the mirror really *was* magical. Because then she could slip into it and hide away. Let her mirror image, the happy girl, the *normal* girl—let that girl go to the prom.

The doorbell rang. Beth drew in a deep breath. She had made her parents promise not to answer it, telling them that she'd spent her whole life picturing the moment where she opened the door to meet her handsome date, Prince Charming come to sweep her away to the ball. She'd made them promise to stay upstairs until called upon, and keep the twins under lock and key so as not to spoil her picture-perfect moment. It was only a half lie.

She *had* spent most of her life picturing this night. She had lain in bed, staring up at the pale pink canopy—the one that was taken down when she got too old, even if, ashamed to admit it, she had wished it could stay forever. The swooping pink fabric made her feel like she was lying down to sleep in some exotic land, a world of silk scarves and magic carpet rides, ladies-in-waiting, Prince Charmings. She had gazed at that canopy, night after night, imagining herself as a high school senior, finally able to escape the dull realities of life in Grace, California, ready to face the world. All grown up.

It'll be fine, she told herself, walking slowly downstairs. This was why she couldn't have her parents in the room. It would take all the strength she had to open the door, to officially begin the night. She wouldn't have anything left over for the artificial smile and the bright tone, the good-daughter act they needed to assure themselves that Beth was still perfect. She needed a moment alone behind the door to close her eyes, breathe deeply, and remember that she was stronger than she looked. She had to be. *I can do this*, she told herself.

The door swung open.

"Whoa. You look . . . whoa."

Beth's throat closed up. She just stood there, staring at the tuxedo, the fresh corsage in its plastic case, the scuffed black loafers, the smoothed-down hair, the black bowtie, impossibly straight. "What are you . . . what are you doing here?"

Reed Sawyer's hands tightened on the corsage case, which crackled as the plastic bent in on itself. His eyes met hers, and, much as she wanted to, she couldn't look away. She'd seen those eyes in her dreams, deep and dark, bottomless. And in her dreams—nightmares, really—they accused her.

But this Reed was real, and there was nothing in his eyes but . . . she wouldn't let herself believe it was tenderness, or affection.

Surely it was just the light.

"I said I'd take you to the prom," he said, his voice the same velvety growl that she remembered. She wanted to touch him. Just his arm, or his shoulder, just to run her fingers lightly across his chest or to straighten the bowtie that didn't need straightening, to reassure herself that he was really there.

"That was last month," she said softly. "Before . . ."

Before he had found out that she was a killer.

It was an accident, she told herself. *I never wanted it to happen.* She was trying to learn to forgive herself. But if it was hard for her to do, it would be impossible for Reed. And why should he want to bother? Reed had only wanted Kaia—and accident or not, Beth had killed her.

"I said a lot of stuff," Reed said.

Beth nodded.

"And I meant it."

Do not *cry,* she ordered herself.

"But . . ." He shrugged. "I said I'd take you to the prom. I keep my promises."

"You went to all this trouble"—Beth gestured at the tuxedo and all of it—"just because . . ." She tucked a loose strand of hair behind her ear. "Reed, you really shouldn't have, I mean—I never would have expected, not after . . ." She took a deep breath and tried to steady herself, or at least steady her voice. "You didn't have to do this."

"I don't do anything because I have to," he reminded her. "But if you want me to go—"

"No!" She reached out for him, then dropped her hand almost as soon as she'd raised it. "Reed, you know how sorry—"

He shook his head. "No more," he said harshly. "You said it enough, and . . ." This time, she had no idea what was hidden in the silence.

And I can't stand to hear it again?

And whatever you say, I'll hate you forever?

And I forgive you?

But he didn't continue, just opened the corsage package and pulled out a single white lily on a thin elastic string. "My dad said I had to get this for you, and since I didn't know what color your dress was going to be, I figured white, so . . ."

"It's beautiful," she told him. "It's perfect." She held out her hand, expecting him to hand her the flower. But instead, he rested his hand beneath her palm and closed his fingers warmly around hers.

Their eyes met again. "Beth, the reason I'm here, the thing is—"

He broke off at the sound of footsteps coming up the walk.

"Beth?" Adam, as always, looked as if he'd been born to wear a tuxedo. He hesitated a few feet away from the doorway, confused.

Reed ripped his hand away. "You're fucking kidding me," he growled, his eyes hardening and his mouth twisting into a scowl. "You work fast, don't you?"

"Reed, wait," Beth pleaded. "We're not together—"

"Lucky him."

"I didn't think you were coming."

"Yeah," Reed snarled. "I got that." He tossed the lily to the ground and turned away. "Forget it." Beth sagged against the door frame, watching him storm down the walkway. *I will not cry*, she told herself. *I will not collapse. I will just*— But she didn't know what she was supposed to do next.

"What was *he* doing here?" Adam asked, hurrying toward the door as if to hold her steady. She waved him away. She couldn't stand the thought of him touching her, not now.

Beth shook her head. "Nothing." The problem was, she didn't *know* what he'd been doing there. "Let's just get out of here."

"Beth, wait." His voice was hesitant, like he was afraid that his next word would set her off. Like she was delicate and could break. "Talk to me. What's going on?"

She shook her head again, harder, feeling the slipknot

brushing against the nape of her neck. "I can't. Seriously, let's just get out of here."

He sighed. "Fine. But first . . ." He clasped both of her hands in his.

She tried to tug away. *Just friends*, that's what they'd said. That's what they both wanted—or, at least, all they could handle. But he held tight.

"You look, uh, really pretty," he said.

She looked down. He was stepping on the lily. "Thanks," she murmured.

He crossed over to her side and put an arm around her waist, just like he always had in the old days. The crushed lily no longer looked like a flower. It was just a broken heap of white, ground into the cement.

"Come on, Cinderella," Adam said gently. "Let's go to the ball."

Stop giggling, Miranda Stevens told herself.

But she couldn't help it.

"Looks like you got something on your dress," Kane said, rubbing his fingers against the soft green silk. "I think it's just water."

She giggled.

"What?"

"Nothing." She giggled again. No surprise: It's what girls did around the great Kane Geary. Miranda had always prided herself on being different, but now she understood. She had to giggle. Not because it was cute, or because she was trying to be more feminine. But because it was ridiculous.

Kane Geary, in a tuxedo, his arm stiff around her waist, posing for the camera.

Kane Geary, prom date.

Kane Geary . . . boyfriend.

You just had to laugh. Or, in Miranda's case, giggle.

"Miranda, what's up with you tonight?" Kane asked. He had started calling her Miranda after Vegas, after the kiss. Before, it had always been "Stevens." But now, things were different.

"Nothing. Really." She rolled her eyes at her mother and slid her finger across her throat, the message clear: *Picture time is over*. And, uncharacteristically, her mother obeyed, hurrying across the expansive backyard to gossip with Harper's parents. Mrs. Grace was brimming with tears over the way her "little girl" was all grown up. Miranda's mother, on the other hand, was just relieved, and—as she never tired of pointing out—shocked that Miranda had scored a date.

Kane turned her around in his arms so they were facing each other, then leaned down and kissed her. He tasted like spearmint and gin. "Have I told you how beautiful you look tonight?"

No need to suck up, she was about to joke. *I already agreed to go with you.*

But she cut herself off. She wasn't his buddy anymore, she was his *girlfriend*—but she wouldn't be for long if she couldn't figure out how to act the part.

"Thank you," she cooed. "And you look really handsome."

He gave her a strange look, then smiled. It wasn't the famous Kane smirk, crooked and mysterious and all-knowing; it was just an ordinary smile. Then his hand was warm against her neck, softly kneading the tight muscles, and she closed her eyes. "And what have I done to deserve this?" she asked, sighing blissfully.

"Nothing," he whispered in her ear, pausing to quickly kiss the lobe. "You can owe me one."

She glanced at him, expecting to see mischief in his face, some deliciously devious anticipation of the IOU, but nothing was there but the placid smile. She smiled back, and then there was silence.

All those years, all that banter . . . and suddenly, they had nothing left to say.

"Maybe, um, we should go check on Harper?" she suggested, tipping her head toward the edge of the backyard where Harper was chatting animatedly with her date and obviously doing a fine job of taking care of herself.

"Good idea." Kane grabbed her hand and led her

across the yard as she tried to keep her sharp heels from digging too deeply into the Graces' finely manicured lawn.

They caught Harper with her head thrown back in authentic-sounding laughter. Only a best friend could have known it was utterly fake. "Jake was just telling me about the time he got drunk off his ass and ended up streaking naked through a PTA meeting," Harper said, gasping for breath. She gave Kane a sharp poke on the shoulder. "Is there a reason you waited so long to introduce me to your only nonloser friend?"

Kane raised an eyebrow. "I like him too much to punish him like that, Grace."

"Very funny." Harper pulled back her lips in a gruesomely exaggerated smile. "So why now?"

Kane shrugged. "What can I tell you? He lost a bet."

Everyone laughed, except for Jake—a dark-haired senior from the next town over who was built like a quarterback and grinned like a talk-show host. "*He* is going to the prom with the hottest girl in town," he said, wrapping an arm around Harper's shoulders. She slipped out of his grip.

"Hotness takes work, boys," she said, grabbing Miranda's wrist. "So *we* are off to make ourselves beautiful, and then"—she shot a look over her shoulder at the horde of eager parents—"we can get the hell out of here and have some real fun." Harper dragged Miranda into the kitchen and shut the sliding-glass door behind them. "Kill me now."

"That bad?"

Harper wandered into the living room and threw herself down on one of the couches. "He's fine. Whatever. I told you this was a bad idea. I didn't want to go."

Miranda snorted. "Like I was really going to let you sulk in your room on prom night. You think I could have any fun knowing you were lying in bed crying about—"

She fell silent under Harper's steely glare.

"I'm over him," Harper said steadily.

"Right. I know." So over Adam that she hid every time she saw him coming down the hall. So over him that every time Miranda—unwisely—said his name, Harper's face flushed red, then turned to stone. "You're totally over him. Which is why we thought—"

"We," Harper cackled. "I love it. Kane Geary has never been a we in his life—I still don't get how you did it."

Miranda flopped down on the couch next to her. "Yeah, I'm a regular superhero."

"The power to leap tall buildings and melt the hearts of ice-cold bastards."

"Just call me Wonder Woman," Miranda said sourly. "As in, I wonder what the hell I'm doing."

"Trouble in paradise?"

"We're talking about *you*," Miranda pointed out. "Jake

is perfectly nice—and, in case you didn't notice, hot. I wouldn't let Kane set you up with a loser."

"He's not a loser," Harper admitted. "He's just not . . ."

Not Adam.

The Eiffel Tower–shaped poster board was peeling off the wall, the sparkling lights dangling from the ceiling had mostly burned out, and the faux champagne tasted like sugar water. So much for Midnight in Paris.

"Isn't it the coolest?" Emma Logan asked, grinning idiotically at her fellow prom princesses, assembled in a neat row of chairs across the stage. "It's like we're really in Paris." She pointed at the river of blue balloons that wound its way around the edge of the gymnasium. "Look, it's like the Thames!"

Harper rubbed her forehead, careful not to accidentally smudge her mascara. "First of all, it's not *Thames*—" She pronounced it as Emma had, rhyming with "James." "And, second of all, that's in London." *Idiot*, she wanted to add, but even though she no longer cared about these girls, or their A-list boyfriends, or the masses of hangers-on who followed all of them around like lost kittens, some reflex forced her to finish the sentence with a graceful, self-deprecating smile, as if apologizing for not being just as dumb.

"God, did you, like, sleep through geography class?" Sara Walker piped up from Harper's other side. "It's totally supposed to be the Seine." She pronounced it "seen." This time, Harper didn't bother to correct her. Nor did she point out that Sara's dress looked more like a potato sack than a prom gown. Except for the color—*that* just looked like cat puke.

The vice principal took the stage, pulling his tuxedo jacket down over his lumpy potbelly. Harper could see the sweat running down the back of his neck. "Welcome to the Haven High Senior Prom!" he shouted into the mic, and, possibly for the first time in his career, he was rewarded with a round of sincere and thundering applause. "Are you all having a good time?"

More cheering. Harper clapped too, bringing her hands together so sharply, her palms stung. The pain helped wake her up.

"Behind me, you see some of the loveliest ladies in all the land," the vice principal said, holding out his hands to stem the drunken wolf whistles. "And tonight, one lucky princess is going to become a queen." A mousy sophomore scurried onstage and handed the vice principal a tiara. From where Harper was sitting, it looked like a jewel-encrusted crown, sparkling in the light like a lattice of diamonds. But she knew better. It was mostly cardboard, paste, and sequins, with a few rhinestones stuck on for good measure.

The sophomore handed him a small white envelope and then, with a wide-eyed glance at the prom court—a look that said, *just maybe, someday, don't laugh, but it could be me*—rushed off the stage. Emma was grabbing handfuls of her dress and twisting them into tight knots while Sara gripped the edges of her chair, her bloodless fingers turning white. Then the vice principal opened the envelope, and every girl onstage sucked in a sharp, terrified breath.

Every girl except Harper, who—unlike the rest of them—hadn't campaigned, hadn't tallied a crowd of friends and admirers who'd promised to vote for her, wasn't darting glances at the competition and trying to convince herself that her smile was brighter, her hair shinier, her breasts perkier, her chances better.

Partly because she just didn't care anymore, or at least she didn't want to.

Partly because she knew who she was, and what she deserved. And so did everyone else.

"So without further ado, your new prom queen is . . . Harper Grace!"

There was a flurry of squealing, and Emma and Sara gave her a hug. They all hated her.

Harper stood up, crossed the stage, and accepted her crown. It looked fake and cheap close up. The metal dug into the skin at her temples. If she kept it on all night, she was going to get a headache.

Harper raised her hand and gave the crowd her best Miss America wave. The warm roar of appreciation that greeted her was almost enough to puncture the numbness—almost, but not quite.

"On to prom king," the vice principal continued, placing a meaty hand on Harper's shoulder. She forced herself not to shrug it off. "Let's see who will be lucky enough to get the spotlight dance with our queen."

And *now* Harper felt her stomach clench. She wiped her palms against her dress and tried not to show that she cared. She *didn't* care, she told herself. Whoever was elected king, that's who she would dance with.

And if it was him, then so be it. She would dance with him, just as she'd done plenty of times before. And she would feel nothing. Because she was over him. Because he had chosen Beth; he had proven that Harper meant nothing to him, or at least didn't mean enough, which was just as bad. She would stand across from him and lace her arms around his shoulders. She would inhale his cologne, that deep, musky scent that smelled like the center of a forest. She would lean in, feel his breath on her cheek, press her chin into his shoulder, and sway. She would let him hold her, let his hands rest warm and solid at her hips, let his body press against hers—only because she had to. Because it was an obligation, the responsibility of winners.

She would do what she was supposed to do, and she would feel nothing. Because she was over him. So she didn't care if he lost—and didn't care if he won.

"And your new prom king . . . Adam Morgan! Come up onstage, Adam, to collect your crown and your queen!" The applause faded away, and the crowd drifted to the edges of the dance floor as a cheesy love song came through the speakers.

You're mine, all of the time.
I belong in your eyes . . .

A spotlight lit the empty floor. And Adam still hadn't appeared. Someone laughed.

"Adam Morgan," the vice principal said again. His hand, still on Harper's shoulder, was beginning to sweat. "Has anyone seen Adam Morgan?"

"Kid's not here!" someone shouted from the crowd.

"King me!" someone else called out. "I got what she needs!"

Harper scoured their faces, looking for his. The music played on.

With you I live,
Without you I cry,
Without you I die . . .

This is pathetic, Harper thought. So stupid. So high school. So beneath her. But the spotlight shined, the music played, and the floor was empty.

Her body on autopilot, Harper walked to the edge of the stage and descended the stairs, keeping her head up and her shoulders back. She crossed the floor, the crowd opening up to let her pass, and found herself in the middle of the dance floor, alone.

She wouldn't cry. That wasn't her style. But inside, where no one could see . . . inside, it felt like something was on fire.

And then strong arms were around her waist, holding her steady, and she was swaying with the music, and, for a moment, everything was as it should be.

But it wasn't Adam.

"Congratulations, Your Highness," the boy whispered in her ear. It took her a moment to come back to herself, to remember. Not Adam. It was her date, come to rescue her.

The boy—Jake, she remembered—held tight. "It was no contest," he murmured. "Compared to you, the rest of these girls are total dogs."

She knew she should say thank you. But she didn't want to speak. She didn't want to be there at all. She wanted to disappear; she wanted *him* to disappear.

He tugged her tighter and pressed his cheek against

the top of her head. He smelled wrong. Like coffee and deodorant. Harper pulled back and looked at his face, really *looked* at it, for the first time that night. It was ruddy and well proportioned, with all the right features in all the right places. His eyes were brown and sparkly, his nose slightly too large; he had a dimple in his left cheek and a cleft in his chin. "Thanks for bringing me tonight," he said, his breath slightly sour from Kane's bootleg gin.

He waited for an answer. Instead, she kissed him.

> *With you I live,*
> *Without you I die . . .*

The numbness descended again, saving her. He rubbed his hands up and down her back, like Adam, but not Adam. She closed her eyes, but there was no fooling herself, no pretending that he was anything but a stranger. No pretending he was anyone else. His fingers cold against her skin, he brushed her hair back, and kissed her, and kissed her, and the song refused to end and he refused to let go.

And it was as she had imagined it.

She felt nothing.

chapter two

"SHUT THE HELL UP!" REED SHOUTED, THROWING his empty bottle against the wall. It smashed to pieces, the glass spraying through the air and clattering against the linoleum. "Just shut up." He leaned forward until his face was nearly pressed into the beat-up couch that smelled like mildew, and tucked his head between his arms, trying to drown out the noise.

To drown out everything.

"Dude, what's your deal?" Fish asked, appearing in the doorway. He was still holding his drumsticks.

"Just give it up," Reed said. He took another swig of the tequila. His head throbbed. Why was even he still awake? The liquor and pot were supposed to knock him out, or at least make things blurry and painless. But his eyes were open, and his mind was too clear.

It was the rage. Nothing had been able to stop it, not for weeks. Not the drinking, not the smoking, not the pills. He was too angry, and whatever he did to try to avoid it only backfired. The drinking fueled the rage. The pot trapped his mind in an endless loop—Beth. Kaia. Beth in his arms. Kaia in the car, broken. Smashed. Beth's lips. Kaia's smile. Death.

And now he had a new image to play with: Beth and Adam.

It was his own fault. He didn't know what he'd been thinking, dressing up like a penguin, crawling back there like nothing had happened, like he could give her a second chance after everything she'd done, like they could start fresh. Maybe he'd imagined that she was hurting too, that he wasn't the only one who lay around all day choking on fumes and cursing everything. It had been a mistake. Just the latest in a long line.

"We're rehearsing, man," Hale complained, unstrapping his guitar. "*Your* idea, before you flaked."

"I'm back now, aren't I?"

Fish threw a drumstick at him. "Yeah, you're back, drunk and stoned, and you didn't even bring any of the good stuff to share. So what good are you?"

"You wanna rehearse?" Reed pushed himself off the couch, then staggered as the world tipped beneath him. He collapsed backward, his head slamming against the wall with a dull thud and a sharp pain. "Let's rehearse."

Hale snorted. "You're worthless like this. Get some sleep."

"Is this a joke?" Reed sneered. *"You're* calling *me* a slacker?" He was the one who always wanted to rehearse. He was the one who booked them gigs, who wrote the songs, who wanted them to go on tour—or, at least, he had been.

These days, there didn't seem to be much point.

He grabbed for a half-open beer, missed, and sent it flying across the room. "Shit! Thassa last one."

"You're a mess, kid," Fish said.

Reed peered up at him, at his stringy blond hair, sallow face, bloodshot eyes, ready to argue. A mess? If anyone was a mess, it was . . .

But he lost the thought. Just like he'd lost everything else.

"I'm sorry," Beth said again. "Really, I'm so sorry."

Adam squeezed her hand. "Stop. It's okay."

Beth leaned back on her swing and tipped her head up to the sky. "It's not okay." She shivered and rubbed her hands along her bare arms.

"Cold?"

She shook her head, but Adam draped his tuxedo jacket around her shoulders. Instead of sitting back down on his swing, he stayed behind her and gave her a gentle push. Her heels skidded across the dirt.

"You can go now, if you want," she told him. "I'm okay. Really."

"And I'm okay here, too."

She didn't try to convince him, even though she almost believed it was true, that if he left, she would be okay—at least as long as she stayed on the playground. These days, it was the only place where she felt safe, the only place where she could quiet all the accusing voices in her mind. Tonight, it had seemed like the only place to hide.

"I can't believe I made you miss your senior prom," she told him. "I suck."

Adam grabbed her shoulders and pulled the swing to a stop. "Don't say that." His voice was low and steady. Insistent.

She scared him, she knew that. After what had happened in Las Vegas—after standing on a ledge, waiting to take that last step, discovering how much she wanted to—she scared herself. It was why she didn't want to be alone.

"Prom's not over yet," she said. "You could still make it, and maybe she—" Beth cut herself off. It was their unspoken agreement. She never talked about Reed. He never talked about Harper.

And neither of them talked about Kaia.

Adam let go of her. He sat down on his swing again and pushed himself off, into the air, back and forth, his body awkwardly large and long, his legs pumping, his mouth open in a silent howl to the wind.

"Why are you being so nice to me?" she asked, mostly because she didn't think he would hear.

But he did. "I just want to."

"After what I did?"

He stopped swinging and turned toward her. "Beth, it's *over*," he said firmly. "You have to let it go. Start over."

She nodded. He made it sound so easy.

Adam suddenly stood up. "Let's dance," he said.

"What?"

He grinned, and in the dark she could still catch a glimmer of the little-kid enthusiasm she'd fallen for years ago. "It's prom, right? Let's dance."

"It's not prom. You're *missing* the prom—to babysit me." Because when Reed had left her house she had burst into tears, even though she had forbidden herself to fall apart all over again. And even though she had forbidden herself to let Adam pick up the pieces, *again*, she had let him hug her, and hold her, and take her somewhere safe.

"So you owe me," Adam pointed out. He reached for her hand and pulled her off the swing.

The bottom of her gown was covered in dirt she'd kicked up on the swing. It didn't matter; she'd never wear the dress again. "There's no music."

Adam laughed. "No way am I singing. Just use your imagination."

She let him grab her by the waist, and then she put her arms around his shoulders and they swayed, listening to the crickets and the rustling breeze. Beth closed her eyes, and again, she asked a question so softly that she assumed—she hoped—he wouldn't hear.

"Do you love her?"

And this time, he didn't hear.

Or at least, he didn't answer.

The official Haven High PTA post-prom extravaganza had it all: a rock-climbing wall, a row of slot machines, a go-cart track, semi-edible snacks from every restaurant in town—and a horde of gorgeous, glamorous, inebriated girls with low-cut dresses and high-octane libidos.

And Kane wasn't allowed to touch any of them.

He wasn't even allowed to look.

"What did you say?" With painful effort, he tore himself away from the forbidden fruit and turned back to his date. His *girlfriend*, he thought, surprised as always that the word didn't incite a shudder or anaphylactic shock. There was instead just a general wave of unsteadiness, like the way he always felt the day before getting sick or the day after getting smashed.

"I said, do you want to go with them?" Miranda asked, nodding toward the guys who were cutting out early, headed for a post-post prom party in the desert. Although, knowing these guys, "party" meant "getting stoned, getting stupid, having lots of sex" and then repeating the cycle until dawn broke. Just what the doctor ordered to wash away the sickeningly sweet taste of prom.

"No," Kane said quickly, taking Miranda's hand. That's what couples did, right? "Unless you want to, Miranda."

"It could be fun," she said.

For Miranda? About as fun as getting a pencil jammed in her eye, and she knew it.

"I'd rather just stay here," he lied. "We haven't gotten to try out the rock-climbing wall yet. It, uh, looks like fun."

It looked like loser central. But at least he was trying. God, was he trying.

She rolled her eyes. "Can I talk to you for a second?"

"Whatever you want," he said. "It's your special night." Now he was making *himself* nauseated. And all he got for his trouble was another eye-roll.

Their hands clasped, she led him through the crowd of seniors stuffing their faces, around the slot machines, and out the back door. The PTA mother stationed there informed them that, once they left, they wouldn't be allowed in. Miranda grimaced. "I think we'll live."

Kane drew in a deep breath. The air inside had tasted like cotton candy and hairspray. It was the taste of feeble love poetry and awkward slow-dancing and virgins hoping against hope to get laid. He'd almost suffocated.

Miranda looked up at him, then down, then up again, then seemed to come to some kind of decision. "What's the deal, Kane?" she asked. "Why are you being like this?"

"What are you talking about, Miranda?"

"I'm talking about *that*," she snapped. "*Miranda?* Since when do you call me Miranda?"

"Okay, *Stevens*," he retorted. "If you want to talk about out of character, since when do you want to hit some skeezy stoner after-party? Since when do you giggle?"

"I do *not* giggle."

Kane raised his voice to a flighty falsetto. "Oh, Kane, let's dance. I just *love* this song. Giggle giggle. Oh, Kane, you're so funny! Giggle giggle. Oh, Kane—"

"Shut up."

"All night long, Stevens. And it's been going on for *weeks*."

"And how about you?" she argued. "Buttering me up

like we're on a reality-TV show and you're lobbying for a rose?" She put on a false baritone. "Why, Miranda, you look so pretty in that dress. Miranda, have you always been so beautiful? Miranda, why would I ever want to look at any other girls when I'm with the most wonderful one there is?"

"I would *never* talk like that," he said indignantly.

"Oh, really? So you were looking at other girls in there?"

"Of course not! Why would I want to when—" He slammed his lips together and glared at her. Point taken. "What do you want from me?" he finally asked. "I'm just trying to be a good boyfriend."

"And I'm just trying to be a good girlfriend!"

They were both silent for a moment. And then they burst into laughter.

"We're doing a pretty crap-ass job of it, aren't we, Stevens?"

"At least I have an excuse," she pointed out. "This is new for me. But you? If you got a dollar for every girl you've been with, you'd be a millionaire . . . and, uh, technically a male prostitute. But you get my point."

"Hey!"

She flinched. "I'm sorry—did I offend you? I didn't mean—"

"Hell yes, you offended me. Thank God." He smirked

at her. "Bring it on." He grabbed her hands and pulled her close to him, loving the way her tiny body fit in his arms. "You're not some simpering bimbo," he reminded her. "You're sarcastic and obnoxious and overcritical—"

"And you're a shallow, insensitive, egomaniacal, self-centered asshole," she countered, grazing her hand across his cheek.

"And you can't resist me," he said smugly.

She grinned defiantly at him. "Sweet-talk me all you want, I'm still not sleeping with you."

"Who said anything about sex?"

"You didn't have to say anything." She raised her eyebrows. "I know you, sex maniac. And I know that you're the one who can't resist *me*."

He laughed. "Forget what I just said. Where's the sweet, subservient, giggly Miranda? Let's get her back here. This one's kind of annoying."

"She went to bed. Guess you're stuck with me." She rose up on her toes.

"Punishment for all my sins." He kissed her.

This is Miranda, he reminded himself, as he often did when he looked down to discover her wrapped in his arms. He still couldn't believe it, and he wasn't sure what was stranger: That now, whenever he saw Miranda, short, loudmouthed, neurotic *Miranda*, all he wanted to do was run his fingers across her skin, brush her red hair away from her sparkling green eyes, and taste-test her lips to see whether she'd opted for strawberry or peach lip gloss that morning. Or, maybe stranger yet, that he'd never noticed any of it before.

Kane was an expert in many things, but girls were at the top of the list. No detail escaped his notice, no cleavage, no ass, no freckled cheek or husky laugh flew too low for his radar. But until last month, Miranda had hidden in plain sight. The brainy one, the perpetual sidekick, the girl with a million complaints, twice as many insecurities, and a permanent membership in the "just one of the boys" club. Or so he'd always thought.

Kane hated to be wrong—but, better late than never, he was now thoroughly enjoying being right.

Her lips were firm and warm, and he rubbed his hands across her back, slipping his fingers beneath the edge of the green satin to massage her smooth skin. He could feel her smiling through the kiss as she ran her fingers through his hair and then rested her hands at the nape of his neck, kneading his muscles, clinging to him.

Miranda Stevens, he thought again, opening his eyes to take in her pale eyelids and the long, reddish lashes that brushed her cheeks. *Unbelievable.*

They finally broke for air, their foreheads still pressed together. Her face was flushed. "We'll figure this out," she whispered. "Right?"

"We'll get it eventually," he said. "We're very smart."

"I am, at least."

"Watch it, Stevens." He grabbed her waist and lifted her off her feet. "Remember, I'm bigger than you."

She reached out and tickled the spot on his neck just above his left collarbone, and he convulsed with laughter, dropping her back to the ground. It was his only weak spot; most people didn't know it existed.

"So . . . now that we're being honest and all that . . ." Her flushed face turned an even deeper pink. "Can I ask a question?"

He gave her a he-man pose. "Yes, I am a male model. Why do you ask?"

She smacked his chest lightly. "Seriously."

"Okay. Seriously."

"Are you . . . sorry? You know. About us?"

Kane couldn't help thinking about the girls still inside the party. Many were, as he knew from personal experience, better kissers. Many were better looking, better dressed. But none were actually better.

"No regrets, Stevens." He kissed her again. There was so much he had to lie to her about—it felt surprisingly good, for once, to tell the truth.

Adam froze midway up the walk. She was sitting on his front stoop, the silver dress sparkling under the porch light, her thick, wavy hair doing its best to escape from an elaborate upsweep. Her heels lay at the bottom of the steps; her toes were painted red.

"Hey." Harper smiled sadly as he approached. It was the first time she'd spoken to him since that night in Vegas.

"Hey."

"Nice tux." She leaned backward, her bare back pressed against the porch steps. "My dress matches your boutonniere." She laughed, once. "Funny."

He sat down next to her, aware of how close their hands were, aware of the space between them. "What are you doing here, Gracie?" he asked softly.

"Congratulations." She reached behind her and handed him a cardboard crown, painted gold and covered in fake jewels. "Prom king."

He laid the crown on the stoop, picturing the night he'd missed, and a terrible thought occurred to him. "And prom queen . . ."

She nodded. "As if there was ever any doubt." There was a shadow of the old Harper haughtiness in that last part, but only a trace, so insubstantial that he wasn't sure it had been there at all.

"Congratulations." The prom king and queen always shared a spotlight dance. If he had been there . . . but he hadn't.

Harper bared her teeth, though it wasn't quite a smile. "Yes, it's a true honor," she said. "I've got everything I want in the world." And again, there was a slight trace of a familiar bitterness, but then it was gone, and she just looked sad.

"Why are you here?" he said again.

Harper looked down, playing with the strap on her small silver bag. "I know she's your ex," she said quietly. "And I know you still care about her, even after—" She swallowed hard. "What she did. You may not believe me, but I even know she's not the only one to blame. I'm not saying she should go to jail. I'm not even saying she should be miserable for the rest of her life. *I* was the one up on that roof with her, Adam. I was the one who—"

"I know, and—"

"Adam, I need you to not talk for a minute, okay?" There was no emotion in her voice. "Just let me say this. Can you do that?"

He nodded.

"I was up on that roof, and I meant what I said to her, and if someone wants to be her friend, fine. Great. Kaia's dead. I can't fix that. And no matter what happens, even if . . ." She drew in a sharp breath. "I can't fix it. She can't fix it. So she gets to move on with her life. Fine. But why you? That's what I don't get, Ad. Why does it have to be you?"

There was a pause, and she looked at him expectantly.

"Now I talk?" he asked.

She nodded.

"She needs me," he said simply. "There's no one else."

Harper rubbed the back of her hand against her eyes, like a little kid. "What if I needed you? What if I told you that I couldn't survive without you, that I was weak and lonely and you're the only person who can make things okay?"

"Is that true?"

Her eyes widened, like she wished it could be. But then she shook her head. "I don't need you. I want you. And you . . . I know you do. I can *see* that you do."

He grabbed her hands and pressed them to his lips.

"I want you," she whispered. "You're *my* best friend, you're *mine*, and I want you back."

"That was your call, not mine," he said. "Say the word, and I'm back."

Harper drew her hands away. "She put something in my drink," she said, too calmly. "She put something in my drink, and I got in a car, and Kaia died. And if that doesn't matter to you—"

"Of course it matters!"

"She should be in jail," Harper said flatly.

He tensed. "You promised you wouldn't say any-thing—"

"Don't." There was ice in her voice. "Don't defend her to me. Don't try to protect her from me. Just don't."

"Harper, I know you're mad, but if you tell . . ."

"*Shut up!*" She smashed her hand against the stoop. "I'm not telling anyone," she said more quietly. "If she goes down, I go down. I was . . . I was the one behind the wheel."

He reached out a hand, touched her shoulder, but she pushed him away. "I'm not *her*," she snapped. "I don't need your pity. I don't *need* anything."

And that was the problem. Harper was strong. Harper *didn't* need him—not the way Beth did. Adam couldn't just walk away from that. Much as he may have wanted to.

It couldn't matter what he wanted. Not after—he shut his eyes, seeing it again, as he did almost every day, the image of her blond hair rising over the ledge, climbing back to solid ground. She'd come so close. . . .

He couldn't let it happen again.

"You can't have us both, Adam. You get that, right? After what she did to Kaia, to me . . . you don't get to be okay with that. Not if you want—" She shook her head. "It doesn't matter. I just need you to say it. That's why I came here, I guess. I need you to look at me and say it. You pick her."

"I'm not picking *anyone*," Adam protested.

"Yeah. You're not." She nodded, but didn't raise her head again. She sat slumped, her chin pressed to her chest a moment, and then looked up, her eyes dry. "So I guess we're done."

"Harper, I wish . . ."

"Just do me a favor and forget we had this little chat, okay?" she asked. "It's humiliating."

"It's not," he said. "I'm glad you came." It sounded so lame. Formal, like he was bidding farewell to a party guest.

"You should probably go inside now." She was covering her mouth with her hands, which muffled her voice. "I'm just going to sit here for a while."

He stood up. "Okay." She didn't watch him walk up the steps and toward the house. She just kept staring out at the street. He paused in the doorway. "Gracie?"

She didn't say anything.

"You look—" He wanted to tell her how beautiful she looked. But he'd already told Beth the same thing. Somehow, it felt like Harper would know. And that would make things worse. "Get home safe, okay?"

"Good night, Adam."

He went inside and, for a long time, watched her through the peephole. But she never turned around, so he never saw her face. She stayed perfectly still. He went upstairs, took off the tuxedo, brushed his teeth, washed his face, and when he came back down, she was still there. He finally went to bed, knowing she might stay for hours.

And knowing that, by morning, she would be gone.

chapter three

"WHO DOESN'T BUY A *YEARBOOK*?" MIRANDA ASKED, pulling hers out of her locker and running her hand across the rich leather binding. "What's wrong with you?"

"A hundred bucks for a picture book filled with people you hate?" Kane argued. "What's wrong with *you*?"

"We survived high school," Miranda said. "We should get to enjoy the rewards."

"There's only one reward," Kane said. "Getting the hell out."

She smacked the yearbook against his chest. "Do you want it now, or what?"

"What for?"

"So you can sign it, jerk. Write me a loving message about everything I mean to you."

Kane leaned toward her and nuzzled his face into her neck. Miranda flushed with pleasure. She'd never expected to be half of one of those PDA couples, but now she couldn't get enough of those DAs, public or not. "How about I save us both some time," Kane murmured, guiding her behind a bank of lockers, "and just tell you right now how much I—"

"Yo, Geary!"

They broke apart as a handful of Kane's ex-teammates loped down the hall. "Dude, awesome yearbook photo," one of them said, flipping his book open and pointing to the photo of an extended middle finger sitting over Kane's name. "Which of those yearbook chicks did you have to screw to pull that off?"

"Hope it wasn't the butt-ugly one," another said, laughing. "Because it wasn't *that* awesome."

"I have my ways, gentlemen," Kane said smoothly. Miranda edged away from him. He didn't stop her.

"Sorry, shorty," the first guy said, leering at Miranda. "Didn't see you down there." He noticed the yearbook in her hand. "*You're* a senior? I thought you were like, a freshman or something."

Miranda had been going to school with him for seven years, and had spent junior year health class staring at the back of his oversize head. Apparently, she hadn't made much of an impression.

"Kane, I've gotta go," she said quietly. "I'm late for class, and I've got this test—"

Kane ruffled her hair—he never remembered how much she hated that. It made her feel like a little kid, which was a feeling that, at five feet tall, she got plenty of. "Stevens here is a total brainiac," he bragged.

Miranda blushed. "Kane . . ."

"Not so smart to hook up with this guy," the other jock said, clapping Kane on the back and laughing. "Now, if you ever want to get with a *real* man . . ."

"Knock it off, O'Hara," Kane said, wrapping an arm around Miranda and tugging her toward him. "She belongs to me."

It was all so caveman. "I don't *belong* to anyone," Miranda snapped, stepping away.

The jocks laughed. "Watch out, Geary. She's tough. Don't let her whip you."

Kane leered. "Not to kiss and tell, gentlemen, but if anyone here's getting whipped—"

"I'm out of here," Miranda said loudly.

He shrugged, barely even glancing in her direction. "Cool. Later, Stevens."

Miranda glared at him. "Yeah. Later." And she stormed down the hall, seething.

He caught up with her just before she stepped into her classroom. She ignored him, but he grabbed the strap of her bag and tugged her back.

"I have a test," she said.

"You're mad."

Miranda glared. "Now who's the brainiac?"

"Why are you being so uptight?"

"Why are you being such a jerk?"

Kane sighed. "I thought we agreed we were going to be ourselves. I was just having a little fun—isn't that what we're supposed to be doing?" He tugged on her ponytail. "You know, I hear that when a guy teases you, usually it's just because he likes you."

She couldn't hold back the smile. "Your friends are idiots."

"No argument here."

"I've got a test," Miranda said. "I'm going inside."

"Hey." He stopped her again and held out his hand. "What about your yearbook?"

It was impossible to stay mad at him. "Write something nice," she warned, handing him the book.

"I'm always nice," he said, wiggling his eyebrows. He leaned toward her. "There's something I forgot to tell you about your test."

"What?"

He kissed her.

And that afternoon, when he finally gave the year-book back to her, she thought about the kiss, about how sweet it had been, how soft and kind and tender, no matter how he was acting. When she read his yearbook entry, her heart plunging in disappointment, even as she berated herself for having stupid expectations—she thought about the kiss.

> *Stevens,*
> *Who knew that mouth could do more than argue? You're a true-blue friend, a red-hot lady, and all that other good yearbook shit. You've got a big heart, and I've got an even bigger . . . you know. So we're both winners.*
>
> *KG*

It didn't mean anything, she told herself. Guys didn't talk about their feelings, didn't write them in yearbooks, no matter what she'd been hoping. It didn't mean they didn't feel anything at all. She didn't need him to say it. She didn't need him to write it.

Not when she had his kiss—that said it all.

Adam balled up the pale blue slip and threw it halfway across the room, right into the trash can. Three points.

A blue pass was never a good sign.

The study hall teacher gave him a sympathetic look, then waved him out the door. And he began the long, slow march to the guidance office, running through the past several weeks in his head, searching for what he'd done wrong. The last time he'd sat in Ms. Campbell's cramped, cluttered office, facing down her Ben Franklin glasses (with hairstyle to match), she had given him a shape-up-or-ship out lecture that culminated in the only persuasive threat in the guidance counselor arsenal: Get your grades up and your shit together, or you won't graduate.

Not in those words, of course.

Hating her, hating school and, most days, hating his life, Adam had still followed orders. Now his grades—reliably mediocre—were, in fact, the only thing he could count on. He opened the door to her office, steeling himself against the cloying taffy scent—with an undercurrent of cigarettes—that always made him choke. Then he put on his best golden-boy smile, ready to convince the counselor that Haven High's record-breaking, all-American pride and joy was back in business.

He needn't have bothered.

"Coach?" he said in confusion.

Coach Wilson was sitting behind the desk, his large frame penned in by the menagerie of windup figures and china figurines that blanketed the surface. "They're doing some construction over in the athletic wing—your counselor said we could use her office for our meeting." The coach stood up. "This is him, our star."

The man sitting across from Coach Wilson stood up and grasped Adam's hand, pumping it up and down. "A pleasure," he said. "The coach was showing me some game tapes, and that shot you got off in the play-offs? *Nice*."

"Uh . . . thanks," Adam said, shooting a helpless look at his coach.

"And your foul-shot ratio is damn impressive," the guy continued, "though we may have to work on your shooting stance—it's a little loose, but that's easily fixed with the proper training. No offense, Coach," he said, turning toward Coach Wilson, who'd settled back into the guidance counselor's chair.

"Hey, you're the expert," the coach said, grinning. "I'm just a lil' old high school coach. What do I know?"

"Enough to beat me eleven-three last time we played," the guy pointed out.

"Oh, that's right!" The coach slapped his forehead in exaggerated surprise. "I forgot all about that."

"Bullshit. It's all I heard about for a month."

"Uh, Coach?" Adam nodded toward the clock. "My next class is going to start soon, and—"

"Where are my manners?" the guy said, indicating that Adam should take a seat. "The name's Brian Foley.

Your coach and I went to high school together, back in the stone age."

"Brian's a coach now at UC Riverside," his coach said, giving Adam a meaningful look.

"Here's the deal, Adam," the UC guy said. "I've got a last-minute spot on next year's squad, and I want you." He tossed Adam a white-and-yellow T-shirt reading UCR HIGHLANDERS. "You've got Highlander written all over you."

"Me? But—I didn't even apply to Riverside," Adam said. "I'm going to State, in Borrega."

The UC coach snorted. "Do they even have a basketball team? Listen to what I'm telling you, Adam. I *want* you on my team. And I can *get* you on my team. Doesn't matter if you applied to the school or not. I've seen your transcripts, I can get you admitted. I may even be able to manage a scholarship. It'll take some doing, but . . . I've seen you play, and you're the guy to play for me."

"You can really do all that?" Adam asked, trying to process. He was going to the state school in Borrega, that had always been the plan. It was an hour away from home, one step up from community college, and everyone he knew would be there too. Harper would be there.

"Adam, my friend, welcome to the wonderful world of college athletics." Coach Foley stretched back in his seat. "I can do pretty much anything I want. And, once you're a Highlander, so can you."

Adam squirmed under the guy's fiercely confident stare. "I don't know . . ." He'd been counting the days until he could finally get out of school and never come back. Moving hundreds of miles away to some strange place where he wouldn't know anyone, and would need to work even harder than he had in high school? What was the point? "School's not really my thing."

"Morgan, be smart," Coach Wilson said. "This is your shot. It's what we in the coaching biz like to call a win-win situation. Don't pass it up."

"He doesn't have to decide right now," the UC coach said, standing up. He leaned over and shook Adam's hand again. "You've got two weeks." He handed Adam a business card. Adam stared down at it, stunned, still expecting the whole thing to be a joke. But the card looked real. And both coaches looked dead serious. "Call me by June fourteenth, if you're interested. Otherwise the spot goes to someone else." He waved good-bye to Coach Wilson and headed for the door, pausing to give Adam one last once-over. "Your coach here is a wise man," he said. "And he's given you some good advice. Be smart, like he says. You're on the foul line now, kid, and you only get one shot."

"I'm really going to miss you," Ms. Polansky said, signing Beth's yearbook with a flourish. Her picture was next to a large empty spot, where Mr. Powell's photo had been yanked days before the yearbook went to press, leaving the staff no time to redesign the page. When they'd set their production schedule, they hadn't factored in the possibility that Haven's newest teacher was living under a false name, on the run from a teen sex scandal.

Beth could have given them a clue. Even now, she could still remember the sour taste of Powell's mouth and feel his fingers digging into her shoulders as he struggled to hold her in place. But she'd kept her mouth shut. Just another mistake.

"I'll miss you, too," Beth told her junior year English teacher, wishing she could slip back in time. Things had been easy when she was a junior; *life* had been easy.

"Oh, I doubt it," the teacher said, laughing. The rare smile made her look several years younger. Although Beth knew that Ms. Polansky had been intimidating Haven High students ever since her parents were in school, she sometimes had trouble believing that the lithe, impeccably tailored woman in front of her was well into her sixties. "Once you get to Berkeley, you'll forget all about us—you'll get a chance to see what *real* teaching is like."

Beth flushed and dipped her head, letting her blond hair fall over her eyes. "I, um, didn't get into Berkeley," she admitted to the woman who'd written her a rave recommendation for her dream school.

Ms. Polansky pursed her lips, then gave a sharp nod.

"No matter, no matter," she said briskly. "Plenty of good schools, and students like you can excel anywhere. If I remember, your second choice was . . . UCLA?"

Beth rubbed her hand against the back of her neck and made a small noise of agreement. She glanced over her shoulder at the door, wishing there was some graceful way she could cut short the conversation and flee.

"And you were accepted, I presume?"

Beth made another noncommittal noise.

"What's that?" Ms. Polansky asked sharply.

"Yes," Beth said, sighing heavily. "I got in."

"Buck up," the teacher told her. "I spent some time in L.A. as a young woman—many, many years ago, as you can imagine—and it's really quite the exotic locale. I'm sure someone like you will have no trouble—"

"I'm not going," Beth admitted. Ripping it off fast, like a Band-Aid. But it still hurt.

"What's that?"

Beth settled into one of the chairs in the front row of the empty classroom, feeling a strange sense of déjà vu, as if any minute Ms. Polansky would start lecturing about Hamlet's motivations in the third act while Beth struggled not to think about whether Adam would like her dress for the junior prom.

"Some stuff happened this year, and, uh, I turned down my acceptance," Beth said. She didn't say the part about how she'd thought there was no point to planning a future when she couldn't imagine living through the next day. Nor did she mention that she had expected to spend next year lying on a couch with her stoner boyfriend, choking on a cloud of pot that would help her forget everything she was passing up.

"Why would you do a stupid thing like that?" Ms. Polansky snapped.

Beth winced. "I'm just stupid, I guess."

"You're the farthest thing from it." Ms. Polansky settled down at the desk next to her. Her voice softened. "What happened?"

Beth shrugged. "I made a mistake."

"Can you fix it?"

"No." Not that she hadn't tried. Her father had tried. Her guidance counselor had tried. But it was permanent; it was over. "I missed the deadline. They'd still be willing to let me in, but . . . I lost my scholarship. And without it . . ." Beth shrugged again. Without the money, there was no way. She'd always known that. It was the reason she'd worked so hard every day, every year, knowing that her only shot for the future was in being perfect. And she'd actually managed it, right up until the very end. When she'd thrown it all away. "I'm thinking about taking some night classes . . . community college or something. . . ."

Ms. Polansky handed the yearbook back to her and

stood up. "Well, then. That's settled. I'm sure you'll find a way to make it work."

"I'm sorry," Beth said.

"For what?"

"For . . . letting you down."

"Nonsense," the teacher said. "You're only letting yourself down."

That made it even worse.

Harper stuffed a limp, greasy fry in her mouth, washing it down with a swig of flat Diet Coke. "Exactly which part of this are you going to miss?" she asked Miranda, who was gazing at the tacky fluorescent décor like it was the Sistine Chapel.

Miranda squeezed closer to Kane, who was stroking her arm with one hand and stealing fries off her untouched plate with the other. "This," Miranda insisted. "*Us.*"

"I see you every day, Rand," Harper pointed out. "And next year, when we get the hell out of here and get our own apartment, I'll see you even more. And as for your boyfriend here"—she jerked her head at Kane—"I could do with seeing him a little less."

"You know you'll miss me next year," Kane said, flashing her a smug grin. "What would you do without me?"

"Celebrate good times," Harper sang tunelessly.

"Your life would be dull and colorless without me," Kane argued.

"Oh, Geary, I know how much you love to be right, so why don't you prove it? You leave and never come back, and I'll e-mail you to let you know how it all turns out."

Kane grabbed a straw from the table, tore off one end of the wrapper, then brought the straw to his lips and blew the wrapper into Harper's face. "Patience, Grace. All good things come to those who wait."

Harper grinned—then spotted the hint of a quiver in Miranda's lower lip. *Stupid*, she told herself. Miranda had been dreaming about Kane for years, and now that she finally had him, he was headed east to college in less than three months. And Harper just had to dredge it up and turn it into a joke.

"I'll be waiting a long time," she said quickly. "Fall feels like forever away. *Graduation* feels like forever away."

"It's only two weeks," Miranda pointed out, picking at her food. "And I just thought coming back here at least once before it's all over—it would be like the old days."

The Nifty Fifties diner, with its peeling movie posters and Buddy Holly tunes blasting out of the ancient speakers, was the perfect spot for nostalgia. Especially since they'd been coming here several nights a week since ninth grade. The fab four: Harper, Kane, Miranda—and Adam.

Now Kane and Miranda were nuzzling each other

and sharing a shake, while Harper sat on her side of the booth, alone.

"You're such a sap," Harper told her best friend.

"Speaking of which . . ." Miranda pulled out her camera.

"No more!" Harper said, waving her hands in front of her face. Miranda had been documenting everything that had happened for the past couple weeks.

"No way," Kane said, trying to grab the camera out of Miranda's hands. She squirmed away. "No need to immortalize another lame night in the world's lamest diner."

"Come on," Miranda begged. "For me?"

Kane looked at Harper. Harper rolled her eyes. "The things we do for love," she said, spreading her arms in defeat. She waved Kane over to her side of the booth. "Come on, let's get this over with."

Kane squeezed in next to her, and they pressed their heads together. Miranda held up the camera. "Think happy thoughts!"

But as the camera flashed, Harper's mouth dropped open and her eyebrows knit together in alarm, turning her face into a fright mask of shock and horror. Because right before the camera flash had blinded her, she'd glanced toward the door. The perfect couple—blond, bronzed, beautiful—had just walked in. They weren't holding hands, but they were a couple nonetheless. Anyone could see it.

They were heading right for her.

"What's *he* doing here?" Harper spat.

Miranda turned around, then looked back at Harper, eyes wide. "I don't know, I didn't—" She suddenly looked at Kane. "Did you?"

Kane tapped his fingers on the table. "I didn't know he would bring *her*."

"Even so, what were you thinking?" Miranda hissed.

"I was thinking *she* wasn't coming," he whispered, jerking his head toward Harper. "Like you told me."

"Then I told you she *was* coming."

"Well, by then, it was too late, wasn't it?"

"You could have said something," Miranda complained.

"I just did."

"Forget it," Harper snapped. "It doesn't matter. It's done. I'm out of here." She stood up just as Adam and Beth reached the table. Beth was wearing a pale-green polka-dot sundress with a white sash around the waist that looked like it belonged at a post-golf garden party—but, fashion don't or not, it still showed off her long limbs and deep tan. *Lawn Party Barbie*, Harper thought in disgust. *And she's finally reclaimed her Ken.*

"Harper," Adam said in surprise. "I didn't know you were going to be here."

"I'm not," Harper said. "This is just an optical illusion. It'll be over in a second."

"You don't have to go just because—"

"Yes." She glared at Beth, who at least had the decency to look away. "I do."

Miranda caught up with her just outside the diner, and they stood in the doorway, the flashing neon casting their faces in blue and red. "Don't go," Miranda pleaded.

"I can't sit there and look at the two of them," Harper said. "You know that."

Miranda sighed. "Yeah. I know. I just . . ."

"Rand, we've got plenty of time," Harper told her. "We can make ourselves sick on greasy crap some other night."

"It just feels like everything's . . ." She shook her head. "I only wanted it to be like it was in the old days, for once."

"This isn't the old days," Harper pointed out. "And maybe the old days weren't so great, anyway."

"Maybe." Miranda gave her a sad smile. "Do you want me to leave with you?"

"I'm fine," Harper lied, grabbing her by the shoulders and turning her back toward the entrance. "Stay here with Kane. Have fun. And if you happen to get the chance to pour boiling coffee in her lap . . ."

Miranda gave her a quick hug. "Call you later. Have a good night."

"Yeah." As if. Miranda went back inside, and Harper began the long walk home. Although it was only a few hours past sunset, the streets were empty, the stores boarded up for the night, and the bars already stuffed with people looking for a quick and cheap escape from the dusty desert night. Walking down the narrow road, the streetlights flickering and the moon hidden behind a cloud, it was easy for Harper to convince herself she was the last person in the world. Or at least the last person who mattered.

Her phone rang when she was only a few blocks from home; she didn't recognize the number. Any other time, she would have screened, but hearing someone else's voice—anyone else's voice—would be better than listening to her own. "Hello?"

"Hey, it's Jake."

She hesitated, trying to connect the name with a face.

"Jake Oberman?" the voice said, and the face became clear. It was a rugged, chiseled face with dark eyes and soft lips, with a shock of dark hair slipping down over the eyes. Jake Oberman, senior, point guard, prom date. Jake Oberman, who had rescued her on the dance floor and then, proving himself the perfect gentlemen, had driven her home, opened the car door for her, walked her to her house, and left with only a quick good-night kiss and not a single complaint that she was cutting short their prom date before eleven o'clock.

"Hey," she said warily. "What's up?"

"I'm in town," he said. "In Grace—you know the Lost and Found?"

"Know it and loathe it."

"Yeah, it's a shithole," Jake agreed. "Which is why I'm getting out. Any chance you want to grab some food?"

"Are you asking me out on a date?" Harper said, a flirtatious tone creeping into her voice. "A little last-minute, don't you think?"

"You aren't one of those Rules girls, are you?" he asked. "Need three days' notice for a date, never call a guy, don't kiss until the third date, all that crap?"

"And what if I am?"

"I'd pretend I didn't think you were a total freak," he said. "After all, I'm a gentleman."

"Right, I can tell," she teased. "But you didn't answer my question. Are you asking me out on a date?"

"What if I am?"

"Then I'd probably wonder what was in it for me."

Jake laughed. She had to admit, he had a good one— hearty, but not forced. And a good, solid baritone, just like his voice. "Free food and the scintillating company of yours truly?"

"*Scintillating?*" she repeated. "Why, Mr. Oberman, are you trying to impress me with your big SAT words and fancy book learnin'?"

"Whatever works," he said. "So, what do you say?"

She had reached her street. She paused on the curb. Her house was much bigger than Adam's, a holdover from the time when the Grace family had ruled the town. Now it was all her parents could do to make payments on their second mortgage. Adam's house was smaller, but the paint was fresh and the lawn neatly trimmed. He worked hard to make it presentable. In the old days, he had mowed the Grace lawn, too, first for some extra spending money and later for an excuse to hang around shirtless while Harper teased him from the sidelines and brought him fresh lemonade.

"Harper?"

"Sorry? What?"

"You, me, a whirlwind romance?" he prodded her. "Or, you know, a slice of pizza."

A few months ago, Harper would have said yes without a second thought. She'd already dated half the guys in the senior class, and most of them weren't nearly as hot as this Jake guy. Kane had good taste, she'd give him that. It could even be fun—he looked like a jock but talked like a human being, which was always a plus. Besides, back then, none of that would have mattered. Harper felt unwanted, Jake wanted her—it was a simple equation.

"Maybe another night," she said, and now she didn't sound flirtatious, just tired. "Rain check?"

"I'll hold you to that," he said.

She didn't have a witty response, and she didn't care, so she just said good-bye and hung up. And although it was only a few minutes past ten, she went inside and went to bed. Maybe what she'd told Miranda was true. The old days were done.

Beth closed the car door and settled back into the passenger seat with a loud sigh of relief. "Well, that was . . ."

"Awkward." Adam stuck the key in the ignition, trying not to replay the night in his mind. It had been a mistake to bring Beth; it had been a mistake to come in the first place. It had, mostly, been a mistake to think that he could make things normal again, just by wishing it.

"With a capital A," Beth agreed.

"I'm sorry." Adam pulled out of the lot, reminded of all the nights he'd come to the diner to pick up Beth after her shift. Back when she still worked there; back when they were still in love.

"Don't apologize," she said. "They're your friends."

"So are you." He reached over to squeeze her shoulder. "If they can't handle that . . ." No one had said so out loud, of course. Beth and Kane had sniped at each other, Miranda, loyal to the bitter end, had glared silently down at the table, unwilling to engage with the enemy. And Adam had tried to keep up a nonstop stream of meaningless conversation without calling attention to the fact that everyone around him was miserable. It would have been hard enough under normal circumstances, but tonight, still shaken from his encounter with the UC Riverside coach, Adam wasn't quite at his best. He hadn't told anyone about the offer; he still wasn't sure he believed it.

"I know," she said quietly. "Thank you." He laid his hand over hers, and she squeezed it. "It means a lot, that you're always there for me."

Not always, he thought, self-hatred rising like bile. *Not when you needed me.* He saw her there again, standing on the ledge, staring down into the darkness, ready to jump.

An old Simon and Garfunkel song came on the radio, and Adam turned it up.

"I love this song," Beth said, smiling faintly.

"I remember."

"Reed always used to make fun of me for liking this kind of stuff, but . . . sorry."

He glanced over at her, then back at the road. "What?"

"I shouldn't talk about him, with you. I mean, it's kind of weird, right?"

Adam shrugged. "Maybe. But not bad-weird. You should talk about him. If you want."

"I don't."

They listened to the music. Beth sang along under her

breath. Her voice was a little thin, but sweet and on key, just as he remembered.

"Okay," he said eventually, pulling the car up to the curb in front of her house. "Door-to-door service."

"Thanks for—you know, thanks," she muttered, fumbling with her seat belt and scooping her bag off the floor.

Adam turned the car off. "Beth, wait." Before, when they were together, she had always pushed him to think about the future. She had wanted better for him than the life he'd planned for himself. And she had always given him the best advice. "Something happened this morning, and uh . . . can I ask you something?"

"Anything." She tucked a strand of hair behind her ear.

"I got called down to the guidance office," he began hesitantly, "and there was this guy there, with the coach. . . ."

She nodded, waiting for him to continue.

But he couldn't. She was depending on him. He could see it in her face. If he was going to leave, he would have to tell her in the right way, at the right time, and this wasn't it. He couldn't say anything, not until he'd made his decision.

"Never mind," he said.

"What? You can tell me."

"No, it's just some stupid basketball thing. It's no big deal. So, I guess, have a good night, okay?"

"Ad, I know you don't want me to thank you anymore,

but—" Beth leaned across the seat and gave him a tight hug. He rested his chin on her shoulder and listened to her breathing. "I owe you," she whispered. "For everything."

She let go, but he held on, pulling away only enough to see her face. It was mostly hidden in shadow. There was a tear clinging to the corner of her left eye. She gave him a half smile. "Déjà vu, right?"

He knew that she was thinking of all the nights he'd dropped her off at home, lingering in the car for one last kiss.

"A lot's changed," he said softly. "But . . ."

"It still feels kind of . . ."

"Yeah."

Beth's eyes were watering. These days, they always were. He could almost see the old woman she would become someday, the worry lines and creases, the sagging of time weighing her down. She wasn't the same girl he'd been in love with. If he'd even been in love. She was watching him, like she was waiting for something.

So he kissed her.

It was light, it was hesitant, and then, almost as quickly, it was over.

She pulled away from him, but not in anger. Just surprise. "What was—?"

"I don't know," Adam said quickly. "I just thought . . ."

"You mean you want to . . . ?"

"I don't know." Adam looked down at his hands. One

of them was resting next to hers, and he inched it over until their pinkies were interlocked, just like he always used to. "Do you?"

"I don't know." She pulled her hand away and started rubbing her thumb across her palm, the way she did when she was nervous. "I mean . . . we could. I guess. If you wanted to."

He had stopped asking himself what he wanted. Because if he couldn't have what he *really* wanted, then what did it matter anymore?

"Maybe we should just, uh, figure it out later," Adam said.

"Okay. I'm, um, I'm just going to go, then." Beth opened the door, then turned back to him. He leaned toward her to give her another hug, but she went in for a kiss, and their foreheads knocked against each other. Beth looked horrified—then started to giggle. Soon they were both laughing. "Okay, I'm really going now," Beth said, gasping for breath. It was good to see her smile again.

"Good night." He gave her a kiss on the cheek, and she left. He waited until she was safely in the house. Then he flopped forward, letting his head thud against the steering wheel. "What are you doing, Morgan?" he groaned. "What the hell are you doing now?"

chapter four

IN THE OLD DAYS, BETH WOKE AT 6 A.M. EVERY DAY, weekends included. There was always too much work to sleep, too many obligations clogging her day to enjoy lounging around in bed until noon the way all of her friends did. But now she didn't care about her work and she'd ditched most of her obligations. There didn't seem to be much point anymore to the whole bright-eyed-and-bushy-tailed act, especially when she dreaded nothing more than the prospect of facing another day. Now Beth stayed in bed as long as possible, persuading herself to get up only by promising that, before long, night would fall and she'd be able to climb back in again. So when the phone rang at 9 a.m. on Saturday, she was still sound asleep.

Her friends would have been shocked—if she'd had any left.

"This is Ashley Statten, from the *Grace Weekly Journal*," the woman said, her voice snappy and staccato, each consonant bitten off sharply to make way for the next. "Is this Beth Manning?"

Her first thought was that someone had talked.

So many people knew her secret, and too many of them hated her. Harper had promised she wouldn't say anything to anyone, but . . . Harper had made a lot of promises. And to date, the only one she'd come through on was her promise to ruin Beth's life. So maybe it had only been a matter of time. And if the newspaper had the story, that meant that the police were probably on their way.

She expected terror to shoot through her, but all she felt was a nearly giddy relief. Maybe it was actually over. She'd thought she would have to carry this burden for the rest of her life—just make it through one day, Harper had said, up on the roof, then make it through the next, but that was easier said than done. She hadn't had the nerve to end things herself, but maybe if the police did it for her—

No. Beth had promised herself she would stop thinking like that. She'd promised Adam.

"Some English teacher from your school called, said you're looking for an internship next year," Ashley Statten continued. "We usually don't do that kind of thing, but I guess your teacher used to be my editor's teacher and he's still scared of her, because he didn't say no." She said all this without pausing for breath, and it took a moment for Beth to catch up. "So here's the deal. This is your lucky morning: You get a trial run, because I'm working on the perfect article for you and I could use some backup. You interested?"

"I, uh . . ." Beth rubbed the sleep out of her eyes and tried to process. "Interested in what?"

"A little slow on the uptake, aren't you?" the woman snapped. "I'm working on an article, the anthropology of high school girls, alpha queens and their beta ladies-in-waiting, soft bullying, climbing the social hierarchy, sort of a *Mean Girls* meets *Coming of Age in Samoa*, with a little of that *Ophelia Speaks* crap thrown in for good measure, the seamy underbelly of America's youth, hometown high jinks, et cetera, et cetera, you get the idea, right?"

"Um, right . . ."

"You don't sound too sure."

"Right," Beth said firmly, scrabbling for a pen to write down *Coming of Age in Samoa* so that once she hung up, she could figure out what the woman was talking about.

"So you help me out on this story, be my inside man,

so to speak, and then we'll see what we can do about next year."

"Next year?"

"Full-time, paid internship at the glorious *Grace Weekly Journal*," Ashley Statten said sarcastically. "Your entrée into the fabulous world of dead-end, small-town journalism—obituaries, housewife gossip, town meetings about whether to tear down the old Crenshaw place, and epic arguments about gas station zoning permits and land use. Work hard and don't screw up, and all this and more could be yours. You in?"

"Yes!" And for the first time in a long time—since before Kaia, since before Adam had broken her heart and Kane had stomped it to bits, maybe since before Mr. Powell had jumped her in the school newspaper office—Beth let herself imagine a future of ink-stained fingers and tight deadlines, rolling presses, last-minute scoops, secret sources, banner headlines, and a byline, a *real*, *professional* byline, of her very own.

Beth Manning.

Staff Writer.

Grace Weekly Journal.

It wasn't Berkeley. But it was something; it was a start.

"I'm definitely in," she said eagerly. "Whatever you want, I can handle it. Just tell me what I need to do."

≈ ≈ ≈

The shapeless black robe made her look like a chocolate doughnut. Miranda shifted toward the right, then to the left, then turned her back to the mirror, craning her head around to try to get a look at her ass. It was undetectable beneath the billowing polyester. That was one good thing, at least—the robe might cover up all the places she went in, but it would also hide the many places she bulged out.

Miranda told herself to stop.

She wasn't supposed to look like a supermodel; she was supposed to look like a graduate.

She arranged the flat-topped cap on her head, flipped the tassel to the left side, and looked again, feeling like she was wearing a costume.

"Oh, you're all grown up!" her mother cried, stepping into the room without knocking. "I don't believe it."

"Believe it, Mom." Miranda rolled her eyes, but she couldn't stop herself from smiling. Was her mother actually experiencing a maternal moment? Unlikely. And yet, that was without question a tissue in her hands, and she was dabbing away at her eyes. Just like a real mother who cared. "Two weeks and I'm out."

"You know, your father and I are just so proud of you," her mother said, coming over to rub Miranda's shoulders. Miranda pulled away. "Our little girl, so smart, so independent, and in the Cal State honors program next year! I have to admit, dear, I had no idea you were so bright."

"I got that," Miranda muttered, taking off her cap and placing it carefully on top of her dresser. She left the robe on. Something about it made her feel powerful, like she could withstand her mother. Or maybe it just gave her a place to hide.

"College is such an enormous step," her mother said kindly. She sat down on Miranda's bed and patted the spot next to her, gesturing for her daughter to sit down too. Miranda stood. "You must be pretty nervous."

Miranda shrugged. "Not really."

"Living on your own for the first time . . ." Her mother shook her head. "It's hard. And not just financially. Maybe if you were more independent, I wouldn't worry so much, but . . ."

"Mom, I've got homework to do, so unless there's something you need—"

"I just need my oldest daughter to be happy," her mother said. "And I've been wondering: Have you given any thought to living at home for another year?"

"*What?*"

"Think about it, Miranda. You don't know how to live on your own. You can commute to classes for a year, and live here, for free, and that way you'll still get to see us, and you can still take care of your little sister in the evenings and help out around the house—"

"You want me to ditch college so that I can be your

nanny?" Miranda asked incredulously. "I'm supposed to junk my life so that you and Dad can keep having 'date night' twice a week?"

"That's an awful thing to say," her mother said. "I'm thinking about *you*."

"You're never thinking about me," Miranda snapped. "You just don't want to lose your servant next year—who else is going to cook dinner and vacuum and do the laundry? Not Stacy, I know that. And not *you*. This is so selfish."

"Don't talk like that," her mother said. "You may think you're all grown up, but I'm still your mother, and this is still your family, and—" She broke off, dabbing at her eyes again to wipe away some fake tears. "And we need you *here*, at least for a little longer. I don't see what's wrong with that. With my new promotion I'm going to be working longer hours, and your sister isn't old enough yet to stay home on her own. We're your family, and we need you—so you tell me: Who's the selfish one?"

Miranda couldn't speak. She was too angry—except for the tiny part of her that wondered if her mother was right.

"Honey, I didn't come in here to fight," her mother said in a more conciliatory tone. "I just want you to think about it. I really think it would be best for you. You've got some more growing up to do, and the thought of you out there on your own—"

"I won't be on my own," Miranda countered. "I'll be with Harper. We're supposed to be going apartment hunting tomorrow, and you want me to just abandon her?"

"She'd do it to you," her mother said harshly.

"What's that supposed to mean?"

"I see more than you think I see." Her mother scowled. "I know what kind of a friend that girl's been to you. What happens next time she pulls another one of her stunts, and you're out there all alone?"

"Just stop. Harper's not going to be pulling any *stunts*." Miranda took a deep, calming breath, but it wasn't quite calming enough. "Can you just leave now? I have work to do."

"I'm not leaving until you admit that I only want the best for you, and agree to think about what I said."

"Fine."

"I don't think you understand how much I've had to sacrifice for you, Miranda, how much I've given up to be a good mother to you, and I don't think it's untoward of me to ask you to make a small sacrifice for me, for your family. I don't think that's out of line."

"I said *fine*. Fine!"

"You'll think about it?"

Miranda sighed. "I'll think about it."

Her mother stood up and walked over to the door,

pausing on her way out. "You really do look lovely in your robe, darling."

"Thanks," Miranda said warily.

"I know how you girls are at this age: You hate things that seem loose and shapeless, but there are times when that can be more a blessing than a curse—am I right?"

"What are you getting at, Mom?"

"Nothing!" she protested. "How about this weekend we go shopping for something special to wear underneath it. A new dress."

"That's okay," Miranda said. "I'm going with Harper."

Her mother raised her eyebrows. "I assume she's the one who let you buy that prom dress?"

"What was wrong with my dress?"

"Nothing . . ."

"But," Miranda prompted her.

"But I just think that you would have looked better in something that wasn't quite so clingy. If you would just let me help you, I could teach you how to cover up your problem areas rather than draw attention to them like—"

"Forget it!" Miranda snapped. "Just let it go. Please."

"You've never been grateful for anything I've tried to do for you," her mother said in exasperation. "I'll just never understand how I raised such an impolite child. You accuse me of only thinking about myself, dear—I suggest you take a look in the mirror."

And when her mother was finally, blissfully gone, Miranda did exactly that.

Not a doughnut, she thought in disgust. *I look like a bonbon. A short, round, bulgy, chocolate bonbon.*

Miranda ripped off the gown and threw herself down on the bed, reaching for the bag of mini Snickers she'd stashed beneath it for emergencies like this one. Talking to her mother opened up a gaping hole inside her, one that could only be filled by massive amounts of gooey chocolate. So much chocolate, in the end, that she would balloon out into the disgusting round mess that her mother saw whenever she looked at her; so much chocolate that she would feel sick, and bloated, and need more than anything to get it out of her, to stick her finger down her throat and lean over the toilet with the faucet running so no one would hear, and choke out all the calories and sugar and words that were weighing her down.

She had promised herself she wasn't going to do it anymore; she had promised Harper.

And if that wasn't enough, there was the thought of Kane. If he ever knew what she did when she was alone and miserable—if he ever saw her hunched over, face pale and sweaty, stomach clenched, choking on the stench, stuffing the empty candy wrappers into her backpack and then throwing them out in the garbage can down the street so that no one, especially her prying, judging, hating mother, would ever know—Kane would be disgusted. Because it was disgusting. *She* was disgusting.

Just one, she thought to herself. *I'll just eat one, or maybe two.* And then she would call Kane, or Harper, and get out of the house. She pulled a candy bar from the bag, tore off the wrapper, and bit into the gooey sweetness. The caramel filling stuck to her teeth, and the rich taste cut through her confusion. She wouldn't think about her mother anymore, or about next year, or the apartment, or how helping her family meant abandoning Harper but keeping her promise to Harper meant abandoning her family. In fact, she wouldn't think at all. She would just taste, and chew, and swallow.

Only one. Maybe two, she told herself, tearing into the second bar even as she chomped down on the first. *Then I'm done.*

Adam faked left, went right, raced for the foul line, and got off a perfect shot. He followed the graceful arc toward the basket—and even Kane had to nod in appreciation at the soft swish.

"Nice. Been practicing, Morgan?" Kane asked, grabbing the rebound. "Waste of time—you know you'll never beat me."

And, in all their years of playing one-on-one, he never had. Adam lunged for Kane, knocking the ball out of his hands and stealing possession. He imagined a horde of screaming fans on the sideline rising to their feet and holding their breath in anticipation as he dribbled down-court, heart pounding, feet slapping the concrete, the ball stinging his fingers as he slapped it down again, and then stopped, rising to his toes, cradling the ball in his finger-tips, tensing his muscles, bending his knees, aiming and, all in a single graceful move, a split second that left no time for thought, only action, thrusting the ball into the air for three perfect, final, game-winning points.

Kane leaped up, slapped the ball away from the basket, cradled it to his chest and, two dribbles later, sunk an easy layup. "That's twenty-one." He passed the ball to Adam, hard. "Game."

"Maybe I let you win," Adam said, grabbing his shirt and water bottle. He twisted off the cap and gulped down a few mouthfuls, almost choking. The sun had turned it into a hot soup. He gave up on drinking and poured the rest of it over his head, closing his eyes as the water splashed across his face and ran down his chest, washing away the sweat. He felt good. Exhausted, overheated, thirsty, defeated—but good. "Maybe I've been letting you win the whole time."

"Then maybe you're a bigger moron than I thought."

"Good game," Adam said, tossing over Kane's water bottle without bothering to warn him of the putrid tem-perature.

"Good for me," Kane shot back. He tipped the bottle back over his mouth and, watching Adam out of the corner of his eye, downed the whole thing in nearly one gulp.

They headed for the parking lot, empty except for Kane's lavishly restored silver Camaro and Adam's beat-up Chevrolet, both parked in the only shade. Adam leaned against the door of his car, the one that was painted a different color than the rest. He was in no hurry to get home.

"I'm gonna miss this," he said.

Kane hopped up on the hood of the Camaro and stretched out like a cat in the sun. "Losing? Don't worry, Morgan, there'll be plenty of opportunity for that."

Adam threw his sweaty T-shirt at Kane's face. *"This,"* he said. "Playing ball here." He gestured over to the other end of the lot, where the empty high school waited for Monday to arrive and its inmates to return. "I might even miss that."

"Drink some more water, man," Kane teased. "You must have sunstroke."

Adam laughed. "Okay. But at least this."

"Dude, don't cry. We've got all summer. Time enough for me to beat you hundreds of times."

"Maybe not," Adam said.

"How many times do you need to lose before you stop denying the inevitable?"

"Not that," Adam said, rolling his eyes. "I mean, I

might not be around all summer. I might have to take off early . . . for training."

Kane sat up. "You joining the marines?"

It had just slipped out. But now that it had, Adam didn't want to stop himself. He had to tell someone. "Some coach from UC Riverside wants to recruit me," he admitted. "Admission, scholarship, a spot on the team— I've got until graduation to decide. Less than two weeks. And if I say yes, I go in July to work out with the team and start some work-study job."

"Are you kidding me?" Kane jumped off the car and slapped his fist against Adam's. "Awesome."

Adam shrugged.

"Wait—what do you mean *if* you say yes?" Kane asked, narrowing his eyes.

"I mean, *if*." Adam leaned back, searching the sky for clouds. He couldn't find any. "I don't know if I want to go."

"You don't know if you want to go to a *real* college, for free, and play on a division-one team?"

"Borrega's a real college," Adam said hotly. "Real enough for me, at least. I know it's not *Penn State*"—he scowled—"but we can't all be brainiacs like you."

"For one thing, you're not as dumb as you pretend to be," Kane said. "Otherwise I wouldn't be wasting my Saturday with you."

"I must be even *dumber* than I pretend to be," Adam

countered. "Otherwise I wouldn't be wasting my Saturday with you."

"Very funny." Kane didn't crack a smile. "So what's the deal? Why do you need two weeks to figure this one out? You shouldn't need two minutes."

"It's complicated," Adam said. "It's far away, and my mom doesn't have anyone else, and it'd be a lot of work and, you know. There's Harper. And Beth."

Kane shook his head in disgust. "Wrong answer."

"What do you want me to say? It's the truth."

"Morgan, what are you doing? You want to be with Harper? Be with Harper. You want to be with Beth—well, that's your mental problem—suck it up and be with Beth. But either way, they're just *girls*—pick one, pick the other one, fine, but don't waste your whole life sticking around for them."

"It's not that simple," Adam said. "You don't know—"

"Hey, I got a girlfriend now. You don't see me ditching Penn State for Stevens, do you?"

"It's different," Adam insisted. "You and Miranda . . ."

"What?"

"Nothing." Kane would never understand what it meant to care about someone; what it meant to have someone depend on you.

"Fine. Forget it. Back to you and your screwed-up life," Kane said, when it became obvious Adam wasn't going to elaborate. "You're telling me you'd give this up for Harper? It's not like you're willing to give up anything *else* for her."

"Don't—" Adam broke off, feeling the anger bubbling in him again. But it wasn't directed at Kane. "You don't know what's going on with the two of us, so don't—don't talk about it."

"I know she's miserable," Kane said. "And you're prancing around with Beth like you don't give a shit."

"Well, I do, okay?" Adam said angrily.

"So freaking do something about it."

"Don't you think I want to?" Adam kicked at his junky car door. It shook with the impact. "I can't."

Kane blew out a short, dismissive breath. "Because of Beth."

"Yeah." Adam slumped back against the car. "Because of Beth."

She hadn't intended to eavesdrop.

She'd just wanted to share her good news—and she wanted to do it without Kane's sneer getting in the way.

Beth had spent the morning in the *Grace Weekly Journal* offices, gaping at the people running back and forth—even on a Saturday—to put together a *real* newspaper. So, okay, there were only three staffers, and the big breaking story was a water main leak on Azure Avenue, but it was a newspaper. And she was a part of it. Ashley Statten, a miniscule woman with a bleached-blond pixie cut and big brown eyes, had given her the rundown of her story—talking even faster than she had on the phone—and then gave Beth her assignment. She was to interview her fellow students and find out, in Ashley's words, "what they want, what they need, who they really are, deep down, where no one can see." If she did it well, she might actually be able to fix the mess she'd made of her future. Next year didn't have to be one long, hideous shift at Guido's pizza parlor, shirking from Reed's hostile gaze and wondering whether the grease would ever wash out of her hair.

And all she'd wanted to do was celebrate it with someone. The newspaper office was only a few blocks from the high school, from the basketball court where Adam played pickup ball every Saturday, so she'd walked over, planning to surprise him. And instead, here she was, hiding behind a tree like some kind of feeble cartoon character, waiting for Kane to leave . . . and listening.

"You don't owe her anything," Kane said. "And if she's trying to tell you different—"

"She's not telling me anything. She just needs me."

Kane peered intently at him, then burst into laughter.

"What?" Adam asked.

"You *are* a moron," Kane said, shaking his head. "Unbelievable."

"*What?*"

"You're hooking up with her, aren't you?" Kane started laughing again.

"Am not," Adam said.

"Come on, Morgan, there's a reason I always clean you out when we play poker."

"It was just one time," Adam admitted. "We didn't even . . ."

Kane bowed with a flourish. "Never bluff the master," he crowed. "So what now? You're getting back together?"

Adam didn't say anything for a moment. He rubbed his forehead with the heel of his hand. "I don't know. Maybe?"

"You know what your problem is?" Kane asked, opening his trunk and tossing in the basketball.

"You?"

"You've got a hero complex. You see a damsel in distress, you think it's your job to rescue her. You don't know how to be with a girl if you're not rescuing her from something."

"I never had to rescue Harper," Adam said defensively.

Kane gave him a pointed look. "Exactly."

Adam opened his car door, glaring. "You have no idea what you're talking about." He got into the driver's seat, but Kane grabbed the door before Adam could shut it.

"I know you feel sorry for her," he said. "Hell, even *I*

feel sorry for her. It's pathetic. But that doesn't mean you owe her anything."

"She's my friend," Adam said stubbornly. "She needs me."

"If that's true, she won't want you screwing up your life for her. Maybe she's not as needy as you think." Kane slammed the door shut, then got into his own car, and they both pulled out of the lot.

Beth leaned back against the tree, then let herself slide down to the ground, the bark scraping her back.

She had known that Adam felt sorry for her. But she'd let herself believe that he was telling the truth when he said he'd stood by her because he wanted to, because he cared. The other night in his car, she had even let herself believe that there was still something between them, or could be.

It was pathetic. Kane was right: She was pathetic. And she was dragging Adam down because she was too weak to convince him to walk away.

Tomorrow, she thought with determination. *I'll tell him tomorrow.* She would persuade him that she was strong, that she didn't need his support. She would convince him that he would be better off far away from her. And whatever came next, she would face it.

Alone.

chapter five

"THIS DUMP IS EVEN WORSE THAN THE LAST PLACE," Miranda hissed, pulling Harper out of the apartment so she could breathe again without choking on the stench.

"It's not so bad," Harper argued. "It could use some cleaning up, sure, but it was a good space, and the building's kind of . . . well, it's got character."

Miranda looked from the peeling paint to the mold-encrusted ceilings to the stained carpet that smelled faintly of urine, and finally back to Harper. "I think you mean it's got characters," she said. "As in, scary guys in chains hanging out on the front stoop who look like characters from *The Sopranos*."

Harper rolled her eyes and headed down the hallway, toward the narrow, musky fire-stairs. There was an
elevator, but according to the dirt-encrusted sign on the
front—the one that looked like it had been hanging there
for years—it was out of order. "I don't think we need to
worry too much about the Jersey mob if we live here."

"Oh, there's no *if*," Miranda said firmly. "This half of
we will under no circumstances be living *here*."

"What about the last place we saw?" Harper asked,
once they were safely back out on the street.

Miranda shook her head. "That stain . . ."

"I told you, it wasn't blood," Harper insisted.

"Says you."

"So what about the third place?"

Miranda wrinkled her nose. "Was that the one with
the shower in the kitchen or the one that smelled like the
town dump and was next to the local Hells Angels head-
quarters?"

"Shower in kitchen," Harper murmured.

"No."

"Then what—"

"And no to the Hells Angel's place too," Miranda
said quickly. They turned left onto the main avenue, and
the campus opened up before them, all sprawling green
lawns and Spanish-style stucco buildings, with real college students hurrying back and forth, backpacks slung

over their shoulders, cell phones—or, in some cases, Frisbees—in hand.

"College," Miranda said in amazement. "Can you believe it? This is really going to be us next year."

"Not if you don't stop vetoing all our apartment options," Harper said.

"Find me a place that doesn't suck," Miranda said, "and I won't veto it." Nor would she sign a lease, not until she decided whether she was moving at all, or giving in to her mother's wishes. But what Harper didn't know couldn't hurt Miranda.

Harper waved a copy of the local newspaper in her face. "We've seen every place we can afford, and they're all beneath your standards. You think *I* want to live in one of these piles of crap?"

"It's almost enough to make you want to stay in Grace," Miranda said, laughing nervously. "You know, live at home for a year, save up some money for a real place. One that doesn't have a pee-stained rug and a meth lab on the fourth floor."

"Please, God, tell me you're joking." Harper plopped down on a nearby bench and flung her arms out dramatically. "Tell me you haven't forgotten our sacred vow to get the hell out of Grace as fast as humanly possible."

Miranda gave her a weak smile. And then her phone rang.

"Hello?" she said, glad for the interruption.

"Hey, gorgeous, any luck finding a palace fit for a queen?"

Miranda smiled, blushing, happy Kane couldn't see her through the phone. It was bad enough having Harper there, batting her eyelashes and fluttering a hand over her heart. "Tell your *lover* I say hello," she whispered, a wicked grin on her face. Miranda turned to face the other direction.

"Maybe if I were the queen of the underworld," she said into the phone, sighing. "It turns out hunting for affordable student housing is the ninth circle of hell."

"That's what you get for picking a school without dorms," he teased. "You'll be squeezed into some apartment too tiny for a decent-size keg, while I'll be . . . well, let's just say they don't call it Happy Valley for nothing."

"So I should be back in a few hours," Miranda said abruptly. She didn't like to think about what would happen next year, when Kane would move three thousand miles away. "What time are you picking me up?"

"Uh, yeah, that's actually why I'm calling," Kane said. "I'm going to have to cancel—something came up."

"Oh." Miranda resisted the urge to ask him what. If he wanted her to know, he would tell her. But he didn't.

"Sorry about this," he said. "I know I promised you we'd finally hit that Mexican place you love, but—"

"Another time," she said, trying to sound like she didn't care. And like this wasn't the fourth time in three weeks he'd cancelled like this, abruptly, mysteriously . . . suspiciously.

"Maybe tomorrow?"

"Maybe." She grinned. "Unless I get a better offer."

"They don't come much better than me," he boasted.

"I'm trying a new thing this week," she said. "Optimism. So I'd like to believe there's still hope."

"There's always hope, Stevens. I'll keep my fingers crossed for you. Sorry again about tonight."

"No problem. Later."

She hung up the phone and gave Harper a rueful smile. "So it looks like I don't have to go back early after all."

"He cancelled?"

Miranda nodded.

"Again?"

Another nod.

"With no explanation, I assume?"

Miranda slumped down on the bench next to Harper. "Tell me he's not seeing someone else."

"He's not seeing someone else," Harper repeated dutifully.

"You believe that?"

Harper paused. "I believe it if you do." Then she swatted Miranda with the rolled-up newspaper. "Look on the bright side, Rand. This means we get to look at more apartments."

Miranda grimaced. "And the day just keeps getting better and better."

"*Goddamnit!*" Reed smashed another bottle against the brick. Impact. The bottle exploded. Glass skidded and swooped through the air, clattering onto the hard-packed dirt. He didn't feel any better.

He never felt any better.

He let himself slouch to the ground. Then he fell back, head thudding into the overgrown grass, arms stretched out. A snow angel. If there were ever any snow. He closed his eyes. It was like snow in his mind. A foggy white dust speckled over his thoughts, burying them in the deep. They jutted up, smooth white shapes, evidence of what had been.

Lost the job.

Lost Kaia.

Lost Beth.

Lost everything.

The pain was still there, still sharp, like someone was taking a baseball bat to his stomach. But he couldn't attach it to anything that had happened or anything that he'd done. It was just there, along with the rage, along with the misery. There without cause, without purpose, and without end.

If he could see the problems—if he could dig his life out of the snow, see it clear again, maybe there would be something to fix. But the way things were, it seemed pointless. Everything seemed pointless. Better to let the snow bury him.

"Dude, what the hell?"

Reed opened his eyes.

A pale apparition loomed over him, blond hair shimmering down.

"Beth?"

An explosion of laughter.

"He thinks you're his girlfriend!" Another body appeared, shoved the first one out of the way. They landed on the ground. Reed closed his eyes again, shut them out. "Dude, you're wasted."

"Am not," Reed mumbled.

Wasted.

That was the word. Everything had been wasted, had wasted away. He'd thrown it away. Or she had thrown it away. He couldn't remember which anymore. Didn't care.

Hands grabbed his shoulders, dragged him up. He stepped, stumbled, lurched, fell again. Arms caught him. Held tight.

"To the couch," someone said. "Help me get him inside."

His feet scuffed across the grass, smearing through the dirt. Reed laughed, though he didn't know why.

"Funny for you, man. You're not the one doing the heavy lifting."

"'S not funny," he slurred. "Sucks. It sucks." The world was too bright, and he was too dizzy. It was better with his eyes closed, when he could wish the lurching, sickening motion away. "Leggo!" he cried suddenly, lashing out. His arm thudded into something with a soft thwap, and someone grunted. Let go. And he sank to the side, almost dropping to the ground, where it was solid and it was still. But then they gripped again, tighter this time, and he was moving.

"Yeah, it sucks," someone said. "At least you got that part right."

They dropped him, and it was soft, and it was cool, and finally, he slept.

"Remember the first time we came out here?" Miranda asked, sipping her Diet Coke.

Harper started laughing so suddenly, she nearly choked on her grilled cheese. "Visiting Kane's brother," she said, after she'd swallowed. "Big man on campus. We thought we were *so* cool, going to our first real college party."

"Party. Right." Miranda giggled.

"There were people and music," Harper said defensively. "That's technically a party."

"People lying on the floor stoned out of their minds," Miranda reminded her. "And lots of Bob Marley."

"You tried pot for the first time."

"And you drank so many wine coolers, you threw up in a bush."

Harper shivered in horror. "I almost puked on Adam— he got out of the way just in time. Not such a successful outing."

"You did hook up with that college guy," Miranda said. "What was his name? Peter? Paul?"

Soda spurted out of Harper's nose. "Patrick!" she exclaimed. "Poor, poor Patrick, with his pierced tongue and his organic deodorant. I couldn't get his stink off me for days."

Miranda sighed. "Things were good back then, weren't they?"

Harper took another bite of her grilled cheese, the house specialty. "What's with all the nostalgia trips, Rand?"

"I don't know. It's just a lot, all at once, you know?"

Harper gave her an exasperated look. "Obviously I don't know, or I wouldn't be asking."

"Hello, graduation? Ring a bell? End of high school, beginning of college, everyone's going away, everything's changing."

"Not everything," Harper counted. "I mean, I know Kane—"

"I don't want to talk about it," Miranda said.

"Okay. Fine. My point is, the rest of us are all sticking around here. Everyone that counts. You. Me."

"Adam?"

"Now *I* don't want to talk about it," Harper said.

"Fine."

They sat in silence as the waitress took their plates away and brought over the thick slices of chocolate cake Harper had insisted they order. Another specialty of the house. Harper dug right in, and, after a moment of hesitation, Miranda followed suit.

"So if every topic is off-limits now, does that mean we're not going to talk at all?" Miranda finally asked.

"Not every topic," Harper said. "Apartments." She pulled out the flyer from the last place they'd seen, a cozy two bedroom a few blocks from campus. "This is it. Big windows, okay kitchen, the shower's in the bathroom where it belongs—and bonus, it doesn't smell like dead bodies. I think we should go back and sign the lease before someone else gets it."

"Harper, I told you, I'm not ready yet."

"But what are you waiting for?" Harper asked, irritated. It was, by far, the best place they'd seen all day—and despite her massive flirting offensive, the owner had offered no assurance that he'd hold it for them. "You need extra time to find something wrong with it? Look, I'll even let you have the bigger bedroom." Then Harper imagined stuffing all of her clothes into the tiny closet. "Well, I'll flip you for it. That's only fair."

Miranda just took another bite of her cake.

"What? *What?* Am I missing something? Tell me what's wrong with it."

"Nothing's wrong with it," Miranda said. "It's great. I can totally see living there with you. But the thing is . . ."

Harper's throat clenched as she waited for Miranda to finish, knowing this couldn't possibly be good.

"My mom wants me to stay home for the year, find a way to commute," Miranda finally said, staring down at her plate. "She just got some big promotion, and she needs help taking care of Stacy, and you know I'm like their free babysitting service, and she laid this big guilt trip on me about how I was abandoning the family and—"

"And you told her she's a selfish bitch and you've wasted enough of your life doing what she wants," Harper finished for her, without much hope.

"And I told her I'd think about it," Miranda admitted.

Harper slumped down on the table, resting her forehead against the cool plastic—at least until she remembered where she was and decided that even dramatic effect wasn't worth physical contact with the million germs skittering across the grimy surface. "Why would you do that?" she moaned, sitting up.

"Because she said it was important," Miranda said. "That she really needs me."

"Where was she when you needed her?"

"Needed her for what?"

"Oh, I don't know. How about needed her to be an actual mother and *not* make you feel like shit every time she opened her mouth?"

"She's not that bad," Miranda said.

"She's worse."

"Look, I haven't made any decisions one way or another."

Harper exploded. "You shouldn't even have a decision to make! You promised me that you were coming next year—we had it all planned out. We're going to Cal State, we're getting an apartment. We have a *plan*. You can't just flake out at the last minute!"

"Stop yelling at me!" Miranda cried. "I'm not doing this to screw you over—" She stopped herself and took a couple deep breaths. "Look, I'm not doing anything at all, okay? Not yet." She stood up. "I'm going to the bathroom, okay? Try to chill out."

Harper looked up at Miranda, then pointedly down at the chocolate crumbs on her empty plate. "Rand, you promised you weren't going to do that anymore."

"What?"

"I'm sorry I yelled at you." Harper tried to look apologetic, even though inside she was still seething. "I didn't mean to get you so upset that you . . . look, you promised to stop, okay?"

Miranda tried to turn away, but Harper grabbed her wrist.

"Promised to stop what?"

Harper tried to stifle her irritation. This was so typical of Miranda, running off to bend over a toilet rather than actually dealing. "You know what I mean," she said, not wanting to spell out all the gross details.

"I'm going. To. The. Bathroom." Miranda spoke slowly and clearly. "It's not a euphemism."

Harper gave her a skeptical look.

"What, you want to come with me and stand outside the stall?" Miranda waited a moment, then shrugged. "Didn't think so. I'll be back in a minute. Don't skip out and stick me with the bill."

Harper smiled sweetly. "Would I ever do that to you?"

Miranda raised her eyebrow—a nasty habit she'd picked up from Kane, who could, of course, say everything he ever needed to with the arch of a single brow. It drove Harper crazy.

Harper sighed. "Rand, you know I'm not going anywhere. We're in this together."

"And by 'this,' you mean . . . ?"

"Whatever happens next," Harper said.

"So that means I'm stuck with you?"

"For life."

Miranda burst into laughter. "*Now* I feel like throwing up."

Harper kept the smile on her face until Miranda was safely behind the bathroom door. Then it fell away. *She* was the one who felt like throwing up, and not through some perverse need to purge herself of chocolate cake. Miranda was right: Everything *was* changing.

Which, now that she thought of it, seemed like an incredibly obvious and overdue observation. But she hadn't given it much thought. As long as Miranda was around, Harper could pretend things were the same as they always were—that *she* was the same as always. But on her own . . .

She was Harper Grace, scion of the Grace family, heir to a proud heritage of haughtiness, social power, lost treasure, and former glory. She was Harper Grace, prom queen, alpha female, arbiter of all things cool, most desired, most likely to get whatever she wanted, no matter who got hurt along the way. She was Harper Grace, the girl to be envied, the girl who saw what she needed and took it, the girl with the power.

Or at least she was—within the confines of Grace,

California, where sophomores worshipped her, bartenders sucked up to her, boys chased her. Where everyone knew who she was and what she stood for.

Who was she here, a hundred miles away, in a town full of strangers? As long as Miranda was by her side, she was still everything she'd ever been. But alone? She could be anyone; she could be no one.

The call came an hour late, but at least it came.

Kane grabbed his coat and keys and drove out to the rendezvous point, a secluded alley on the edges of town, behind a bar that had closed its doors a year before. The space had never been sold to anyone else, so it sat dark and empty, just waiting for shady characters to show up and conduct their shady business. It was safe and secluded, but mostly, Kane liked it because it established the appropriate atmosphere. It was his second favorite thing about this whole business: the ominous darkness, the way it made him feel edgy and dangerous and completely in control.

His most favorite thing, of course, was the money.

And it was rolling in.

His San Francisco connection had come through, and the shipments of pot candy—Buddafingers, Puff-a-Mint Patties, Rasta Reese's, an infinite variety of chocolate delights—came through every week, right on schedule, arriving in unmarked boxes filled with treasure. Chocolate gold, as he thought of it. Because once word got around town that a new dealer was in the game—a dealer with connections and with the perfect, untraceable product that could be consumed anywhere, in public, in class, even at home under the most doting daddy's watchful eye—the masses had arrived on his doorstep.

Not literally, of course. He was careful to keep his identity well hidden, and made himself available only to the most trustworthy of those in the know. He made sure that whatever they had on him, he had twice on them. There was nothing on paper, nothing to connect him to the product, or the buyers, or to any illegal activity at all. Nothing except the candy bars themselves, chock full of illegal delights. And Kane kept those under lock and key.

This guy went by "KC" and dressed like a '90s rapper. Kane didn't care. He just cared about getting paid.

"It's all here?" he asked, when the envelope had changed hands.

"You don't have to count it, man," the guy said, hands shoved in his pockets and shoulders hunched. "You can trust me."

Kane sneered. "Right." He opened the envelope, leafed through the bills, did some quick mental math, then nodded. "Okay, you've got yourself a deal." He pulled a box out of his trunk. "Fifty bars. Should get you through the next week."

The idiot took the box and started to walk away without looking inside.

"Count them," Kane said. "I don't want you to start thinking you can trust me."

He counted—and, though Kane doubted the guy could make it past ten without using his toes, he counted all the way up to fifty, saluted, and then faded back into the night.

Kane stuffed the cash into his back pocket and got back into his car. Five hundred bucks. Not bad for a night's work. His phone rang again, just as he was about to start the car. Kane cursed. If the little twerp was trying to hit him up for more bars, or had some feeble complaint about the product—but then he glanced at the screen.

"Hey, babe," he said smoothly, bringing the phone to his ear. "You and Grace make it back without killing each other?"

"Barely," she said. "So . . . have a good night?"

He could hear it in her voice: She wanted to know. She was worried about where he'd been, what he was doing, why he wasn't with her. He couldn't blame her—but he also couldn't tell her. She'd never understand. And he refused to feel guilty about lying. That's who he was, and she'd known that from the beginning.

"Yeah, nothing big," he said. "Just had to do some stuff for my dad. You know how it is."

"Yeah," she said, in a voice that admitted no, she did not know how it was. "Well, I should probably go. I've to get some homework done for tomorrow."

"Two weeks to graduation and you're still doing homework? You're such a nerd."

"What's that make you?"

A nerd-lover, he was about to quip, but cut himself off just in time. Lovers, they were not. And *love* . . . it wasn't a word he wanted coming out of his mouth, in any form. "Just lucky, I guess."

"Nice save," she said dryly. "See you tomorrow?"

"I'll be the guy standing in front of your locker with a dozen red roses," he joked.

"I'd settle for some black coffee and a low-fat muffin."

"Split the difference?" he suggested. "How about a dozen carnations and a jelly doughnut?"

"'Night, Geary."

"Later, Stevens. Sorry I missed you tonight." And it was true, he thought as he hung up the phone. The wad of cash in his pocket felt good, and the evening had gone exactly as planned. But if he could have told Miranda the truth, if she could have been there to admire his work, and then to celebrate . . .

He cut himself off. He couldn't trust anyone with his secrets, not now. He couldn't afford to. And Miranda wouldn't get the beauty of his operation. She might try to stop him. Then he'd have to give up the business—or give up Miranda.

And he didn't see any reason why he should have to choose. He was Kane Geary, which meant he was used to having it all.

When he woke up, Fish and Hale were sitting a few feet away, staring. They looked unusually sober. Reed felt unusually tired and unusually sick—and he was pretty sure he was still a little drunk.

"What?"

"Dude, we need to talk," Fish said.

Reed's head hurt. He tried not to move it. "Talk about what?"

"About you."

"What is this, some kind of intervention?"

Hale glared at him. "This is serious, dude."

Reed snorted. That hurt his head too. "Like you've ever been serious."

"We're going on tour," Fish said. "After graduation."

"We talked it over," Hale said, "and we agreed."

"*We?*"

"Yeah, the band," Hale said.

"Since when does 'the band' not include me?" Reed asked.

"Since you stopped giving a shit," Fish snapped.

Reed sat up, despite the way it made his stomach lurch and the world spin. "Are you kidding me?" he asked. "Who's the one who always wants to rehearse? Who's the one who writes all the songs? And who's the one—ones— who sit around and get stoned all the time?"

"We're not kicking you out of the band," Fish said. "We're just telling you. We're going on tour after graduation. Three months, ten states. We'll sleep on the road. Hale's already got us a couple gigs."

"This was your idea, man," Hale said. "Remember?"

Reed remembered. He'd been stupid enough to think that they had a future—even though they never rehearsed, and they were always stoned and, more to the point, even though they sucked. It hadn't been his idea, not really. It had been Beth's. *Go on tour*, she'd urged him. *If you really want to make this thing happen, work at it. Get better. At least give it a try.* Beth was all about hard work. Except in her own life, apparently. Then she just wanted to take the easy way out.

Reed winced, and fumbled around in his pocket for another joint. But he was all out.

"What's the point of a tour?" he asked. "We suck. We're always gonna suck. Just let it go."

"And stay here for the rest of our lives?" Hale asked. "I'd rather die."

"There's stuff out there," Fish said. "There's *girls* out

there. And we're going. Get your shit together and come with us."

"Or what?" Reed asked.

"Or stay here, and we'll get a new singer." Fish stood up and, a beat later, Hale did too. "She's not worth it, dude. She's just a girl."

Reed didn't know if he was talking about Beth or Kaia. Fish probably didn't know either.

"It's not about a girl," he said. "It's . . ." But he didn't know. It was buried, and he was too tired to dig for it. Maybe it *was* just about a girl. But what did that mean? That he should forget her? That he should move on? That he should take her back?

She doesn't want to come back, he reminded himself. *She's back with her ex.*

Beth was the one who'd moved on. Beth, who should have stayed miserable and alone forever after what she'd done to him—and what she'd done to Kaia—had moved on. And Reed couldn't hate her for it. He couldn't hate her for any of it.

"So you're really going on tour?" he asked, lying back down on the couch.

"*We're* going," Fish said. "You know you want to get the hell out of this town."

Get the hell out. It sounded good. It sounded *right*. Reed took a deep breath, filling his lungs to capacity. It felt like the first deep breath he'd taken in a long time. His foggy head began to clear. Maybe he could do it. Clean up his shit. Figure out what to fix, what to forgive, and what to forget. Mind clear, soul free, he could start moving again. Get off the couch and off the booze. And get the hell out of town.

chapter six

"GUTTERBALL!" SOMEONE SHOUTED GLEEFULLY IN the background. But halfway down the lane, the ball veered away from the gutter and smashed into the cluster of pins. One after another tipped and wobbled, finally clattering to the ground. But two held their ground, separated by too much empty space.

"Shit," Kane muttered, collapsing onto the bench while he waited for the ball to return.

Miranda was waiting for him, her expression quizzical. "You okay?" she whispered.

Kane grunted. "I'm wearing shoes that probably have some other guy's toe mold growing on them, wasting a night with"—he glanced over his shoulder, where several of the guys from the basketball team were building a precarious tower of empty beer cans—"the goon squad. And now I've got to pick up an impossible spare. So yeah, I'm fine."

Miranda gave his upper arm a gentle squeeze. "That's not what I meant."

Kane shrugged her off. "I'm up," he said, reaching for his ball.

He lined himself up, took a few practice swings and, in his mind, mapped out the path the ball would need to take. Then he was ready. Arm drawn back, three loping steps, arm swinging forward, swift and smooth. Release. The ball flew from his fingertips, cracked against the wood, skidded down the varnished lane—and sailed through the empty space between the two pins.

This time, Kane didn't curse. He couldn't pretend to care about bowling, of all things. Not that night. He just fell back onto the bench and gave Miranda a wry grin. "Not my night, I guess."

She looked like she wanted to say something, and he steeled himself. That was the thing about girls. Always wanting to talk. Especially if they spotted a weakness, some chink in the armor. That's how it started: They slipped a finger through and widened the hole, just a bit, then a bit more, until, if you weren't careful, they eroded the protective covering entirely, and there you stood before them, naked.

And not in the fun way.

But Miranda didn't say anything. She just leaned against him and put her head on his shoulder.

Kane spent the next hour trying to decide whether to make up an excuse and ditch out on the night. He hadn't wanted to come in the first place, and under normal circumstances, he never would have agreed to it. A night of bowling with "the guys"—and their simpering girlfriends, half of whom Kane had gotten to first. It was a perfect storm of shit, but it was also the path of least resistance. And on this particular night, he didn't have the energy to resist.

As the boys broke for nachos, Miranda once again tipped her head toward his. "Want to get out of here?" she murmured.

They were in the parking lot before the guacamole was gone.

"Sorry about crapfest," Kane said, once they'd reached his car.

Miranda shrugged. "I told you before, I *like* bowling. Much as I suck."

"So why'd you want to leave?"

"You just looked . . ."

Kane tensed.

"Like you didn't want to be there," Miranda finally said.

Kane hunched over the steering wheel, his fingers gripping the ignition key. He didn't look at her. "Why'd you ask me that before? If I was okay?"

Miranda's hand fell lightly on his shoulder. "I know something's wrong," she said. "But you don't have to tell me."

Kane swallowed hard. Was he losing his touch? He'd filled the night with the requisite number of shrugs and smirks, burying his mood in the standard assortment of casual quips. No one should have been able to guess. No one else *would* have been able to guess.

Certainly another girl wouldn't have seen through the act. But another girl—at least the kind he was used to—wouldn't have known him so well. Or at all.

"I'm going to drive you home," he said abruptly. Her hand stayed on his shoulder.

"Okay."

They drove in silence. Miranda didn't ask why they were cutting the night short, and Kane realized he almost wanted her to. He tested a response in his head:

It was my mother's birthday yesterday. My father forgot. My brother forgot.

Which left me alone to celebrate. Just me and that ugly green vase on the fireplace where we keep her ashes.

I skipped the cake.

Kane would have laughed if it weren't so pathetic. He just couldn't say it out loud, even if he'd wanted to. The type of girl he was used to would listen to his sob story with tears in her eyes, and reward his sensitivity with a shower of kisses. But that type of girl would never hear this story. No one would.

Kane couldn't stand to be around other people, not when he was feeling like this.

But he made a sharp U-turn. "Let's go to my place."

Miranda looked at him in surprise. They almost never went to his place. "Sure."

What are you doing? he thought. Better to get rid of her, and sooner rather than later, before he said something stupid, something he would regret later. That would be the smart move.

But he didn't want her to go.

They ended up in his bedroom. Kane sprawled on the bed, flat on his back. Miranda curled up next to him, her arm thrown across his chest. The night before, he'd lain there alone, a half-empty bottle of scotch on his night-stand, the stereo blasting at full volume. This was better.

They didn't talk.

They always talked—it's what they did best. They bantered and sparred until Kane lost his train of thought staring at the pink flush rising in Miranda's cheeks and he stopped her latest rant with a kiss. She didn't let him get away with anything; except that night, she let him get away with shutting up.

"You remember in first grade, how we got to bring in cupcakes or something for the class on our birthdays?" he asked suddenly.

Miranda nodded, her chin digging into his shoulder.

"When it was my turn, my mother sent me in with a big box of strawberry cupcakes," he said. "Can you believe that? Freaking *strawberry*. What kind of first grader eats strawberry frosting?"

Miranda knew what had happened to his mother. She had to know, because she'd known him since they were toddlers—she'd been there. But he never talked about his mother, not to anyone. And Miranda knew that too. But she didn't mention it.

"I like strawberry frosting," she said quietly.

"That would make you the only one." Kane barked out a laugh. "Nobody wanted to eat them. The teacher had to send them all home with me at the end of the day. I could've killed her, you know? My mother. It was so stupid. *Strawberry*. I threw them all on the floor or something and locked myself in my room. I was such a little shit."

"Geary, you were six," Miranda pointed out. "That's what six-year-olds do."

"She never yelled at me," Kane said. "She never said

anything about it, and never told my dad. When I finally came back downstairs, the kitchen was clean and there was a birthday cake waiting for me. Chocolate frosting."

Miranda propped herself up on an elbow and looked at him closely. Kane readied himself for a nauseating outpouring of sympathy. It would be his own stupid fault.

She smiled. And then she kissed him, once, softly. "You were six," she said again. "And from what I remember, you were a spoiled brat. But it was your birthday . . . and she was your mom."

Kane shut his eyes for a second and closed his arms around Miranda. He wanted her there, he realized. It wasn't just that he didn't want to be alone or was too lazy to make up an excuse to get rid of her; it wasn't that she was a decently hot girl willing to climb into bed with him. It was *Miranda*, and he didn't want her to go.

That should have concerned him. There was a slippery slope between wanting and needing, and his sledding days were far behind him. The alarm bells should have been ringing. But they were silent.

He shifted onto his side, leaned in, and kissed her. She sighed as he pulled her toward him, their tongues tangled, their bodies twined.

"Feeling better?" she asked, a hint of a laugh in her voice, when they finally broke apart.

Kane raised an eyebrow, and this time he wasn't faking the smile. "So far, so good," he said, lunging for her again. "But definitely still room for improvement."

They'd been at it for an hour or so when the phone rang. Kane let go immediately and sat up, grabbing for his cell. "Sorry," he mouthed, "I have to . . ." Miranda shrugged, waiting quietly as he hunched over the phone

Finally, Kane punched the phone off and gave Miranda an apologetic look. "You're going to hate me, but . . ."

"Don't say it."

"I've got to take off." He leaned in to give her a quick peck on the lips, but she twisted away. Maybe it wasn't fair to be mad, not when he was obviously having such a crappy day, but it also wasn't fair for him to leave like this, abruptly and without explanation, *again*. She'd forced herself all night not to ask him what was wrong, even though it was obvious something was. And that had been the right choice. But how many things was she supposed to leave unspoken?

"How about Saturday," he suggested as they walked out to the car. "We can spend the day together and finish what we started. . . ."

"We've got Harper's graduation party on Saturday," Miranda reminded him.

Kane groaned. "That's not a *party*, it's some kind of PTA-approved freak show."

"Then it's too bad you promised to go, isn't it," she said, climbing into the passenger seat. He sighed and got in next to her.

"You're mad."

She shook her head. "Just drop me off and go wherever it is you're going." Kane's Camaro was in the shop, and Miranda had offered him her Civic for the week—but that was before she knew he was going to ditch her yet again and head out for . . . wherever it was he went after he got rid of her.

"Look, I'm *sorry*, but I've really got to—"

"It's fine," she said. If he could keep his moods to himself, she could do the same. "Whatever. Let's just go."

"So now you're going to sulk?"

"I'm not sulking."

He darted a hand out and began tickling her, running his fingers lightly along her neck. She shivered and bit her lip to suppress the giggles, then smacked his hand away.

"Definitely sulking," he concluded. "I'll make it up to you, okay? Tomorrow night we'll—"

"I'm not *sulking*," she snapped. *Now or never*, she told herself. Miranda's first priority was to protect herself, and that meant getting the truth, whatever it was, on her own terms. Which meant *now*. "Where are you going, Kane?"

"It's private," he said, pulling the car out of the lot and turning onto the road that would lead them back to Grace.

"So private, you can't tell me?" she pressed.

"I'm supposed to tell you every little detail of my life? I didn't realize that was how this was going to work."

"It's not going to work at all if you keep ditching me to sneak off with some other girl." Miranda sucked in a sharp breath and pressed her hands to her lips. She hadn't been meaning to go that far.

Kane turned to look at her. "Is that really what you think?"

Fiery red with embarrassment, she stared straight ahead. "Can you just watch the road?"

Instead, he pulled over to the shoulder and turned the car off. "Stevens, look at me. Is that what you think I'm doing?"

Miranda shrugged. Think and fear were two different things. But it was a yes on both fronts. What else could it be? "I don't know," she mumbled. "Maybe."

"Well, it's not."

She couldn't help herself. She snorted.

"What?" he asked.

"Of course that's what you'd *say*." She gave him a wry smile. "It doesn't mean you're not doing it."

"Stevens . . ." He brushed her hair away from her face and ran his fingers lightly across her lips.

"There's no other girl," he said firmly.

"Then what?"

"I can't tell you. You wouldn't approve."

"Why? Because I'm so naïve and uptight?"

His hands began crawling across her again, this time working their way up her thigh. "You weren't so uptight a few minutes ago. . . ."

"Kane!"

"Fine, fine, your loss." He took his hands away and, giving her a pointed look, placed them firmly on the steering wheel at ten and two o'clock, just like a good boy. "Better?"

Not exactly. But she nodded, anyway.

"It's just not your kind of thing, okay?" he said wearily. "You're going to have to trust me."

"They say every good relationship's built on a foundation of trust," Miranda mused.

"My point exactly."

"So . . ."

"So . . . ," he echoed, when she didn't speak.

"So take me with you," she said firmly.

"What about trust?"

"Earn it." Miranda grinned defiantly and, reaching for the steering wheel, rested her hand over his. "And maybe you'll find out you don't know me as well as you think."

Kane's eyes darted toward his watch, and he sighed. "Fine. You want to go, we'll go. But don't say I didn't warn you."

"Geary, everything about you says 'Danger, stay away,'" Miranda said as he laced his fingers with hers. "If I listened to warnings, don't you think I would have started with that one?"

Kane squeezed her hand and brought it to his lips. "It's not too late."

"Perfect," Beth muttered, giving the side of the car a sharp kick. "Just perfect." Not like it was a surprise: It had only been a matter of time before her parents' ancient Volvo gave up the fight. If the noisy clunking of the engine hadn't given that away, the goopy liquid dripping out of the exhaust pipe and the smoke that occasionally rose from the hood would have offered a substantial clue. Beth had just hoped it would happen when she wasn't driving.

But things didn't usually work out like that—as in, for the best. So she was the one behind the wheel when the car puttered to a stop, warning signs flashing, smoke pouring out of the hood, and the engine mercifully shutting down before it exploded, or whatever cars did when they'd reached their final resting place. Which, in this case, was the parking lot behind Guido's. She was tired, she was filthy, and all she wanted to do was get home in time to take a long bath before Adam picked her up for . . . well, it wasn't a date. Not quite, at least. But that didn't mean she wanted to reek of garlic and onions when he arrived at the house.

Beth called information to get the number for a tow truck. After putting her on hold for ten minutes, the man at the garage told her it could take two hours for someone to arrive.

"You can't come any faster?" she asked.

The guy on the other end of the phone grunted. "Got one driver out on a job, and the other's not in yet. He'll get there." And then, before she could say anything else, he hung up. So Beth waited in the parking lot—a safe distance from her car, in case it decided to explode after all—and hoped someone she knew would show up for a slice of pizza and offer to fix her car or at least give her a ride home.

Be careful what you wish for, Beth's father, the platitude king, liked to say.

The mud-spattered pickup pulled into the lot and parked just a few feet from her. There was nowhere to hide.

"Trouble?" Reed asked, leaning out the window.

A line from an old movie floated through her head. *Of all the pizza joints in all the towns in all the world, he walks into mine.*

Beth shook her head. "I'm fine."

He got out of the truck and walked past her and into Guido's. She considered her options. There was run—but to where? And then there was hide—immature, which wasn't a problem, but also unfeasible, which was. There was nowhere to hide, except in her car, which seemed both uncomfortable and unsafe. Especially given that more smoke was pouring out of it than ever. She supposed she could just start walking home—but what if, by some miracle, the tow truck actually arrived early? If she wasn't there to greet it, the guy would drive away again, leaving her sad little Volvo to rot.

So when Reed came out of the pizza place, she was still standing there, trying to decide what to do.

Reed walked past her again without pausing, without even glancing in her direction. He opened the door to the truck and got in, and only then did Beth realize she'd been holding her breath. The engine rumbled, and the truck sped toward the parking lot exit—then screeched to a stop.

He leaned out the window. "Get in."

"What?"

"You're stuck," he said. "Get in."

Beth tucked her hair behind her ears and tried to smile. "I'm fine. The tow truck is coming soon, and I have to wait around for it, so . . ."

"And who's gonna be driving the truck?"

"How am I supposed to—oh." His father worked there, she remembered. And Reed filled in for the drivers sometimes, to pick up extra cash.

"You're stuck with me either way," he said. "Get in, I'll drop you, then go back for the car."

Defeated, Beth crossed to the passenger side and, climbing in, breathed in the familiar aroma of leather and motor oil. "Thanks."

He didn't answer, just shifted into drive and pulled out of the lot. The radio was on, but she couldn't hear the music over the thunder of the engine. For several minutes they drove in silence. *This isn't so bad*, she thought. It was hard; it was painful, sitting there so close to him, knowing she had no right to ask him anything, to know how he was doing or how he was feeling, much less to reach over and touch his hand. His fingers were caked in grime. It was painful, all right, but she could handle it. The ride wouldn't last forever.

"You switch your shift?" he asked suddenly.

"What?"

"You didn't used to work today."

"Oh. Right. After everything that happened, I just thought I should, um, stay away. From . . . you."

"You could have just quit," he pointed out.

"I need the money, and—"

"I didn't mean you should have," he said. "I didn't mean anything."

"Oh."

His hair was sticking straight up, like he'd just rolled

out of bed. It was wildly curly and tangled, like if she stuck her hand into its nest, she might never get it out.

"Doesn't matter, anyway," he said. "I'm out of here in a week. The band's going on tour."

"Really?" She knew she sounded bright and chirpy—and that was good. She didn't want to let on how it made her feel, the thought of him leaving town. She didn't have the right to feel that way anymore. And really, what was the difference? Whether he was in Grace or across the country, he was still out of her life. For good. "That's so great!"

He shrugged. "Yeah, I might not go. I don't know."

"You have to go," she insisted. "The Blind Monkeys are nothing without you."

"Yeah. Maybe."

There was another awkward silence. This time, Beth broke first. "I'm sorry about the prom. I really didn't think you'd still want to go."

"It was stupid," he said. "I should have . . . called. Or something."

"Look, Adam and I, we're not—"

"None of my business," he said quickly.

"I know, but I feel like I should explain."

"I don't care!" he shouted.

She flinched.

"Sorry," he said. "Can we just let it go?"

Beth turned her face toward the window and squeezed her eyes shut, listening to the rumbling engine and wishing the ride would end.

"Beth . . . I gotta ask you something."

"Okay."

"You don't have to tell me." He rustled his hair, leaving it wilder than ever. "But I need to . . . I have to ask."

"Anything," she promised. She knew there was nothing she could tell him that would help, much less fix things, but she could tell him whatever he needed to know. She owed him that much.

"Did you hate her?"

"Who?" Beth asked, afraid she knew.

"Kaia. I just, I need to know."

Beth sighed and leaned her head back against the coarse, grimy seat. "I wish I could say no, but . . . yeah. I guess I did. I thought I did. But I swear, Reed, I never meant for it to happen."

"You keep saying that," he said harshly. "So what *did* you mean?"

"I don't understand."

"What the hell were you doing? Why would you spike Harper's drink? What did you think would happen?"

She took a deep, shuddering breath. Thinking about everything that happened was nearly impossible, even when she was lying in bed, curled up under her blankets and trying to fall asleep. Revisiting it here, with *him*? It was torture. But she would do it, because she had to.

It helped that he was watching the road. Beth knew she wouldn't be able to say what she was about to say with his wide, dark eyes watching her.

"I was with Adam," she began, because everything began with him. "We'd been together for almost two years, and things were . . . not perfect. But good, you know? Then Kaia showed up, and at first, everything was okay, but . . ."

Beth told him everything. The way Kaia had mocked her, torn her down—and Adam had just ignored it. The plot Harper, Kane, and Kaia had concocted to tear her and Adam apart. The pain of hearing that Adam had lost his virginity to Kaia—had slept with her while he and Beth were still together, supposedly in love. And the glee on Kaia's face when she spilled the secret, ruining Beth's life with a few words and an icy smile.

"I just wanted to win," Beth admitted. "For once, I didn't want to be the one who played by the rules and got screwed. I wanted . . . I wanted her to know how I felt. I wanted . . ." She shook her head. "I don't even know. I don't know what I thought would happen. I didn't care. I just wanted her to *hurt*." Beth realized there were tears running down her face. This was the first time she'd said it out loud, and for a moment, she was back there. She felt the hate.

"But I never thought she'd get in a car, or that Kaia . . . you've got to believe that," she pleaded. "I never meant for her to—" She forced herself to choke the word out. "Die."

And then she lost it. Beth pressed her hands against her face, trying to stop the tears, but they flooded out. She'd thought she was past the worst of it, but now it was all back and the wounds were just as fresh. Nothing had changed, she was still lost and alone, she was still a killer. Kaia was still dead. Her eyes filled with tears, her hands shielding her from the word, she couldn't see Reed, didn't know how he was reacting. She knew he didn't say anything to try to comfort her—and he didn't touch her.

She finally caught her breath, wiped her dripping nose on her sleeve, tried to rub the red out of her eyes, and then, finally, drawing her courage, dared to look up. The truck had stopped, and Reed was watching her. "Thanks."

Beth didn't trust herself to speak. She just nodded. They were parked in front of her house, and she realized he was just waiting for her to get out and leave him be.

She opened the door.

"I'll tow your car over to the shop," he said. "Someone'll call you and let you know the damage."

She nodded again. Then, forcing herself, said, "Thanks for making me come with you. You could have just left me there and—just, thanks for not abandoning me in the parking lot. For, you know, wanting to help."

For a moment, it looked like he was going to say something, but then the moment passed, and another, and then she got out of the truck and slammed the door, tears springing to her eyes again. She rubbed them away furiously.

"I wouldn't have left you there," Reed said. She whipped back around to face him through the open window, but he was staring in the other direction.

She waved, even though she knew he couldn't see her. And then he drove away.

They pulled up to a small barnyard, and Kane turned off the ignition. "Just remember," he warned Miranda. "You asked for this."

Miranda peered out the window at the dark, empty land surrounding them. "I think I can handle it."

He led her down a gravel walkway and over to a penned-in area. Three shadowy figures stood just outside the gate. When they got closer, she recognized them. Mark Walker and Jesse Lopez, two guys from the basketball team. And next to them, bending over and fiddling with something in the pen—

"Harper?" Miranda asked incredulously.

Harper whirled around. "You brought *her*?" she asked Kane.

Kane shrugged. "She said she wanted to come, so I figured."

"What's going on?" Miranda asked, looking back and forth from her boyfriend to her best friend to the guys who were unlocking the gate and leading something out on a leash, something that looked like . . . *a pig?*

Jesse Lopez handed the end of the leash to Kane, and Mark Walker led two more out of the pen, trying to hand one leash to Harper, who stepped back, holding up her hands in defense. "No way," she said quickly. "No way. I'm here in a supervisory capacity only. The pigs are *your* deal."

"What's going *on?*" Miranda asked again, louder this time. She glared at Kane. "You drove me all the way out here because you're . . . stealing pigs?"

"Not stealing," Kane said. "Borrowing. We have full permission of the owner."

Jesse raised a hand sheepishly. "It's my uncle," he explained. "I told him we'd have 'em back in a few days."

"And what are 'we' doing with them in the mean-time?" Miranda asked, gaping as the fattest of the pigs began nibbling at Kane's shoelaces.

"You want to tell her?" Harper asked.

"Senior prank," Kane said, giving her a boyish grin. "We're keeping them in my yard for a couple nights, then when the time is right . . ."

"We set 'em off in school," Mark said, nearly salivating in anticipation. "And that's not even the best part."

Miranda cocked her head and turned to Kane, who was certain to be the one responsible. "And what, exactly, is the best part?"

"We draw numbers on them," Kane said proudly. "Piggie numbers one, two, and four."

"Where's number three?"

"That's the beauty of it," Harper explained. "It'll take them long enough to catch the first three pigs. Imagine how much time they'll waste looking for the fourth one—the one that doesn't exist!"

Miranda burst into laughter. "This is the dumbest thing I've ever heard."

"Welcome to the wonderful world of senior pranking," Harper said wryly. "It's a dirty job, but someone's got to do it." And, as Miranda knew, that someone was traditionally an elite group of seniors, handpicked by the previous senior class for their cunning, deviousness, ruthlessness and, most important, their cool factor. She should have realized that Harper and Kane would be at the top of the list.

"So what are we waiting for?" Miranda asked, taking one of the pig leashes out of Mark's hands. "Let's get these oinkers on the road!"

They led their livestock back into the darkness and, with some coaxing and—in the case of the largest pig—a fair amount of pushing, grunting, dragging, and cursing, got the pigs safely loaded into the back of Mark's pickup truck. As the others were securing the pigs, Kane pulled Miranda aside into the darkness.

"It's supposed to be a secret," he whispered. "That's why we didn't tell you. Plus, I didn't want to drag you down in the mud with me."

"I'm glad you did," she said, rising on her toes and giving him a quick kiss on the cheek. "If you're going to wallow in the mud"—she glanced down at her hands, which were streaked with grime—"why do it alone?"

"You never cease to surprise me, Stevens," he marveled.

"And you never cease to underestimate me, Geary," she said, slugging him on the shoulder. He grabbed her arm and spun her around so her back was pressed against his chest, wrapping his arms around her waist and resting his chin lightly on her head. She was a perfect fit. "When are you going to figure out that you can trust me?"

"You're not the one I'm worried about," he said softly.

Miranda turned around to face him and buried her head in his chest. His arms tightened around her, and she closed her eyes, savoring the moment.

She didn't ask what he'd meant.

"So tell me again why you can't interview me, Ms. Professional Journalist?" Adam demanded. He was sitting on the floor of his bedroom, his back against the bureau and his feet kicked up against the wall. Beth was straddling the desk chair.

Both of them had, without mentioning it, avoided the bed.

"Conflict of interest," Beth said. "And I'm not a professional journalist. Not yet. If I screw up this story . . ."

"You won't screw it up," he said firmly. He'd been saying it all night.

Six months ago, it wouldn't have been like this. Beth would have thrown herself into the new project with determination and surety, vowing to impress the newspaper staff so much, they offered her a job on the spot. Adam didn't have to wonder what had happened to that Beth. He knew.

She stood up and walked over to the window, which faced the backyard. It also faced Harper's bedroom, which was why, these days, he usually kept the blinds down.

"Adam, I need to—" She stopped, her back to him.

"What is it?" he asked, when she didn't continue.

But she just shook her head. "Nothing." She'd been doing it all night, starting to say something, then cutting herself off in the middle as if she'd lost her nerve. Or maybe he was just projecting, because he'd been doing the same thing. The UC Riverside coach had called again today, checking in on his progress, wondering if he'd made a decision yet. He hadn't. And, much as he would have liked to talk it over with Beth—the *old* Beth—he knew this one couldn't help him. She probably couldn't handle hearing about it in the first place. So he kept his mouth shut.

"You've been really great tonight," she said. "Thanks for taking me out."

"We had to celebrate!" he said. "This is huge."

"Yeah. Maybe." She turned back to face him. "Do you want to go outside for a while? Sit on the rock and . . . talk?"

"No," he said, too quickly.

She blanched, and turned quickly back to the window. "Oh. Of course not. I should probably just get out of here. I'm sure you've got stuff to do, and . . ."

"No. It's not that."

Adam saw her shoulders heave with a deep, shuddery breath, then another. He stood up and crossed the room to join her at the window. The light in Harper's bedroom was on; he suppressed the urge to close his blinds. What were the odds that she was watching? He tilted his head, leaning it against Beth's. "It's not that," he said. "I just . . . I don't want to go outside, okay?"

He couldn't take Beth out there to the rock, to his and Harper's place, the long, flat rock that lay on the boundary between their properties, where they'd spent so many hours of their lives lying side by side talking about everything that strayed across their minds. Where they'd shared their first kiss, complete with awkward fumbling and entangled braces—and where, this year, they'd shared far more than that. Even if Harper never spoke to him again, that place would still belong to the two of them.

Adam turned slightly, and so did Beth, until they were facing each other. He watched her eyes, pale blue and glittery, like a pool of water at dawn; she didn't look away. He didn't know who leaned in first. It just happened. One moment they were standing apart, their arms resting on the windowsill, lightly touching, Beth's lips, covered in pink gloss, slightly parted and curling up in a half smile. The next moment, they were kissing. Adam had time to think about the silhouette their faces would make in the window, shadowy lips connected, shadowy hands pressed against shadowy faces—if anyone was watching. And then Beth pushed him away.

"I'm sorry," he said, confused. "Did I . . . ?"

"No. I shouldn't have." She stepped away.

"I thought it was what you wanted," he said helplessly.

"You thought . . ." She sighed, and slid down the wall into a sitting position, curling her legs up against her chest. "I heard you. A couple days ago in the parking lot. With Kane."

"What are you talking about?" Adam slumped down next to her—keeping a few inches of space between them.

"I know you're only hanging out with me because you feel sorry for me," she said, her voice thin and flat.

"I don't know what you think you heard, but—"

"Please, Adam. Just . . . I heard you." She turned to look at him, and she wasn't crying. Her lips weren't trembling, nor was her voice. "Can't you just admit it?"

"Fine." He hated this. Hated everything about it. "I guess I feel kind of sorry for you. But that's not all of it."

"I know." She sighed heavily. "You think you owe me. I heard that, too. And I guess . . . I already knew. It's the way you look at me. Like you think I'm going to break or something. You're scared of what will happen if you walk away. I knew that. I just . . . I didn't want to know. You know?"

He couldn't deny it.

"You'd rather be with Harper," she said. "And you should be."

Adam shook his head. "That's not going to happen."

"Only because you're with me," Beth said. She touched his arm, lightly, and then dropped her hand back onto her knees. "Because you think I'll fall apart if you're not here. But that shouldn't have to be your problem."

She was giving him an out. And he was tempted to take it. But. There was always a but.

"But it's true, right? What happens if I ditch you, like everyone else?"

She sniffled, and looked down. "I'd be fine."

"Now who's lying?"

"I don't want to need you," she said in a choked, angry voice. "I don't want to be that girl, some weak, broken thing dragging you down."

"You're not," he assured her.

"I should be stronger than that."

"You will be," he promised. "But for now . . ."

"Yeah. For now." She pressed her hand to her mouth and made some noise that could have been a laugh or a sob. "So here we are."

Adam scooted over a couple inches and looped his arm around her shoulders, pulling her toward him. She didn't resist. He tugged her closer, and she laid her head against his shoulder while he stroked her arm, gently, rhythmically, up and down, up and down. "Here we are," he echoed. And they sat like that for a long time, eyes closed, bodies together, without moving, until Beth felt strong enough to go home.

chapter seven

THE CONVERSATION WENT LIKE THIS.

Harper: "No. There's no way. Just *no*."

Amanda Grace, Harper's ever-doting mother, torch-carrier for the Grace family heritage, and president of the Haven High PTA: "I'm not asking you, I'm telling you."

Harper, her arms folded: "Then I'm not coming."

Richard Grace, without looking up from his newspaper: "You're coming."

Harper: "Is it your goal in life to humiliate me?"

Amanda Grace: "I'm not asking you to stand on the roof and sing the national anthem. I'm just asking you to be there."

Harper: "And to smile, and make nice, and pretend I don't hate every single person there."

Amanda Grace: "Yes, that, too."

Harper had stormed up the stairs, defeated. And then she had managed to put the whole thing out of her mind. Until the invitations arrived. As if things weren't bad enough already. The invitations were made from a thick card stock, dyed pale blue and dotted with tiny green and lavender flowers. *Con-GRAD-ulations!* they announced, in tacky pink letters. The "o"s had been turned into balloons.

Amanda Grace was displeased. She had requested something tasteful, but the result was half bridal shower, half kiddie birthday party, and all awful. She sent them out, anyway. And then *Harper* was displeased. Because her mother sent them out to everyone. Every single person in the senior class. Including Lester Lawrence—or Lawrence Lester, Harper could never remember which it was—who would probably bring his pet crickets. Including Ellen Blumenthal and Margaret Cheever, who still worshipped the Powerpuff Girls. Including the ditzy cheerleaders and the boneheaded jocks and the math club losers and all the guys she'd ever hooked up with and all their former and current and jealous girlfriends.

Including Adam.

"It doesn't matter if you don't like them. This party

isn't for you," her mother reminded her as Harper stood at the edge of the kitchen, waiting to make her grand entrance into the backyard where the detestable masses had invaded her only remaining sanctum. She was wearing a black slipdress with a red sash and a plunging neckline that her mother complained was too dressy and too dark for the occasion. Harper didn't care; she felt dark. And she figured she might as well look hot.

Her mother handed her a bowl of cheese curls. "This party is for your class. It's a celebration." There was steel in her voice. "So *smile*."

Harper smiled, prepared herself, and stepped outside.

"Hey, Harper, your house is so great!" burbled some girl who, under normal circumstances, Harper would pretend didn't exist. She smiled and elected not to comment on the neon monstrosity the girl was wearing as a dress.

"Awesome party," some loser surf-talked, giving her a "hang ten" wave as if the nearest ocean weren't hundreds of miles away. Harper ducked her head, dropped the cheese curls on a nearby table, and barreled across the yard toward Miranda and Kane. The happy couple looked disgustingly content in their little corner, playing with each other's hair, gazing into each other's eyes, and pretending the rest of the world didn't exist. It was gross, but it was better than nothing.

"Thanks for coming," she muttered, taking a quick swig from Kane's ever-present flask.

"Rockin' party," Kane said sarcastically, nodding toward the pastel streamers Amanda Grace had hung from the trees and the old speakers that were pumping out some kind of 90s hip-hop in a feeble attempt to seem hip.

Harper sighed. "It's a good thing high school's ending in a week, because I'd never live this one down."

"Look on the bright side," Miranda pointed out. "No one whose opinion you care about is dumb enough to show up." Harper had done an efficient job of spreading the word that the event would be about as thrilling as a PTA bake-off, and suggested that her fellow A-listers hold out for Savannah Miller's party a few nights later. Savannah was a drab nobody who'd barely registered on Harper's radar since seventh grade, when the two of them had been stuck together for a history project and Savannah had irritatingly refused to cheat. But she was rich, and her parents were out of town, which—thanks to Harper's help—opened the possibilities for true greatness. Let Amanda Grace have her garden party; Harper would have a raging night to remember. Even if she had to have it at someone else's house.

"Yeah, that's the good news," Harper said. "The bad news is that every single loser showed, and now we're stuck with them."

"*You're* stuck with them," Kane corrected her. "We're

putting in our face-time, and then"—he tapped his watch and winked—"it's time for some oink-oink."

"I never thought I'd say this," Harper said, "but I'd rather be wrestling pigs in the high school gym than here stuffing my face with cheese puffs and pretending these people don't make me sick."

"Don't worry, Grace," Kane said kindly. "Every time we look at those pigs, we'll be thinking of you."

"You're such a sweetheart." Harper looked over his shoulder, scanning the faces in the pathetic crowd.

"He's not here," Miranda said quietly.

Harper turned back around. "What are you talking about?" But she couldn't fool Miranda.

"It's still early," Miranda said hopefully. "Maybe . . ."

Harper shook her head. "It doesn't matter. Let's snag some of those miniquesadillas before they're all gone, okay?"

And Miranda, thankfully, let it drop.

Harper managed to keep up a steady stream of chatter for the next two hours, standing at the fringes with Miranda and Kane, picking apart the wardrobes and personalities of their fellow seniors as Harper pretended she wasn't keeping one eye fixed on the gate, waiting for Adam to walk through it. But then Miranda and Kane left, and it was a lot harder for her to pretend she wasn't miserable.

The later it got, the harder it was for her to convince herself that he might still show. People were starting to leave, and the only new arrivals in the last hour had been—

"No." Harper gaped at the entry gate. "Oh, no, I don't think so." She stormed across the yard and planted herself in front of them, hands on hips, fierce scowl on her face. There was nothing she could do about her mother, and there was nothing she could do about Adam, but *this* was a problem she could handle.

"What are *you* doing here?" she asked in disgust, staring down her two sophomore clones: pathetic, brainless twits who dressed like her, talked like her, and wouldn't leave her alone. In the beginning she'd been flattered—after all, you couldn't fault their taste. But the monkey-see, monkey-do act had gotten old a long time ago. "This is a *senior* party."

"We know!" the one on the left said, nearly clapping her hands with excitement. She'd dyed her hair since Harper had seen her last, and her curls were now the exact shade of brown with reddish streaks that Harper saw in the mirror every morning. Harper's nickname for her—Mini-Me—had never seemed so apt.

"We can't believe it!" That would be Mini-She, the best friend, whose arm was covered in the same thin jelly bracelets Harper had worn for a few weeks back in May before getting sick of the look. "It's so sad that you're graduating," she moaned. "We're going to miss you sooooooo much."

"I said, what are you doing here?" Harper asked again, knowing she would have to get them out before her mother spotted them. In Amanda Grace's book there was only one thing tackier than crashing a party: making a scene by tossing out the crashers.

"Do you mind?" Mini-Me asked. "We just wanted to come and tell you how much we're going to miss you next year."

"Soooooooo much," Mini-She added, sounding even more cowlike than she had the first time.

It was perfect, Harper thought. A symbol of the disaster her life had become: her two clingy, sycophantic clones crashing the lame excuse for a party that Harper would have done anything to escape, while the only person she had really wanted to be there never bothered to show up. Suddenly, she was fed up—with her oppressive mother, with the losers invading her backyard, with the pride that wouldn't let her make things right with Adam, and, most of all, with the Minis, these girls who had plagued her all year long, who wouldn't give her a moment of peace. *Enough*, she thought. *This is finally enough.*

"Get out," she said coldly. "You're not welcome here."

"But, Harper," Mini-Me whined, "I know we're not seniors, but we thought since we were your friends—"

"My *friends*?" she sneered. "You think I'd ever be friends with someone like you? Someone who can't even come up with her own identity, so you have to steal mine?" She started to laugh. "You're not even *good* at it." She pointed at Mini-She's hideous floral miniskirt. "I wouldn't wear that rag to take the trash out. I wouldn't even *use* it as a rag to wipe the bathroom floor."

Mini-She's lip wobbled, and Mini-Me took a step backward, her eyes wide. "We just wanted to . . ."

"Wanted to what?" Harper asked. They didn't answer. "Wanted to *what*? No, I didn't think you'd come up with anything, because you don't want anything—how could you? You're nobody. You're clones. You're cheap knock-offs. You only want what you think I want." She shook her head, as if in pity, though she felt none. "I'd tell you to get lives of your own, but somehow, I just don't think you can handle it. But here's an idea: If you've got to steal someone's life, make it someone other than me. You got that?"

The girls were frozen, unwilling to speak but afraid to look away.

"I said, *You got that*?" Harper repeated angrily. "Get out of my face and find someone else to copy. I can't deal with it anymore. It's too pathetic. You're too pathetic."

If they'd gotten angry, she might have felt guilty. She might even have apologized. If they had yelled back, or even rolled their eyes and turned silently, walking out with their chins up and their shoulders back, Harper might have realized that she'd misjudged them. She might have reminded herself that even though they acted like mindless clones, they *did* want something: her friendship. She might have felt the way she had at the beginning of the year: sympathetic. Flattered. Even—if they had shown the slightest hint of rebellion or self-preservation or dignity— a little impressed.

But they didn't. Mini-Me turned red. Mini-She stared at the ground. And then Mini-Me actually said it. "I'm sorry." And they spun around and skittered away.

The adrenaline flooded out of her. She felt like shit. And she wished she could take it all back. Not because she felt guilty, or because she'd been cruel. But because Mini-Me and Mini-She had worshipped her. They'd wanted to *be* her—which made them proof that she was someone worth being.

And now the proof was gone.

Heather Martinez, age 17, interview #1

Q: If you could do high school all over again, what would you do differently?

A: I'd never hook up with Rodney, that's number one. Asshole. Did you hear what he said about me to—

Q: I mean, in the broader sense. You know, if you could change what high school was like.

A: Oh. Yeah. Um, I guess maybe I wouldn'tve taken Spanish, because that French teacher guy was pretty hot, you know, before he disappeared. And I would've . . . well, maybe I would've studied a little, you know, actually gotten some decent grades so I wouldn't have to go work at my mom's store after graduation and I could actually get out of here, you know? Do something.

Q: What would you do?

(Interviewer note: Subject doesn't answer for several minutes.)

A: Maybe . . . this is gonna sound kind of stupid, but . . . maybe be a teacher?

Q: Why is that stupid?

A: You know. What kind of idiot comes back to school once they finally let you out? I always used to say that, after graduation, I'd never walk into a school again. And . . . yeah, I guess I won't.

Kyle Chuny, age 18, interview #4

A: I didn't think you knew who I was.

Q: We've gone to school together for fifteen years. Why wouldn't I?

A: I don't know. I guess . . . no one ever seems to know who I am. It's like all these kids that I used to hang out with in elementary school, now they blow past me in the hall like they don't even know me. I asked this girl out once, right? I knew she was going to say no, but I figured whatever, right? This was last year. So I asked her to the junior prom. And she just looked at me like I was crazy, and she was like, "Aren't you a sophomore?" Then she

just started laughing. And when I told her I
was a junior, she laughed even harder.

Q: Does it make you mad?

A: Whatever. It's just high school, right? And now
it's over. And I figure in college, things'll be
different in college. People will be different,
you know?

Q: Why?

A: What do you mean? It's college. College
people.

Q: Aren't college students just high school
students one year older?

A: No, no way. It's like a whole different thing in
college. Everything's different. It has to be.

Barbara Morris, age 18, interview #6

Q: Will you miss high school?

A: Yeah, of course I will. I'm totally psyched for
college next year, but everyone here is so
great. I'm never going to make friends like this
again. I mean, I know everyone talks about
how you meet all these great friends in college,
but can they ever really know you? How can
anyone really know you if they don't know
where you came from? It's not like your friends
from home—nothing will ever be like that.

Q: So you're going to keep in touch with them?

A: Yeah, we made a pact. We're going to text
every day, no exceptions. It's going to make
it easier to leave—knowing that there's
someone out there, someone who knows who
you really are.

Q: Does that mean you're nervous about college
next year?

A: No. Definitely not. I've been waiting for this

my whole life. I've got it all planned out.
I'm going to major in political science, write
for the newspaper, then get into a good
law school, make law review, and become a
constitutional lawyer. Who knows, maybe I'll
even make it to the Supreme Court.

Q: Sounds like you've got it all figured out.

A: It's not hard, when you know exactly what you
want.

Ashley Statten looked up from the interview notes
that Beth had carefully prepared for her. "What the hell is
this?" she asked, throwing them down on her desk. "Is this
some kind of joke?"

Beth shifted her weight from one foot to the other.
Ashley hadn't offered her a chair. The newsroom was
pretty dead—everyone else had headed home to enjoy
their Saturday night, but Ashley was scrambling to meet
her deadline and apparently wanted Beth to share in
her misery. "If that's not exactly what you needed, I've
got a lot more," Beth said. She'd spent hours the night
before transcribing all her interviews and pulling out the
moments that she thought were most revealing. Telling
herself that this was the start to her journalism career. It
was almost enough to assuage the sickening feeling she
got listening to all these seniors talking brightly about the
future. It seemed like everyone else was looking forward
while Beth was still stuck in the past.

"More? Spare me." Ashley stood up and walked over to a metal filing cabinet against the side wall. She pulled a digital camera out of the cabinet and brought it over to the desk. "I knew this was a bad idea," she muttered. "What would someone like you know about *real* journalism?" She waved the camera at Beth, who took it in confusion. "You know how to use this thing?"

"Um, I guess so. But . . . use it for what?"

Ashley glared at her. "Look, another time, maybe, I'd sugarcoat this, but I don't have the time, so let me be blunt. These interviews suck. They're tepid, they're boring, they're totally off-topic. You let your subjects ramble. You don't press them on the hard questions. You don't get *anything* juicy out of them. To be honest, I just don't see much journalistic instinct here. And your subjects? Where are the alpha girls? Where's the head cheerleader? The star quarterback? The school slut? Where's my story?"

"I can do better," Beth said quickly.

"I doubt it," Ashley said. "But that's moot. I don't have enough time to send you back out there, and lucky for you, I've got most of the material I need from my own interviews. But here's the good news, for you, at least. My editor has a real hard-on for that English teacher of yours, and she thinks you're God's gift to journalism—which means that unless you burn the place down, you're probably going to get that internship next year. So here's all I need you to do. Take the camera. Hit a party—there's one coming up on Tuesday night."

"How do you know?"

"Because *I* actually did some investigative reporting," Ashley said. "Maybe you've heard of it? Look, I'd go myself, but"—she gestured down at her tailored gray suit—"obviously I'd have a little trouble blending. So it's on you. Take some pictures—and no more of this 'best times of our lives' crap. This story is about the dark side of high school, and I want you to get me some good-girls-gone-wild pics to go along with it. From what I hear about Haven parties, shouldn't be too tough. Think you can handle it?"

"We'll see." Ashley waved Beth away like a mosquito and turned back to her computer. "Do even a mediocre job and you'll get your precious internship, whether you deserve it or not. But, Beth?"

Beth paused on her way to the door, wondering if even a real journalism internship would be worth facing Ashley Statten day in and day out. "Yes?"

"Don't screw up again."

"I think number four belongs in the principal's office," Miranda said, holding steady as the pig jerked forward on its leash and squealed in frustration.

"And *I* think my girlfriend's a criminal mastermind," Kane said, trying to kiss her. She squirmed away.

"Not in front of the pig," she teased.

They crept down the dark hallway, the distant pitter-patter of little footsteps telling them that pigs number one and two were already well on their way to causing trouble. When they reached the central administration office, Kane brandished a key.

"Do I want to know where you got that from?" Miranda asked.

Kane shook his head. "Probably not."

He let them into the office, and they released the pig, slamming the door shut before it could escape. Miranda burst into nervous giggles—she still couldn't believe she was doing this: trespassing, smuggling livestock, defiling school property. It was so *not* her. But it was Kane, and she was pretty proud of herself for keeping up. With only a minimum of nervous questions and heart palpitations.

"You're sure there are no security cameras?" she asked as they slipped toward an exit.

"This is Haven High, not the Pentagon," Kane said. "Trust me, I've done this plenty of times."

"Why—no, never mind." She rolled her eyes. "I don't want to know."

"Again, probably not." Suddenly he froze, and grabbed her, raising a finger to his lips. Miranda's mouth formed a silent O of horror as she heard the footsteps. Not scuttling pig patters, but solid, heavy steps. Headed in their direction.

"Is there someone there?" a deep voice called out, and a weak flashlight beam broke through the darkness.

"Shit," Kane whispered.

Miranda was shaking. One week to graduation, and now . . . what would her mother say if she got thrown out of school?

Kane grabbed her arms and squeezed tight. "Calm down," he whispered. "We got this. When I say the word, just run for the exit. Fast as you can. Okay?"

Miranda shook her head. "We have to hide. Maybe . . ."

"*No. Run,*" Kane mouthed. "Trust me?"

She nodded.

"What are you kids up to down there?" the security guard came into sight. "Hey, hey you—get out here!"

"*Now!*" Kane mouthed, and Miranda ran.

"What the—?" They slammed past the security guard before he could stop them and burst through the exit.

"Keep going!" Kane shouted, and Miranda sprinted across the field and down the hill to the parking lot, flinging herself into the passenger seat of her car while Kane leaped into the driver's seat and peeled out nearly before she'd managed to slam the door.

"Go!" she screamed. "Go!" She didn't breathe again

until they were safely out on the main road, lost in the flow of Saturday night traffic. "You don't think he saw the car, do you?" she asked. "If he caught the license number . . ."

"Did you get a look at that guy?" Kane asked scornfully. "Probably burst an artery halfway out the door."

"Be nice," Miranda chided him, but it did make her feel better to think of the guard's potbelly and the way his footsteps had fallen behind them so quickly. They were safe. And they'd pulled it off.

Kane pulled into the empty lot of a shoe store that had closed hours before. He turned the car off.

"What are we stopping for?" Mirada asked.

"This." He turned to her, grabbed her face in both hands, and kissed her, hard and deep. "We did it."

"We really did, didn't we?" Adrenaline was shooting through her. Her hands were tingling, and she felt like her head was about to pop off. "I can't believe I did that. It was—we could have gotten in so much trouble, but . . ."

"It was worth it, wasn't it?" Kane asked, with a knowing grin.

"Totally. It was amazing." She touched his cheek, rubbing her fingers against his jawline. "*You're* amazing. I never would have . . . before. I just mean—this is incredible. Being with you. I've never been so happy, and sometimes I just think, it's like everything I've ever wanted is finally—" She cut herself off in horror.

Kane didn't say anything.

You scared him away, she thought furiously. *It was the perfect moment, and you ruined everything.*

"I didn't mean, I just meant, you know, we had a good night, and—" She was babbling, trying to fix it, but it couldn't be fixed. It was ruined. "You know, it's just cool, hanging out and all, and I'm just a little wired from the criminal activities and—"

"Come here," he said, drawing her into his arms. "I had fun too," he whispered, and kissed her again. Maybe he hadn't understood what she was saying. Maybe he had chosen to ignore it. Or maybe this was his way of saying that he agreed, that they *weren't* just having fun, that this was something more for him, too. Miranda didn't know. She just knew that she'd almost screwed everything up and yet he was still there, still real, kissing her, holding her and, even with her arm wedged against the glove compartment and the gearshift digging into her thigh, she was happier than she'd ever been.

She would just have to be more careful. She couldn't afford to risk telling him how she really felt, that she was falling in—

No, she couldn't even afford to *think* it. Not yet. She would just be patient, and maybe someday *he* would say it. And then she could let everything out and stop worrying that she would do something to make him leave. It hurt—the worrying and the waiting, always expecting that something awful was about to happen—but she was willing to give it time. She was willing to trust him. She just hoped she could trust herself to stay silent.

Kane could never find out that she was falling in love.

It's not too late, she thought, knocking on the door. *You can still run away.*

But then the door swung open.

"Oh, Harper!" Adam's mother leaned toward her to give her a hug. Harper could smell the whiskey on her breath. "So charmin' to see you." The slur in her words was so slight, it might not have been noticeable to someone who wasn't looking for it. But when it came to Adam's mother, Harper was always looking. "C'mon in."

"Actually, could you just let Adam know I'm here?" She didn't know why she didn't want to go in the house. It wasn't just Mrs. Morgan. The idea of being trapped in there with him . . . she couldn't do it. So she waited on the porch as Mrs. Morgan called her son downstairs.

"I'm juss having a lil' drink," Mrs. Morgan said in her heavy Southern accent. "Y'all sure you don't want to come in and have some?"

"I'm fine," Harper said. Adam's mother always made her vaguely uncomfortable. Maybe because she had never been able to forget the day she'd walked into Adam's kitchen and discovered his mother lying on the kitchen table . . . with their seventh-grade math teacher lying on top of her.

"You kids have fun," Mrs. Morgan told her son when he finally arrived in the doorway. She pinched his cheeks, which he endured, as he always did. "Don't you do anything I wouldn't do." She was still cackling as they closed the door in her face.

Adam blushed. "You know my mom, she's just . . ."

"Yeah." Harper swallowed hard. "You didn't come."

"What?"

"To my party. You didn't come."

Adam looked like he didn't know what he was supposed to say. "I just figured you wouldn't want me there."

"I don't get why you would—"

"Harper, you made it perfectly clear that you don't want me around."

"And you know why," Harper snapped.

"Yeah, I do. So unless you changed your mind . . ."

"You know I can't—"

"Fine." Adam turned and opened the screen door. "We can't keep having this same conversation."

She grabbed his arm. "Wait."

They paused like that, her fingers wrapped around his bicep. She missed the feel of him. "I don't want to fight." Harper didn't know why she couldn't stay away from this place. "Can we just . . . take a break from all that?" she asked finally. "Pretend like none of it matters, just for tonight?"

"Temporary truce?"

She nodded, and they shook on it.

"Backyard?" Adam asked, and headed around to the back before she could answer. He just knew what she wanted. He knew her.

They lay on their backs on the wide, flat rock, their arms splayed out and almost touching, but not quite. Harper had always loved lying next to someone, listening to their breathing, a silent confirmation that she wasn't alone. Adam's was slow and steady. She wished she could put a hand on his chest and feel its gentle rise and fall. "Remember when we built the fort?" she asked. They'd propped some cardboard and wooden planks against their rock, then pillaged the Grace family linen cabinet and strung up Amanda Grace's antique silk sheets as tarps.

"I thought you were going to be grounded forever," Adam said, chuckling.

"You would have rescued me," Harper reminded him. They had come up with a secret plan, involving a ladder, two skateboards, and enough supplies (candy bars and Gatorade) to last them several days "in the wild." Fortunately, the grounding had only lasted a week; they'd never had to run away.

"That's my specialty," Adam said. "Remember when we 'camped out'?"

Harper snorted. "I can't believe I let you talk me into that." In sixth grade, they had pitched a tent in the back-yard. Adam told ghost stories, while Harper complained about the bugs. "So gross."

"And when that cricket climbed into your sleeping bag . . ."

"Ew!" Harper squealed, and jerked her limbs as if she could still feel the insect skittering up her body. "Don't go there. I can't even *think* about that."

"Hey, I saved you, didn't I?"

She smiled, glad that it was too dark for him to see her face. "Yeah, I guess you did." He had gotten rid of the cricket, dried her tears, and talked her out of going inside. Then he'd promised to stay up all night, "guarding" her. It was the only way she'd been able to fall asleep.

"Things are really ending, aren't they?" she said. "I mean, high school, living at home, all that." But that's not what she meant, not completely.

"Yeah." He was quiet for a moment. "Next year . . . This place, it seems like nothing ever changes. But now . . ."

"Everything's changing." She turned over on her side and watched his face, silhouetted in the moonlight. It suddenly seemed so stupid, the way she'd pushed him away,

just for trying to do the right thing, just for trying to protect someone else. He was Adam Morgan, that's what he
did: protected. Rescued. Saved. It was why she loved him.
So why couldn't she just get over it? Harper inched her
hand across the cool surface of the boulder until her index
finger brushed up against his wrist. She was so close. If
she could just stop hating Beth so much, if she could just
ignore that part of his life and accept that she didn't get to
have *all* of him . . .

She moved her hand, feeling like she was pushing
an enormous weight. Her muscles strained—her heart
strained—and then it was done. Her hand rested on his,
their fingers merged together. He didn't move. "Adam . . ."

"I might go away to college next year," he said suddenly.

She took her hand away.

"What?"

"A recruiter came. A basketball coach, from UC
Riverside. He offered me a spot on the team, and a scholarship, and . . ."

Say congratulations, she told herself furiously. *Sound
happy. Be happy.*

"UC Riverside," she said instead, her voice thin and
flat. "That's, like, hundreds of miles away."

"Yeah. It's a five-hour drive."

"So are you . . . when do you leave?"

Adam sat up and rubbed his hands across his face. "I don't know if I'm going yet. I haven't decided." He turned to her. "What do you think?"

Stay, Harper thought, wishing he could hear. *Stay for me.*

She shrugged. "Your call. It sounds really . . . great. For you."

"Maybe." And without warning, he reached for her hand. She let him take it, let him press it between his palms. A warm tingling rose up her arm. "Gracie, I don't want to leave with the way things are. . . ."

Leave. He was leaving.

She pulled her hand away and climbed off the rock. "I have to go home," she said without emotion. Every feeling she had was locked up tight, because if she let even one dribble out, the floodgates would open.

"Now?" Adam jumped off the rock as well and tried to take her hand again, but she stepped away.

"It's late. I should—I have to go."

"I'll walk you home," he said, sounding almost desperate.

"No." And she said it firmly enough that he didn't protest.

He was leaving her, she thought, as she waved good-bye and walked slowly through the darkness. She was in no hurry to get home; she just needed to get away. At least for tonight, she had to leave him first.

chapter eight

"YOU SURE YOU WANT TO DO THIS?" ADAM ASKED.

Beth took a deep breath and grabbed her camera. "Want to? No. But let's go."

They threaded through the crowd, Beth snapping pictures and feeling like a total loser.

"So whose house is this?" she asked as they stepped into the entry hall. It stank of beer.

Adam shrugged. "Who cares?"

"Yo, Morgan!" someone called, and it was echoed by shouts from all over the room. A few guys from the basketball team hurried to knock fists with him and boast about their keg stands.

"Hey, Adam." A cheerleader named Brianna draped herself around his neck. He pried her off. "Going to miss me next year?"

"Sure."

"Because I'm going to miss you," she whispered, almost crawling up his arm. "Want me to show you how much?"

"Not really." Adam shook her off and turned to Beth. "Sorry about, uh . . ."

She shook her head. "Don't worry about it." She wasn't jealous. At least, not in the normal way. But she couldn't help noticing the way everyone turned to look at Adam as he passed by, their faces lighting up when he smiled or waved. Everyone wanted to talk to him, to touch him, even just to be acknowledged by him. Beth, on the other hand, was invisible.

She snapped a couple more pictures, but she couldn't figure out where to point the camera. Whenever anyone caught sight of her, they froze and stuck on a pained smile. Something told her Ashley Statten wouldn't approve.

"Want a drink?" Adam asked, nodding at the keg. Beth shook her head. "Yeah, I probably shouldn't, either."

"I can drive home," Beth offered. But he just shrugged. He hadn't wanted to come in the first place, even though everyone claimed this would be the best graduation party in years. But Beth hadn't had the nerve to come alone.

A tall, dark-haired senior Beth didn't recognize approached them, slapping palms with Adam. "Yo, Morgan, haven't seen you since the season ended."

"Hey, Jake," Adam said, his first genuine smile of the night making an appearance. He turned to Beth. "This is Jake, he's a point guard for Crestview—almost beat us out for the championship this year."

"*Almost* being the operative word," Jake said ruefully. "And this would be?"

"This is Beth," Adam said, "my, uh . . ."

"Nice to meet you," Beth said quickly, shaking his hand.

"*The* Beth?" Jake raised his eyebrows. "Nice to meet you, too." He tapped Adam on the shoulder. "Listen, there's something I need to ask you, but maybe we should talk somewhere else?"

"It's okay," Adam said. "She's cool."

Beth wasn't sure whether that meant he trusted her to hear anything—or he didn't care what she thought.

"Yeah, okay. So . . ." Jake shifted his weight and scratched the side of his head, stalling. "The thing is, you probably know I took Harper Grace to the prom, right?"

Adam's jaw muscles tightened. Jake wouldn't have noticed, but Beth did. "Yeah, I heard."

"So when I went, I didn't realize the two of you were . . . you know."

"We're not," Adam said quickly.

"Right. I just wanted to check in with you, because . . ."

Beth didn't want Adam to realize she was staring, but she couldn't look away. He didn't look angry or upset. He looked . . . still. Like he'd put a tight lid on his emotions and he wasn't going to let a single one of them bubble to the surface.

"I thought I'd go for it," Jake finally said.

A muscle at the corner of Adam's eye twitched. "Why tell me?"

"I just wanted to make sure you were okay with it. You know, bros before hos and all that. Not that Harper's a—I didn't mean—"

"It's fine," Adam said. He grabbed Beth's hand, squeezing it so tight that it hurt. "Good to see you, Jake."

"You too!" Jake said, too heartily, but Adam had already turned away, dragging Beth into the surging crowd.

"You okay?" she asked hesitantly, not sure if she wanted to hear the answer.

"Fine," he growled. "Let's go find the keg."

"Did Isabelle Peters always have such pretty eyes?" Kane asked, nodding at the quiet, first-chair violinist who was leaning against the mantel and falling out of her low-cut red corset top.

Miranda followed his gaze. "Those aren't her eyes," she said sourly.

"I'm going to go say hello," Kane said, staring shamelessly. Miranda stared too, wondering how the girl could breathe.

"Do you even *know* Isabelle Peters?" she asked, but Kane was already heading across the room. Miranda hurried to keep up, feeling like a fool. She'd been following him around all night, even though he'd barely spoken to her, much less looked at her. She told herself he was just in a bad mood.

Apparently, his mood had cleared just in time for him to flash a brilliant smile at Isabelle Peters, who blushed so deeply, her face clashed with her shirt.

"That was a beautiful violin solo you did at the spring concert this year," Kane said. Both girls gaped at him.

"I . . . I didn't know you were there," Isabelle stammered.

"Neither did I," Miranda said pointedly, since as far as she knew, Kane hadn't attended a school concert since giving up the trombone in the fourth grade.

"It was mesmerizing," Kane said. He took Isabelle's right hand and laid it across his left palm, running his right hand lightly over her fingers. "To think that your ordinary hand could create such magic . . ."

"Um—um—" Isabelle ripped her hand away. "I should,

uh, I have to go find my, uh, boyfriend. He's somewhere, I should, oh—" She was still muttering to herself as she hurried away.

Miranda couldn't help but laugh. "I guess your magic was too powerful for her," she teased.

Kane scowled. "What's that supposed to mean?"

"What? I was just—"

"What are you, jealous?" Kane sneered. And this wasn't the playful smirk she'd grown to know and love. This was full-blown disgust. "So now I'm not allowed to talk to other girls at all, is that it?"

"What are you talking about?" Miranda asked.

"You don't own me, you do realize that, right?"

"Why would I want to own you?" Miranda reached out for him, for his hand, his shoulder, but he pushed her away. "Kane, what's going on with you tonight?"

"Nothing." He rolled his eyes. "How about we stop analyzing everything I do for once, okay? I'm getting a drink." He turned away from her and headed abruptly toward the keg.

"Nothing for me, thanks," Miranda said sarcastically, knowing he couldn't hear.

She sat down on one of the couches, narrowly avoiding a puddle of spinach dip that was seeping into the brown leather. The party swirled on around her. Miranda waved to some friends, but couldn't muster up the will to actually talk to any of them. Not even Harper, whom she spotted by the dining room table, holding court over a gaggle of admirers but, at least to Miranda's trained eye, sulking and miserable. Harper was the last person she wanted to talk to right now, since she would have had to admit that her boyfriend was treating her like crap, and Harper would have wondered why she was putting up with it.

Maybe he's finally figured out I'm not good enough for him, Miranda thought.

But it wasn't her own voice she was hearing. It was her mother's. Inside her own head. And the self-pity and self-doubt backed off, replaced by outrage.

You don't deserve this, another voice pointed out. This one was Harper's, and it was angry. *Why are you letting him treat you this way?*

Miranda stood up and stalked into the kitchen, where a herd of frat-boys-in-training were working on their keg stands. Kane was, as usual, standing off to the sidelines, watching the action. And to an outside observer, it was obvious what was going on: The guys were performing for him, even if they wouldn't have admitted it to themselves. Trying to impress him, just like everyone else.

"Kane, can I talk to you for a sec?" she asked, tugging at his sleeve. *Don't ask—tell.* But there was difficult, and then there was impossible. Miranda was doing her best.

"Kinda busy here," he said, without taking his eyes off the pathetic keg action.

"Busy doing what?"

"Who wants to know?"

"How about your *girlfriend*?"

And now he did look at her, and she recoiled, because there was nothing in his eyes but scorn.

Steady, her inner Harper cautioned. *Hold your ground.*

Better fix this before he dumps you out with the trash, her mother's voice argued.

Miranda almost laughed. Was she going to lose her boyfriend and her mind all in the same night?

"Kane, this sucks," she finally said. "I'm ready to go home."

He looked at her again, like he'd forgotten she was even there. "Cool. Good luck finding a ride."

Miranda opened her mouth, but nothing came out.

It's your car—let him *find a ride.* But he was the one with the keys, and she was too embarrassed to force the issue.

Stay. If you walk out now, you might not get another shot. But she couldn't. She couldn't do that to herself, not even for Kane.

"Fine. I'm out of here," she spit out. "Have a good night."

Kane smiled at her for the first time that night—no, more like leered. "Oh, I will."

He wasn't drunk enough, not yet. But the beer tasted like ass, the punch rotted his teeth, and his stomach was staging a mutiny.

Having fun yet? Kane asked himself, and even his mental voice was sardonic. A party packed with hot girls, free booze, empty bedrooms, drunken seniors willing to do almost anything now that the end was in sight—it was supposed to be everything he'd ever wanted, but he could barely muster a smile.

And you know why.

Kane told himself to shut up. He'd never been the kind to be bothered by inner voices; no point in starting now.

He pushed through the crowd and burst out onto the front lawn, which was mostly empty—all the action, more illicit by the minute, was out back, shielded from prying neighborly eyes. It's where Kane should have been. But he stayed in the front, walking the perimeter of the lawn, trying not to think.

And then he saw the perfect excuse to shut down his brain.

Harper. In a silver halter top and knee-high red leather boots with stiletto heels, leaning against a tree, looking hot and miserable. Looking like she didn't want to be alone.

"Hail, Harper, full of Grace," he greeted her, propping an arm against the tree trunk just over her head so that their bodies were only a few inches apart.

"Geary," she said wearily. "Just the man I didn't want to see. Where's Miranda?"

"I am not my girlfriend's keeper," he intoned solemnly.

"Just full of bullshit tonight, aren't you?"

"I aim to please," he said proudly. "Speaking of which, you're looking pretty pleasing yourself, Grace."

"Yeah, thanks."

"No." He touched her chin gently, then ran his hand through her wavy hair. "I mean, you look *good*. You're in a different league from the rest of these girls. You always have been."

"What the hell are you doing?"

He didn't know what he was doing. He was drunk, he told himself, so it didn't matter. It didn't count. He grabbed her hand. "Tell me you've never thought about it, Grace. You, me—who else deserves us? Who else can understand our evil genius?"

She looked up at him, her lips moist and shimmery, slightly parted, giving him that look, and he was sure it meant desire. It meant *go*.

He lunged in for the kiss. And he must have been even drunker than he thought, because when she thrust out her arms and pushed him backward, he stumbled off balance and slammed into the ground, ass-first.

"What's wrong with you, slimeball?" she asked, standing over him. There was no anger on her face or in her voice. Just . . . Kane refused to acknowledge that it was pity. She wouldn't dare.

"I'm fine, thanks for asking," he said, examining his limbs and joints with exaggerated concern. "No major injuries."

She sat down next to him and gave him a light shove. "Obviously you must have hit your head at some point."

"Funny."

"I get what you're doing," Harper said.

He gave her what was supposed to be a withering stare, but Harper wasn't much for withering. "I wasn't aware I was doing anything."

"Miranda told me what she said to you on Saturday night. All that schmoopy stuff about how happy she was."

Kane grimaced. What was it with girls and their bottomless need to *talk*? Couldn't some things be left unsaid?

"She said she was afraid she screwed things up and scared you off, but then you were great about it and convinced her that everything was okay." Harper clapped him on the back. "I didn't want to be the bearer of bad news, but . . ."

"But?"

"But I know you, Geary, and I know you've got to be freaking out."

Kane didn't respond.

"It's just like you to freak out in such a pathetic, piggish way." She laughed. "What were you thinking—that you'd come on to me, I'd tell Miranda and she'd break up with you, and it would save you from the horror of having an actual relationship?"

"Maybe I just thought you looked hot," Kane said.

Harper grinned. "You thought right. But I know you, Geary. Even you aren't *that* sleazy."

Kane sighed and leaned back on his elbows, tipping his head back so far, it nearly brushed against the grass. "So . . . are you going to tell her?"

"Do you want me to?"

She's just a girl, he reminded himself. *I should be able to take her or leave her.*

But he didn't want to leave her, and that's what scared him.

"No," he admitted.

"Then I won't. But keep in mind I'm not doing this for you," Harper said. "And if you screw up again—"

"I know."

"I think you're terrible for her," Harper told him. "But . . ."

"But?" he prompted.

"But who am I to know anything?" she asked, flopping forward and resting her head in her hands. "Look at me. I'm totally screwed up."

Kane knew she wouldn't have admitted it to anyone else—and probably wouldn't have admitted it to him, either, if he hadn't just entered into her debt. It was why he respected her. "You look pretty good, from where I'm sitting."

Harper laughed bitterly. "Yeah, well, from where I'm sitting, it looks like my life is crap. Everything that's happened this year . . ."

"Kaia," he said quietly. They never said her name, not anymore.

She nodded. "You'd think I'd be dying for this year to end, but . . ." She glared at him. "Swear you won't tell anyone, ever."

He held up a hand like he was swearing in at court. "Scout's honor."

"Like they'd let you into the Boy Scouts," she scoffed.

"Hey, I got six merit badges!" he said defensively. "And was working on a seventh . . . when they threw me out for hitting on the Scoutmaster's wife."

"Pig."

"Thank you."

"I'm terrified," she admitted. "Next year, leaving

everything behind, everyone . . . it scares the shit out of me." She looked at him nervously, waiting for some response to the bombshell.

"No, it doesn't," he said.

"Geary, I'm baring my soul here. You don't get to tell me I'm wrong."

"You're not scared," he argued. "You're Harper Grace. Nothing scares you."

"Yeah, right." She looked over her shoulder. "Where are the cameras, Dr. Phil?"

"You need some self-actualization crap?" he teased. "Repeat after me: I am Harper Grace, and—"

"Shut up." She punched him lightly on the shoulder. "This is serious. I'm telling you how I feel."

"And I'm telling you to shove it." Kane was starting to feel like himself again. It was so much easier to have all the answers when you were dealing with someone else's life. "You're not scared. That's just your excuse not to go after what you want."

"And what is it I want?"

He gave her a disappointed look and clucked his tongue. "Grace, I thought we were being honest here."

"I don't—"

"Three days to graduation," he pointed out. "Clock's ticking. If you want Adam, he's right inside. Just go get him."

"Right inside with Beth," she reminded him.

Kane smacked the ground. "Get over it! So he can't get Queen of the Blands out of his system. Since when do you just accept that and walk away?"

"Since he chose a murderer over me," Harper murmured. "He had his chance. I can't go chasing after him. And even if I did, soon he won't even . . ."

"What?"

"Nothing."

Kane sighed. "Look, I don't know what your problem is, and it's not like I'm qualified to hand out relationship advice. Maybe you're right, and you can't have him. It doesn't mean you should just lie down and play dead."

"So what do you suggest?"

"Since when do you need my suggestions?" He grabbed her by the shoulders and gave her a sharp shake. "Forget about Adam—go find someone else. Or a bunch of someone elses. Have some fun again. You may not have noticed, but we're at a party."

"Yeah, you seem to be having a hell of a good time."

"We're talking about you," he said. "And you love parties. Last I checked, you love men. And, most of all, you love the idea of getting the hell out of Grace, CA, and starting your real life. It's all you've been talking about since first grade. So don't tell me you're scared. Just figure out what you really want, and go get it. You're Harper Grace. That's what you do."

Harper gaped at him.

"What?" he said finally. "Did I sprout a third eye?"

She balled up her fist and he flinched, half expecting her to punch him again, but instead she just rapped sharply on his chest. "Why, Tin Man," she said, dripping with sweetness, "I do believe you may finally have grown a heart."

"Great," he said sourly. "Does that make you the brainless scarecrow or the gutless lion?"

She wiggled her legs in the air and clicked the heels of her red leather boots together. "Get a clue. I'm Dorothy."

Kane stood up and brushed off the grass. "Then click your heels together for me a few more times, would you? Because I'm heading home."

"Kane—" She jumped up and grabbed his arm.

"Yeah?"

"What you said . . . thanks. But as long as we're dishing out the advice—"

"Who said *we* were dishing out anything?"

"As long as we're dishing out the advice," she said again, louder, "here's some for you. I may need to go after what I want, but you . . . all that crap you think you want?" She jerked her head toward the party, toward the girls and the booze and the drugs and the fun. "Do you really want it more than what you've already got?"

Kane shook off her arm. "I'm going home, Oprah. So unless you want to come along . . ."

"Don't throw away something good just because you think you can do better," Harper said quietly. "And I'm not just saying that for her. I'm saying it for you."

"So what do you think? Ad? Did you hear me?"

He shook his head. He hadn't heard. He still wasn't hearing. He was just seeing. Her.

Adam wasn't trying to watch her. He was trying *not* to watch her. But she was everywhere, and he couldn't stop himself. It was like he had an internal radar that *pinged* every time Harper glided across his field of vision.

Ping. There she was, moping in a corner.

Ping. There she was, fending off Jake Oberman.

Ping. There she was, disappearing out the door—and he'd hoped she had left for the night, that he was finally going to get some relief.

But then she returned, a wide smile on her face. She strode across the room, with purpose, toward him—he thought, at first—but then past him, to Jake. Adam watched. He couldn't help it. Harper didn't even notice. She was on a mission. Jake looked up, smiled. Harper grabbed a fistful of his shirt, tugged him toward her. They kissed.

Ping.

"Adam, what are you . . . oh." Beth's voice trailed off.

Harper had obviously caught Jake by surprise, but it

hadn't taken him long to rally. They were locked together, Harper up on her toes and Jake's long fingers roaming across her back, veering down, cupping her—

"Bastard!" Adam hissed, and took a step. Then stopped himself. Beth put a hand on his arm, and he forced himself not to shake it off. His blood burned. How dare he—how dare *she*? And right in front of him . . . Adam knew he wasn't allowed to be angry.

He didn't care.

He wanted to storm over there, grab Harper out of Jake's hands, punch Jake in the gut, sling Harper over his shoulder, and run away.

Maybe punch Jake in the gut *and* face, he thought, watching the guy practically undress Harper while everyone watched. But then definitely grab her and head for the hills.

Maybe she's drunk, he told himself. *Maybe he's taking advantage, and she needs rescuing*. But Adam, better than anyone, knew that Harper wasn't drunk. After all, he'd been watching her all night. He'd counted the beers, followed her steps, monitored every move out of the corner of his eye. She wasn't drunk. Not yet, at least.

And when had Harper Grace ever needed rescuing?

No, he didn't want to save her. He just *wanted* her—and he hadn't realized how much, until right now.

"Ad? Are you okay?" Beth asked.

It was only then that he remembered she was there. She was there with *him*. He couldn't run across the room and . . . do anything, not with Beth by his side. Was he supposed to abandon her to pull some caveman stunt that would probably just make Harper laugh?

"Do you want to take off?" she asked.

He ripped himself away from Harper and Jake and turned to face his date—not allowing himself to wonder whether he was here with the wrong girl. He was here with the one he had to be with. And it's not like Harper had given him much of a choice. "Don't you have to stay?" he asked, though he did want to leave, and now, before he did something stupid. Or would it be stupider to do nothing? He glanced at Harper again, who had finally detached herself, at least for the moment. She looked strange, and it took him a moment to figure out why. She looked happy. "Shouldn't you stick around? You know, the picture thing?"

Beth gave him a weird look. "I gave my camera to that guy Mike, from the basketball team, don't you remember? It was your idea, you said I'd get better pictures that way, if I handed it off?"

Adam shrugged. He'd been too busy watching Harper to pay attention to much else. "Right. Sure."

"I should probably stick around and keep an eye on it, but . . ." She rested her hand against his lower back, offering him support. "It doesn't matter. If you want to go."

"You can stay," he offered. "I'll grab a ride—"

"You shouldn't go alone," she said. "I'll come."

She was trying to support *him*. Adam almost laughed. While he'd been standing there thinking about ditching her to go make some kind of scene with Harper. Harper, who had barely looked in his direction all night long.

I'm an idiot, he thought angrily. *A selfish idiot.*

Harper was the one who'd forced a choice, and Adam had made it. Now they both had to live with the consequences. Adam had promised himself that he would stand by Beth no matter what. And if "no matter what" included Harper sucking face with some asshole from Crestview, well . . . there was nothing he could do about it. Not without breaking his promise.

Adam had broken enough of those for one year.

"So should we get out of here?" Beth asked.

He slipped his hand around hers, and she gave it a gentle squeeze. "Let's go home."

The noise burrowed into her, spurted out of her, swung her around, and sent her sailing. Not just the music, a rocking beat that made Harper want to fling her arms wide and spin, bashing her head back and forth, her hair flying. It was everything. The shouts, the cries, the laughter, the hoots, the hollers, the giggles, the whispers and murmurs and drunken shrieks all mixing together into a single voice and it was *her* voice, and Harper sensed that if she opened her mouth, it would all flow out of her, the excitement, the wild, the *party*.

The life of the party. The phrase finally made sense to her. The party itself was alive, a churning mass of twisting bodies and toothy grins, and Harper was at the center of it all, letting it raise her up. What had she been doing, slinking around in corners, wasting her chance to touch and taste everything the party had to offer?

There was the boy, Jake, and it felt so good to be wanted again, to know exactly what to do to make him need her—and then to leave him behind, begging for more. She couldn't give it to him; she couldn't waste any more time on one person. She owed it to the party to be free, to be wild, uncontained and unrestrained. She let the motion of the crowd carry her, let the glasses pass through her hand, slugged back their contents, swallowing the warm, bitter liquid until it made her brain buzz.

She didn't drink to forget or to lose herself or to hide—she drank because it was there, and *she* was there, fully, finally, and she wasn't wasting it, not anymore. She could do anything, and she could do it on her own, without him, without anybody, because she was Harper Grace and that was all she needed to be happy.

And when hands grabbed hers and pulled her up onto a table, she followed their lead and shined under the stares and the cheers, and the flashes in the crowd made her feel like a star, like she had an entourage and a fleet of paparazzi just trying to catch up, and now they had, and she was going to give them a show. The music surged and she sang along, because she could, and pulled off her shirt and swung it in the air because it was hot and so was she and because she wanted to—and that's what the night was about. And then Jake was up on the table next to her, he'd found her again and his kiss was even better the second time around.

"I need you," he whispered, and she couldn't hear the words but she could read his lips, and it felt good to be needed, but she didn't need him—didn't need anyone—so she kissed him again and then pushed him away, off the table, because it was hers alone. It was her party, it was her night—she was Harper Grace, it was her world, and she was finally ready to stake her claim.

chapter nine

KANE STOOD ON THE DOORSTEP, HOLDING HIS FIST a few inches from the door. There was still time to change his mind and make a quick getaway. He could end this thing right here and now before he got in any deeper.

He knocked.

Miranda's mother opened the door, and Kane did his best to smile. Mrs. Stevens, on the other hand, was beaming. "It's so wonderful to see you again," she gushed. "I hope Miranda's taking good care of you—you've been so good to her."

Kane nodded. "Is she home?"

"Miranda!" She bellowed a couple more times and, finally, there was an irritated response.

"What?"

"Come down here. It's your boyfriend!"

Silence. Mrs. Stevens gave Kane an awkward smile and patted him on the shoulder. "She's probably just getting a late start this morning. I'll go up and see what the trouble is."

"I can come back another time . . ."

"No! Oh, no!" She pulled him inside and slammed the door behind him, as if afraid he'd escape, then bustled upstairs. A few moments later, Miranda appeared.

She didn't say anything to Kane, didn't even look at him as she walked past, opened the door, and stepped outside. He didn't move, not until she turned around and glared. "Are you coming?"

Kane followed her out.

"I can't talk when *she's* breathing down my neck," Miranda muttered. She leaned against the porch railing. "What do you want?"

Kane paused. Smooth-talking was, of course, his specialty—but suddenly he didn't know what to say. "I thought you might want your car back."

Miranda pursed her lips. "I said you could have it for the week, and you can have it for the week. I don't say things I don't mean."

The implication was clear: *Unlike* some *people*.

"Can we go somewhere?" he asked, squeezing his fist around the keys. The metal bit sharply into the flesh of his palm.

"Where?"

"Just . . . you know. For a drive." He needed to talk—but if he was behind the wheel, he could say what he needed to say without looking at her. And she wouldn't be able to leave.

"Fine."

They walked to the car and though he hurried to open her door, she anticipated him and got there first, shutting it without a word. He got into the driver's seat, and they pulled away.

"I'm sorry about last night, Stevens," he finally said, once they'd gotten onto the open highway. "I was an asshole."

"The biggest," she agreed. "What gives?"

Kane tried one of his patented adorable grins. "Can I plead temporary insanity?"

Miranda turned her face away, staring out the window at the empty desert streaming by. "If you don't want to be with me, just say it," she said, with only a hint of a waver. "You don't need to put on this elaborate show. If you want to break up, let's break up. It's fine."

"It's not fine." He didn't take his eyes off the road, but

he reached across the seat and took her hand. "Stevens, it's *not* fine. I don't want to break up."

"Then *what*?" she asked, putting his hand firmly back on the gear shift. "You can't just treat me like crap and then show up the next day and pretend nothing happened."

Focus on the road, he told himself. *Just pretend she's not even in the car.*

"I got freaked," he admitted. "All that stuff you said, I just . . . I got freaked."

"Oh." They were both quiet for a moment. "Because you thought . . . Kane, I wasn't trying to, I mean, it's not like I said—" She took a deep breath. "I'm not trying to pressure you. I really didn't mean anything."

"Don't say that." He pressed down harder on the gas pedal, wishing he could outrun the conversation. Or just fast-forward a few minutes so that he wouldn't actually have to live through it. "I'm glad you said it. You know, that this is making you happy. That we're—I'm glad. This is good, Stevens. What we've got here?" He took her hand again, and this time she let him. "It's good. And I don't want to screw it up."

"You didn't," she said softly.

"I wish I could . . ." Kane sighed. "I'm just not that kind of guy. We're not going to sit here and talk about my feelings and shit. I don't do that."

Miranda laughed, and the sound made something in him unclench. He relaxed his hold on the wheel. "Don't you think I know that? Kane, I've watched you spout Shakespearean sonnets to impress some illiterate who thought you wrote them yourself. Do you really think I'd believe you if you started telling me that my lips were like rubies and comparing me to a summer's day? Do you really think I *want* that?"

"So what *do* you want?"

"Nothing," she said. "I'm not asking anything of you—I mean, it would be good if you never treated me like crap again, but that doesn't seem like too much to ask, right?"

"I think I can handle it," Kane said. He knew he should push her harder—she had to want something more from him. Or if she didn't, she should. She deserved to demand something from him, from their relationship. But if she was going to pretend otherwise, he wasn't going to press the issue. "So am I forgiven?"

Miranda raised his hand to her lips and began kissing his fingertips. "Somehow I suspect you'll find a way to make it up to me. . . ."

He was about to suggest one when the cop car appeared in his rearview mirror, its siren blaring.

Kane glanced down at the speedometer. "Damn." He veered toward the side of the road and pulled to a stop, mildly irritated at the prospect of a ticket—until he remembered what he had in the trunk. Then, suddenly, a ticket seemed like a small price to pay.

He wiped his palms on his jeans and then rolled down the window. *Just give me the ticket and walk away*, he silently implored the cop. *Nice and easy.* Miranda had already pulled the registration out of the glove compartment and handed it to Kane, giving him a sympathetic smile, like they had nothing to worry about but a minor inconvenience.

"You know how fast you were going, son?" the cop asked, his sunglasses so large, they nearly covered up his pencil-thin mustache. Kane didn't recognize him, which meant he wasn't one of the usual traffic cops. He took a closer look at the uniform, feeling bile rise in his throat—state police?

"I'm very sorry, Officer," Kane simpered, handing over his license and registration. "It won't happen again."

"This your car, son?"

Kane resisted the urge to tell him to shove the "son" talk. *Play nice*, he warned himself. "It's my girlfriend's car, sir." He nodded at Miranda.

The cop tipped his hat to her. "Then maybe your *girlfriend* can tell me why there's an empty bottle of beer in the backseat."

Oh, shit. "I don't know how that got there," Kane

said quickly, which was true. He'd given some guys a ride home the night before, and one of the idiots must have used the car as his own personal dump truck. "Really."

"Sure you don't." The officer's lip curled up in a sneer eerily similar to the one Kane usually wore. "But all the same, I'm going to have to ask you two to get out of the car so I can take a closer look."

"I don't think you have the right to—"

"Kane!" Miranda hissed. "Just let him do his job so we can get out of here."

He nodded and gave her a tight smile. They climbed out of the car and were escorted to the cop car, where they were told to stand still and watch as the cop searched Miranda's Civic for more contraband. Kane berated himself with every curse word he'd ever learned. How could he have been so stupid?

"Chill out," Miranda whispered. "It's going to be okay. I don't think they can do anything to us for an empty bottle."

And then the cop opened the trunk.

Game over.

"Well, well, well," the cop drawled. "What's this you've got in here?"

"What?" Miranda asked. "I don't have anything in there—" She started toward the car, but the cop held up his arms.

"I'm sorry, but I'm going to have to ask you to stand by the car, miss," he said, looking not the slightest bit sorry. "In fact, judging from what I see here, I think I'm going to have to run you both down to the station."

"What's he talking about?" Miranda asked Kane, looking panicked. "What's in the trunk?"

Kane didn't say anything. Miranda leaned against him and put an arm around his waist. He couldn't move, not even to comfort her. Not even to step away.

The cop approached.

"Sir, I don't know anything about something in the trunk," Miranda said nervously, her face flushed.

"Well, maybe that's true, and maybe it isn't, but someone's got to be held responsible. How about you, son?" His eyes bored into Kane. "You know anything about what's in that trunk? You want to take responsibility?"

This was his chance.

Actually, his *chance* had been that morning, when he could have taken the large cardboard box of pot candy out of the trunk *before* driving over to Miranda's. His chance had passed him on by. This was just his moment to minimize the damage. As the cop said, to take responsibility. Kane's gaze drifted down to the guy's holster, which contained a real gun. Kane talked big, but he'd never been this close to a gun before, so close that he could have reached out and made a grab for it.

The cop was drawing out a pair of handcuffs. At least those, Kane was familiar with. But before, he had always been the one holding the key. The cop swung the hand-cuffs back and forth, and Kane imagined how they might feel on his wrists. Miranda's arms tightened around him, and he could feel her shaking.

This was his moment.

"I'm sorry, Officer, but I have no idea what's in that trunk," he said, meeting the guy's eyes with a suitably apologetic smile. "This isn't even my car."

With only a couple days to go before graduation, school had become pretty much optional, which meant that Beth was free to drop the camera off at the *Grace Weekly Journal* offices midday. She was eager to see the journalists in action, struggling to meet their deadlines—but unfor-tunately, the office didn't seem that much busier than it had over the weekend. Everyone she passed had a bored, sleepy look on their face as if they'd just interrupted a nap to do a few minutes of work before falling back asleep again. It didn't matter, she told herself. So what if it wasn't the *New York Times*? It was a start.

Ashley Statten, at least, looked wide awake. She leaped out of her chair when Beth approached, grabbing the camera out of her hands. "Finally! The article's all set and ready to lock, I just need the photos." She hooked the camera up to her computer and began flipping through the images as Beth hovered nervously over her shoulder.

"Can you not do that?" Ashley asked, glaring.

"What?"

"I can't really concentrate with you standing there and—oh, forget it." She grabbed a few sheets of paper from her printer and shoved them into Beth's hands. "Why don't you sit over there, read this, and be quiet."

"What is it?" Beth asked.

Ashley rolled her eyes. "I can't imagine why you aren't already a prize-winning journalist, what with those stellar investigative skills." She tapped the top of the page. "As this rather large clue in the shape of a headline will tell you, it's an advance copy of the article. Enjoy."

Beth settled into the designated chair and began to read.

BEAUTY AS THE BEAST:
THE RISE AND FALL OF A HIGH SCHOOL DRAMA QUEEN

By Ashley Statten
Photos by Beth Manning

Harper Grace and Kaia Sellers had it all. Beauty. Popularity. Power. High school remains the country's last monarchy, and at Haven High, Harper Grace and

Kaia Sellers reigned as queens. But no golden age
lasts forever. Camelot ended with a tragic car crash
that left one girl dead and raised endless questions
about the disturbing underbelly of Grace's youth
culture. Allegations of student-teacher liaisons, blackmail, and drug use abound—and at the center of it all
stand two girls, picture perfect, their glossy hair and
pretty smiles hiding the dark truth.

Beth gasped and, her heartbeat quickening, skimmed
through the article, which got worse with every sentence.

"She's a royal bitch," one senior, who preferred to
remain anonymous for fear of retribution, claimed
about Harper Grace. "She's got no soul. Ask anyone.
She thinks we all worship her—but that'd be like
worshipping the devil."

How did she get all this? Beth wondered, incredulous
as she read Ashley's rundown of Harper's and Kaia's misdeeds, including a step-by-step explication of how Harper
had, over the years, clawed her way to the top.

Ilana Hochstein, a psychologist specializing in the
behavior of modern teens and author of the recent
book *Out of Control,* asserts that "High school girls

can be ruthless—they're masters of manipulation,
backstabbing, anything you can think of to get ahead,
they've done. There's rarely physical violence,
but the emotional damage done can be far worse."
Experts agree: Adolescent girls are weapons of mass
destruction. And the cauldron of Haven High—a perfect storm of sex, drinking, and misbehavior—offered
the perfect setting for Harper Grace and Kaia Sellers
to practice their craft.

Beth tore through the rest of the article, terrified she
was going to see her own name, but it was nowhere to be
found. Just more sociological spewing about alpha females
and the corruption of modern youth, all spiced up by tales
from Haven High's very own "dark side," as personified
by Harper and the dearly departed Kaia.

"Perfect!" Ashley exclaimed suddenly, enlarging a
couple of the photos on her screen. "Maybe you've got a
future in photography."

Beth didn't recognize the images—they must have
been taken after she'd left, because certainly, she would
have remembered this.

In the picture on the left, Harper stood on a table, top-
less, waving her shirt in midair, her mouth open as if in a
silent scream. The picture on the right was similar, except
that she had her tongue jammed down some guy's throat.

"I should caption this 'Portrait of the artist as a young slut,'" Ashley said, laughing, "but I guess that wouldn't fly with this crowd. What do you think, Beth? This is your world, after all."

"I don't—I think—" Beth stopped. If she got the internship, Ashley might be her boss. *If* she got the internship. If she didn't screw up and start pissing people off. If she just kept her mouth shut and let this go.

But even Beth wasn't that weak.

"I think this is libel," Beth said, slapping the pages down on the desk. "It's a total hatchet job. You can't just say this stuff about people—I mean, Kaia's *dead*, and Harper's just—she's a *person*. You can't just write this about her like she's not going to read it. This will kill her."

Beth expected the reporter to defend herself. But she just leaned back in her chair and smiled. "What do you care?"

"What do you mean? I care because—it's wrong. You can't write something like this and call it journalism. It's character assassination."

"What do I mean? I mean, what do you care what happens to Harper Grace? Didn't she ruin your life? Isn't she your worst enemy?"

Beth's eyes widened.

"Oh, I know everything," Ashley said snidely. "It's called journalism. You should try it sometime. I asked around, I know what she did to you. And what you did to her—"

Beth gasped—how could Ashley have found out about the drugs she'd slipped Harper? And if she knew, and she knew about the car accident . . .

"That stupid gossip flyer," Ashley said, making a tsking noise. "I don't know why you thought that was going to work. But then, I guess that's why girls like Harper and Kaia walk all over you, isn't it? I'm thinking about making this part of a continuing series—maybe part two should be an exposé of the high school underclass. What do you think? You could give me an exclusive."

"You can't print this," Beth insisted. "I won't let you."

Ashley stuffed the pages and her notebooks into a drawer and shut down the file on her computer. "I don't see how you're going to stop me," she said calmly. "It's a done deal. In fact, with photos like these, I think it's pretty much guaranteed a page-one spot for our graduation edition. And just think—it's all thanks to you."

"I don't know anything about it!" Miranda said again, tears streaming down her face. "Why won't you believe me?"

"Because it's your car, miss," the detective said. "Which means that unless you can prove someone else put the contraband in there without your knowledge, it's your responsibility."

Miranda moaned. None of this seemed real. Not the tiny dark room with the long mirror along one wall, or the rosy-cheeked bald man sitting across from her informing her of her rights. Not the reddish rings around her wrists from where the handcuffs had chewed into her skin, or the sore muscles in her back from sitting in that chair, in that room, for hours, answering every question the same way.

I don't know.

But didn't she know? Didn't she know who *must* have put the box of pot-laced candy in her trunk—a big enough box, the man had helpfully informed her, to indicate intent-to-distribute, which apparently activated some kind of mandatory sentencing guidelines. In case she was found guilty, of course.

Sentencing guidelines.

Intent-to-distribute.

Guilty.

She was trapped in some horrible made-for-TV movie about good girls gone bad, and surely any moment now someone would arrive to change the channel. Surely, to be more specific, if the box belonged to Kane, then he would claim it. He wouldn't let her take the fall.

Take the fall. There was another line she'd heard only in prison movies. If this did turn out to be real and not some overly vivid nightmare from which she'd soon wake, she was going to need a whole new vocabulary.

"I'm sorry to inform you of this, miss," the man said politely, grabbing her arm and pulling her out of the chair. Her legs barely supported her. "But you have the right to remain silent. Anything you say can and will—"

"Wait," Miranda said desperately. "I didn't do anything. Please."

But the man had continued through her interruption, and was already at the part about court-provided attorneys.

What about my right to a phone call? Miranda wondered through her horror. *When does he get to that?*

But he never did. First there was the fingerprinting. She'd done it once before, in third grade, as some kind of state-supported missing-children program. *Get your kid in the system,* the teachers had advised, *and you'll always be able to find her.*

They'll always be able to track me down, Miranda now thought. If, for example, she went to prison, then escaped. She'd be in the "system" forever.

She told herself to stop running movies in her head and start figuring her way out of her mess, but there was no way out. The man's grip on her arm was firm. He grabbed each finger in turn, pressed it into the inkpad, then smashed it onto the little white piece of paper. Then they dragged her away, her hands still stained with black.

It was picture time.

Just like when she'd gotten her driver's license, she stood on the blue tape square, in front of the white screen, and stared at the tiny box camera. *Am I supposed to smile?* she thought stupidly, but then the camera flashed, and it was over.

"We've got to fix up a cell for you," the cop told her, not harshly, but not gently, either. "You can call whoever you need to, then Carrie here will take you into the waiting area until we're ready."

Miranda started trembling. *This isn't real, this isn't real, this isn't real,* she repeated to herself, her lips moving, though no sound came out. She forced herself to stop thinking about where she was and what came next, because if she did, her mind would tear apart, she could feel it already, straining, fault lines crackling across the surface. She just needed to obey orders and put one foot in front of the other. Survive.

The pay phone was sticky. Miranda held it between two fingers and tried not to touch it to her ear or mouth. They gave her a couple quarters.

Harper didn't answer the phone. And Miranda couldn't bear to leave a message. Not this message.

The next one was worse.

"Mom?"

"Miranda, where are you? I was expecting you back hours ago, I need to run out and your sister can't stay here by yourself, and you're just off with your boyfriend somewhere? I thought we'd talked about responsibility—"

"Mom!" Deep breaths, Miranda told herself. Just say it. "Something . . . happened."

"Was there an accident?" her mother asked, and Miranda was surprised to hear the concern in her voice. It sounded almost . . . maternal. And it gave her a little courage.

"I'm actually, uh, down at the police station," she said quietly, humiliated.

"What happened?" The concern was gone.

"We got stopped. For speeding. And, uh, the cops found some, uh, drugs in the trunk—but they're not mine!" she said quickly, before her mother could ask.

"Oh, Miranda, what have you gotten yourself into?"

"Mom, I told you, it wasn't—"

"Something like this could ruin your future," her mother complained. "How many times have I told you to *think* before you act?"

"That's what I'm trying to tell you, Mom, I *didn't* act. I didn't do anything."

"Then why did they arrest you?"

"I don't know!" Miranda shouted. "But why don't you take my side for once in my life and *believe* me!"

"Don't you take that tone with me!" her mother

snapped. "Now you see where that kind of disrespect for authority will get you."

"You think I'm in *jail* because I talk back to my mother too much?" Miranda asked incredulously. The familiar rhythm of their mother-daughter sniping was actually helping to calm her down. It was comforting to know that even *here*, her relationship with her mother was a constant. Constant dysfunction—but beggars couldn't be choosers.

"What I think is that this whole thing is extremely disturbing."

"You think *you're* disturbed?" Miranda forced herself to stop. She lowered her voice. "Look, Mom, I need a lawyer—I need to get out of here."

"Do you know how much that would cost?" her mother asked. "Won't they give you one for free?"

"I guess, but—" The cop had explained that would probably take at least another day; Grace wasn't Los Angeles, with public defenders lining the court hallways, waiting for the next defendant to pop off the assembly line. There were only two or three lawyers who served regularly across the county, which sometimes meant long delays. Especially when the case was so minor. It didn't feel minor to Miranda. "Mom, I need to get out *now*. I can't stay here—I can't sleep in a cell!"

"It won't be so bad," her mother said. "You have to learn that your actions have consequences. I'll talk to your father—I don't know how I'm going to break this to him—and we'll talk to you in the morning."

"Mom, *please*." She was disgusted with herself for whimpering, but there was nothing she could do about it.

"Oh, don't be so dramatic. It's one night, it's not going to kill you. We'll work it all out in the morning."

"Mom—!"

Dial tone.

Carrie, receptionist-cum-prison guard, escorted her to the "waiting room," which was really just a narrow room with peeling yellow walls about the size of her bedroom. It was filled with rows and rows of chairs, like a bus terminal waiting area, but they were all empty. All except for one, in the corner.

She sat down in a seat against the left wall. Carrie sat across from her. "I'm supposed to cuff you," she said. "But I think it's okay. Not like you're going to run, right?" She laughed.

"Right," Miranda agreed, managing a weak smile.

Carrie nodded toward the back corner. "You can talk to him, if you want." When she smiled, the thickly applied bright red lipstick made her look a bit like an evil clown.

Miranda didn't want. But apparently Kane did. He slid into the chair next to her, then flashed Carrie a winning smile. "Is it okay if we talk privately for a minute?"

Carrie blushed. "Sure, I guess that'd be fine." She

moved a few seats away, never taking her eyes off Miranda.

Kane put his hands on her shoulders and began to massage. She wanted to knock them away, but she couldn't move.

"I'm so sorry," he whispered. "Are you okay?"

"It was you, wasn't it?" she asked coldly. "They're yours."

"Stevens, I never expected this to happen—"

"Tell them the truth," she pleaded. "Just get me out of here."

He leaned closer, his lips against her ear. She shuddered at the touch. "This isn't such a big deal, Stevens. It's your first offense, you'll get off with a slap on the wrist, trust me."

"Funny, it feels like a big deal to me."

"They're just doing this to scare you, I promise. They're bored, and this gives them a chance to play big-city cop for the day. But nothing's going to happen to you; I won't let it."

"And how are you going to stop it when you're at home in bed tonight and I'm here, *behind bars*?" She glanced down at his fingers—no ink. She was alone in this. And he could give her all the massages and whispered assurances he wanted, but he wasn't going to change that. He *could*, but he wouldn't. She understood that now.

Or rather, she knew it. She would never understand it.

Something incomprehensible blared on Carrie's walkie-talkie. She held it to her ear, then nodded. "I gotta take you back now," she said apologetically, gesturing for Miranda to stand up. Kane stood too. He tried to give Miranda a kiss, but she turned her face away.

Carrie gripped her upper arm and guided her toward the door. "You can check back tomorrow about bail," she told him.

"Miranda, it's going to be okay," Kane said. "I promise."

His face looked different than she'd ever seen it. Without the smirk and the arched eyebrows, it looked naked. Defenseless.

"I'm going to fix this," he said.

The dam burst, and tears streamed down her face. She didn't want to look at him, but she didn't want to look away because when he left, she would be alone. And soon there would be bars.

"Miranda, *look at me*," he insisted. "Believe me. It's going to be okay."

"Kane—" She gasped for breath. "Please!"

Please do the right thing.

Please sacrifice yourself to save me.

But if that's what she wanted, she'd chosen the wrong boyfriend. She knew that as well as he did. At least, she did now. Miranda had always claimed she knew Kane, knew what she was getting into. But secretly, she'd always thought she knew better. That beneath the blasé bluster, there was something real. Something good.

"I'm sorry," he said, his voice husky. "*Miranda*, I'm sorry." And then, as Carrie pulled her through the door, he turned away first, like he couldn't watch them take her away. "I just can't."

"Don't give me that bullshit!" Harper screamed, and there was a thud that sounded like she was throwing her entire body at the door. "Let me *in*!"

Kane grabbed his shoe and threw it at the front door, wishing it was Harper's head. "I told you, I'm busy. Go away."

"Busy? Your girlfriend's in *jail*, asshole! Now *let! Me! In!*"

Kane sighed and opened the door. Maybe this was his punishment. If so, it wasn't nearly what he deserved. But it was a start.

"Why are you here, Grace?" he asked wearily, settling down into one of the living room couches. Not the couch he'd been lying on for the past three hours, staring up at the ceiling and wondering what the hell was wrong with him. It was time for a change of scenery.

"Good question, Geary," she spit out, pacing back and forth. "Why *am* I here? Why aren't I at home sleeping off my hangover? Why did I get dragged out of bed to go visit my *best friend* in *prison*?"

"You saw her?" he asked, leaning forward. "How is she?"

"No, asshole, I didn't see her, they wouldn't let me until tomorrow. They're big on the rules there, you know, in *prison*."

"Stop saying that. It's not prison. It's just the police station."

"It might as well be prison. Is she locked in a cell? Are there bars? Is she stuck in some shithole sharing a bunk-bed with a hooker?"

"How am I supposed to know?"

"Exactly." Harper stopped pacing and glared down at him. "You wouldn't know. Because you're not there. *She* is. And you just let it happen."

"What makes you think this is my fault?"

"*Drugs* in her car? Intent to distribute?" Harper kicked at the couch, narrowly missing his legs. "They're *yours*, Geary. What kind of a loser lets his girlfriend take the fall for him?"

As if he hadn't been asking himself the same question for hours.

He shrugged, and composed his face into the perfect image of apathy. "Look, Grace, whatever Miranda has or hasn't done, there's nothing I can do about it. It's not my problem."

"Not your *problem*?" Harper sat down across from him and leaned forward, no longer shouting. "Not your problem, Kane?" She shook her head. "I knew you were slime, but I always thought . . . what are you doing? How are you letting this happen?"

"Don't," he warned her, with an edge to his voice. "Don't try to pretend that you wouldn't do the same thing."

"Of course I—"

"Oh, please." He sneered at her, letting his anger rise because it was the only thing that would wash away all those other, messier emotions. "You and I are the same, Grace. We look out for ourselves. We take what we want, we don't care who gets hurt. You treat Miranda like shit whenever it serves your purposes, so don't come in here acting all noble."

"It's not the same."

"It *is* the same. We're the same. The only difference is, I *own* it. You like to pretend that you're better than all that, but when it comes down to a choice between your happiness and someone else's, don't tell me you don't choose your own. Every damn time. You want to call me slime? Take a look in the mirror sometime, Gracie, because it's oozing out of every pore."

Harper's face had gone white. She stood up. "You disgust me."

"That doesn't make me wrong."

She slammed the door behind her, and he was alone again. Kane opened his fist. He had been clutching his phone ever since he'd left the police station. With one call, he could end this. End it for Miranda, at least.

But for him, it would be the beginning of hell. There was no case against her. Charges would never stick. The car had been out of her possession for days. A fine, maybe. Community service, even. But nothing big. Nothing major.

Kane, on the other hand, already had a juvenile record. A trivial one, just minor infractions, but a record nonetheless. And Kane had connections—which, under the wrong circumstances, could become witnesses. Kane had everything to lose.

Miranda would be fine, he told himself. He'd find a way to fix things, without destroying himself in the process. He couldn't do that, even for her. He couldn't do it for anyone.

It doesn't make me evil, he told himself. *It just makes me human.*

Self-preservation was a fundamental human right. More than that—it was an obligation.

He wished he could be that guy, the one who could dial the number, confess to his crimes, and save the day. For the first time in his life, he wished he was someone else, someone nobler, someone braver. Someone better. But he wasn't.

This is who I am, he thought, finally putting down the phone. *Whatever it costs me.*

But this time, he wasn't the one who would pay.

chapter ten

WHERE DO YOU SEE YOURSELF IN TEN YEARS?

It was a standard yearbook question, and everyone knew you were expected to supply a standard yearbook answer. The public answer—the short, snappy, wholesome answer that would appear next to your photo and send the message to your parents, teachers, friends, and enemies that you were normal. It was the generic answer, the nothing-to-see-here-folks quip that the eye skimmed over, it was "I'll be married with 2.5 kids," it was "I'll be a millionaire," it was "I'll work for my daddy's accounting firm," or "I'll win the lottery and buy the high school and turn it into a bowling alley," or "I'll be hanging out at the Playboy Mansion with my good friend Hef."

And it was a lie.

Because if you had enough brains to actually graduate from high school, it meant you'd never be stupid enough to tell the truth, to expose the dirty little secret of who you really were—and what you really wanted.

Harper lies under the silken canopy, her legs bare, her skin glowing, her neck draped with jewels.

"You may approach," she says languidly, when she hears the knock.

Adam rushes to her side, dropping to his knees and clasping her hand. He presses it to his lips. "I thought I would die without you," he says.

"You were only gone a day."

"One day too many." He caresses her cheek. "Every hour was agony. Every minute was a stake through my chest."

"So you missed me?" she asks, favoring him with a smile.

"It was as if a chunk of flesh had been torn away, as if someone carved out my heart and threw it on the ground," he says. He grabs her hands, and she rises to her feet. The kiss is magical.

"I love you," he tells her, his arms still around her. "I love you more than I ever thought possible. I'll love you forever."

"And if I ever asked you to do something for me, to give something up—"

"No sacrifice is too great," he says. "I would do anything for you. I would rather die than see you hurt."

"So I have your complete devotion?"

He kisses her again. "You have everything of me there is to give."

Harper rubbed the tears away from her eyes and tried to focus on the road. Kane was wrong: They weren't the same. They couldn't be. She was selfish, she knew that. But there was nothing wrong with wanting things. And there was nothing wrong with demanding what you knew you deserved.

She didn't want Adam to be her servant, didn't want him to throw away his life for her. She just wanted to come first—she wanted him to love her more than he loved Beth, more than he loved basketball, more than anything. Yes, she wanted all of him . . . but only because she loved him so much.

Only because she was ready to give him all of her.

So Kane was wrong. It wasn't the same at all. Whatever she did, she did for love—love of someone else. Kane only loved himself.

Kane settles into the Jacuzzi, raises a glass of Cristal, and thinks how much he loves his life. It isn't just the thirty-room McMansion or the seventy acres of surrounding grounds, complete with tennis court, stables, swimming pool, and artificial *waterfall. It isn't the seven-car garage with its rotating line-up of Porsches, Ferraris, Bentleys, and the one constant: a mint-condition Aston Martin Vanquish, retail value $228,000, that does zero to one hundred in ten seconds flat.*

The hired help is a plus, the butlers and maids and chauffeurs and chefs and masseurs whose job depends on keeping Kane happy and ensuring he never lifts a finger for himself. And the women . . . he has to admit, the women are a big part of it, the internationally renowned beauties, the starlets, the heiresses, the modern-day Helens of Troy who fall at his feet and beg for his attention, who primp and pamper him and, when he gets bored, go gentle into that good night without so much as a wrinkle-inducing pout.

It is all that—but it is also more.

It is the power. It is knowing he can pick up the phone, or merely nod his head, and he can redeem a life—or destroy it. He commands legions. He is loved by the masses.

He is feared.

Kane threw his phone against the wall. It made contact with a loud crack, then clattered to the floor, a shattered piece of casing sliding under the couch. He had a plan. He knew the way his life was going to unfold; his every action was coolly calculated to bring him one step closer to the goal. *Stay cool*, that was the key. Cold, rational, disengaged. Keep emotions out of it. Stand on the sidelines, observe, interfere only when necessary, and only when the outcome is guaranteed.

Never, ever get involved.

These were rules he lived by, and they had their purpose.

He needed to protect himself if he was going to get what he wanted—and he *was* going to get it. What else mattered in life, if not that?

Something else. A whisper in his ear. *Something more.* He brushed it away.

The impulse to help, to save, to sacrifice, it was childish, he told himself. Immature. *Do the right thing*—it was a joke. Right and wrong were relative. He was the constant.

The plan was the constant. He had to think long-term. He had to forget Miranda and keep his eye on the ball.

"Keep your eye on the ball," Adam tells the fan, a seven-year-old who gazes at him with adoring eyes. The kid's shirt reads: I WANT TO SLAM LIKE ADAM. And you can tell from the look on his face that he does—he wants to do everything like Adam. Just like the rest of the country. His face on the cereal boxes, his name on the sneakers, his jersey in the hall of fame, and a championship ring on his finger—it's because he's the best, not just on the court, but off.

"Keep your eye on the ball," he says again, "that's all it takes."

The kid nods eagerly. Adam signs his basketball and moves on.

"The Humble Hero," they call him on TV, not because of his three-pointers, but because of the way he rescued that woman from a burning car and saved that child from drowning in a lake. He has paid for a young girl's heart transplant and endowed a homeless shelter. He does what he can, saves who he can, and asks nothing in return. The sports writers love him for loving the game. The talk show hosts love him for loving the world. The fans love him for being Adam Morgan, star athlete and model human being, selfless and charitable. Heroic.

They love him without knowing him, without needing to know him.

But back home, there is someone who does know him—someone who loves him not because he's good, but because she can't help it. She doesn't need his charity. She doesn't need his help, or his advice, or his endorsement. She doesn't need to be saved.

She just needs him.

Adam closed the blinds and stepped away from the window. Maybe Kane was right, and he had a hero complex. But what was so wrong with that? What was wrong with not wanting to be selfish? With wanting to fulfill his obligations?

He lay down on the bed, staring up at the ceiling. There was, of course, one very obvious thing wrong with it. He was miserable.

Not that he would have admitted it out loud. But alone, in his room, the window overlooking Harper's bedroom on one side, and the official offer from UC Riverside on the other, he finally had to face facts.

This sucked. She was probably over there right now hooking up with some other guy, and he was thirty feet away, struggling not to be selfish and not to make the wrong choices.

And, because it couldn't be said enough, he was alone.

They like me, they really like me, she thinks, alone in the spotlight, a model for the masses. The master of ceremony unveils the plaque, and it is official: She is the newest member of the Haven High Hall of Fame.

"Beth Manning was a model high school student who has grown into a model adult," says one of her former teachers.

"We're all so proud to have produced such an amazing alumna," says another. "I wish we could take the credit, but she was a lovely, kind-hearted, brave, brilliant, perfect student from the day she walked into the building right through the day she walked out."

"I want to be just like you when I grow up," one of the students tells her. "I mean, you're like Mother Teresa—you know, with better hair."

The love of her life is watching from the front row, his movie-star eyes filled with admiration. "Was my speech okay?" she whispers as she sits down next to him.

"It was brilliant." He kisses her. "You're brilliant. Everything you do amazes me."

"How can you say that," she asks, "when you know who I really am?"

"I can say that because I know who you really are," he tells her. He gazes at her, his dark, unruly hair flopping down over his eyes. She pushes it out of the way for him, and he grabs her hand. There are black flecks of grease under his fingernails. "I know everything about you," he says, his voice warm and hoarse, a little scratchy, like he has just rolled out of bed. "And I love it all. The good and the bad. I love you." He takes her shoulders and turns her around to face the cheering crowd. "Everyone does."

Beth had always wanted to be liked. And she'd done everything she could to make it happen. She'd made the beds, done her homework, kissed her boyfriend, smiled at teachers, babysat her brothers, said please and thank you, bought on sale, arrived on time, looked before she leaped, followed the rules. Almost always followed the rules.

It hadn't worked.

Then she'd broken the rules, and that hadn't worked either.

She couldn't stop hearing Ashley Statten's cold voice:

"I don't see how you're going to stop me." It was almost a dare.

No one liked her. And maybe it was time she stop caring. Maybe it was time she ignored the rules, and what people thought, and even what *she* wanted. Maybe getting people to like you was actually beside the point.

Harper, for one, was never going to like her. And the feeling was mutual. She'd get no credit for sabotaging the article, no credit for saving Harper from public humiliation. If she did it right, no one would ever know. But maybe she had a better reason to want to help. Maybe she had a responsibility. Maybe she needed to prove to herself—not to her teachers, not to her friends, not to the boy who was never going to look at her again with anything but disgust, but to herself—that she could stand up for something, for someone, even if it was hard, or especially then.

Maybe she just had nothing left to lose.

"Nothing to lose, baby!" Reed shouts, and dives off the stage, splashing into a sea of arms. He lies on his back as the fans hand him off, struggling to touch his shirt, to feel his arm, to grab a lock of his hair, a piece of the legacy, a touch, a taste, a whiff, anything, of a rock god.

They float him back to the stage and he leaps up, grabs his guitar, and plunges into the sound, and behind him the band rocks out and he sings. He sings that song they've been waiting to hear and the sound of their cries drowns out the music, but it's music to him, because they're the ones who make all this possible—the Top 40 singles, the platinum records, the Music Video Awards, the cover of Rolling Stone, *the mansions, the recording studio, the movie deals, the Fender Strat in his hand and the groupies waiting backstage—the sex, the drugs, the rock-'n'-roll.*

He loses himself in the music because he's got nothing to lose—he is the music, it's all he cares about, all he loves. There's no one to let him down, no cares, no pain, only him, on his own, with his guitar, his voice, his songs, and his music. It's the only way to live.

Reed slammed his hand down on the strings. What was the point in rehearsing? He was playing like shit. And he knew why. He couldn't stop thinking. He couldn't stop worrying, and wondering, and hating her, and missing her.

He just wanted to forget.

He'd tried alcohol. He'd tried pot. And now he'd finally, after too many weeks of avoiding it, tried his guitar. They were all useless.

"Just stop!" he shouted, pressing his hands against his head like he could squeeze his brains out through his ears. That would be the dream. Nirvana. To finally stop thinking, stop *hurting*. He closed his eyes, willing it to all go away, disappear into a blinding white emptiness, to leave him with the ultimate dream, an empty mind.

A peaceful fog.

A merciful haze.

A blank.

She is . . .

She has . . .

She wants . . .

Nothing. Blank.

Miranda lay on her side, huddled up on the thin mattress, staring at the metal door—there were no bars, it turned out, but plenty of locks—that separated her from the outside world. And, because it hurt her too much to think about how she'd ended up there, she tried to think about where she was going.

She drew a blank.

Oh, she could mouth generic sentiments all day and all night, she knew all the right things to say, to paint a picture of her very bright future. She knew what she was *supposed* to want—the job, the husband, the kids, the oh-so-wonderful life—but when it came to what she actually wanted, she was clueless.

Who had time to think about that? There had always

been something else to do. Take care of her sister; obey her mother. Tend to Harper and solve the latest melodrama; chase after Kane. Miranda knew what her best friend wanted—she could write a book on the subject, and it would be a long one, given the hours she'd spent nursing Harper through every down, celebrating every up, analyzing to death every everything. And she'd tried to figure out what Kane wanted—tried to be the perfect girlfriend, sweet yet witty, undemanding, understanding. She'd spent years trying to catch him, and once she had, all she could think about was pleasing him. And look how far that had gotten her.

It was two nights before her high school graduation, and while the rest of the world was celebrating their bright and shining future, she was alone in a jail cell staring at a blank wall and a dead end. She felt empty, like she'd given everything she had to everyone else. And now that it was just herself, she had nothing left.

chapter eleven

BETH WRAPPED THE T-SHIRT AROUND HER FIST. SHE
stared at the window, gathering her courage. There were
no lights behind the building, so all she could see was the
narrow tunnel illuminated by her flashlight beam.

What if there's an alarm? she asked herself, her inner
voice tight and panicky. These days, her inner voice lived
in a constant state of panic, and she was tired of listening to it. She took a deep breath, drew back her fist, and
punched the glass as hard as she could.

It bounced off with a dull thud.

Hysteria swept in, and Beth began to laugh. It always
worked in the movies. A single punch, a satisfying crack,

shards of glass exploding inward, and then her hand, protected by the T-shirt padding, would reach in and unlock the window, lift it up, climb through.

She punched the window again, kicked it twice, then sat down on the ground. Defeated.

She'd overcome her nerve, her nature, and her last vestiges of common sense—only to be defeated by Plexiglas. All hail the wonders of the modern world.

"Am I interrupting something?"

She nearly screamed when she heard the voice, then again when she recognized it. And she couldn't help but wonder whether this was all a dream. Didn't it seem more likely that, after trying her best to find a solution to the Ashley Statten problem, she'd just given up—like always—and gone to bed? That now she was dreaming a life where she played the action hero—albeit a failed one?

It seemed a more logical explanation. Because what was realistic about Beth Manning sneaking out in the middle of the night to break into the *Journal*'s offices . . . and what made sense about Reed Sawyer showing up to watch her do it?

"What are you doing here?" she asked, turning around to face him. It was too dark to see anything but the dim outline of his figure, and though she had the flashlight, she chose not to turn it on. It seemed better to do this, whatever this was going to be, in the dark.

"What are *you* doing here?"

"I'm, uh . . ." She had prepared an elaborate excuse for herself, just in case she got caught, something about leaving her driver's license in the newsroom and needing to get it before the next day so she could drive her ailing grandmother to a doctor's appointment—but she'd lied to Reed enough. It was dark, it was late, she had failed, and—except at the end, when he'd walked away—Reed had always been the one person who hadn't judged her. He wouldn't turn her in. He probably wouldn't even care. "I'm breaking into the newspaper office." She sighed. "Or at least, I was trying to. Turns out breaking and entering is harder than it looks."

"Oh."

She waited for him to ask why.

"You want help?"

Beth flicked on the flashlight. She needed to know if he was mocking her. He squinted in the sudden light—but there was no smile on his face.

"Don't you want to know *why* I'm breaking in?" she asked.

"Is it a good reason?"

"I think so."

"Then no." He jerked his head toward the back door, then started toward it, pausing only to turn back and ask, "You want my help or not?"

She hurried after him. He pulled something out of his pocket and started fiddling with the doorknob.

"You know how to pick locks?" she asked incredulously.

He shrugged. "Not so tough."

Before she could ask *how* he knew, or *why*, they were inside. She hesitated in the doorway.

"Why are you here?" she asked him.

And maybe because she had told him the truth, or because it was even darker in the newsroom than it had been outside and he didn't have to see her face, he told the truth too. Or at least, what sounded like the truth. "I needed to see you," he said. "So I drove over to your house—but then I couldn't. So I just sat there. And when you drove away . . ."

"You followed me."

"Pretty much."

"Oh."

"You want to know why?" he asked.

She was afraid to say yes.

"I should probably do this and get out of here," she said quickly, turning the flashlight on again and heading for Ashley Statten's desk.

"So what are we doing?"

"Reed . . ." It was comforting to have him there—but that wasn't good enough. "You should go. I don't want to get you in trouble."

He shook his head. "I'm not leaving you alone here. So I can stand here and watch . . . or I can help."

So Beth gave him the flashlight and had him go through the drawers searching for Ashley's notes and hard copies, while she broke into the computer system—which, fortunately, didn't require anything more than finding the password taped to the inside of Ashley's top desk drawer— and deleted all traces of the article. Then she found the right camera, pulled its memory card, and deleted the incriminating photos.

"I think we got it—"

"Shhh!" Reed froze, and flicked off the flashlight beam.

Beth trembled in the dark as someone fumbled with a set of keys just outside the front door.

"Run!" Reed whispered. They took off for the back exit.

But the front door swung open too quickly. Beth dropped down behind a desk, holding her breath. She heard heavy footsteps, and the room burst into light—and then a deep, angry voice boomed out. "Stop!"

Caught. She knew she should be panicking or terrified, or at least in tears, but she was just calm. It was all over now. And there was a silver lining: At least she'd had time to destroy the article. Whatever trouble she got into, it would be worth it.

Beth gritted her teeth and prepared to stand up, when—

"You! Stop! Are there more of you?"

Reed's answer was calm and matter-of-fact, like he did this kind of thing every day. "No. It's just me."

"Dad, we need to talk."

Kane's father dropped his briefcase in surprise. "Why are you sitting in the dark?"

Kane didn't have an answer. His father snapped on the light.

"Working late again?" Kane asked sardonically. The only thing his father worked on past closing-time was his secretary.

"You know it." His father grinned and offered him a palm to slap; Kane declined.

"Something happened," Kane said. "I need your help."

"Hold on, not until I help myself." His father, as usual, veered straight for the liquor cabinet and poured himself a glass of scotch. He offered the bottle to Kane, who shook his head.

"Not tonight."

His father raised an eyebrow and took a sip, then sat down across from Kane. It was the same spot Harper had occupied a few hours before. "Girl trouble?"

"Not exactly." Kane leaned forward. "It's Miranda—you've met her, I think. We've been, you know. A few weeks now."

His father chuckled. "Sounds like girl trouble to me."

He leaned over and slapped Kane's knee. "It's about time, too—it's been a long time since you've needed any of the old Geary wisdom. So what's the deal with this girl? Is she hot?" He laughed again. "Look who I'm asking—of course she's hot."

"I don't need your . . . wisdom," Kane said, trying to suppress his irritation with the aging-playboy act. "I need your lawyer."

Kane's father sank back into the couch, the smirk wiped off his face. "What did you do?"

What did *I do?* Kane asked himself, but didn't wait for the answer. That was a completely separate issue; the problem now was helping Miranda. And Kane had to believe that whatever he had or hadn't done was irrelevant.

"The cops pulled us over for speeding and found a stash in her car," Kane said. "Just pot, nothing big, but you know these cops—"

"All too well," his father said, scowling, and there was a pause long enough for them both to remember the time Kane had narrowly escaped prosecution for his fake ID business—escaped only because his father's skills in bribery and blackmail rivaled his own.

"They're not going to let it go, and her mother's being a total bitch about the whole thing, and if she gets stuck with some incompetent public defender . . ." He refused to think about it. "Can you just hook me up with your lawyer? I can pay you back, eventually." Although now that his prospective cash flow had dried up—half his product was impounded at the Grace police station, and the rest of it wouldn't be seeing the light of day for a long, long time—he didn't know how.

"You want me to lend you *my* money and *my* lawyer so you can get your deadbeat girlfriend out of jail?" his father asked incredulously. "And in this fantasy world where I enable your juvenile delinquency, am I offering bail money, too?"

"You don't have to be such an asshole about it," Kane said, trying not to get angry, and failing. "She's not a juvenile delinquent."

"No, just a drug dealer," he said snidely. "And an incompetent one at that. When are you going to learn that you have to stop hanging around with people like this, son? Surrounding yourself with bad influences. It's idiotic. You're better than that—you've got a future ahead of you."

"What if I were to tell you that I was the bad influence, and that I was the one—"

"I'm going to stop you right there, son, because in the hypothetical I think you're about to propose, you'd find yourself with a criminal record, probably a felony, and there's nothing I could do about that, lawyer or not. That means no Penn State, no future, no nothing."

They stared at each other, and Kane knew that his father knew. Knew and was willing to stay silent, as long as Kane played along. Kane looked away first. "That's why I need to help her," he said quietly.

"And I'm your father, which is why I need to help you. And the best way to do that is keeping you as far away from this mess as possible. This girl's not your responsibility—I see no reason for you to get involved."

"What's wrong with you?"

"I'm your father," he said. "I'm just trying to do what's best."

"You're choosing *now* to be a parent?" Kane asked, outraged. "After everything?" After all the late nights, and the girls, and the drinking, and the lessons in manipulation and emotional blackmail, after all the buddy-buddy midnight oversharing his father had forced in a pathetic effort to pretend he was still eighteen? After leaving Kane and his brother to raise themselves, forgetting to stock the refrigerator or enroll them in school or do any of the things any normal parent would file under "what's best," he was choosing *now* to pull a Father Knows Best and lay down the law?

"Don't give me that weepy bullshit!" his father shouted. He stood, too. He was still several inches taller than Kane. "You know I did the best I could for you boys. After your mother—" He slammed down the glass of scotch. "I did everything I could."

"Yeah, you were a stellar parent," Kane drawled. "Father of the year."

"I gave you what you needed," his father said coldly. "I taught you boys what matters in life. I taught you how to look out for yourself. That's all you need."

"Lucky for me," Kane said. "Because that's all I got."

Miranda had never understood claustrophobia. Until now. Now she got it, the way the air hung heavy and the walls closed in, the thoughts battered her brain—*What if there's a fire? What if the ceiling collapses? What if? What if?*— worst-case scenarios of doom and destruction through which she would suffer alone, trapped by four windowless walls and one padlocked door.

So when the key turned in the lock and the door swung open, her heart sang. And even though they weren't there to set her free, or tell her that her mother had decided to love her after all, but only to march her down a hallway and into yet another dark, closet-size, locked room, even then she felt a little bit better.

Because sitting across from her, his hands folded on top of a thin manila file and his face composed into a rigid smile of professional competence and faint empathy, was a lawyer. And that meant hope.

Her escort didn't handcuff her to a chair or stand guard with his gun drawn. He just sat her down and walked out, closing the door behind him, and Miranda could, if she really tried, savor the illusion that she was in some other little room, far away, having a polite chat with a pleasant stranger. At least until the lawyer opened his mouth and launched into a litany of terrifying terms—sentence, felony, misdemeanor, arraignment, circumstantial, worst-case scenario—pausing occasionally to wipe his runny nose on a soggy handkerchief, the same handkerchief he used not once, but twice, to wipe away imaginary smudges on his horn-rimmed glasses.

And then, all too quickly, he was standing up and shaking her hand, and telling her he'd see her in the morning.

"But you just got here," she protested. "Aren't you going to get me out? What about bail? I can find someone to—"

"I thought they'd already explained all that to you," he said, sniffing. "We can't even start on the bail process until the morning, and then there's the question of arraignment, and getting onto the docket, and I think the judge is out with some kind of"—he sneezed—"bronchial infection."

Miranda knew it was irrational, but she couldn't let him leave, not until he'd promised her that he could fix this. "Look, I didn't do anything. You're going to help me prove that, right? Please?" She knew she sounded pathetic, but at this point, she didn't much care.

The lawyer slid the file into his pleather briefcase with a sigh. "Melissa—"

"Miranda."

"Of course, of course. I can't make you any promises, but no one wants to go to court on something petty like this. It's a waste of everyone's time. I'm sure we can plea them down to a few misdemeanor charges, some community service—"

"Are you not listening to me?" Tears of anger spurted out of the corners of her eyes. "I didn't *do* anything. I can't let people think I'm a drug dealer, I can't have that on my record. You have to *fix this*."

"Melinda—"

"*Miranda.*"

"It's late," he said, flicking his eyes toward his watch. "I only came by because they said you were having a meltdown. I just wanted to run through the basics with you. We'll talk more tomorrow. I promise."

"I'm screwed, aren't I?" she said, not meaning to whisper but unable to muster enough air to speak in a normal voice.

The lawyer gave two sharp raps on the door, and it swung open at his command.

"We'll talk tomorrow," he said again. "I'm sure we'll figure something out. Trust me."

Miranda just hung her head and let the cop waiting

outside escort her back to her room. Her cell. She was done trusting people. It was a mistake. Why else was she here?

You know why you're here.

She sat down on her cot, wide awake, willing the door to magically swing open and set her free. But it stayed closed, trapping her with her thoughts.

It's your own fault.

She hadn't trusted too much. That would have been understandable; that would have been forgivable. Miranda picked up the thin, lumpy pillow and squeezed it between her hands. *Trusting* would imply that she had been naïve, that she had been deceived.

But that wasn't it at all. She'd known exactly who Kane was, *what* he was. And she had allowed it. She had never demanded he be anything more than the selfish, self-centered, arrogant jerk he'd proven himself to be, time and time again. She'd let Kane be Kane, and she just went along for the ride, afraid to ask for anything more.

That wasn't blind trust. It was just stupidity.

She punched the pillow, and then, because it didn't make a good thud and it didn't hurt, she punched the wall. Hard. Pain shot through her knuckles and up her arm.

She had let this happen to her. Just like she let *everything* happen to her.

She let her mother push her around, call her an ungrateful daughter, berate her, insult her, and then demand that Miranda be available to her every beck and call.

She let Harper lean on her, interrupt her life with melodramas sometimes tragic and sometimes petty, cry on her shoulder—and she let Harper push her around, and use her, abuse her, and basically do whatever she wanted without thought or concern about how Miranda would feel.

Miranda stayed silent, because what if she spoke up and asked something for herself and the answer was no? What if they left her one by one, because they found out who she really was—fat and ugly and boring and needy? What if she ended up alone? She'd let the what-ifs eat her up inside and, instead of standing up for herself, stayed quiet, tended to other people's needs—and, whenever it got to be too much, locked herself in the bathroom and threw it all up.

Because, sooner or later, some things just need to come out.

She disgusted herself.

She punched the wall again, and again—then stopped abruptly, bringing her fist to her mouth, sucking on her stinging knuckles.

Enough.

Enough hating herself. Enough *hurting* herself. Enough swallowing other people's shit with a happy smile. Enough keeping quiet. Enough fear.

When she got out—and she *would* get out, she told herself, one way or another, she would ensure that Kane didn't get a chance to ruin her life—things would change. *She* would change. She would fight. She would move out of the house, whatever her mother said. Figure out what she wanted—and get it.

She would start a new life.

And this one would be her own.

"You want to tell me what you're doing here?" the man asked. From where she was crouching, Beth could only see his shoes. But she recognized the voice: It was the editor in chief.

Reed didn't say anything.

"I could have just had the cops come check this out, you know," the editor said. "But I wanted to see for myself who was trying to break into my newsroom."

Reed still didn't speak.

"So you're going to answer me, kid." The editor got louder. "And tell me what you're doing here. *Now.*"

There was a long silence.

"Fine, then. I'm calling the cops. Enjoy prison."

Beth didn't let herself stop to think, because if she

had, she might have chickened out; or her legs, already weak and quivering, might have rebelled and refused to stand. So without thinking, she stood and revealed herself. "Don't call the cops," she pleaded, squinting in the bright light. "Please."

The editor in chief gaped at her. He was gripping a baseball bat. "Aren't you the new intern? What the hell are you doing here?"

She could have made up an excuse, but he was going to find out eventually. "I broke in and erased Ashley's article," she admitted. "It was a personal attack on . . . a friend of mine, and I—I know it was wrong, but I had to. Reed—" She winced, realizing she should never have said his name. "He had nothing to do with it. He found me here, and he was just trying to stop me, I swear."

Reed looked at her like she was crazy.

Don't say anything, she pleaded with him silently, hoping he could still read her eyes. *Just shut up and let me do this for you.*

The editor shook his head in disbelief and, with a long sigh, put down the bat. "You broke into my newsroom to destroy one of my stories? I suppose you're expecting me to compliment you on your moxie or something?"

Beth just pressed her lips together and waited.

"That's not how things work in the real world, young lady." He took off his glasses and rubbed his eyes. "But your teacher thinks you walk on water—and while she's obviously wrong about that, I don't want to humiliate her by getting you arrested. Which doesn't mean there won't be consequences."

"If you have to call the police, please just let Reed get out of here first," Beth pleaded. "I swear, he's not involved. He was only here to talk me out of this. Please."

"You're not really in a position to be asking for anything right now," the editor said sternly. "But . . . I'm not calling the cops."

Beth felt all the adrenaline leak out of her body. As the crisis moment passed, the fear returned.

But something else came with it: pride. Because this time, she hadn't given in to the fear. She'd done what she needed to do, and that had to count for something.

"You're fired, obviously," the editor snapped. "And I'll be informing your school about this. And your parents. We'll let them decide how to deal with it."

"Thank you," Beth said, surprised to discover she wasn't crying. "Thank you so much."

"Don't thank me, just get out." He looked down—and Beth realized that beneath his long coat he was wearing pajama pants. "I'm going home to bed."

Beth and Reed, without looking at each other or speaking, filed out of the office. The editor locked up behind them, glared at Beth for a long moment, then stalked away.

"Thanks," Reed said quietly. "You could've just stayed down and kept your mouth shut. So . . . thanks."

"I couldn't let you take the blame."

"You could have," he said. "You just didn't."

They walked down the dark street together. Beth's car was parked a block away, and Reed's was just behind it.

"I followed you because I was worried," he said suddenly.

"What?"

"Tonight. When you left. I thought—I don't know. It was late and it seemed like . . . something was wrong. I just knew."

They paused on the sidewalk between their two cars.

"You were worried about me?" Beth asked, not sure what she was supposed to think.

Reed laughed; she'd missed the sound of his laugh, warm and scratchy at the same time, like a wool blanket that had been in the attic for too long. "Crazy, right? What kind of trouble could you be getting into?"

She smiled up at him, and though she was sure it was too dark for him to see, he reached out his hand and almost touched her cheek. His arm fell away just before it made contact. "You don't smile enough. Anymore."

"I didn't know you were watching."

Reed shrugged.

"I'm not back together with Adam," she said, then felt stupid, suddenly feeling like she'd said exactly the wrong thing. "I mean, I know you don't care, it doesn't matter, I just thought . . . I wanted you to know. We're not together."

"Okay."

They watched each other, and she thought how strange it was to look at someone's eyes without looking away, how it made you feel so connected to the other person and disconnected from everything else, all at the same time.

"So . . . ," he finally said, still staring at her.

"So . . . I should probably, um . . ."

"Beth—" He raised his hands and cupped her chin, so gently, and she leaned forward and for a moment she thought, no, she *knew* it was all going to be okay, the world was somehow going to give her all the things she wanted but didn't deserve, Reed had finally found a way to forgive her, he still loved her, she could see it in his eyes, how much he wanted to go back to what they used to have— and then he bent her face forward and kissed her softly on the forehead. "Good night."

chapter twelve

SHE DIDN'T GET IT. AND SHE CERTAINLY DIDN'T believe it. Not at first. Not when the cop opened the door to her cell and escorted her out—not, this time, with a grip firmly clamped around her arm, but with a smile, and a small wave of the hand to indicate she should follow behind. Not when they brought her to a counter marked PROPERTY and gave her back her watch and her purse. Not even when she followed the cop into the lobby and he nodded toward the door and said, once again, "You're free to go."

Miranda just stared at him. "I don't understand. What happened?"

The cop smiled implacably, though only the lower half of his face moved. His stare stayed cool and emotionless. "I can't discuss details of a current investigation."

"But it's an investigation of *me*!" she protested.

The cop shook his head. "Not anymore."

And that's when she saw him, heading down the hall in a familiar direction, toward the doors that locked only from the outside. His fingertips were smudged with black ink.

"Kane?" she said wonderingly. "Kane!"

The woman guiding him down the hall—Carrie, the same one who'd shepherded her around the night before—paused and looked back at her. But Kane just stared down the floor as if he hadn't heard.

Miranda followed him with her eyes, expecting to feel some stab of sympathy—after all, she knew where he was headed, and what he was facing. But she felt nothing. Not even curiosity about what had happened, how he had ended up in the dark, narrow hallway while she faced an open door.

He wasn't her concern, not anymore. She had to focus on herself.

And on that front, it seemed, things were starting to look up.

Miranda tested out a smile, and although the cop didn't react, it felt good on her face. "I can really leave?

Just . . . go? You believe me, that I didn't do anything? This is over?"

The cop nodded. "Everything's been cleared up. Sorry for your trouble." He didn't sound sorry; Miranda didn't much care. She was out of there, out of danger, and suddenly everything seemed lighter, brighter—*easier*. All the vows she'd made to herself the night before, lying in the darkness, desperately hoping she would have a chance to fulfill them, they all seemed ridiculously easy. What was facing down her mother or sticking up to Harper, compared to prison?

"I can leave," she murmured to herself, wanting to scream it out loud, wanting to sing. But she just walked quietly toward the door and, savoring the power, the *freedom* that came with the simple gesture, opened it.

"Miranda, wait!" a woman called.

For a moment, Miranda was tempted to run. Her heart slamming, she knew, deep down, that a mistake had been made and the woman had arrived to correct it, to drag her back inside, into the dark, lonely, locked cell— that unless she fled, far and fast, she might never get her chance to leave again.

"I have something for you," the woman said. It was Carrie, and she was smiling—this was a real smile, one that crinkled the corners of her eyes and made them sparkle. "From your boyfriend—"

"He's not my boyfriend," Miranda snapped, and saying it out loud wasn't nearly as painful as she'd expected it to be.

"Oh. Well. Anyway, he left you this." She held out a piece of paper, folded over a few times into the size of a playing card. Miranda recognized the familiar scrawl covering both sides of the page.

She didn't want to know what he had to say for himself, but she took the note and slipped it into her back pocket. "Thanks."

"He turned himself in, you know," Carrie said.

Too little, too late, Miranda thought bitterly. She pressed her lips together and gave Carrie a tight nod. "They said I can go now."

"Of course you can—and make sure you have a great day!" Carrie said in a chirpy voice that matched neither the situation nor the setting.

Miranda grinned back and did her best to muster equal levels of perkiness. She could feel the note bulging in her pocket, but it didn't matter; it was already part of the past. "Thanks," she said again, meaning it this time. Her smile grew wider as she grasped the doorknob and, once again, pushed the door open, this time stepping through without looking back. "I think I will."

Haven High loved scandals and hated Beth, which meant word of her criminal trespasses made the rounds at lightning speed. By the time Adam woke up the next morning, he had six voice mails and four text messages gleefully alerting him to the second-best gossip of the night. He didn't even get out of bed before reaching for the phone.

"Are you okay?" he asked as soon as she'd picked up.

"I'm fine," Beth said, sounding strange. Not like she was lying, though. And maybe that was the strange part— she really did sound fine.

Adam sat up in bed, tossing back the covers. His bedroom faced southeast, and by midmorning this time of year, it was boiling. "Is it true? You broke into—"

"I don't really want to talk about it," she said, without emotion.

"Right. Okay. But . . . are you in trouble?"

He could hear her sigh.

"Well, I'm grounded until forever," she said lightly. He knew it was the first time she'd ever been grounded, or, as far as he knew, punished at all. "But I don't think the school can get me into much trouble. What are they going to do, suspend me?"

"Was that a *joke*?" he asked incredulously. Graduation was only a day away; soon the entire senior class would be suspended. Permanently.

"Not a very good one, but I guess so. Why? You don't think I have a sense of humor?"

"No, I just thought . . ."

"You thought I'd be curled up in bed weeping, wondering how I was going to go on?" she suggested. "Or maybe you thought I had some kind of breakdown last night and went psycho, what with the whole breaking-and-entering thing?"

"Well . . ." He laughed a little. "Sort of. So . . . you want me to come over or anything? Keep you company?"

There was a pause. "Do you *want* to come over?"

"I will, no big deal," he said, though he'd had other plans for the day. Well, not plans, not quite, but something he wanted to do, or at least wanted to think about doing, something that could have been important. Something for himself. "If you need me to."

"Try again, Ad. Do you *want* to? Honest answer."

He hesitated. Just because she said she wanted his honest answer didn't mean it was true. Did he owe her the lie? Or did he owe her the truth?

"I didn't think so," she said, before he could answer. "And I don't need you to. I don't need you to feel sorry for me anymore, Ad, or to stick by me because you think I can't deal on my own."

"I told you, that's not—"

"I know, I know," she said quickly. "It's not the only reason, but it's a reason, you said it yourself. Don't lie now."

Who *was* this girl, the one who sounded so much

like the Beth he used to know, calm and confident and in control?

"What do you want me to say?"

"Nothing. You don't owe me anything anymore. We're friends. You've been an amazing friend, Ad, but you don't have to . . . you don't have to worry about me. Not anymore. I'm okay. Or I'm going to be. I should have been okay a long time ago, but . . . better late than never, right?" She laughed nervously as he tried to figure out what she was talking about.

"Time's running out, Adam," she said. "Don't waste it on me."

"This isn't about—"

"It's always been about her," Beth cut in. "Even when we were together, everything was always about her."

"No," he protested.

"It doesn't matter anymore," Beth said. "That's over now."

"Beth—" There was too much he wanted to say, too many regrets about the things he'd done and the things he hadn't said and the way everything had ended up, completely screwed up and broken, so much pain that it seemed like, if he tried, he could trace it all back to one bad decision. His own.

"I loved you, too," she said quietly. "I hope she makes you happy. You deserve that."

Adam didn't know what he deserved, but as he hung up the phone, he knew that he had to stop asking himself the question. Just this once, he would go after what he wanted. She was less than a hundred feet away, maybe lying in bed thinking about him—maybe, though it made Adam sick to imagine it, she was thinking about Jake Oberman, or some other guy who'd managed to weasel his way in.

It didn't matter, he told himself. He'd wasted time, but he had to believe he hadn't missed his chance. He just needed to find a way to persuade her. A big way, something so dramatic, so romantic, so unforgettable that she wouldn't be able to walk away again—something that would, in one stroke, overcome everything that had come between them this year, that would make her see the truth, and believe it: He wanted to be with her.

Only her.

He just hoped it wasn't too late.

Harper rushed over to Miranda's house as soon as she got the call, and when the door opened, she threw herself around Miranda and squeezed.

"Um, choking," Miranda gasped after a few moments.

"Shut up." Harper realized her face was wet with tears. She didn't care. Miranda was home safe, and that's all that mattered. "Are you okay? Tell me you're okay."

"Okay. But. Can't. Breathe," Miranda teased, trying to break free. Harper just squeezed tighter.

"If you think I'm ever letting go, you're crazy." She did let go, eventually, but only once she'd forced herself to stop crying. By the time Miranda saw her face, she wanted everything to look normal and casual. Not to mention happy. "What can I do? Do you want to go lie down? You must be tired. I could bring you some of your favorite foods, or we could watch one of those lame movies you like, or—"

"I'm not an invalid," Miranda protested. She glanced over her shoulder, a scowl darkening her face. "Let's just get out of here, okay? I don't want to be stuck in the house with *her*."

"Anything you want." Harper grabbed her arm and dragged her to the car. "Tell me everything. Unless you don't want to talk about it. Do you want to talk about it? Whatever you want, okay?"

Miranda just rolled her eyes and headed for the car—Harper's car, of course, since Miranda's was still impounded at the police station. "We can talk when we get to wherever we're going. Let's just . . . let's just relax and enjoy, okay?"

So they were mostly silent for the ride. Harper cued up Miranda's favorite playlist, a mix of Top 40 songs from the year they were in ninth grade, and drove toward what she promised Miranda would be "the perfect place."

"The *Fun Zone?*" Miranda asked incredulously, as the car pulled to a stop outside the garish pink and green building, its sign shouting its mission statement—FUN! FUN! FUN!—in six-foot-tall neon. "You brought me to the Fun Zone?"

"We don't have to go in if you don't want to," Harper said, wondering if she'd done exactly the wrong thing. "I just thought . . . you know, you've been so into the nostalgia thing lately, and I don't know if you remember, but—"

"Of course I do." Miranda giggled. "Remember when we hid ourselves under those little colored balls and your mom thought we'd disappeared?"

Harper burst into laughter. "She almost had a heart attack, and she kept yelling that someone needed to—" She cut herself off. It didn't seem so funny anymore.

"To call the cops," Miranda finished for her. "It's okay, really."

"I thought I'd be grounded forever after that one," Harper said ruefully.

"It felt like forever," Miranda said. "A month is a long time when you're nine years old."

For years, the Fun Zone had been their birthday tradition. It was a dark, noisy zoo filled with video games, rides, cheap pizza, and screaming kids: every parent's nightmare and every child's dream. Harper and Miranda had only been allowed there on special occasions and so, twice a year, for each of their birthdays, they'd made the pilgrimage to kiddie nirvana, slapping quarters into slots, pushing joysticks until their thumbs cramped, stuffing themselves with pizza and cotton candy and, always, toasting each other with chocolate milk shakes and pledging that they would be best friends forever.

The tradition had died out sometime around age twelve, when suddenly nothing without shopping or cute boys or makeup had qualified as much of a fun zone. At least for Harper. Miranda had always talked of the place fondly, while Harper mainly remembered it as a greasy stink-pit of sweat and noise. But this was Miranda's day. Harper had turned off her phone, cancelled her plans, and was ready for some serious girl-on-girl bonding.

"This is perfect," Miranda said, beaming. "Let's do it."

The Fun Zone wasn't that crowded, and they were able to find a table where they ordered their regular pepperoni pizza and, of course, two chocolate milk shakes. Harper half expected Miranda to object to the milk shakes and steeled herself not to comment, not today. Today Miranda could eat—or not eat—whatever she wanted. But Miranda just smiled and let the waitress walk away.

"Place hasn't changed much," Miranda observed as a screaming seven-year-old ran past her chair, his younger sister hot on his tail.

"Fun, fun, fun!" Harper said sarcastically as they both ducked a water gun spray.

"Okay, so it's not quite heaven on earth anymore," Miranda admitted. "But it's good. Thanks for thinking of it. And for, you know, being here."

Harper wanted to grab her and hug her again, but she held herself back. "I wouldn't be anywhere else, Rand," she said, more seriously than she'd ever said anything in the Fun Zone. "I hope you know that."

Miranda nodded. The waitresses returned with their milk shakes, and Harper lifted hers in the air. "To you," she suggested.

"It's bad luck to drink to yourself," Miranda protested. "Besides, we should stick to our old toast, don't you think? It's tradition."

"We're not ten anymore—" Harper began, then caught the look on Miranda's face and shut herself up. "Okay." She struggled to remember the familiar litany. "To you and me, best friends forever, until hell freezes over—"

"Until pigs fly," Miranda chimed in.

"Until Niagara Falls."

"To infinity and beyond."

Harper hesitated before the traditional last line, then smiled and clinked her glass against Miranda's. "Till death do us part."

They played a few of the arcade games and even tested out the ball cage—before getting tossed out for being over the age limit—but eventually had to admit to themselves that some things just aren't so much fun anymore once you're all grown up. (Although Miranda *did* enjoy beating Harper on the retro Ms. Pac-Man machine, a feat she'd never managed to accomplish as a kid.) All too soon, they found themselves back at the table, picking over their pizza crusts and ordering a second round of milk shakes.

Harper propped her elbows on the table and gave Miranda the Stare. "Okay. Tell me. Are you okay? Do you want to talk about it?"

Miranda closed her eyes and for a second she was back there in that cell, and she *did* want to talk about it, but suddenly she couldn't get the words out. Her throat closed up, her eyes teared, and, beneath the table, her knees began to tremble. And maybe it was better not to push it. Why wallow in bad memories? It seemed self-indulgent and depressing, especially since Harper was trying so hard to cheer her up. She smiled, hoping it looked real. "I'm fine, I swear, it was no big deal. Sort of an adventure. I'm sick of thinking about the whole thing. What's going on with *you*?"

Harper wrinkled her nose. "Really?"

"Really. Any movement on the Jake Oberman front?"

Harper looked dubious but then shrugged, and launched into a typical Harper Grace monologue. "We were actually supposed to go out today, but I blew him off, and I have to admit, I'm not that sorry about it. I mean, I don't know, Rand, he's totally hot and all, and he seems like a nice guy, but . . ."

Miranda zoned out. She couldn't focus on Harper's love life, not when her own was . . . well, what love life?

That was over now, and she didn't want to feel sorry about it, she wouldn't *let* herself feel sorry about it, but when she thought about Kane . . .

The letter was still in her pocket. She half wanted to read it, but she knew that once she did, she wouldn't be able to forget what it said. Whatever it said. There'd be no going back. So for now, it was still folded up. Untouched.

And Harper was still talking. *Nothing ever changes*, Miranda thought. *I go to jail, and she still can't shut up about herself for one minute—*

And whose fault is that?

"I'm not fine," she said suddenly.

Harper's mouth snapped shut. There was an audible click as her teeth banged together.

"I'm not fine, and it *was* a big deal," Miranda said, swallowing hard. She stared over Harper's shoulder at some kid who was rubbing chocolate cake all over his face. "It was horrible. I thought I was—I don't know. I just didn't think I was going to be able to handle it. And I thought I was going to prison or something, and it all just . . ." She wasn't crying, but she had that hollow, shivery feeling in her chest that told her it was only a matter of time, so she stopped talking and pressed her face between her hands, like she could somehow squeeze out all the bad thoughts.

"Thank God!" Harper exclaimed.

Miranda looked up at her in surprise.

"No, I don't mean thank God it was horrible," Harper said. She reached across the table and grabbed Miranda's hand. "I just mean thank God you want to talk about it. You were really freaking me out with all that 'I'm fine, I'm good, happy happy, joy joy' stuff. So what was it like?"

"You really want to know?"

"No, Rand," Harper said sarcastically. "I want you to sit here and listen to me talk about what I watched on TV last night, because that's oh so much more important."

Miranda took a deep breath. "Okay, well, the first thing is, it turns out I'm a little claustrophobic. . . ." And she told Harper everything, starting from how terrified and ashamed she'd been when the handcuffs went on, to the horror of being fingerprinted and searched, to the night she had spent alone in her cell, counting the panels in the ceiling and wondering how she would survive another hour, then another. And then there was the worst moment of all, the realization that Kane was to blame—and that he was leaving her there alone to face his consequences.

"That asshole," Harper said, hatred in her voice. "I still can't believe he did that to you. I could kill him."

"He did turn himself in," Miranda protested weakly.

Harper looked horrified. "Rand, please, *please* don't tell me you're thinking about forgiving him. Or that you actually feel sorry for him or something."

"No. *No.*" And she wasn't lying, she knew that. "I just . . . I don't hate him. Is that weird? I know I should probably hate him. Or miss him. Or something. But I'm just . . . I don't know. Numb."

"Maybe you're in shock," Harper suggested.

"Maybe. I kind of hope not." She shook herself as if she could fling away all the unpleasant memories that coated her skin like the scent of the jail cell, which three showers in a row hadn't managed to wash away. "So I guess I'm single again." She laughed softly, amazed she was able to find even a bitter humor in the situation. "Looks like we better get cable next year, since it seems like I'll be putting in some serious couch-time."

"Next year?" Harper said, leaning forward. "You mean . . . ?"

"I mean next year in our apartment," Miranda said, grinning. "If you're still looking for a roommate, that is."

Harper looked like she was going to explode. "Really? You're sure? We're getting out of here together?"

"As soon as humanly possible," Miranda confirmed. "And I promise, I'll try to keep the 'why, oh why am I single?' whining to a minimum."

"I wouldn't worry about that," Harper said, "since I'll be whining right along with you."

Miranda raised an eyebrow—at least she'd gained one useful skill from Kane. "What about Jake?"

"I don't think it's going to happen," Harper admitted. "I wish I could, but I'm just . . ."

"Not over Adam?"

Harper looked down and began playing with her straw, stirring the remnants of the milk shake round and round in the bottom of the glass. "I don't think he's the kind of thing you get over," she said finally. "But *it's* over. I get that now. And I think . . . I think I can be okay on my own."

Now Miranda was the one to reach across the table. "You're not on your own."

Harper squeezed her hand gratefully. "Aren't I the one who's supposed to be comforting you?"

"Given that you're just as screwed up as I am, I think this can be an equal-opportunity comfort session," Miranda teased.

"Hey, at least I'm not a felon!"

"That's ex-con, to you," Miranda corrected her. "So you don't want to mess with me."

"Ooh, are you going to shiv me or something?"

Miranda laughed. "Someone's been watching too many episodes of *Prison Break*."

"What else was I supposed to do?" Harper asked. "*Someone* wasn't available to play with, and life is somewhat dull when you're not around."

"Yes, I know, you can't live without me," Miranda teased.

"You're right." Harper grinned. "And since it's all about me, after all, thank God you're back."

Miranda raised her glass. "I'll drink to that."

Adam was sitting on her doorstep.

She almost missed him in the dark.

"Your phone's been off," he said, when she came in range.

"I was with Miranda." Harper tried not to betray her surprise. "Did you need something?"

"How is she?" he said. "Miranda."

Harper shrugged. "You know Miranda. She says she's okay, but . . ."

"If she's not, she will be," Adam said. "She's tough."

"Yeah . . . I hope so."

Adam dangled a piece of black fabric from his hand. "I need to blindfold you."

"You need to—what?" She took a closer look. "Is that a *sock*?"

Adam blushed. "It's the best I could do. It's clean."

"You want to blindfold me, and then . . . ?"

"It's a surprise." He stood up, brushed himself off, and came over to her, putting his hands on her shoulders. "Trust me?"

Harper couldn't stop the smile. "Always."

But she stopped him just as he was about to tie the long, black sock around her eyes. "You *sure* it's clean?"

He didn't answer, just tied it tight and then took her hand and led her through the darkness.

"Watch your head," he warned, guiding her into a car. His hands were warm and firm, one gripping her arm, the other flat on her lower back. She didn't want him to let go, but then he did, and a door slammed. Another opened, and she heard him get in next to her.

"I hope you're not expecting me to drive," she teased.

"I got it from here," Adam said, and started the car.

Harper hated surprises, as she hated anything out of her control. But she didn't ask any questions. She didn't want him to think she was actually enjoying this. So instead she sat quietly, listening to his breathing, which sounded very loud in the dark.

It was hard to keep track of the time when she had nothing to measure it by but the sound of his breathing, the gravel crunching under the tires, and the wind rushing past. But it didn't feel like very long before they had arrived.

Adam opened the door for her and guided her out, then put an arm around her waist and, with his other arm, took her hand in a strangely formal gesture. At first, she took tiny, hesitant steps, worrying that she would catch her heel on something and pitch face first into the ground. But the farther they walked, the more certain she became that Adam wouldn't let her fall.

Another door opened, and they were inside, her feet clicking on tile. The smell was familiar, but she couldn't place it, and she wasn't trying too hard. It was better to just coast on the warm, safe feeling of Adam's arms, because she knew that all too soon, he would let go. And then he did.

"Ready?" he asked.

More than ready. "You tell me."

"One more thing." He left her standing there alone, and it was disorienting, almost terrifying, standing in a strange place surrounded by darkness, not knowing who or what might be watching. So disorienting that she was about to rip the makeshift blindfold off herself, surprise or no surprise—and then the music started.

> *I belong in your eyes,*
> *I lose myself in you.*

It was a slow song, a love song.

With you I live,
Without you I cry,
Without you I die.

Harper almost gasped. It was the song that had been playing at the prom, as she stood alone, waiting for her prince.

Adam slipped something onto her head, then took off her blindfold. The first thing she saw was his eyes, green and sparkling and misty soft. Then the dimple that appeared whenever he smiled. Next the cheesy cardboard crown on his head, painted gold and lined with sequins.

And, finally, she pulled her eyes away from him and realized they were in the school gym, surrounded by streamers, balloons, sparkling lights, and a fake Eiffel Tower.

"You did this?" she whispered. He nodded. "How—Adam, what's going on?"

He took a step closer, then another, and looped his arms around her waist. "I'll explain everything, but first, can we dance?"

And, despite her vow to protect herself, to forget about Adam, to move on, she put her arms around him, leaned her head against her shoulder, closed her eyes, and lost herself in his embrace.

"You made me the prom?" she murmured. They

swayed gently with the music, barely lifting their feet off the ground.

"I got some friends in high places. Or at least, on prom committee."

"But why?" His shoulder was so soft, and, just like she remembered, she fit perfectly into the dip where it met his neck.

"I should have been here." Adam stroked her hair. "I wish I could go back. But . . ."

"But you can't."

"I thought maybe, just tonight, we could go back and pretend this whole year didn't happen—"

Harper stopped dancing and, though she hated to do so, pushed him away. "Adam, what is this, really? Because if this is just pretend, if you're just having one night of fun before—" She took a deep breath and drew herself up very straight, trying to make her voice as hard as possible. "What is this supposed to mean?"

Adam, who hated talking about—well, pretty much anything that didn't come with a scoreboard—didn't look away. "It means I want you, Harper. And not just for tonight."

"So what changed?" she asked, afraid to let herself believe him. "I suddenly *need* you more than Beth does? Did my spine disintegrate? Because I must have missed the memo."

Adam's hand grazed her cheek. She didn't push him away.

"I don't care if you need me," he said. "I need you. I *want* you. When you made me choose—"

"Maybe I shouldn't have," she admitted quietly, though it went against her principles to admit a mistake.

He shook his head. "Beth is my friend, she needed help. But you—"

"I never need help," Harper said bitterly. It was a tired old song, and by now she knew the words by heart. "I'm strong. I can stand up on my own. Blah blah blah."

He grabbed her hands in his. "I was going to say, you're more than a friend. You're my best friend. You always have been, Gracie. You're everything."

Harper sighed, still hearing Kane's words ringing in her ears.

We look out for ourselves
We take what we want.
We don't care who gets hurt.
We're the same.

"I don't need to be your whole world," she said, trying to convince herself as much as Adam. "I just . . . I need to matter. I need to know you're on my side, and I know you *say* you are, but it seems like there's always something else more important—"

"Harper, look at me."

As if she could look away.

His gaze was fierce, and his eyes too bright, as if covered by a sheen of tears. But that was impossible. This was Adam. "You matter," he said. "And there is *no one* else. I will always choose you. I need you. Do you believe me?"

She wanted to. She wanted to so much. But then what? What would happen the next time she needed him and he wasn't there? What would happen when he left?

He always left.

"I choose you, Gracie." His eyes were wide, and his hands were trembling around hers. And she realized maybe he was frightened, too. "I love you."

Maybe it doesn't matter what happens next, she thought. *He's here now.*

"I love you, too."

Harper didn't close her eyes. She wanted to see his face as it drew closer, watch his eyes close, his long lashes brush her cheek, his hands cradle her face.

He tasted the same.

She sucked at his lips, stroked the soft skin at the nape of his neck, massaged her fingers through his hair. Everything else fell away, except for the feel of his body pressed to hers.

And the feel of his lips.

Time passed, and they couldn't let go. They had waited too long; they were too hungry for each other.

And then more time passed, and their lips finally parted but their hands stayed clasped as they walked out of the gym and back to the car. They could have stayed there, or found a private place on the side of the road, or driven to that spot behind the ravine where people sometimes went when they needed an escape. It was the desert—there were plenty of places to be alone.

But instead they drove home, and without speaking—without separating—they walked into the backyard and climbed onto the rock, *their* rock, and although the sky was clear and the moon was only a sliver, they never noticed the stars.

They were still there, on the rock, Harper's head on Adam's chest, cradled in Adam's arms, when dawn lit up the sky with a new day. And even then, they might have stayed, happy, entangled, together—were it not for a previous engagement.

"Good morning," Adam whispered, kissing her on the forehead.

She kissed him on the lips. "Good morning. Ready for this?"

"As I'll ever be."

But neither of them moved. They just lay there, side by side, hands clasped. Their caps and gowns waited inside, and soon enough they'd get up, change, pose for proud parents, prepare themselves for everything to end.

It was early. There was still time to kiss. Time to hold each other. Time to savor their beginning.

chapter thirteen

IT'S BEEN SCIENTIFICALLY PROVEN: NOTHING IN this universe is more boring than a graduation ceremony. Even when you're the graduate. *Especially* when you're the graduate, sitting in the 104-degree heat, sweating through the robe that only an hour before had made you stop in the mirror and gape at yourself, thinking, *Can this really be me?* The same robe that had made you pause in conversation with friends to think, in amazement, *This is it.* There may have been a moment of gravitas, of sober recognition, before the ceremony began; it may even have leaked into the grand march onto the football field, as the familiar chords of "Pomp and Circumstance" kept strict four-four time and made the whole thing seem like the closing scene of a bad movie.

But by the time the speechifying really got under way, the robe had turned into a portable sweat lodge and the only thing marking the rhythm of the principal's droning was the loud snoring coming from the third row.

Adam grabbed his cap, tilted his head back to get a good look at the cloudless sky, and prayed for rain. He was supposed to be sitting up onstage, the better to accept his award from the athletics department, but he liked it better here, hidden by the crowd, Harper by his side, no one to see when he yawned or made faces or tried to avoid his coach's questioning stare. As the valedictorian rose to start her speech, starting out with some pretentious quote about reaching for the stars, Adam finally gave in to the inevitable. He closed his eyes.

Beth sat at attention, trying not to pretend she didn't care that she wasn't up there in the salutatorian's seat, waiting to deliver her speech and prove to the world that she was . . . well, second best, which was still pretty good. She'd been in the running until October, when everything, including her grades, had overshot the cliff and done a Wile E. Coyote plummet to the bottom. At least she was starting to dig herself out of the hole and walk away.

Reed would have been sitting several rows behind her, if he'd followed the orders about alphabetical seating, which seemed unlikely, since no one but Beth had bothered. Maybe he would have been staring at her—or, more likely, staring blankly, bored and stoned.

But he wasn't there at all.

Adam dozed on Harper's shoulder as the principal droned out the names, waking only to clap for her, and then again to ascend the stage and pick up his own diploma. But Harper listened to every name. Powers, Ramirez, Resnick, Richards, Sambor, Sauer, Segredo . . . Solomon.

Skipping right over it, as if Kaia Sellers had never existed, as if there wasn't an empty chair where she should have been, smoothing down her hair and making snide comments about everything and everyone in her sightline. And there *was* no empty chair, no pause where her name should have been, not even a cheesy memorial that would have made all the posers fake cry while making Harper want to vomit. There was just that split second between Segredo and Solomon, one second for Harper to fill in a silent name and let herself imagine for one last time how things might have been different, how they *should* have been different. Adam squeezed her hand, like he knew, and she realized that maybe she wasn't the only one.

Then came Spiers, and Starrow, and finally Stevens, and as Miranda shook the principal's hand and smiled out at the crowd, Harper pulled herself away from the past, stood up, and cheered.

And Miranda didn't just smile at the crowd, she looked hard, searching for the face she knew wouldn't be there, even as she told herself that he wasn't her problem anymore. He was home, she knew that much. Whether he'd skipped graduation through choice or necessity, she had no idea. He hadn't tried to contact her.

But there was the note, the note that late last night she'd finally set down on her desk, smoothed out, and, knowing that she should probably light it on fire, read slowly and fearfully, and then read again. And again.

It began, *What I should have written in your yearbook.*

It was one page long, handwritten, front and back.

I was too afraid to tell you the truth, it said.

I wasn't good enough for you, it said, further down. *But you made me better.*

I never let myself feel this way about anyone, it said.

I didn't know what to do.

I was scared.

And also: *You're stronger than you look. I'm the opposite.*

It said *I'm sorry* five times.

I want to say please don't hate me, it said. *That would be a very me thing to say.*

But, *Please hate me,* it said.

It said *thank you* once, but it didn't say for what.

The word *love* appeared only once, at the end.

I wish I could have meant this the way you deserved. But I mean it the best way I can:

Love,

Kane.

There was a loud cheer, and a flock of black caps took flight.

It was over.

Harper couldn't keep her hands off his bare skin. It was warm, like something was burning just beneath the tan, taut surface. She pressed her hand flat against his abs, then ran her fingers lightly up his chest, tickling his neck. He laughed, then lunged toward her, nipping playfully at her ear, her nose, and then tickling his fingers across her neck and back until she convulsed in giggles, shaking helplessly in his arms.

It was a secluded spot in the desert, hidden from non-existent passersby by a small grove of Joshua trees, which meant absolute privacy to enjoy themselves—and each other.

As the laughter drifted away, they lay still, spent, tangled up in each other.

"I wish we could stay here all day," Harper mused, kissing his bare shoulder. "And all night . . ."

"You're the one who wanted all the group festivities,"

Adam reminded her. "I would have been perfectly happy—"

"I don't want Miranda to be alone," she said. "Not tonight."

"I know." He curled himself around her, lightly stroking her bare arm. "It'll be fun."

"Speaking of alone . . . ," she said hesitantly. She'd promised herself that she would do this, but now that the moment had arrived, she wasn't sure she could go through with it. But Harper Grace had never backed away from a challenge. "If you want to bring Beth tonight . . . you should. Invite her along, I mean."

Adam gave her a sharp look. "Are you serious? You want me to bring *Beth*?"

"Of course I don't *want* you to," Harper said, recoiling. "But . . ." She reached for his hand and laced their fingers together. "I'm trying, okay? If you need this, I'm trying to be okay with it."

He raised their linked hands to his lips and kissed her fingertips. "You're amazing," he whispered. "How did we waste so much time?"

Harper winced. It wasn't her favorite topic, not now that she was racing the clock. She'd been waiting for graduation for so long—and now that it was here, all she could think was, *One month, and then he leaves me again.*

"We have time," she murmured, nestling into him,

wishing that every inch of their bodies could be in contact at once. "Just not enough."

"Maybe more than you think."

Harper sat up. "Did they push back the date you have to leave?"

"Maybe . . . maybe I'm not going."

"What?"

Adam sat up too, cracking his knuckles one by one as he did when he was bored or nervous. "I'm calling the guy today to give him my decision, and I've been thinking . . ." He shook his head. "Maybe it's not such good idea. It's so far away, and you know me and school." He made a sour-milk face. "Not a perfect match. And you and me, we only just—" He put an arm around her shoulders. "I don't want to leave. Not now."

Everything had already been almost perfect—and now the *almost* had vanished. Without her having to wheedle, manipulate, lie, cheat, beg, or do any of the other things she'd always tried in the past when life had threatened to sweep her in the wrong direction. It had just happened, with no effort whatsoever. Adam was staying true to his word: He was choosing her. It seemed almost too good to be true.

And it is. She didn't want to hear the voice, but it was persistent, and it was loud. It was her own.

"You have to go," she told him, confused by the words

coming out of her mouth. Since when had she developed a conscience? And what would this disgusting voice of righteousness have to say in a few months, when she was lying in an empty bed missing Adam, miserable, alone? What would it say when Adam found some nubile, overly flexible, morally challenged Riverside cheerleader to occupy his time while Harper was waiting for his phone call hundreds of miles away?

"You have to go," she said again, pushing away thoughts of the future. "This is too big, it's too much. You can't give it up for me."

"It's not just for you," he protested. "It's, you know, it's far away, and a lot of . . . okay, it's for you. But it's for me, too. I don't want to leave you."

"And I'm not letting you stay," she said, trying to sound tough. "You're not that dumb, Ad. You can't walk away from something like this. This is your future."

"Who are you, my guidance counselor?"

Who was she?

His new girlfriend, who would miss him too much to bear, who deserved more than a few weeks to actually be happy before he ripped her heart out again?

Or his old friend, his best friend, who knew what was right for him—and knew that she couldn't get in the way?

"I'm the one who knows you better than anyone else," Harper said. "That's what you're always saying, right?

And I know this is what you really want. This is what you need. You have to go for it."

"Then come with me!"

She could see past the eagerness right through to the desperation, and the knowledge that it wasn't going to happen.

Even so, she let herself imagine it for a moment, just picking up and driving across the desert with him, landing in Riverside, finding an apartment, a part-time job, living in sin (and watching her mother's head explode as a not-so-trivial side benefit), having Adam around every day, every minute, whenever she wanted him, close enough to touch.

She gave herself that one moment to live in the fantasy. And then it was back to real life.

"I can't do that to Miranda," she told him. "We've got plans. And . . . *I've* got plans. I can't just follow you. Even if . . . even though it would be amazing." She tipped her face forward so that their foreheads kissed. "One year. There are vacations, and we can visit each other on the weekends, and . . . maybe it won't be so bad." She wasn't trying to convince him. She was trying to convince herself.

"One year," he echoed, touching her face like he was trying to memorize its shape. "We can do that."

"And after that, if we're still together—"

"We *will* be," he said, with more certainty than she

could allow herself. But maybe that was okay. She was sure of only one thing: If it all went wrong again, she would fight for them—and maybe this meant he would fight too.

"I'll miss you," she said, eyes closed tightly so that no emotion—or anything else—could leak out.

He touched her lips. "Smile," he said. "I'm not gone yet."

Four weeks. It wasn't enough time. It wasn't fair.

But—she kissed him, hard, and wrapped her body around his—it was better than nothing. And it would have to do.

Don't expect anything, Beth reminded herself, creeping slowly up the path. She clutched the letter in her hands, trying to envision how this would go—how it should go. She could hand it to him, then run away. Or she could ask him to read it while she stood there, watching his face for some hint of understanding. Or maybe she should just set it down on the doorstep and leave without making him face her again.

That was probably the right thing to do, but just this one last time, Beth allowed herself to ignore that. She needed to see him. She needed to explain why she had written the letter—it wasn't because she hoped to excuse herself or even explain herself. She wasn't trying to get him back. She just wanted to help him understand what she'd done to him—and to thank him, for everything he'd done for her.

They'd been together for such a short time, but somehow he'd managed to crawl inside her, to *change* her. It was all in the letter—all that, and another apology. Not for the way she'd hurt Kaia, but for the way she'd hurt him.

His father answered the door. At least, Beth assumed it was his father; they'd never met.

"Is Reed here?" she asked.

"You just missed him," the man said.

"Oh." Beth tried not to be too disappointed. "Can I, um, leave this for him?"

The man wiped his hands on his pants, smearing a streak of black grease across the worn denim. He took the letter. "He'll be gone a few months, but I can hold it for him, if you want."

"Gone?" Her voice squeaked. "Gone where?"

The man shrugged. His hair was lighter than Reed's, and gray at the temples, but it was just as curly. "With his band somewhere. They took off in the van, said they were going on tour. Didn't want to hear my opinion on the topic. And I got one."

"Oh."

Don't cry, she told herself. She took the letter back. "Do you have an address or something? Somewhere I can . . ."

But the man shook his head. "Don't know where he went, don't know when he's coming back. Sorry."

Do not cry.

Reed was gone. It was over. Not that it hadn't been over before. Not that he hadn't been gone—but this was different.

Why hadn't he said he was leaving so soon? Beth wondered. When they'd stood there in the dark, all those things going unsaid—if she'd realized that this was one of them, she might have . . .

What? she asked herself bitterly. *What would be different?*

And the answer: *nothing*.

Maybe this was better. Seeing him only reminded her of what she couldn't have. And letting herself believe that he would still be watching out for her, protecting her, jumping in to save her from herself . . . that was just another sign of weakness. And she was done with all that.

She started her car, then hesitated. Adam had invited her out with him—with "us"—for the night. And despite her grounding, it was tempting. No one would want her around, she knew that. Not even Adam. But being hated and ignored might still be easier than spending the night alone, staring into the empty future.

No.

She'd promised herself she would stop making the easy choices. She wouldn't crash Adam's celebration just because she couldn't stand to spend the night alone. So she drove home.

And by the time she got there, she'd almost convinced herself that it didn't matter that Reed was gone for good. Then she saw the van parked at the curb, and knew she'd been lying to herself once again.

He was leaning against it, waiting.

For her.

Beth ran to him, then stopped abruptly when she was about a foot away—knowing that if she went any farther, she wouldn't be able to stop at all.

"Hey," she said, cool and casual.

"Hey."

"Yo, Beth," Fish called, hanging out of the van, a skinny goth girl with blue-streaked hair and black lipstick clinging to him. Something about her looked vaguely familiar. "Did you hear? We're going on tour."

"Gonna be rock stars, baby," Hale said, waving from the driver's seat. He had a goth groupie of his own, almost identical to the first, except that her streaks were purple. She waved as if she knew Beth.

"Tell Harper we say thanks for the advice!" the groupie chirped.

"Yeah, and that she was right. We needed a change. Uh, dude," her friend added. Then, in sync, they turned toward their rock stars and commenced with the PDA.

Reed touched her arm. "Want to walk?"

Beth nodded, and they started slowly down the sidewalk, both looking at the ground.

"So you're leaving?" she asked.

"Yeah. For a while."

"That's great." But she couldn't muster up much enthusiasm.

He shrugged. "We'll see. Could be good, could be . . . well, you know the guys."

"Yeah." She smiled weakly. "Well, good luck, I guess."

"You too. So . . . you sticking around here for a while?"

The awkwardness was almost physically painful. Beth couldn't believe there had been a time when they'd spent hours together without noticing the time pass. And now they'd been reduced to pitiful small talk? The raw, angry silence between them had almost been better—at least it meant that there was still something between them, that they weren't just strangers with nothing in common except a miserable past.

"For a while," she replied. "I figured I'd take a few classes at State and save up some money, then reapply to Berkeley. I'll do whatever it takes to get in this time." It was the first time she'd said it out loud, and she was surprised to hear that it sounded like a solid plan. For the first time, she began to believe it might work.

"That's cool," he said. She winced at the tone; she knew when he was trying to be polite. "You will."

"Thanks. So . . ." She waited for him to explain why he'd come.

"Yeah. Uh, good luck with all that, I guess."

"You too. With the tour, and everything."

"Beth, before I go . . ." He stopped walking, and she turned, waiting for him to continue. "I didn't want to leave without . . . you know. Saying good-bye."

"I'm glad," she said softly. "I'll miss you."

There was a pause. "I miss *you*," he said. "That's what I wanted to tell you."

She couldn't speak.

"And also . . . I forgive you."

"Reed, you don't have to—"

"No. Just let me—" He shook his head. "I know you didn't mean for it to happen. And . . . I get why you had to lie. Why you thought you had to. I'm not even . . ." He took a step toward her and raised a hand, awkwardly, then dropped it again. "Maybe I'm not even sorry. That you did. The two of us, we . . ."

"It was amazing," she said, and no amount of telling herself not to cry would prevent the tear from dripping out. She wiped it away before he could see. "And I ruined everything."

"No."

"Yes."

"Well . . . okay, yes. But—" He touched her face with

the back of his hand, running his nails lightly down her cheek. "It's over. Let it go, okay? I'm trying to. I just—I want you to be happy. Let yourself be happy."

"I want to," she whispered.

Reed glanced back at the van. "I should take off."

She nodded. "How long will you be gone?"

"Don't know. A while."

"I wish . . ."

"Yeah. Me too." He smiled his crooked smile, and then his arms were around her, hugging her tightly, and she leaned against him one last time, pressing her face into his neck and breathing in the rich, deep smell: coffee, cigarettes, and beneath it something warm and sweet, like almonds roasted in honey. "I'm not mad anymore," he said softly, squeezing tighter. "I'm not. I just—I can't be with you. Not after . . . not yet."

"I know."

"Maybe someday," he whispered. "Maybe things will be different."

"Maybe," she breathed, even though they both knew it was a lie. And maybe whatever was between them wouldn't have lasted, anyway. Maybe as time passed, and she'd gotten stronger, she would have remembered herself, and the two of them wouldn't have worked. Maybe. But she didn't believe that, either. She still loved him. She just couldn't have him.

Her maybes were just pretty ways to disguise the truth. There was only one maybe she could cling to: *Maybe* it would be okay. Maybe she would move on, and stand on her own, and let herself be happy.

Maybe it was possible.

"I don't want to let go," she murmured.

"Me neither." But then he did, only a little, enough to see her face, and then he leaned in and kissed her, as softly and tentatively as he had the first time, when he'd been afraid of hurting her and she'd been too weak to push him away. So she'd let him get hurt instead.

This time, she was stronger.

"Good-bye, Reed," she said, still so close, she could feel his lips brushing against hers. And she let him go.

"You sure you want to do this?" Harper asked, hesitating with her finger on the doorbell.

Miranda smiled ruefully. "I don't know about you guys, but I'm kind of partied out."

"Yeah, but there's plenty of other stuff we could do—" Harper began.

"We're doing this," Miranda said firmly.

Harper looked skeptical, but Adam pressed his hand over hers, and the doorbell rang.

Miranda tried to freeze her face in a neutral expression, and waited for the door to open.

"What are you guys doing here?" Kane asked. He looked normal enough, if more casual than usual in jeans and an old T-shirt. "If you came by to lecture me—or threaten me," he added, looking at Harper, "good timing. My dad just left, and we wouldn't want the ranting and raving to let up for more than a few seconds."

"Get over yourself," Harper said, pushing past him into the house. "We're crashing your pity party, Felon Boy. And we brought reinforcements." She nodded at Adam, who pulled a bottle of Champagne out from behind his back.

Miranda didn't say anything, just stood slightly behind the rest of them, listening and waiting. She couldn't quite look at Kane.

"How you doing?" Adam asked, throwing himself on one of the couches.

Kane shrugged. "Out on bail, sporting the latest in felon fashion"—he raised the cuff of his jeans to reveal a black electronic ankle bracelet—"you know, same old, same old."

Miranda still wasn't looking, but she could feel his eyes on her.

"Can I talk to you for a minute?" he asked quietly.

Miranda shrugged. "I guess."

Harper grabbed her wrist. "You need backup?"

"I think I got it," Miranda said, and followed Kane

into the kitchen. She realized it was kind of odd, how little time they'd spent in this house while they were dating—not to mention all the years they'd known each other.

I keep people out, he had written in his letter. *It's all I know how to do.*

Miranda leaned against a marble counter. Kane stood across from her, looking uncharacteristically awkward and unsure of himself. He rubbed the back of his neck, fiddled with the cuff of his shirt, then finally spoke. "Miranda, I'm really sorry—"

"You don't have to apologize again," she told him. "I get it, you're sorry."

"It was horrible."

"Unforgivable, really."

"And you must hate me."

"Utterly," she agreed, the corners of her mouth creeping up at the edges. It wasn't because she suddenly found him irresistible, or because standing here facing him she was ready to fall for his charm and forgive his every sin.

That's what she'd been afraid of—it's why she hadn't wanted to come. And why she'd had to come.

But it wasn't happening. She finally met his eyes, and for the first time he wasn't Kane Geary, cool, charismatic, charming Greek god with the perfect body and irresistible smile who could get away with anything. He was just Kane, the guy she'd known forever, the guy who'd made some mistakes. Whatever power over her that he'd once had, it was gone.

And now she let her mouth widen into a smile, because she'd passed her first test. She had faced him, and she was still in control. She was free.

"Miranda, if I could go back, if I could—"

"Save it, Geary." She hopped onto the counter, enjoying the sensation of being above his eye level, rather than several inches below. "You did it, and it sucked, but you did the right thing in the end. If you hadn't—" She shivered, imagining what it would be like if she were the one locked into a metal bracelet, facing court dates, trials, sentencing. . . . "Anyway, thanks for that."

"I should have done it sooner," he said.

"Damn right."

Kane leaned against the counter next to her, his hand next to hers. They didn't touch.

"So what happens next?" she asked.

"Penn State's over," he said, tipping his head back as far as it would go and then expelling a long, angry breath. "Even if they don't revoke my admission, well, let's just say my dad's not going to be shelling out massive amounts of tuition money for me anytime soon. He's not too happy right now."

"I'm sorry." And it was even a little true. "I know how much you wanted to get out of here."

"I still might," he said with a bitter laugh, "if the cops get their way." He sighed. "But it seems like my dad's lawyer's going to get the case kicked. Insufficient evidence, illegal search and seizure, something. I don't know. I haven't really been thinking about it."

Miranda raised an eyebrow. "What else is there to think about?"

He turned toward her, and he didn't have to say it out loud. For once, his eyes actually gave him away.

"Stevens, I . . . you have to know . . . I . . ."

Part of her was tempted to let him keep torturing himself, blurting out nonsensical phrases in that strangled voice. Maybe if she waited long enough, he would actually choke out a sincere sentiment or two, much as it pained him.

But she didn't need it, not anymore. Besides, sweet and sincere didn't really become him.

"I don't hate you," she said finally, putting him out of his misery. "I'm not even that mad anymore. Promise."

"So I've still got a chance?"

"With me?" Miranda jumped off the counter, laughing. "A fat chance," she said. "Very, very fat. Like sumo wrestler fat."

He smiled wryly. "I had to ask."

"I'm glad you did." And then, like it was nothing, she rose up on her toes and gave him a quick kiss on the lips, allowing herself a split second to remember other, better, longer kisses and everything that had come with them, then stepped back, surprised at how easy it was. "Look me up when you get out on parole," she teased, "and we'll see if you're a changed man."

The famous Kane Geary smirk made its first appearance of the night. "Stranger things have been known to happen, Stevens. You never know."

"Never" was the right word, she told herself, because he'd never change. And she'd never let him back in, or anyone like him. She wouldn't be that stupid again. Whatever he said, now or later, she finally knew better. She'd made herself a promise, and she was sticking to it.

But there was that smile, and those eyes . . . and his letter.

Never, she told herself firmly. *Never again.*

Then again—cue smirk—stranger things have been known to happen.

"So, what are we toasting to?" Kane asked, pouring the champagne into his father's best glasses. "Maybe to not getting sick off this cheap drugstore booze?"

Harper smacked him on the shoulder, not so lightly. "Maybe to the fact that your friends are willing to put up with a soulless sleazebag like you for one more night?"

Kane gave her his sweetest, smarmiest smile. "So

you're saying we're friends again? I better go write it down in my diary. I've been so worried about losing my BFF."

She raised an arm to smack him again, but Adam caught it in midswoop and pulled her into his arms. "How about to finally figuring things out," he suggested, giving Harper a knowing smile.

Miranda grinned and raised a glass. "That works for me."

Harper's hands tightened around the glass. She leaned her head back against Adam's chest and watched Miranda stretch out as Kane, for once, watched *Miranda*, darting glances at her when he thought no one was looking. There was an empty glass sitting on the liquor cabinet—*one for Kaia*, she thought, *who should've been here*.

She had known the people in this room for most of her life, and she knew them better than she knew anyone, saw them more than she saw her own parents, day after day, year after year. She knew the way Miranda looked when she was about to sneeze, the arm Kane preferred using when he was trying to tickle his latest conquest, the song Adam hummed to himself when he was working on a math problem or setting up the perfect three-point shot—and they knew just as much about her.

And they put up with her anyway.

"It's all over, isn't it?" she said suddenly. "Nothing's going to be the same after this."

Kane looked at her like she was crazy. "Would you *want* it to be the same? Do you not remember . . . everything?"

"It hasn't been the best year," Miranda pointed out.

"See, even the nostalgia queen agrees with me," Kane said.

"It's kind of been the worst." Adam leaned down to kiss the top of her head. "At least, until recently."

"I know, but . . ."

But it wasn't true. Or, at least, it wasn't the whole truth. Things had been hard—things had, at times, been impossible—but no easy fight was worth winning. It wasn't that she had no regrets; it wasn't that she would have done it the same way all over again. It wasn't that she thought it had all worked out for the best. Some mistakes you couldn't fix, no matter how much you wanted to. Some things you couldn't get back.

It wasn't that she had forgotten the year's failures, the nights she'd lain in bed staring into the dark, willing herself not to cry—and it wasn't even that the triumphs were so sweet that they overpowered the flavor of defeat. It was that they had been through so much—too much—and they had still ended up here, celebrating, victorious. Together. They had battled and bloodied one another, they had kept secrets, broken hearts, lied, betrayed, exiled, they had walked away, said good-bye and sworn it was forever, and somehow, every time, they had mended, they had forgiven, they had survived. Some mistakes could never be fixed—some, but not all.

Some people can't be driven away, no matter how hard you try. Some friendships won't break.

"It wasn't the best year," she admitted. "But it had its moments. *We* had our moments."

Kane smirked. "Since when did you become Little Miss Sunshine?"

Harper leaned into Adam, who wrapped his arms around her waist. "Since I got a clue." She pressed her lips together and swallowed hard. *Graduation only meant the end of high school*, she told herself, *not the end of everything.* There was no need to get weepy or to bathe in nostalgic schmaltz. Even if she was surrounded by the only people who'd ever mattered to her; even if this was the beginning of good-bye. She was Harper Grace, and her eyes would stay dry as she raised her glass. Her hand would *not* tremble. And her voice would never break.

"To survival," she said, and it wasn't a suggestion. "Whatever it takes."

Miranda nodded and clinked her glass against Harper's. "And to sticking together."

"Even when we should know better," Kane added, raising an eyebrow.

Clink.

"To never giving up on each other," Adam said.

Clink.

Harper drank last, waiting for the rest of them to tilt their glasses back. She wanted to fix the image in her mind, to remember them celebrating. She wanted to remember them happy. And then she brought her own glass to her lips and tipped it toward her mouth, the fizzy champagne sharp on her tongue and icy cool as it trickled down her throat.

To surviving, she thought, as Adam's arms tightened around her. *To whatever comes next.*

To us.

TURN THE PAGE FOR A LOOK AT ANOTHER
BOOK BY **ROBIN WASSERMAN**.

HACKING HARVARD

*T*his story is not mine to tell.
  It is, however, true—and I'm the only one willing to tell it.
It begins, like all good stories, once upon a time.

"I'm in."

The shadowy figure slipped down the hall, infrared goggles giving the familiar surroundings an eerie green haze. Dressed in head-to-toe black, a mask shielding his face, he would have been invisible to the security cameras if his partner hadn't already disabled them. Five minutes, blueprints from the firewalled Atlantis Security site, a pair of wire clippers—and the job was done.

Snip! Good-bye, cameras.

Snip! Farewell, alarm.

Still, he moved slowly, carefully, silently. The operation was just beginning. Anything could go wrong.

The target was twelve doors in, on the left. Locked, as they'd expected.

Good thing he had the master key.

The equipment was stashed in a closet directly across the hall, secured behind a no entry sign, official-looking enough that no one had dared enter. He wheeled out the cart, grimacing at the squeaky wheels. No matter. There was no one to hear. The next security patrol wasn't scheduled for another three hours, thirty-two minutes—and reconnaissance indicated that the night guard almost always skipped his three a.m. rounds in favor of a nap in the front office.

If anyone else approached, the perimeter alert would make sure he knew about it.

He pushed the door open and surveyed the target. It would be close, but they'd get the job done. He crossed the room, taking position by the wall of windows. Thirty seconds with the whisper silent drill, and the lowest pane popped cleanly out of the frame. He attached his brackets to the frame, threaded the high-density wire through, waited for the tug from below and, when it came, locked everything in. That was the easy part.

He turned around, his back to the empty window, and closed his eyes.

Visualization, that was the key.

He'd learned it from the masters. James Bond. Danny Ocean. Warren Buffet. See the plan unfold. Visualize the details, the problems, and their solutions, the eventual prize in your hand. Believe it—then do it.

It sounded like self-actualization, Chicken Soup for the wannabe winner crap—but it worked.

He closed his eyes. He saw. He believed. He knew.

And then, with a deep breath, Max Kim got to work.

Once upon a time, there were three lost boys.

One was a Robin Hood, in search of a cause. One a Peter Pan, still hunting for Captain Hook. The third a Prince Charming, bereft of his queen.

There was, of course, an evil prince.

An ugly duckling.

A moat to cross, a tower to climb, a citadel to conquer.

And finally, there was a wicked witch. But we'll get to me later.

Because in the beginning, it was just the three of them: Max Kim. Isaac Schwarzbaum. Eric Roth. The Three Musketeers. The Three Amigos.

Three Blind Mice.

"Janet Pilgrim, October 1956. Betty Blue, Miss November. Lisa Winters, December." Schwarz forced himself to breathe evenly. The familiar litany helped. "June Blair, January 1957. Sally Todd, Miss February. Sandra Edwards, in the red stockings"—Breathe, he reminded himself—"March. Gloria Windsor . . ."

He'd almost regained his calm—and then he looked down.

Hyperventilation ensued.

Again.

One hand gripped the edge of the roof, the other hovered over the wire as it ran through the pulley gears, hoisting its load, ready to bear down if anything slipped out of place. But he wasn't worried about the equipment. He was worried about the ground.

His earpiece beeped, and Eric's voice came through, crystal clear. "Another load, coming up."

"Hurry, please," Schwarz begged. "Being up here is not good for my asthma."

"Schwarz, you don't have asthma."

Oh.

Right.

The excuse worked wonders for getting out of the occasional stepfamily touch football game, as Carl Schwarzbaum could barely be bothered to remember that his oldest son still drew breath—much less which bronchial maladies kept that breath labored and far too short for football.

Eric, on the other hand, paid attention. Which made him significantly harder to fool.

"You ready to receive?" Eric asked.

Schwarz nodded. "Roger." He drew in a deep, ragged breath, then leaned over, arms outstretched, waiting for the metal cage to appear out of the darkness. Max was still inside, preparing more loads for Eric, who would pack them securely and send them on their journey to the roof.

Where Schwarz waited. Trying not to look down.

It's only two stories, he reasoned with himself. Not bad at all. Not dangerous. Not worthy of a panic attack. Not enough to make him dizzy and short of breath, to make his chest tighten and his palms sweat inside the rough leather gloves.

"Dawn Richard, May 1957," he murmured. "Carrie Radison, pretty in pink. Jean Jani. Dolores Donlon. Jacqueline Prescott, Miss September. Colleen Farrington, in the bubble bath." It helped, like it always did, like a bedtime story he told himself, chasing the monsters back into the shadows. "Miss November, Marlene Callahan, behind the door. Linda Vargas, by the fire. Elizabeth Ann Roberts, January 1958, a very happy new year."

Just two stories. Not a long way down.

He could estimate the height and his mass, calculate the impact velocity, apply it to the standard bone density and tensile quantity of his muscles, calculate the probability of tears, breaks, demolition. Rationally, he knew that two stories was nothing.

But in the dark, the ground was impossible to see.

And it felt substantially farther away.

From the Oxford English Dictionary:

Hack, noun, most commonly meaning, "A tool or implement for breaking or chopping up. Variously applied to agricultural tools of the mattock, hoe, and pick-axe type." First usage 1300 AD: "He lened him a-pon his hak, wit seth his sun us-gat he spak."

I just wanted to understand. After it was all over, I just wanted to know what I'd missed, to get why it had meant so much. This didn't help.

Other options:

"A gash or wound made by a cutting blow or by rough or clumsy cutting."

"Hesitation in speech."

"A short dry hard cough."

Most uselessly: "An act of hacking; a hacking blow."

And then, inching closer to paydirt, the seventh usage: "A spell of hacking on a computer . . . an act of gaining unauthorized access to a computer system." First use 1983.

I showed Eric. He laughed. The date was ridiculous, he said.

The definition was useless, he said.

The term hack had been co-opted—falsely, offensively, clumsily—by the mainstream media, who thought writing about computer hacking masterminds would sell more papers.

He said.

According to Eric, hacking in its pure form stretched back centuries. It wasn't restricted to a single medium. It was more than a methodology. It was an ethos.

"This is your problem," Eric complained, tapping the computer screen. The Che Guevara action figure perched on top tilted and swayed, but declined to topple. Max had given it to him for his last birthday—"a revolutionary, for my favorite revolutionary"—and while it was intended as a joke, his prized position atop the computer screen suggested that for Eric, the mini-Che was equal parts entertainment and inspiration. "The OED is an outmoded technology." He leaned over my shoulder, his forearm brushing against my cheek, and closed the window. Then, reaching around me with the other hand, so that I was trapped between his freckled arms, he opened Wikipedia and typed "hack" into the search box. "It's dead, like the Encyclopædia Britannica. A bunch of old white guys sitting in a room deciding what's true—it's a dead end. That's what this means—" He brushed his hand across the top of the monitor fondly, like it was a family pet. "The end of gatekeepers, the end of the fossilized *system that depended on an 'us' and a 'them,' the knowledgeable and the ignorant. Communal knowledge, that's what matters now. Not what they want us to know, but what we want to know. That's the future."* He *glanced up from the computer, up toward me. Behind the glasses, his eyes were huge. "Information wants to be free."*

"Schwarz is losing it," Eric whispered. Thanks to his improvements, the mics were so sensitive that they picked up his every word. "Let's speed this up."

"Code names only," Max reminded him. "We don't know who might be monitoring this frequency. And whose idea was it to stick Grunt on the roof?"

"Mine. And it was a good one." Eric flipped channels back to Schwarz, hoping he was right. "You still with us up there?"

"Susie Scott, Sally Sarell. Miss April, Linda Gamble. Ginger Young on the bed. Delores Wells on the beach, Teddi Smith, Miss—"

"Schwarz!"

"Ready for Phase Three." The voice was pinched and nasal, with a hint of a whine. As usual. "Can you, um, please go faster?"

"We're working on it."

And back to Max.

"Last load," Max confirmed. "Hoist it up, Chuckles, and I'll meet you and Grunt on the roof in five."

Eric began unhooking the metal grips and threading the wires back through, winding them in a tight coil. His cheeks burned in the wind. Unlike Max, he wore neither all black nor a mask for their missions, trusting the darkness to protect him—and, failing that, trusting the intruder alert sensors, which could never fail, because he had designed them himself. Max dressed for drama; Schwarz dressed however Max told him to. But Eric dressed for efficiency, flexibility, comfort, and speed. A gray T-shirt inside out, its faded message pressed to his skin: IF YOU'RE NOT OUTRAGED, YOU'RE NOT PAYING ATTENTION. His lucky socks, sneakers, Red Sox cap, and cargo pants—stuffed with lockpick, RF jammer, micro-scanner set to the police frequency, pliers, extra wire coils, a house key. He carried no ID. Just in case. If he missed something on the scanner, if their detectors failed, and a car pulled into the lot without advance warning, if someone, somewhere, heard something, and a cop appeared, there was always the all-purpose backup plan.

Ditch the equipment.

Forget the mission.

Run.

"Explain to me again why I have to be Chuckles and you get to be Cobra Commander?" Eric asked Max, hooking the line to his belt and giving it two quick tugs. There was a grinding sound, and then the ground fell away beneath him as the mechanism hoisted him up. He grazed his fingers against the brick facade; it scraped and tickled as the wires hauled him up to the roof.

It was nothing like flying.

"Because you always make me laugh," Max replied in a syrupy sweet voice. "At least, your face does."

"You're hilarious."

"Chuckles is a noble leader of covert operations for the G.I. Joe team," Max said. "You should be proud."

Eric snickered. "And you should stop playing with dolls."

"They're not—"

There was a pause. Eric hoped he wouldn't have to hear the lecture again, the one about eBay and nostalgia items and untapped gold mines. The one that comprehensively—just not convincingly—explained why Max had a pristine collection of Pokémon Beanie Babies on his top closet shelf.

"Never mind. Suffice it to say, that's why you don't get to pick your own code name," Max said. "You don't have the proper respect. Consider this your punishment. *Chuckles.*"

Eric scrambled over the edge and, with a thin sigh, planted his feet on the rooftop. Schwarz had already hurried over to the opposite edge, to get started on Phase Three. "So what'd Schwarz do to deserve Grunt?" Eric whispered.

"*That's* not a punishment. That's a description. Ever catch him with one of those vintage *Playboys* he loves so much?"

Eric made an exaggerated retching noise and flicked off the sound. Now if only, he thought, staring at Schwarz and wincing as he pictured what he desperately didn't want to picture, he could shut off his brain.

Max was the one who finally explained it to me.

"Hacks. Not pranks. Never pranks. Pranks are for idiots." He had his back to me. I'd interrupted him in pursuit of his other passion, hawking eighties nostalgia crap on eBay. That afternoon he was downloading photos of his latest acquisitions, a full collection of My Little Ponies, complete with Show Stable and Dream Castle. He'd pieced it together for a total of

twenty-seven dollars, and planned to resell it for at least three hundred. Just another day at the computer for Max, who believed that if you didn't clear at least a five hundred percent profit on any given transaction, you just weren't trying.

"Pranks are for amateurs. Live-action jokes with a total lack of sophistication and purpose. Not to mention sobriety." Warming to the lecture, he spun around to face me, skidding across the hardwood floor toward the couch. It was crimson-colored, like everything else in the Kim family's house. I sprawled across it, my feet up on the side, shoes off, to keep Dr. Kim from having a heart attack on discovering I had scuffed his fine Italian leather. Max warned me that my socks would get Maxwell Sr.'s forehead vein pumping just as quickly.

They were a deep, rich, dark, true blue. A crayon blue. An M&M's blue.

A Yale blue.

So I took my socks off too.

"Prankers have no vision," Max complained. "Saran Wrap on the toilet, cows in the lobby, dry ice in the pool, chickens in the gym. . . ." He rolled his eyes. "So what? What's the point? Gives us all a bad name. Even a good prank—even the best prank—is just funny. And then that's it. Over. Forgotten. But a hack . . . you're playing in a different league. Higher profile. Higher stakes. Higher calling." His eyes glowed. I'd seen the look before, but only when he was talking about money. Always when he was talking about money.

"TP cubed," he said. "Target, planning, precision, and purpose." He ticked them off on his fingers. "That's what we have, and they don't. Worthy targets, long-term planning, technically sophisticated and precise *execution—and a noble purpose. You want to make a statement, stand up for the right side. You want to take someone down who really deserves it."*

"And you want to be funny," I added.

He glared at me like I'd just set fire to his My Little Ponies. "Funny's beside the point. In 1961, the Cal Tech Fiendish Fourteen got sick of the annual invasion of Pasadena by football-crazed morons. So they hacked the Rose Bowl halftime flip-card show. They fooled two thousand University of Washington students into flipping over cards that combined to spell out CALTECH. There were more than ninety thousand people in that stadium. Millions more watching live on TV. You think they were going for funny?" His face twisted on the word. "It wasn't about making people laugh. It was about achieving greatness."

"Where's the higher purpose in screwing up a halftime show?"

Max sighed, then turned back to his computer. "Forget it. Maybe it's a guy thing."

I glanced toward the stack of My Little Ponies.

He was lucky I didn't have a match.

It took longer than expected, but by two a.m., Phase Three was completed.

Max stepped back, spread his arms wide, and gave the rooftop assemblage a nod of approval. "A masterpiece, boys. We've done it again."

Five rows of small desks and chairs faced an imposing, kitchen table–size desk and padded black office chair. Behind it stood one blackboard, complete with wooden pointer and blue chalk. Corny motivational posters hung from invisible walls—rows of fishing line strung at eye level. And, hanging above them, the pièce de résistance: one oversize, battery-powered clock, so that when Dr. Richard Ambruster, the desperate-for-retirement history teacher and current tenant of the now empty room 131, eventually found his classroom, precisely re-created on the Wadsworth High roof, he would be able to calculate his tardiness down to the second.

In his twenty-two years of teaching high school, Richard Ambruster had found only one thing in which to take any joy: giving detentions. Speak out of turn? Detention. Request an extension? Detention. Miss a homework? Detention. Refer to him as "Mr." rather than "Dr."? Two detentions.

But the crown jewel in his collection of detention-worthy offenses was tardiness. Thirty minutes or thirty seconds late, it didn't matter. Excuses, even doctor-certified ones, carried no weight with him. "My time is valuable," he would tell the unlucky latecomer in his haughty Boston Brahman accent. "And your time, thus, is mine." Cue the pink slip.

Two days before, a bewildered freshman, still learning her way around the hallowed labyrinthine halls, had foolishly asked an upperclassman for directions to room 131. She'd ended up in the second-floor boys' bathroom. Ten minutes later she'd slipped into history class, face red, lower lip trembling, sweat stains spreading under either arm. She hadn't gotten two words out before Ambruster had ripped into her, threatening to throw her out of his room—out of the school—for her blatant disregard for him, his class, his time, his wisdom, and the strictures of civil society. As she burst into tears, he shoved the pink slip in her face and turned away.

And for this, Eric had decided, Dr. Evil needed to pay.

The freshman was blond, with an Angelina Jolie pout . . . and eyes that seemed to promise misty gratitude—so Max was in.

Schwarz didn't get a vote, and didn't need one. He just came along for the ride.

In the morning, Ambruster's howl of rage would echo through the halls of Wadsworth High School, and Eric would allow himself a small, proud smile, even though no one would ever discover the truth about who was responsible. In the morning, Max would try to scoop up his willing freshman and claim his reward, only to get shot down yet again. In the morning, Schwarz would wake up in his Harvard dorm room, which, two weeks into freshman year, still felt like a strange, half-empty cell, and wish it was still the middle of the night and he was still up on the roof with his best friends. Because that was the moment that counted. Not the morning after, not the consequences, not the motives, but the act itself. The challenge. The hack.

The mission: accomplished.

So what was I doing while they were scaling walls and freezing their asses off for the sake of truth, justice, and bleached-blond high school freshmen?

I was raising my hand, I was doing my homework, I was bulking up my résumé, I was conjugating French verbs, chairing yearbook meetings, poring through Princeton Review prep books, planning bake sales, tutoring the underprivileged, memorizing WWII battlefields and laws of derivation and integration, exceeding expectations, sucking up, boiling the midnight oil, rubbing my brown nose against the grindstone. I was following the rules.

As a matter of policy, I did everything I was supposed to do. And as far as I was concerned, I was supposed to be valedictorian.

Except I wasn't.

At least, not according to the Southern Cambridge School District. Not when Katie Gibson's GPA was .09 higher than mine by day one of senior year. All because in ninth grade, when the rest of us were forced to take art—non-honors, non-AP, non-weighted, a cannonball around the ankle of my GPA—Katie's parents wrote a note claiming she was allergic to acrylic paint.

I got an A in art.

Katie got study hall.

My parents threatened to sue.

And, only once, on the way into the cafeteria, because I couldn't stop myself:

Me: "Is it even possible to be allergic to acrylic paint?"

Katie: "Is it even possible for you to mind your own business?"

Me: "Look, I'm not saying you lied, but . . ."

Katie: "And I'm not saying you're a bitch, but . . ."

Me: "What's your problem?"

Katie: [Walks away]

By the second week of senior year, the truth had sunk in. I wasn't going to be the Wadsworth High valedictorian. Salutatorian, sure. Number two. Still gets to give a speech at graduation. Still gets a special seat and an extra tassel. Probably even a certificate.

But still number two. Which is just a prettier way of saying not number one. Not a winner.

Then, in late November, something, somewhere beeped. A red flag on Katie's record, an asterisk next to the entry for her tenth-grade health class, indicating a requirement left unfulfilled, a credit gone missing. She could make up the class, cleanse her record, still graduate—but not in time for the official valedictorian selection. She was out.

I was in.

The rumor went around that I'd given the vice principal a blow job.

Eric held out his hand, palm facing up. "Give it."

"What?" Max's beatific smile didn't come equipped with a golden halo, but it was implied.

"Whatever you've got in your pocket," Eric said. "Whatever you took out of Ambruster's desk."

"What makes you think I—"

"Excuse me?" Schwarz said, his voice quaking. "Can we get down off the roof now?"

"You can go," Eric said. "But he's not leaving until he puts it back."

Schwarz stayed.

Max rolled his eyes. "You're crazy."

"You're predictable."

"Clock's ticking," Max said, tapping his watch. "If the guard shows up after all and catches us here . . ."

"It'd be a shame. But I'm not leaving until you put it back." Eric stepped in front of the elaborate pulley system they'd rigged to lower themselves to the ground. "And you're not either."

"You wouldn't risk it."

"Try me."

Schwarz's skittery breathing turned into a wheeze. "I am sorry to interrupt, but I really do not think we should—"

"Schwarz!" they snapped in chorus. He shut up.

Max stared at Eric. Eric stared back.

And after a long minute of silence, Max broke.

"Fine." It wasn't a word so much as a full-body sigh, his entire body shivering with disgruntled surrender. He pulled a folded-up piece of paper out of his pocket.

"Next week's test questions?" Eric guessed.

Max grunted. "And the password to his grading database. You know how much I could make off this?"

"Do I care?"

Max sighed again and began folding and unfolding the sheet of paper. "So how'd you know?"

"I know you," Eric said.

"And just this once, couldn't we . . ."

Eric shook his head. "Put it back where you got it."

"You're a sick, sick man, Eric," Max said. "You want to know why?"

"Let me think . . . no."

"It's this moralistic right/wrong bullshit. It's like you're infected. Don't do this, don't do that. Thou shalt not steal the test answers. Thou shalt not sell thine term papers and make a shitload. Thou shalt not do anything. It's a freaking disease."

Eric had heard the speech before, and he finally had his comeback ready. "Oh yeah? I hope it's not an STD, or I might have given it to your mother last night."

Schwarz snorted back a laugh, and Max, groaning, shook his head in disgust. "First of all, I think the term you're looking for is yo mama," he said. "Second of all . . ." He pulled out his cell phone and pretended to take a call. "It's Comedy Central. They say don't quit your day job."

"Put the test answers back, Max."

Max glared at Eric, but slid the paper back into Ambruster's desk. "If you'd just get over it, we'd be rich by now."

"If I didn't say no once in a while, we'd be in prison by now."

"Excuse me?" Schwarz began again, timidly.

Once again, the answer came back angry and in unison. "What?"

Schwarz spread his arms to encompass their masterpiece, the orderly silhouettes of desk after desk, the inspirational posters blowing in the wind. "It is beautiful, isn't it?"

It was.

Three proud smiles. Three quiet sighs. And one silent look exchanged among them, confirming that they all agreed: Whatever the risk, whatever their motives, whatever the consequences, this moment was worth it.

"Now can we please get off the roof?" Schwarz led the way down, holding his breath until his feet brushed grass. And a moment later, the three of them disappeared into the night.

It was their final dry run, their final game in the minor leagues. Max was the only one who knew it, because Max already had the plan crawling through his mind, the idea he couldn't let go. He hadn't said anything yet, but he would, soon—because up on that roof, he decided it was time. The hack on Dr. Evil had gone so effortlessly, with almost a hint of boredom. It was child's play, and Max was getting tired of toys.

He knew the idea was worthy.

He knew the plan was ready—and so were they.

I wasn't there, of course. But I've pieced it together, tried to sift the truth from the lies, eliminate the contradictions. And I've tried to be a faithful reporter of the facts, even the ones that don't make me look very good.

Maybe even especially those.

The three of them agreed not to broadcast what they'd done. But much as I know now, close as I've gotten to the center of things, I'm still not one of them, not really. And that means that I never agreed to anything. I'm not bound. I can do what I want—and I want to speak.

So like I say, this isn't my story to tell, but it's the one I've got. And all it's got is me.

ABOUT THE AUTHOR

ROBIN WASSERMAN is the author of *Hacking Harvard*, the Seven Deadly Sins series, the Cold Awakening trilogy (*Frozen, Shattered, Torn*), *The Book of Blood and Shadow*, and *The Waking Dark*. She lives in Brooklyn, New York.